PRAISE
for

March 1917

The Red Wheel, Node III, Books 1–4

"*The Red Wheel* and *The Gulag Archipelago* have been called Solzhenitsyn's two 'cathedrals.' You cannot fully understand the horrors of communism and the history of the 20th century without reading them."

—*New York Journal of Books*

"Despite its relentless focus on political events, *The Red Wheel* paradoxically instructs that politics is not the most important thing in life. To the contrary, the main cause of political horror is the overvaluing of politics itself. It is supremely dangerous to presume that if only the right social system could be established, life's fundamental problems would be resolved. Like the great realist novelists of the nineteenth century, Solzhenitsyn believed that."

—*The New York Review of Books*

"Solzhenitsyn crafts 655 brief chapters in which diverse actors, unaware of what others are doing, blindly shape events. . . . [His] novel allows us to glimpse those deeper meanings and elusive powers."

—*Wall Street Journal*

"Only a great work of art like *The Red Wheel* can convey the soul of a lawless mob that has lost all sense of measure. . . . This action-packed account, beautifully translated by Marian Schwartz, tells the story of one moment in which the failure of good men to act made all the difference in the world."

—*National Review*

"A work that combines deep civic and spiritual wisdom, literary art of high quality, and dramatic history that informs and instructs, *The Red Wheel* deserves a readership that is receptive to its enduring lessons. With the publication of the whole of *March 1917*, those lessons are much easier to discern."

—*Law & Liberty*

"Histories tend to collapse events into a single narrative; Solzhenitsyn insists on plurality. He explodes the Russian Revolution back into myriad voices and parts, disarrayed and chaotic, detailed and tumultuous. . . . In *March 1917*, Solzhenitsyn attempts the impossible and succeeds, evoking a fully formed world through episodic narratives that insist on the prosaic integrity of every life, from tsars to peasants. What emerges is a rich history that's truly greater than the sum of its parts."

—*Foreword Reviews*

"[A] magisterial depiction of the long, slow collapse of the Tsarist regime in which everybody gets a voice, but nobody feels that he or she can prevent the worst of it. Eerily prescient for the binary confusions of the present."

—*VoegelinView*

"*March 1917* is haunted by 'what-ifs.' Indeed, Solzhenitsyn suggests, the revolution was less likely than other outcomes, and all retrospective attempts to describe it as inevitable are fallacious. In his view, events might just as easily followed a different course. As we contemplate what transpired, we regret the Russia that might have been."

—*The American Scholar*

"This is the principal work of the Nobel laureate's life, to which Solzhenitsyn dedicated several decades and into which poured all his thoughts about the senseless chaos of the modern and postmodern worlds, all told through the prism of that most contingent of events, the Russian Revolution."

—*The New Criterion*

"If Aleksandr Solzhenitsyn's *The Gulag Archipelago* presented a mindset-changing view of the history of the USSR, the historical novels that make up his epopee *The Red Wheel* are a counterweight to the heroics of the October Revolution."

—*The Russian Review*

"Solzhenitsyn relives and recreates how it all happened in Russia in the second decade of the twentieth century, and he does not allow this pivot of world events to be bastardized by the clever hindsight of historians and the comfortable value judgments of our time."

—*The Spectator*

"This third installment of *The Red Wheel*, Aleksandr Solzhenitsyn's narrative of the events leading to the Russian Revolution, is remarkable in its complexity. The novel presents a polyphonic kaleidoscope of people, places, and events, some real, some fictitious."

—*Society Journal*

"The best historians and novelists—and Solzhenitsyn was first and foremost a novelist—narrate history through the eyes and ears of the participants who don't know the outcome of the events they are observing and participating in. In *March 1917*, Solzhenitsyn presents events through the characters' perspectives and perceptions at the time, not in hindsight or years afterward."

—*Asian Review of Books*

"Progressive historians have whitewashed the Revolution into a 'people's revolution,' inspired by the benevolent and charismatic Lenin and founded on the humanitarian Marx's principles of equality. In truth, the Revolution wasn't even supported by a majority of the proletariat. Aleksandr Solzhenitsyn's recently translated *The Red Wheel: March 1917* . . . [is a] sobering antidote to this naïve view."

—*Claremont Review of Books*

THE RED WHEEL

A Narrative in Discrete Periods of Time

NODE I
August 1914 (Books 1–2)

NODE II
October 1916 (Books 1–2)

NODE III
March 1917 (Books 1–4)

NODE IV
April 1917 (Books 1–2)

The Center for Ethics and Culture Solzhenitsyn Series

The Center for Ethics and Culture Solzhenitsyn Series showcases the contributions and continuing inspiration of Aleksandr Solzhenitsyn (1918–2008), the Nobel Prize–winning novelist and historian. The series makes available works of Solzhenitsyn, including previously untranslated works, and aims to provide the leading platform for exploring the many facets of his enduring legacy. In his novels, essays, memoirs, and speeches, Solzhenitsyn revealed the devastating core of totalitarianism and warned against political, economic, and cultural dangers to the human spirit. In addition to publishing his work, this new series features thoughtful writers and commentators who draw inspiration from Solzhenitsyn's abiding care for Christianity and the West, and for the best of the Russian tradition. Through contributions in politics, literature, philosophy, and the arts, these writers follow Solzhenitsyn's trail in a world filled with new pitfalls and new possibilities for human freedom and human dignity.

Aleksandr Solzhenitsyn

APRIL 1917

THE RED WHEEL / NODE IV

(25 April–18 May)

BOOK 1

Translated by Clare Kitson

UNIVERSITY OF NOTRE DAME PRESS

NOTRE DAME, INDIANA

Published by the University of Notre Dame Press
Notre Dame, Indiana 46556
www.undpress.nd.edu

Translated from book 1 of books 1–2:

“Апрель Семнадцатого” (1)
© A. I. Solzhenitsyn, 1991, 2009

“Апрель Семнадцатого” (2)
© A. I. Solzhenitsyn, 1992, 2009

Published in the United States of America

Library of Congress Control Number: 2025934557

ISBN: 978-0-268-21052-6 (Hardback)
ISBN: 978-0-268-21054-0 (WebPDF)
ISBN: 978-0-268-21053-3 (Epub3)

GPSR Compliance Inquiries:
Lightning Source France, 1 Av. Johannes Gutenberg, 78310 Maurepas, France
compliance@lightningsource.fr | Phone: +33 1 30 49 23 42

Publisher's Note

April 1917 (consisting of books 1–2) is the start of a new phase in *The Red Wheel*, Aleksandr Solzhenitysn's multivolume historical novel on the roots and outbreak of the Russian Revolution. If the first three nodes together comprise the "Revolution," the fourth node, *April 1917*, showcases the "Rule of the People."

The first node, *August 1914*, ends in the disastrous defeat of the Russians by the Germans at the Battle of Tannenberg in World War I. The second node, *October 1916*, offers a panorama of Russia on the eve of revolution. *August 1914* and *October 1916* focus on Russia's crises, revolutionary terrorism and its suppression, the missed opportunity of Pyotr Stolypin's reforms, and the souring of patriotism as Russia suffered in the world war. The third node, *March 1917*, recounts the revolution as it unfolds in Petrograd, as riots go unchecked, the Tsar falters and abdicates, but both the state and the numerous opposition leaders are incapable of controlling events.

The fourth node, *April 1917*, captures the division and helplessness of Russia's first revolutionary rulers, paving the way for the victory of the ruthless Bolsheviks later that year. The action of the present Book 1 (of two) is set during April 11–May 5, 1917, and presents a shift towards a more radical revolution and political turmoil. The provisional government comes under fire for its "bourgeois" capitalism and continuing commitment to World War I. Bolshevik leader Vladimir Lenin returns from exile and delivers his April Theses in Petrograd, actively sowing seeds of division. He declares that the Revolution is not complete and openly calls for civil war, outlining a radical plan to overthrow the Provisional Government and seize power for the Soviets. Amid the chaos and rising tide of Bolshevism, the elements of resistance, and decency, slowly begin to awaken. Book 2 of *April 1917* is to follow.

The nodes of *The Red Wheel* can be read consecutively or independently. All blend fictional characters with numerous historical personages, usually introduced under their own names and with accurate biographical data. The depiction of historical characters and events is based on the author's extensive research in archives, administrative records, newspapers, memoirs, émigré collections, unpublished correspondence, family records, and other contemporary sources. In many sections the historical novel turns into dramatic history. Plots and subplots abound.

The English translations by H. T. Willetts of *August 1914* and *October 1916*, published by Farrar, Straus and Giroux in 1989 and 1999, respectively, appeared as Knot I and Knot II (the latter titled, per Soviet Russia's calendar reform, as *November 1916*). The present translation, in accordance with the wishes of the Solzhenitsyn estate, has chosen the term "Node" as more faithful to the author's intent. Both terms refer, as in mathematics, to discrete points on a continuous line.

In a 1983 interview with Bernard Pivot, Aleksandr Solzhenitsyn described his narrative concept as follows: "The *Red Wheel* is the narrative of revolution in Russia, its movement through the whirlwind of revolution. This is an immense scope of material, and . . . it would be impossible to describe this many events and this many characters over such a lengthy stretch of time. That is why I have chosen the method of nodal points, or Nodes. I select short segments of time, of two or three weeks' duration, where the most vivid events unfold, or else where the decisive causes of future events are formed. And I describe in detail only these short segments. These are the Nodes. Through these nodal points I convey the general vector, the overall shape of this complex curve."

Dates in the original Russian text were given in the Old Style, according to the Julian calendar used in Russia until 1918. In the English translations these dates have been changed, in accordance with the author's wishes, to the New Style (Gregorian) calendar, putting them thirteen days ahead of the old dates. The March 1917 revolution thus corresponds to the February Revolution in Russian history (Old Style), just as the revolution that placed the Bolsheviks in power in November of that year is commonly referred to as the October Revolution.

* * *

The English translation was made possible through a generous anonymous donation to the Solzhenitsyn Initiative at the Wilson Center's Kennan Institute, which is gratefully acknowledged.

The maps and the Index of Names have been adapted and revised from the versions in the French translation, *La Roue rouge*, Quatrième nœud, *Avril dix-sept*, tomes 1–2, with the kind permission of Fayard and approval of the Solzhenitsyn estate.

Contents

CALENDAR OF REVOLUTION / xix

INTRODUCTION: 11 APRIL – 24 APRIL

DOCUMENTS – 1 / 1
George V's secretary to Foreign Minister Balfour.

DOCUMENTS – 2 / 1
Ambassador Buchanan to Minister Balfour.

CHAPTER 1 / 1
The war and Social Democrats in Siberian exile. — Irakli Tsereteli. — Return to Petrograd. — Tsereteli changes the EC's platform. — Pressure on Milyukov at the Liaison Commission. — Death of Chkheidze's son. — The Provisional Government's declaration of 9 April.

DOCUMENTS — 3 / 10
Address by the Provisional Government concerning desertion.

CHAPTER 2 / 10
Vera Vorotyntseva over Easter. — At the Kadet congress. — Prince Evgeni Trubetskoy in the Public Library.

DOCUMENTS — 4 / 18
Appeal of the Provisional Government to soldiers concerning the railways.

CHAPTER 3 / 19
What is the secret to taking power? — It would not come. Other EC leaders squeeze out Steklov. — Beginning of the All-Russian Conference of Soviets. — His report on the Provisional Government as a battering ram and a maneuver. — Constrained in advance by the pathetic resolution. — Shaking up the debate. — Resolution is rephrased. — Plekhanov arrives.

CHAPTER 4 / 32
Prince Pavel Dolgorukov. His trip to regiments at the front.

DOCUMENTS — 5 / 36
Guchkov's appeal concerning desertion.

CHAPTER 5 / 36

Stankevich. Problems of convening the Constituent Assembly. — How the Conference of the Soviets proceeded. Questions racing by. — Debate on the war. — How *Izvestia* is run. — Lenin's group at an EC session. Argument about passage through Germany. — Frictions between EC and government. A storm at the EC. — Stankevich's report concerning *Izvestia*.

DOCUMENTS — 6 / 45

Guchkov's order against arrests of officers.

CHAPTER 6 / 46

Victory in March for Himmer's ideas. — Zimmerwaldists suffer a defeat at the EC. — Himmer at the Conference of the Soviets. — Plekhanov crashes. — Lenin's welcome at Finland Station. — His speech the first evening at Kseshinskaya mansion. — His speech at the Social Democrat "unifying" session. — Welcoming Chernov and company. — Redirecting his energy into *The New Life*. — Not a chicken in every pot, but spiritual freedom!

CHAPTER 7 / 58

Sasha Lenartovich chooses his party. — Where he does not agree with Kamenev. — Lenin's welcome. — Sasha's impressions of his first speech. — Discipline at the rallies in front of Kshesinskaya mansion.

CHAPTER 8 / 66

(Rule of the people in Petrograd: fragments)

25 APRIL–1 MAY

CHAPTER 9" / 77

(the press on Lenin, 17–29 April)

CHAPTER 10 / 82

Vorotyntsev at GHQ. — They just don't see the extent of the collapse. — The army has no leader. — Idea of an officer congress. — Soldiers' movement to save the army. — Giving up their Crosses. — For the government and against the Soviet. — But government misses the opportunity. — Alina moves to Mogilev.

CHAPTER 11 / 89

Gessen and Gredescul evaluate current events. — What about Lenin? — Young pupils' daring.

CHAPTER 12 / 93

Kerensky indispensable to Revolution. — Visit to Tsarskoye Selo. Unexpected impressions of the Emperor. — Clemency toward Ivanov. — Attacked by *Izvestia*. Kerensky triumphant over Soviet. — Tsarskoye again. Royal couple separated. — In a flash: Kronstadt, greeting Grandmother, Conference of Soviets. — On behalf of the Prime Minister. — Delegations, delegations.

— Ministry of Justice matters. — Unpleasantness. — In Reval with Grandmother. — With Western socialists in Petrograd. — Impulse toward foreign policy. Milyukov detestable. — Scene of wrath. — Forestalling the note to the Allies. — Worries on 25 April. — Have a talk with Lenin? — He reunites the royal couple.

CHAPTER 13 / 112
(Rule of the people at the front: fragments)

DOCUMENTS — 7 / 119
Ambassador Paléologue to the French Ministry of Foreign Affairs.

CHAPTER 14 / 119
Guchkov ill again. — His trip to the South and to Minsk. — Resolutions from military units encourage him. — And undermine him. — The Minister of War in humiliation and powerlessness.

CHAPTER 15 / 127
Lenin's first steps in Petrograd. — How to answer the social patriots. — Direct danger. — Failure at Izmailovsky Battalion. — Instilling party unity in his crew. — Accurately calculate whom to target. — The right way to speak about war and peace. — Lenin in a storm. A sense of timing. — Grotesque stupidity with the high schoolers.

CHAPTER 16 / 140
(Rule of the people in the provinces: fragments)

CHAPTER 17 / 145
Yurik Kharitonov's military games. — No way for him to take part in the war. — Studies at school fall apart. — The Don floods. — An incident by the showers. — The flood broadens into disaster.

CHAPTER 18 / 151
Alina in Mogilev. — Approach and anguish.

CHAPTER 19" / 154
(from the bourgeois press, to 27 April)

DOCUMENTS — 8 / 164
Resolution of the Provisional Government on the protection of sowings.

CHAPTER 20 / 165
Milyukov becomes the target of the left. — Lenin comes to grief. Mensheviks addled. — Albert Thomas parrots the Soviet. — Forced to compromise: not a note to the Allies, but an address to the citizens of Russia. — Horse-trading over the text. — Ambassadors' reproach. — President Wilson's incautious statement about the Straits. — Kerensky and the EC encroach on policy. — The government's humiliation on the day of the martyrs' funeral. — Kerensky's fabrication: the note is being drafted.

DOCUMENTS — 9 / 177
French minister Thomas, while in Petrograd, to French ministry of foreign affairs.

DOCUMENTS — 10 / 177
German State Secretary Zimmermann to German Ambassador in Bern Romberg.

CHAPTER 21 / 178
EC concerns. — The danger in electing a separate garrison bureau. — Ninety in the EC already. — Current EC business in leaders' absence. — Military Congress must be nipped in the bud! — Prevent Lenin's arrest. — Fight over an EC bureau. — Scandal surrounding Steklov.

CHAPTER 22 / 184
(Rule of the people in the countryside: fragments)

CHAPTER 23 / 192
How to smooth things over with Alina. — Vorotyntsev pores over GHQ documents of the war years. — How to exit the war now? — An alliance of military men?

CHAPTER 24 / 200
General Gurko takes measures for the Special Army. — Taking command of the Western Army Group. — Disaster on the Stokhod. — General Gorbatovsky's plan. — Guchkov in Minsk. — Gurko seeks ways to direct the front. — How the Minsk congress opened. — And what it came to. — Mutiny at a Red Cross congress.

CHAPTER 25 / 210
Likonya.

CHAPTER 26 / 210
(Rule of the people in Moscow: fragments)

CHAPTER 27 / 213
Disabled veterans demonstrate. — At the Tauride Palace. — Violence against cripples.

CHAPTER 28 / 219
Alekseev confirmed as Supreme Commander. — But control is lost. — Ashamed in front of the Allies. — Proposal for a military congress. — Alekseev signs committee Regulations. — Proposal for army commissars.

CHAPTER 29 / 227
Klim Orlov in the Soviet of Workers' Deputies. — The debates held there. — Volynians want to arrest Lenin. Stop them!

CHAPTER 30" / 235
(from the socialist press, to 30 April)

CHAPTER 31 / 241
Chernega back at his battery after the Minsk congress.

DOCUMENTS — 11 / 247
Autonomous Schlüsselburg.

CHAPTER 32 / 247
Difficulties of the grain monopoly. — Shingarev makes speech after speech. — Missing the Sowing period! — Land redistribution?—miscalculation, there is no land to redistribute. — Committees, committees. — Shingarev sees his family off to the countryside.

CHAPTER 33 / 254
The campaign against Lenin turned out to be serious. — Forced to answer the resolution of the Executive Commission. — Lenin's speech at the soldiers' Soviet in the Tauride Palace. — Lieber's speech.

DOCUMENTS — 12 / 263
From German ambassador in Bern Romberg to Imperial Chancellor Bethmann-Hollweg.

CHAPTER 34 / 263
Guchkov's naval matters. — And army matters. — Hostility with the Soviet. — A conference with their leaders. Hopeless. — A ministerial session. — Milyukov's note adopted.

CHAPTER 35 / 272
(Rule of the people on the railways: fragments)

DOCUMENTS — 13 / 276
Exchange of telegrams between German general headquarters and the military attaché in Bern.

CHAPTER 36 / 276
Milyukov at pointless sessions of the government. — Demands from the periphery, disintegration of the country begins. — Imperial heritage on Milyukov's shoulders. — They demand the note to the Allies. — Milyukov composes it. — The ministers discuss it and adopt it. — "1 May" in Petrograd. — Milyukov's ride about town.

CHAPTER 37 / 289
How the Vyazemskys got to Gryazi station. — At Lotaryovo all was calm. — But look at Usman, look all around! — Prince Boris at peasant assemblies. Peasants come to congratulate him with 1 May. — What is to come?

CHAPTER 38 / 298
Conundrums facing the Minister of Justice. — How Kerensky slid out from the Kronstadt incident with Pereverzev. — Difficulties faced by the Extraordinary Commission of Inquiry. — How dignitaries are kept at the Peter and Paul Fortress. — Kerensky before and during the holiday.

CHAPTER 39 / 308
Andozerskaya observes the revolution. — No, nothing funny about Lenin. — At the First of May demonstration.

CHAPTER 40 / 311
Plekhanov. Revolutionary from a young age. — The tribulations of émigré life. — A defender of the homeland. — His return to Russia. — His speeches at the Conference of the Soviets. — *Unity* against Lenin. — But no invitation to the government . . . — And refusal by Executive Committee.

2 MAY – 5 MAY

CHAPTER 41 / 321
The Sevastopol Miracle. — Kolchak makes for Odessa. — Trip to Petrograd. — At Guchkov's. — To Reval? — Anna Safonova.

DOCUMENTS — 14 / 330
Exchange of telegrams between German foreign ministry and the ambassador in Bern.

CHAPTER 42 / 330
Political babes in arms. — The separate layers of the Russian officer corps. — The situation at GHQ. Vorotyntsev in the First of May procession. — At home. A name-day party?

CHAPTER 43 / 335
Alina envious and hurt.

CHAPTER 44 / 337
Ambassador Paléologue's secret removal. — "Concert-meeting" at Mikhailovsky Theater. — Speech by Albert Thomas.

CHAPTER 45 / 343
Himmer's program, the only correct way to resolve the issue of war. — Distrust of Milyukov, their confrontation at the Liaison Commission. — Himmer's passion for his paper, *The New Life*. — His rage at Milyukov's note.

CHAPTER 46 / 350
Lenin subdues his party's Petrograd conference. — Overjoyed at Milyukov's note. — But it's too early, we're not ready for an uprising.

CHAPTER 47 / 356
The note is read at the Executive Committee. — Turmoil.

CHAPTER 48 / 361
Stankevich at Kerensky's early in the morning.

CHAPTER 49 / 363
General Alekseev visits the Northern Front. — Arrives in Petrograd.

CHAPTER 50 / 365
Fyodor Linde's youth. — Linde convinces the Finland battalion committee to march.

CHAPTER 51 / 370
Kornilov tends to garrison business. — His meeting with General Alekseev.

CHAPTER 52 / 374
Alekseev invites Kolchak for a meeting.

CHAPTER 53 / 376
Executive Committee wavers. — News of the Finland Battalion.

CHAPTER 54 / 381
Current agenda of the Provisional Government. — Session with General Alekseev.
— Alarm over regiments on the march.

CHAPTER 55 / 387
Regiments standing in Mariinskaya Square.

CHAPTER 56 / 391
The Provisional Government rejects Guchkov and Kornilov's proposal to call on loyal troops.

CHAPTER 57 / 393
Speeches before the regiments on Mariinskaya Square. General Kornilov calms them.

CHAPTER 58 / 396
General Alekseev's press conference.

CHAPTER 59 / 398
(Petrograd streets: 3 May, late afternoon)

CHAPTER 60 / 402
Useless gathering of the Soviet. — Stankevich's speech.
— Bolshevik call for overthrowing the government. — Chernov tries to calm things down.
— Explosive debate. EC loses control of the Soviet.

CHAPTER 61 / 410
Evening in front of the Mariinsky Palace. — Ministers arrive and make speeches.

CHAPTER 62 / 418
How Prince Lvov gathered the evening conference. — Incident with correspondents.

CHAPTER 63 / 421
(Petrograd streets, toward nightfall)

CHAPTER 64 / 425
Night in front of the Mariinsky Palace.

CHAPTER 65 / 428
Joint nighttime session of the Provisional Government,
the Executive Committee, and the Duma Committee.

CHAPTER 66 / 436
Lenin's calculations. — Insurrection now?

CHAPTER 67 / 440
V. M. Chernov's past life. — The current state of the SR party. — Chernov's article on Lenin.

CHAPTER 68 / 445
Alekseev visits Kornilov, early morning.

CHAPTER 69 / 448
Kolya Stanyukovich with friends in the morning on Nevsky Prospect.

CHAPTER 70 / 451
Tereshchenko patches everything up with Tsereteli.

CHAPTER 71 / 454
This is the Acheron flowing! — Two nighttime appeals by the Kadet party.
— The Public Library decides to march.

CHAPTER 72 / 458
(Petrograd streets: 4 May, afternoon)

CHAPTER 73 / 462
Panic in the EC: working Petersburg is in revolt. — EC leaders on the Field of Mars.

CHAPTER 74 / 465
Engineer Lomonosov on the square in front of Kazan Cathedral.

CHAPTER 75 / 468
In the training detachment of the Volynian battalion. — Kirpichnikov and friends want to arrest Lenin. — Wandering the streets. — Scrum with workers, shots fired along Nevsky.

CHAPTER 76 / 481
Milyukov puts the brakes on the "Clarification." — Provisional Government business. — Kornilov bursts in: authorized to maintain order?!

CHAPTER 77 / 485
Newspaper article about the demise of the *Empress Maria*. — How it had happened. — Kolchak's fault, too? — Kolchak's visit with Plekhanov. — Another worker march; shots fired along Nevsky a second time.

CHAPTER 78 / 488
Kolya up and down Nevsky Prospect. — The central Petersburg public comes together. Delight.

CHAPTER 79 / 491
Mikhailovsky military school batteries refuse to appear when summoned by General Kornilov.

CHAPTER 80 / 494
Andrusov and Grimm on Mariinskaya Square in the afternoon. — Speeches by vice-ministers. — Rumors of shooting along Nevsky. — Investigation begins immediately!

CHAPTER 81 / 499
(Petrograd streets: 4 May)

CHAPTER 82 / 503
Executive Committee waits and is powerless. — The shadow of Counterrevolution? — "The Seven Dictators" to ensure troops do not leave their barracks. — The government's Clarification arrives, EC agrees to it.

CHAPTER 83 / 506
(Petrograd streets: 4 May, toward evening)

CHAPTER 84 / 509
Lenin sends Kollontai to the Soviet plenum to save the situation. — Presidium is happy with the Clarification and silent about the shooting. — The course of the speeches. — Kollontai's speech. — Message about another shooting. — But no one names the Bolsheviks! — So resume the attack.

CHAPTER 85 / 520
Crowd in front of the War Minister's residence. Ministers gather. — Ministers among themselves: emerging unscathed?

CHAPTER 86 / 523

Nighttime shootings at the corner of Nevsky and Sadovaya.

CHAPTER 87 / 527

Lenin: we survived the evening, the night, and seem to be finding a way out. — Urgent Central Committee resolution in the morning. "Down with the Provisional Government" is an adventurist slogan. — Punish the ladies at the central telephone exchange. — Morning papers: the bourgeois press takes fright; the Soviet press sensible. — As for the Bolsheviks: we do not support plotting and violence! — Take stock of our mistakes. — Postpone civil war for the moment.

DOCUMENTS — 15 / 532

From German diplomatic correspondence, regarding a new transport for émigré revolutionaries.

CHAPTER 88 / 532

Milyukov: won too great a victory! — Did not let the Revolution perish. And stood his ground. — But the Kadet Central Committee retreated. — In the government Milyukov is alone, again.

CHAPTER 89 / 537

The Duma Committee is sidelined and forgotten. — Shulgin languishes from inaction. — Kadets have failed to realize their defeat. — Socialist newspapers lie about the street events. — Shulgin prods the Duma Committee to set up a pseudo-parliament. — Vinaver's plans for a celebration of the First Duma.

CHAPTER 90 / 543

Steklov's authority keeps falling. — Steklov's path to Lenin. — The beginnings of a negotiation with Germany on a separate peace.

CHAPTER 91 / 546

Ksenia and Sanya. Their meeting.

MAPS / 551

INDEX OF NAMES / 563

Act Two

Rule of the People

The way out . . . is but one—revolution, a revolution both bloody and ruthless. . . . We shall be more consistent than not only the feeble revolutionaries of '48, but the great revolutionaries of '92; we shall not waver if we find that . . . we must spill three times more blood than the Jacobins. . . . With full faith . . . in the glorious future of Russia . . . to be the first to consummate the great cause of socialism, we shall let out but one cry: "To the Axe!"

"Young Russia" proclamation, 1862

Calendar of Revolution

3 April
- Rout of two Russian divisions on the river Stokhod
- German Ministry of Foreign Affairs demands from the Finance Ministry another 5 million German marks "for political aims in Russia"
- Fritz Platten, instructed by Lenin, enters into secret communication with the German ambassador in Bern

6 April
- Good Friday in the West
- United States declares war on Germany
- German government grants permission for Lenin's group to travel in isolated carriage

7–10 April
- Kadet Party congress in Petrograd

9 April
- Lenin-Zinoviev group departs Zurich for Germany. German ambassador in Bern: "It is of the utmost importance that the German press entirely ignore what is happening."

11–16 April
- All-Russian Conference of Soviets in Petrograd

12 April
- Lenin's group sails to Sweden. Emperor Wilhelm orders: should Sweden not receive them, send them through the Eastern front instead

13 April
- Plekhanov arrives at Finland Station

14 April
- Lenin's day in the Swedish backwoods, shielded from biographers (meeting with Parvus?)

15 April
- First day of Orthodox Easter

16 April
- Lenin arrives at Finland Station

17 April
- Lenin, at the Tauride Palace, issues his "April Theses" on consolidating the revolution

21 April
- Chernov, Deutsch, Avksentiev, Savinkov arrive at Finland Station

Introduction:
11 April–24 April

DOCUMENTS — 1

6 April

GEORGE V'S PRIVATE SECRETARY STAMFORDHAM TO FOREIGN MINISTER BALFOUR

. . . He must beg you to represent to the Prime Minister that from all he hears and reads in the press, the residence in this country of the ex-Emperor and Empress would be strongly resented by the public, and would undoubtedly compromise the position of the King and Queen. . . . Buchanan ought to be instructed to tell Milyukov that the opposition to the Emperor and Empress coming here is so strong that we must be allowed to withdraw from the consent previously given to the Russian government's proposal. . . .

DOCUMENTS — 2

13 April

AMBASSADOR IN PETROGRAD BUCHANAN TO FOREIGN MINISTER BALFOUR

. . . I agree with you entirely. . . . It will be far better if the former Emperor does not proceed to England.

[1]

It cropped up suddenly and the Social Democrats in Siberia had to deal with it: Tsereteli, who within the space of two days had become the master of Irkutsk, was asked whether the munitions trains that had arrived from Vladivostok should be allowed through to the front. "Of course," cried Tsereteli, without a moment's thought. "Let them through!" This was the birth of what would, within a few weeks, come to be mocked as "revolutionary defensism."

The war! How the Siberian exiles had discussed it, pondered over it in those years. All were united in their passionate opposition to this mad war, which was especially pointless for Russia, since she was in no need of even the tiniest territorial acquisition. But their hope that the socialist parties of Europe would take up the fight against imperialist tendencies in their own countries had come to nothing: incredibly, it transpired that the working class there felt more kinship with the national policies of their ruling classes than with the international objectives of the proletariat. Only we Russians were free of all that! And we did not want to be as short-sighted, pragmatic, lacking in principle as our brothers in the West. However, there was little hope that this war would come to an end amidst popular uprisings—so which side should we support? From Europe came publications saying that Lenin was openly advocating a "reverse nationalism," wanting and striving for Russia's defeat. But the socialists in Siberia (such as Tsereteli and his party comrades Dan, Voitinsky, Weinstein, Hornstein, and Yermolaev, as well as the like-minded SR man Gotz) took the line of absolute neutrality. (That is to say that they would, of course, have sympathized with the Western democracies, but what if it meant that with them Tsarism would also triumph? That would be terrible. The only hope was that the deep-rooted interests of the Russian bourgeoisie could not be reconciled to an autocracy and would undermine it.)

And suddenly—revolution! And this war was its inheritance. The Russian socialists were suddenly transformed—from a persecuted opposition with no responsibilities they suddenly became the masters of a land in revolution. And that brought about a psychological change, a new attitude toward the war. They had still not formulated it theoretically, but it was suddenly seen in the actions of Tsereteli.

At the 15 June 1907 session of the Second State Duma, when it was already clear that either the arrest of the Social Democrat faction or the dissolution of the Duma was just a few minutes away, Irakli Tsereteli, a young man who had not finished university but was already leading the Moscow student body and the SD faction in the Duma, had, at 11pm, been given the floor. The clean-limbed young Georgian, with a nobility, an elegance to his movements, an independent set of the head and big, dark eyes, leapt to the platform for the last time and, in a voice sonorous with rage, castigated this government of summary courts martial, this celebration of unbounded violence that had subjected the Duma to the bayonet. On that day the vast autocratic State had seemed impregnable and eternal; and our chests, especially his chest, already suffering from consumption, seemed doomed to be crushed.

But now, less than ten years later, news flowed into the capital of Siberia, Irkutsk, to its barely conscious inhabitants and its far more alert exiles, in private telegrams of congratulation—news of the unthinkable and very sudden crumbling of this accursed autocracy. They had been expecting anything at all—except this! Until then the political exiles had only been able to seethe with rage in their private apartments or, in summer, at their dachas, when their groups argued about the tenets of socialism (though they had sometimes published journals, and Gotz had managed to produce a regular Zimmerwaldist newspaper). But now suddenly they were, in just three days, acknowledged as the sole authority here. Tsereteli had taken immediate charge of the Committee of Social Organizations, established an eight-hour working day, addressed the garrison lined up on the square before the city duma, and then had the troops march past him while they bellowed a delighted greeting to the committee and a reluctant one to the commander of the Military District.

You had to live this change to fully grasp it—this change in fortunes after six years in prison (hard labor had been commuted to a prison term on account of Irakli's poor health), followed by four years of exile in Usolye. (The exile, though, had not been too hard and had been fruitful. Sixty versts by train from Irkutsk and you could travel there any day of the week—but it was still permanent, irrevocable exile unless you fled abroad.) And now suddenly this fairytale event, the instant crumbling of the age-old order (but wasn't this success too easily achieved to last?), this state of exhilaration, an unrelenting tension.

But from the very first days there was also an acute anxiety as to the fate of the revolution. There was not in fact an understanding with this yelling mass of soldiery: this was not the working class but a force of nature without defined social ideals—it was not even conscious of what was happening, and it harbored within it the dangers of both anarchy from the left and counterrevolution from the right. The Russian Social Democrats had learned long before, from Marxism, that the revolution could not leap from Russia's semifeudal regime to a socialist order in a single bound: for the moment the most they could possibly achieve was the democratization of the country on the basis of bourgeois economic relationships. But this so sudden bonding with the working class of millions of armed soldiers was luring the socialist parties into the most extreme experiments, to impose the will of the socialist minority on the whole country—possibly leading to an explosion, to counterrevolution and to the disintegration of the revolution.

By the tenth day of this frantic, sleepless Irkutsk existence, Irakli had already begun coughing up blood and had to take to his bed. What a blow, for his health to fail at that most glorious moment of his life. Friends and family cabled calling him back to Georgia but, no, he was desperate to get to the heart of the revolution! The "Second Duma train" set out from Irkutsk to Petersburg, and was met at every station by excited crowds: the people were looking for leaders. But Irakli continued coughing up blood for the whole journey and did not leave the train to make speeches, but stayed in his compartment discussing quietly with members of local soviets.

To outstrip the slowly moving train, they would swoop up the Petrograd Soviet's *Izvestia*, coming from the opposite direction and bringing news ever fresher, like so many quenching gulps of revolution. It was already clear that the authority of the Soviet was far greater than that of the Provisional Government. The trenchant articles in *Izvestia* demanded mistrust of the bourgeoisie, but some articles contradicted others. Who was writing them? Who was printing them? It seemed that the Soviet did not have its own clear program. He longed to arrive as soon as possible, to put an end to this chaos and uncertainty! Now, when the revolution was moving on from negative to positive tasks, what was most needed was a clear program, especially regarding the regime and the war. With joy and pride they read and reread the Manifesto of 27 March, that international word so longed for throughout the war by exhausted masses all over the world. Of course, this did not mean reckless defensism. But neither was the overthrow of the Provisional Government to be desired. And how hard it would now be to explain to the working masses in Petrograd that, notwithstanding the indisputable victory won by the revolution, they must moderate their demands; to show them how important it was to maintain the intangible, elusive influence of technically trained educated circles.

And Tsereteli said as much in a speech on the very first evening of his return to the now unrecognizable Tauride Palace, from which he had been snatched and sent into exile. And afterwards "Old man" Chkheidze gently chided him, for we had not yet spoken out in such blunt terms, had not yet ventured to formulate so clearly the Executive Committee's position on the war.

Not that he was especially old then, though he had welcomed Irakli as a son: he was only fifty-three, but worn out. He was absolutely drained and gave of himself when speaking at public events (during the days of the revolution he even forgot his walking stick). Yet in ordinary conversations he would be circumspect in his views, with none of that revolutionary flint and steel. And he still needed strength for the great future that awaited him: for judging by his position now it was almost certain that Chkheidze would become chairman of the Constituent Assembly, if not the future Russian president.

Tsereteli, like all members of all the Social Democratic factions in all four Dumas, was immediately given a consultative vote in the Executive Committee. And once there he saw within two days that he could carry the Committee with him. Until that time the most prominent figure there had, it seemed, been Nakhamkes-Steklov. But he, it turned out, had been the one publishing the muddle-headed, confused *Izvestia*. And, despite his prominence, on closer examination he was clearly incapable of serious political work. (Kerensky invited Tsereteli to meet him privately in Sokolov's apartment and complained, in some agitation, that Steklov and other left-wing members were systematically discrediting him. But he could not bring himself to take measures against them—he would have liked others to do it.)

The Siberian Zimmerwaldists had arrived with warm feelings toward the Manifesto of 27 March, for in truth it accorded with the principles of the revolution: both the struggle for a democratic peace and, at the same time, the defense of the country. But the nimble, hairsplitting, perceptive homunculus Himmer-Sukhanov, who turned out to be the author of the Manifesto, was now busying himself engineering a volte-face and orienting the EC toward the single objective of peace, with no concern for defense of the country. He had collected signatures supporting this policy, and at the thronged EC session of 3 April the little man, irritated, coldly reprimanded his bulky comrades: the Executive Committee had not fulfilled the duty it had undertaken in the Manifesto and was not fighting the imperialism of the Provisional Government, but instead accommodating itself to the Milyukov-Guchkov war ideology. He did not reject defensism outright, contending rather that any activity with the aim of strengthening the army would divert us from the struggle for peace, and he therefore urged that all our forces should be oriented toward that struggle. Anyone who wanted could pursue defense without us, but we must launch a mass campaign in the army and among the working class against the imperialist policies of the Provisional Government.

In his three days in Petrograd Tsereteli had certainly noted some muddle-headedness in the actions and sudden enthusiasms of the EC, but even so he looked around now in amazement. Were they, without even trying to reach agreement with the Provisional Government, proposing to remove it forthwith? And was no one going to stand up to that corrosive gnome?

But this was not a gnome! Above the smoke-filled EC room hovered the terrorism of the mad internationalist extremists, and the others did not dare raise their voices to argue with them. So Tsereteli, quivering with indignation, with all his Siberian fearlessness and with ten years of prison and exile behind him, rose to his full—and massive—height and began:

"The revolution must not allow its conquests to be crushed by outside forces! In the conditions of the Russian revolution it is wrong to equate defensism with support for imperialism! Who is to defend the country *before* peace is concluded? The defense of our land is not alien to us and it is not an accommodation with the government: it is one of the fundamental tasks of the revolution. Russian democracy has never yet had such power within the country—but that means, as well, accountability to mankind."

He articulated these ideas now with one turn of phrase, now with another, not at all briefly and perhaps not in the best possible form—and he saw the expressions of the EC members change. But he himself did not yet understand the power of the explosion he had set off.

This launched two days of stormy debate. Faced with his impartial Siberian sobriety the Bolsheviks were at a loss, and even the narrow-minded Shlyapnikov, with his crude, working man's hatred of the bourgeoisie, could not find the courage to repeat his call to overthrow the Provisional Government and replace it with a government of workers and peasants. (Time was slipping away—they were losing their opportunity to fuse with the Bolsheviks into a single party! There was no one there to discuss it with—if only Lenin would arrive soon!) And the half-paralyzed Lurie, whose infirm lips, eyelids, and facial expressions always lagged behind his energetic ideas, just patiently explained to the inexperienced Siberian that the whole of Europe was ripe for peace and all that was needed was a bold appeal. Audacity would, as Danton said, save the revolution!

But how loud now were the voices of the sincere defensists, who had until then been kept down! Bogdanov dared to point out that Germany had remained silent, Europe as well, and no one had even reacted to our Manifesto, and they were all fighting! Gvozdev warned that if we remained silent on the subject of defense someone would stir up the soldiers against us. (These two Workers' Group men were particularly sharply criticized by the left for their collaboration with Guchkov.) And Goldman-Lieber made a fiery speech, both revolutionary and defensist, saying the principal danger for our revolution was from Germany. Now old man Chkheidze also inclined toward this view, and Skobelev, easily roused, started talking about a "teaming up of the state and the revolution." And more, and more, and practically everyone who spoke turned out to be pro defense. (And it was impossible now to imagine which of them had conceived and signed the "Order No. 1.") Bramson fervently lamented our rout on the Stokhod (which had just taken place, on the first day of these discussions). Lieutenant Stankevich also joined in, of course: every time the question of peace is raised it demoralizes the army; a soldier is only steadfast in marching and fighting as long as no one puts the possibility of peace into his head, and in European armies this is not tolerated; so how on earth can we dare to launch a "campaign for peace" in the army? The common soldier isn't there to talk about peace; Himmer's resolution is only helpful to the Germans. But even Tsereteli's resolution—with two battle-cries in parallel, defense as well as peace—is already demoralizing the army. (Stankevich was very forthright, perhaps too forthright, and he emitted a whiff of something alien to our socialist party psychology—he was not one of ours, or not entirely so.) As for Chaikovsky, tall, lean, old but well-preserved, from the populist socialist and cooperative movements, he went as far as to heap praise on Tsereteli for his fighting spirit on behalf of the state, and warn that anti-defense prejudice must be banished from the soviets, and that the enemy had occupied ten of our provinces—yet now they were trying to talk us into peace. And the retaking of Armenia, he said, had nothing to do with imperialism—and Russia's need to control the Straits stemmed from its legitimate aspiration to have access to the open sea. Tsereteli even had to defend himself from these panegyrics from the right. No, he told Stankevich, the army had become a factor of politics and could not now be removed from the tasks of the revolution or the peace campaign within it.

But the internationalists were given such a battering that a wider picture began to take shape: a new, rational majority, such as had never been seen before, was forming in the EC and changing its very face.

And it must have been because he sensed this irreversible tide that Nakhamkes came up with a sensational intervention. That butcher, who had thirsted for the blood of the top generals and ranted in *Izvestia* that GHQ commanders should be tried in a court of law and hanged, that prominent, imposing, broad-shouldered, bearded coward now changed tack to side with the majority, declaring himself a supporter of active defense. (The truth is that he was never really left or right but the embodiment of a "case by case" politics. And, seeing the inexorable formation of a new majority, he hurried to become a member.)

So the Bolshevik-Himmerian left front was crumbling. All they could do now was resort to cunning: ask that the resolution should include the struggle for peace as an ideal and, after the vote, feign an understanding that the following day we would be opening up the nationwide campaign for peace and against the imperialist government . . .

No, sir! First we, the Liaison Commission (Tsereteli, so prominent, so important from the first day, was already a member of this too), would negotiate with the government.

This was all Himmer muddying the waters. His position since the very first days of the revolution had been crafty and complicated: to allow bourgeois members into the government, hobble them with fetters manufactured by the left, and immediately set the people against them—but in a way that would not immediately topple them. Such a tangled plan could be maintained in Himmer's head, but in the great mass movements of real life it could not. And for this reason, the game he had been playing in March was already up.

On 5 April, at the magnificent funeral for the martyrs of the revolution, Tsereteli traveled through the million-strong crowd in a vehicle he shared with Vera Figner. She was greeted with such warmth along the whole route that it seemed as if everyone knew her personally: many approached and pressed her hand. Her eyes sparkled with happiness: a liberated people remembered and was paying honor to that comrade-in-arms of Zhelyabov and Perovskaya! Irakli was deeply moved—he had not expected young revolutionary faith and enthusiasm like this from the countless demonstrators!

But what an irony! It was not on any ordinary day but on that particular day of national solemnities, one night after the EC had, with such great difficulty, overturned the internationalists and moved to support national defense—it was on that day that Milyukov gave his brazen interview about the dismemberment of Austria-Hungary, about the expulsion of Turkey from Europe, and about the Straits. Was he mocking the revolutionaries, and the Manifesto of 27 March?

That evening the Liaison Commission met at the Mariinsky Palace, with the government. (Skobelev and Nakhamkes brought thick briefcases with them, but they were stuffed with newspapers and useless documents.) Tsereteli studied the faces and mannerisms of the ministers—he had met none of them before. He decided they were, for all their surface amiability, circumspect underneath. There was nothing to be done about it—they were representatives of the bourgeoisie and he would have to be on his guard. He was struck by the kindly Prince Lvov, who appeared to be totally uncomprehending. What *war aims* could we be discussing, he wondered, when the Germans are on our land? And who in the world doubts the democratic nature of our policies? Tsereteli, although a new boy here, tried immediately to puncture the egotism of that class: how was it possible not to take the mood of the people into account? If there was unrest in the factories or in the army it was only due to a lack of clarity regarding the aims of the war: everyone feared the war might be prolonged for the sake of aims that were foreign to them. The Soviet could only exert influence on the tired masses if it instilled into them the confidence that any new victims would die only to save the country, not to conquer new territories—and the government should publish a declaration on this matter, for then it would be easier too for the Soviet to mobilize workers and soldiers to defend the revolution against an outside enemy. Tereshchenko and the energetic Nekrasov said in response that they were happy to receive the Soviet's support for national defense. And then it seemed to Tsereteli that, by saying this, Milyukov's cabinet colleagues were already distancing themselves from him (as Kerensky put it, and publicly, the following day). But Milyukov launched into the same old song, with professorial aplomb: Russia, he said, needed to maintain the trust of its allies, and they might interpret a declaration such as the EC was demanding as the beginning of a move toward separate action on our part; and the foreign minister could not take on himself the responsibility for any such act.

In a word, it was clear that he was not in agreement with defense alone—he wanted to grab something for Russia.

But surely the ministers had to see that, logically, they could not stand their ground without an agreement with the Soviet? And Tsereteli, with new force stemming from his conviction: we are certainly not demanding steps that could lead to a rupture with the Allies. Russia must declare that she has renounced plans for any conquests and then go to her allies with a proposal to revise their plan of action. Even if we cannot persuade them by diplomacy, we shall have some effect on them through a press campaign.

Tsereteli was inspired by this vision of a way out. This was a way—unexpected, unusual, honorable—for Europe to escape from its unprecedented war!

Skobelev joked, not unintelligently:

"Was it not you, Pavel Nikolaevich, who, when speaking against Stürmer from the Duma platform last year, explained to us how difficult, how extraordinarily tricky and tough it had been to persuade England to acknowledge our claims on Constantinople? So why do you think they'd be so piqued if we renounced those claims now?"

Milyukov countered with a reproach: the European socialists were not responding to the Manifesto.

But he was not after the truth—it was only a subterfuge. "Right!" exclaimed Tsereteli, knowing how convincing he was with eyes blazing. "Right. Let's assume we don't fare well in Europe—but still the whole country will pull together, and that is our greatest strength!"

And now Guchkov, who had remained silent, mistrustful and hostile, said:

"For the sake of army unity, I agree."

Shingarev's endorsement came from the heart: Your faith is infectious! I agree—as long as you can unite the masses behind our national defense. But can you guarantee that?

He could not answer on the strength of ardor alone. Of course no one could give guarantees in advance where millions of soldiers were concerned. (Especially when we ourselves had already ruined things—only better not say this aloud.) But the inclination of the majority among revolutionary democrats was to support it.

But Milyukov alone was still refusing to budge, unmoved, uninspired. And when he dug his heels in, he could not be dislodged.

It was decided that the government would discuss the matter once more and try to formulate a declaration.

Two days later the Liaison Commission went to the Mariinsky Palace again. Milyukov sat, impenetrable, while Lvov read the government's draft declaration. It seemed right, almost, the tone was right—but . . . no. It avoided any clear answer on the principal point. "No nation's patrimony to be taken from it"—that was too vague: whose patrimony was Galicia? Armenia? Maybe even Constantinople? So you must say, clearly, *Russia renounces the seizure of foreign territories*—full stop.

Milyukov was immovable: he blocked them all. They had, he said, already made the maximum possible concessions. And as for the point at which a direct approach is made to the Allies, the foreign minister must reserve that decision for himself.

Fine, he could agree—it would even be better to start with a declaration, to the people, to increase enthusiasm here at home. But you must *clearly renounce* territorial conquests.

Just when had Milyukov acquired all the techniques of a diplomat? Not a direct approach, but one arrived at by a roundabout route: you interpret the text your way and the Foreign Ministry in its own way.

None of this doublespeak! No interpreting! We must change the direction of our foreign policy in full view of the nation! *Without* that correction the declaration is unsatisfactory—and we'll make it known that the Soviet's and the Provisional Government's views are unreconcilable!

A gaping chasm lay between them. The majority of ministers—and even Guchkov—understood that, for the sake of unity, they would have to give in. But their bourgeois minds were paralyzed by an ingrained conviction that the old war aims had been legitimate.

They argued and argued. Around midnight Chkheidze was called to the telephone. He returned, the life drained from his face, his legs barely able to carry him, and sat down again at the meeting. Tsereteli, sitting next to him, asked in a whisper what had happened. His wife had called. Stasik, their only son, had been playing with a gun at a friend's house and had injured himself, seriously. "Well go home!" But Chkheidze, his gaze wandering, retorted that the fate of the revolution was being decided. How could he leave?

But . . . his son??

So he stayed, stayed at the meeting—his hair sparse and straggly around a bald patch, an untamed growth of bristles on his cheeks and round his lips, and an unkempt beard—and stayed till the end, trying to participate and complaining to no one!

Who would have thought it, such iron restraint from a tired old man!

They finished at two in the morning, though still without agreement. Irakli took his fellow countryman home, for his arms and legs had grown very weak.

On the staircase they met the stretcher bringing home the lifeless body of his son.

He had died during that final hour of the meeting. Nikolai Semyonovich slumped over the boy's forehead.

The following day the Executive Committee decided unanimously, with no debate, to consider the government's declaration unsatisfactory.

A great, unbridgeable rift had opened up. The immortal February revolution was splitting in two!

At that very moment the telephone rang—and Prince Lvov informed them that the government had accepted the amendment and he would send it over.

It arrived. It was entirely, word for word, the same text that had been rejected—what an obstinate fellow, that Milyukov!—but after "No nation's patrimony to be taken from it" the Prince had added by hand in pencil—the pencil none too sharp—"no forcible seizure of foreign territories."

They had wrung it out of them!

What a shake-up there would be in the views of the world's fanatical, imperialist bourgeoisie! It was 9 April: the *first* time any warring power had renounced all seizure of lands!

DOCUMENTS — 3

FROM THE PROVISIONAL GOVERNMENT TO THE PEOPLE

17 April 1917

. . . By decision of the Provisional Government dated 31 March full immunity from prosecution is granted to anyone drafted into military service up through that date, but who have evaded serving . . . and equally to soldiers and sailors who are currently on the run or on unauthorized leave, except those who fled to the enemy—as long as they voluntarily join up with their units by 28 May. All such persons will be freed from judicial measures and penalties, even if they had, prior to 18 March, committed deceptive actions, attempted self-injury . . . intentional damage, squandering or misplacing the public property or arms issued to them. . . . Anyone who fails to appear by 28 May will answer according to the full extent of the law.

. . . to all citizens of Free Russia—with an appeal to aid in the directing of such persons to their units. . . . Let those, whose husbands, sons, and brothers are honorably serving in army ranks, come to the aid of local authorities and help them to gather up. . . . Let shame come upon anyone who, on account of faint-heartedness . . .

Prime Minister Prince *Lvov*
War Minister *Guchkov*

[2]

In the big cathedrals they were also celebrating the Easter midnight service that year in the open air, on the parvises. At Our Lady of Kazan and at St. Isaac's they held, as usual, splendid pontifical services—with a congregation of aristocrats, members of the diplomatic corps, and even of the new government. And you could get into St. Isaac's this year without a pass. But Vera was not tempted to go, for, having grown up in Moscow, she could not come to love the Petersburg cathedrals—her soul was not at ease there.

So she attended the Easter matins in her own church, St. Simeon's, with her nurse and, responding to the joy of the service, prayed to the Lord to give her strength in her sadness.

Before, she had thought it would be hard to make up her mind. To make up her mind to refuse Mikhail Dmitrievich.

But no—the hard thing was living with that refusal, afterwards.

Yes, the human race is too weak to live without that lantern to light our way: God knows everything we do and even think and, after death, so too do the people on whom we have wished ill. And we cannot hide; we cannot hide.

But there again, Vera would probably not have found the strength to make that decision if everything around her had not seemed to be unraveling. Together with the long-awaited, boundless joy of the revolution something else had also burst in, treading on its heels, even pushing it aside; a disorderly, reckless, permissive, shameless **now everything is allowed**. (But why? How come . . .?)

And that was another reason why, at this moment, Vera could not possibly seize her happiness, steal it from *those two*, even with them putting up almost no opposition.

At this moment particularly she could not, in the midst of this new current.

But that was nonsense—it was nothing to do with that.

In the heavenly radiance of the singing at midnight matins, Vera seemed to be plucked from the earth and swept higher, beyond herself, as if to join the angelic host, and sensed that she was approaching this decision rationally, willingly, and even joyfully.

Indeed, there was no other way.

People do find the strength even to renounce a free life altogether, for the sake of their soul—of their spirit.

And so it was with Vera: the grief of that renunciation would remain, maybe forever.

And for *him* . . . her decision would bring him no relief.

Did she make the decision on his behalf?

But there was no other way.

In some areas there was, in the streets, a great deal of shooting into the air that Easter night—by soldiers or drunks or pranksters—and there was panic among the faithful with their candles.

The Neva ice had broken during Holy Week. Snow-fringed ice floes drifted past, the left bank was now clear but ice still clung to the right. With a sharp wind blowing in from the sea, excess water was flooding in and breaking the ice. And the temperature was settling back to freezing at night. But, just in time for Easter, the warm days blew in, the snow rapidly melted, and water poured off the dirty streets. (And for the first time the melted snow made the water supply muddy—something had gone wrong with the purification at the central pumping station.)

On Bright Monday night there had even been some warm rain and by Bright Tuesday it was almost summery. Vera and a colleague went off in light coats for a walk in the park in Lesnoi and heard chaffinches there and larks, already back after the winter.

Just an ordinary *walk*. As if her heart were not held in an iron clamp.

But both there and back—through a totally unswept, uncleaned Petrograd (only on Nevsky Prospect had they started sweeping), with an overall layer of rubbish in some places and, in others, piles of it not collected, but with red flags everywhere—they had to go on foot. People hung in clusters on the trams and hundreds thronged around the stops—there were no queues, just crowds—and men, both soldiers and civilians, rushed to scramble on, jostling, shoving the women aside. The militia with white armbands stood, indolent, nearby. There was nothing they could do, nor did they want to!

The people in charge and the newspapers were already grumbling that too much time had been lost since the revolution and that now this inopportune Easter holiday was interrupting the tempo we needed everywhere. *Speech* urged citizens to take the initiative and shorten their own holiday at this inconvenient moment. But all the same the typesetters stopped printing newspapers for a few days, mail was not delivered, and letters from Moscow were taking two weeks to arrive. It was rumored that millions remained unsorted at the post office.

Vera was fasting this year on the fifth week of Lent—but a special kind of pleasure came her way for four days starting on Palm Saturday: she was given a guest ticket to the Kadet party congress at the Mikhailovsky Theater. And what a relief it was, to take leave of her inner burdens, to forget them, as if they did not exist.

It was all very festive! People said it was the troops of Russian liberalism on parade. Everyone of any celebrity in Russia was there, many of them in the presidium, and almost all the ministers, but they were late and then arrived separately—Milyukov, Manuilov, then Shingarev, each greeted with a flurry of applause, interrupting the speaker. (Only Maklakov came in unnoticed and took a modest seat below the journalists' boxes.) The congress delegates (three hundred and something—for some towns had not been able to send anyone—plus about fifty from the Central Committee itself) were seated in the yellow seats in the stalls, the Petrograd party members in dress circle boxes, the luxury boxes were crammed with journalists and in the upper circle, between the rows of light fittings, were guests. There was even a sentry at the theater entrance (but he was alone and just for show—he never stopped anyone coming in). The lobby was decorated in Kadet party green, and students, both boys and girls with green armbands, checked tickets and showed people to their seats. Most of the delegates were mature in years, greying, with bald patches and the fine, respectable faces of lawyers, doctors, civil servants, zemstvo men.

To open the congress, up stepped the strapping, bull-headed Prince Pavel Dolgorukov, but much of the general enthusiasm evaporated when he started reading from his notes with a stammer. First everyone stood to honor the memory of those who had given their lives for the people's freedom. Then—for the first time in the history of Kadet congresses!—Dolgorukov proposed three cheers for the army and a telegram to General Alekseev. Then Vinaver was elected congress chairman and he read out more telegrams, to the Allies and to President Woodrow Wilson. And he read out a telegram from "the party's Nestor," Petrunkevich (who could not be there in person but asked that his voice be counted in support of the democratic republic—well, well!). And telegrams were immediately read out from the congress to Petrunkevich and Korolenko. Then they gave the floor to the slight, genteel Kokoshkin for the first report—which had the delicate mission of demonstrating why, when a constitutional monarchy had remained in the Kadets' program for twelve years, and rightly so, the time had now come to install a republic and, what's more, a democratic republic.

And Kokoshkin gave this demonstration: the Kadets had kept the monarchy before only because of the political conditions of the time in terms of the understanding of the masses, but now this symbol was no longer of any use to the population, since the monarchy had, during the war, discredited itself by standing against the Fatherland. And this most decisive change of program was easily approved on the spot by a storm of applause and then by the raising of delegates' cards. Professor Lossky even went as far as to say that now even the Octobrists would have to become republicans, but bourgeois republicans, whereas we are democrats and, if you like, even socialists. (A frisson—maybe fear—ran through the hall.) But we reject social revolution: we, as Fabians, are for a society of evolutionary socialism. And the fiery Mandelstam from Moscow, always such a leftist, declared that the division of the Kadets into left and right was over, that the party was henceforth united and that it was time, for the sake of accuracy, to call it "republican-democratic," and that it was an utterly erroneous prejudice to think the creation of a republic presupposes that the people need to have lived a long cultural and political life.

Two months earlier the Kadets had been saying nothing of the kind, but now, yes, it was apparently beyond doubt. And the tall, stately Prince Evgeni Trubetskoy (it was comical to hear Manuilov call him "Comrade Trubetskoy")—his features noble, his fresh complexion belying his over fifty years, deep in thought as if alone, even on the platform addressing the hall—also maintained that Russia's form of government was already decided, by life itself, and that all they had to think about was how to shore up the republic against the military threat and against anarchy.

But what then would be the role of the Constituent Assembly? There may have been any number of brilliant orators in the party, but it was Kokoshkin that they sent up again with a report on the Constituent Assembly—where, in that fragile body, was there so much resolution? And he explained persuasively how complex the process of formulating election principles and regulations was, and that the elections themselves would be even more complex in a country unprepared for them—and that was no four-month job. So they had to be patient.

On the second day of the congress there were many local reports, all similar in nature, about how exactly power had passed into the hands of the people in some places. But it was Rodichev who really shook up, fired up the congress. He mounted the platform already in full flow, ecstatic: "Centuries from now the nations of the Earth will remember 1917!" And, his voice thundering, his pince-nez gleaming in the light of the chandeliers, he carried his whole audience with him, not giving them time to mull over his individual phrases. The only reason the enemy had not reached Petrograd was that the English fleet had come to our aid, and how many English and French bones were buried at Gallipoli, opening the way for us to reach Constantinople, and we must not dare renege on obligations to our allies. "Russia is with us! Do not be thrown off course by the cries of overbold elements! Know how to counter them! Future centuries are watching us!"

And **how** he spoke! The hall was stunned. Vinaver shook Rodichev's hand: "Russia is proud of you! You have captured the hearts of thousands!" And, at Trubetskoy's suggestion, the congress resolved to publish millions of copies of the speech. (But, strangely, when Vera read the newspaper reports of that speech the following morning, it was long, with few, if any, ideas. Such is the power of oratory!)

There was an unexpected hitch when the Orenburg delegate had an objection: "We Russian Muslims love Turkey and we don't want her destroyed," and if the party did not change its view regarding the Straits, then the Muslims would turn away from the Kadet party. There was puzzlement among the presidium, but who came up to reply? The resourceful and uncompromising Kokoshkin again! Islam, he insisted, had nothing to do with it. Mecca itself had revolted against Turkey and the Straits were now under the control not of Turkey but of Germany, and if we refused to redraw the map of Europe, refused the pressing needs of our grain trade, our people's verdict would be a harsh one.

Politics was certainly not the main thing in Vera's life. But there, amidst the stucco and velvet of that hall, below that ceiling with its cupids, the political atmosphere was heating up as never before, as if those seated there needed no oxygen, no birds on green boughs—they needed nothing but the triumph of Kadet green, of their color. So many brilliant minds, and all collected in a single hall at the same time. It could hardly have crossed her mind that these were all men who actually chose female companions for themselves and who were not at all indifferent to women—no, it was as if their intellects alone glided like swans through the dense, electric air, and whatever the subject of the speech it was always interesting. And the main thing was that the decisions made in this hall would constitute the fate of Russia for the immediate future.

On the third day Vinaver addressed the topic of authority and humbly thanked the Petrograd garrison for the revolution. We must sustain this revolutionary zeal, he said, and for its sake we must reconcile ourselves to some temporary disorder during the transition period. We must maintain our vigor and fend off all threats from the forces of counterrevolution! This is the motto of our principal tactic of the moment. But the Soviet of Workers' Deputies is overstepping the boundaries of criticism and beginning to interfere directly in the functions of government. Our Central Committee has twice told the Soviet, both in writing and in person, that its "orders" are sowing the seeds of a discord bordering on madness and crime. And anarchy is already flaring up in various parts of the country. Public opinion must raise its head and speak out more loudly.

But people immediately, and confidently, started correcting Vinaver. Prince Shakhovskoy, thin, gloomy, with a pointed beard, said that by proclaiming the republic we were actually moving closer to our neighbors on the left and differences of opinion were melting away; and their minimum program exactly coincided with our current program and they were very reasonable people. And we should form a bloc with them. And even the peasants, those amorphous strata of society, were in essence no great distance from Kadet principles, but the parties of the left were recruiting supporters from that group more rapidly and we also had to organize some propaganda. Ignorance reigned in rural areas and they already wanted to divide up the land. The only thing we could not accept was the Bolsheviks' maximalism, but even the Bolsheviks were becoming more reasonable by the day. And the impulsive Mandelstam spoke again, saying how close we were to the parties of the left and how immeasurable the virtues of the Soviet of Workers' Deputies.

But the argument was interrupted. At that moment Milyukov appeared, accompanied by loud ovations—and Mandelstam, his constant left-wing challenger, greeted him as a dear and wise leader, and this elicited even more delight from the hall.

A great ovation too for Nekrasov—who was young but also growing into a leadership role. Proudly, resonantly, he vowed that the Provisional Government might perish but it would never surrender. (Ovation.)

And Milyukov again, in response, declared that on 12 March the fate of the overthrow had hung by a thread, but that even outside the Progressive bloc people with statesman-like minds had been found, that the Soviet of Workers' Deputies was showing an extraordinary facility for organizing the masses, and that that offered the best possible hope for the future. And the

Soviet would soon be supplemented with people with experience from abroad, and they would help in our uphill struggle.

It was then resolved that a monument be set up in Moscow to the immortal Muromtsev, and that the remains of Herzenstein be transferred from Finland to Russia. And the provincial delegates thanked the Central Committee for the policy it had adopted, and the Central Committee thanked the provinces for their support, and Vinaver thanked the ministers individually and then the whole congress and especially the Kadet youth—and so what if our enemies say we are changing our program as we go: only the dead never budge.

And when he had brought the congress to a close people did not disperse for a good while, but shouted congratulations to the Central Committee, the congress organizers, and the ministers.

But of all the speakers on all four days Vera was most affected by Prince Evgeni Trubetskoy. He had spoken maybe four times, once each day, so unlike his customary reserve. Once it was about the republic. Another time it was about the revolution in general, on a philosophical level. Our revolution, he had said, has a rare spiritual beauty. The Great French Revolution saw Jacobinism and the guillotine, while we have completely abolished the death penalty! And this brings the Kadets closer to their neighbors of the left. And while there is in the country a single, unified frame of mind, a single, unified inspiration, why should we not unite all the revolutionary parties? That is the very essence: our revolution is not based on class, it is not bourgeois—it is owned by the whole nation, and this national character of the Russian revolution is seen even more clearly in the provinces than in the center, and it is worth taking a trip out and immersing oneself for a while. (He had just visited Kaluga province.) And he spoke once more, this time saying that it was not at all hard to expose the demagogy of the Bolshevik slogans. We must explain to the peasants that the expropriation and distribution of land without payment would attract large numbers of newcomers into the countryside—workers, domestic servants, petty clerks—and the peasants would get not more land but less.

And, based on his recent impressions of Kaluga, he issued a particularly significant warning:

"The backwaters of our rural areas, untouched by education, do not express their thoughts very clearly. Perhaps this is also because today going against the general current is not always without its dangers. They beat about the bush, but we have to listen closely, so as to anticipate any problems. I imagine the problems may not be monarchist sentiments so much as monarchist doubts: how are we to live now, without the Tsar, without the police . . .? There is scary talk of the 'red cock' rising in the countryside—but in actual fact country people would far rather have order than violence."

But in the general hubbub, the rapid succession of events, the diversity of the congress, these words flashed past as if unheard and no one referred to them after that. But Vera was very receptive to his ideas. Because our whole future was, she now saw, in the countryside, in what country people did. Because of the speaker's voice, his noble, thoughtful, undemonstrative way of speaking. And also because he was, simply, the idol of the librarians on Aleksandrinsky Square, a man of acknowledged genius, a philosopher—there were few alive to match him.

A few days later he came into the library again and it happened to be Vera who went to get the books he had ordered. They stood, sorting them out at the end of the counter, while two colleagues a little farther away tried to listen, so interesting was Evgeni Trubetskoy to everyone there. He was very well-disposed toward Vera—though when he was too deep in thought he might not recognize her, or might take her for someone else, or might take cover behind an absent-minded, meaningless smile. It was said of Prince Evgeni's late father that he was so distracted that he would sometimes not blow out the candle by his daughter's bed but blow at his daughter instead. It ran in the family—that family of philosophers. But this time the prince was absolutely intelligible and attentive. Vera reminded him of his splendid words at the congress, about the country people. He looked at her trustingly, his thoughtful blue eyes gazing at her for almost a full minute. Perhaps he did not see her?

But he did see her. He said, suddenly, "I myself had not expected the rural situation to make such a deep impression on me. It's not my Kaluga trip that's affecting me now, but my childhood memories. It's strange, you know, but this month, this time of great events, it's as if I've been living more in the past. I . . ." Was he hesitating? "I came to Petrograd for sessions of the State Council, but then came the revolution. And in the Hotel de France, on Morskaya, to the music of machine-gun fire . . . proclaiming the birth of the new Russia . . . I was for some reason immersed in contemplation of the old Russia, of the dear departed . . ." He closed his eyes. When he opened them, they were even more blue, deeper. "Our link with the departed must always be preserved. And I, in my room, to the sound of shooting, with all the hullabaloo, wrote for two days without stopping, recording my recollections."

Lucky he wasn't at the Astoria, thought Vera.

"I started with my earliest childhood, with my grandfathers, my grandmothers. My grandfather Pyotr Ivanych's Akhtyrka was a magnificent Empire-style estate, for show, not for living. We lived crowded into just one little wing of it—but what a palace, overlooking a dammed-up section of the Vorya, an island, boats . . . and what a park! A century old, with arbors and little bridges with birch-wood handrails. Akhtyrka has remained in my heart like a symphony. . . . Every path in the park, every clearing, every bend in the river seems to *make a sound*. Each place has its individual motif, and the musical form is inseparable from the visual."

Vera stood motionless, so that he would not stop, so that he would say more, so that no one would interrupt.

"And in the reception rooms hung a large number of dark, smoke-blackened, not even well painted portraits of my ancestors, sporting medals and sashes or else with hunting dogs, in gilt frames. And I could not bear them. And after my grandfather died I shot an arrow into the portrait of Emperor Aleksandr Pavlovich in purple robes and with a polite, but sour, smile."

Evgeni Nikolaevich's dark brown hair was combed smooth, not a hair out of place, his little beard and moustache met, forming elegant curves, and the whole of his aristocratic face was very calm, unfurrowed by any grimace, any irritation—like an open field for his thoughts (although Vera had once seen him bent double, laughing helplessly).

"After the abolition of serfdom, my grandfather lived another ten years, but he was in a state of shock. And on our patronal festival in July he would arrange a ceremonial sortie onto the great portico, sit in an armchair, and watch as locals rushed up the drive. The boys and young lads scaled soap-smeared poles, trying to reach harmonicas, caps, and red belts, and slid down one after the other without reaching them, until some quick-witted ones quietly rubbed their hands with resin. When all those presents were gone, they started distributing beads, headscarves, and ribbons to the women and girls. They would form a neat line, coming forward one by one to kiss grandfather's hand, which lay on a cushion, and receive their present from the other. But the gifts were only for his former serfs, so two of the former wet-nurses were stationed by the queue, allowing only their own through, and sending outsiders on their way.

"Must it not have been degrading—for freed peasants?" ventured Vera.

His expression was tender, pained.

"As for us children, we were up on the portico, flinging gingerbread into the crowd and laughing as the boys rolled around in the sand to reach it. And . . . I deliberately aimed the gingerbread at their heads . . ."

DOCUMENTS — 4

APPEAL OF THE PROVISIONAL GOVERNMENT

17 April 1917

Soldiers! We have overthrown the old regime, for it was an arbitrary and violent reign . . . no order can prevail where someone else's rights are being trampled at every turn . . .

Now such order is especially necessary on the railways. And yet, from many railways, reports are arriving of lawless and violent actions that groups of soldiers permit themselves to take against passengers and railway personnel. Windows are broken, reserved seats in passenger carriages are commandeered, the carriages themselves are being overfilled to such an extent that their springs buckle and their axles crack. Personnel are threatened and made to perform actions at direct odds with rail safety, and there was an incident where the engineer, under threat of bloody reprisal, was forced to set course for a washed-out section of track.

Soldiers! You must clearly understand. . . . Show yourselves to be fully worthy of the freedom you have obtained . . .

Prime Minister Prince *Lvov*
War Minister *Guchkov*
Transport Minister *Nekrasov*

[3]

Living by the precepts of our spiritual heroes—Chernyshevsky, Dobrolyubov—in years gone by we could only screw up our eyes before the luminous vision of our future in a socialist Russia. And the approaching joy of that transfigured world was so very much greater than our, your, my life that no thought of the self ever wormed its way in: no "what role will I get then?" "what job exactly?"

But now suddenly that distant Ideal had arrived! It was already, confidently, advancing across Russia! And now the question arose quite naturally: what kind of position shall I occupy in this new order? Now, in this long-awaited time of fervent national joy under the wing of the Revolution, it is so much more vexing if your comrades reject you and do not allow you the influence on events commensurate with your abilities as a leader of the far left.

When we study history, it all seems so simple: a resolute individual arrives and takes power, as if power were sitting waiting for him. But when you reach into real life and stretch out a pair of hands that are by no means weak, to take that power—it won't come! It will not be taken!

What's the problem? What special methods, what special qualities are needed?

In earlier ages you needed a mastery of cold steel, which meant you needed strong shoulders and must ride a horse. But now here you are with broad shoulders and they're of no use. Perhaps theoretical ideas and the ability to expound them quickly and clearly? But history shows us that we do not need to master these personally—it's enough to have such a person nearby, someone like Himmer.

So what is it? Timing? Divining the right moment for every step, when to move a short way, when to cover more ground? But what moment could have been better than 12 March, going into the not yet created Executive Committee of an as yet unborn Soviet of Workers' Deputies? And leading negotiations with the future government—and placing a proprietorial hand on the table in the guise of approval: "Exist!" . . . but on our terms. What higher post could there be—not the government, but above the government, for it was you who created that government and allowed it to exist? Since the very first day, what position could possibly have been stronger? In the whole of Russia only Kerensky could compete, but he was not supported by the Soviet. So surely the moment had not been missed?

Key positions? But you did have the best positions, the two very strongest: you have in your hands, yours alone, *Izvestia*—the face of the Soviet, even more visible all over the country than the Soviet itself—and the Liaison Commission, the lever that really steered the government. And you were there, one of the five EC members, and yours was the foremost voice there, disdainfully dictating to ministers. The Executive Committee kept expanding, so a bureau had to be elected, with seven members—including you.

And it was *you* who came up with the now celebrated formula for support of the Provisional Government, "insomuch-insofar." Someone had to read out the Manifesto to all the peoples—and it was you who read it out from the high dais. Someone had to receive ever more delegations from the front, without counting the hours, and to personify for them the whole Soviet—and that person was you.

But would power come to you? No, it would not.

Either, in the Liaison Commission, Chkheidze or even that ninny Skobelev would object in front of ministers that he had given his personal opinion, not that of the Soviet. Or someone would challenge him in front of military delegations. How could they be made to fall into line? Nakhamkes did not know. He could not do it.

And there was Lieutenant Stankevich, a complete stranger to the proletariat, who had pushed his way into the EC and would take well nigh every opportunity for nitpicking criticism and started finding fault with *Izvestia*. And it was not just him: a whole intrigue was developing against *Izvestia*.

He grew wary. He had to think about strengthening his position. But just then, as if on cue, Tsereteli arrived. And that was a catastrophe, a turning point for the whole Executive Committee. Thanks to his earlier Duma fame, Tsereteli walked straight into both the EC and the Liaison Commission without need of an election (and it had already become cramped there with six members, so someone would have to be pushed out) and he started talking everywhere in such a rich, confident voice as if he had been a member of everything from the first day, as if he had known and foreseen all these situations in advance.

And Steklov-Nakhamkes realized that he had allowed those happy weeks to slip away—and with them the chance to take charge of Soviet power and then maybe the whole of Russia. He had let it slip. What had he lacked? Sharp wits? Daring? *How* is power taken? Well just go and try.

Does it need genius? True, you're not a genius. We can't all be geniuses. It's very hard to remain on a peak.

This is when he regretted that he had, all these years, been vacillating, *unaffiliated*—neither Menshevik nor Bolshevik, nor anything else. All his life he had stood apart, never joined groups, and he had felt this gave him freedom. But now it turned out that he had no support, no party colleagues, nor even any friends.

And along with Tsereteli had come Gotz as well. Then Dan. And Liber. And the addition of more and more leaders was, bit by bit, squeezing out the original leader, Steklov.

Tsereteli suddenly launched a polemic against Himmer on the question of war and peace, and with an asperity that was not customary in the Executive Committee. He was moving fearlessly toward a rapid split between the center and the left! And the opportunists on the right came to his support. And what about Steklov? Was he in danger of being marooned with an ousted minority? That would have put an end to his political career. And he decided on the spot to take a giant step before the ice floes split apart entirely, to step onto the bigger one. So he supported Tsereteli's view that we had to strengthen our defense, reinforce the army.

He had never yet been infected with the syphilis of social patriotism. But now he had exposed himself to it.

He had made a jump for it, but it looked like the confident step of an unhesitating individual who really knew his mind. (Though in actual fact a great deal of uncertainty had stolen into that corpulent frame.)

He was counting on this step to maintain his place in the leadership group, with Chkheidze and Tsereteli. But no! Yet again he was let down by that curse of non-affiliation. They had to select the ten members of the presidium for the All-Russian Conference of Soviets (the Conference, as a supreme parliament of Russia, was needed to shore up the Petrograd Soviet)—and from the Executive Committee leadership came Chkheidze and Skobelev, from the Mensheviks Tsereteli, Bogdanov, and the Muscovite Khinchuk, from the SRs Gotz—and who did Steklov represent? No one. And he did not get in. (And whoever gets nominated gets confirmed. What free elections could there be in that hall? What did this crowd understand?)

In that month of revolution, this had been his first major failure. Not being elected to the front row. (Throughout the last weeks he had thought that at the first Congress of the Soviets they would elect him chairman of the All-Russian Executive Committee. That would be like the President of Russia. And the present Conference was leading up to that Congress. But now . . .)

A main speaker? But on the subject of war and peace it was Tsereteli again, who was already leading the pack. Only the policy toward the Provisional Government was recognized as being Steklov's as of right: so that would be his report. And that report was now his principal battering ram. He worked on it, mostly at night, composing hard-hitting phrases! At the Conference, from among the delegates' seats (he had not managed to get into a box in the White Hall), his bulky presence observed all the comedies of the first day: the ovation to the Grandmother, her vacuous speech, how she "entered this temple of Freedom," and how they carried her from the hall on her chair. Half a day was lost at the funeral of Chkheidze's son, and in the evening serious debate was again interrupted by Kerensky—who leapfrogged every queue, every rule—and what pathetic drivel he came out with: "I am confident that our confidence and my confidence," "I entered the Provisional Government not because I wanted to be there but to carry out the will of those who sent me." But he, the swine, "did not want to be" in the Provisional Government only because he feared his colleagues in the Soviet and most of all he feared Nakhamkes, who sensed it: he even avoided meeting him in the corridor. But he was shameless—a real Khlestakov, easily scrambling over or sliding round obstacles, an example to us all! And now he could not move without accolades being heaped on him. He had even claimed the Grandmother as his prize, and wove into his speech at the station the fact that he had traveled to the Lena, practically to where she was exiled. She had never even seen him, but "Dear friend Kerensky," she had said, "we love you and shall die together with you!" (Given her age, this promise was not worth a lot.)

This was exactly the kind of light touch that was lacking in the heavyweight Nakhamkes.

Thanks to the multitude of delegates from the front, the Conference of Soviets began convincingly in favor of continuing the war (he had been right to jump to the other ice floe), with no one arguing except a few Bolsheviks. But not even the Bolsheviks then dared explain clearly what they did want, and Kamenev and Nogin both said there would be a worldwide uprising of the proletariat and the war would come to an end. But what if there wasn't?? This omission was noticed by the whole Conference, including the simple lads in army greatcoats.

But it was also quite clear that Tsereteli was unduly exaggerating our "victory over the bourgeoisie" and the unity now achieved with the government. He was even giving his argument an opportunistic slant: the government itself, he said, had now taken a decisive step along the path indicated by democracy and was renouncing its imperialist ambitions. But, *wer "A" sagt, muss auch "B" sagen.*[1] And now Steklov was left with no other line to take at the Conference than to support Tsereteli: yes, a defeat at the front would be the end of the Russian revolution. He spoke in the discussion—five minutes, since he was a rank-and-file speaker, not a leader or a main speaker, but he said what he needed to in the five minutes: that Tsereteli had developed the arguments brilliantly and that it was at *our* prompting that the government had taken a very significant step, while Kamenev's resolution was no more than a general outline of internationalist principles, and did not provide an answer to the burning questions of this particular moment.

Could he count on having at least neutralized Tsereteli where *his own* report was concerned?

The leadership of the EC was so rushed and so overloaded that they did not check in advance what the main speakers would be saying, nor even

1. He who says "A" must also say "B" (German).

their main points, and this is what Steklov had been counting on. And now his non-affiliation came to his aid: he didn't have to tell anyone his ideas. However . . . the Executive Committee had been thinking ahead, and for each principal report it had ratified in advance the future resolution that we would be putting to the Conference. And they had voted through a resolution that the government would "by and large" merit support "insomuch-insofar"—Steklov's own formula! But with it they had tied Steklov's hands. This resolution was not at all what he wanted to say or how he wanted to place the emphasis. Now he had to decide: was he going to tell them everything he had been burning to tell?

And he decided he would. The resolution tied his hands, but in Russia, in Petrograd, there was no balance: the government was no good—it could not stand on its own two feet. The resolution tied his hands, but he could construct his speech with such passion that the Conference itself would reject the resolution and charge forward in the wake of the speaker! The speech itself, and the full extent of this maneuver, were under his control. Then it would all depend on how successful he was. But he would shake them up, both the hall and the Executive Committee! Nakhamkes did not need to fabricate his passion: it had never abated throughout the whole war, seething within that broad chest as he lay low under the temporary guise of purchasing officer for the Union of Towns. It was that passion that had, not long before, guided his pen as he wrote for *Izvestia* the articles "GHQ, center of counterrevolution" and "Rebel generals." This passion furrowed his brow when anyone so much as mentioned the names Guchkov or Milyukov in his presence. He believed, indeed he knew, that counterrevolutionary plots were being ceaselessly hatched in every military HQ, every cellar, and in the very heart of the government.

So was he now, after Tsereteli's presentation saying the government was being kind and cooperative, going to attack it and proclaim it the enemy?

He had to!

The EC would be furious! But also powerless, if he could carry the hall with him.

It would be the speech of his life. He could take revenge there and then, and regain the leadership.

It was only by recreating those heady days of mid-March that he could be seen at his full stature. It occurred to him that he could show the assembly that scrap of paper, little more than wrapping paper, on which, in big letters, he had written his historic nine points for the government. Before talking about the "policy toward the Provisional Government" he needed to explain how he had *created* that government.

And so he mounted the well-known Duma platform in the celebrated White Hall. (The only pity was that it was late—ten in the evening.) Before him was not the Duma, but something more powerful still.

"Comrades, we sometimes hear complaints that the Soviet is too soft, I would say too indulgent, toward the Provisional Government. Some even criticize it for accepting the very creation of that Provisional Government instead of somehow trying to assume the government's place."

(Were people saying this? Perhaps it was only the Bolsheviks. What people were actually saying was that the Soviet was paralyzing the government.) Well, then:

"I should like to tell you the story of this relationship and, even if highly schematic . . .,"

And—he had opened up the way for his fiery tale. Now there materialized, ever more animated, pervading the air of the hall . . .

". . . that celebrated late-night session. And here, comrades, is—" and he pulled from his jacket and unfolded . . . "the celebrated historic document on a scrap of cheap paper . . . our nine demands . . . which the Provisional Government copied, almost word for word—and neither the majority of the Russian population, still less the whole of the European and wider international press knows this—copied almost word for word into its celebrated program."

(Can you hear over there, you ministers?)

And he raised the crumpled paper and patiently showed it to every part of the hall, turning it over back and forth. For this was his king pin, his certificate of leadership.

"Here is that document! I shan't pass it round the hall in case it gets lost—for we shall be presenting it to the history museum." (What a delightful thought.) "If you like, I can read it out, but then I shall exceed the half-hour I've been allotted."

Voices from the hall: "Yes please! Please!" And the presidium had to keep its counsel.

And Nakhamkes felt himself come alive again, on the summit that had eluded him before. He began reading slowly, point by point, as he had originally written it—and as Milyukov had corrected it, in pencil, here and there . . .

". . . They wanted to impose the Romanov monarchy on us, on the victorious Russian democracy. Milyukov in particular was insisting that the heir, Aleksei, be proclaimed emperor, with Mikhail Aleksandrovich as regent. . . . But the Russian people, the author of our revolution, had instructed us to declare that the only form of government it would recognize was a democratic republic. So you can imagine how astonished and how indignant we were to learn that Guchkov and Shulgin were going to GHQ to conclude some kind of agreement with the Romanovs. I am rushing ahead, but I must tell you that our Soviet ordered its commissars to stop the train that Guchkov and Shulgin had requisitioned."

Loud, enthusiastic applause! The power of the Soviet!

"Unfortunately, these gentlemen somehow slipped through and did . . . well, you know what they did. But, as one of our comrade soldiers wittily expressed it, Mikhail Aleksandrovich 'came round to our point of view'. . ."

But, if the working class was so powerful, why did the Soviet not seize power as—and this is now clear—it should have?

". . . We heard rumors that five regiments were descending on us from the north and General Ivanov was bringing twenty-six troop trains from the south. Shooting was heard in the streets and we thought it likely that the inadequate forces surrounding the Tauride Palace would be overwhelmed. We were expecting them to arrive at any moment and, if not shoot us, then haul us away . . ."

The listeners were hooked. Success! The second half-hour was now slipping by, but Chkheidze did not dare signal to the speaker.

"But that is not the issue. We had no psychological urge to put ourselves in the place of the privileged, enfranchised classes—for radical revolutionary parties cannot be part of a bourgeois government while a capitalist system is still in place."

Now the secret story had been told—now on to times less distant.

"But after the very first days we became aware that the government was sometimes acting without our supervision and that there was some delay in fulfilling our demands, and in the speeches of some ministers we caught an undesirable tone. We thought we needed to apply some pressure, and told them we considered it absolutely necessary to move on to practical steps: to publish a law declaring all generals who would dare lay their sacrilegious hands on the achievements of the revolution to be enemies of the Russian people and outside the law. And we were promised that such a decree would be issued. But, comrades, it has not yet been issued."

Nakhamkes was now on his favorite hobby-horse, his fury with the generals, and getting carried away, even mixing things up to his heart's content: yes, he was writing articles on the subject in *Izvestia* and putting his foot down in the Liaison Commission, but no one had ever promised him anything, and even his colleagues in the Soviet were looking askance at him. But here he was, his powerful voice in full flow and no one corrected him from the presidium—and the uneducated delegates from the provinces and from the front were now imbued with that same fury: treacherous generals, double-crossing generals, their names obviously well known. And the Provisional Government was sparing them?

"But when General Ivanov—who had led several trainfuls of troops against revolutionary Petrograd—was, outrageously, released, freed without the knowledge of the Soviet . . ."

That blow was aimed at Kerensky, but the latter was powerful and could not be named; but here was another, attacking the most hated figure of all:

". . . Life has persuaded us that we need a permanent body to apply pressure on the government and, most of all, on the activities of the Minister of War, who is still causing us—and perhaps you too, comrades?—extreme apprehension."

This was heart-stopping talk. What—the Minister of War too? He was a traitor too??

"Until very recently he did not even make an appearance at the general sessions of the Council of Ministers when we went there with our demands, and I have to tell you that three-quarters of our questions concerned the Minister of War. We are receiving information from the front the whole time, and it is no secret that among the high command the old regime's Augean stables are not getting the energetic cleaning they need."

Applause! Yes! Yes!

Now he was hitting hard! With all the force he could muster! He was unconsciously copying Milyukov's speech—so successful, so influential—of 14 November, delivered from this very dais five months earlier. But now it was against Milyukov's own circle.

Who would be thinking about procedures now? Who would be allowed now—be it even that feeble chairman—to interrupt?

Was Nakhamkes thinking he could, right there at the Conference, bring down Guchkov, and the rest would happen of its own accord and they would arrest GHQ? What really infuriated him was that the heads of the principal generals had not yet rolled! If we're going for them, then let's do it properly, let's settle our scores with those generals, those swine, show them no mercy!

He had the whole hall in the palm of his hand. And what is revolution? It's exactly this, moving the masses, the masses who have not yet settled, not yet lost their impetus. And a single speech can do it! Just a nudge! Just a phrase!

But which?

"To arms, citizens!"? "Get them!"?

It wasn't enough. . . . Something was lacking. . . . He himself was lacking something. Ingenuity? Daring? The courage to make that leap?

And in his head the plan for this report was getting in the way—how much he had not yet said, what he'd missed and should go back for . . . (But in the end it would, no matter what, inevitably slide toward that pathetic resolution . . .)

It wasn't right. He was no Danton.

And yet, with renewed energy:

"It's no secret to us that, as life returns to its normal course, counterrevolutionary forces are certainly starting to gear up as well! That campaign of slander and insinuations that the bourgeois press is waging against us . . ."

"Anonymous members of the Soviet"? Under the lash with all those yapping little nobodies! Start trembling!

". . . There is some kind of *unifying center* sending out signals and slogans, as if on command. You know the celebrated campaign against Order No. 1? You know the attempts to discredit the Petrograd garrison—which had given the signal for freedom to all—under the pretext that it was here dodging military service, while it was actually safeguarding our freedom? It was absolutely obvious that counterrevolutionary forces were beginning to cluster round a certain *center*, still hidden for the time being, and preparing to attack revolutionary democracy from the rear!"

Now, thundering:

"And we *know* this organizational center of counterrevolution!! But we shall not name it for the moment. That is for later. It must be repulsed. And I hope this conference will make its authoritative voice heard, will say the time has come for the Provisional Government to repudiate this campaign—and then we shall see how much we can trust that government from now on."

This platform, if a little lower than the last, was still excellent—he could still cry "To arms!" But he did not have that lightness of touch, that daring. And why that heavy body, that ponderous voice, that laborious structure to his report?

But the structure was not at fault—it was the speaker himself who had lost his way, lost his forceful train of thought, and looped back to those first, fiery days of the revolution.

"And Order No. 1 was the authentic creation of the masses, of the people! Of the soldiers themselves!"

Applause. So the hall had been with him the whole time, following him!

The hall was following him and he had to lead it on vigorously, on to the attack! But his undisciplined mind somehow got caught up in that *dual power* question that the bourgeois papers were droning on about, and he started explaining dual power in detail. (It was nearly midnight—Chkheidze was beginning to nod off, but did not interrupt him.)

"Those shameless slanderers! When Order No. 1 was promulgated no Provisional Government yet existed—and what was that weak Duma committee? Who elected it? It was the pale, feeble creation of the upper echelons of society, while our Soviet had sprung from a broad, wholesome mass, a hundred thousand strong."

The language of all those running the Soviet was already so firmly fixed: they never uttered the words "Executive Committee" aloud, but always "the Soviet." The Soviet, with three thousand members, had broad shoulders.

"What should we understand by the term 'dual power'? It is not dual power, but legitimate oversight by the people, to force the government to take into account the demands of its revolutionary people."

One theme completed. But somewhere on the way he had mentioned the Romanov dynasty—and his mind, not firing on all cylinders, had clutched at it as a real godsend—yes, the Tsar, of course!—and he hauled in that line:

". . . This dynasty is the most pernicious, the most noxious of all. . . . We were receiving information that negotiations were under way with the English government to let Nikolai and his family leave the country. And when we heard from our comrades the railway workers that two special letter trains were moving toward Petrograd carrying the Tsar and his family, we suspected that arrangements had been made for him to get to England via Tornio. What were we to do? Take fright at the specter of dual power or take the most energetic measures to stop the tyrant's flight?"

A storm of rapturous applause! They were roaring!

And this was the last lofty platform from which he could launch the attack, and change the history of the whole Russian revolution! And again he whipped up that ardent mid-March atmosphere! And the hall was putty in the speaker's hands!

But Nakhamkes lacked true genius—he had cut this platform off from his previous bridgeheads instead of merging it in with the counterrevolutionary underground center and with the mutinous GHQ and those generals whose heads had to roll, right now, the whole lot of them.

And in the meantime he was into the third hour of his historic speech and it was past midnight. And he felt that mandatory resolution weighing like a millstone round his neck. There was nowhere else for him to soar. And even his bull-like neck began to droop, his voice to weaken. And, lower and lower:

"I hope you will adopt the resolution that I have the honor of proposing in the name of the Executive Committee. '. . . Recognizing that the Provisional Government . . . is demonstrating its intention to pursue the path indicated . . . emphasizing the need for constant action from the Soviet to urge it to embark on the most energetic struggle with the forces of counterrevolution . . . recognizes that it is politically expedient to support the Provisional Government *insomuch-insofar* . . . unswervingly toward a consolidation of the achievements of the revolution . . .'"

Shortly before one in the morning Chkheidze managed to mumble that the Conference was breaking until the next day, but the EC members rushed to their room and indignantly, furiously berated Steklov: how dare he distort everything? They surrounded him, a pack of little men, though the tall, slender Tsereteli was the same height as Steklov and his dark eyes were blazing.

"How did he dare?" It was hardly worth asking. It had been said and could not be unsaid. Steklov steadfastly protested his innocence. Tell me what I did wrong—how did I depart from the resolution? The revolution is pitiless: it has to save humanity's highest values without regard to individuals. But for *those* individuals, of the Provisional Government, history has already sharpened its axe.

And the Bolsheviks supported him. They were very pleased.

And again he was saved by his non-affiliated status: he had betrayed no party.

Discussion of his report continued the following morning. More than a hundred and twenty angry delegates had registered to speak. They were not such simpletons sitting in the hall as might have been assumed on the basis of the greatcoats (there had actually been a good few veteran socialists among them). Many had seen it immediately, and that's where they began. Comrade Steklov's report was *against* the Executive Committee's resolution and the conclusions he had drawn from the whole history of relations with the government were diametrically opposed to the resolution, and the speaker had not said a single word that supported it. After Comrade Steklov's report, that resolution was totally unsatisfactory. The speaker had painted a clear enough picture of the nature of this government and that picture troubled us greatly. The resolution clearly bore no relationship whatsoever to Comrade Steklov's report, and if he had been actually aiming to give us a resolution contradicting his whole report he could not have done any better. (Applause.) The speaker can congratulate himself on his success.

And it was true—he could! They had understood him! That was just what he wanted. And the Executive Committee looked like fools.

For two days—three sessions—the tide of debate on Steklov's speech rolled on (he'd really shaken things up!) and only Gendelman, a Moscow SR man, attacked him viciously. It had not, he said, been a cogent analysis but a series of anecdotes to entertain his audience, which for a responsible public figure was quite inadmissible: just a few minor facts, and Comrade Steklov won applause for stopping Nikolai Romanov being taken abroad. And what about the object of silence? Why not name that center of counterrevolution, if it is known . . .? But Eltsin came back at him immediately, every bit as heated. So what if the speech was of an entertaining nature; that doesn't matter, it's the facts Comrade Steklov quoted that matter—no one has refuted them, so we can draw our own conclusions!

And it seemed to Nakhamkes that he had indeed outplayed the Executive Committee! Soldiers and provincials were speaking and, the less sophisticated they were, the more they had taken his speech to heart. No! We must tell this government that they are our political enemies and we cannot trust them! We consider that we alone—we, here—are the legitimate authority of this revolutionary people, and the Provisional Government is there to execute current tasks. We, the army and the working class, have the right to determine Russia's future and we shall only allow the government to act on a temporary basis, as long as it is fulfilling our own program. Ab-solute mistrust of a government that was not born of our revolutionary democracy!! Applause! The tide of revolution must rise higher and higher—we must not allow it to ebb! Our resolution must be a manifesto to the people—and not the one we were given! If any task stands before us, it must be to *seize power* and establish a revolutionary government!

Was that not enough? What more could a speaker wish for? He had stirred up more than he could have expected.

But there was more! Another push, and another! And look:

"Comrades! It's time to stop playing hide-and-seek! If our government really thinks it is not autocratic but appointed by our revolutionary nation, it has to *make an appearance here*! It must account to us all, to revolutionary Russia!"

Had he done it? Had he won? Was this the tragi-heroic moment of the Great Revolution?

The chairman was already putting a motion to the five hundred delegates in the hall:

"We have a proposal to call the government in its entirety, here, to this hall, to explain to us the matter we have discussed and shed light on the entirety of its activities."

And of course they'd come, the wretches! They wouldn't dare not to!

But then, from the presidium:

"We can call the government whenever we like. And if necessary we can go even further. But at this moment the Executive Committee does not consider it necessary."

Tsereteli's opportunist henchmen had taken over at the EC . . .

There was shouting back and forth around the hall.

Tsereteli parried the blow by churning out for the delegates, in great detail, yet another new theory, maintaining that the Provisional Government represented a very reasonable type of bourgeoisie, which had made an enormous concession as regards foreign policy and was working willingly with the Liaison Commission.

And the delegates from the front, too, were coming up with hare-brained ideas:

"Comrades, we must not make a show of pressing the government, of summoning it. We could press and press and easily crush it completely. We mustn't get drunk on power. We have to remember that we here are not the whole of Russia, and these revolutionary times will not last for ever. A different time will come."

So there were two schools of thought in the discussion as well.

"Allow me to put it to the vote, this proposal to summon the Provisional Government."

The vote was tense.

Rejected.

It had fallen through. They'd gone too far with that "government making an appearance."

So it had fallen through.

The great moment of the Russian revolution had evaporated.

The sessions were cut up, with interruptions, and during the pauses the factions were humming with activity, buzzing about, either flying off into separate little rooms or congregating in a crush, the blockheads, railing at "Steklov's disgraceful, disruptive action! The resolution's been discredited now! Now we'll have to move even further to the left!" (While the hulking Steklov stood there and endured it.)

And they rephrased the resolution. They muddled it up, lengthened it, broke it down into separate points—and it gradually became stricter and more unforgiving to the government and, bravo, there remained no hint of any independence for it. (And Kamenev, satisfied, withdrew his, Bolshevik, resolution without a vote.) But what was this: *by and large to support the government??* The Mensheviks and SRs were getting on better and better, and coming to arrangements. The Mensheviks found a certain comfort in the fact that the Provisional Government would, despite everything, remain as it was: there was no need to overthrow it, and the Soviet would not have to take upon itself the responsibility of power—which Dan had greatly feared.

And whose job was it to go up and humbly submit this resolution from the dais? The original speaker, obviously.

Of course, he'd be happy to read it—he had, in general terms, won it. But not to the degree he'd needed. There had not been a coup—though he had rendered the government impotent. And he had without a doubt consolidated his own position.

And he stepped up, a strapping figure, and in a loud, powerful voice—though without great fortitude in his breast, or any fire—read the revised set of points. And he added his own observation, his last hope of again sparking rebellion in the hall.

"By and large, the government has fulfilled its obligations—under constant pressure from us. But the forces of counterrevolution are not slumbering."

But the victory was not as complete as he had wanted, and he had to make a gesture toward Tsereteli.

"Although the government too could, in certain circumstances, repulse counterrevolutionary propaganda . . . the Provisional Government stands to the left of the Kadet party. We cannot talk about its failure or ineptitude. For the moment there is no point discussing its replacement by a democratic government even further to the left."

Voices were raised:

"But that's a new resolution! We need a break!"

"This," Steklov replied, joylessly, "is the same resolution. The Executive Committee has done no more than attend to the instructions of the Conference and rework the text."

Another happening that cut into the sessions was the arrival of Plekhanov on the evening of 13 April: a ceremonial welcome was required.

The leaders of the EC left the Conference for the station and that night was lost. The following morning they extended the Conference from three to six days and continued discussing Steklov's report—and did not even begin debating the remaining ten or so questions.

Plekhanov's arrival was expected by many socialists—and Burtsev with particular fervor—to produce some kind of miraculous turning point in the revolution. The Great Man was coming! He'd decide the matter! He would now intervene forcefully in this political struggle, make authoritative pronouncements on all the burning questions! A red-letter day for the entire Liberation movement! A crowd of ten thousand or so gathered at Finland Station, the public thronging the whole length of the platform, women with red roses, and, in front, a line of soldiers and militia with rifles. On the command "present arms," the Marseillaise was played—and Tsereteli, Skobelev, Chkheidze, and Burtsev emerged from the carriage holding aloft . . . a small, haggard old man, dazed by the welcome. In the reception rooms Chkheidze, much cheered and even beaming (to the extent he could since the death of his son), greeted the arrival of the Father of Social Democracy in Russia, who would bring peace to the divided Social Democrat family. Then some more speakers, all on the same subject: thanks to his great knowledge and authority, Plekhanov would at last unite all of Russian Social Democracy. But he could barely muster the strength to reply that he had no doubts about Russia's radiant future, which was now imminent. And again they held him aloft, carrying him toward the crowd outside and into the motorcar taking him to the House of the People.

Nakhamkes did not follow, not expecting a brilliant speech (and indeed there was no speech at all). He had already understood, there, at the station, that this exhausted old man was nothing like the one who had stood firm in Switzerland fifteen years before: Nakhamkes had at that time almost worshipped him. But no, he had nothing more to contribute. He would hold no sway.

And this was confirmed the day after next, when he was taken to the White Hall for the Conference, collected his strength, and raised a feeble voice to deliver his address. And what a feeble address it was! He mentioned Lassalle and, for some reason, Vogt and even Darwin, raised the dust of times past, spoke of his literary talent and his past militancy, and of how he had foreseen everything about the Russian working class, and how all the seeds had been sown by the Great French Revolution. . . . Sown, yes, they'd been sown—but Plekhanov, as he mumbled his address, had not grasped the dynamics of the situation here, and how it was awaiting firm direction. He even boasted of being a *social patriot*, which sounded tactless.

The old man was behind the times. Overtaken by the revolution. He was no longer a leader.

[4]

Right up to this war, Prince Pavel Dmitrievich Dolgorukov had been a convinced pacifist: he had even chaired an international pacifist convention in Stockholm. Although wars had broken out in the previous decade—Russo-Japanese, Balkan, Italo-Turkish—they had seemed like spasms of man's previous rancorous existence, or misunderstandings not cleared up in time by sluggish diplomatic processes. But errant humanity had finally achieved the triumph of Reason by the early twentieth century, and it could now be seen spreading all over the world!

The breakout of this war in Europe had shocked the prince profoundly, like a shell scoring a direct hit on his soul, filling him with black, swirling despair. Oh no—that age of Reason had certainly not been reached: there was a long way to go yet! And what forces of evil and perfidy, previously hidden, were now revealed within the Central Powers! Now Prince Pavel was serving the defense of Russia as best he could: he wept over our 1915 retreat and was then gradually overcome by the anger pervading the whole country, at the Myasoedov wasps' nest, the Rasputin goings-on, and the fact that Tsarism had ceased to be our bulwark against the external enemy, had not worked for victory as it should have, and had perhaps even been hypocritically working for our defeat, perhaps even in close association with Wilhelm. And, in response, in a solemn, tacit agreement between all the active forces in Russia, anxious for her future as a sovereign power, a healing, wonderfully bloodless national revolution was born, now clearing away all obstacles to Russia's victory! The people had rebelled in the name of an ideal shared by the whole nation, and the revolution was the authentic child of the whole nation. It was a sure sign: since the country had taken the change of power in its stride, it meant the idea had come of age deep inside people.

And for a good two or three weeks Prince Pavel's heart had resounded with the peals of Easter bells. He had remained jubilant right up to the Kadet party congress in early April—the greatest triumph in a hundred years for the party and the whole of Russian society—and he had lined up with the other leaders on the stage of the Mikhailovsky Theater before an enthusiastic audience. And Vinaver proclaimed the party's fundamental task: to repulse the counterrevolutionary forces of the right.

But it transpired that already, even before that, voices had been heard in Petrograd and Moscow, at first unheeded but then more and more disappointing. People began to say publicly that the revolution had not been a spontaneous urge for an ideal shared by the whole nation, but only a continuation of the revolutionary efforts of a century, and that its aim was to free the nation of "bourgeois elements," to democratize not only the social order but also all property relations, down to the smallest estate, the family hearth, the orchard, the little wood, the horses, farming equipment, the land itself, the great industrial enterprise and the tiny workshop. And they started cursing even us, radical progressive circles, as "bourgeois," along with all wearers of bowler hats and starched collars, making no distinction between wartime profiteers and selfless zemstvo activists, between the Black Hundreds and Milyukov, or the socialist Plekhanov, or the young ladies strutting around in high heels. After all our fervent espousal of the public cause, this slap in the face, this "bourgeois"?

Wake up, fellow-countrymen! Are we really the villains of our fatherland? Is this the time for class interests to supplant our common ideals? To remain passive in the face of our patriotic duty? We have to moderate our appetites! We have to work for the motherland!

Over the high days of Easter it had seemed that, despite all this, conciliation filled people's hearts. Prince Pavel had celebrated the holy night in the Kremlin, exchanging Easter greetings with all the people in Cathedral Square. And he had spent the whole of Easter week in Moscow. But, no. The calm turned out to be short-lived, and the most alarming news started coming in from the front. Prince Pavel was used to visiting the front: during the Japanese war he had represented a medical organization set up by the nobility, and in the current war he had visited several times as a delegate of the Union of Towns (he had been exempted from military service on account of his eyesight, though his twin brother Pyotr was serving). And now Prince Pavel had been commissioned by the Duma Committee to make a tour of the Western and Southwestern fronts—and left the day after Thomas Sunday. (It was still cold—he wore a beaver coat and hat.)

In the train (where for some reason they had done away with sleeping berths—had the Russian population increased, or the distances shrunk?) were large numbers of military men: officers returning from convalescence and soldiers either from leave or, in some cases, they seemed to be returning deserters who had been coldly received at home in their villages and now preferred the settled, military life, with army rations, to that of a vagabond. The trains trundling past in the other direction were jam-packed with rowdy soldiers, singing, whooping, and directing taunts and foul language at those traveling gloomily past them, toward the front.

In truth the auspices were terrible—even worse than the rumors reaching Moscow. How on earth could the national revolutionary ideal have become, in the space of forty days, distorted into its total antithesis? Despite everything, we had always felt that Russia was our hearth and home. But now everything, everywhere, was like a public back alley.

First Prince Pavel visited Krasnov's Cossack division, which was showing no signs of falling apart: the Cossacks were highly disciplined, parading, barking out "Good day sir!," "Hurrah," and they held the deputy aloft.

But from then on he encountered nothing like that. Regimental commanders were distraught, no longer the masters of their regiments. Tears glistened in the eyes of old generals and grizzled officers. The officers' position was terrible. Sometimes they advised Prince Pavel not to address the regiment at all, but he would order them to assemble, climb on to a tree stump, and begin: "Christ is risen!" And, despite everything, from many hundreds of throats would come the response: "Indeed . . ." And from that the Prince would go on to say that the Moscow Easter chimes were still sounding in his ears and that he brought to the regiment not only greetings from the State Duma but also Russia's heartfelt hopes. And then, so that they would not believe the mendacious slogans doing the rounds, he went on to say that it was impossible to pursue trench warfare without advancing. And sometimes his speech so touched them that they took a collection for the government: caps were filled with silver rubles and even St. George Crosses (and the Prince was always astonished—were they not sorry to lose those?). Or else they asked "But why do people say . . .? We've heard that . . ." And went on to quote from socialist leaflets. Or they were hurt: how could it be that they were serving their country, fighting, getting injured and killed, while back home the land was to be divided up? And sometimes, specially if it was getting dark, and usually from the back rows, cries would be heard: "We've had it with fighting! Make peace now and we'll get off home!" "It's easy for you to talk—you can roll up here and then go home! What about us in the trenches giving the lice a feast?" "Why listen to him—we're not going to advance anyway!" But if he asked them to come closer to explain, the back rows would stay put. The officers stood, eyes downcast—a pitiful sight.

So had the concept of national honor also become a "bourgeois superstition" now? At this of all times, after the overthrow, when we had a unique opportunity to draw closer to our allies, were we to be pulled apart from them?

And this was how his feelings were seesawing, from one regiment to the next. Either all was lost or it was still possible to put it all right.

But in the Yelets Regiment he was faced with a singular situation: the regiment had thrown out its commanding officer, who had taken refuge at corps HQ, and a young company commander had been elected in his place. The corps commander begged the Prince to go and talk some sense into the regiment: if he could arrange it, the old commander would return—if only for a few days—and the self-appointed leader would be removed and then a more fitting replacement immediately appointed. The Prince went. The self-proclaimed leader did not even make an appearance and all the officers were hesitant and fearful. Via the most senior officer and in the name of the government and the Duma, the Prince managed to muster, if not the whole regiment, at least 350 or so men. He began the meeting with the Paschal greeting, told them of the discipline he had seen in the Cossack regiment, and said they must hold on until the Constituent Assembly without breaking military regulations—and he said nothing about their removing their commanding officer. "Can I tell the government that you will not be listening to foolish people and you will not abandon your duty? That you will stand firm for Russia and freedom?" "Yes indeed. We'll stand firm." They dispersed. The Prince went in search of the self-proclaimed commander. This was not easy—the latter was hiding. The Prince explained that he had come with no authority of any kind, as a voluntary intermediary, and that he was talking as one Russian to another, and he advised him to present himself to the corps commander, for otherwise the Yelets regiment would be entirely disbanded. The upstart was dogged: "If anyone can maintain discipline in the regiment it's me and only me."

"But even Order No. 1 confers no right to elect commanding officers—that's the first step toward disintegration. Later some demagogic clerk will come along and take your place." "It wasn't my idea, they elected me." This got them nowhere.

When the Prince left, his driver told him the men had thought the deputy was coming to arrest the commander they'd elected, and they'd come to meet him holding hand grenades, just in case.

*
* *

The soldier of today
He won't fight, come what may.
He doesn't want the war—
He likes his freedom more.

DOCUMENTS — 5

APPEAL TO THE SOLDIERS OF THE ARMY IN THE FIELD

20 April 1917

Soldiers! . . . Mass desertion is starting to become dangerous. . . . Criminal appeals are being spread in the army about the supposedly imminent redistribution of land that . . . Soldiers! Do not weaken the army by abandoning its ranks, do not believe rumors. The land question will be resolved only by the Constituent Assembly. . . . Today, abandoning army ranks constitutes apostasy from the principles of the freedom so recently won.

War Minister A. *Guchkov*

[5]

Stankevich had volunteered, and eagerly, to draft a report on the Constituent Assembly for the All-Russian Conference of Soviets. He had thought a great deal about the Constituent Assembly, even before this.

But for many years who among the Russian intelligentsia had not been thinking about it? Who had not proclaimed those stirring words? In the darkest days of Tsarism they had risen before us like a crimson sun—ushering in an era of freedom and happiness. Of course, we had been influenced by historical reminiscences—starting with Rousseau's idea of the Social Contract and, in 1789, the Estates General declaring itself the Constituent Assembly and vowing not to disperse until it had produced a constitution. (But our State Duma, though an elected body, was not that brave.) It is true that, among the masses, there was little understanding as to what it was all for, but in the upper strata of society it had penetrated minds and so mesmerized people that even Mikhail Aleksandrovich had unequivocally abdicated in favor of a Constituent Assembly, which was assumed to be indispensable.

But no one had created it yet. And there had never been one in all Russian history.

What would it do? Well **everything**, it seemed. It would set everything straight in Russia. There appeared to be not a single aspect of life where hopes were not vested in the Constituent Assembly, hopes that **It** would settle everything. Not only the constitution, not only relationships between Russia's peoples, but also all issues relating to land ownership, all societal relationships, all state laws, and, come to think of it, all the current forms of multiple authority, the current war, and the future peace.

When would that Assembly be convened? In mid March even learned jurists like Kiesewetter had been saying it would be in a month or two. By mid-May, then. A week later the Provisional Government had told the Executive Committee that it would be convened by mid-summer at the latest. But the EC had thought that too late and tried to speed things up. (The Bolsheviks were in more of a hurry than the rest: they were particularly anxious lest the Assembly be delayed and revolutionary fervor cool.) But having pondered over the difficulties of holding an election when 10 to 12 million of the most active members of the population were in the army, might it not be better to put it off until after the war, when it could proceed calmly? And now, at the Kadet party congress, Kokoshkin had declared that it was wrong to assume it was possible to convene the Assembly even in four months, in mid-August. What sort of elections could be held at harvest-time? How could peasants leave their villages to vote? Stankevich also thought it impossible now to manage it any earlier than September. So in early April, a month after the revolution, the government had decided to start convening in the meantime a Special Conference to draft the Electoral Regulations, with sixty or seventy of the best jurists and representatives of civil society. And this Conference would certainly take more than a month to work out the best possible arrangements and send out consultative questionnaires to all political and social organizations. Would the conditions be the same for eligibility both to vote and to stand for election? Would it be a majority or a proportional system? How many members should the Assembly have? At what age would people have the vote? What about the residency requirement? How would servicemen vote—in their electoral constituencies or their military units? And what if their units are in combat? (And now there were already demands that deserters should not be deprived of the vote.) And by the time that Special Conference, itself every bit as cumbersome as a parliament, had collected everything and processed it, and the electoral rolls had been drawn up and appeals considered, and election campaigning had taken place so that no one would complain that the will of the people was not properly reflected—by that time we'd be well into autumn and, with Russian roads impassable at that time of year, no country people would leave their villages to go off and vote. . . . So . . . should we put it off till winter?

The Constituent Assembly was fervently desired but, if you looked at it a bit more carefully . . . in Russia, which had never known such elections, which was at war, and had just been destabilized by a revolution that had left no local self-government functioning . . . how could country-wide elections be organized, without even local authorities in place? So, before all this, local authorities would have to be elected. And that would need electoral regulations, electoral rolls, appeals, campaigning . . .

Previously our dreams had not featured such considerations.

In recent weeks Stankevich had studied the problem closely. And when he was entrusted with this report, he thought it right not to conceal all those difficulties from the

Conference of Soviets. Yes, he must say, the Constituent Assembly will be the crowning glory of the victorious edifice of the revolution, the complete embodiment of the principle of popular sovereignty. It will be the establishment of a totally new state. But at the moment we do not have even the basic units of local authority that we need to organize elections. And we must not close our eyes to the fact that the nations comprising Russia will not appear at the Assembly in a companionable crowd, but will harbor old resentments, make their old demands, which are at times mutually exclusive. And now a war is raging. And now there are clarion calls from the countryside regarding land! And we have a food crisis. And the transport system has broken down. Any one of these problems would require all the attention and vigor of a fully prepared and businesslike legislative assembly—which our totally inexperienced assembly will not be. At what age will people have the vote? Everyone agrees it should not be under twenty—but eighteen-year-olds are also bearing arms. How can we discriminate at the polls between comrades in arms who all go off to die as equals? And if an eighteen-year-old soldier votes, then how can we refuse an eighteen-year-old mine worker? And how can we refuse refugees, victims of the war, the right to vote? But how would the locals react to them being given the vote? (Also, the refugees are demanding that their ballots be sent away for counting at their previous addresses.) The participation of women seems beyond doubt—this will be seen in the world as our greatest achievement. But democratic voices are telling us that most Russian village women are still weeping over losing Nikolai Romanov from the throne. And they'll outvote all of us. And the village women are all under the influence of the clergy. (But then again, if the elections are concentrated into a few centers in each district, what woman is going to leave her cottage and children and travel to the city to vote?) The villages are benighted and could have some surprises in store for our revolution. And how can we run a universal secret ballot with mass illiteracy? If we could manage the task of educating our benighted masses, we would not fear a chance result in an election. But, on the other hand, if we keep putting it off, people's revolutionary enthusiasm will fade. And there's another danger: that the illiterate mass will be taken over by small, well-organized groups. (And *Izvestia* is suggesting that even in the army "worthy candidates may not be found" and proposing that the army, and every district, be given the right to elect not their own candidates but others, from the cities, substitute delegates.) The whole future of freedom in Russia is staked on this card: how are we to organize these elections?

And another thing: *where* is the Assembly to be? The case for Moscow is being pressed hard. Public figures are making speeches about it, newspapers writing about it: it must be Moscow, they say, our first capital, for there alone can you feel the authentic pulse of Russian national life, and it alone is forever dear to the Russian heart. Petrograd is a city of civil servants, international in nature, of an alien climate, situated on the fringe of Russia, far from its centers of production. And it is in conflict with Russia, has never enjoyed the country's trust; for it was only that way that the Court could develop, so like the German court, with its cosmopolitan breed of bureaucrats, its stultifying foreign approach toward all the benign initiatives of the zemstvo system in Russia. But to move the Constituent Assembly out of Petrograd would mean reorganizing the whole administrative apparatus, a mass of technical problems—and anyway, not a single one of the socialist parties wants that.

And while we are cudgelling our brains over all these problems and dragging them out, life goes on and we must come to some decisions. And now the Provisional Government has, without a Constituent Assembly, just ratified an act giving Poland its independence. No small step.

Stankevich intended to say all this in his report. But there was another aspect, and he did not know whether to mention it at the Conference of Soviets and, if he did, how. For these were the Soviets themselves. How would they behave in elections to the Assembly? They would, of course, not be indifferent. At the very least they would be monitoring the elections—but how impartially? Most probably they would be campaigning and maybe actively participating. In which case they would determine the entire composition of the Constituent Assembly. For the Soviets also claimed to embody the whole nation, and why would they want a second such embodiment in the form of the Constituent Assembly? One would invalidate the other. By the time the Assembly was ready to invalidate the Soviets, the latter would already have had their cadres, accustomed to being in charge, skilled at exercising that power—would they now abolish themselves?

In which case, what was the point of this whole report?

Stankevich decided to give just a hint of this. A word to the wise.

But as the Conference proceeded, his presentation became squeezed into the very end, and it passed unnoticed, with no repercussions. There was now no time for anything, least of all any discussion, so that matter, the Constituent Assembly, flew past like an express train that hardly anyone even notices. And when it came to voting on the ready-prepared resolution, fewer than half the delegates remained—the rest had gone off for Easter. But not before voting through a proposal that the Soviets should be financed by the state.

The reason everything was so rushed was that the Conference had been launched with no planning and run unintelligently. The first day had been almost entirely swallowed up by speeches of welcome and then accompanying Stasik Chkheidze's coffin to the station, on its way to Batum. And then two hours or so spent waiting for the Grandmother, then listening to her words, gracious and sincere: "We are all children of the one nation, why have we started quarrelling?" They had brought people in from distant regions, extended the event to a week and heaped up an impossible number of issues and sections; and no one could make sense of anything. (A fine rehearsal for the Constituent Assembly.)

But at the same time, what a lot there was to observe, to learn from, to test our policies. It really was the people, fired up by the revolution—here they were, they came! Fewer workers and a lot more soldiers—the whole Duma hall was in military hues, and the gallery was jam-packed with them. And their faces were good, fearless, no baseness, no pretence. Of course, they were not eloquent. Their thoughts were, in most cases, diffuse—they were, rather, feelings, and unclear at that, and not put into sentences. But sometimes a little soldier with a booming voice would leap up and not mince his words, speaking in commanding tones and without hesitation. And everyone would listen intently.

But in the presidium were only civilians, ten party leaders. And the speakers bounding onto the platform the whole time were certainly not simple folk: they already knew propaganda by heart. The same people were even coming up to speak twice, three times, especially party people—Pumpyansky, for example, who had managed to present himself as a delegate from Chita (elected by telegraph, perhaps?) and, from Moscow, the Bolshevik

Nogin and the SR Gendelman—and each one, without fail, would trot out "We, representatives of the working class . . ." Dozens of ordinary lads were excluded from the discussions, while the majority of delegates sat silent, only mumbling or applauding. And they had no power over the resolutions, which were agreed by party factions behind the scenes.

So was that how all people's movements were led? Was this a forum of the people?

On the subject of the war, however, there were two dozen speakers and two sessions. Stankevich followed these intently. Very clear voices were heard, the voices of front-line soldiers: "The fatherland is in danger." This was not just talk—it was the cry of a sick heart, a cry of despair. Our soldiers were demanding a clear answer: the war is continuing, so what are we going to do? Men are already refusing to go out on reconnaissance. The Bolsheviks can't imagine what it's like in the trenches—they're in their golden dream of the brotherhood of nations. We don't need other people's territory, but we won't give up our own—we'd rather all fall on the battlefield and block the Germans with our chests! (A storm of applause in the hall.) Someone from the Special Army: we must stand firm till we have an honorable peace! Why is the idea of an immediate peace being raised behind the lines and not at the front? We need to think some more about what's best for us. Could it be to carry on suffering in the trenches?

The Bolshevik reply: Why carry on fighting? Are we serving the English and French bourgeoisie? And someone yelling from the hall: well who are the Bolsheviks serving? Get out! We don't want you here! And Skobelev was barely able to calm the hall. The next Bolshevik, of course, mumbled that yes, we'll defend the country as long as you tell us to, but it'd be best to end the war as soon as possible.

The wiles and ruses of the Bolsheviks were easy to see. Even with the few representatives they had there they took up a third of the discussion, and still it was not enough for them. But, having lost the resolution, they now channelled their efforts into amendments. Nogin alone proposed three in a row, infuriating the hall to such an extent that there were calls of "Get him off! We've had enough of the Bolsheviks! We're fed up with them!" And all their amendments were rejected.

But that presidium of civilians, those "representatives of the working class" without a single worker, and Tsereteli first among them, was fearful of any other possible amendments, such as the possibility of an offensive—so they passed the whole resolution on a single vote, in the form they had prepared in advance.

And thus Stankevich observed the "flood of democracy" and the way masses were led.

Passions ran high around Steklov's forceful speech. Fulminating against the Provisional Government was, of course, nothing new: in a good few factories and army units socialist agitators were abusing it in the choicest language, and on the front the soldiers' meetings were abuzz with the regular topic: should they or shouldn't they trust the government? But with this presentation Steklov had gone much further: it had provoked the hall like a red rag to a bull. And he had thrown in a real firebrand when he said the Provisional Government was counterrevolutionary and called Guchkov a *sinister force*, a label that not long before had referred only to Rasputin's circle. And the trusting minds of the soldiers were soaking up these descriptions of their Minister of War.

That was enough! Steklov had to be cut down to size! It was the only solution. The surest way would be to pull *Izvestia* out from under him.

There was plenty to be said about *Izvestia*, as would be plain to any member of the Soviet if he took the trouble to look a bit more closely, more soberly at it, at the Soviet's own publication. The paper was, basically, not being *run* by anyone, and Comrade Steklov was not burdening himself with the job. There was no system, no search for content—what was published was a jumble of whatever happened to come along. It gave no understanding at all of what was happening in Russia, for there was practically no news from the country as a whole, and as for international events—don't even ask, there was simply nothing to read. And in the midst of that meager fare, suddenly a long article: "The aims of social legislation in Finland"—whatever for? Or a page and a half would be given over to some rally in London, but no further word about England ever again. Or an anonymous teacher would suddenly write in with a detailed criticism of the newly constituted council of the Ministry of Education. And not a word about education after that—or about any of the other ministries. There was no differentiation between important and unimportant items. You would find, closely juxtaposed, reports from the depths of a Russian province, from Stockholm, and then the province again. Some important piece of telegraphed news would suddenly appear, three weeks late. You could not even say it reflected the life of the Soviet of Workers' Deputies itself (you could read about all meetings of the Soviet far earlier and in far more detail in the bourgeois newspapers). Once a month the EC minutes would suddenly appear, also five days late. On 5 April the EC gave in to public pressure and revealed the names of its members, which no one in Russia had previously known. But Comrade Steklov took his own decision to delay a further six days. (And almost all the members decrypted their pseudonyms, but not he—he still listed himself as Steklov). So what did the paper actually consist of? It was the most boring, unreadable selection of monotonous appeals, salutations, resolutions, minutes of regimental meetings, all printed one after the other, whatever was sent in by some bumpkin, while the editorial staff didn't do their job. There was a headline: "At a regional conference." But up to the very end of the article there was no mention of which region or which party. Lines were missed out or transposed. There were glaring misprints: the declaration issued on 9 April by the Provisional Government was dated one month earlier. What a mess. And it was on the basis of *Izvestia* that the whole country was judging the Petrograd Soviet, that strange, outlandish authority now in charge—and what conclusions was it drawing? The image was shameful. And amid this greyness would appear, from time to time, solid chunks, inflammatory articles by Nakhamkes himself, always unsigned but always easily identifiable by their heavy-handed style, the unequivocal tone and crude expressions used.

Stankevich was sure he could bring down Nakhamkes at the EC—it was all too clear. He had been promised a slot to speak at the very first EC meeting after Easter, on 17 April. But at that meeting Lenin suddenly appeared, having arrived in scandalous fashion the previous day. He had brought his brood too—Zurabov, Zinoviev with his effeminate voice, and Shlyapnikov, who had become a fixture there—and all three started addressing the meeting, one after the other, about an issue that was not on the agenda, the situation of the émigrés in Switzerland. (They spoke, while the bald, crafty, extremely unpleasant Lenin sat at the back, by the wall—he remained silent, as if pulling invisible strings.) Zurabov and Zinoviev were not even speaking on their own behalf—and absolutely not to whitewash the Bolshevik leader and their own journey through Germany—but, so they said, on behalf of the "internationalist comrades in Switzerland." It was they who were asking the Executive Committee to press the Provisional Government to open negotiations with the German government to allow all the remaining political émigrés to travel across Germany in exchange for German prisoners of war currently in Russia.

This request was unexpected and staggering. "Pressing the Provisional Government" was nothing new to the Executive Committee and it was ready to press them any time. But . . . pressing the government to enter into direct negotiations with Wilhelm?? That was very clearly outrageous—but what objection could they have to the spirit of internationalism? Under its previous leadership, the EC would have been floored, as were now Chkheidze and Skobelev, while Nakhamkes sat stolidly to one side and smoothed his beard happily. And neither did Himmer come up with a new idea. And Stankevich, though certainly indignant, did not feel he had the right to answer first; and besides, he would not be able to maintain a sufficiently internationalist tone and could spoil everything. What saved the situation was Tsereteli's presence there now, having so swiftly attained power and a leadership role. You could not say he had a sparkling brain or was a polished speaker—he had neither attribute—but his heart was true, his instincts accurate. He sized up the situation rapidly and was the first to answer, cleverly turning the situation around. The Executive Committee was, he said, already the object of sinister propaganda. And if we were to pass such a resolution our enemies would use it against us to their own benefit. Rumors would be rife that we are in cahoots with Wilhelm and that Germany would be sending revolutionaries to us for their own ends. (Which was also a sideways swipe at Lenin.)

Lenin, already squint-eyed, began squinting even more while, in the wake of Tsereteli, Bogdanov also plucked up courage and bluntly exposed Lenin's real intent: the bourgeoisie had already begun a campaign against Lenin for traveling across Germany—and could take aim at us too. Let the government look into getting the émigrés home through France and England. We should *condemn* anyone taking the law into their own hands and traveling through Germany!

Now Lenin could no longer bear his backstage role, jumped up, and, in a voice shrill and spiteful, and with an impairment in his speech, started justifying himself: they had made no commitments to Germany; the plan for their journey had been proposed by Comrade Martov, and all negotiations had been led by Comrade Platten; and the political aims of the German government had nothing in common with the objectives of the Russian revolutionaries. Rather, the Executive Committee itself was fueling the insinuations and slander. If it wanted to put an end to the bourgeois lies it should instead be passing the resolution proposed by Comrade Zinoviev.

Taking responsibility for the resolution and thereby whitewashing Lenin's clique. Of course.

There were also a few soldiers in the Executive Committee. And one of them jumped in immediately, stating baldly that all of them were against anyone traveling through Germany and against any such resolution.

And no matter how much the Bolsheviks continued to insist, their resolution was not passed. However, the Executive Committee agreed to explain all their arguments in *Izvestia*. So all in all the EC was shown to be weak: it had not condemned their passage through Germany.

The meeting had gone on longer than planned and Stankevich's report was postponed till the next day. But the following morning's *Izvestia* featured not only a long (and anonymous) article by the Bolsheviks, "How we traveled back," justifying their actions, but also an extremely sympathetic piece, clearly by Nakhamkes himself, about Lenin's arrival. (*Izvestia* had never shown such warmth to anyone else.) So Stankevich understood that Nakhamkes, under pressure in the Executive Committee, was looking for allies among the Bolsheviks. Already, of all the speeches at the Conference of Soviets, the only ones he had printed prominently, as separate articles, had been Kamenev's. But that day he had devoted four of the eight pages to his own rabble-rousing speech against the government.

Stankevich went to the new session, on 18 April, in an even more determined frame of mind. But even at that new session they did not start with *Izvestia* but with the Liaison Commission's report. Since the storm over Steklov's speech criticizing the Provisional Government, there was no more inflammatory issue in the EC than its policy toward the government. And who was to speak on the topic yet again? Comrade Steklov, of course. And he, it seemed, was intending to win now the battle he had lost at the Conference. The meeting the previous evening at the Mariinsky Palace had been extremely tense. The EC had told the ministers how unhappy they were at not being informed of the appointment of Alekseev as Supreme Commander. And why was Guchkov's purge of the high command taking so long? And an Executive Committee commissar must be allowed to check all telegrams leaving GHQ. (And the ministers, for their part, had wanted to find out what the EC thought about Lenin's passage across Germany and the EC had refused to talk about the matter, but Milyukov had been intransigent: Platten's action, he said, had been inimical to the Russian state.) In addition to that, in Petrograd Kornilov was continuing to swear in troops, which was putting the revolutionary units who had refused to take the oath in an untenable position; and worst of all, the government, which had previously dragged its feet on this, had now flatly refused to pay the ten million rubles for the Soviet's expenses. So relations had become impossible and required decisive action!

Today at the EC meeting, Himmer jumped in. Yes, he said sharply, relations are not good, but all the EC does is note the government's high-handed behavior, to no avail, and always accepts it as a *fait accompli*. We do not react forcefully enough when they refuse our requests. That affair with Platten: it sets an unacceptable precedent! We must use all our authority to ensure he is allowed into Russia from the Swedish border. We must blow this whole situation open to the public gaze. We must keep minutes of every step in our interaction with the government.

The judicious Tsereteli disagreed. He felt the government was very cooperative on a good few issues. The EC itself had not accepted the exchange of émigrés for prisoners of war, and there was no good reason to blow the situation open. We could achieve more via a less official route.

The Bolsheviks and the Interdistrict man Krotovsky demanded both a split from the government and a public exposé. We must abandon this principle of "preserving the government" and press especially hard to get Platten to Petrograd. The time has passed when we needed to support the government! It's ignoring us more and more. We must refuse our support, and publicly!

Three days earlier, at the Conference, the exact same people had passed a resolution supporting the government, and now a whole group was being marshalled (with Nakhamkes, again, in the lead) to attack the government and bring it down. This ordinary EC meeting threatened to become the key moment of the whole revolution. And Stankevich, forgetting about *Izvestia*, was about to jump in and defend Tsereteli—when Bogdanov adroitly intervened. He pointed out that the EC had weakened itself by taking up the cudgels and being defeated on the least advantageous issues. With a part of the army already sworn in, it was foolish to raise the question of abolishing the oath, and doomed to failure; and a similarly foolish, losing proposition to risk our necks for the exchange of prisoners of war, or for Platten, trailing along after Lenin's group, which had taken no account of the interests of the Russian revolution, only its own wishes. And complete stupidity to engineer public exposure of the fact that we were not to be given ten million in state funding. We'd have no support from the public.

Tsereteli indicated that the discussion should be brought to a close at that point because it had all just been settled at the All-Russian Conference. But no, to hell with the Conference and any thought of order—now they were almost brawling (clearly the Bolsheviks and Nakhamkes had colluded on this—today they intended to overturn that decision). The Bolsheviks dug their heels in, but even the moderates Bramson and Dan had lost their heads seeing the luster of the ten million slipping away from them. And Krasikov was shouting again for the Liaison Commission's negotiations to be minuted and for the ministers to sign all the minutes (making utter pawns of the ministers!). But even Nakhamkes was alert enough to object that in that case the ministers would become too cautious in negotiations, which would certainly do us no favors, while Himmer was embroidering on that idea of the minutes in scathing terms, envisaging sworn minutes-takers, a notary with two clerks. There was shouting and bickering from all sides—and in the midst of the hubbub Chkheidze not only lost control of the meeting but also lost his head, old and feebler as it now was since burying his son a week previously, and in a moment of lightheadedness proposed to do away with the Liaison Commission entirely and that no one should have meetings with the government, all communications with them to be only in written form. . . . The meeting, stunned, fell silent. Bramson was among the first to recover. This would deprive us of all the benefits of face-to-face contact, he said. Fine, let's not have minutes, but the Liaison Commission members must take notes without the ministers seeing. (On their knees, under the table, then?)

Krasikov's proposal failed by the tiniest of margins, Bramson's passed.

And now, with everyone in total disarray, came Stankevich's report on *Izvestia*. During the brawl it had crossed his mind that the timing was bad again, the moment had passed, it would not be appropriate. But he stood up and, with his magnificent self-control and a cold scorn, raked the stout Nakhamkes over the coals, raising several bursts of laughter from the whole, exhausted group. And laughter more than anything can kill. Nakhamkes, after his attack on the government, was not expecting a hit from this side, in this form. The editors of *Izvestia* were summoned and started distancing themselves from Nakhamkes and letting the cat out of the bag about the chaos reigning in the editorial office. Tsereteli supported Stankevich. Nakhamkes, now discouraged and incoherent, was pleading his cause and showing himself in an even less favorable light.

A commission was appointed, of Stankevich, Dan, and Himmer, to investigate the editing of the paper and reorganize it. (Follow this through to the end, Stankevich decided.)

But there was also a moment of comedy. Brandishing that day's *Izvestia*, Stankevich ridiculed the editors' call to identify and apprehend the authors of anonymous leaflets, when they themselves were always writing anonymously. But there was some puzzlement among the Executive Committee: they supported the editors.

"Strange to say," mused someone aloud, "even we need our own counterespionage operation."

DOCUMENTS — 6

ORDER

20 April 1917

. . . Various local executive committees are conducting arrests of officers, who are being replaced with other persons with neither the knowledge nor acquiescence of senior commanders. . . . I cannot allow such arbitrary actions. I recommend that any questions pertaining to justified grievances against commanding personnel be brought to the attention of senior commanders, so that a thorough and all-encompassing investigation might determine the degree of culpability of each particular person.

War and Naval Minister A. *Guchkov*

[6]

The original sin of our revolution was Russia's peasant system. Because of this, the forces of socialism were inadequately manned. When the population had thrown off its Tsarist fetters, was sprinkled with the life-giving water of revolution, and could have worked marvels of autonomous creativity, it was—both in the provinces and in the army—malign, bourgeois elements that took the initiative. And was a peasant in an army greatcoat really going to understand proletarian demands like an eight-hour day? For such norms did not exist either on the front or in the villages. And in early April the soldiers were being incited—by appeals to their self-interest—against the workers, who, they had been told, did not want to work and were ignoring the interests of the front. This was an extremely dangerous moment for the revolution, when military delegations descended on factories to check on the work! The very fortress of the revolution found itself under threat from the elemental force of the peasantry. And a great deal of tact was needed to counter this atavism of the soil and the elemental, primitive, but objectively unavoidable chauvinism of those inarticulate masses, and set about the real work of socialist enlightenment: pulling the armed peasant out from under the age-old power of the bourgeoisie and allowing the blinding rays of revolutionary pride to permeate him. But even in the Soviet the majority had the peasant's narrow-mindedness, the peasant's opportunism. And so it began—an assault by all the socialist parties on the mind of the peasant-soldier, through newspapers, leaflets, missions to the front, rallies, and, at the Tauride Palace itself, meticulous work with all the military delegations arriving there (and there were more and more of these) analyzing current revolutionary issues: they must win the support of the silent masses. And it must be said that, in late March and early April, the Executive Committee had been the embodiment of that striving for proletarian democracy: if it did not enlighten and convince everyone, it used its authority to force everyone to follow its lead. The soldiers became reconciled to the workers' demands and the dangerous battle for the army was won. The army ended up in the hands of the Soviet and now there were no more jackals of reaction, no more patriots for hire, no Thiers or Cavaignac there to strangle Russian democracy! By mid-April revolutionary power had reached its peak—and it was all in the hands of the Soviet.

And Himmer was triumphant, maybe more so than all the rest. He considered the March events to be almost entirely his own achievement (although outsiders were oblivious to this, did not understand it). And that was why he kept a jealous and responsible eye open for events taking a wrong turn, always drawing on the creative resources of his political and socialist thinking to correct it.

Within a month we had, with Zimmerwaldist slogans, conquered not only the front-line forces but also the army reserves, and now all the power was in our hands. We were winning the battle! But—would the Soviet know how to exploit this march toward victory? That was the question.

The slogan "The revolution continues!" was intolerable to the Provisional Government. Those endlessly despised, evil, bourgeois hypocrites, all slaves to their fat money-pouch and boulevardier existence, now flung themselves into preaching *Burgfrieden* at home and defense of the fatherland abroad. But what was this "defense of the fatherland" if not the odious smothering of the revolution? Under the flag of defending the fatherland, or even "defending the revolution," the classical ideology of imperialism that we knew so well was showing through. The "freeing of Belgium, Serbia, Armenia, Kurland, and Poland" was not at all necessary to bring the war to an end, but was a pretext to bring the army to heel—to snatch it from the Soviet.

And what was extraordinary, Himmer discovered, was that even their intellectual leading lights such as Milyukov could be inherently incapable of understanding that! Something had happened a few days before: during a break in the Liaison Commission meeting, Himmer had said to Milyukov, "The revolution has gained the breadth that we wanted and you didn't want. You failed to secure the political dictatorship of capital. You have no real, practical power against democracy, and the army will not go over to you." And Milyukov had replied, with an expression of absolutely genuine sadness: "How can you put it that way? The army should not be coming over *to us*, but fighting on the front. You can't really think our policies are class-based, bourgeois? We're just trying to stop everything unraveling irremediably." Himmer was staggered: Milyukov seemed to be genuinely *unaware* that his policies were class-based—yet he was the leading figure of Russian imperialism and an architect of the World War!

Even partial concessions on the question of peace would have led to the merciless dictatorship of capital. If the revolution did not end the war, then the war would strangle the revolution.

This was why Himmer's anxiety had not abated ever since 27 March, since the publication of his brainchild, the Manifesto. He had already, that very day, dealt Chkheidze a sharp reprimand (which the latter had been unable to answer) for his unauthorized defensist comments from the platform of the Sea Cadet Corps: ". . . we shall not let go of our rifles; we shall defend our freedom to the last drop of blood."

But Tsereteli had arrived and ruined everything, revealing for all time his petit bourgeois essence. And to think that he had, until that day, been considered a leading Zimmerwaldist. Everyone in the Executive Committee was simply stunned—such trenchant speeches in support of the war had never been heard there, and even enemies of Zimmerwald involuntarily adjusted to the new wind that he brought.

Since that moment the issue of peace had been withdrawn from the sphere of the mass struggle and moved to that of an agreement in camera: Tsereteli was received with honor into the Liaison Commission. And it was there that Milyukov's well-known, evasive declaration of 9 April was born—as if it were not already clear that no bourgeois document had any value; that any real concessions would have to be wrung out of them not by peaceable agreement but through pressure by the masses.

It would have been possible to put things right at the Conference of Soviets, if a combative, class-based resolution on the war could have been passed there, and Himmer and Lurie had managed to get into the commission responsible for drawing up that resolution. But now that an opportunistic streak of possibilism had appeared in the workers' movement it would not be easy to get rid of it. Supported by the gutless Chkheidze, Tsereteli had taken control here too, and the Conference had approved the 9 April declaration. (However, they did put into that resolution not "defense of the fatherland" but "defense of the revolution.")

At the Conference Himmer, seated in the government box, had been disturbed by the large number of army delegates he saw. It was with particular distaste that he observed the ensigns, clearly Kadet lawyers in disguise, all brazenly speaking "in the name of the such and such army" or "such and such corps." The presidium had been elected without any changes—it remained as the EC had planned it. And conspicuous in the group was, of course, Tsereteli, slender, with large, soulful eyes, who commanded such attention when he spoke. His looks and manners were unquestionably noble, and when angry his magnificent voice rang out and a blue vein stood out on his forehead. And, with his Caucasus temperament, he would gallop fearlessly toward any precipice. Of course he was an outstanding leader of a human herd, but as a political thinker he was insignificant, obsessed by a primitive, utopian idea. This very well-known Social Democrat had no real proletarian platform, and this was plain at every step of the way.

Indignant at Steklov's furious speech, the right-wingers of the EC had met at one in the morning to appoint a co-speaker representing the opposing view. And who had been saddled with that task? Himmer! Himmer resisted: he was a revolutionary, not a compromiser! (He personally had nothing against the threats Steklov had leveled at the bourgeoisie. In fact, there should not just be threats but action too!) However, the whole EC was counting on Himmer, as their political theorist and writer. So, to get out of doing the job, the following morning he had to present his main points to the EC, namely: the Provisional Government is a class-based organ of the bourgeoisie and the Soviet is a class-based organ of democracy, and between them an irreconcilable class struggle is unavoidable. However, the form of this struggle could, for the time being, be not the overthrow of the government but pressure, control, and mobilization of our forces. Kamenev strongly approved of these points, but a snap EC meeting, with Tsereteli leading the way, had rejected them decisively. Thus Himmer was spared becoming co-speaker.

That tense struggle, with night and day coalescing, had lasted the whole of March and all through the Conference of Soviets in mid-April. He ate his dinner wherever he could, and spent the night more often than not nearby, in the Peski district, in the home of a revolutionary friend, for he could not get to his own home on the Karpovka after midnight. And one night, as the exhausted Chkheidze, Dan, and Himmer were being driven to their apartments, they were all three suddenly startled to see a large crowd marching. All carried lighted candles and they were all singing. What kind of demonstration was this? The EC had not arranged it and not been informed of it. What did the marchers want?? But the driver reminded them that the following day was Easter. Ah . . . Easter . . . It had completely slipped their minds.

Himmer was of course proud of his status—unaffiliated, one of a kind, standing alone (and his preferred technique in campaigning was to recruit support before a vote by approaching people one by one in corridors). But now he was also assailed by melancholy: just why was he fated to be one of a kind and utterly alone? It was impossible to continue the struggle without solid allies—he had to join forces with someone. With Steklov he was having no success at all. He would very much have liked to form a bloc with Kamenev: their aims coincided most frequently. But Kamenev was not sufficiently combative. The problem with the revolutionaries was that few of them were working conscientiously to develop a revolutionary socialist culture. But Kamenev actually was, and this was what made him so likeable, while the other Bolsheviks were totally worthless. And apart from the Bolsheviks there were Lurie and Shekhter, who were combative, but they were just not up to scratch—and Krotovsky was even worse—while Erlich, Rafes, and Kantorovich were social traitors. Should he search among the SRs? (But they were far weaker these days.) Aleksandrovich was exceptionally combative, a seething mass of anger, but when it came to theory he could not string two words together, and he was a poor public speaker, only ever coming out with the same threats: "They'll see when Gotz arrives! . . . when Chernov arrives!" But Gotz had arrived, and what had they seen? The younger Gotz was made of different stuff than his immortal elder brother. He was no theoretician, no independent thinker, nothing like a leader of men, and his public speaking was vacuous. He was no more than a technician, an organizer. But Dan had also returned, and been elected to the EC. Himmer had had high hopes for him as well since he was, despite everything, an outstanding figure in the International, and his whole life was infused with Social Democracy. His class instinct was true and he had a good theoretical turn of mind, though it must be said that he was not a brilliant writer or a first-class speaker. But his background as one of the founders of Menshevism and a pillar of the Liquidator group showed his true colors. Exiled in Siberia he had looked like an Internationalist—but on his return, in the EC, he had immediately joined forces with Tsereteli. So Himmer had no one.

The tone of the Executive Committee meetings was clearly becoming more and more unpleasant. The small, resolute Zimmerwaldist group—Himmer himself, Steklov, and one or two others—having launched the Soviet on a revolutionary course, had now been squeezed out and were no longer steering its policies. The great flowering of late March, that radiant time when the revolutionary line had dominated, was over. The composition of the EC was drifting in a petit bourgeois direction, tacking between the proletariat and the plutocracy, and an intellectual, narrow-minded majority had gained the upper hand—*right-wing mamluks,* as Himmer and Lurie had labeled them. Who could have imagined, in those fiery days of March, such a perfidious turn of events, imagined that our own defensists would pile in to form a conciliatory petit bourgeois dictatorship over the Soviet, a dictatorship that would push the revolution into a quagmire? Instead of that government of the franchised classes capitulating to the Soviet, was it the revolutionary policies of the Soviet that were capitulating?

But something even more dangerous was afoot: on the evening of 13 April Plekhanov was being met at Finland Station after his time abroad. Himmer was extremely wary of the damaging role the opportunist and social patriot Plekhanov could play in the future of our revolution. So he stayed aloof from the welcome ceremony and did not go to the station with the other EC members. But then his curiosity got the better of him. How could he not, despite his reservations, just take a look? So he went to the House of the People on Kronverksky Prospect, where they were to bring Plekhanov from the station. Because of his arrival, there was no working session of the Conference of Soviets that evening but, to keep the out-of-town delegates and the Petersburg Soviet occupied, they had been brought to the great auditorium of the House of the People. Chkheidze and Tsereteli had announced the imminent victory march of world revolution, after which the leaders had gone off to the station leaving on the stage, as a presidium, a few nameless soldiers—and there began an endless stream of salutations from unwashed representatives of the provinces and military units, and from Poles, Cossacks, Latvians, Jews, and Estonians. All of them had now had enough of salutations and started babbling away about whatever came into their head, and the hours were passing without anything happening. Himmer sat in the hall among the audience. By now there were even impatient voices raised against the EC: why had they been brought here? And, to make things worse, the train was late, and at the station there were a great many speeches by leaders saluting the elder leader, while at the House of the People the same old salutations were dragging on longer and longer. Then, from the station, all the EC members went home, except Chkheidze who alone, stumbling with fatigue, accompanied Plekhanov to the meeting. He led the old man forward, from behind the theater scenery, and introduced him: he was banished, but now he's back, to complete the work of freeing Russia! And a noisy ovation rose from the audience, which then subsided into attentiveness. And Plekhanov could have captured the whole hall, soviets of the capital, the provinces, and the army, with just one energetic speech, the speech of a leader. And after that he would have done a great deal of damage. With bated breath they awaited the old man's words. But he, worn out, stood motionless toward the back of the stage. Looking, in his fur coat, like a stuffed animal, he no more than bowed and uttered not a word. And Himmer was delighted: no, Plekhanov would not lead them; it was too late; he was not up to it. (Two days later they took him to the White Hall, to the Conference of Soviets, and again Chkheidze proclaimed, somewhat foolishly, that "Nikolai the Bloody wanted to be banished to England or farther, but we said 'no, just you wait here a while, till Georgi Valentinovich, our dear, banished teacher and comrade, returns.'" And Plekhanov, holding the Western socialists by the arm for support, made a speech in a weak voice—no, it made no impression. He'd grown weak. He was no danger. Anyway, he fell ill immediately afterwards.)

But, three days after Plekhanov, Lenin arrived!

Then Himmer's heart started pounding unbearably. The two had certainly disagreed at times, and Lenin had even vilified him as a "vacuous chatterbox, and we have plenty such in our bourgeois parlors"—though he had softened since the beginning of the war, now calling him "one of the better representatives of the petite bourgeoisie." But despite these insults, so strong was the left-Zimmerwaldist tendency in Lenin, so incomparable the revolutionary force he exerted, that Himmer's secret dream was to find in Lenin himself that most solid of allies! But now they were expecting a very nasty bourgeois campaign against Lenin for crossing Germany, and Himmer was planning, in the newspaper he was launching with Gorky, a riposte to those shopkeeper patriots, that sea of petit bourgeois banality emanating from the boulevard press. **What else** was Lenin to do? **What other** route remained open for his return to the homeland, thanks to friend Milyukov, who had blocked the Allies' frontiers to the antiwar revolutionaries? Faced with the dirty politics of those servants of the Allies' capital, the émigrés' conscience was clear!

Again the EC presidium members, Chkheidze and Skobelev, set out for Finland Station, and did not take Himmer. But he was so anxious to meet Lenin, that he went on his own.

The square in front of Finland Station was overflowing with vast crowds, just about allowing space for trams to pass, but nothing more. There was a mass of red flags and a great gold-embroidered banner of the Central Committee of the Russian Social Democratic Workers' Party. Military units were lined up, and plenty of them: these were not just a few odd soldiers—the Bolsheviks, masters of organization, had somehow managed to get them there. Bands were playing in different parts of the square, a good number of cars were rumbling and sputtering and there were even the intimidating hulks of two or three armored cars. And from Simbirskaya Street came yet another monstrous form, this one exuding light: a searchlight was advancing (and this was the first time Himmer had seen one in motion), swaying and shooting bands of light across roofs, houses, pillars, wires, trams, and human figures.

The farther in you went, the more rigorous were the Bolshevik procedures. Not everyone was allowed into the station—there was a great deal of checking at the entrances. Not everyone was allowed on to the platform either, and almost no one was granted access to the imperial reception rooms. On the platform, under an awning, they had built several arches and garlanded them with red and gold, and hung flags from them, inscriptions, slogans. Sailors were lined up in two rows ready to present arms, and at the end of the platform, where Lenin's carriage would come to a halt, were a band and members of the Central Committee and Petrograd Committee, holding flowers. Some of the most important people had traveled out to meet the train in advance, at Beloostrov.

All these arrangements were absolutely correct: Lenin's reception had to be all the more triumphal given that he was about to be vilified for his passage through Germany.

Showing his EC membership card, Himmer was able to see everything, penetrate all barriers, even into the imperial reception rooms, where he was the only EC member who had not been officially invited. Chkheidze, who had lost his son a few days earlier, sat downcast, confused, lost in a dream, while the eternally cheerful Skobelev was, as usual, beaming and joking. But Tsereteli had refused to come, on principle.

This time the train was even later and they had waited a long time. But now the locomotive's lights were approaching and from the far end of the platform the Marseillaise rang out, accompanied by cries of welcome—and a group began walking down the platform to the sound of the music, between the two lines of sailors. You couldn't tell what kind they were, but there were quantities of flowers. And in the front, Shlyapnikov was bustling about like a master of ceremonies: "If you please, comrades, if you please! Let us through, comrades! Let us through!" Chkheidze and Skobelev took up their positions in the middle of the imperial reception room.

Lenin was borne aloft by strong hands right up to the entrance. He did not walk in but trotted in briskly, as if not arriving from the train but running to catch it, wearing a black bowler hat—and Kollontai presented him with a magnificent red bouquet. Another thirty or so people went in after him, including one curly-headed, gawky young man, and he was given a bouquet as well, but much smaller. And the Bolsheviks locked the door now, to stop any unwanted members of the public getting in from the platform. And the door from the station concourse was locked too, but this was a double-wide glass door, and there were a great many people pressing up to it, looking in.

In the middle of the room Lenin, still in movement, almost bumped into Chkheidze, an unexpected obstacle, and stopped. Possibly, when he recognized Chkheidze, someone he had been cursing for many years now, he would not have paused there, but Chkheidze, from the depths of his melancholy, launched into a welcome speech. It contained few joyful turns of phrase, however, and already by the third sentence he was heard to say that for the defense of the revolution the forces of democracy must not move apart but must draw together, march in serried ranks, and that the Executive Committee hoped these aims were shared by the man they were now welcoming.

But Lenin, keyed up by his reception, paid not a moment's attention—not even for the sake of appearances—to the lecture he had just received, and did not even look at Chkheidze, instead taking a rapid, confident glance to and fro while straightening the flowers in his bouquet, looking up at the ceiling moldings, then around at the people present, in search of an audience. Reckoning that there were, in fact, enough, plus the curious faces watching through the glass door, he addressed his reply to them:

"Dear comrade soldiers, sailors and workers! I am happy to greet, in you, the advance guard of the worldwide proletarian army! The predatory, imperialist war is the beginning of a civil war across Europe. The dawn of the socialist revolution has begun to fire up the whole world! Long live the socialist revolution!"

Himmer began to tremble: however could he himself, in his everyday struggles on behalf of the Russian revolution, have missed this pan-European process? It was as if a flame had been brought up close to his face. What was this? The fire of revolution was already taking hold, and everywhere? It was staggering! And how Zimmerwaldist! How very, very Zimmerwaldist . . .

But with this, the speech was at an end and no events developed afterwards. Lenin paid not an iota of attention to the Executive Committee (nor did he notice Himmer among the others), and now they were already opening wide the glass doors for him and he swept out on to the front portico and down into the square accompanied by thousands of voices crying out, several bands, and searchlights.

Lenin streaked past like a comet! Like a comet that totally bewitched Himmer and carried him away in its tail, in the very end of its tail, behind everyone else: he did not witness its arrival anywhere, did not witness any speech—he only wanted to melt in, to melt into the very end of the procession which was, incidentally, heading toward the Petersburg Side, where he himself lived. But when they arrived at Trinity Square he did not turn off toward his home, on the Karpovka, but walked to the Kshesinskaya mansion itself. It sparkled, with lights outside as well as in and with a multitude of red banners, and from the balcony Lenin, now hoarse, was coming to the end of a speech, certainly not his first:

". . . the annihilation of peoples to profit the exploiters. . . . Defense of the fatherland is a spurious slogan—it is the defense of one group of capitalists against another."

How direct, how blunt, how fearless! Solemn truths about the war, absolutely uncamouflaged! But also, how very undiplomatic, crude even. Yes! This was the way to move the mass of soldiery rapidly toward political consciousness—but also perhaps to call down on oneself a violent chauvinist reaction.

And Himmer was drawn further in—he wanted more, to see more, to touch . . .

Two sturdy workers stood guard at the gate. A third was questioning, inspecting, deciding who could come in. Himmer showed his EC membership card and they let him in. Then, further on, some Bolsheviks he knew from the EC (and the gawky fellow he had seen arriving with Lenin turned out to be Zinoviev), introduced him to the still-excited Lenin, who recognized his name. "Ah, Himmer-Sukhanov, yes of course. We've crossed swords in our time!" And he was even invited up to the first floor to join the Bolshevik generals for tea (and it was not every EC member who would have been invited, not just anyone). And Himmer felt better and better among them, close to Lenin as he bathed in the glow of victory. Himmer had to pinch himself—he could not believe it. Was it a dream? Might this even be the end of his constant journeying, his quest? Why not? With the Bolsheviks, especially the likeable Kamenev, he had very few differences of opinion, not on the main issues, and they almost always voted the same way. Over tea Lenin, not mincing his words, attacked the Executive Committee and all the Soviet's policies—which had drifted so far to the right since the Manifesto of 27 March that this criticism was richly deserved. Lenin was particularly hard on Tsereteli and Chkheidze, which was correct, but also on Steklov, which was unfair, calling him "the quintessential social lackey." In the meantime, they were being urged to finish their tea, since about two hundred Bolsheviks, from Petersburg and from the Conference of Soviets, were now assembled on the ground floor. They wanted to greet Lenin again and were expecting a political discussion with him. Himmer also squeezed in. And there was not in fact a discussion but a whole speech, clearly well prepared, honed to perfection. Each point had bedded into Lenin's thinking long before and been asserted many times. But now he slammed his message home with a ready, overwhelming force. And . . . what a speech!

The Bolsheviks just listened, spellbound, open-mouthed. And on to Himmer's small head with its mop of matted hair all the power of this speech, so very new, came crashing down like a rock slide. He was absolutely stunned. Even he, Himmer, could not grasp all the twists and turns in the speech! And then, trudging home through the nocturnal streets, he was scratching his head, trying to collect his thoughts and assemble some objections.

It was a lightning strike, that speech! Forces of nature, hitherto dormant, had now arisen, a spirit that would destroy everything, which knew no doubts, no minor human problems. The worldwide socialist revolution was ready to break out from one day to the next. The crisis of imperialism could only be resolved by socialism and only by a civil war. The opportunists in the Soviet, the *revolutionary defensists*, could do nothing practical to achieve peace for all. (Lenin had rejected them too, all of them, consigned them to the enemy camp! It made your head spin.) The Manifesto of 27 March had boasted of the "revolutionary power of democracy," but what kind of power was it, when an imperialist bourgeoisie was installed at Russia's head? Capital cannot be overthrown by manifestos. (And he was burying Himmer's

Manifesto too, under the same debris!) What kind of freedom was it, if the secret treaties had still not been published? What kind of freedom of the press if the printing facilities remained in the hands of the bourgeoisie? The Soviet was that of "workers' deputies" in name only: it was run by social patriots, servitors of the bourgeoisie. As a very first step we had to make this petit bourgeois Soviet proletarian. Then we would have no need of a parliamentary republic, no need of a bourgeois democracy, no need of a government even. We would have a republic of Soviets of workers', soldiers' and *farm laborers'* deputies! (He'd made no mention of peasants' deputies, and that was impressive!) And so, mind-boggling fragments poured out. The land? Immediate "organized seizure" everywhere. The factories? Armed workers would both work on the shop floor and be running production. And he had inveighed furiously against the European socialists, even those who were actually battling their bourgeoisie, but their efforts were too feeble, and even against the right Zimmerwaldists: only the *left* Zimmerwaldists were guarding the interests of the proletariat and the worldwide revolution, and all the rest were traitors to the working class! And the very name of Social Democracy was now tainted with treason!

Himmer's weak legs could barely carry him as he wove his way along Kamennoostrovsky Prospect, deserted at that time of night. A "Republic of Soviets"—what did that mean? A system of free communities? And what was to be done with that stupid peasantry? Would—oh dear—would Soviets of workers and farm laborers really be able to build socialism against the will of the majority? With our petit bourgeois structure and our splintered, backward peasantry, how could we expect to see a worldwide socialist revolution? Yes, of course! Lenin was a thousand times right to say that the worldwide revolution was approaching. But declaring it in the abstract, with no practical application to today's political situation, was only throwing the real possibilities into confusion and even harming them. Even harming them grievously. There was a captivating audacity in the way Lenin took no notice whatsoever of the Social Democrats' program. But he had not demonstrated an understanding of the real state of affairs in Russia. And there was, in his speech, no concrete analysis of the socioeconomic conditions necessary for socialism in Russia. Why, actually, there was no economic program there at all, was there? How could it work without one? . . . No, it would not be possible to ally himself with Lenin, for he was overstepping all reasonable boundaries.

No, Himmer was not cut out to be a member of any party. He was too much of a Lavrov, too much of a "critically thinking individual."

The following day, 17 April, he was to hear that speech again. Before the Conference participants dispersed, at the Tauride Palace, a long-awaited unifying session was called, bringing together all the Social Democrats—Bolsheviks, Mensheviks of all hues, and those unattached to any faction—with the aim of creating a single SD party. Dzhugashvili was listed to speak for the Bolsheviks. But now, of course, Lenin rushed there at full pelt. If the Conference had not already finished, his inflammatory ideas would have been disgorged there. But now there was an even greater irony: at the *unifying* session, he launched into an irreconcilably divisive speech causing the worst schism the party had ever known in the previous sixteen years. And the more violent the reactions of his audience, the more intransigent the phrases he slung their way.

Poor Goldenberg, who had put the most effort into unifying the Social Democrats, was almost reduced to tears by Lenin's speech denigrating all and sundry. The Social Democrats in the Semi-Circular Hall of the Duma were at first stunned, but then started interrupting, protesting, venting their anger: "He's raving! He's just a rabble-rouser!" And the Bolsheviks applauded all the more, and the enraged Bogdanov shouted, "That's disgraceful, applauding that balderdash! You bring shame on yourselves! You are Marxists, after all!" The entire *unification* agenda had gone by the board, and all the other speakers—Dan, Voitinsky, Lurie, Yudin—used their time only to challenge something Lenin had said. Tsereteli argued heatedly that if they had seized power in the first days, they would already have been crushed; that they must not proceed on the basis of what could be seized but of what could be secured. The annulment of the treaties with the Allies would have led to the total destruction of the International. Goldenberg declared that Lenin had staked his claim to the throne left vacant thirty years before by Bakunin, the outdated remnants of a primitive anarchism and a leap into open anarchy, and had raised the flag of civil war within Social Democracy itself. Steklov said, and Himmer thought to himself, that the Russian revolution had passed Lenin by, but that when he had acquainted himself with the situation in Russia he himself would give up those ideas. (Himmer did not want to speak against Lenin, but he thought that certainly, in an atmosphere of real battle, Lenin would quickly become acclimatized and discard most of his anarchic ravings.) In response, of the Bolsheviks only Kollontai spoke and she was met by laughter and derision. Lenin declined to make any concluding remarks or answer the objections (and this was his constant weakness, face-to-face disputes without any preparation). In the corridors the Bolsheviks were whispering here and there that, yes, Ilyich's ideas were abstract and "if anything we're closer to you than we are to him." But aloud they did not dare. And fifteen or so Bolsheviks even walked out in protest, outraged by Lenin's behavior.

But even then it was not the end of the prominent émigrés returning! Five days later Chernov too, leader of the SRs, was met at Finland Station. Again, Himmer went.

Well, the SR welcome ceremony was inferior to that of the Bolsheviks in terms of both organization and pomp. Although there were, in the square, both military units and columns of workers, and youngsters were crowded together on the platforms of six-ton trucks, there was less order and no searchlights were in evidence. On the station platform, reusing the same arches, they had replaced the Bolshevik slogans with "Land and freedom" and "In struggle we gain our rights." Kerensky came to meet Chernov (and his adjutants had called out to the crowds in front of him, "Citizens! Make way for the Minister of Justice!"), but the train was even later this time, and Kerensky did not wait, leaving Zenzinov in his place. The imperial rooms were packed: entrance was open to all and the public there was, by and large, educated. There was a mass of people wanting to speak, to greet the SR leader, and an impromptu commission was set up to decide, amidst noise and squabbling, who would be allowed to speak and who not.

Chernov appeared, exuberant, constantly smiling all round. It was the smile of a strong man. Now he was given an enormous bouquet and, amid cries from the crowd and to the strains of the Marseillaise, he managed, with difficulty, to make his way through to the imperial rooms. During the first speech from the party, Himmer saw, through the undulating crowd, that Chernov was accompanied (and this had not been announced beforehand) by old Deutsch (a constant compromiser, dangerous given his longstanding authority—he would support Plekhanov), Fundaminsky, Avksentiev and another trim figure dressed in the English style, who turned out to be Savinkov. What was he to do? The EC had not entrusted him to welcome *them*, and he personally had no inclination to do so: he decided to address Chernov alone. Himmer gave his welcome speech (and he had to address Chernov as the "great theoretician of socialism from the very heart of the revolution") a combative slant, focusing on the most important thing: how appreciative the EC was of Chernov's merits in supporting *internationalist* (read Zimmerwaldist) socialism and adding that now, within the revolution, these positions were *in mortal danger*—but that we would defend them from enemies both without and *within*! Chernov was very happy to reply, but he did so at such length that it took its toll on everyone squashed in there. He also revealed a strange mannerism, a coquettish way of rolling his eyes. Then everyone went out into the roar of the square and he gave another speech there (standing, from a motorcar), and the SR bosses (accompanied by armored cars) proceeded to their headquarters on Galernaya, most probably not for a stern policy speech, but to make merry in the style of their voluptuous leader.

But, shaken as Himmer was by Lenin's extreme schismatical leanings, he was equally disappointed to note that Chernov showed no intention of excluding any group, wanting instead to unite all the populists. What? Must this mold also accrete to Zimmerwald? It seemed, however, that Chernov was affecting more optimism and assurance than he actually felt.

Himmer despaired! The leading theoretician of the EC had no allies, nor any application for his energy. Now he decided to redirect it into his newspaper, *The New Life*, which he would be bringing out now, in a few days, not so much together with Gorky as under cover of that illustrious name. And close to *Pravda*'s line, but not locked into it, he would trace the true path of the revolutionary flame. And there would also be the great names of culture: Romain Rolland, Benois, Lunacharsky . . .

(And he must not forget his scholarly standing either, not forget how decidedly different he was from that group of grey party men of the EC brotherhood. A few days before, as it happened, someone had come up with the plan for a ceremonial opening of the All-Russian Association of Positive Knowledge and invited scholars, writers, and notable figures, including Himmer. And he had made a speech. Firstly, for the sake of modesty, he had expressed a reservation: "It is, of course, not up to us, the unskilled laborers of culture, to . . ." but then went straight on to lay out before the scholars the program of the revolution:

"The workers' movement and democracy's struggle are guided least of all by the ideal of well-being, and are not concerned that there should be a chicken in every pot: they aspire to the emancipation of mankind and its entry into the realm of spiritual freedom.")

[7]

It was strange, how Sasha Lenartovich's fate had become linked to the Kshesinskaya mansion. He had been among the first to enter it, hot on the heels of the fleeing owner, and since that Bolshevik meeting in the little hall with the fountain he had visited ever more frequently: he already felt at home there. (But the Cavalry administration he now shunned entirely. He had collected his wages for March, but for April it might by this time be awkward—though many were happy to take theirs.) He was driven not by the sentiment, now so fashionable, that was prompting any doctor or lawyer, fattened up by his bourgeois comforts, suddenly to declare that he had always been in favor of freedom and had even suffered for it in his youth, and is leaving the Kadets for the Populist Socialists—if only for the sound of the word "socialism." No. Ever since 12 March when he had stormed the police stations, Sasha had wanted to take an active, and ever more active, part in the revolution! It was what he'd been waiting for and living for, this revolution! But it was only in earlier times that solitary fighters like his uncle Anton could shine. Nowadays a lone fighter could do nothing of note—he had to join the ranks. But Lenartovich had joined no battalion: the Officer-Republicans had achieved nothing, so what was left? A political party? But the parties were all pretty feeble as well: only the Bolsheviks were effective. And they had more backbone than the Interdistrict group.

That backbone was provided by a score of forceful, fearless, even if young lads, such as Solomon Roshal. Sasha admired Roshal who, though still a student, had gone all out to bring the maritime fortress and naval base round to his cause. And the Bolshevik leader Lev Borisovich Kamenev, on the other hand, was sensible, well-balanced, thoughtful, and very likeable. He had chatted to Sasha once for half an hour and won his heart completely, even though not convincing him on every issue. In personal conversations everything Kamenev said seemed impeccably consistent. But when speaking in public (at the Conference of Soviets Sasha, in the gallery, had heard him several times), perhaps in response to impatient outbursts from the opposition, or perhaps it was in the nature of public speaking, tiny fault lines of contradiction would form, widen as if on the surface of a balloon being inflated, and become visible. So Sasha still had some doubts on major issues.

Firstly, the war. Kamenev did not seem sufficiently firm in his conviction that this damned war must be finished with as soon as possible, and definitively; though neither had he ever been heard to say it was permissible to carry on fighting. He proposed to press the Provisional Government into getting all the warring parties to negotiate—but how long was that going to take? As a result Kamenev became known as a benign dreamer, whose golden dreams would be rudely interrupted by the crash of German artillery. No! Sasha longed for total resolve, for an idea blazing with passion or, as some were calling for, a flaming torch of shared insurrection, to be passed across the battle fronts! It was the only way to have done with this war!

Secondly, about the Provisional Government. Although Kamenev did not go along with the impatient types who said the government must immediately, right now, straight away be overturned, neither did he have a single good word to say about it. He said that not one member was trustworthy, that they were class enemies, and that we wouldn't lift a finger to support them; that nothing could tempt us to join the government and we would keep it under every kind of oversight. But how, in that case, could this government govern? It was, despite everything, our first revolutionary government, our major achievement! He was proposing instead to unite around the Soviet—but the Soviet was not a government! "The proletariat must accede to power": that idea was also very unclear to Sasha. The working class was being inflated into some new "His Majesty," about whom it was forbidden to voice the slightest criticism. Another demonstration of a well-known truth of historical materialism: that ways of thinking are conservative, lagging behind ways of life.

And yet, no matter what issues still needed clarification, Kamenev's quiet dignity, tact, and intelligence made him far superior to the expansive, simple-minded Shlyapnikov and the sluggish, obtuse Stalin. As for Muranov, the less said the better.

And what were they to make of Lenin now? The Bolsheviks, proudly loyal to their center abroad, had tensely awaited his arrival, all full of hope but some also on their guard. At that same Conference of Soviets Nogin had read out Lenin's telegram from Switzerland, saying that England would on no account allow him or the other internationalists through and that the Russian proletarian revolution had no worse enemy than the English imperialists and their stewards, who would stoop to any deceit or baseness. And now, on the morning of 16 April, news arrived at the Kshesinskaya mansion, quite unexpectedly, of a telegram sent from Sweden: Lenin and his companions were on their way and would be in Petrograd late that very evening. Amazing! How on earth had he suddenly managed to get out, fool the English, and be wafted away, as if through the air? From a few discreet conversations, Sasha discovered that he had traveled through Germany. Some found this extremely worrying: how would it be seen by the masses, by public opinion? But Sasha was not the slightest bit worried: it was excellent! Quite right too! He could imagine that burning impatience—he'd heard a lot about Lenin's character. Yes, he'd been quite right! Why bother with frontiers and governments, when the time had come to have done with this whole war! And now, like a fiery meteor, he was heading this way!

They heard about it on Monday morning, but as this was the second day of Easter no newspapers were published: no one was working anywhere and they could not even get an announcement printed. And it would have been too late anyway. Yet Bolshevik headquarters decided they must organize a massive, splendid welcome. But how were they to round up the people? They sent messengers out to the Vyborg, Neva, and Petersburg Sides and Vasilievsky Island to tour round, mustering a crowd. They phoned Kronstadt and were told that the ice would be starting its springtime drift any moment now but they would still send a small delegation. It was also, of course, Easter in all the barracks: there was, it seemed, no way detachments could be assembled and brought along. Midshipman Ilyin, with the terrifying sobriquet of Rodion Raskolnikov, undertook to find some sailors—and he did indeed bring to the station a detachment from the 2nd Naval Depot. Lenartovich was sent to the Peter and Paul Fortress, since he'd been there before. And, talking to the people there, together they came up with a brilliant idea: to mobilize the Fortress's searchlight crew for the welcome. They would send two searchlights to the station, two along the route to Trinity Square, and the others would illuminate the Square from the Fortress towers, to meet the arrivals. Three of the armored cars kept in the Kshesinskaya yard would go as well. As evening fell the heavens opened, which might well have deterred those interested in attending. But the rain stopped and the crowd did not have to be assembled till eleven, so they managed in time. The workers arrived, some with rifles. Several thousand people were crammed into the square, and searchlight beams scanned the dark, overcast sky and the station. An impromptu welcome, but a great success!

Sasha did not go onto the platform but stayed in the square outside, with the searchlights. Many in the crowd did not even know who Lenin was, but waited for him all the same—and now he was about to appear! As they came out on to the station steps, some lads from a detachment of the workers' militia raised their rifles into the air. Lenin climbed onto the seat of a car to make his speech, but he was not visible. So they lifted him onto the roof of an armored car. Now Sasha was quite close and could hear and see him, in a pool of light, perfectly.

He had had high expectations of Lenin but at first he was disappointed: he was unattractive, constantly fidgeting, waving his arms around all the time, and his voice was flat. But *what* he was yelling—that was a different matter!

". . . to greet you, representatives here of the victorious revolution, you, the advance guard of the worldwide proletarian army! We are on the threshold of a pan-European civil war! The hour is near, when the German people will hear the call of our comrade Karl Liebknecht and turn their bayonets against the exploiters! Germany is already in a state of ferment!"

Extraordinary! He had just come from Germany—he knew what he was talking about. This was a dream come true!

"The whole of European capitalism could collapse any time now, if not today then tomorrow. The Russian revolution, your great achievement, has struck the first blow against capitalism and is ushering in a new era! Long live the worldwide socialist revolution!!"

A new way was opening up! The surest way to end the World War. At last it had reached the consciousness of the European masses too.

Everyone, whether they had heard him or not, shouted "hurrah," rifles were raised again, Lenin climbed down into a car and set off slowly, the crowd pouring into the street after him; and the armored cars slowly moved off, with searchlights swinging their blinding beams.

Many walked all the way to the Kshesinskaya mansion, jamming the whole street and half the square, and waited for another speech. And Lenin, hatless, almost totally bald, came out onto the little first floor balcony and from it he yelled the same speech as before, his right hand slicing into the air like a spade. Roshal, in a student cap and sailor's pea jacket, had just made it in time and came out onto the balcony with Lenin, to shout "hurrah" on behalf of the Kronstadt contingent.

Then, after the senior figures had had their tea on the first floor, all the leaders came downstairs to the small, white marble hall with a piano, near the winter garden. There were ornate ceilings, vases, stucco moldings, but in place of the ballerina's white silk-upholstered furniture, they had dragged in crudely produced chairs and benches, and somehow a hundred and fifty or so Bolsheviks managed to squeeze in. And they all listened devotedly (more devotedly than Sasha) to their leader's speech.

Sasha, now up close and with good lighting, was even more disappointed with Lenin: he didn't cut a heroic figure, most unprepossessing. And on top of that he had a speech defect and his eyes, eyebrows, and lips looked Mongoloid for some reason; his domed head was abnormal, disproportionate, and his teeth were crooked, uneven, and damaged—but there was something stronger, something more intense than Lenin himself, which blew through his being as if through a conduit, then swept you up and made you fly.

It was not passion in his voice, no, not that, but it was as if some powerful machine were advancing ineluctably, carving itself a path. There were no oratorical flourishes, just the force he exerted on his audience. Everything he said against the war was splendid: most of all it was the promise of immediate world revolution that would catch you up in the whirlwind. But what nonsense was he saying about power? Power should have been seized by the proletariat and the poorest peasantry in the very first days, but they had been scared of their own shadow. And now . . . you could not trust the likes of Milyukov and Guchkov and there was no point even trying to convince them of anything, for they were capitalists and were, with their billions, crushing the life out of the whole nation. We should not, he said, be congratulating one another on this bloodless revolution, for revolution was no firework display but a fight to the death against the exploiters. We had before us a war against the parasite classes. He said of the "government of capitalists" what, until now, only the benighted types on the Vyborg Side committee had been blathering on about, except that Lenin did it more trenchantly and more intransigently. But what, Sasha wondered, would happen if we overturned the government right now? What if we *seized* everything, "starting with the banks, so as to propel mankind forward"? We'd have total anarchy and the end of the revolution! And the most surprising thing he said was that on no account should we unify with any of the socialists. The speaker was even prepared to sever relations immediately with any who did wish to unify! What folly. Why ever split our forces into smaller and smaller factions?

It was, of course, aimed primarily at Kamenev. But the latter sat unperturbed and at the end—it was already three in the morning—he summed up very diplomatically: we can agree or disagree with the speaker, but in any case the brilliant and acknowledged leader of our party has come back—and together with him we shall advance toward socialism.

Sasha's brain was working feverishly. He had never experienced a night like this. Hounding Milyukov? But that was playing on his audience's basest instincts—and Milyukov was Russia's pride and joy. It was a wild concoction of real nuggets and mistakes. He was calling for a great leap, immediately, but without any firm foothold. His frantic energy and the coherence of his argumentation captivated his listeners. But his program and his picture of the future were nevertheless unclear. Sasha had seen this in the deep puzzlement spreading over many faces. So was there to be a struggle within the party? Kamenev had said confidentially that he was convinced that after three days in Russia Lenin would see things differently.

The rank-and-file Bolsheviks were perplexed. They were all accustomed to seeing Lenin as their leader, and how could they manage without him—how could they cut off their own head? If you spoke out against Lenin people called you a Menshevik, an opportunist. A new split in the party now would be its downfall. And he was repeating over and over that if anyone reached out so much as a finger toward the defensists this would be a betrayal of international socialism. Unifying with them would be treachery and if this happened we must go our separate ways—and he preferred to remain in the minority. Why, throw out our Social Democrat sign like so much dirty laundry and call ourselves the Communist party.

The following day, apparently, at the Tauride Palace, his only supporter had been the beautiful Kollontai. (It was strange, unnatural even, that she should be the one to share all his ideas, and so exactly. A couple of days later, his enemies started spreading a little rhyme: "Lenin says that black is white, Kollontai says, 'Yes, that's right!'")

The coherence in Lenin's statements was reflected in the cohesion, increasing by the day, among the Bolsheviks. Sasha continued to frequent the Kshesinskaya mansion. He was struck by the realization that, for them, it was less important to perceive which of Lenin's individual ideas were right and which wrong than it was to take action—concerted action.

It gave Sasha a very unpleasant feeling. So unquestioning! Such unthinking devotion to the cause! But on the other hand he too was looking for a solid structure. Without that attitude, no solid structure could be achieved.

Oh well, there was still time to observe.

And how were they going to win Petrograd over? The leaders had decided there were too few of us to cover the whole town, and the Vyborg Side was the only part where we had the advantage. So we would not go anywhere. We would initiate a permanent public rally here at the mansion, with speeches from the balcony, and the listeners would stream in. The street widened out toward the square: there would be room for all comers. They fixed a red flag on the balcony, with the legend "PC-CC RSDRP" in gold, and draped the windows of the winter garden in red. With the feminine tracery of its latticework, the mansion-cum-palazzo had a cheerful, playful appearance. And the springtime scent of plants in bud. Nearby was a rare sight, the soaring minaret and faience cupola of the mosque, and on the other side the Peter and Paul Fortress. The Neva, the city's lungs, ran close by. And every day, all day long and late into the evening, it was rally after rally, speech after speech from the balcony. "Lenin's Hyde Park," a nice little property, scoffed *The Russian Will.*

A motley audience would assemble there: simple folk, soldiers, injured men from the military hospitals, urban bourgeois, lordly types in expensive collars and hats, and ladies, and junior officers, all there out of curiosity—which was what the party had been banking on. Even a deacon in a cassock might find his way in and shout up from below: "Lvov is a Kadet party puppet! We, the clergy, want to send delegates to the Soviet of Workers' Deputies!" Mostly people listened quietly and were happy to believe what they heard: "It's a good thing he didn't come by sea—they'd have drowned him." And, from a woman wearing a black lace kerchief: "I didn't know England was that underhand." And if someone in the crowd, convinced by the press attacks, shouted, "You lied from the moment you got off the German sealed train!" then from the balcony would come a vigorous response: "Those pressmen'll get their comeuppance! We'll teach them to set soldiers against workers!"

During the day the crowd was smaller, torpid, and not over-inclined to argue. They had the party program explained to them in detail. The housing question? Yes, the building of people's palaces will have to be delayed due to a lack of iron and concrete. But, for the time being, requisitioning premises from the bourgeoisie will help. We'll have to ask those living too well to tighten their belts a bit. (Applause. The crowd liked that.) Theaters will be free, a far cry from paying twenty rubles for Chaliapin. (Shouts of approval.) Taxes? There'll have to be taxes, but they'll be paid by the richest, specially the property owners.

But it was the war that really fired everyone up. Those gentlefolk of the "People's Freedom Party," being driven around, lounging in their carriages—the war was their good fortune: without it they'd have lost the Straits. Rodzyanko had eight million acres in Ekaterinoslav province. It was to hold on to that land that he wanted to send Petrograd men to the front. Let anyone who thinks going to the front is so pleasant take himself off there! (The soldiers liked that—they'd spread it all round town.) In Russia there are more than two million coppers, city police, gendarmes, and detectives—let them go off to war! (Howls of delight.) And Guchkov should stop trying to frighten us with a Wilhelm offensive! Put an end to the war! No confidence in the Provisional Government!

Sasha, of course, had no trouble seeing the fallacy here (we had five to seven times fewer policemen than they had in England or France) but, but . . . if you wanted to join these ranks you had to pay for it. He himself never addressed the people, and it was not because he was shy: he could not, out of his own mouth, articulate such idiocies or rack his brains for instantaneous, crass rejoinders to the calls from below. But he helped organize everything. There was no doubting the revolutionary daring in all this.

Kollontai's addresses to the soldiers were effective. They listened attentively.

"What does the government tell you about land? They propose you should wait? But things like that you don't just wait for—you take them. Remember the example of the French revolution: they took the land and took a bayonet to the landowners. I'm not suggesting you bayonet them all, but . . ."

Toward evening the crowd, now lit by streetlights, increased to four hundred or so, and they shouted more boldly. And they had to be handled more firmly. There was always a chairman on duty on the balcony to run the rally. A lad from the front came out with: "We need men in the trenches, and they're sending invalids spitting blood and with fingers shot off. So we shouldn't oppose sending the Petrograd garrison to the front!" And back came an immediate response from the Bolshevik side: "Don't fall for those sob stories! Refuse Guchkov's order to send out reinforcement units!" A student from the crowd: "And what does the Soviet think of that?" "You can't speak from down there. Sign up to get on the speakers' list." So he sent up his question in writing—and it went straight into the waste bin. Trustingly, they gave the floor to a corporal, and off he went: "I've got the George Cross. There'll be no peace while the Kaiser's on the throne or he's dictating peace conditions. My brother's at the front and my parents at home are both sixty and I don't shout 'down with the war.' I don't want Germans lording it over us. So don't you and your Lenin go shouting the praises of those Prussian Junkers!" And, from below, Bolsheviks placed in the crowd for the purpose shouted, "Comrades! Let's arrest him!" and the chairman immediately withdrew his right to speak.

Another time they gave the floor to a student, who also turned out to oppose Lenin, and even put on an uneducated manner of speaking, with "or mebbe" and "killin'." He was silenced and removed from the balcony. Protests were heard from the crowd, and the chairman shouted, "Quiet! Only our people can speak! This is our platform! If you don't want to listen to us, you can leave." If someone from the crowd shouted something critical of Lenin the response would be immediate: "And who are you then? A social bourgeois? A social provocateur? We're calling the militia. Fancy a trip down to the commissariat?" And they'd go downstairs immediately to give their people back-up. Either they'd throw the troublemaker out or grab him, bring him into the house, where there were more guards, and draw up a charge sheet in the name of the "Combat Organization of the CC": "Spoke, without permission from the chairman, in inflammatory terms." And if he still didn't pipe down he'd be threatened with arrest. Scared, he might not reveal his name. (On the Vyborg Side they were already used to this: there anyone speaking out against Lenin was simply beaten up.) An engineer had the floor: "Lenin's not a patriot!" And they came back immediately: "We have to draw up a charge sheet!" And he was taken off to the commissariat for questioning.

These procedures were of course crude—no better than under the Tsar—but without them the rallies would have collapsed and that would have been that. No way of doing it without that discipline.

And these measures were, strangely enough, very helpful: in the environs of the Kshesinskaya house dissident voices were silent and Suvorin's spiteful *Little Gazette* actually admitted to its readers that it was dangerous to walk past that particular mansion. So that was the way to do it!

Sometimes Lenin himself spoke—not too often, but always full of rage. He would rush around the little balcony in a frenzy, gesticulating so wildly that he seemed in danger of toppling over the balustrade. "I'm not even going to answer the scum who are yelling that I've sold out to Germany! And we're spilling our blood for the English and French bourgeoisie! Milyukov says so himself: we have interests in common with the Allies!" Or else he would tell his listeners point-blank, "You are within your rights to take back what the bourgeoisie stole from you. The Provisional Government is a gang of bloodsuckers—the power should be in the hands of the Soviet."

Everyone, including Sasha, was stunned by the extreme nature of his language. Maybe Lenin was becoming unstable, had succumbed to his own rhetoric? And there was that gesture, too, that had appeared: he would raise a clenched fist.

The day before, the Sunday, a demonstration had been organized, to protest outside the Allies' embassies, with the anarchists joining in too. But a large detachment of militia had stopped them on Trinity Bridge.

However, Sasha was quite taken with this bellicose atmosphere and he took part, contributing the authority of his military appearance and conduct. (He was also given the job of liaison with the 180th Regiment on Vasilievsky Island, where there was already a Bolshevik committee.) He knew that Lenin had raised a few hackles, and not only among the bourgeois newspapers: at the university and the Bestuzhev Courses too his tactics were hotly disputed. All this could not immediately, or very clearly, be accommodated in the mind: Sasha had experienced this for himself. But since Lenin's arrival he was now quite sure that Milyukov and Guchkov were indissolubly bound up with the continuation of this war. And this was an attraction for Sasha, a promise of victory: for in the midst of that lack of focus, those contradictory opinions dividing the Petrograd public, a small but close-knit force with the right idea of an end to the war could be victorious! The whole thing depended on some well-directed pressure. There were rumors that, at the Conference of Soviets, people were saying the Provisional Government were usurpers. That was of course true. But what about the Executive Committee of the Soviet? Were they not equally usurpers?

And, if they were, in what respect did the Leninists have any fewer rights?

Sasha was seized by the urge to take part in another great movement, just as he already had, during those March days.

Although, alas, he had heard that his brother-in-arms in the storming of the Mariinsky Palace, cavalry captain Sosnovsky, had been unmasked as a common criminal. Could that really be true?

[8]

(RULE OF THE PEOPLE IN PETROGRAD: FRAGMENTS)

* * *

Apart from the Cossacks, no one in Petrograd refused to attend the "funeral for the martyrs of the revolution," the first funeral in Russia in a millennium without a cross and censer: nine hundred thousand people trudged along in a daze to shove the extraordinary red coffins into trenches while a band played. The Cossacks stayed in their barracks: their conscience would not allow them to bury people without priests. But by the following day concern was already spreading among the simple people and the soldiers: "No good'll come of it! That's the devil's work, burying people like that! God'll punish us!" And a day later the soldiers' deputies in the Soviet were given permission for a requiem. They asked the clergy of Our Savior on the Spilled Blood to conduct the service on the Field of Mars.

And during the second week after Easter frequent processions from various churches made their way there.

* * *

In March all the yardmen stopped clearing snow from the streets and sanding them when it was icy. Snowdrifts developed in the middle of streets even in the center of town. Then the military authorities sent reservists from the Volynian, Pavlovsky, Preobrazhensky, and Izmailovsky Regiments and the Grenadiers to clear the ice from the streets, and detachments from the Semyonovsky Regiment to the railway depots, because the unloading of freight cars had all but ground to a halt. And lads from the Moscow and Lithuanian Regiments to do the actual unloading.

When the snow thawed, mixed with the horse manure it had become a chocolate-colored slush, and when it dried up the streets remained dirty. Bits of paper, cigarette boxes, and sunflower seed husks are lying around everywhere. In courtyards the cesspits have not been cleaned, due to a shortage of sanitation teams.

* * *

On upper floors the water pressure is no longer adequate (whereas it was previously). So tenants are unwilling to pay their full rent. The mayor has appealed to them to save water by partially blocking the taps on the lower floors with lead and not all taking their baths on Saturdays. The cost of water will be doubled, so that people will use less.

The water supply staff have demanded a million-ruble pay raise from the City Duma.

* * *

In the raw spring weather, the queues in front of bread shops and bakeries are as long as they were before the revolution. People start to queue in the middle of the night. The bread ration cards do nothing to reduce the queues, since not enough bread is being baked anyway. There's a limit on the amount issued to a single person, even if that person comes with more than one ration card—which makes the cards pointless. A family divides up the ration cards and sends members to queue in two different places. And again they go from the Vyborg to the Petersburg Side looking for bread.

Soldiers are constantly impinging on the queues for bakers' shops, sundries shops, and methylated spirit sellers, by forming their own separate soldiers' lines, which move faster, so there's nothing left for the main queue. The community governor's office has called on the soldiers to remember that all citizens now have equal rights. The women in the queue use some very ripe language to tell the soldiers their mutiny has only made things worse.

* * *

In Petrograd it has already, since March, been hard to spot any soldiers actually *standing* guard: all sentries now sit on chairs or stools with their rifles leaning against a wall. On the way to his post a soldier never neglects to stock up on sunflower seeds and cigarettes.

The soldiers are always being either taken to demonstrations or kept in their barracks for meetings and rallies. The streets are full of soldiers out enjoying themselves. But the more practical among them go off to supplement their pay with a job on the side: they sell newspapers or sunflower seeds, knock together portable hawkers' stands, sweep the streets, or become porters or militiamen.

* * *

When soldiers encounter officers on the streets of Petrograd, by and large they not only don't salute—they don't even take the cigarette from between their teeth or their hands out of their pockets. However, one in ten does still salute, which only makes things more troublesome for the officers: they have to keep a watchful eye on every soldier they encounter so as not to miss one of these pedants. It would be far simpler if no one saluted anymore.

Some officers have started going round without epaulettes on their greatcoat (only keeping them on their tunic).

* * *

Many passersby no longer sport red emblems. On the pavements and at hawkers' stands people sell smutty little brochures about the Tsar, the Tsaritsa, and their "bedroom secrets."

The magazines have photographs showing the Tsar now, clearing away the snow and chatting affably. Sometimes two of his daughters are with him.

* * *

More and more trams are taken out of service due to overloading and poor quality repairs. (The workers have sacked some of the tramway engineers as well as the director of the power station.) To remedy the situation, the Municipal Board has altered the traditional, age-old Petersburg routes: many of the longer-distance routes no longer go through the city center. And no trams will now run along Nevsky Prospect between Mikhailovskaya Street and Znamenskaya Square.

Moreover, to speed up the turnaround, sixty stops have been removed. They have also, in their haste, taken out the route linking four train stations.

So all hopes are pinned on the cabbies, then? But they've started charging exorbitant prices: from Baltic Station to Nikolaevsky Station with luggage costs the same as three hundred versts by train in second class.

* * *

All the office workers ignore their bosses and spend their time chatting, or on the streets demonstrating.

The post is no longer delivered five times a day, as before, but only twice. You're lucky if your morning paper arrives by eleven in the morning and not at nearly five in the evening. The postmen pocketed their customary Easter tips but didn't work for the four days of Easter. The mailboxes are now emptied twice a day instead of eight times. Previously, when you sent a letter or telegram you knew exactly when it would arrive. Now it's totally unpredictable.

And because at night households, fearing burglars, have stopped opening their doors when they hear a knock and "Telegram!" the night-time delivery of telegrams is also discontinued.

* * *

In recent weeks Petrograd has surpassed Moscow in the number of congresses it hosts. It is, after all, the capital. The Kadet Congress. The All-Russian Conference of Soviets. The All-Russian Teachers' Congress. The Trudovik Congress. And congresses of the Bund, Cossacks, Women Doctors, Army and Navy Doctors, Military Pharmacists. As well as a good many celebratory tributes of various kinds. And conferences of the minor parties.

* * *

And, still, ever more demonstrations stream toward the Tauride Palace, specially on Saturdays and Sundays. In recent weeks the Tauride has seen demonstrations by Muslims, Jews, Buddhists, teachers, apprentices, orphans, the deaf and dumb, pharmacists, midwives, and prostitutes. Once several thousand soldiers' wives arrived and announced their demands from the platform of the White Hall: a doubling of rations for soldiers' wives, equality with officers' wives, and equality between common-law wives and legally married wives (that is, they should receive rations). "Palace grenadiers" arrived, old men who had served in the Russo-Turkish war. Three hundred or so high school pupils arrived (skipping classes) with massive red placards proclaiming, "Greetings to the Provisional Government" and "End the school year now, without exams!" A woman with a resonant voice made a speech in favor of immediate peace with no annexations or indemnities and she was applauded. A Caucasus fighter from the Native Division, brandishing his dagger, promised to throw the Germans out of Russia and not to lay down his arms—and he was applauded too.

And there was a procession of churchgoers of some kind singing psalms. They carried red flags and banners with the words "Christ is risen! Long live the free church! For a free people, a democratic church!"

And when, exactly a month after the revolution, the training detachment from the Volynian Battalion, led by Sergeant Kirpichnikov, arrived to make their mark, it was a weekday, no one was expecting it, and no one could be found to receive them except Ramishvili.

* * *

All over town there are rumors and more rumors: due to the collapse of the Baltic fleet, the Northern Front is exposed and the Germans might arrive in Petrograd at any moment.

Among the people, discontent over the new order is growing, but they discuss it only in whispers: it's dangerous. In prosperous circles they've been waiting for some miraculous deliverance, but no deliverance materializes. What good are appeals from the government when half the country is illiterate? If only a strong individual would appear, he would save everything! But no such individual appears. Some even say what about the Germans then, perhaps they'd be better? People are starting to move, making for somewhere more peaceful: Moscow, Kiev, the south, abroad. Some, but fewer, are moving their capital to Europe before it's too late. Others say that's despicable.

* * *

It's still possible to leave by train in third class, especially to Moscow. But for first and second class and sleeping berth tickets at Nikolaevsky and Vindava Stations you have to queue for days, and there's a roll-call morning and evening. At the municipal ticket office on Bolshaya Konyushennaya Street there's a queue of more than five thousand people, and you have to spend several days there (the Municipal Board has posted guards and allowed fires at night). At the end of April they started giving out not tickets but vouchers, for the purchase of tickets in the second half of May. Sleeping car berths were discontinued altogether and replaced by standard seats.

People have started leaving town on the roofs of trains, and one hundred versts out on the Moscow-Vindava route several people lost their grip and were fatally injured.

* * *

The factory owners have paid their workers for all the days of the revolution and the day of the funeral for the martyrs and undertaken to pay the workers elected to positions in soviets of deputies, food supply committees, and factory militias. But there are more demands: to increase wages four and five times higher. Workers at the Triangle Factory are demanding a six-hour working day and supplementary pay for every past year of the war.

Searches at all factory gates have been discontinued.

* * *

Delegations of soldiers have started arriving from the front and going round factories to check on the work. The workers have changed their tone completely: now they'd be ready to work a fourteen-hour day, except that there's a shortage of raw materials and fuel. In truth, it's not hard to fool the soldiers at the factory: they have no idea.

But the men of the Finland Regiment's reserve battalion, on the other hand, are threatening to eliminate the newspaper publishers who print stories saying work is going badly at the munitions factories.

* * *

The legend of the terrifying black motorcars has continued to circulate in Petrograd all March and through to mid-April, frightening inhabitants and militiamen. At night, the latter shoot anyone who fails to stop. State Duma deputy Baryshnikov was driving around with defective headlamps. On the corner of Shpalernaya and Tauride streets, near the Duma, militiamen riddled his car with bullets.

In the middle of the night the community governor had a phone call from Suvorovsky Prospect reporting that four militiamen had been killed by a passing black motorcar. In fact one of its tires had burst and the militiamen had dropped to the ground to avoid the gunfire.

* * *

Karp, Shulman, and Shechte, deputies of a sub-district militia commissar, behaved extremely rudely to a visitor. She filed a complaint to the "provisional court." But the court found in the men's favor.

Wages in the new militia have been set two or three times higher than in the old police force. But they have not even been trained to use their weapons. During Holy Saturday night, one militiaman loading his revolver shot another; in the Vasilievsky Island tram depot a militiaman was showing one of the conductors his Browning, a shot rang out, and the conductor dropped dead. And yet another militiaman, aiming at a mad dog, sent a bullet through the chest of a track guard and injured a greaser. And the dog ran off.

* * *

Near Nikolaevsky Station a well-known con man, Shimansky, was arrested. During the first days of the revolution, wearing an officer's uniform, he had been appointed a commandant of some kind and then, when unmasked, he ran off with a gang of ruffians in a motor car. And in the evenings he would burgle apartments under the pretense of searching them.

In the Tauride Palace a sailor, Gushchin, was arrested with a forged authorization to obtain food supplies for a non-existent guard of a hundred and forty men. He had received those supplies several times. The document certifying him as a deputy in the Soviet also turned out to be forged.

A member of the Petrograd "flying squad of the revolutionary militia," Shmukler, sent the Skorokhod factory a spurious requisition on behalf of the squad and received thirty pairs of shoes free of charge, which he sent to his father, a provincial shoe salesman. But the fraud was uncovered, quite by chance.

* * *

On the corner of Nevsky Prospect and Sadovaya Street an official in the criminal investigation department recognized three young militiamen with armbands, who were standing guard there, as criminals given long sentences under the old government. Their documents proved to be authentic, but they still ran away when an attempt was made to detain them.

And Justice of the Peace Okunev, who had previously been responsible for underage offenders in the Petrograd jurisdiction, now recognized in seventeen- and eighteen-year-old militiamen the faces of his old charges.

* * *

In the Aleksandrinsky Theater an expensive bronze watch in a case was stolen from the director's box.

On the eve of Thomas Sunday ruffians found their way into Trinity Cathedral on the Petersburg Side. They stole chalices, crowns, and icon mountings and plundered the candle box for money.

At Finland Station one night three goods wagons were pillaged and expensive goods and parcels, just arrived from abroad, were stolen: boxes of gold and silver watches, silk, worth more than half a million rubles in total.

Someone even broke into the treasurer's office in the community government building and took money and documents.

Over a two-week span in April approximately three hundred apartment burglaries were reported.

* * *

On the evening of 26 April numerous telephone calls came into both the Vyborg Side militia and the Moscow Battalion at the same time, reporting that the old regime's civil servants held at the Kresty jail were being set free and the prison guards had been slaughtered. Large contingents of the militia and the Moscow soldiers were immediately dispatched to the Kresty. Nothing of the kind had happened there, but as they were there they ferociously conducted checks of the cells, banned the detainees from walking in the corridors and reduced the number of parcels they could receive from outside.

It transpired that the calls had been made by a gang of thieves, who had spent those hours robbing the Vyborg Side.

* * *

Timofei Kirpichnikov was given an appeal to the citizens of Russia to sign: ". . . to serve the Provisional Government with the utmost dedication . . . I call on you, my fellow-citizens, for a second time, to perform a hard task. We are being urged to betray the cause of our noble, free allies, to buy the gratitude of the German Social Democrats. . . ." Then, by order of General Kornilov, he was awarded the St. George Cross (to conform with the rules for the medal, a story had to be concocted that he had attacked some police machine guns) and promoted to warrant officer. The brigade commander kissed him warmly, in front of the ranks, and Kirpichnikov promised to die for freedom if necessary. Then they took him to the teachers' congress, where he made a speech and the teachers raised him aloft to the strains of the Marseillaise.

But then Astakhov, the ensign from the Volynian Regiment, proved that on 12 March he, in his army greatcoat, had lined up with the insurgents. He was then promoted to second lieutenant and the battalion committee elected him battalion adjutant.

* * *

Around the graves, the Field of Mars is deep in mud, rubbish, cigarette butts, and sunflower seed husks. Someone has smashed a chain and a little iron post is lying around.

Where is the solemnity of the great national funeral? Neither flags nor wreaths remain. There are collection boxes, without any kind of inscription. And a single, small plate with "Pilgrim, revere this place: here great Russia was born." A peasant stops, crosses himself at length, and throws a postage stamp into the collection box (stamps pass for currency now).

* * *

The assembly of Petrograd domestic staff, two thousand women, has voted to demand from their masters an eight-hour working day and a pay increase (to parity with civil servants). Otherwise there'll be a general strike.

* * *

Men from the front-line regiments come to the reserve battalions: send those reinforcement units! Petersburg agitators set off for the Volynian barracks: don't listen to the delegates, don't you go to the front. It's a provocation!

There was a new fashion in the reserve battalions, to send reinforcements consisting of volunteers only. Fifteen or so companies of this kind were assembled from army regiments stationed on the outskirts of town, from the Jägers and the Izmailovsky and Volynian Regiments, and finally the Oranienbaum machinegunners also scraped one together. In his order of the day Kornilov would warmly salute the units as they left. They would set off to take the train with revolutionary banners and bands playing, accompanied the whole way by jubilant crowds.

* * *

In the Moscow Battalion a rally was convened. They had calculated that Guchkov intended to deploy fourteen thousand men from Petrograd to the front and twenty-one thousand to work on farms—Latvians, Estonians, St. George Cross holders. . . . These orders are a threat to the revolutionary cause. They gave the floor to an ensign who had just arrived from the front. He was very agitated: "I'm a peasant's son myself. But first we've got to defend our homeland." The chairman of the meeting, a civilian, answered: "Of course, the position on the front is difficult, but what are fourteen thousand soldiers to them? But for the Petrograd garrison it would be a great loss. We'll be of more help if we do something radical instead of sending reinforcements that melt away on the front line: let's finish with this war." The reservists willingly agreed to this and carried a resolution on behalf of the battalion: until a precise and definite order came from the Executive Committee of the Soviet, they would not send men from the battalion either to the front or to work on farms.

* * *

During the night of 24 April there was a confrontation between Leninists and anti-Leninists on Znamenskaya Street and it came to fisticuffs. Several of the latter group were detained and taken to the Aleksandr Nevsky district commissariat. But a crowd gathered and defended them—and they were released.

* * *

Passing the Kshesinskaya house when Lenin was speaking from the balcony, an army doctor, L, a member of the Luga Soviet, started voicing objections. He had barely uttered a few words when some sailors bounded out of the Kshesinskaya house, grabbed Doctor L by the scruff of the neck and dragged him off to the nearby Modern circus, which was empty except for a few other "objectors" who were under arrest.

But a Luga soldier had seen this from the crowd, ran to the telephone exchange, and phoned Luga to report it. The Luga executive committee phoned the Kshesinskaya house straight away and demanded the arrested doctor's immediate release: otherwise they would now send a large detachment to throw the Bolsheviks themselves out of the palace. And five minutes later Doctor L was free.

* * *

Beyond the Narva Gate, newspaper sellers have their "undemocratic" (non-socialist) papers snatched out of their hands and burned on the spot.

There have already been demands for a four-hour working day. And there are threats to pelt the future Constituent Assembly with grenades, if it "goes against the demands of the masses."

* * *

Petrograd is rife with disturbing rumors about Kronstadt: it is behaving like a separate state; there are incessant assaults and murders; people have not gone back to work. Constantly, in the papers: government commissar Pepelyaev has been there, even Kerensky has been there, and both say the rumors are a provocation, spread by enemies of Free Russia; life in Kronstadt has gone back to normal; productive work is going on there; their defenses are in excellent condition and officers have the full trust of the sailors. Of course, warned Pepelyaev, passionate opinions are sometimes voiced, but passions are gradually yielding to reason. . . . And even General Kornilov went and reviewed the troops. The papers say he "took away with him a most gratifying impression."

But: there were sixty officers shot in the first days, and of the two hundred and six arrested it seems a hundred and twenty-six have been released and eighty are still under guard. (And for a spot of fun the sailors take them out and watch them sweep the streets. And in the reserve barracks' guardhouse where they're confined, they're taught to sing the International.) Kerensky has ordered a special commission to be set up under prosecutor Pereverzev, to check which others of the Kronstadt officers can be released and which should be transferred to Petrograd for investigation. Pereverzev already visited Kronstadt with the same task before Easter but was not allowed to carry out any investigation. Now he has gone for a second time, taking with him a private note from Kerensky: Admiral Maksimov is asking for Captain Almqvist, a Finland Swede, to be released as soon as possible. Pereverzev obtained his release on Saturday, 21 April.

That evening, at the naval officers' club, an Estonian concert was under way, and the Executive Committee was meeting nearby. Suddenly a rumbling, shouting crowd dragged in Almqvist and his father, who had been seized on their way out of Kronstadt. The frightened Committee members announced from the front steps, "We're summoning the commission of inquiry straight away. If they're at fault we shall deal with them however you see fit!" Cries of: "Arrest the whole commission! They're in cahoots with the officers, they're traitors, bourgeois! Execute the prosecutor!" They arrived. Pereverzev, a fearless advocate in Tsarist trials, including the Potemkin case, now told the story in detail, about Kerensky and Maksimov—but there was a cocking of guns. He was not allowed to finish: they wanted to hoist him up on their bayonets. One young man, wearing a Psychoneurological Institute cap, was in a particular frenzy. The sailors called him "Doctor Roshal." The Executive Committee managed, with difficulty, to persuade them to allow a night to consider the matter. In the morning there would be a meeting in Anchor Square and judgment would be passed on the commission. That night they decided that the commission had made a series of errors (it had, with the agreement of the crews, released another three officers, all now re-arrested), its members would resign voluntarily and be released to return to Petrograd. Here in Kronstadt they would set up their own commission of inquiry (with the participation of "Doctor Roshal").

In the morning they not only had to spend a long time trying to persuade the angry crowd to release the commission. They also had to wrench from their grip both the Almqvists—who were being taken for execution on Anchor Square, the father along with his son.

* * *

"When you arrive in Kronstadt, the air is different!" (Bakasheva, a Bestuzhev student and a Bolshevik).

* * * * *

Joy supreme, joy reigns
In the heart of a reborn nation.
Our victory cry circles the world:
Brotherhood, love, liberation.
(Draft of a new national anthem)

25 April–1 May

[9'']

(The Press on Lenin, 17–29 April)

That the leaders of left-wing parties should hasten to their homeland is eminently desirable: they should be where the action is. But the circumstances in which the Bolshevik leader arrived must provoke, to put it mildly, some puzzlement. No citizen of Russia can think it possible to accept favors from the enemy. This elementary rule of political ethics is acknowledged by all socialists and it behooves those who preach the end of the war at any price to be particularly scrupulous in this respect. They should have asked themselves why the German government was so ready, so eager to render this unprecedented service. And however could they bring themselves to accept this kindness? It was either total alienation from their homeland or a show of bravado. The way to the heart and conscience of Russia does not lie through Germany.

(*Speech*)

. . . Germany is behind our lines! Traveling through Germany, they enjoyed more than just diplomatic privileges: their luggage was not searched, their passports not checked. They would not have been allowed through if this had not been advantageous to Wilhelm.

(*New Times*)

Letter to the editor. Protopopov held talks with a private individual—and what a fuss people made then. Lenin concluded an agreement with the official German government—with the government that is poisoning Russians with noxious gases and sinking hospital ships. Even if England flatly refused to let you through, you had no right to negotiate with Germany . . . you have no right to talk about your internationalist sentiments.

Tarasov, First-year cadet in the Mikhailovsky Artillery School

Individuals with no motherland are stirring up the sea of our public opinion and shouting themselves hoarse with demands for the army and the people to lay down their arms before the Germans. They are not even traitors, for a traitor must have a motherland to betray. Why did Lenin's anonymous, thirty-strong band need to tear along in German railway carriages if not to lend a hand to the Germans? Like his German hosts, Lenin is shouting about the "criminal governments of France and England" and, of course, not a word about Hindenburg or Wilhelm.

(*Evening Times*)

. . . Even before this, associates of Parvus's institute were allowed to travel from Switzerland through Germany . . .

To hell with you and your Zimmerwald! To your ear that German word is more resonant than the word Russia. After our victory you'll be a laughing stock: you'll have to beg a lift back through Germany . . .

(Boris Suvorin)

. . . Of course Lenin is no provocateur and has not sold out for German money. The sealed carriage is a laughable detail. Lenin cannot discredit the idea of socialism.

All those tittle-tattlers in the papers have invented malignant gossip about the passage through Germany. But in *Pravda* we see more and more frequent appeals for order and calm. We must welcome *Pravda* as an organ of peaceable socialist propaganda . . .

(D. Zaslavsky, *The Day*)

On 17 April Lenin was the loser in a skirmish with Tsereteli. He has not changed since 1906. Those who remember that distinctive figure in rallies at the time of the First State Duma will now immediately recognize "the unyielding one": that same distinctive head, the same rushing about the platform, never standing still for a minute, running and jumping the whole time; the slight speech defect, but also a particular eloquence, all aiming to engage the masses with slogans they can understand. More demanding individuals cannot be satisfied by this, but at rallies, where it is not logic and reason that count but brutal attacks and demagoguery, he is a dangerous adversary. His plan is completely divorced from real life. It is fanatical. He is raising the flag of civil war between the various strata of our democracy. He has not garnered wild applause, but he does have some support.

(*Stock Exchange Gazette*)

. . . In reply, Tsereteli told Lenin that he was not taking into account the balance of power. In the particular conditions in Russia, the proletariat would not have been able to hold on to power had it seized it. A dictatorship of the proletariat would attract strong protests from a significant section of the population. Our proletariat has set off along the only proper path, a universal rather than a class-based path. As Lassalle said, individuals can be wrong—classes, never.

The listeners' sympathies were entirely with Tsereteli.

. . . First impression of Lenin's arguments: an émigré has arrived, who understands nothing of the conditions in Russia . . .

The sooner the Bolshevik faction reveals its true nature, the better. The Russian Bolsheviks are excluding themselves from the revolution.

(*Morning Russia*)

He's none too bright, we know,
So Germany's no foe
And civil war's the aim
Of that disordered brain.
"The courteous Hun's our friend:
I got home in the end.
For favors they await,
I traveled back in well-sealed state!"

(*New Times*)

. . . If there is no civil war, one will have to be invented . . .

. . . Lenin is dear to the Germans precisely as a man of conviction, who cannot be dismissed as a provocateur. But he is worse than any provocateur, his demagoguery is unconscionable (though he personally may actually have a conscience) . . .

. . . His demagoguery is particularly dangerous today, when the masses are still feeling burnt from the revolutionary flames and any rough handling is painful.

. . . Under any system that kind of rabble-rousing is an ordinary criminal offense.

. . . And if the lists with the names of Chernomazov and Malinovsky had been burned, like the documents in the District Court, would they now be yelling in *Pravda*? They have no motherland and they would not think twice about betraying their own father . . .

. . . After an absence of many years, to return to the nest with the sole aim of defiling it . . .

Lenin is proposing to topple all the thrones: English, Japanese, Italian—but only those of our allies.

Lenin is now in Petersburg. He is very skilled in practical questions of domestic policy: he is the top expert in Russian agrarian matters, his name familiar to every peasant since 1905. . . . Lenin is a communist and this is why his words will penetrate the heart and soul of the Russian peasant, who is already in tune with communism.

(*Vossische Zeitung*)

Since 1905 he has immersed himself totally in party disputes on tactics and moved further and further away from authentic Marxism. . . . His proposals for "fives" and "tens" in 1905 were the product of his unruly nature. . . . He has declared himself a communist, a proponent of civil war—and around him is an intellectual vacuum (while Plekhanov is surrounded by a throng of followers who are true believers). But he will be useful in a negative way; as a shining example of what we must not do . . .

(*Russian Will*)

. . . To Lenin's credit, he does not play games with terminology: he calls a spade a spade. . . . His oratory, unfortunately, works well on the mind of the masses . . .

. . . He is calling for battle not only against the Provisional Government but also against the Soviet of Workers' Deputies: he dislikes its composition . . .

His very first address was, politically, highly significant: he took all the ideas of Bolshevism to their logical conclusion. The Russian socialists have turned away from him, manifesting a healthy political instinct . . .

. . . People have started wondering whether the red flag is now not enough for him, whether he now wants Bakunin's black flag. No, Lenin will never be his equal. Bakunin was, despite everything, a true Russian.

. . . What kind of anarchists are the Leninists, if they have set up their own police station at the Kshesinskaya house and are drawing up charge sheets?

. . . Lenin will not take power, but he will make Free Russia's birth pangs harder to bear. The Provisional Government cannot possibly be overturned because it is supported by an agreement with the Soviet . . .

. . . a shady gambit . . . Around Lenin is a void, silent as the grave. Lenin's return to Russia will do him no good—he might end up taking the same route back to Switzerland . . .

. . . Lenin has already crossed the line into buffoonery, and it is hardly appropriate to engage in argument with him. Lenin's declaration is not even worth condemning. We should just forget about this noisy, incendiary anarchy . . .

. . . Is Lenin dangerous or not? For the moment it is hard to say: the ordinary people are not very enthusiastic. The domestics in the capital, for example, are saying a spy has arrived—the Germans let him through . . .

. . . "Down with the war!" they shout, those naïve maniacs. We should see the funny side of their commandeering the Kshesinskaya palace: nothing will come of that mob. . . . People are according Lenin too much significance, exaggerating the danger he represents.

. . . But even so, we must not use force to crush the Bolsheviks.

. . . We are beginning to see harassment of the supporters of a certain tendency of socialist thinking, the leader of which is Lenin, and on the part of *Russian Will* this harassment is escalating into incitement to violence . . .

(*Workers' Gazette*)

The basic feature of Lenin's program is its primitivism: there is the proletariat and there is the bourgeoisie, with the petite bourgeoisie hovering between them. He *cannot demonstrate* that the seizing of power by the proletariat is in the nature of our revolutionary movement. Neither can he show that the peasants are interested in permanent revolution and the dictatorship of the proletariat. (The Paris Commune was not supported by the peasants.) Lenin does not have a broad political program but, instead, some sort of murky plot. Lenin is helpless on political theory: he is leading the working class into disaster.

(Kantorovich, writing in *The Day*)

. . . He is silent on the matter of the Constituent Assembly. . . . But how does he think he can establish a republic without police, a standing army and a civil service?

. . . Lenin proposes, in place of the war, "the overthrow of all the capitalist governments in the world." Does he think that will take less time? It would be quicker to take Berlin than to force the whole planet to convert to a socialist system.

. . . At many rallies the Leninists are electrifying crowds running into the thousands.

. . . If in his opinion the bourgeoisie, down to the most humble of the petite bourgeoisie, as well as the whole of the intelligentsia must be deprived of rights, then why give rights to the peasants? It is sufficient to give rights only to the "poorest peasant" category. He has started saying as much . . .

G. V. Plekhanov's organ, *Unity*, proposes that the "counterrevolutionaries of the right" be "relocated from the land of plenty in the south to the cold of the north" and that battles with the "counterrevolutionaries of the left," as he describes the Leninists, be verbal only. All this is very good. But we must condemn, and in the strongest terms, Plekhanov's words about "Lenin's appeals for fraternization with the Germans, with the aim of overthrowing the Provisional Government." Is Mr. Plekhanov giving any thought to the influence of such words in an atmosphere of revolutionary zeal and still burning passions?

(*The People's Cause*)

. . . And look at the conditions under which the Bolsheviks are proposing to initiate civil war in rural areas: the villages and hamlets are without men, the fields are not sown, the country is collapsing, especially the transport, famine is reaching the towns, the war continues. . . . The political ravings of revolutionary lunatics—and they even want to be handed social revolution in Europe! Instead of securing the promised peace they are turning it into a pipe dream.

(*The Day*)

. . . Lenin has dissociated himself even from his own party (from Kamenev), thereby helping unite all the socialists . . .

. . . The danger has emerged from the front that everyone thought was absolutely secure: the left flank! "Permanent social revolution" translates into Russian as "violence, come what may" . . .

. . . Leninism is counterrevolutionary. The ideological junk of Leninism will muddy the waters of the river of Russian liberty.

. . . To Lenin's irresponsible agitation there can be only one response: society's contempt.

. . . The Russian people will make a laughingstock of Lenin, and Germany will not get her reward . . .

. . . The Bolsheviks' public appearances have a positive side: they are making people with any common sense keep their distance.

. . . An individual uttering such idiocies is no danger. It is a good thing he came: now he is in full view. Now he will demolish his own arguments.

. . . You spineless chickens, why are you frightened of the Bolsheviks? Can you not live without a scarecrow? The Bolsheviks are a type we have known for a long time: they will cave in the first time they face a practical problem. Leninism is a typical product of mechanistic reasoning and loud slogans with no substance. The organized masses will never follow him; the popular masses will reject him.

(M. Osorgin)

. . . People are screaming at Lenin in a frenzy . . . as if he really were a creature from hell. What are we to do, pelt him with rotten eggs? Lynch him? In times past, Lloyd George also railed loudly, against the Boer war—and where would England be now if they had lynched him then?

(*The Day*)

. . . The issue here is not Lenin himself. The man in the street needs a concrete figure on whom he can vent his hostility to a revolution that has vastly overextended itself. So he is venting it on Lenin, who has become the target of the bourgeois press . . .

* * *

HE'S BEEN A ROVER—NOW HE WANTS TO TAKE OVER

* * *

[1 0]

Vorotyntsev had been at GHQ for two weeks now and even, fortunately, in the Operations Section: Svechin had done well.

But it was not the GHQ he had pictured from afar: it had gone into slow motion, like a care home for invalid generals. Generals and senior officers were now accumulating at GHQ, having been condemned to death in their units or just thrown out by the committees (some for nothing more than a German surname), or else removed by Guchkov and now on the sidelines. Some requested a new assignment, farther away from their previous units, and some asked for nothing and were willing to stay. While others, who had been pushed out of their previous post, were now arriving and looking to carve themselves a path, to gain an audience with the new upper echelons.

It was terrifying, the crowd of generals and colonels that had come together here: was GHQ becoming a rubbish dump?

And it was here that Vorotyntsev had been transferred.

But GHQ was no more sick than the whole Army was now.

The men that fate had brought together here had plenty of time to talk. And what dreamers they had among them, with precise plans for rapidly "saving Russia."

"Saving" it, so simply that it seemed none of them had yet understood the *extent* to which Russia was already collapsing. A fiery Galaxhad seized us in its tail and was pulling us along! And here they were, expounding on who was responsible for what had happened and who should be reassigned to which post. And how good it would be to restore the Emperor to the throne.

We were too weak even to stay upright in this whirlwind: however could we do any *saving*?!

But those who won't see don't see.

Just as, last autumn too, they had not seen that we had to get out of this war! Get out!

What could be done now? And with whom?? Impossible to say.

Svechin had just managed to transfer Vorotyntsev to GHQ when he promptly disappeared: Guchkov had assigned him to lead a corps. He'd not wanted to go, but he could not refuse: this was no generous promotion, like that offered Vorotyntsev, but an ordinary job transfer.

He had left, saying there was no point specially thinking up a way out: the service itself would show them what to do.

"No, my friend," retorted Vorotyntsev. "This service won't show us anything any more—the days of true service are long gone. We're sunk. Now we have to put our energy into finding some unconventional solution. But who could do it? There's no one."

Svechin had left, and there was no one else at GHQ who was close, no one to confide in.

A leader! Oh for a leader! A quick-witted, intelligent, energetic general who would immediately inspire loyalty in the Army and a willingness to follow him! Then everything would be resolved! To such a leader, such a savior, Vorotyntsev was ready to offer unconditional devotion. And how many times in military history such leaders had appeared when needed. But not now, not here.

Things with us were so bad that there was already no one.

Toward Easter, Alekseev had been officially confirmed as Supreme Commander, a role he had, in effect, occupied since the Tsar's abdication, and even before. But he was never a leader, only a conscientious, hard-working staff officer. And this is what he remained. And, it seemed, with less drive than ever, dispirited: in a word, crushed. Or did that grizzled, round, honest, unassuming head know, contain, so much that Vorotyntsev could not even imagine? No, that did not seem to be the case.

What about Gurko? He had, after all, accepted the Western Front.

But not GHQ . . .

(And Lechitsky had gone for good, retired the week before.)

In mid-April, at the same time as Vorotyntsev, General Denikin had arrived at GHQ and, on 18 April, taken up the post of chief of staff to the Supreme Commander. But although he had previously commanded the "Iron Division," no iron, no firmness of any kind was evident in him but, rather, a softness inappropriate for a general. He showed great caution at every step, underlining the fact that he was, all things considered, a supporter of civil liberties and a sensible republican system.

As if ideas **of that kind** had any relevance today.

Immediately after Easter Guchkov, traveling to the South, had not left the train at Mogilev but met Alekseev and Denikin in his carriage, and then nominated the Supreme Commander's new quartermaster general to succeed Lukomsky: Yuzefovich. Lukomsky was no loss, but neither was Yuzefovich a great find.

In short, all the leaders at GHQ were coming and going impotently, seeing no clear course of action to follow. And Brusilov and Ruzsky exuded that same impotence, although Sakharov had now been removed. (And he was no great loss either: Shcherbachev would be more decisive. But what could the Romanian Front decide?)

Gurko . . .??

No. The time had come to stop waiting for orders and do something themselves.

He had to do something himself.

But—what . . .?

When in extreme danger, under fire, in the thick of the battle, there's just one thing you must never do: hesitate. You have to move. If you have barely advanced, then retreat—but after a sizeable advance the only option is forward!

But what now?

Now, among the officers at GHQ, a movement had indeed emerged: now they were all forming their own soviets, convening congresses, for only that way could they get their voice heard, have any influence on Russia. But no one hears a united voice from the officers. Why should officers be denied what everyone else had? So they had to create an organ that could speak on behalf of all active duty officers. Let's say, a "Union of Army and Navy Officers." And for that they had to convene a congress. At GHQ, in May. They had set to it with extraordinary enthusiasm (the GHQ contingent having no combat duties): some were drawing up an appeal to this congress, others the program of the future Union, and a third group was already sending out notices and invitations to all units and HQs, by telegraph and post. (And to the Petrograd officers too: they could come as guests.) The task of the Union, as they saw it, was to transform the army, even while engaged in military action, to preserve its power. They must prevent the army disintegrating as a result of the soldiers' mistrust and the false ideas being spread, and rapidly develop among the officers themselves a sense for the superior interests of the state as well as some political education—especially since soon, even while continuing to wage war, the army too would be voting in the Constituent Assembly elections.

"Transform the army"! Was that all? But cooking on ice isn't done in a trice—Vorotyntsev had known that saying since his Zastruzhe days. Having the front-line forces take part in the Constituent Assembly elections while continuing the war, for example.

But you never know, perhaps this absolutely legal Union of Officers might allow us, the officers who had survived, stayed firm, to assemble, unite, and . . .? But they were also drawing up the program for the future Union, and it said, ". . . in the spirit of the principles advanced by the revolution, we believe in and pledge our obedience to the Provisional Government. . . ." But what else could the harried officers write? And after that, of course, came ". . . the only way of consolidating our civil gains lies in total victory."

They were talking to the fiery whirlwind in the language of the parlor.

Stationed at GHQ, he could not refuse to join this Union in the future, but no matter how hard that nice "little captain," Lieutenant Colonel Tikhobrazov, tried to persuade Vorotyntsev to add his signature to the appeal to the congress, the latter refused. Neither did he join the "provisional committee" that had been set up on the spot.

How blind they'd become! They'd all been caught up, sucked into the same massive, all-consuming vortex that had swallowed up the Tsar: how were they to win the war? How were they to "consolidate civil gains" by victory over Wilhelm when the latter was overjoyed by our revolution. Our roads were about to dry up, yet he was not on the offensive, was he? Did no one want to see?! (Or were others thinking the same way as Vorotyntsev but not voicing their thoughts?)

This was one of the first gifts bestowed by the revolution: having to hide our feelings. Even if everyone now understood that it was not possible to continue fighting this war, they would all dance around the bonfire proclaiming that the victorious war was finally about to start.

Vorotyntsev was stuck at GHQ, like an axe in dough.

What ill fate was this? There was nothing he could save, nowhere to apply himself. And when the revolution was releasing human molecules to jump about freely, he could only toss about with them, helpless.

But hold on! Since the beginning of April there had in fact been a salutary, and far-reaching, movement to be seen—on the part of the soldiers! The soldiers themselves had seemed to be aghast and recoiled in the face of ruin. The Army itself had begun to step back from the abyss. A flurry of resolutions from military units and speeches from soldiers' delegations had started to appear and gain ground—and they had seemed more extraordinary than the first acts of violence, the first uprisings. And these resolutions could not have been adopted entirely without the agreement of the mass of soldiery.

And the content of the resolutions? Well, naturally it was: Be more stringent in checking the exemption lists for people dodging conscription! Don't let the *bourgeoisie* stay safe away from the front, take the *capitalists* off the exemption lists! (The words were not theirs, but the sentiments were.) And send the reserve garrisons to the front—don't keep grinding us down till our forces are totally drained! And: give equal privileges to the Guards and the army (which was only right), and increase the soldiers' pay and financial aid to their families. (They were asking for less than they were giving.) And they sounded challenging, even menacing notes directed at the workers, who in all the brouhaha had managed to snatch for themselves—while the country was at war—an eight-hour day! Less speech-making in the factories and more shells!

But now some city-dweller had lobbed another idea into the army: in addition to their life, they should offer the new government—which was nothing like the old, treacherous one—the gold and silver from their chests, to wage the war. And this idea spread through the front-line units like an epidemic: to give up their St. George Crosses, silver and gold, and give up their medals (and then their gold and silver coins, and any hard cash). And the men unpinned from their soldiers' tunics their proudest possessions (which they had once received under the sign of the cross), for which they had been ready to make a disproportionate sacrifice, to lay down their lives—and threw them into anonymous collection bags. Units were handing over St. George Crosses by the casketful, by the boxful. The Tsarskoye Selo hussar regiment alone gave five hundred crosses and medals. To Vorotyntsev this was as heart-breaking as if he himself were handing in a decoration: they were so easily giving up something so sacred! All the newspapers had now published several such reports, with photographs (unbearable!) of soldiers standing in line to give up their crosses (they were, though, looking dispirited). At first the boxes were being accepted by the ministers themselves, with a few words of thanks, but then they tired of this and arranged for the boxes to be sent direct to the Ministry of Finance. But in the units the soldiers decided to go even further: they voluntarily reduced their bread ration and refused their sugar money—and all to help the beloved Provisional Government.

And who was it for? What was it for? How pitiful, our Russian innocence! And how pitiful people's naïveté—when seen alongside the hideous acts that were being committed. There it was, the soul of our people.

Those ministers and newspaper literati, who had never had shells raining down on them or run through minefields, what did they understand of the extent of these soldiers' sacrifices? For them this was just an adornment to their propaganda.

But the main idea in the resolutions from the front was: no orders to the army from any body except the Provisional Government! We pledged our allegiance to that government and we do not acknowledge any other authority! That oath must not be touched! (This was aimed at the Soviet, which had abolished the oath.) Our loyalty is to the Provisional Government alone! It must not be put under pressure!

The 6th Army was blunt: no one is to visit the units unless they're sent by the Provisional Government. As for the 7th Army, it was: we unconditionally deny any legislative power to the soviets and put our lives at the disposal of the Provisional Government with the aim of toppling German militarism. The 1st Petrograd Uhlan Regiment: we give our oath before God always to defend the interests of the Provisional Government! And the 1st Nevsky Regiment: the Soviet of Deputies must not publish its resolutions with the heading "Orders," so as not to cause trouble among the soldiers, and it must call itself the "Soviet of the Petrograd Garrison." The 10th Army addressed the Soviet direct: please do not issue your own, independent instructions to the army. The 105th Division: the orders and circulars issued by the Petrograd Soviet cannot be considered binding on the Russian people or the army in the field, for without discipline there is no army, but a rabble. And the Kuban Cossacks: we will not allow any opposition to the Provisional Government on the part of the Soviet! (And when there were resolutions in favor of the Soviet, they were from small units, insignificant little groups.)

The soldiers on the front were getting over the shock of the revolution delivered by Petrograd and the seductive possibilities that had flooded in, and were returning to the age-old sobriety of a peasant people. It was amazing how much good sense remained within the army: how could there still be so many patriotic voices?

It made you wonder: maybe we weren't too exhausted to continue the war after all.

And it was in this massive change of heart among the soldiers, in this elemental movement of the soldiers' conscience that the Provisional Government could have found support during the weeks before Easter.

Vorotyntsev knew very well that, with any ill-educated mass, it was always possible to come to an agreement as long as you explained things clearly and boldly—and did not miss your opportunity.

And the government's *Herald* published, published more than the other papers, in every detail and in a bold typeface, all these resolutions, for the edification of the populace and the edification of some outsiders too. But the ministers themselves were so inert that they were incapable of taking that edification on board for themselves, of grasping these never-to-be-repeated two or three weeks, of profiting from the non-deployment of the Petrograd garrison to restore the army in its wrath and its pride. Did they think everything would be achieved by nothing more than the publication of some resolutions? They did not understand the fluidity of the current situation, for such initiatives to prevent total ruin would last no longer than do fine days in March, and they had to seize the opportunity; or it would be swept away into the louring storm. No! They were hearing all of this at the Mariinsky Palace and immediately undermining the support as it arrived there by responding publicly, and in print, that the Soviet of Workers' Deputies would in no way, no way whatsoever, restrict the authority of the ministers.

How were we to understand this pitiful government giving itself over to the control of some faceless socialist mob? Why were they taking directions from out of the shadows? Was their own authority becoming illusory?

After Easter this surge of enthusiasm on the part of the soldiers had waned from lack of support, and the corrosion continued.

But—Guchkov?! He was in this government. Could he really not see, not understand the opportunity they were missing! It was high time he called on one or other of these loyal regiments to get rid of that Soviet gang!

He had issued a handsome decree for Easter: when recruiting for responsible positions, it said, the old regime had bypassed highly talented people, enthusiastic, energetic, with a forceful character and firm convictions. The system must be radically altered, we must give such posts to young people whose energy has not been sapped. . . . I sincerely believe that the best people will lead the Army and Navy along the right path . . .

Until recently Vorotyntsev had dreamed the same dream.

But what had come of it? Guchkov had thrown himself with gusto into purging the generals. What a shambles! Already not only bad generals had been cleared out, but average and good ones were gone too; and every second division was now run by someone new, ignorant of the situation.

Yet at times of such tumult it is the status quo that preserves momentum.

And how abject, how feeble was the tone of all his orders—not orders, in fact, but requests to the soldiers. And what was he doing, leaving his central command post (as the Tsar too had so disastrously left GHQ on that fateful day) and rushing round the distant front lines? What was he doing in Kishinev, in Odessa? How was he helping? And his every phrase alluded to how the old government had led the country to its downfall. How they all loved recollecting their sufferings and their services to the country. Did he think this would save the situation? Placate his enemies?

The night before, on the way back from the South, Guchkov had passed by GHQ without stopping, apparently sick. (If only he could talk to him personally, now! But he had passed on by . . .)

No, the Army had no leader.

Where was the authority? What was needed now most of all was some strong authority. And even while setting no store whatsoever by this Provisional Government, even then . . . if only it were at least firm!

Vorotyntsev had never before experienced such constant, tense wandering in the unknown as in recent weeks—and never had his deliberations so rapidly borne fruit.

Where should the action be launched? Where but at GHQ? There was no other choice. They already had their backs to the wall.

Hic Rhodus, hic salta!

Vorotyntsev would have felt far less constrained now if he had been alone, living a bachelor life in the officers' hotel. But it had not turned out that way: Alina would not hear of him living alone in Mogilev now, and she had moved there immediately, with some of their belongings following after, even though finding an apartment would be cumbersome given the current influx of refugees into the town. If things had been as before, Georgi would of course have vetoed the plan and Alina would not have insisted. But after all that had happened recently a downright refusal was impossible: it would immediately have aroused suspicions, looked as if he was seeing someone here. And set off another marital storm, another breakdown even worse than before. That was all he needed! But this way all her anxiety, her distress, should gradually abate. It wouldn't carry on indefinitely.

Indeed there was room for some relief that everything had come to such a peaceable conclusion. In Mogilev Alina had not once reproached him or said a word about Olda, not even mentioned the name. Nor had she in her letters over the previous six weeks. And his trip to Petrograd in March had not been discovered—it actually seemed unreal. Thank God for that! Georgi just had to avoid stirring things up, not rock the boat, not reopen old wounds. He could not think back without a shudder to those November days at the guesthouse. Alina had been quite unprepared for that blow—it could have destroyed her. It felt as if, in that slender throat, he was strangling what was dearest to him.

Of course their life was not as before. How much had been missed out, now irretrievably lost. But if she was trying to make peace, harmony, then he had to help her.

And surely she must have understood the times they were living in . . .

[11]

"Could it really be, Iosif Vladimirovich, that the old government was right, that we Russians are not sufficiently mature to handle freedom? That we're blind to our greater civic duty, that we see only the freedom to do what was previously forbidden? Does our Russian mentality really acknowledge no other freedom than loutish desire?"

"I can agree with you, Nikolai Andreevich, in one respect only. It's clear that not only were the dirty old beggars' rags—which Russia has now thrown off and burned—feeding decay and pestilence into the pores of our Russian organism. We have to surmise that malignant juices from the organism itself were also saturating the rags. Yes, our people have been poisoned, and the poisoning has gone on for centuries. Its ignorance, its prejudices were for too long nourished by Tsarism, and have become an integral part of us. And now of course there's a danger that, thanks to the ignorance of our masses, that still fragile flower of freedom could perish."

Gessen and Gredescul, two professors, two editors-in-chief—of *Speech* and *Russian Will* respectively—had met that morning in the library and could not, of course, take their piles of books and immediately go their separate ways but stayed, engaged in debate, by the counter.

The somewhat stout Gessen, with rounded eyebrows above round, gold-rimmed spectacles, was developing his thesis.

On the other hand, he felt, the springtime joy of the revolution was itself having a powerful curative effect on the nation's soul. Suddenly another side of Russia's soul had also been revealed: the spirit of the ancient popular assemblies, still alive, even after five hundred years of autocracy. It was a trust not in individual figures but in the multitude, in the many present at the assembly, the deployment of the people's independent initiative. Like grass in spring, life was bursting out everywhere, irrepressible. Russia was melting in the fire of incandescent ideas and ready for casting into completely new forms.

He spoke with poised conviction:

"This is Russia's second baptism, in the font of liberty, and she'll be wholly imbued with it, through to the innermost recesses of the soul, as they say. Anyway, how was the revolution itself possible? Does that not testify to the unprecedented maturity of the people? Since the beginning of this war a political consciousness had been growing rapidly within them and has smashed the shell of autocracy."

The slight Gredescul's neck was twitchy in its starched collar, his eyes, behind the spectacles, restless, tenacious, caustic:

"But we should not be too indulgent of our people, our sphinx. It proved astonishingly easy to destroy the old, yes. But will it be as easy to build the new? Where did this centrifugal particularism come from? It's totally understandable on the part of oppressed nationalities, but why classes, too? Why cities, villages, military units, professions, individuals? Pursuing group interests, they're losing all sense of the whole, and this could crush our freedom."

"Yes, freedom has pampered them, that's true," agreed Gessen, not too worried. "But who wouldn't be dizzy with success when the eight-hour day was introduced with such magical ease here, while in the West it's still just a dream? Yes of course, we have to bring home to them that, while we'd all like to be up on deck, with a view of magnificent shores, no—we have to get down to menial work, down into the hold! This depends on us, Nikolai Andreevich: now, more than ever before, we must 'go to the people,' spread the word. A propaganda not of revolution though, but of enlightenment. Over the past ten years, we've educated people on the topics of sexual love, impressionism, futurism, cubism . . . but we forgot our 'daily bread' of democracy, and now the revolution has taken us by surprise. And I'm telling you, it's actually very good that questions and dangers are looming up before us, because we had encountered no opposition and it was beginning to alarm me."

"Well as far as I'm concerned, Iosif Vladimirovich, these extreme claims by the socialists, which had always delighted me, have started to worry me. What they are planting in the people's minds now is nothing like education. They're forgetting that the overthrow belonged to our whole nation, that individual groups should not lay claim to power. Say what you like, but the Soviet of Workers' Deputies is acting totally irresponsibly toward the Provisional Government. How can they maintain that Soviet power is acknowledged by the whole of Russia? And what are these commissars from the Soviet doing with the ministers? They walk around like Roman tribunes. But workers constitute five percent of the Russian population! And the intelligentsia entered the revolutionary arena before any hint of a 'proletarian consciousness' had appeared. And as for the army—they came in last of all. And apart from the intelligentsia no one was ever ready to take power. But now they're pointing fingers at the intelligentsia and calling it 'the bourgeoisie.'"

"Now there I'm with you. The old regime never feared revolutionaries: what it did fear was a civic constitutional democracy. They never sent us off to hard labor; but how they hated us! We were moved not by passion but by reason. Only we could—and still can today—calmly weigh up a situation and proceed with confidence."

But no, that did not reassure Gredescul: he was shifting his head from side to side on that restless neck, although his collar was actually quite loose.

"But even so, if the socialists recognized the Provisional Government—and they didn't have to recognize it—then logically they must also give it the means to realize its democratic program."

Gessen, like a kindly, slightly eccentric schoolmaster, smiled warmly and smoothed his great moustache:

"We're all looking for enemies everywhere, and so we end up attacking our brothers-in-arms. Revolutionary thinking is always full of suspicion, founded and unfounded. But all the same, the Soviet is the government's brother-in-arms."

"But what about Lenin? His refrain is already 'down with everything'—and he says it openly. Down with the whole lot, including the government and the war."

"Oh, Lenin again! But where's the danger in him? What can he do with his little band of maniacs?"

"Oh, don't be too sure! When everything's on the move, and moving centrifugally. . . . We should definitely ban Leninist propaganda as treasonable in any case."

"Oh! Oh! This pains me!" Little wrinkles had appeared on Gessen's plump, tautly smooth face and even on his extensive bald patch. "And to hear this from you! Those are the extreme ideas of your *Russian Will*. And then won't the reactionaries be overjoyed. Do I need to remind you that the means we adopt in our struggle must be equal to the noble principles of justice and liberty?"

"Justice and liberty, Iosif Vladimirovich," jumped in Gredescul, excitable, irritable, "but not to the extent that . . ."

"Ah, well," replied Gessen, absolutely calm, "excuse me, but there you're pandering to the views of the average middlebrow. Can the solution possibly be violence? Are we nostalgic for the old police constables? Pining for law and order, someone to obey, someone to be in charge? The man in the street sees imaginary dangers on all sides. It doesn't occur to him that if for a moment he stopped being a slave and became a citizen, then half his tribulations would immediately disappear. The government has moral force. It's effective because it relies not on troops, the militia or the courts, but on organized public opinion. 'The inaction of the government'? Today that reproach makes no sense. Before, we were within our rights to blame the old government for everything; but now Russia's fate is in our own hands—each one of us."

Gessen smiled, seeking the approbation of the silent ladies present.

"But would Leninist propaganda be possible if it encountered a massive outcry on the part of the public, a surge of popular indignation? How does the city dweller respond to Lenin? The curious go and listen, shrug their shoulders, and make no move to oppose him—and this is it, the craven practice of the slave. Lenin's agitation activities can be blamed on the nation itself and on society."

No, Gredescul did not agree, and wriggled his neck again. But he scooped up his books and turned to go into the reading room.

But at that moment the librarian Maria Mikhailovna, a lady in her middle years, was approaching rapidly, agitated and choking in her tight collar. Not noticing her eminent guests or, on the contrary, actually hurrying to say her piece while they were still there, she pressed her fists to her temples, one hand clutching a handkerchief.

"My God, what on earth is going on? What is going on?"

"What is it?" asked Gessen, concerned.

She started telling her story to the company at large. Her elder son, an eighth-grade high school pupil, was a member of the newly created board running all secondary educational institutions: a kind of government of all the Petrograd high schools covering all independent public activities. And yesterday they had learned that, defying the leadership and ignoring the refusal issued by the board, the younger pupils, aged twelve to fifteen, had been going round all the high schools, stirring the pupils up, telling them that today, Wednesday, they were not to go to classes but to the Kshesinskaya mansion for a mass demonstration—against Lenin. And now there was a struggle to win over the mass of high school students. The board, having conferred with the adults and with Kerensky, categorically forbade them to go—but the younger students had insisted, fixed the time and place to assemble, and, can you imagine, they went! And among them was Maria Mikhailovna's younger son! And what were they going to run up against there? There was no way of knowing what the Leninists might do!!

"Ye-e-s," said Gessen to the mother, extending that vowel sympathetically and screwing up his eyes tightly behind his spectacles. "We must just hope their meeting with Lenin does not happen. Lenin's benighted audience is enough for him: he must not poison the minds of children, whose experience hasn't yet generated an antidote. It's bad enough that the idea of such a demonstration occurred to schoolchildren at all. Children have no business fighting, with Bolsheviks or anyone else."

"And Kerensky himself forbade it!" exclaimed the distraught mother. "But they . . ."

"And a very rational decision on the part of the board. What can the street, in the ferment of revolution, give children? Nothing but depravity."

But Gredescul liked the children's forthright approach:

"I think it's a noble idea!"

"That's because there's no son of yours there!" retorted the mother.

But Gessen came back, puckering his lower lip into the form of a scoop:

"Yes, their feelings are understandable. These children of the revolution have been seized by revolutionary fervor, but their fervor is impulsive: they're running to attack Lenin as to a fire. These last few weeks they've imbibed so many sensations of freedom, so many political emotions, that they're impatient to be heard, along with everyone else. But they have nothing ready to say, except 'down with'; but the walls of the mansion will not fall at the sound of 'down with.' You can't jump from Ilovaisky's schoolbook straight into a battle with Lenin. What are they going to do, throw the book in his face? You won't bring him down with a book. It's too early for them to don the citizens' togas from their fathers' coat-hooks. The future belongs to our children, but you can't leapfrog straight into the future, like jumping over the skipping rope in a gymnastics class."

Today, Vera had heard, the Ladoga ice had started coming down the Neva. It always broke up later than the Neva ice, with an interval between, sending down massive white-green blocks. By the bridges and at river bends there were blockages, apparently. She must go and look.

A fragment of the eternal majesty—here before us, here after us.

[1 2]

Revolution is a magical red vortex. And anyone wanting to soar within it and not burn his wings (or break his legs) must have an innate skill for virtuoso flying across chasms and balancing on fragile, pliant, lofty bridges with no handrails. (This skill cannot be cultivated artificially.) And it is daring, confidence, sincerity, generosity of heart, and an unerring split-second impulse that win the day.

And Kerensky had made the intoxicating discovery of all these qualities in himself!

Even before this, the earth had not had a strong hold on him, and he had taken flight before. But that roaring pillar of fire, the revolution, had lifted him, carried him off, further and further! And nothing but victories! Nothing but peaks!

The prize of the revolution was liberty. But **who**, by his decisions, amnesties, smashing of shackles, must make this liberty a reality? The Minister of Justice. And that was Kerensky. **Who** was called on to bring together, delicately, tumultuous revolutionary democracy and the timid circles of the franchised classes, allowing the Provisional Government to be formed and to function? The hostage of democracy within the government. He was this as well. **Who** had to keep constant watch, eagle-eyed, on the ministers from these franchised classes and correct them immediately or else, losing patience, divert an area of their authority to himself? The incomparable, the only darling of democracy. This too was Kerensky. And **who** had, daily, to explain to revolutionary Russia in the most vivid terms everything that was going on? An inspired orator, he did that too. **Who** must hold back the Acheron, the outbursts of rage in the Soviet, outbursts of hate among the sailors? The first flower of the revolution. This too was Kerensky. And ***who*** had to shake up the Senate, the courts, the judicial statutes and create a redoubtable Extraordinary Commission to loom over all the villains of the old regime? Clearly he, the Prosecutor-General, did.

It was also clear that the hated tyrant, the baleful Tsar who had crushed Russia and sat atop corpses—now that he had toppled from the throne and slid down from the heights—into whose hands must he, by law, fall, if not those of the Prosecutor-General?

But this had not happened immediately. The Tsar's arrest had been carried out by the military authorities, and the Minister of Justice had not—despite his burning secret desire to rush to the palace himself—found time in the mad spin of the first weeks to take over complete responsibility for the captive Tsar from Guchkov and Kornilov. (But he had to. It would not be right to leave this nerve center in their hands.) Late March had been so hectic (and politically so complex), that he could not even find the few hours needed to take a drive out to Tsarskoye Selo.

When the Prosecutor-General did at last focus his attention on the fate of the Tsar, it was at the very moment when the most worrying news started coming in: the guards had learned from the palace footmen that commandant Kotzebue was spending a great deal of time visiting Vyrubova and, what's more, talking in a foreign language. He'd also been observed handing the imperial family letters with the seals still intact. There were rumors, too, emanating from the imperial servants, that papers were being burned in the palace. All of this could amount to, quite simply, preparations—for a plot? An escape? And Guchkov was becoming ever more sluggish, passive, helpless: so the moment had come to grab the Tsar out of his hands! And Guchkov was not even putting up any resistance. Over the course of twenty-four hours the blow was struck: Captain Kotzebue was dismissed and on 3 April Kerensky, with his trusted, democratic lawyer Korovichenko, raced off to Tsarskoye Selo.

He tried to look as official, cold, and menacing as possible. A chauffeur from the royal garage drove him in one of the ex-imperial cars. To make more of an impression, on this occasion he wore a shabby pair of cowhide boots, which had been procured for him in workers' circles a few days earlier, and a cross-buttoning workers' shirt. He mustered an entourage from among the "delegates" to go with him in two other cars. His tour of the palace started at the kitchen, and he made his first speech to the palace servants, telling them they were now serving not the Tsar but the people, and they must keep a close eye on the palace prisoners. Then he looked round the pantries, cupboards, and cellars. He addressed the guards. Then he questioned the servants working in the living quarters about the large quantity of paper ash that was being cleared out of the stoves. He calculated that, by that time, reports would already have reached the royal couple, and they would be sufficiently worried. It was strange, but he too felt a growing anxiety, but of the kind he could usually, with a bit of ingenuity, dispel. Now at last he would march resolutely toward Nikolai Romanov—without the barrier of thousands of generals and dignitaries—and dictate to him the will of the Revolution. He went in. It was a small room where, around a small table, the whole imperial family rose to meet him, hunched up, somehow, as if expecting him to lob a bomb at them. And Kerensky suddenly wavered. For this grim tyrant suddenly turned out to be not at all terrifying, even though in military uniform, but with a gentle, bewildered smile. And his whole mien was bewildered, resigned, as he walked toward the Prosecutor-General, his hand slightly raised for a possible handshake. Among those present now were none of those delegates, these eyes of the Soviet, in whose presence the minister had been so menacing an hour before; and Kerensky confidently stretched out a hand to the Tsar. The hand he met was soft: there was no asperity in the handshake, and on the Tsar's face played an acquiescent, apologetic smile, and his eyes, even on that overcast day, were blue. Question, answer, a few more words—they sat down, had a brief conversation, and Kerensky cast an observant eye over them all. Well, the children were certainly sweet. Only that she-devil Empress's chilly demeanor hadn't thawed, but what else could you expect from her. But as for the Tsar, well he was nothing like a monster, with those surprisingly guileless eyes and pleasant smile, and there was no sign that he was stupid, as everyone had chorused, over and over. And Kerensky actually had to restrain himself, to avoid softening and staying longer. They talked for ten minutes or so. Kerensky asked, among other things, whether it was true, as the German newspapers were saying, that Wilhelm had several times advised the Russian Tsar to adopt more liberal policies. The Tsar made no attempt to evade the question, and gave a straight answer: "Quite the opposite, in fact. But he did start trying to advise me, though he never understood Russia's situation." Kerensky was so charmed that he called him not "Nikolai Aleksandrovich" but "Sire," and a couple of times even "Your Majesty."

He forced himself to bring the visit to a close and summoned his trusted Korovichenko and introduced him to the Tsar. But as he left, he sent word to arrest Vyrubova immediately, not allowing her to see the imperial family again, and to take her to Petrograd.

The whole procedure and the trip were a great success, and no crisis would have arisen if Aleksandr Fyodorovich had not, in that same period, again demonstrated his magnanimity. He was passing the ministerial pavilion of the Tauride Palace, where there were still some prisoners, and decided to drop in. And he discovered there the elderly, newly arrested General Ivanov. And the old man touched him deeply: this honest soldier had served Russia for half a century, had never in any way sought to ingratiate himself with the Emperor, had taken every possible measure to ensure that his punitive expedition against Petrograd would not succeed, was devoted to the people and was himself of simple stock. But he was now suffering deprivations ill-suited to his years. And why? What was his crime? Without giving it too much thought, Kerensky took it upon himself to issue an order: the general was to be made to sign a declaration of loyalty to the Provisional Government and an undertaking not to leave Petrograd, and then be allowed to go home.

But this humane gesture would cost him dear. The following day, 7 April, the Soviet's *Izvestia* published a most malicious article (clearly the work of Nakhamkes, who had taken possession of the paper) claiming "great astonishment" that such a dangerous enemy as General Ivanov, who had marched on Petrograd as a dictator and was facing the prospect of execution without trial, should now be suddenly freed? What has the "monitoring personally by the Minister of Justice" got to do with this? You cannot decide things in this free and easy manner.

And his scouts were telling him that, at the Executive Committee, they were talking about summoning the Minister of Justice to explain himself.

This immediately cast a shadow over his irreproachable visit to Tsarskoye Selo as well: did it not seem that there too he had offered protection to enemies of the revolution?

Any other minister, and even any socialist, would have been at a loss—but not the tribune Kerensky. He saw immediately (inspired thinking!) the correct leaps he needed to cross the chasms—leap, leap, and keep your balance! And, repeating the magnificent performance that had been so successful on 15 March and gained him a position in government, he now rushed headlong to the Tauride Palace. But not to justify himself to the EC—he was not so artless: his approach had always been to ignore them completely. He rushed straight into the White Hall of the Duma, where the soldiers' section of the Greater Soviet was in session, and was met with applause. And he leapt onto the familiar platform. (Again an extreme measure, but the situation, for one with a keen sense for such things, required an extreme measure.)

He had not, for a long time—or, rather, he had never—prepared speeches. They would come together of their own accord as he reached the platform: this was his revolutionary genius. And phrases even occurred to him while he was already in full flow, appearing unexpectedly, even to the speaker himself. First he would marshal some support:

"Comrade soldiers! All my time has been taken up with my work. And I never had any misunderstandings with you. But now rumors have been started by people with evil intentions, who want to sow discord among the democratic masses. For five years, I denounced the old regime from this platform. I know the enemies of the people and I know how to deal with them: I have had to spend a great deal of time in the dungeons of Russian justice."

One might have thought from this that he himself had served time in the ravelins. But he went on, even more extreme:

"I have long demanded, here in closed-door Duma sessions, the abolition of the salute and measures to improve the soldier's lot. I spoke fearlessly here of the old regime's denial of rights, and fought, to the point of collapse, for the human rights of the democratic masses . . ."

Brilliant: you toss out "to the point of collapse," and just at that moment you really do start feeling close to collapse, and the audience can see that. And you are seized by uncontrollable emotion and your voice rises, and a pirouette occurs of its own accord, and a flight from one aerial platform to another:

"And now, when I have all the authority of the Prosecutor-General, and no one under arrest can be freed without my agreement," (a storm of applause) "people appear, and dare to express mistrust of me. They suggest I am acting indulgently toward the old government and . . ." (onto the attack now) ". . . members of the imperial family. I warn them: I shall not allow any such mistrust of me or any such insults to the whole of Russian democracy in my person!!"

And there it was: "**the whole of**"! And, all but ready to rip from his chest his well-fitting, one-of-a-kind jacket:

"I ask this of you: either exclude me from your ranks . . ." (the soldiers' ranks) ". . . or give me your unconditional trust!"

There was an immediate storm of applause and he had the soldiers' absolute trust. But that was not enough: now he had to pick his way along that crest:

"Yes, I have released General Ivanov, because he was old and sick and the doctors confirmed that he would not survive so much as three days where he was. But he is under my supervision, in a private apartment. I am also accused of leaving several members of the imperial family at liberty . . ." (This was not quite the accusation. It was not "several" members who were free, but all thirty of them apart from the clumsy Maria Pavlovna, but this maneuver was needed as a little security barricade and so that they would not interfere in his relationship with Tsarskoye Selo. Also, you have to understand a crowd: no matter what turning he took now, no one would dare challenge him.) ". . . So you should know that the *only* ones who have remained free are those who fought Tsarism." (This included Nikolai Mikhailovich and the three Grand Dukes who had married morganatically.) "Dmitri Pavlovich is free because he killed Grishka Rasputin."

And now it was as if the whole dynasty had whirled past us and we were at the crucial point:

"There must be no room for mistrust. I was at Tsarskoye Selo. The palace commandant now is someone I know well. The garrison has promised to execute my orders only. And I shall not leave my post until I have nailed down the certainty that there will be no regime in Russia other than a democratic republic!"

Ovation! They rose to their feet.

"I entered the Provisional Government as the representative of *your* interests. In a few days a document will be published, declaring that Russia renounces all aspirations to territorial conquest." (They were at that time still dragging the document out of the obstinate Milyukov, but it's certainly true that Kerensky's efforts were contributing, and the masses need to know it.) His voice was tensing now, ready for a new peak: this is the revolutionary instinct. "Comrades, I am working myself to the brink of exhaustion, but I can do it only as long as I am trusted. And now that people have appeared, wanting to sow discord in our ranks, if you want me to I shall work with you. But if you do not want this, I shall leave. I want to know: do you trust me or not? If not, I cannot work with you."

It was more than just an ovation. The hall was shaking from all the applause. And voices cried, "Please! Please! Work with us! We trust you! The whole army trusts you!"

Kerensky had expected, never doubted this response and now, as a final farewell from the platform:

"Comrades, I did not come here to justify myself. I came only to declare that I shall not allow myself to be the object of suspicion, even if it comes from the whole of Russian democracy."

And again, a storm of protestations of trust, and the orator was not feeling well (on the highest peaks of inspiration, some mechanism would fail in his head). Aleksandr Fyodorovich was supported and lowered into a chair and drank some water. His voice, now weaker, returned:

"I shall work for your good, to the point of exhaustion, comrades! And if you have any doubts, come to me, day or night, and we'll always reach an understanding."

And, accompanied by a burst of salutations, Kerensky was lifted, in his chair, and borne aloft from the hall.

Nakhamkes was defeated. And the Executive Committee was defeated. But still, for their total defeat, now he had to pass their rooms, not even popping in to say hello: he didn't need them. He had to shake their dust from his feet; he had no more business at the Tauride Palace! (And those EC members who wanted to sow discord were crushed so thoroughly that, via Sokolov, they were now making contact for a private meeting: "Aleksandr Fyodorovich, you really should not, must not neglect the Executive Committee in this cavalier manner." "But comrades, I cannot, practically and technically, seek your agreement on every step I take, and pressure from you is making my position in the government impossible. Ministers are liable simply to give up and leave." He would not sever relations, however: for it was his connection with the Soviet that kept Kerensky's position within the government secure.)

But even this was not all. By no means. This was only part of the pirouette. He wouldn't have time that day, but the following day he must hurry to Tsarskoye Selo! The Prosecutor-General was cut to the quick. What? *He* was not firm enough? (And it was all the more hurtful because, deep inside, he himself felt it was true: no, he was not firm enough!) So he would immediately increase the severity of their conditions. Muravyov had reassured Kerensky that some terrible incriminating evidence against the Tsar was about to be revealed any moment now in the Extraordinary Commission. And it was important that the Tsar and Tsaritsa should not manage to cook up a scheme and that she should have no opportunity to influence her husband. A good idea! And the next morning, before Tsarskoye Selo, he went to see Buchanan and asked him not to press his government to speed up the Tsar's departure to England: he could not possibly leave the country for at least a month, not until the examination of documents was completed. (And in his heart he was thinking: "Yes, and things will be easier that way. In a month, the situation for his departure will be far calmer, if the Tsar turns out to be innocent. But what if . . .? What if . . .? Oh . . .")

But although the Prosecutor-General had rushed there to administer punishment, he observed palace etiquette, not bursting in to see the Tsar before the lackey had announced his arrival to the master of ceremonies and the Emperor had expressed himself "graciously disposed" to receive the visitor. There was a nice idea in this: he would not imprison the Tsar in the Peter and Paul Fortress, not humiliate him, not confine him to a hovel, to the wretched life of a pauper. He would make the royal family into museum figures, housed under glass: he would leave them their gilded prison and all their servants (though no laundress would be able to leave from now on without a visa from the Minister of Justice), and retain all the palace ceremony, even the footmen with their ostrich feathers. But the family would be constantly observed from the outside, while no sound from them would reach to the outside.

He announced it: the Tsar and Tsaritsa would now be separated. They could meet only at the common table, always in the presence of officers of the detachment guarding them and, furthermore, they may talk only in Russian and only on general subjects. (His original intention had been to separate the Tsaritsa from her children, but her lady-in-waiting, Naryshkina, had come to him—unbeknown to the imperial couple—to ask permission to leave the palace, regretting that, in the heat of the first moments, she had stayed. Nevertheless, she objected to the Empress being torn apart from her children: it would be too hard on her.) Also, at the changing of the guard both of the royals would have to show themselves to the departing and the newly arriving guard; but this could be portrayed tactfully, as presenting the commanders of the two guards detachments.

He was amazed how calmly the Emperor took everything. Incredible self-control! But Kerensky, feeling embarrassed, explained to him that all this was not with any serious aim, only to appease the Soviet of Workers' Deputies: the pressure from left-wing elements was quite unbearable. And he slipped into "Your Majesty" again. But he also wanted to frighten him. There were, he said, incriminating documents concerning certain high officials. The Emperor replied, calmly: "But perhaps these documents are forged?" Kerensky also spoke, separately, to the Tsaritsa, in the form of a semi-interrogation: in what way did she seek to influence her husband and interfere in governing Russia? But he felt her answers were absolutely truthful, and nothing incriminating could be gleaned from them. And the children were very sweet. Kerensky's feelings were contradictory and awkward for him: a terrible, revolutionary trial was needed—and he felt sorry for them.

But even that wasn't all: a genius of the revolution was bound to feel pulled in all directions. From Tsarskoye Selo he went straight on to Kronstadt, which was seething. (Had there been murders there . . .? Was there a mutiny dragging on?) Once there—a speech at the Soviet of Sailors' Deputies: "Our freedom is in the hands of Kronstadt!" Was all the terror down to that nice student Roshal, that neuropsychologist now wearing sailors' trousers? Kerensky greeted him with a kiss. And back to Petrograd in a flash. To the press: "I have just returned from Kronstadt. All attempts to set us against them will founder on the understanding of our now mature people. The Baltic fleet is reborn and will not betray Russia!" And a report to the government: in Kronstadt absolute peace has been restored, absolute unity between sailors and officers: these rumors of officers being harassed are false. (And there were not, in fact, so very many killed.) And this too, placed in all the newspapers: "The Minister of Justice has instructed the Extraordinary Commission of Inquiry to pay special attention to the case of the Tsar." Also, to all the newspapers, a piece denying that he himself had interrogated Vyrubova: what nonsense, another malicious rumor. (They could also construe it as a kind of collusion.) And now, like a comet, off to the station, where the much-loved *Grandmother* was finally—only now!—due to arrive. He would give her a bouquet of red roses: "You are the Empress of Russian liberty!" Take her to the imperial rooms of the station—and make a speech. And take her by car to the Tauride Palace and in front of the Executive Committee, now pushed to the sidelines, another speech: "Three years ago, when I was on the Lena . . ." (on assignment, as a lawyer) "Grandmother was there too, guarded by the gendarmes. And now I am so proud to be meeting our beloved Grandmother here today!" And, together with Chkheidze, carry her, in her chair, out of the hall. And host a luncheon in the ministry for Grandmother and Vera Figner (what symbolism!). And the mild-mannered

Prince Lvov also came, to greet Grandmother. And then Kerensky must rush back to the Tauride Palace for the Conference of Soviets, make his entrance, interrupting the speaker, to a crescendo of applause (that produces the best effect, when they stop what they're doing and applaud), and make another speech: "To the whole of democracy I bring the heartfelt salutation of the government. I could not get onto the list of speakers, despite the need I feel to be among you. We are all here together, old comrades in our struggle against the old regime."

And only with that was his three-day pirouette complete. And the Prosecutor-General was no longer vulnerable to attack from any side.

And that very evening—how absurdly dense the time had become—he would receive from Prince Lvov, who was leaving for GHQ, the style "on behalf of the Prime Minister." (That he, the hostage of democracy, and no other should be signing "on behalf of" Prince Lvov! He was surely going to end up as Prime Minister: his was a rising star.) And the following morning he would already be receiving, in the name of the government, delegation after delegation from the front. (This suited Kerensky very well.) And he would be exchanging kisses with a delegation from the St. George Battalion, with which he'd become acquainted during his visit to GHQ.

And that evening, back at his ministry, receive deputies from the Conference of Soviets again, so as to make a more lasting impression on them. (And so the Executive Committee failed to conduct this Conference without Kerensky. At the Conference it was said of him, for example: "We should not attack, torment that heart, which burns for the good of its people. To offend that man would be a crime, comrades!")

And he would have carried on whirling about like a magical star: he could manage it. But then Easter rolled along, with a natural pause of several days, causing even the revolution to take a break. And Kerensky really did need a rest—from the government, from the Soviet, from speech-making, from his family—and he wanted to go off for a few days, incognito, to a sanatorium in the environs of Moscow (with the prospect of an interesting encounter). But he was careless enough to mention it to someone, and the very next day it was in the papers. The plan was ruined. But anyway, the Moscow environs were a long way to go. So he would go to Finland. And in that case—why not look in on Helsingfors and, o revolutionary heart, why not address the Sejm? (For Finland had not behaved entirely properly with respect to Russian democracy.) He was given a bouquet—he thanked them with a kiss: "This is the most precious thing I have received in Finland."

On returning from his Easter break (and discovering that Plekhanov and Lenin had arrived and Chernov and Savinkov were expected any day now) he was immediately sucked back into that hungry vortex. You don't get a moment to recover your breath, when you're being propelled up and up, to ever greater heights! And what was the key to this extraordinary success? It was, of course, that Kerensky possessed a unique combination: brilliant revolutionary flair, a clear socialist consciousness, and a very deep sense of patriotism. And this was why he could charm people: everyone, from all schools of thought, like a whirlwind. (What a remarkable destiny!)

In the early days, he did not mix the different episodes together. For example, on the way back from Finland, at Beloostrov station, he was unfortunately stopped by the border police: it seemed he had no documents on him. What a joke! (This episode too, like everything he did, got into the papers—so much for hiding away to have interesting meetings! They didn't stop Lenin, but they stopped Kerensky. What a joke!) The officials at the border crossing telephoned Petrograd and then offered the minister earnest apologies for the inconvenience caused, while he, for his part, praised them for their vigilance. (But he was, because of this, late for the SR conference—and it was important for him to be seen among the SRs, since he had, since March, been using that designation.) After that, things became very muddled. For some reason he was at the Petrograd Municipal Board—and made a speech there. And at the teachers' congress—another speech. And somehow he came to be at the railwaymen's congress. What reminiscences could he share with them? He talked of how, during those March days, they had pinned down the ex-Tsar on the rail network. But also (with an eye to the future, to ward off a hysterical reaction from the Soviet!): "There are attempts to engender alarm among us, but we have nothing to fear from counterrevolution and no need to take any special measures against the representatives of the old government and the old regime. Our struggle was against the regime, not against any particular individuals: they have already suffered enough, been sufficiently humiliated and dragged through the mud of people's contempt." And he truly did feel this way, especially remembering the Tsar and his children. And, his voice beginning to tremble: "As Minister of Justice, I want the Russian revolution to show that the triumph of democratic ideals is not bound up with violence!" (And then Vyrubova's parents rushed up to him asking that she be released because she was ill—but he refused. Grand Duchess Maria Pavlovna also sent a petition, from Kislovodsk: this woman was yet another complication.)

He also found time to write to the SR newspaper, urging them to remember the behest of Nikolai Turgenev and put up a monument to the Decembrists, not just anywhere but on the wall of the Peter and Paul Fortress. And he would make up for what he had missed with the SRs by attending the Trudovik congress, in the Hall of the Army and Navy. And the congress had been, it seems, fairly tedious until . . . like a thunderclap hitting that stifling atmosphere, into the hall ran Kerensky, honorary chairman of the congress. And took the floor immediately! "I came to express my personal gratitude to you for the friendly attitude I enjoy in your midst." And he explained why, five years before, he had agreed to stand for election as a Trudovik, even though he had felt himself more akin to the SRs: because all groupings among the socialists should now unite into a single bloc. "Trudovik comrades," (and here his voice modulated) "these five years have left an indelible mark on my life! Our common experience is momentous for the whole cause of Russian and world democracy." And even (he led up to this delicately: it could be useful for Lenin): "We and the Social Democrats were, for all these years, consistently more true to the policy of renouncing seizure of territories than some European socialists were. The destiny of our country is now being forged, perhaps for centuries to come . . . The paramount idea of socialism is absolute reverence for man and his distinctive character. We shall build our state on two principles: labor and man. We have before us the supreme mission of demonstrating the value of socialism as a system of government . . ." And, while the actual chairman was adding something, Kerensky was already moving rapidly toward the exit via a lateral colonnade and everyone was jumping up and another storm of applause broke out, cutting the chairman short. And from the hall and from the neighboring rooms joyful, animated groups spilled out onto the grandiose marble staircase or waved from the galleries alongside it, and boys and girls, forgetting their hats and coats, leapt out into the street to accompany their Kerensky. (An idol to the young, especially.)

And now it was off again, somewhere else, where he also had to speak, apparently in support of the Freedom Loan: "Democracy now prevails in our country: in other words, all the people are in charge. And I am firmly convinced that the people will welcome the loan. I have faith in the people's intelligence! In our popular masses lies an inexhaustible treasury of wisdom! The Russian nation will take its fitting place among the democracies of the world!" And again, straight off somewhere else: "Back in August 1914, in the State Duma, I declared my belief that Russian democracy would win the battle for liberty! And I believe the whole world will respect our principles. Let us throw off from our hearts the remains of our old enslavement and our fear of some mythical counterrevolution." And off somewhere else: "We have laid not only all our thoughts and feelings, but our whole life at the feet of the masses, the workers and peasants of Russia." Aha! Now he knew where he was: at the Mariinsky Palace, greeting another of the military delegations: "You, in your soldiers' and sailors' uniforms, are the custodians of our life. Spread the word: I would not have joined the Provisional Government if the land question had not been at the top of the agenda. But I did join, and I don't regret it, because there I met honorable men and we shall do our duty, leading the country toward the Constituent Assembly and preparing her to embrace the freest regime in the world. As long as we are in our posts and while I am in the ministry, there is no threat to the freedom of the Russian people!" And now he was kissing the deputies of the Special Army (its Guards "have boundless confidence in him"): "Now the Russian army has been given freedoms of a kind no other army in the world enjoys." And now they brought him five hundred gold and silver George Crosses and medals from the Guards Hussar Regiment. And now a Kuban Cossack captain brought greetings from the units at the Persian border.

But how many matters there were concerning the Ministry of Justice as well! In forty days he signed forty legislative acts and orders, all exceptionally humane. On top of all the amnesties, there was also a decree revoking punitive measures against the Zemgor members suspected of counterfeiting, bribery, extortion, and misappropriation of supplies; another suspending measures to collect on promissory notes and all legal action on monies owed; and the lifting of exceptional and intensive security measures—he also, however, set up revolutionary courses to train up prison guards. (And, what's more, every day he found time to relieve a few figures in the legal world of their duties, without waiting for the leaden-footed decisions of the Senate.) A deputation of soldiers even came to see him here at the ministry, about, as it turns out, land. They asked that landowners should not, for the moment, be allowed to sell their land, especially to foreigners. "Fine, I'll pass this question on to the Minister of Agriculture. You'll be notified." "But how is it that you, an SR, are receiving people in a hall with Tsars looking down from the walls?" Kerensky looked around and blushed crimson with embarrassment, for his careless staff did not take down a portrait of Aleksandr II. "Yes, yes, we'll take it down tomorrow! No, today!" How was he to attend to everything, find time for everything? Now he had to rush off to a night session of the Provisional Government. (You drive fast through Petrograd at night—the militia have shot at you before.) Lvov not there? Then sign a decree about fuel, or whatever else may arise. Discontinue the allowance for right-wing members of the State Council (but mustn't stop paying left-wing members). And now the head of counter-espionage asked for his department to be protected from the Soviet, which wanted to disband it, as if the struggle with Germany were irrelevant. Reinstate it! But then he discovered that a good few people are appearing at various offices and pressing to have their needs met, citing an opinion or verbal instruction from Kerensky. The scoundrels! Issue a rebuttal to the press: they must produce written documents. And now someone slipped in a request from Admiral Maksimov to free some Finnish captain in Kronstadt. Here you are—and he signed. But, two days later, another eruption in Kronstadt: they'd seized that captain, who'd just been freed, and come very close to hanging the prosecutor who'd been sent there, Pereverzev. Damn that Kronstadt, and that Roshal! They were never going to get Kronstadt under control, because even the Petrograd Soviet was frightened of it.

All the more reason to speed off now to the Baltic fleet! To Reval. With Breshko-Breshkovskaya: that would make an impression! (Grandmother was particularly necessary to him there, to confirm his status as a long-standing SR member.) The two days were, one could say, a constant round of ovations and demonstrations, starting as they approached the town. Reval was a sea of red flags and they were welcomed at the station by a large crowd, delegations with bouquets, and an honor guard. (Kerensky reviewed the line, shaking the hand of every sailor, soldier, and officer.) Grandmother, modestly dressed, with a blue shawl, unselfconsciously exchanged kisses with the representatives of each group. In the car they were strewn with flowers, and Kerensky felt compelled to stand up and give a speech about the Grandmother's services to Russia. Then Grandmother also stood up in the car. First they went to the Russian market: there, Kerensky proposed that they should all honor the memory of the combatants, and assured the crowd that the achievements of the Russian revolution would never be taken from them. "Our SR party, the party of chivalry, truth, and honor, has always been known for its candor and openness." Then to the Katharinenthal Palace, now seat of the Executive Committee of the Soviet, for a speech. To the seamen's club—a speech there too. (Throughout the whole of each public speech, you are always aware of the joy you bring to your listeners. But Nakhamkes's *Izvestia* stubbornly ignores all of Kerensky's speeches.) A luncheon at the naval officers' club, and speeches from both the guests. To the City Duma: "You will soon realize that the Russian people and the Provisional Government will unite the whole world . . ." And that evening, a meeting at the Estonia theater. The following day, to the fleet, a tour of the ships. And a handshake for everyone. The fleet was completely battle-ready. "In your complex task, you cannot manage without officers: so keep them safe. But if you detect that your officers are not sympathetic to the revolution and have leanings toward the old system, well in that case we'll deal with them and show them no mercy."

He returned to Petrograd in a state of total exhaustion. "I am quite overwhelmed by the general enthusiasm shown me by the Army, Navy, and civilian population of Reval . . ." The sailors had kneaded and crushed his right arm to such an extent that now he had to bandage it up and wear a sling. (But this produced an even better effect: like an injured soldier, back from the front.)

If that had been all, if there had been only that . . . But what about the Western socialists?

Immediately after Easter, French and English socialists started arriving. And Kerensky, keyed up as he already was, now reached fever pitch. This was a unique opportunity to achieve, in a single inspired move, four objectives: to win the heart of socialist Europe; convey to Europe via these arrivals his position on this war; to keep the new arrivals away from the Executive Committee and take over the guests' care for himself; and use them to edge Milyukov out of foreign policy (and then cut him off completely), liberating it for himself. (It was extraordinary that he did, for some reason, want to run foreign policy as well!)

The Western socialists arrived—and Kerensky became quite a natural figure in matters of diplomacy. Ambassador Paléologue invited him to a luncheon. There, with the openness appropriate to a festive meal, Kerensky spiritedly revealed to the assembled company things that could not be spoken of plainly in public discourse: Yes, we, the Russian socialists, and, yes, I personally agree with continuing the war! But the Allies must now revise their peace plan and accommodate it to the concept of our Russian democracy. Otherwise we're in an awkward position—you're familiar with the Soviet's manifesto . . . (This manifesto, causing offence to our allies by betraying Western democracy, had upset him personally, but nowhere could he dare say that openly.) In short, the allied governments should renounce annexations and indemnities—or something of the kind.

And the following day, distancing himself from Milyukov, he delivered an official address to the newly arrived socialists at the Mariinsky Palace:

"I am *alone* in the cabinet, and my opinion does not always chime with the opinion of the majority. I am a *hostage*." But, in the voice of a man with considerable power: "Until now you did not hear the voice of Russian democracy. But, *comrades*, you must know that Russian democracy is, at the present time, master of the Russian land. We have decided, once and for all, to cease all forays into predatory imperialism. And our enthusiasm comes not from the idea of fatherland but from within our dream of brotherhood among all nations of the world. And we shall defend to the end our government's declaration of 9 April," (in fact it was Kerensky who had insisted on it) "as well as . . ." (there was no avoiding it . . .) "the Soviet's manifesto. And under no circumstances shall we allow a return to predatory objectives in this war. And we expect you to show the same decisive influence on your bourgeois classes as well. After all, it is from you, the French, that we always learned revolutionary enthusiasm and from you, the English, great tenacity."

And the following day, of course, he hosted a reciprocal luncheon, in the Ministry of Justice. But they were not very malleable. Even the gloomy, sharp-tongued Cachin, apparently fairly left-wing, even he defended the bourgeois French government, saying he had no intention of trying to influence it but would instead tell the Soviet of Deputies that without victory there could be no free development of nations, and that the time had come to settle, *definitively*, the destiny of all the nations.

Two days later, however, another French socialist arrived, Thomas, who was already a minister. This one turned out to be more receptive to the intoxicating revolutionary atmosphere of Petrograd: "Yes, this is Revolution, in all its majesty and beauty!" He talked of ineffable joy in his heart and fervent hope, and was won over, captivated by Kerensky's personality. And Kerensky sensed, ever more clearly, that he was the master of foreign policy too. The only impediment was his ignorance of foreign languages. But he had already addressed a Russian audience several times, defying the opinion of the Foreign Minister, once stealing a march on him by declaring that Constantinople should be internationalized. And, at the Conference of Soviets, saying that if Russia were the first to amend her war aims, then all the powers would have to change their own—it was clear as day. But it was not only Milyukov's policies that Kerensky found so detestable. It was, even more, Milyukov himself: his doctrinaire erudition, dogmatic self-assurance, multi-layered insincerity, and the way he played at being leader of the whole of educated Russia. Kerensky sensed in him a haughty critic, an enemy, and his antithesis. And at almost every meeting they were exchanging jibes, while in private, with no secretaries present, it would almost come to blows, once provoking a real scandal. Milyukov had dared to say, or rather mutter almost inaudibly, that German money was one of the factors contributing to the March coup and *everyone knew it*. Kerensky did not just start quivering with indignation: he allowed that quivering to take him over, and worked himself up into an intoxicating fury, because he had realized in a flash (all this was intuitive, spur-of-the-moment, no rational judgments) that there would be no better or more effective moment to deliver the blow. And he did not challenge Milyukov's statement, did not exclaim—instead he screamed: "Wha-at?? Wha-at did you say? Say it again!!" But Milyukov did not blench, and stubbornly repeated that abomination. And then Kerensky—even he was trembling at this dazzling eruption of his fury—did not exclaim, but screamed, launched himself with a howl: "After what Mr. Milyukov dared to say in my presence, slandering the holy cause of the great Russian revolution, I have no wish to remain here one minute longer!!" And he snapped his briefcase very noisily shut, banged it down dramatically on the table (perhaps he was overdoing things here) and flew like an arrow out of the meeting room. What an effect! And he knew they would run after him: Tereshchenko and Nekrasov were already running. But he was not going to be stopped! And he climbed into his car and went off to his ministry. (And went to bed. The next day Prince Lvov arrived with a guilty air, to try and talk him round.) And this was a winning blow, which pulled Milyukov down a whole notch and strengthened his own position.

Kerensky was too busy to devote himself exclusively to foreign policy but, ever vigilant, even in this whirl of activity he could not fail to note that the pause since the 9 April declaration had been too long: Milyukov wanted, on the sly, to restrict himself to a declaration to the Russian people, without sending an official note to the Allies, so as not to tie his hands for the future. This game had to be derailed. Milyukov's hands would have to be tied. Already, at the Liaison Commission (which Kerensky hated since, by its very existence, the EC was expressing mistrust of its "hostage"), Chernov had begun asking for that note to be sent. And now Kerensky had a brilliant idea! It had come to him last night, and today he put it into action: he simply informed the press that the government *was drawing up* a note to the Allies, and that it would, *in a few days*, be published. Superb! The next day, 26 April, it would be in the papers. Let Milyukov try and get out of it then.

Kerensky had a superabundance of energy (despite his occasional blackouts). Thanks to this, he was already directing foreign policy and had already started imposing his will on the army. Stealing a march on Guchkov, he had already, in March, proclaimed via the press that we needed a younger body of generals and only then could we go onto the offensive with enthusiasm. And then he even suggested forming two separate ministries, a War Ministry and a Naval Ministry (so that he could snatch at least one from Guchkov). In recent weeks Guchkov had been looking more and more sorry for himself, a wimp, a wet rag capable of less and less—while Kerensky went from strength to strength. He was ascendant, and started to see for himself the destiny of a Joan of Arc, as savior of the fatherland! The stars above moved inexorably, leading Kerensky to have to take control of the Army.

And look at today: a delegation from the 7th Army had arrived at the Mariinsky Palace. Guchkov, as usual, was either away from Petrograd or ill. And Prince Lvov was not at all keen to attend. So who was to welcome them in the name of the government? His step firm, his pace brisk, into the rotunda (feeling himself quite the military man, and with his arm in a black sling) strode Kerensky. The delegation was lined up, the captains interspersed among the men, and the minister passed down the line, amiably shaking each of them by the left hand. The pleasant, cultured Lieutenant Stepun spoke on behalf of the delegates: "Mr. Minister, sir! You are for us the living incarnation of unity and solidarity: no wonder you are the link bonding the Provisional Government and the Soviet of Deputies. But can this unity penetrate through all the layers of the life we are now creating?"

The question could not have been more apposite! And somehow the whole situation had become so favorable, so uplifting that Kerensky felt the impetus to make a speech that would soar (and the reporters hurried to record it):

"Yes, the primary task of the Provisional Government is to further the unity of our nation at this crucial moment of its life. And there is no threat to our fulfilling this task. We are ten of your comrades, ordinary citizens. We took upon ourselves a heavy burden, a massive responsibility at a moment of the utmost devastation—and we must not allow our front line to be penetrated and our freedom taken from us. In fulfilling these tasks we need the criticism and the oversight of the Soviet of Soldiers' and Workers'

Deputies, the people, Russian democracy. So do not be perplexed by stupid gossip spread by the enemies of freedom: we *want* this oversight. We are taking all decisions in contact with the Soviet and are happy when it gives us directions of any kind. If there are disagreements between us, they are only about what to do today and what to defer till tomorrow. We have not yet arrived at the era of a dictatorship of the proletariat: we are in the era of national revolution. And there is not, and cannot be, a desire on the part of the Soviet to provoke a civil war. I believe in the people's intelligence: I believe they will take the path to salvation, not to destruction, for no one could want his own destruction. I believe there is, in the popular masses, an inexhaustible fount of political wisdom and creative energy. We believe that constructive tasks and not party slogans will triumph. The people will understand that it is not possible for the new power to create everything, immediately, out of nothing."

How peerless his balance on such pliant bridges! Every day fighting with the Soviet, every day he had to praise it skilfully, or else be swallowed up. Kerensky saw at once, in that little delegation, the whole of the Russian people, listening to him with honest eyes, and at once he was talking to the whole nation.

What could be of interest to the people? An eight-hour day? It's the norm for all the workers, so yes. But for our national defense we need to strain every sinew. If, now, we don't give the army everything it needs, it's because we cannot. But in the case of the old regime it was because they didn't want to. The old regime left everything in disarray. (Railing at the old regime was always a winning topic; something to unite us all.) And how about land?

"I am a convinced supporter of the motto 'land and freedom.' The people must be given both in full measure. But until the Constituent Assembly no one has the right . . . Not a single square foot of land will be assigned to anyone until all the people have had their say, and especially the army, which has spilled . . ."

And here it comes, the emotional pinnacle:

"Few people realize the immensity of the events we are living through. For centuries, we were accustomed to waiting and receiving nothing, but now we want to receive everything, not waiting so much as a day. But turning a despotic monarchy into perhaps the most perfect republic on earth is not a task to be completed in a few days."

And now this:

"In the headlong rush toward our goal, we must beware of overshooting that goal and seeing it not in our hands but behind us! The end result depends on our restraint, on keeping a cool head."

No, here is the pinnacle, only now did he himself see it:

"No counterrevolution is possible, for no one is insane enough to want to rebel against the will of the whole of the army, the whole of the peasantry, the whole of the workers' democracy—against the wishes of Russia. And if someone did try to rebel, where would he find supporters? No guns would be fired, no trains would run and that mad attempt would never emerge from the study into the street. And if it did emerge, those madmen would be eliminated on the spot."

Now on to the war? How would he invigorate the combatants? Ah!

"Go back to the front and do your duty—your almost unendurable duty! We demand it! And anyone who does not heed this demand will be made to recognize that we have a right to our place in the world, and we shall give up that right to no one. Let them not think that free Russia means collapse, that democracy means anarchy. Anyone who thinks that way is wrong and has already been proved wrong! Why, there is not one soldier, not one sailor, from any state in the world, who has such rights as you have! But rights bring obligations . . ."

He was tired. But while things were going like this he really could not stop. So he also talked about the cradle of democratic freedom, and inspected lines of happy delegates, left hand outstretched—and more, and ever more. Today, 25 April, was an ordinary weekday, and what a typical day for the Prosecutor-General, crammed full of worries like sardines in a can. In the morning there was a troubling report in the newspapers: the 12th Army delegates feel that detaining the Tsar at Tsarskoye Selo is too lenient, and are demanding that he be moved to the Peter and Paul Fortress. (And again he suspected this was a Nakhamkes maneuver. A threat! He'd have to rush over there and take measures. Today.) But who was pressing to see the minister now? A deputation from the student municipal board. What is it, my dear young people? It turned out there was propaganda targeting high-school pupils, calling on them all to go to the Kshesinskaya mansion and demonstrate against Lenin today. The student self-governing board had ruled that this must be stopped: it is not a matter for high-school pupils. But the younger pupils wouldn't listen and the board needed the support of the popular revolutionary leader.

"Ah . . ." Kerensky could only smile. "Ah, that Lenin." And, sternly: "Yes, I *forbid* this demonstration! In a free country we must have free speech, and the Bolsheviks have that right: they fought against Tsarism as we all did. Tell the high-school pupils that I forbid them to go! Freedom must come into our schools, but pupils must not leave the school premises in search of it. We can manage on our own, believe me!" (And what if Lenin set his armed guard on them? What then? The children must be protected and stopped from going to Trinity Square.)

Oh dear! That Lenin! All that unnecessary racket he'd made trundling through Germany. And what for? All he'd done was to undermine his authority in the eyes of the masses. But no route for the return of amnestied emigrants had been formally banned, and Kerensky had been the first in the government to derail Milyukov's efforts to keep Lenin out of Russia. Yes, he'd received plenty of protests from the Petrograd public, wanting him to take measures against Leninist agitation, but he was proud not to have taken any such measures: we ourselves had to be worthy of the freedom we had proclaimed! For that matter, why not visit Lenin personally there, in his den, and explain everything to him? He'd been cut off from Russia and living in a totally isolated environment, he was seeing everything through the lens of his own fanaticism; and he had no one nearby to help him get his bearings. As two prominent socialists, surely they could find a common language? (And all the more, given that, deep in his Zimmerwaldist heart, Lenin was of course right—right!) Besides, he and Lenin were fellow countrymen, both from Simbirsk. When Sasha Kerensky was six years old, his father had signed seventeen-year-old Volodya Ulyanov's high school diploma.

But no, he felt uncomfortable about going. Firstly it would, despite all that, mean humbling himself and, secondly, he might get publicly insulted. Lenin would do something like that.

And now there were some more socialists here: today Kerensky was giving a luncheon at the ministry in honor of Albert Thomas, and Chernov, who arrived a few days ago, was also invited. (Chernov was considered the leader of the SRs, though Kerensky didn't think him much of a leader.) And of course the beloved Grandmother! And at the lunch there was—again—such an understanding with Thomas! Such fellowship!

But duty tugged the Prosecutor-General into his car—and off to Tsarskoye Selo, to the town hall, where the garrison committee representatives and the military units were already assembled. Comrades, do not let these ill-informed demands of the 12th Army trouble you. At the moment it's not possible to move the ex-Tsar to the Peter and Paul Fortress. He cannot escape from here: you yourselves are guarding him. And communication with the outside world from the Aleksandr Palace is impossible. I have personally inspected everything and I am, personally, supervising everything. The commandant here is Lieutenant Colonel Korovichenko, whom I know well.

Some complaints: in the palace the officers in the guard detachments are being turned into drunks. And in that condition they could be bribed.

It turns out that, following Court tradition, the heads of detachments are issued half a bottle of wine each from the imperial cellars on the day they're on duty.

So that's what's going on! Fine, we'll stop distributing bottles. And let's increase the guard too.

Peace restored. What now? Drop in at the palace?

And while dropping in, a quick visit to the Emperor?

They talked for nearly an hour. Say what you will, His Majesty is a charming fellow.

And he doesn't complain about anything, despite being kept apart from his wife for two weeks. But the investigation has still brought no promising leads, not even hints. Well then, let's reunite them, that'll be fine. And Kerensky lifted the ban.

He raced back at top speed. It was already dark.

The whole time he was twisting and turning, flying this way and that but, in a strange way, it was thanks to this that he acquired ever more strength as a revolutionary leader.

He searched his memory: wasn't there something else today? Yes, he'd promised to go to the Koussevitzky concert. All right, he'd go—that was important too. He'd have to say a few words, something appropriate to the occasion.

[1 3]

(RULE OF THE PEOPLE AT THE FRONT: FRAGMENTS)

* * *

The powerful ice drift along the Dvina broke the underwater telephone lines linking our right bank to our position on the left. It was impossible to get a boat across the river, and the only means of communication left was flashing a lamp on and off. But there was a cable suspended over the river, and a soldier from a technical train unit, Aleksandr Loshchinsky, undertook to cross the river hanging from the cable and pulling a telephone wire across. The Germans shot at him, but he was unhurt and reached the other side! Everyone on both banks was watching, and they took a collection as a gift. And General Radko awarded him the St. George Cross.

* * *

The heavy flood on the Dvina forced both sides to take shelter from the swell. For four weeks there was a lull. Just before Easter the water retreated, but there was another lull. The German Landsturm troops were constantly raising white flags and leaving their trenches, waving their arms, waving their caps, and meetings were happening everywhere. Sometimes they managed to exchange their sausage for our bread and give our men leaflets, and no perfidious shot was ever fired. Then sometimes our artillery would disperse them with a warning salvo. The infantry threatened artillery batteries with a barrage of hand grenades if they tried to prevent fraternization.

Artillery Lieutenant Colonel Burya went to an observation point and bullets whistled past him. His own side's infantry was firing at him.

* * *

That year the two Easters came one after the other, first the German, then ours a week later. In previous years too the gunnery had fallen silent over the Easters, but this time—absolute peace for a fortnight.

Even before that, their reconnaissance men had been hurling leaflets to just in front of our trenches, and some were also dropped from an aeroplane: "Russian soldiers! You should know what our Chancellor has said about peace. Only we are not interfering with you, so do not interfere with us." In other words, don't expect Wilhelm to abdicate as well.

And then, in all sectors, they climbed out of their trenches with flags both white and red, waving their caps, and invited us: come out, step beyond your barbed wire, and we can get together in no man's land.

Well we liked that. We went.

Didn't the priest teach us that all men are brothers?

* * *

But in the Carpathians, in the 18th Corps, the Germans came to our trenches one afternoon for some amicable fraternization. Clearly they did some reconnaissance too, noting the positions of the machine guns that day (for they were moved regularly). And that very evening they opened fire and scored direct hits.

* * *

When a delegation from a reserve battalion arrived from Petrograd, the Moscow Life Guards on the front line became very exuberant. In the evening, after the oath of allegiance to the Provisional Government, an unruly, tipsy crowd of soldiers surrounded the officers' club and set up a menacing growl: "Arrest them!" Not all of them. It turned out they had a list of eleven officers. "But what for?" asked the regimental commander, Major-General Halfter, who had just arrived in a carriage. They shouted out their answers: They're too strict, they're loyal to the deposed regime, they're against the new order. The major-general could think of nothing to do but arrest them himself and he moved off to Division HQ with the officers around his carriage and thirty or so armed men following like a detachment of guards. There, with the officers in the HQ yard, the men kept watch over them. But Captain Rykov came out of HQ, onto the top of the steps. He was from their Moscow Regiment, and since that morning he had been at HQ on business. "What are you doing here?" "Standing guard." "Guarding what? Get out of here, you scum!" The bewildered soldiers retreated and went back to the regiment, grumbling. But the officers refused to go to their units if the soldiers responsible for the mutiny were not punished in accordance with martial law. But the divisional commander could not do this. And the doomed officers left the regiment and set off to work on an auxiliary supply train. They had a phrase for it now: "in view of current circumstances." To take these officers' posts, the men elected different officers and the Guards Division staff officers ratified their appointment.

* * *

Ensign Krylenko of the 13th Finland Regiment, having already addressed his own regiment enough, now went to the neighboring regiment, the 11th, for permission to speak at a rally there. Since he was a Social Democrat, they could not refuse and they called the rally for Easter Monday. And this is what he said: The Austrians we are facing are an open, honest enemy. But there is another enemy, who is dangerous because hidden: the enemy within, supporters of the monarchy and the restoration of the old regime. They are quietly gathering their forces to plant a knife in the back of the revolution. These enemies are also to be found among the officers and generals from aristocratic backgrounds.

And he talked for two hours, finishing with:

"Long live the world revolution to come!"

He wiped his forehead with a dirty handkerchief and jumped down from the table. The regimental commander walked up to him, embraced him and kissed him warmly.

* * *

The officers, full of hope, welcome the arrival of Duma delegates: perhaps they'll bring the men to their senses, improve their mood. But the soldiers are saying: here's another bourgie turning up, another speech, all he wants is our blood, he wants us to climb over the barbed wire while they take things easy on the home front.

But when it's a delegate coming not from the Duma but from the Soviet, the command cannot forbid it. "There's a tannery where I come from and all day long I'm in the stench and dirt tanning hides, but the profit goes to the boss. Shouldn't I, the worker, get as much as the boss? Shouldn't the profits be divided equally? Now we have freedom and equal rights in everything!" His speech was punctuated by cries of approval, laughter, guffaws.

They often come in soldiers' uniforms too: "Peace to the peasants' huts and war on palaces! War is the destruction of the people. Germany's tired too. We and the German people will make peace, a fair peace, and we'll do away with the army. The land will go to those who work it."

And why wouldn't we believe a soldier? We've got to go and organize our lives. Otherwise, why talk about "freedom" if it's only for those left alive after the war? If there's freedom and they're promising land, then why should we die and not enjoy that new life?

"If the Provisional Government doesn't walk shoulder to shoulder with the Soviet then we'll get rid of it! And send Nikolai to the Peter and Paul Fortress!"

* * *

The officers' behavior varied. There was one, spent the whole war avoiding the fighting and now appeared in the regiment, getting officers to pledge funds for a revolutionary library for the men. Another, an acting official who once wept on receiving a cigar-case from the hands of Grand Duke Mikhail Aleksandrovich, in April raised a pennant by division headquarters that reads, "Long live the democratic republic!" while all the time scheming to get for himself the senior adjutant's job.

* * *

But despite all this, on the front there's still a "revolutionary time lag" relative to the ferment in the rear. Technical and automobile units are the first to disintegrate. The cavalry, still as smartly turned out as ever, is disdainful of the infantry, where things are now lax. And the latter call the cavalry "oprichniks" and "officers' flunkies."

* * *

Three students from the Petrograd Technical Institute came to the 8th Army to agitate, to drum in the need to persevere in the struggle against the Germans. The soldiers, their minds already made up, came back at him:

"If you're so keen on fighting, just get some rifles and stay here in our trenches."

* * *

In an infantry regiment of the 18th Corps, an excellent officer on the battlefield had a bit too much to drink, lambasted the revolution out loud, and sharply criticized the behavior of his men. In reply, they shot him in the back and even abused his body. Then Commissar Oberuchev, a populist ever since his youth, later an SR, arrived:

"You killed an officer in the meanest, basest way. And the killers are standing here now, among you. We shan't seek them out and they'll escape trial. But I am sure that in a short while they will present themselves to the authorities of their own accord and say 'We're the ones who killed the Lieutenant, put us on trial! It's weighing on our conscience and we can't live like this any longer.'"

The men fell silent. Not a word.

It'll be a long wait . . .

* * *

Now some cavalrymen too, who've been demoted to the trenches, turn up at a meeting: "We don't agree with the way we're being used. You might as well just draw lots to assign the squadrons."

In April, even in the Preobrazhensky Regiment, men are refusing to go and cut down trees to repair the trenches, which have been eroded by flooding. Lieutenant Disterlo barely talked them round.

* * *

Two battalions of the 611th Regiment, which had been assigned to move into position, lined up fully equipped. The chaplain held a service, after which the soldiers opened fire, into the air: we don't want to go! (And some were also firing in the direction of the officers, above their heads.)

Sometimes men threw whole boxes of cartridges into the river: whatever happens, we won't be fighting.

* * *

The 126th Rylsk and the 127th Putivl Infantry Regiments were ordered to take parallel routes to relieve units of the 12th Division. The Rylsk Regiment, after a day's march, held a meeting that night and sent delegates to find out: why was no other regiment of their 32nd Division marching with them, along the same route, and why had the Putivl Regiment taken a different route? And why had they been sent two days earlier than proposed? And why were the officers on horseback? And was it true that the regimental commander had left the front? Having established that the commander was still there, they started asking him if it was true that the Rylsk Regiment was going to crack down on the 12th Division, and that the latter had already laid mines under the bridges. The next morning and half the afternoon the regimental commander exhorted the Rylsk troops to move off, but they expressed their lack of confidence in him and in the company and regimental committees, and voted to send elected representatives from all companies straight to Corps HQ to question whether the instructions being issued were just and wise. And for the time being they would stay where they were and thus hold a celebration of freedom.

* * *

New reinforcements arrived for the 26th Corps on the Romanian front. The corps commander himself, General Miller, came out to meet the arrivals, saw they were wearing red bows and ribbons and told them to take them off—they were not part of the prescribed uniform. "You're not girls, wearing those ribbons!" Cue for a mutiny. In a great mob they arrested the general and led him away to the guardhouse. And no one in the corps lifted a finger.

Message from Army HQ: the divisional commander is to replace the corps commander and launch an investigation. General Miller is to be released and sent to HQ to make his personal report.

* * *

As long as the 2nd Combined Cossack Division was on the front line it remained surprisingly disciplined, even after Easter, and not a single deputy turned up there; and the new newspapers, for some reason, never came their way either. But at the end of April the Cossacks were taken off the front line for a rest, and the rot rapidly set in in their ranks. They started holding rallies. They demanded that the savings money be shared out equally. They wanted the stock of new army uniforms—which were supposed to be worn in the year to come—to be issued immediately for everyday wear, even though those they were wearing were in good condition. And the 16th Don Regiment personally took new uniforms from the storerooms and dolled themselves up in them, and the other regiments followed suit. And they wore red bows. They demanded more leave. Cossacks—yet they stopped regularly grooming and even feeding their horses! They demanded that the officers shake hands with each of them: "We're officers too, and just as good as them!" And they loafed around and hit the bottle.

* * *

The 2nd Caucasian Grenadier Division received an order to move from the reserve into combat positions. The regimental committees held a meeting together with the divisional committees and decided to summon the corps commander to explain why it was their division and not the 1st that was being sent to a critical sector. The following morning the corps commander, General Makhmandarov, presented himself to the ranks of his division and explained. But his answers did not satisfy them. And Ensign Remnev, with a mob of soldiers, removed both the corps commander and the divisional commander, and appointed the bewildered General Benescul as corps commander: and he dispatched the 1st Division to the combat positions.

* * *

Lenin's opinion: "Soldiers taking the initiative and removing their commanders? Useful and necessary in every respect."

* * *

The soldiers settled down to playing cards (previously it had been forbidden). But what could they gamble with? Well, why not gamble away state property? And they organized parties and dances. The reserve kitchens were turned into distilleries. (They filtered the alcohol through gas masks, thus ruining the masks.)

Soldiers away on leave either never come back or are extremely late.

In the artillery, horses have started disappearing. What is going on? It turns out that while the horses are at pasture, deserters buy them from the team drivers, so as to get to the station—if not all the way home—as quickly as possible.

At eight versts from the front line, you wouldn't know it. An aimless crowd of infantrymen is wandering around the villages and roads. Some walk locked in an embrace, very drunk and singing in rasping voices. They stop officers they meet on the way and talk to them very loudly.

By the end of April, no fewer than a thousand men had disappeared from the 11th Finland Regiment (where Krylenko had spouted his rhetoric)—and there was no one to replace them. "They're all going home—why should I stay? People are saying there'll be peace now."

Recently captured German prisoners say Germany won't attack now because in a month the Russian army will be in total chaos.

* * *

Cossack captain Shkuro and his adjutant went into a Kishinev restaurant. A dishevelled gang of infantrymen burst in and lounged about, not removing their caps and yelling abusively. Shkuro went up to the soldiers and told them to remove their caps and behave properly. They argued. The captain threatened to summon an armed detachment. Then they tumbled out into the street to drum up a mob to destroy the captain. The adjutant just had time to phone their Special Kuban Detachment. The angry mob threatened to smash up the restaurant if the captain didn't leave. Shkuro left, his revolver cocked: "I can bring down seven of you. I won't be taken alive!" The crowd, bawling, swearing, ordered him to go with them to the commandant's office. Shkuro replied that he would go of his own accord but he'd shoot the moment anyone got too near him. And they walked the length of one block in that way—but there was a clatter of horses' hooves and along the cobbled street a squadron of Cossack cavalry came at full gallop! And another! Half-dressed and barefoot, horses unsaddled; but they had sabers, daggers, and rifles with them.

"Now get into line, you bastards!" yelled the round-headed Shkuro in a booming voice.

And that whole slovenly mob swiftly formed into lines and stood to attention. (The Cossacks were behind them.)

He thanked the Cossacks and told the mob:

"You're a gang of hooligans, not warriors defending the Homeland."

* * *

In the 40th Corps, leaflets are passed round:

"Brothers! We beg you dont sign up for this law they want to kill us with it, they want to attack, you mustnt go, they dont have the rights they used to, the newspapers say we shouldnt attack anywere on the front, the brass want to kill us. Theyre traitors, our ennemy among us, they want to go back to the old law. You know all the generals had their pay docked, now they want to kill us, when we get up to the barbed wire theyll knock us off there, we cant break through enemy lines, anyway theyll nock us all off there, I do reconnissance I know the enemys got 10 rows of metal spikes and barbed wire twisted round and machine guns every 15 paces. Weve got no reason to attack, its no use. If we go forward theyll kill us and no one will be left to hold the front. Pass this on brothers and write it down yourselves, do it quick.

Respecfully *forest*"

* * *

From the "Officer's Prayer," a hand-written poem of spring 1917:

Courting death, we fought for our country,
While at our backs came a hundred shots.
Thank you kinfolk, thank you, our brothers,
Thank you dear capital. thank you, Kronstadt!

DOCUMENTS—7

26 April
MAURICE PALÉOLOGUE, FRENCH AMBASSADOR IN PETROGRAD TO THE FRENCH MINISTRY OF FOREIGN AFFAIRS

Encrypted telegram

. . . Grave as the possible break-up of the Alliance may be, I still prefer that to the consequences of the equivocal negotiation that the socialist party is, I am told, readying itself to propose. In fact, if we did need to continue the war without Russia's participation, we could derive several benefits of very considerable value from the victory, at our lapsed ally's expense.

[1 4]

Counting from Mikhail's abdication, today was Guchkov's forty-first day as a minister. That was all. And of those days he had spent almost eighteen traveling, on various missions. And of those he had been ill for almost a week.

Illness! What a curse! He had spent his whole life rushing around in fine health, from Manchuria to Greece and the Boer Republic, his whole life in combat, in duels, in public debates on his way to the upper echelons of government—only to be downed now, his knees giving way, his strength abandoning him. And it was particularly disappointing that he had fallen ill before he'd even reached Kiev: while meeting the Southwestern Army Group staff he had told the deputies that he could hardly walk. But in that damned, filthy Jassy—in the very south, and it was already late April—the weather had suddenly turned, and there was a chill rain, adding a heavy cold to his problems. The following day, he arrived in Odessa with a temperature of 39.5 and a stack of work awaiting him. And he'd summoned Kolchak from Sevastopol, but could not muster his thoughts for a proper discussion. It was in Odessa that one of Guchkov's main War-Industry Committees was at work, and now he had a debt of gratitude to repay, and from the station he dragged himself to look round an exhibition of arms production by the Odessa factories, and the minister was "presented" with a cannon carriage. And then to the hotel for a banquet with the War-Industry Committee. And the mayor of Odessa gave a speech about Guchkov's role, and Guchkov, in his reply, stressed all the incredible obstacles that the old regime had put in the way of the committees. And representatives of the students and the Ukrainians and the Poles came to make speeches, and Guchkov replied to one of them that we'd become used to fearing Odessa, there was always some kind of conflagration there—but our fears had been groundless and everything here was on the right track. He would have liked to stay in that hotel, in that heated room, till the end of his stay. But he could only have the smallest of his planned meetings there. One with the Odessan generals, with General Marks reporting on how he had buttressed freedom in the Odessa Military District without even the tiniest pogrom ensuing; then a meeting with the special commissioners for food supplies; then with the members of the Municipal Board on the hygiene situation in Odessa. (He'd seen quite as much as he wanted of Jassy and Kishinev, swarming with people, without bathhouses, without disinfection. On the Romanian Front there was typhoid.) And there was almost no time left for the most important meeting, with Kolchak, who had now arrived. Now he would have liked to go to bed, and the doctor was insisting on it. But no. He had to go, as planned, to address the staff officers of the Military District there, tell them that the revolution had been necessary to save the motherland. And, ceremoniously, to promote to the rank of ensign the volunteer Seifert who, being politically suspect, had been prevented from moving up under the old regime. But at least this was indoors. But then he had to go out—he couldn't refuse—and review the garrison troops on the Camp Field. First and second year cadets lined the route, aeroplanes circled in the gloomy sky, and across the field were dozens of red flags instead of battle colors. He got out of the car and greeted and thanked the troops—with whatever voice he could manage. But that was still not everything: after that, and it was nearly evening now, to the Platon Pier, where the naval crews and staff were lined up for his inspection. He greeted them, received their reports, and made another speech, telling them to serve for the sake of our reborn land. And that was still not everything: they took him by launch to a warship where on the deck Guchkov greeted a crew of freedom-loving sons of the Black Sea fleet, and then had to sit through a dinner, where he could not eat a thing, and then leave for the station to the strains of the Marseillaise, with crowds of people in the streets, under the rain. Even at the station there were delegations, deputations, and, his last hope: to spend twenty-four hours lying down in his carriage until he arrived at GHQ.

But the sickness spread, there were complications affecting his heart, and at Mogilev he could not even visit GHQ, only, in the middle of the night, see Alekseev and Denikin in his carriage: the latter was now his great hope. They discussed Guchkov's purge of officers on the Romanian Front, starting with Sakharov, and the Southwestern as well, with the number of generals removed now reaching a hundred and forty odd. (He'd wanted to get rid of Ruzsky from the Northern Front as well, and replace him with Kornilov, but Alekseev opposed this.) Denikin objected to such a massive purge: surely he had not been mistaken about Denikin? But Alekseev had been in post for a year and a half, he knew the job, had grown into it: he would surely manage. He implored them both to strengthen the army and hold it firm. And to strain every sinew and start the offensive in mid-May, even at the risk of only modest success.

And the train had continued its slow progress, finally getting Guchkov to Petrograd yesterday evening. He'd gone straight to his ministerial residence and to bed. And despite all the audiences, meetings, documents that awaited him, despite the directives he should have been issuing, his doctors had canceled everything for today. He spent the whole day in bed, inert, his strength gone, seeing only those closest to him, Novitsky and Filatiev, but not for long. (And not calling for Masha.)

Prostrate and unable to work. Prostrate and, in his head, scrolling through that trip, those meetings, those speeches, and already muddling up exactly what had happened where. He was sure it was in Jassy that he had met the King of Romania and the Romanian ministers (there was precious little left of their country now). And the deserters' executive committee was negotiating with the garrison committee and demanding an extension of the deadline for returning to their regiments, while they pillaged the town. There was no holding them. This was in Kishinev. He remembered well the conference at Sakharov's HQ, where he removed fourteen generals on the spot. And it was there too that the soldiers' deputies had explained to him why they had arrested General Keller: he had told them to take away the red flags and obstructed demonstrations. (So as to save the old man, he'd had him sent off to serve under Kornilov.) Now Brusilov's and Gurko's HQs were getting muddled in his memory. And where was that ovation? Everywhere. But especially, of course, at the Minsk soldiers' congress: the square outside the theater was packed and so was the theater and it was there, he thought, in the foyer after his speech, that he'd exchanged kisses with some of the officers and men. And had he looked at some new machines somewhere else, apart from Odessa? Yes, in Kiev, at the Arsenal. There'd been problems with the supply of equipment, and he'd given orders—there and everywhere else. Also in Kiev, he'd dropped in at the Monastery of the Caves to pay his respects. (For a minister, it was a necessary gesture.) And in Kiev as well there were deputations of Poles, Ukrainians, and Jews. But the speech in the engineering school—was that there, or somewhere else? And in military hospitals? He'd visited those in various places, and thanked those who'd paid their duty to the fatherland in blood. And for some reason he'd been at nurses' conventions—yes, twice, in different towns. He'd talked some bosh about how he couldn't imagine the front without nurses and long may they continue their selfless labors and not get distracted by abuse from corrupt elements. (Everything in the army was going to the dogs and it had reached the nurses too.) And somewhere they had carried him shoulder-high to the car. Several times. And somewhere he'd inspected mess tents, dressing stations, hospital trains, and, at Birzula station, a troop train going to the front. But all those stations were getting very muddled: on the way, he'd left the train at several of them to make a speech. And what a lot of speeches! To hundreds of cadets, soldiers, sailors, to Soviet deputations, to crowds of railway workers and whatever other group turned up.

He did speak, didn't he? What did he say? He hadn't prepared these speeches, so it was whatever came into his head at the time. (He'd always considered himself a good speaker, but now he'd discovered something: before, his speeches had been for the elite, for the intelligentsia, for the Duma; but the mass of simple people needed something quite different, and now he couldn't find the right words. But the main thing was not to succumb to pessimism and disappointment.) What he'd repeated over and over, he thought, more than anything else, was that the revolution had been necessary to save the motherland. (Even he needed that assurance, so the people must need it even more.) The overthrow was, for Russia, an act of self-preservation, the only means of saving itself from destruction. From his work on the War-Industry Committees, Guchkov could testify to the fact that the old regime had led us to the brink of certain ruin, and it was terrible to think what would have happened to us without the revolution. We'd already realized, eighteen months before, that we had to put an end to the old regime, no matter how many lives it cost and even if it needed a violent coup. But that was not necessary: the old regime turned out to be rotten to the core. That was why the overthrow occurred naturally: because everyone had already realized we could no longer live like that. And now, after the turmoil of those revolutionary days, the people have rapidly taken themselves in hand and the life of the whole country is already getting back into the flow of constructive work. But if we *don't* take ourselves in hand (this speech was somewhere else) then all the enlightened achievements of the overthrow will fall away. Now we are approaching military triumph, after which we shall embark on the reorganization at home, on the principles of liberty and equality. But now we must not put all the blame on the government, as we did on the old regime. Now every one of us is responsible for his country's destiny, and if we can all be inspired by this realization and rally together around the Provisional Government . . . I know that the Russian people are a nation of miracle-workers, and the upheaval we have lived through will not do us any harm. Abandon all discord, away with needless suspicion—just put all your efforts into defeating the enemy, the enemy alone; for the Germans are already at the point of exhaustion in this struggle. Now, when our citizen combatants boldly look each other in the eye, discipline in the army will become even stronger and more deep-rooted . . .

But when he'd felt really ill, his words had sounded plaintive: help the Provisional Government—it has a heavy load to bear. For the time being, organize yourselves as best you can . . . And he found himself saying things he certainly didn't think: the Soviet of Workers' Deputies is full of love for Russia. We are united with them by this love and a burning thirst to preserve our freedom. Of course, as with all those who possess inner freedom, there are differences of opinion on certain questions. And at the Minsk congress he'd made a real slip of the tongue and called on them to "crush now that other, internal, enemy!" instead of "external." And they'd printed it like that in the papers, not even putting in the commas. So the way it came out, he had called on them to crush the Soviet of Workers' Deputies . . . (Which wouldn't be so bad, actually.)

And on the days when he was not traveling, he would look at the piles of telegrams on the tables at the ministerial residence, telegrams expressing loyalty, from the army, the navy, and the home front. (That upstart Gruzinov was proclaiming: "God grant that the native Muscovite who is now the first Minister of War of Free Russia may hear, amid the thunder of cannon from the Kremlin walls, the victory cry of our first capital city . . ." Nonsense, of course, but nice to hear.) And almost hourly a deputation, if not three or four, from the front would be awaiting him in the reception area, and the minister would receive them in groups of up to five at a time. On the rare days when he went to the Mariinsky Palace, even there government meetings were interrupted by insistent delegations, and groups of ministers would go out to talk to them, listen to them, and be handed their units' resolutions. These resolutions were, of course, composed by the few educated men in the army, and written by ambitious clerks—but still the army's state of mind was clear to see in them.

We beg you, do not stop the war until we have total victory, only please give us good chiefs. And surely the new Russia should not be branded a traitor? That was the treacherous will of the old government. And we won't forget the millions of common graves where our brothers lie. And what would we say to the hundreds of thousands of cripples? That their sufferings were in vain? "Down with the war": that's the slogan of traitors to the cause of freedom. Treacherous hucksters are stabbing us in the back. The Latvian riflemen declared: if peace is concluded we'll disobey orders and carry on fighting. And the Siberian riflemen, standing next to them, agreed! And as for the Finnish riflemen: the reserve units from Petrograd and Moscow don't want to go to the front, and that's deeply insulting to us in the trenches; we're a revolutionary army too, and if we'd deserted the front would we now have freedom?

In fact, criticism was coming in from many areas, berating the government for not deploying the Petrograd garrison to the front.

But when you're here, on the Moika Embankment—well just you try and deploy them . . .

And when they talked about the factories, the tone was menacing. It's no son of the motherland who demands money from the government, when we're dying in our combat positions. We have lead raining down on us twenty-four hours a day and it's your workers' sweat that's supposed to save the soldiers' blood. Every hour that you're not working is paid for in the lives of your comrades at the front. We demand that work in all the factories must immediately start running at full capacity! (And why just in the factories? They were already demanding an eight-hour working day in weapons repair and in digging reserve trenches as well!)

And sometimes they were even more direct, even more insistent, and Guchkov was surprised to discover that these delegations from the front understood things about the Soviet of Deputies that the government had never dared say aloud. The 15th Siberian division: we call on the Soviet to dispel the fallacious rumors that it is trying to usurp the power of the Provisional Government. And, even more trenchantly: the Soviet supports the Provisional Government only "insomuch-insofar"—what does that mean? They're deliberately destroying our country by doing that! We hear vague rumors that that political group, the Soviet of Workers' Deputies, can't even agree among themselves, and they're putting out directives that contradict each other. So we have to ask them to publish, immediately, a list with the names of the Executive Committee—we don't know who any of them are!

Delegations and resolutions were all very well—but none of the ministers, not even Milyukov, would be willing to start speaking this kind of language. But even those resolutions were contradictory. Suddenly there would be an order to set up a strict rota for time on the front line, *taking no account of the personal views of the unit commanders*. Or: when nominating candidates for command roles, the appraisals must be accompanied by the result of a secret ballot among the subordinate ranks. Which meant the officers would, in effect, have to stand for election. And another problem: while the delegation was making its way to Petrograd, or the resolution was in the post, *there*, there, in the units, something would already have had time to change. Now, while Guchkov had been traveling around the fronts, he had been able to see this for himself: something different was going on there. This **something** was going even further than the resolutions made a few weeks ago. And even these same delegations only spoke this well if they began at the Mariinsky Palace or the Minister of War's residence. But if they started from the Tauride Palace, then the Soviet would somehow manage to work on them rapidly, so that the same delegations started saying the exact opposite. Just now, in the time Guchkov had been traveling, the Soviet had succeeded in assembling at the Tauride Palace some kind of "conference of front-line units" a random group of these visiting delegations, who claimed to represent the whole of the army in the field. The conference was run by three individuals, Liperovsky, Lopukhovsky, and Klopovsky—not a well-known name among them—and a resolution, supposedly of general application, was carried: subjection to discipline and order must not extend to those cases where *soldiers are obliged to take political steps not in accor-*

dance with their convictions as citizens. And, it went on, a proposal must go to the Executive Committee (no mention of the government) to send *commissars* with the broadest possible powers to all the front lines and all the armies, and the Provisional Government must be required to recognize these commissars!

So now everything was unraveling, with no common axle to hold things together.

And from the 12th Army, commanded by Radko, whose initiatives Guchkov himself had approved, four hundred officers—the Soviet of Officers' Deputies led by the Latvian colonel Vatsetis—sent Guchkov a declaration saying that they doubted the candor of many of their commanders and staff officers, who might attempt sabotage. And, they said, if those officers were not yet in direct contact with the enemy it was only because they feared being discovered! But in their hands combat units were badly allocated, reserves were not sent to where they were needed, instructions were confused, commands came late. And the officers were suggesting that their longstanding senior commanders were responsible for all this! What a dangerous distortion of Guchkov's own idea for reform. If his mass purging of generals had made even the officers now start suspecting every general, then how were the troops to be controlled? And now these four hundred troublemakers were proposing that the government should watch the generals closely, follow their every step, have its own eyes and ears on the spot—its own commissars present in each army.

So they wanted commissars there too.

The government could send out commissars, of course, but to help the generals, not to spy on them! And espionage was precisely what those four hundred, from lieutenants up to colonels, were proposing: "to be guided by the social organizations of progressive soldiers and officers" (*progressive soldiers?*—we've not seen those in all of military history!) and receive from them "the most accurate information not only on the actions and behavior, but even on the frame of mind of all persons in command"! And they went even further: within the executive committees, *informant sections* of four to six members were to be set up, and these sections would rule on the dismissal of officers, the replacement of staff officers and the recognition of their activity as harmful. They stopped just short of taking the direct power to dismiss them: they would report to their army group commander-in-chief and to the Minister of War. That was the way the revolution was unfolding!! And Radko, open-hearted (or else he'd lost his mind), was passing this mess on to Guchkov . . .

When, where, in which country did anything like this ever happen? This covert power with a total absence of responsibility! The Soviet of Deputies was like a privy councillor, who cannot be refused. Like another Rasputin, a collective Rasputin. No—it was even more brazen, for at their teeming, jabbering Conference of Soviets two weeks ago, they had declared Guchkov himself a "dark force," a Rasputin, and said he was more or less a friend of the Romanov dynasty, because he had visited the Tsar to collect his abdication!

And how was he to respond to all this? How was the Minister of War to counter these unusual expedients employed by parties or soviets? With meetings of some kind, lobbying, conferences? Should he answer them? That would be humbling. Or not answer? That would be to repeat the monarchy's error: they never answered, and they were destroyed.

The Conference of Soviets had decided to "firmly repulse any attempt by the government to remove itself from oversight by our democracy." They called their gang a "democracy."

Before, when Guchkov had dreamed of his future part in governing Russia, he'd never imagined such humiliation.

And those poor, poor "persons in command"! The Reval officers were proposing to *forget all the wrongs* done them by the sailors during the "period of mistrustful relationships" (when officers were being executed) and had only protested, plaintively, that sailors' interference in officers' operational work when in action was not acceptable and, even more plaintively, neither was their interference in the officers' personal lives because the officers were—even more plaintively—citizens with full rights *too*.

And the Minister of War was also receiving letters from some officers saying that the army simply did not want to fight and we had to end the war: otherwise it would be disastrous.

And Guchkov didn't even dare (for fear of offending society!) remove the officers who had found jobs in the Union of Zemstvos and the Union of Towns from their posts. He could only *fervently urge* them to go back to the front and be replaced in these home front roles by officers now unfit for action.

He even issued an appeal saying that, in accordance with his earlier Order No. 114, soldiers were allowed to visit theaters and cinemas and travel in any class on trains, *but not without paying*, "as was, apparently, assumed." The defenders of the fatherland must, on the contrary, show a good example and obey the rules.

And another one: in the first days of the great events in the renewal of our country, many cars were taken by various persons from state-owned garages; but they are in urgent need of these vehicles in the army and I call on you to return what has been taken and to let us know where there are damaged cars.

The Minister of War was also receiving demands for political rights to be accorded to enemy prisoners of war in Russia: the freedom to travel within their locality, freedom of assembly, and the freedom to live in private apartments. And Guchkov was obliged to explain in the press that this would be contrary to the concept of captivity and would be unfair, because our prisoners of war in Germany were being held in harsh conditions.

And how many concerns the minister had, which did not rise to the level of public appeals or announcements. Out of soldiers with little training, he had to create agricultural teams to help the food supply committees. And now, from his ministerial position, Guchkov began to see that his War-Industry Committees were charging unreasonable prices for military equipment: those prices, both for the army and the navy, must of course be lowered—and for that he had to set up another two new commissions. And the original Military Commission, languishing with nothing to do (useless, hanging in the air, a hybrid from the days of the revolution), had now thought up an activity for itself and started investigating a denunciation, according to which two major monarchist organizations had been formed in Petrograd. (But it was impossible to dissolve this commission, for it was also a sort of creature of the Soviet.) Stacks of anonymous denunciations were brought to the ministry, requiring another explanation in the press: Russia was now free and there was no reason to fear anyone. And that an anonymous denunciation, even if true, may not be investigated. Yet he himself was, anonymously, working on a secret task: how was he to remove the self-styled admiral Maksimov from the Baltic fleet? He had taken it on himself to increase the sailors' allowances, he was pandering to them, and they stood firmly behind him and would never allow his removal. But in the meantime the fleet was falling apart.

And something else: the army was tearing itself to pieces centrifugally, by nationalities. The Poles had detachments and they were demanding to merge into a separate army, and the Ukrainians were demanding separate detachments and regiments.

A bundle of sheer horror.

As for Guchkov, he'd lost his energy. He'd exhausted himself in all this traveling, starting with Pskov, to see the Tsar.

He had always been buoyed up by combat, combat *per se*, by the very fabric of combat, by living it—but it was all different now.

He was flat on his back, his heart beating erratically, his head was heavy and he didn't want to look—to look at those papers awaiting a decision. He could not even concentrate on a single clear idea.

What would happen with the army, with the war?

He'd have to count on a miracle.

[1 5]

In the train crossing Finland Lenin was thinking, quite seriously, that once across the border they'd all be arrested and taken off to the Peter and Paul Fortress. The humorist among them, Radek, had been left behind in Stockholm and the remaining bland group of comrades was planning how to behave under interrogation. The far-sighted Germans had already, of course, at the Swiss border, had them all sign an acknowledgment that: "I am aware that the Russian government is threatening to view anyone traveling through Germany as a traitor. I take upon myself the political responsibility for this journey." After all, from a distance the Provisional Government seemed far more powerful than it did up close.

But at Beloostrov, when they saw, under a fine drizzle and electric lighting, the crowd of Sestroretsk workers who had come out to meet them, Lenin instantly realized that he'd already won! There would be more difficulties—but he had already won! They carried him aloft into the station building to make a speech. He said a few words, conserving his energy, but inside he was rejoicing. (The workers asked whether they should give up their arms. He said that for the proletariat arms were now absolutely essential.) And as always, without the slightest pause, he instantly and entirely shed his previous frame of mind and took on another: he brought Kamenev into his compartment to give him a dressing down regarding *Pravda*'s political line, and at Sestroretsk he did not even leave the train but sent Zinoviev to make a speech. (His sisters and members of the Bolshevik Central Committee and the Petersburg Committee were there to meet him, but he'd see them later: in the last three weeks Kamenev had distorted the party line in extremely damaging ways.)

The stunning reception at Finland Station, with the guard of sailors, the bewildered Chkheidze, searchlights, armored cars, the crowd, was only further confirmation of what he had already grasped two hours earlier. And Lenin, far from surrendering to heedless joy, now gathered his strength to do battle for his dispirited party, which had been led into a mire of compromise. There was a speech that night to his people, another speech to his people the following day at the Tauride Palace, and he was invited to the unifying session there. He gave those unifiers a bloody nose: we're not socialists like you anymore, we're *Communists*! He had to lay that unification to rest! He'd already known all those social patriot swine would be baring their teeth, but he hadn't expected his Bolsheviks to be so lost, so uncomprehending of his program: he was accustomed to more obedience from them. He'd have to work on that. So uncooperative were they that, to the delight of Tsereteli and friends, he had to qualify his stance: I am not speaking on behalf of the party but expressing my personal opinion.

Of course the first thing they had to deal with was the criticisms regarding the journey. So while at the Tauride Palace they also went to a meeting of that odious Executive Committee. Realizing that he himself would be an irritation to everyone there, Lenin sat meekly by the wall, as a prompter, nominating Zinoviev and Zurabov to speak in his place. (Zurabov had not crossed Germany with us: he had joined us in Stockholm. But he was very angry with Milyukov for blocking his passport at Copenhagen, and that anger was extremely productive. Our vulnerable point was that nowhere had we been refused a visa, but Zurabov had been refused!)

We immediately adopted an aggressive tone, not trying to justify ourselves but instead putting pressure on the EC to push the Provisional Government to allow future émigré groups also to travel through Germany. And to stop the slanderous bourgeois attacks on us all! And in fact we won the day over the EC: the EC not only did not dare utter a word of condemnation of that journey—it also resolved to try to get permission from the Provisional Government for all émigrés of all persuasions to return! And in the Liaison Commission they avoided discussing the journey with the government. Another victory! Now the EC had been drawn in with us, they afforded us some protection, even if they weren't our allies—and they were smeared along with us. (And Lenin would never again set foot in there: he had no more business with them.)

And victory at the EC meant victory too at *Izvestia*, and they agreed to print "How we traveled back." So we were accepted in the Soviet press—another victory! And yet another trump card: the plan had been proposed by Martov! The Provisional Government had not answered our telegrams. (And if they never arrived that wasn't our fault.) The honest socialist and internationalist Fritz Platten had taken on the planning. It was an extraterritorial carriage. (The Russian bourgeois press, wanting to insult us, started calling it "sealed." And that suited us fine, especially since it meant there'd been no collusion with the Germans.) An approval protocol had been signed by the French and Swiss socialists and the Pole Bronsky, and now the Swedes signed as well. And those internationalist comrades said to us that "if Karl Liebknecht were in Russia now, Milyukov would be happy to allow him back into Germany! So your task is to go to Russia and struggle there against both German and Russian brands of imperialism!" And we think those comrades were right.

And some diversionary tactics: Chernov, for example, traveled back via England and at first they turned him back. Both the English and the Provisional Government are to blame for putting obstacles in the way of returning émigrés: the Allies are using lists acquired from old Okhrana agents! Now we demand that interned Germans be freed in exchange for us. And we demand reimbursement of the costs of the journey, which we paid ourselves! And something else: why do no newspapers any further to the left than *Speech* cross beyond our border?

This beginning was simply outstanding, and Lenin was already thinking the issue of the journey was now finished with: let's get on with other revolutionary matters! But it was nothing of the sort. The malicious, murky, filthy anti-Leninist slander was only just starting to flare up in the bourgeois press, and in the street as well, once the workers' and soldiers' consciousness had been bombarded with it. And the surprise was not that the hate campaign was being led by all the chauvinistic Great Russian riff-raff, but that Plekhanov and his crazed, dirty, slanderous tactics, with a whiff of the pogrom about them, should have joined the fray. (We'll have our revenge on Plekhanov: "he sold out to the bourgeoisie, went over to the capitalists' side." We'll see whose cry is the more resonant: "sold out to the Germans" will sink without trace if we really promote the internationalist aspect, but no one will forgive an alliance with the bourgeoisie.) But the SRs' paper, *The People's Cause*, was spouting all that "political infamy" and "political indiscretion" cant along with all the others: they of all people could have exercised some restraint. But those pitiful socialists were not, of course, the problem: the important thing was not to let the brains of the masses slip away from us. Now, for example, some small fry, a 4th front-line ambulance detachment from some front or other, was demanding a public inquiry into the circumstances in which Lenin's journey was arranged.

Well, those had to be supported: they were an honest voice among the chorus of slanderers! Yes, yes! And we immediately set off down this, the honorable path of honorable people: we reported on our journey to the Executive Committee. So why, now, comrades of the 4th front-line detachment, are you in such a hurry to brand those who traveled through Germany as "traitors"? Yes, yes, we want that too, a public inquiry at last! And right away. So let's have it, avoiding all the corrupt press and addressing the minds of the masses directly: an "Appeal to soldiers and sailors" (he'd started writing it yesterday and finished it today). The capitalist newspapers are lying shamelessly, insinuating that we enjoyed some kind of special handouts from the German government. The capitalists are lying, spreading rumors that we had a meeting in Stockholm with the German socialists, that we support a separate peace treaty with the Germans! We want peace for *all* peoples, through the victory of workers of *all* countries over the capitalists of *all* countries! But why do émigrés, languishing abroad as a result of their struggle against the Tsar, not have the right to draw up an agreement for the exchange of Germans for Russians *without* involving the government? And why did Milyukov not let Platten into Russia? They're so shameless now that not a single newspaper has reprinted the *Izvestia* article, "How we traveled back." Because our report exposes the finaglers! And how could Plekhanov's paper dare not to reprint the resolution of the Executive Committee? It's anarchic, their lack of respect toward delegates elected by the majority of soldiers! And it's the infamous tactic of a pogrom-maker! At one time Plekhanov was a socialist, but now his pogromist methods have been exposed!

Nekrasov has suggested publicly that "exhortations to violence ring out from Kamennoostrovsky Prospect." Immediate response in *Pravda*: "The minister has a preference for obscure allusions: you are lying! It is Guchkov who preaches violence, threatening to punish those who would unseat anyone in authority. But our job is one of *clarification*: shedding light on all the errors of the revolutionary-defensist frenzy."

Not a moment on the defensive! Constant attack! Deny and stigmatize one hundred percent. Scare them by labelling them! Sully them so they can never clean off the filth!

Let them all curse us. The more the merrier! It's causing a sensation—exactly what we need! It was what Lenin wanted, to throw them into disarray.

But not a chance! Those knights of the stinking slander, especially those from the *Russian Will*, had kindled such a bestial hatred of Leninists among ordinary citizens that it would take more than just one decent polemic in the press to get clear of it. Soldiers from the Moscow Battalion wanted to storm the editorial offices of *Pravda*. And then there was a rumor that in the Volynian Battalion they wanted to arrest Lenin. After that some sailors from somewhere or the other wanted to do the same (and those who had come to welcome him at Finland Station now retracted their welcome, saying they hadn't known *who* they'd been welcoming). We had to ask for Executive Committee protection again. Those three plots were foiled in time, but of course you never know where and when a fourth will arise. And then what? If a large detachment came along it would have no trouble storming the Kshesinskaya house. If they seized it, they'd tear us to pieces, nothing could be easier, because with this government you can't expect the law to protect you. And what's particularly dangerous is: what if someone threw a bomb into the mansion from outside? They'd bury thirty people on the spot! We have to get the Soviet to provide some protection for the mansion! Here's what we need: to set up guard posts ourselves outside the house, manned round the clock—we're particularly vulnerable to bombing.

(It makes you wonder . . . Dammit! Perhaps we shouldn't have traveled through Germany? He'd expected a democratic prison term but he never thought they'd set the Black Hundreds on him. So he gained a month? Or maybe only two weeks? But, on the other hand, what about the U-boats . . .? But then again, he wasn't late for anything, everything happened on time, and now some cash to keep us alive has already begun to flow in via Hanecki, and the day after tomorrow we're launching the *Soldier's Pravda* and the *Voice of Pravda* in Kronstadt.)

But, help! How are we to protect ourselves from a direct pogrom? We must write, now, immediately, another appeal: **Against pogrom-makers!** And again addressing the workers, the soldiers—even the whole population of Petrograd. We are appealing to the honor of the revolutionary workers and soldiers. We have been vindicated by the leaders of the Soviet and they cannot have done it out of fondness for us. Down with the heroes of persecution and deception, who are hiding that resolution of the Executive Committee! They have the gall to refuse to reprint "How we traveled back" from *Izvestia* and want to sow discord among our people. They have organized several exchanges of Russians and Germans for rich people—so why can they not arrange such exchanges for the émigrés? We are absolutely not in favor of violence: we want *clarification* and respect toward the Soviet of Workers' and Soldiers' Deputies. We want to explain to members of the Soviets that all the power must remain in the hands of the Soviets. We have been informed of threats of violence toward us, of bombing. If we are subjected to violence, we shall hold the editors of the *Russian Will*, *Speech*, and *Unity* responsible! Kerensky's paper, *The People's Cause* (run by democrats whose democratic conscience has now awoken), has already described them as pogrom-makers. The community of revolutionary democrats has supported us in a calm, restrained and estimable form. Comrade soldiers and workers! You will not allow the people's freedom to be tarnished by pogroms . . .!

Expressing yourself in an appeal, in a leaflet, where the writing is like a simplified newspaper article, is easier. But now a unique situation had arisen, where it was possible, necessary, and almost unavoidable to address the masses directly, to speak to them. But ever since '05 he had suffered from an anxiety about public speaking. At that time Lenin had rarely spoken in public, and then only before small audiences. But now he had to overcome it! He went to the Izmailovsky Battalion with Zinoviev, and then hastily agreed to address the Grenadiers two days later. But his appearance at the Izmailovsky was, in effect, a fiasco. As he stood up, surrounded by those hundreds of soldiers (from the Kshesinskaya balcony it was different—he could sense, in his back, the support of his people), those obtuse faces, unaccustomed to either his terminology or to discussions . . . how was he to talk to them? The problem was not *about what*, for he would repeat his theses and articles from *Pravda*, but *how*? As he articulated phrase after phrase about international imperialism, about capitalism, he saw no reaction on the faces. And, in an attempt to get through to them, he inadvertently referred to Wilhelm as a crowned brigand, which he had never done since he arrived (and which was tactically inopportune—better to keep quiet about Germany for the moment), and he distanced himself from immediate peace at all costs: the Bolsheviks are not calling for that. And now: the Provisional Government must be toppled immediately! The people must be armed, every last one of them: it is they who will install the order we need! But neither did this sweep the crowd along with him. So: we must immediately seize the property owners' lands! Don't trust anyone, rely only on your own experience, and then Russia will progress with resolute steps toward the liberation of all humanity!

No. His address had failed miserably: it had not even produced any cries of protest. It was a disaster. But now Zinoviev began to speak, his voice resonant. They paid more attention, and he spoke more easily. Well, well. There was a new orator among us!

Now that promise to the Grenadier Battalion started weighing on his mind. There was to be a debate, speakers from the Kadets and SRs—on no account must he show his face there. He could get himself into a fine mess and lose all his authority at one fell swoop! There could be all sorts of surprises and provocations. (But . . . in a flash he saw where public meetings were needed and would be successful: near bakers' shops, by queues. One agitator could speak for five minutes and win over a hundred or so women, persuade them that a woman's duty was to demand the immediate return from the front of their husbands, sons, and brothers!)

But the bourgeois public was so terrified by the figure of Lenin that today their press came out with a pack of lies about him addressing an audience of five thousand yesterday, from the roof of the Modern circus, just nearby on Kronverksky Prospect. There had certainly been such a rally, but without him. (And there were calls for the mansion to be seized and sacked. The militia had arrested twenty or so ringleaders.) He had a little laugh at the thought of himself on that roof. It was a typical error on the part of that liberal gang, their fear of Lenin. Yes, they feared him!

But he had to learn public speaking. He could master that. There'd be no handsome poses, no graceful phrases: but he'd have to get them hooked, find something that touched people to the very core and repeat it, repeat the same thing over and over, like hammering in nails. And—job done!

But there was something to do even before that. Even in these unbelievably barbaric conditions, hounded, with pogroms imminent, and embroiled in that political storm, he had to bring unity to his party, to the crew of his own ship. And that came before everything else. Without it there'd be no advance in any area. The masses are never capable of acting independently in times of crisis: they need leadership from small groups from the central institutions of our party. We must, urgently, train leaders to work on the masses. And all those who came to that welcome outside Finland Station could certainly be potential supporters. But we need to finish working on them. Within our ranks, though, there's a most worrying situation. With the arrival of Kamenev, *Pravda* has shown a marked swing toward Kautskyism, and that demoralizes the ranks to a dangerous degree.

Lenin called meetings, talked to discrete groups and had confidential discussions with individual comrades, either in Stasova's apartment or at his sister Anna's place—to straighten out people's thinking (the choice is yours: either you're a loyal servant of the proletarian cause or a traitor to socialism, toadying to the bourgeoisie!). And talked about the same thing with his sisters on visits to Volkovo Cemetery, to the tomb of their recently departed mother. For they were also, of course, two party members, and two reliable votes were important—not to be sneezed at. (But the relationship with Inessa had deteriorated to such an extent that, before he left Switzerland, he could not even ask her to translate his farewell "Letter to the workers of Switzerland" and he'd given Karpinsky the job.)

At first everyone recoiled, even his closest party comrades: his theses seemed like madness to them all. At the Petersburg Committee there were two votes in favor and thirteen against. But he was certainly no lonelier now than he had been in 1908: we'll weather this and we'll prevail! In the Russian air Lenin learned quickly, but even so he'd made no concessions, either in his program or in his policies. He felt the wind of revolution constantly buffeting the sails, pressing on, further and further—but the others, it seems, felt this was enough for the moment. But a rekindling of the Russian revolution is inevitable. This is just the beginning!

After the slogan "Down with autocracy" so suddenly became a reality, the proletariat found itself with no watchword in store to follow it. How about "Transition to the socialist revolution"? Having started the revolution, we must carry on! The proletariat should, of course, have seized power at the very beginning. We must not forget that, in revolutionary times, the limits of the possible expand a thousandfold. What sort of Bolsheviks are fearful of a battle-cry urging civil war? How can we, while acknowledging the class struggle, not understand that this must inevitably become a civil war at certain points? No! Either you accept the civil-war slogan or you remain with the chauvinists! We're preaching civil war and channelling all our efforts in that direction.

Well, one could say, instead of "civil war," "revolutionary mass action"—it makes no difference. The "civil peace" slogan is just petit bourgeois whining: we must incite in every country a hatred of *its own* government. You may object that the workers are not ready. But the question is not what the workers are ready for now, but what we have to *ready them* for. When the masses succumbed to the fervor of revolutionary defensism, it was more proper for the internationalists to oppose that mass fervor than to "want to stay" with the masses. For a certain time, we have to be in a minority opposing the mass fervor! This is why the propagandists' work is now of central importance. We must—skilfully and carefully, of course, by bringing clarity to their minds—lead the proletariat and the poorest peasant sector, the farm laborer deputies, toward the sovereignty of the Soviets. ("Farm laborer deputies"—they were the tool we'd use to penetrate the amorphous mass of the peasantry.) We have to place before the masses something simple for them to grasp. Soviets are simple. We are not calling for a parliamentary republic—that would be a backward step now—but a republic of Soviets, throughout the country from top to bottom! (We'd have to seize the Petrograd Soviet, and that would settle the whole question of power.) No support for the Provisional Government. From the first stage of the revolution, on to the second! The Paris Commune was too slow in introducing socialism. Control over banks, the merging of all banks into one: this is an important step toward socialism. We'll have to eliminate the standing army, the police, the civil service—and the people, armed to a man, will themselves take on the entire management of the country.

Kamenev now emerged as the main adversary, uniting everyone who was opposed and speaking out in *Pravda*. The news that Kamenev found Lenin's actions disruptive had even found its way into *The Day*. Yes, he was in effect becoming a traitor. If nothing else, this was damning enough: how could he dare, only two days before Lenin's arrival, vote in favor of the joint resolution at the Conference of Soviets without denouncing the class-based nature of the Provisional Government? That was disgraceful and unforgivable! And he has a social traitor's fondness for the SRs: he makes concessions to them. He's too inclined to smooth over differences and lacks the daring to destroy. And if necessary we'll start blackening his name right now. (And he won't be able to withstand it, he knows that.) He's an opportunist, but he's capable of obedience. And when all's said and done, there is no past, only the present: the people who are useful today.

Two days after Lenin's arrival, Shlyapnikov had been hit by a tram and was now in hospital. He, in fact, had made no serious errors, but all the same he'd have to be retired: he wouldn't be able to manage in this new period. He was a transient figure.

A regular change of executive personnel is natural and necessary. The essence of successful political leadership is an ability to see into the future and see where the enemy is currently weakest, where the blow is to be leveled *now*, not yesterday and not tomorrow. But that effort drains you, almost totally, and the only other possibility is to send people who are ready, obedient, like-minded, in whatever direction has opened up. And you need a great many different people: you cannot do everything yourself and anyway you cannot have all the skills needed. But at the moment when you've made your decision and, like a hypnotist, you are passing the current of your will into the one who is to act—at that tense moment no opposition, no disagreement, no doubt is permissible in the person receiving that current. That would cause a shock, as if from that same current, and throw him apart.

Ah, Malinovsky! Now there was the campaign against Malinovsky as well: documents had been found, showing that he'd been collaborating with the Okhrana, and now people were bringing up the fact that Lenin, along with Zinoviev and Hanecki, had covered for him in *Pravda* and vouched for his political honesty. (And Lenin had indeed laid the way for his return to the party: he had, for instance, said in the *Social Democrat* in January that all accusations that he was a provocateur had been dismissed by a party tribunal as utter rubbish but that, languishing in a German prison camp, he'd had no chance to defend himself. Now they blocked all the copies that had not yet been distributed.)

What means do we adopt? The way is clear: the workers must demonstrate wonders of organization, to win victory in the second stage. Are the masses fearful of moving on to overthrow yet another regime? Do they fear more hardships? Then they must be pushed across that threshold. How? Undoubtedly, by the creation of a workers' militia, a Red Guard! It has already been initiated and we need, urgently, to strengthen it. A Red Guard is the definitive solution to the question of an armed uprising! *The era of the bayonet has arrived!!* (But for the public the answer is: we are creating it to resist the re-establishment of the monarchy and any attempts to snatch our promised freedoms.)

And, a separate matter: support for revolutionary Kronstadt. The Bolsheviks must take control there! (Tomorrow some Kronstadt sailors are coming to campaign in Petrograd against the harassment we're suffering.)

And: no moves toward unification with socialists of any persuasion. They're all petits bourgeois and all they do is waver and get in the way of our bringing clarity to the workers' political awareness. I'm ready for an immediate split from any member of our party who wants unification! Of course we Bolsheviks want unity. Of course we do. But around *our* program. We are ready to bring together all who are able, at this moment, to commit to the socialist revolution!

For ten days he worked on his people to this end, sometimes one to one, sometimes in groups of three or four, to produce the majority he needed. And some new party members sprang up there, people whose names he had never heard of in Switzerland, such as Tomsky and Kossior, and every one of them said he had his own opinion! But, reckoning up, he saw he already had his majority. Tomorrow we're holding a conference of city Bolsheviks and we'll make sure the resolutions we need are adopted. In ten days or so we'll be holding an All-Russian Conference (he had sent some of his people to the provinces to be sure of the right election results). We'll get a general pledge of loyalty—and the party will close ranks.

We have to calculate our attacks accurately, work out who's the next target. And deliver the blows thick and fast.

First in line come the liberals and the Provisional Government! The Kadet congress was a gathering of helpless buffoons. (Congresses, congresses—let them babble themselves to death.) And the voice of the Provisional Government trembles with each word it pronounces: in response to the mass desertions, Guchkov doesn't dare threaten punishment! Ha! Against agrarian unrest they're totally helpless. And they've already hobbled themselves with that declaration of 9 April. But that doesn't mean we have to soften our attack. No, we must hit harder! And set the masses against them: just look what a giant step they've taken, from savage violence to the most delicate deception! We mustn't allow them even the tiniest of transgressions: Pokrovsky and Kokovtsov, for example, have joined the board of a bank. We now need to yell: *ministers yesterday, bankers today?* And how many banks are Guchkov, Tereshchenko, and Konovalov involved with today? The bank employees must collect documentation on them. The bourgeoisie overthrew the Tsar so as to preserve their own dominance by imperialist means. But by deciding to continue the war they accelerated the Germans' actions, which will result in their own overthrow. The Provisional Government must be **overthrown**: it's an oligarchy, a bourgeoisie—it will give us no peace, no bread, no freedom.

But also: the Provisional Government cannot be overthrown as long as it's supported by an agreement with the Soviets. That means we must stir up the masses right now, against both the current, rotten "democracy" and the current majority in the Soviet, who have succumbed to the deception of this government of bourgeois gangsters. Because of insufficient consciousness, the Soviet is of its own accord ceding power to the bourgeoisie, and the leaders of the Soviet are clouding the political awareness of the workers. (Having brought down the autocracy, they think that's enough. Not one of those idiots is making any effort to hold on to power.) The Petersburg workers have a particular hatred of traitors: we must do all we can to maintain and strengthen those feelings.

And we must train all our firepower on the troika running the Executive Committee: Chkheidze, because he is, officially, its chairman, and Tsereteli and Steklov because in reality they are the leading figures. (Skobelev doesn't count: he's just a pawn.) And every time, in every article, we must attack those three: they've adopted the Louis Blanc stance, the deeply harmful, social patriotic Kautsky position! (Kerensky is another Russian Louis Blanc, an extremely dangerous agent of the imperialist bourgeoisie and a classic example of a traitor to the revolutionary cause. And a mouthy good-for-nothing—but don't attack him for the moment. He's too popular with the masses.) Petits-bourgeois leaders, those so-called Social Democrats, only lull the masses and smother the revolution with their honeyed words. The Mensheviks are Judases: they've given in to the imperialism of the Entente! (In actual fact, the Mensheviks are no kind of opposition, they have no real organization, and, like the SR party, are in disarray, and their rejoinders in the press are feeble. But that's where we have to focus our party work in Russia now: we have to pour vinegar and gall into the sweet water of Social Democrat ideology. As for the anarchists, they're another matter. Their slogans are almost ours, but they would make dangerous allies—they formulate their ideas too crudely. And if we don't ally ourselves with them, we won't have to share leadership with them.)

The next job is to provoke a *split* within the Soviets; to separate the proletarian, anti-defensist elements from the petits-bourgeois and peasants advocating support for the bourgeoisie. And to smash Social Democracy, which is destroying the revolution! And here's the best battleground of all: we must sink the Freedom Loan! That's what the masses will understand best: don't give any money! All the socialists are just mumbling about it inarticulately, so our success is guaranteed. We'll say in *Pravda*, in large print: "Soviet's resolution on the loan: Rejected!" (and, in a smaller font, "Draft resolution proposed by the Bolsheviks"). And yesterday in the Soviet the Bolsheviks spoke against the loan as much as they wanted to, while the Mensheviks didn't even dare open their mouths.

But at the front-line congress in Minsk we lost: there, the Bolshevik voice couldn't make itself heard. The war question is, of course, a hard nut to crack.

In principle it's clear: the decisive factor in the political life of Russia now is that the soldiers are tired of the war. It would be suicide for our party to pretend that after the autocracy was overthrown the war became defensive. Even winning back Kurland is an annexation and an attempt to crush Germany. No support for the war that Milyukov, Guchkov, and friends are conducting! The Provisional Government is the same kind of imperialist body, but cleverer: their renunciation of annexations is just words. They must publish all the secret agreements and declare them null and void!

But those foolish social patriots, publishing their manifesto, they're also deceiving the masses with their mendacious prattle about going to the bourgeois governments to discuss peace: this is deceiving their own people. And we must make sure people know that if chauvinist revolutionaries were to triumph in Russia then we would be *against* defending *their* fatherland. Appeals will have no effect on imperialist governments: the Russian revolution must instead offer an example to the German workers—by our actions.

But appealing to the Germans to depose Wilhelm is also a betrayal of socialism. (A bond with the Germans? No one could prove it and people wouldn't believe it. And for the masses it's more important to finish the war and be given land.) The idea of conquering the imperialism of other countries is one we always reject. First of all we need to bring down the likes of Guchkov and Milyukov at home and only then call for action by others. And second, the English and Italian kings have to be deposed as well, at the same time—why only Wilhelm? And, everywhere, power must be handed over to the working class. We do not accept the argument that our pro-defeat policy is shoring up kaiserism: this is exactly what we have to do, contribute to the defeat of *our own* government. Those who write "against high treason," "against the disintegration of Russia" are on the bourgeois, not the proletarian side. The proletarian cannot level a blow at his government on the basis of class without committing "high treason," without furthering the disintegration of the "great" power of which he is a citizen.

But with the masses in their current state of mind, we must not reveal the proletarian stance too openly. We cannot say bluntly that we agree to a separate peace. (A story had swept through all the German newspapers claiming that, in Stockholm, Lenin had said we'd soon be signing a peace treaty, if not a general peace, then a separate one. People simply cannot hold their tongue.) To tell the truth, we are encountering some ill will from the mass of uneducated soldiers. Patriotism is a result of the economic conditions in a nation of petty proprietors. Well, we'll have to teach our propagandists to express themselves more carefully: are we really telling people we can end the war immediately, throw down our weapons and not defend our country? We've never proposed thrusting our bayonets into the ground while the enemy is ready for combat. We've been misunderstood! We're only saying that we have to put an end to the war as soon as possible!

That's the right way. Not only must *Pravda* not report *everything* we're thinking and doing, but even our very close associates must not know *everything*.

Lenin had spent his whole life (twenty years, thirty?) in narrow confines, boxed in, underground, in a small circle squeezed on all sides, his possibilities limited. And now there was a sudden million-fold increase in the available space, immediately extending to the whole of Petrograd, Russia, even Europe! How, how could he be sure of not making careless mistakes (which he already had, to a certain extent)? For every tiny wrinkle was also increased a million-fold and immediately seen by everyone. But he was not the far-left flank of the Social Democrats, he was the center of events. People had not understood that yet.

It was a storm! (Symbolically, they'd had to weather a storm crossing the Baltic Sea.) And in a storm you need to do everything at once: keep the boat moving steadily in the right direction (at the helm of all the parties, all Russia, and the whole world), while lashing everything in the boat down so it doesn't get thrown around, and making sure the whole crew is working relentlessly and without errors.

In Sweden, it seems, we did a very good job (and the setup there is certainly no less important than it is here). It was a brilliant idea to leave an office there, manned by Radek, Hanecki, and Vorovsky, to send us funds via secret channels and for propaganda going to the West. (We still have to establish a courier service to them, and do it with the greatest precision and caution.) It's important for the West to be constantly informed of *our* sense of Russian events. The left-wing Swedish socialists have also undertaken to get our propaganda from Stockholm into Europe: they have been, and still are, very useful, and fine comrades, even though they've not yet achieved revolution in their own country. (But if both Sweden and Switzerland are moving toward it, then you can imagine how things are simmering away in Germany and Austria!)

Parvus is right: it's money, money, and yet more money! And now it's needed even more than before. Mass action is unthinkable without substantial finance. And already the sums first received are such that we could not have collected the amount by even the most successful expropriations. And there'll be more! Guaranteed.

It's important that our partners' work, too, should be free of errors. For the moment, the Germans are playing their part brilliantly: not only are they not moving on the front, but they've also been making peace overtures to Russia. This makes our activities a great deal easier. If they would also publicly renounce any annexations (and Romberg has promised to work on this), how much easier it would be for us! But would they really renounce them? They'll take fright, the stinking, imperialist cowards.

But if we don't make peace with them, they'll crush us along with the others.

But (flying off into a spiral of reflections), *but* there is no one capable of fully appreciating (Marx could have done) how he, Lenin, will in fact *outplay* the German General Staff! Even if he gives away a little bit of Russia, it won't be for long. Because then he'll awaken in Europe the forces that will sweep away that Kaiser-ridden Germany! When they made that agreement with us, they weren't thinking straight.

As yet, we've not managed to rock the boat seriously. To start with, things are harder. But later everything will go famously.

A sense of timing! As yet he was a nobody: he had no positions in Russia. But now he was already foreseeing not just victory but also the amount of time he'd need: three months! Within three months of the day he arrived, he'd be able to take power!

But, dammit, how on earth can you plan anything? Yesterday those little fools from the high schools forced their way to the Kshesinskaya mansion—only two hundred or so, it's true, and the other thousand, or thereabouts, were kept back by details of soldiers in the streets. Trinity Bridge was barred by the militia, which stopped the columns joining up and passing. (But people are saying that some of the military detachments wanted to join the high school students.) The two hundred, though, forced their way past the guards right up to the house. Children! And they started whistling, shouting "down with the Bolsheviks," "down with Lenin," and demanded that Lenin himself come out onto the balcony to talk to them. Some of our soldiers went to chase them off—but they wouldn't go.

What a ridiculous situation. Were we to go down to them? That would have been useless, grotesque. (And what if one of those boys had got a pistol out and started shooting? Whose responsibility would that have been?) We announced from the balcony that Lenin wasn't here. And suggested the children should organize a meeting in their school and some Bolsheviks would come and show them the integrity and nobility of our plans. (All these children know is "down with," but we must work on them: we can talk them round.)

But they didn't believe us. And for four hours they refused to leave! And Lenin had to sit there like an idiot, like some small fry, when he should have been leaving. He had to wait till two o'clock, hiding away in secret to avoid the children. Unbelievable stupidity—they ruined his whole day. He'd have to work some more on his timing . . .

What a mess! Pathetic . . .

[16]

(RULE OF THE PEOPLE, IN THE PROVINCES: FRAGMENTS)

* * *

In the Uralsk-Moscow train, the passengers maintain a wary silence on what has happened. At the Volga crossing a group of officers had made some disparaging remarks and were detained at the jetty and interrogated. After Saratov the carriages had filled up with soldiers on their way to no one knows where. People are saying that in **Kirsanov** the bourgeois and top officials have been beaten up and a Kirsanov Republic formed.

* * *

In many homes, in many towns, portraits of Kerensky have appeared. But the money and currency stamps in circulation are the same as before, with images of the Tsars, and ordinary people don't know which way to jump: they'd better be more circumspect, in case the Tsar comes back.

* * *

In **Penza**, after the peasants' congress, the provincial marshal of the nobility was arrested, along with all members of the zemstvo board.

In many areas, self-governing "executive committees," "public safety committees," and "people's will committees" were formed during the revolution. They function in parallel with the self-governing municipal administrations, argue with them and remove them, along with representatives of the central authorities. They seize buildings, requisition goods and transport, and change statutory prices.

* * *

At the Almazovo mine, in the **Donets Basin**, the executive committee arrested four engineers and mine foremen. Workers in the whole Basin want their pay doubled.

* * *

In **Sergach**, the town committee has initiated searches and started requisitioning provisions in private houses, "to supply the rural population."

In **Sychevka** (near Rzhev), population 10,000, the inhabitants were stirred up by agitators, who told them they'd all soon be getting cheap bread and firewood and soldiers on the front would be sent home. Then a group sixty or seventy strong embarked on mass house searches, looking for reserves of flour, cereals, and sugar. Among the members of search parties were also well-known thieves. A soldier with a bayonet would station himself at the door while the searchers would ransack drawers, armoires, chests, attics, and cellars.

* * *

During Easter Week, in **Minsk**'s Market Square, a crowd gave some ex-policemen a terrible thrashing and left them unconscious and bleeding profusely. The militia took them off, but the following day a crowd got together to smash up the militia station as well.

Here and there local executive committees debar priests from conducting services and even take it upon themselves to "defrock" them.

* * *

Some men in soldiers' greatcoats appeared in **Volchansk**, saying they'd been sent from Petrograd to remove the old authority. They gathered a crowd for a public meeting, where they decided to depose and arrest the district commissar, Kolokoltsev, an old Volchansk zemstvo member. They turned the zemstvo premises and his private apartment upside down, but could not find him. Then these stray soldiers commandeered arms from the depot and careered off in zemstvo cars, searching the district for Kolokoltsev. They tracked him down, but at a few hundred feet from their prey the pursuers' car hit a post. They fired at him but missed. Then they set off to sack his estate and then to Kharkov, to demand his arrest. One of the "soldiers" turned out to be a high school pupil in disguise.

* * *

A Captain Kaminsky arrived in **Kostroma** and presented the garrison chief with an order from the State Duma saying that he'd been sent there as a commissar of the Provisional Government and the garrison was to cooperate with him in arresting supporters of the old regime. He organized a meeting of soldiers and workers in the municipal theater and demanded that the Municipal Board release four hundred gallons of alcohol for the needs of military hospitals. This seemed suspicious and he was arrested. They found on him seven official stamps, including those of the Duma and the Provisional Government.

* * *

An assembly of typesetters from the **Tiflis** printing works decided that they themselves should look through the newspaper articles and send any that were suspect off to be examined.

In **Simferopol** a local intellectual, accompanied by some soldiers, appeared in one of the town's printing presses, arrested the owner, and, under threat of arms, ordered the printing of a leaflet saying all shops were being taken out of their owners' control and were now municipal property. Then they posted these on walls along the streets.

* * *

In **Vladikavkaz** the Soviet decided to increase tram workers' pay and bring in an eight-hour day. The head of the tram service, a Mr. Laurent, said: either you raise the fares or you give us free electricity. They bundled him out of the depot in a wheelbarrow and put him under house arrest. The tram workers went on strike, as did the power plant workers, and the town was plunged into darkness. The Soviet of Workers' Deputies supplemented the city duma with sixty "democratic representatives" who had no understanding of municipal administration and whose only concern was to increase all employees' pay and squeeze homeowners. They introduced high salaries for the militia, who could not be dismissed without permission from the Soviet. And Comrade Gonsky, Soviet commission chairman, accepted offerings of cash and in kind for getting people jobs in the militia. Defense lawyers have taken over and run all the judicial institutions.

* * *

One Kolokolnikov, head of the **Tyumen** Executive Committee, angered by articles in the local paper, *Yermak*, sent a detachment of two officers and a dozen men to the apartment of its publisher, Afrosimov, to arrest him. He was sent to jail and then, with an armed escort, to the regional commissar in Tobolsk, who condemned him to exile in Surgut territory. And the *Yermak* printing press now started printing the *Executive Committee Izvestia*.

* * *

On the outskirts of **Yaroslavl**, some Ingush attacked a girl. Austrian prisoners of war intervened to defend her. Then the Ingush started manhandling the Austrians, but some soldiers came to their defense. There was a bloody brawl, with seven Ingush killed.

* * *

Five hundred and six detainees in the **Smolensk** hard-labor prison persuaded the authorities to send them to the front. First of all the regional commissar, Tukhachevsky, let them out to march around town with a band and arrange a rally. Then a medical commission gave them a rapid examination, and three days later they were already in a troop train taking them "to defend the homeland." On the way, they would run off.

* * *

In **Tiraspol** eighteen prisoners awaiting indictment strangled some of the warders, tied up others, grabbed their weapons, and escaped.

In **Bendery** it became common for people to distill freely available methylated spirits into vodka. Crowds of disorderly soldiers bore down on the market, dictated the low prices they would pay, and then chose the provisions they wanted to buy. After them, civilians started doing the same thing. A crowd of looters made for the suburb of Gisca, broke into and pillaged wine cellars, "to stop the Germans getting it," then drank themselves into a stupor. After that they started breaking into local houses and there were cases of women being raped and children molested, and there were some murders. Cavalry detachments arrived from Odessa.

* * *

In **Kiev** the regional congress of German, Austro-Hungarian, and Turkish prisoners of war demanded that the eight-hour working day should also apply to them.

A congress of Ukrainian nationalists was held there as well, and they demanded autonomy for Ukraine without waiting for the Constituent Assembly. And with all those matters to think about they forgot to take measures against the flooding of the Dnieper. Trukhanov Island was submerged up to the attics, many barges broke away from their moorings, and at the Chain Bridge they collided with a passenger steamer. The municipal power plant was inundated with water twenty feet deep, the generators stopped working, and the town was left in darkness. The next day the authorities requisitioned candles and paraffin from small shops and distributed them, via local precincts, to those in greatest need. No newspapers were printed, and the town was awash with rumors.

* * *

Pupils of a commercial school broke into the **Kamenets-Podolski** City Duma. They accused the Duma of being too half-hearted in its reforms and demanded the removal of the mayor, Turovich. Turovich took off his mayoral chain of office, left the Duma, and killed himself.

* * *

Since the middle of April, **Odessa** has suffered an epidemic of robberies and break-ins, because in the major cities of the south three and a half thousand criminals have been released from prison all at once and most have congregated in Odessa. And since the police force there was abolished no one has been protecting people's property. One young woman, whose husband was away at war, spent half the night firing through her window to keep three armed robbers at bay.

With the permission of the new authorities, an open conference of criminals from the Odessa jail was held in the Saratov café. There were about forty of them: their leaders were Grigori Kotovsky and Aron Kinis. Kotovsky said:

"We are sent from the prison fortress to urge everyone to unite in support of the new order. We must be rehabilitated, be trusted, and be freed. We represent no danger to anyone: we want to give up our recent occupation and return to laboring peaceably. Let us all unite in the struggle against crime! We can achieve total security in Odessa, even without a police force. We need to raise a support fund."

People agreed with the speaker. A collection was started. A lenient regime was instituted in the prison, and prisoners had no trouble getting permission for an outing into town. They began to disappear. Inside the prison, they found a way into the cellar where alcohol for the prison hospital was kept, got blind drunk, broke into the apartment of the assistant prison governor, and sacked the place, making off with valuables worth 50,000 rubles and then disappearing. During the period of "self-government," a great deal of prison property was plundered: medical utensils, bed linen, and leather goods.

Kotovsky, who was free to absent himself and go into town on community matters, also disappeared.

* * *

In **Taganrog**, in the early hours of 25 April, a band of miscreants killed the three members of the Vitonov family and a woman who happened to be spending the night. They hanged their victims one after the other and tortured the old man to find out where he kept his money.

* * *

In **Nakhichevan-on-Don**, during daylight hours, a mob including a good few soldiers approached the monument to Catherine II, who had settled Armenians in the town. "The woman who enslaved our peasants has no place here! Let's melt her down for shells!" Two of them clambered over railings and up the figure, put a rope round her neck, and the mob, whooping and whistling, pulled her to the ground, destroying the railings in the process. They dragged her toward the Don to throw her in, but she was heavy, over two tons, and they could not reach the river. So they rushed to the Municipal Board, demanded the portrait of Catherine that hung there and slashed it to ribbons. The Nakhichevan Armenians were affronted.

The Rostov and Nakhichevan city dumas were dissolved and the Rostov Executive Committee forbade their members to leave town, in case they went and complained to the government.

* * *

In **Korsun**, in Simbirsk province, a crowd of soldiers and townspeople gathered by the monument to Aleksandr II, which had been erected at the peasants' expense. Speakers addressed the bust: "You may have given us freedom, but you robbed us of millions in exchange for the land." And they destroyed the monument there and then.

* * *

In **Kazan**, on the morning of 27 April, the large freight warehouses at the station burned down. The losses amounted to millions.

* * * * *

Come summer lightning, set
Our backwaters alight!
Just watch—the glow will lift
All Russia out of night!
(from the newspapers)

[1 7]

All the games Yurik Kharitonov played as a child, no matter how far back you go, would turn into a battle. Once someone gave him a set of dominoes. The pieces were dainty little things, with edges bevelled to a sharp angle, so that if you jogged one piece with another, it could be flipped over. He almost never played the way everyone else does, but conducted duels and whole army battles between the pieces. Any piece turned over, with the dots facing upwards, was counted as dead. There were some particularly stable pieces, which were rarely overturned, and these he recognized in advance, not by the numbers of dots but by tiny distinctive features in the wood grain on the reverse. And he gave them the names of his favorite heroes from books, all of them broadsword- and rapier-wielding warriors, and had them lead troops into battle and face each other in fencing contests. He spent long hours engrossed in these wars, and never tired of them.

He had discovered the same beveled edges on the bone chips that Mama kept in a casket and used when playing *preference*. There were long chips, square ones, and round, of all colors, and if with a long chip you pressed the edge of a short one, it would jump a long way. At first Yurik and a friend would play tiddlywinks, making the chips jump into vases, or seeing whose chip could jump farther. But he soon realized that all the red, white, green, yellow, and blue chips could be led into battle against one another like regiments, surmount obstacles and take towns, with any chips that were covered being considered dead. And Yurik conducted many wars of this kind as well.

He himself was the arbiter, dispensing life and death, but he would, unconsciously, inhabit the personages of his favorite heroes—thus making himself a military commander as well. If he happened to find himself at home alone, he would march around in front of the long mirror on a cupboard front, attack the mirror, blowing an imaginary trumpet and beating an imaginary drum, and then accept the delight and gratitude of the inhabitants he had liberated.

It was the same with his *World Atlas*. For all his love of geography and traveling, Yurik started using the atlas primarily to conduct military action. He would draw, in pencil, sinuous front lines, and then position his troops to break through, imagine battles, and, depending on their result, erase those front lines and replace them with others. He even liked leading his own troops into a desperate situation and then heroically saving them at the last minute. Although the atlas contained all the countries, seductive oceans, and islands, Yurik never led his troops into battle for such distant prizes: all his battles took place within Russia and even, notably, the southern parts, closest to home. For some reason, it was this kind of war, here, that attracted him and made sense to him.

After his older brother, Yarik, had gone off to military school, Mama extracted a vow from Yurik that he would work conscientiously to graduate from modern school and become an engineer, as Dmitri Ivanych had done. Yurik liked his modern school and also liked the idea of becoming an engineer—all his passion for the military was a kind of hidden secret, a second, invisible life that no one else needed to know about: he didn't even let his friends in on these childish games—games it was already shameful to play past the age of ten. But he sometimes played them even at thirteen.

This was his secret: or perhaps the ineluctable destiny of men, all men, no matter who they are, what their profession, to make war at some time in their lives—and for this even to be the most important thing.

Yurik was preparing to become an engineer—but the only death he imagined for himself was in battle! This was the only desirable and worthy death, not the usual way, all sallow, propped up on inflatable pillows amid a musty smell of medicines, and spitting into a little jar. Yurik had no aptitude whatsoever for writing poetry, but the image of that glorious death—under a loyal flag, for a just cause, already pierced by several lances and still advancing with his broadsword—formed such a radiant image in his mind that, at twelve years old, he wrote a whole page in his school exercise book, couched in semi-verse, entitled "How I Would Like to Die." This too he kept to himself.

That was before the war, when no one was even thinking about it. Then, suddenly, it broke out. Yurik would run along on the pavement, down Sadovaya, alongside the troops as they marched to the station, and sing along loudly with their bands. He loved them all, all those marching off to war, and would so have liked to go with them! But this was absolutely impossible: not because Mama had forbidden him even to think about it—Mamas are always forbidding things and holding their sons tight—but because no one would have accepted him, being only twelve years of age at the beginning of the war. Tsarevich Aleksei, who was two years younger than Yurik, was being photographed all the time in military uniform, but that was just pretend: he didn't fight, of course. Sometimes in magazines names were briefly mentioned, or sometimes he spotted photographs of young soldiers, but very rarely. He could not tell where they were, and they did look older than Yurik. Such strokes of luck were probably rare—the rest were sent home.

And so the war had carried on for two years, two years with the front line wavering from one side to another, and Yurik was still only fourteen, slinging his satchel onto his back every day (even this, by the way, had something of the soldier about it) and walked to Cathedral Lane, to his little school, the Popkov Modern School, near the post office. He loved every classroom here, each in its different way, and the small hall where they would play tag during breaks, and the unusual staircase there, cast iron for some reason, which during breaks would resound under the onslaught of pupils' footfalls (while there were small blocks fixed to the handrails to stop boys sliding down). He linked batteries in the physics lab, poured liquids from one test tube to another in the chemistry lab, slid a pointer across the school's large wall maps (he knew all the geography with his eyes closed and sensed the whole Earth as well as he did the floor under the grand piano that he had so thoroughly explored), or else he would peer absent-mindedly out of the window, at the narrow, crowded Cathedral Lane below. He would note with particular interest the injured men, bandaged up, if any walked past, and often thought about the war: it was strange that a really big war had come his way but there was no way for him to take part, no matter how long it lasted.

And now, deep down, he felt this was meant to be. Yes, it was Russia's Second Patriotic War, massive and necessary, and his older brother was fighting, yet even so for some reason it should not concern Yurik Kharitonov: it deceived him. Not because it was going badly—he was, in fact, particularly fond of hopeless wars, since heroes were especially necessary, but for some other reason: this was not *his war*, not the war in which he was needed, the war he had always dreamed of. (Though after such a bloody conflict, what other war could visit the Earth any time soon, to be *his* war? It was unlikely.) So he stopped yearning for it and just studied, just lived.

But then his brother arrived home, on leave! And Yurik attached himself to his sibling, wanting to be with him as much as possible, and listen constantly to his stories of the war! But the war, although perhaps retaining its primary meaning, exalted and valorous, showed itself in Yarik's stories to be leaden, implacable, ponderous, a thousand miles from the easy elegance that Yurik had pictured. His enthusiasm cooled even further.

But then revolution also broke out! For two weeks Rostov, and the Kharitonovs, were aquiver with excitement: Mama and Zhenya shed tears of joy and all their acquaintances rejoiced. Yurik would have succumbed to the jubilation and entirely forgotten about war, but here too Yaroslav managed to cool his younger brother's ardor. The revolution could, he said, bring with it the disintegration of the army. And then, having left, he wrote (don't tell Mama) that he himself had been insulted by soldiers in the train—they'd tried to pull his epaulettes off! Yuri shared his brother's humiliation, quivering with anger. So what state was this war really in now?

And there was another consequence of the revolution: teachers began to read newspapers out to the class and talk about the joyous future awaiting them, and no one needed to prepare any lessons. At first, pupils could organize political meetings during breaks, and then even hold assemblies instead of classes, elect a self-governing body and delegates to the teachers' council. And at Peter the Great School they held assemblies, sometimes for pupils of all Rostov's classic high schools, sometimes those of its modern schools. They made speeches, demanding equal rights with their teachers, and a purge of the superintendents and inspectors. Senior pupils also signed up for a citizens' militia with, at its head, an ordinary student. Yurik also signed up: in the militia he'd sometimes be able to wear a real rifle slung across his shoulder! But so many hundreds of students and high school pupils signed up that, although they were divided into companies and then into groups of ten, there was nothing but pandemonium and feather-brained pranks with nothing military about them. And Yurik left. Then there was a rumor making the rounds that examinations were to be either totally suspended or reduced by half and the academic year shortened, and now you could skip classes with no repercussions. Yurik was most unhappy with this new, disordered state of affairs: a large part of his life was becoming a wasteland, leaving a holiday that was, somehow, stolen. Even in the high school run by his very strict Mama, discipline had become far more lax, and there too they held pupils' assemblies and elections, and Mama wasn't angry, didn't forbid anything and considered all of that quite correct. In fact at home, at the dinner table, for two weeks the only talk was of the new freedom, the new community governor elected by the people—one Zeeler, who was also a Provisional Government commissar—and of how to get rid of the old, conservative city duma (which had no intention of being dissolved).

Another thing about those weeks: Rostov had always been noted for its robberies, but now they'd become too frequent, and even took place in daylight hours. When robbers were caught the authorities had trouble wresting them from frenzied Rostov lynch mobs. And something never seen before: all the banks were now protected by soldiers standing on sentry duty, and armed units patrolled the town.

You could quite lose your bearings in all the muddle that spring, but in Rostov that season was also marked by a force of nature: a flood such as not seen on the Don, people said, for thirty years! Anyway, nothing like it had happened in Yurik's life. First, the thaw caused the Temernik to rise and flood the square in front of the train station, cutting it off from the rest of the town. Then the Don also began to rise and overflow, and rise again and overflow again—and in the last week of April and into May a seascape appeared. From the high slopes on the right bank, from the top floors of the stepped-back buildings of Vorontsov and Konkryn streets, you could not see the opposite bank with the naked eye, nor even with binoculars. The flooding, they said, covered fifteen versts. Green Island was flooded, even to the very tops of trees, and Bataisk, Elizavetovka, Olginka, and Koysug were submerged. Then news started coming in of something terrible in Starocherkassk: five hundred houses washed away?! And total devastation, too, in large numbers of Cossack villages upstream. But the water was rising even farther, posing even greater threats. Each day brought a few such reports. In two places the tracks between Rostov and Novocherkassk had been washed away and the trains had stopped running. And Taganrog was flooded! And nearby villages were deluged and quantities of cattle fodder destroyed.

And another reason, probably, why Yurik was so carried away by this elemental event was that it drew off an anguished craving from his heart: his craving for girls.

This spring Yurik's longing had become simply unbearable. And if he happened to chat to one of the girls he knew, he could not act naturally—not with any of them. And he would dream of them, first one, then another, then a fifth and a seventh, none for very long, promoting her to his ideal. Or just dream of an ardent kiss. Yurik generally liked to jump, run, swim, fight, take cold showers, and had always considered himself agile and sturdy. But this feeling he had for girls, nothing else, washed over his body like a debilitating fog, a sensation of which he'd never known the like, and he was reduced to sitting and lying down, incapable of the slightest activity. Everything in his life—morning, the school-bell, books, food, his boat, the spade, his skates—summoned him to get up and go, but just this one thing was eating into him like an illness, robbing him of his strength.

And it was now, in this tumultuous month, that Yurik had an incident. He had stayed late at the scouts' association on Taganrog Prospect as it was his turn to clear up the hall after everyone had left. Then he went down into the basement, to the showers. Usually a big, noisy crowd showered together. But this time—he had not even turned on the water when he heard someone else on the other side of the partition, in the girls' section. Someone who was also alone, arriving late. He could hear perfectly because, he realized, the partition only reached a couple feet short of the ceiling. And barefoot, without a sound, he started moving along it to look for a crack, any crack. And he found one! And it was perfectly wide enough to see, directly facing the crack, an open door leading to the girls' changing room. And there, there . . . was Mila Rozhdestvenskaya, the doctor's daughter! He recognized her immediately. And she was undressing by a bench—undressing completely! Yurik thought his heart would burst. It was unbearable. His mind went blank for a moment. But he suddenly saw that he could climb up this partition—he could see sufficient toe-holds—and, just under the ceiling, pop over soundlessly and then, perhaps, simply jump down, descend suddenly in front of her and . . . let fate take its course! She'd probably bolted the back door of her cubicle so no one could come in. And, not in the slightest ashamed to appear naked before her, he would ask her frankly, beg her for caresses. They knew each other fairly well, so she shouldn't be too scared. But did he really know her before now? It was only since this glimpse through the crack that Mila had become close to him, incomparably closer than all the other girls in Rostov. She had eclipsed everything else! And he climbed like one possessed, but stealthily, for he might still be heard as she had not yet turned the shower on either.

His head was already near the top of the partition when he stopped. He wasn't scared, no. Nor had he despaired at the thought that she might send him packing: if she did, fine, he'd just climb back the same way. By now he felt joined to her by this secret, a secret that she, in a moment, would share. Everything in him was burning, throbbing, his legs were shaking but he managed to stay in position. But now that he was almost at the ceiling, on the point of crossing over, he had a sudden thought: but it's dishonorable—she's defenseless. And what if she hasn't bolted the other door? What if someone comes in from that side? He took fright, not on his own account but on hers: what would people think of her after that?

He could not bring himself to do it. He'd changed his mind.

He started climbing down, quietly.

And Mila had turned the shower on, so it was noisy now. And she wasn't standing opposite the crack any more.

Yurik bit his hands, powerless, full of self-contempt.

But now, during this massive flood, Yurik got some air, began to forget; was not in such torment.

What a sight. The flood had washed away the dam and continued across the meadows where the Vladikavkaz line ran, beyond the big bridge! Any moment now the link between Russia and the Caucasus would be broken! Then . . . Hurrah, it was broken! The bridge on the eighth verst, between Bataisk and Zarechnaya was carried off, and now train passengers had to cross a hanging bridge. In Bataisk the waters rose to window level and people took refuge in goods wagons. When it was windy, veritable rollers would be whipped up on this sea. But might the water also bring down the massive Rostov Bridge? (Yurik hoped it would, as long as there were no trains on it at the time!) The water was also advancing on Rostov's main station and people and draught horses were mobilized to save the warehouses at the goods station. At the port, workshops, the gas works, offices, depots, a portion of the electricity plant were all inundated! Not to mention that barges, timber, and little boats had been carried off all over the place. (Yurik and his friends had managed to drag their boat almost into town, up a slope, in time.) All the steam launches, all the dinghies from yacht clubs were mobilized (new authorities had not been found yet, so soon after the disbanding of the city duma). Yurik and his friends also went to help, loading here, shoveling there, having completely forgotten what was left of their classes.

Any Rostov boy worth his salt was a good swimmer, oarsman, and fisherman, loved the Don, and spent many a day on the water. But none had seen such water as this in his whole life and even strong men were at their wits' end. (Yurik was at great pains to stop his mother discovering he was going off zigzagging against the wind in the flooded area, so he washed out the bottoms of his trouser-legs and dried them. But at home no one noticed anything: they had their own excitement. Yurik's sister Zhenya had had a baby, Misha, another nephew for him.) By now there was nothing river-like, lake-like about that great expanse—it was a real sea that had rolled into Rostov! You felt your lungs pumping—it was like speeding off in a motor boat!

Clearly, there was nothing good about all this, but a certain joy coursed through his veins. For some reason, we are pleased when misfortunes arrive, even colossal disasters: even if it happens to me, to us. Look, they're transporting cows in little boats, and railway passengers have to take steamboats to Azov. Splendid! There's something seductive about it. Something sweet in disaster.

[18]

Perhaps Alina shouldn't have left Georgi in March and gone to Borisoglebsk. It was a mistake. She should have met him face to face to hear what he had to say for himself. But once she had left, on the other hand, she shouldn't have written to him. She'd flown off the handle. Susanna was right. But how do you not fly off the handle when your heart burns with the pain of an open wound?

But Susanna thought the situation more serious, more dangerous than it actually was. She didn't know, after all, how scrupulous Georgi was—not at all like most officers in that respect. When he did something bad, hurt someone, he always suffered pangs of conscience, begged for forgiveness, and wanted to put things right.

It was quite clear: his unfaithfulness was the result of estrangement, of missing his wife's company. She had always filled his life—and she must do so again, after the war. She must encircle him with her presence.

And then, suddenly, Georgi was transferred back to GHQ! The hand of fate. (Though it would, of course, have been even better if they'd sent him back to Moscow Military District HQ.) And Alina, without a moment's hesitation, decided to abandon her Moscow life and the concerts already lined up—and go to him in Mogilev, be constantly by his side, and re-establish an unbroken rhythm in their married life. That continuity was the most important thing. She must create a cozy, even if temporary, home life in Mogilev.

It would have been crazy, of course, to move all their furniture. And finding an apartment in that overcrowded town was certainly not easy. But it turned out that the Korzners had distant relatives in Mogilev and, at dear Susanna's request, they agreed to rent the small furnished annex in their garden to the Vorotyntsevs. Organizing the housekeeping here was, of course, far harder, but it was almost spring and they wouldn't need to keep the stoves going. Of course, some things had to be altered, moved, re-installed, brought here from their Moscow home. It was a lot of fuss and bother but it was animated, happy. Alina worked furiously. Her energy was unbounded, as long as there was something for her to organize.

But now that complicated business of setting things up was done, and suddenly a terrible apathy, a void, had crept up on her.

No, she absolutely must not give up! She must hold on.

As Susanna saw her off, she was insistent: Alina must resist the urge to deliver a hurricane of reproaches, resist her deep-seated hunger to unburden herself. For a squall of even the most just accusations could only make things worse—even ruin everything. Far better to pretend the crisis had passed, was forgotten, the relationship with that odious woman was finished, severed, and for good: and to accept what he said as totally sincere, feign acceptance and belief, and just keep an eye open from now on. But, added Susanna, she must also be cheerful with him, easygoing. (Just try it, with such a wound, such pain in your heart . . .!)

There was even an upright piano in the annex—but it was horribly out of tune. However had they let it get into that state? Barbarians! And in an unfamiliar town it's not so easy to find a good piano-tuner. She was unlucky with the first one: he started shaving the hammers—badly. She found another tuner, who used some ripe language about the poor job done by the first, shaved some more and fixed the problem. The whole exercise cost her a good bit of time and worry. But now, here too, music began to flow! (How she would have loved her own grand piano here!) Now Alina could not be without music, not for so much as a week: after everything she'd been through, how else could she relieve the strain, when her lips were condemned to silence? It was only by daily music that she could pluck herself from bouts of apathy. And these were to be the sounds that enveloped her husband as he walked in. It wouldn't matter whether or not he noticed which particular piece she was playing: the purity of the music must cleanse his soul, now sullied by his philandering.

"You know," she said, meaningfully, and it sounded good, "whatever happens in the world—wars, revolutions, thrones toppled—a man must not ruin himself, not destroy his *soul*."

And at that moment she looked at him, concentrating hard, putting into that look everything she had promised not to express openly. He shuddered, accepted the look—and looked away. It had met its mark, reached deep into him. She had seen that.

But music was not the only thing. Here, in this enforced provincial seclusion, she could get a lot of things done, completed. Should she, for example, organize her photographs, put them in albums? And take new pictures as well: GHQ would be a once-in-a-lifetime experience. But she must not be so downhearted. She had to be carefree. And yet, no matter how hard she tried, suddenly the memories would return, that whole chain of trials and humiliations would stretch out before her, his raptures over that jade—and her whole being seemed to be pierced by red-hot rods, her hands became weak, and she was all fingers and thumbs.

Soon she no longer felt her usual, healthy self. A kind of weakness the whole time, yet with no illness. She noted the condition in her diary.

Even just the memory of being rejected was a fiery hell! And she couldn't confide in anyone—how could you tell someone about such contempt on the part of your husband? It had all burst out once already, when things were at their worst, to Susanna—she'd already opened up too far in front of her. But now Alina's pride demanded that she should not lose her husband in full view of her friend.

She had to hold on, hold on! She must cry in secret; that would help. But for how long?

And could she put everything to rights now, in Mogilev? So that he, in his free half-hours, would talk to her about army matters—the people, relationships, obstacles, successes?

But as for her news—he didn't expect any and didn't ask. He didn't try to guess what her wishes might be, think about fulfilling them. But it is, of course, in the small signs of attentiveness that love resides. When going out or coming in, he would contrive to kiss Alina on the cheek, unless she offered insistent, waiting lips. True, he was clearly not finding it easy to get over recent history. He had suffered, and that helped a bit: if he suffered, it meant he loved her.

But again she started wondering: how much did he really need a wife? He arrived home late at night, collapsed, and fell asleep—and didn't know that she would lie, hunched up in a little ball, crying quietly.

Perhaps, despite everything, he was still secretly communicating with *her*? She had no way of checking whether he was receiving letters from her at work. Up to now she had never found anything in his pockets. But he could of course be leaving them at work. Alina was on the alert, waiting for him to mention, casually, an unavoidable trip to Petrograd "on army business." She would, of course, go with him, but she wouldn't tell him that immediately: first she'd see how he went about asking her blessing for the trip. Other officers traveled—at GHQ it wasn't hard to invent a pretext. But no.

There was no such mention. So it was credible that *that* relationship was, if not finished, at least in abeyance.

Alina understood that her life, so changed now—and no, it was certainly not as it had been!—was telling her to reflect, to penetrate the mystery of what had happened. That time, at the guesthouse, he had been in such a low, weakened state that he would have told Alina everything, what it was about her that had been so alluring. And, much as he tried to reassure her—she and the other one were, he said, different, inhabiting different spheres of life—but in the most intimate respect they were bound to intersect, be compared, a preference would form. But she hadn't asked: her pride wouldn't let her. He had even, by his infidelity, deprived her of any spontaneity with him. *What* did you tell her about me? And of course her tormented heart was goading her on: how on earth could she get involved with you and suffer no distress from knowing you were married . . .? Could you have done what you did if you'd known the price I'd pay for the suffering you caused?

And even her spirited openness had to be stifled in his presence! But she had resolved to hold on.

How to keep busy? What should she do? She had a nice idea: to take on something else—she'd brush up her French. She found a teacher, just two blocks away, Esfir Davydovna, an acquaintance of her hosts, who agreed to give lessons at a bargain rate in her home. Alina had always liked learning, more than anything else in the world: she really enjoyed it. "Let's do it together," she urged Georgi. "It'd be interesting to study together!" But he didn't have time, and anyway he still remembered a fair bit of his French. "Well why don't I go over my lessons with you in the evening?"

He did not just work days, but every evening as well, and Sundays too: how much were they going to see of each other? By moving to Mogilev, Alina had doomed herself to total seclusion.

Alone for days at a time, how was she to prevent it all coming back, eating away at her? How to avoid going mad . . .?

[19'']

(FROM THE BOURGEOIS PRESS, TO 27 APRIL)

DESPERATE SITUATION IN AUSTRIA.

STRIKES AND UNREST IN GERMANY.

POPULAR UPRISINGS IN BULGARIA.

The Germans are extracting fat from corpses . . . to make margarine.

The Russian army's failure on the Stokhod is to a certain extent obscured by the historic significance of the Anglo-Russian encounter in Mesopotamia.

. . . Surely the Russian people's age-old longing for Tsargrad cannot be considered a military conquest. It was instilled into us by our cultural, defensive goals: we cannot live without access to the outside world. Tsargrad is the key to universal peace.

London. *The Times* writes that: the overthrow "has breathed a new warmth into the traditional friendship which unites" Russia to the United States, . . . Russia's chief Allies will "watch the course of the Revolution with affectionate solicitude."

The President of the Board of Deputies of British Jews has talked, in a public speech, of the Russian Jews' duty—out of gratitude for their liberation—to assist in continuing the war.

The funeral for the martyrs of the revolution, in Petrograd, was a parade of the spiritual and moral force of our revolution. Who among us did not catch his breath as he watched those orderly columns! We could not fail to be affected by that emotional tension, that very particular, heartfelt sincerity . . . the magical perfection of the organization . . .

. . . The Russian Republic is destined to succeed. It was born to live! The swallows of universal liberty are already soaring in the spring air.

We cannot but admire the moral, spiritual, that is the religious, majesty of this revolution. Truly, faith has moved mountains. We are experiencing something akin to the events of two thousand years ago, when two of the Lord's disciples, on the road to Emmaus . . .

(Filosofov)

The Deputy Minister of the Interior, D. Shchepkin, has told correspondents that: "The country is becoming calmer by the day. All fears of possible agrarian unrest have now been addressed. Throughout the whole country the population is now tranquil on the land issue. And the Soviet of Workers' Deputies is not causing any friction with the Provisional Government."

Contrary to various rumors, absolute discipline prevails in the Russian army on the Romanian Front.

(Speech)

Deserters located in the province of Kishinev are in places getting organized and, via delegates, conducting negotiations with garrison committees. And at the same time having no respect for private property.

. . . The army is emerging from the pain of the cataclysm more unified, stronger and more enthusiastic.

(Stock Exchange Gazette)

Gen. Shuvaev has addressed the divisional committee in friendly and frank terms. He made a spirited appeal to the soldiers' civic sensibilities, urging them to help the Provisional Government and stop selling their boots and uniforms. In response a speaker announced that the army would tighten its belt for the good of the fatherland. The general, deeply moved, kissed the speaker warmly.

Gomel. Over 2,000 deserters, with banners proclaiming, "Down with desertion in Free Russia," went to the commandant and asked to be sent to the front immediately.

Kremenchug. A deserters' rally was held, organized by the Soviet of Soldiers' Deputies. The deserters vowed to defend with their lives the freedoms that had been won and protect them from counterrevolutionary attacks.

. . . The revolution has certainly caught the peasantry unawares, unprepared for great, epoch-making tasks.

(Russian Will)

Odessa district . . . increased grain supply. Many peasants are donating grain for the army's needs and refusing payment.

On 14 April, an eight-hour day was introduced throughout the **Donets basin**.

Kiev. At the home of Brodsky, a local millionaire, the most prominent representatives of the Kiev Jewish financial world met to discuss how they might solemnly mark the coming of the new order and liberation of the oppressed Jewish people. At the meeting more than a million rubles was collected. They resolved to raise a further four million from local Jews and set up a model People's University.

. . . In the name of the hundred thousand–strong Jewish community of Ekaterinoslav, we shall give our utmost, defend with our life the flag of the democratic republic.

JEWISH OFFICERS. Authoritative sources are reporting that in June 2,600 Jews are to be promoted to the rank of ensign.

(Stock Exchange Gazette)

Odessa . . . It is vital that the regimental committees unmask and arrest those agitating against the decree permitting Jews to become officers . . .

The Metropolitan of Moscow, Makari, has been arrested on the initiative of the Moscow Soviet of Workers' Deputies, and one has to acknowledge that this action was indeed the right one.

(Speech)

A. F. Kerensky is having to involve himself in every detail of the Tsarskoye Selo palace prisoners' life. Even dismissing cooks and washers-up cannot be done without A. F. Kerensky's authorization.

(New Times)

The Social Democrats, representing neither the nation, nor even the majority of the nation, are in practice ruling the Soviet and, via the Soviet, the whole territory of the Russian state.

(New Times)

In the Soviet of Workers' Deputies there are lawyers, associates who were, before the revolution, better known in nightclubs than in the ranks of the struggling proletariat.

(Stock Exchange Gazette)

. . . The congress of Soviets taking place now is a kind of "ecumenical council" of believers, the source of prodigious marvels. One cannot fail to find spiritual support in what has happened there. . . . Do not fear the Germans, do not fear *Pravda*: people who have a "golden dream" cannot be Russia's enemies. "Bolshevik excesses" are the bugbear of today's shopkeeper types.

(Filosofov)

The very suggestion that a separate peace is possible after the revolutionary coup is utterly absurd. Even Bolshevism, even *Pravda*, which has ballooned before our frightened eyes, and even Lenin himself have never mentioned a separate peace. All these rumors about a separate peace are a deliberate lie to discredit Russian democracy. No one dares insult the Russian people with such a suggestion. It is the revolution that has breathed new life into the slogan "war for liberty."

Kiev, 21 April. Yesterday, a Ukrainian congress opened here, a regional constituent assembly. . . . The Central Rada is to work up a draft statute for Ukrainian autonomy within the framework of a Russian Federative Republic. Grushevsky, the chairman, said that: "We know about the chauvinist intentions of irresponsible figures in the Ukraine, but we are dealing with them as national criminals." In response to the representative of the Kiev garrison, the Social Democrat Vinnichenko said, "The separatist tendency can be considered dead: Russia is more dear to us than she is to you." Levitsky, the head of a workers' cooperative, complained about harassment by the Poles: "Ukraine is not a part of Poland! The Poles are organizing their regiments, but not sending them to the front. They're keeping them here, in the hope of troubles in Ukraine. Hands off our territory!"

On the day of the funeral for the martyrs of the revolution, there were several brazen lootings of Petrograd shops . . .

METHYLATED SPIRIT. The Ministry of Finance has decided to fortify the methylated spirit, to curtail the widespread practice of drinking it.

EXAMINATIONS CANCELED for pupils graduating elementary schools and secondary school pupils moving up at the end of the year.

Jewel robbery . . . M. Kshesinskaya reported the theft of gold and diamonds worth several hundred thousand rubles to the chief of criminal investigation militia. The burglary took place during the days of the revolution. All her safes were broken into . . .

Bublikov appointed one "Captain Sosnovsky" (Iosif Rogalsky) head of security at the Ministry of Roads and Railways. He made all the staff give him all their gold and silver medals. He took as his assistant an out-and-out con artist, who was being investigated in connection with breaking and entering. Together with another assistant he carried out a successful "search" at the home of a millionaire. After a few weeks he disappeared.

The EXTRAORDINARY COMMISSION OF INQUIRY is earnestly appealing to anyone who discovered machine guns on rooftops during the days of the revolution or apprehended police staff with machine guns, to present themselves as soon as possible to give witness statements. No reports based on rumor alone please.

In **Moscow** there is an acute shortage of fodder and horses are dying.

In **Ekaterinoslav** too the memorial to Catherine II has been pulled down. It had been proposed to install it in the municipal museum, but the population demanded that it be sent for melting down into shells.

Yalta. There has been a massive influx of dignitaries, aristocrats and grand dukes here. Nikolai Nikolaevich is at liberty and walks around town alone, distributing sweets to little boys and cigarettes to Tatars. One can sense the intense propaganda on the part of both secret and open monarchists.

BI-BA-BO CABARET, near the Art Theater. Opening of: **GRISHKA AT THE SALON** and **THE TSAR'S FANCY WOMAN**.

For sale: **EMPIRE HALL**, due to owner departure. **URGENT**.

We pay **TOP RATES** for diamonds, pearls, gold . . . A. *Fistul, jeweller.*

VILLAGE GIRL NEEDED as chamber maid.

Little boy to give away for lack of money.

FREEDOM LOAN. Appeal from the Provisional Government
TO YOU, CITIZENS OF GREAT, FREE RUSSIA, TO YOU WHO HOLD DEAR THE FUTURE OF OUR HOMELAND . . . A POWERFUL ENEMY IS THREATENING TO RETURN OUR COUNTRY TO THE DEFUNCT REGIME. . . . WE MUST SPEND MANY BILLIONS TO SAVE THE COUNTRY . . . AND TO FINISH BUILDING FREE RUSSIA ON THE PRINCIPLES OF EQUALITY AND JUSTICE.

MASSIVE STRIKES IN BERLIN

The Cologne Gazette: The current war has become a war against the concept of monarchy. Five monarchs on the Allies' side have already lost their crowns or their possessions: in Belgium, Serbia, Romania, Montenegro, and Russia. The Greek throne is also shaky now. The World War is taking on more and more the aspect of a great European revolution, even bigger than that of 1848.

The English troops are seventy km from Jerusalem. . . . All the allied armies will participate in the taking of Jerusalem.

We have to hope that the new, free Russia, will put an end to public holidays, in view of the gigantic job of work facing us, and leave only Sundays. Religious holidays, with the exception of Christmas and Easter, are a personal matter. The new Russia should be particularly worried about public holidays. If pre-revolutionary inertia and sloth set in again, it will mean certain counterrevolution.

(New Times)

(*From a resolution of the Dno garrison:*) There must be no privileged units like the Guards and the Petrograd garrison. We must consider it a criminal act for reserve units slated for the front lines to instead remain at the rear. It is a treacherous stab in the back for our comrades on the front line. In Petrograd and everywhere else on the home front it is time to put an end to the celebrations and demonstrations. . . . Workers thinking of their personal interests must not forget about the army.

A general assembly of the 86th Infantry Regiment . . . with an appeal to those of our comrades who, at a moment of joy for all Russian working people, have absented themselves from the Regiment. . . . Come back, comrades, by 13 May and we shall extend a welcoming hand. But if you turn away from us we shall demand that you be brought to trial.

The new Ministry of Agriculture cannot manage to implement the vital agricultural measures already mapped out by the old regime. And the main centers of consumption are still living on old reserves . . .

(Stock Exchange Gazette)

. . . At the time of the peasants' congress of the province of Samara, the roads round Samara were impassable due to the spring thaw and delegates were unable to attend: so the congress was made up predominantly of city dwellers . . .

THE FREEDOM LOAN. People! Hear this! This is Mother Russia extending a hand in entreaty. Come, people, come in force, come in your droves! Give as much as you can! Money, bring money for the government! You are lying, you damned Germans—may you choke on your lies!

(Amfiteatrov, *Russian Will)*

A Jewish committee for the success of the Freedom Loan has been set up: Kamenka, Baron Ginsburg, and Sliozberg. The committee has decided to telegraph the representatives of Jewish communities in America, England, France, Holland, and Italy, asking them to form similar committees to float the Loan in their countries.

The French Jews, headed by Baron Rothschild, have underwritten a sum of 1 million rubles to the Russian Freedom Loan. Baron Ginsburg was charged with delivering this announcement to the Ministry of Finance.

At an assembly of the Jews of Moscow, subscriptions to the Freedom Loan totaled 22 million. In Saratov, at an assembly of the Jewish community, 800,000 was collected.

A telegram was received, via Sliozberg, from the most prominent American Jews to the Russians: "The Jews of America count with confidence upon their brethren in Russia steadfastly supporting the new Government, which has received, general, whole-hearted approval in this country. Russia's cause is now become the cause of human liberty and hence of Jewish freedom . . ."

On the order of the chief of staff of Moscow Military District, Gen. Okunkov, over three hundred Jewish students have been enrolled as first-year students at the Aleksandrovsky Military School.

". . . you understand," said Colonel Gruzinov, "that in the event of counterrevolution my head would be the first to roll."

These terrible words about Gruzinov's head come back to me every time I think of what would happen to the Jews in the event of a successful counterrevolution! The Jews must, come what may, consolidate the achievements of the revolution without counting the sacrifices. That is the be all and end all. Otherwise, all is lost. If the government has insufficient finance for the war . . . The abhorrent spawn of counterrevolution must be crushed at inception. The very seed must be destroyed. This requires money and Jews must give it without even counting.

(D. Aizman, *Russian Will)*

. . . Counterrevolution hides away in secret lairs. The old regime has left behind strong and tenacious roots, which must be pulled out immediately . . .

(Stock Exchange Gazette)

. . . Until the Constituent Assembly everyone must be equal and there must be complete freedom of propaganda. . . . But in fact we have seen the emergence of a revolutionary aristocracy, which is allowed to do what it likes and can twist the country round its little finger at will. . . . Let us act out of love, in peace and unity, with fasting and prayers, as we did in 1613 . . .

(Moscow Gazette)

. . . And what became of those millions of "True Russians" that Dr. Dubrovin tried to scare us with . . .?

ENEMIES OF THE PEOPLE ARRESTED, 25 April. Yesterday people freed a few days ago were re-arrested . . .

TO THE PETROGRAD SOVIET OF WORKERS' DEPUTIES
Telegram. Copy to the whole of the Russian railway network.
Other newspapers please re-print.

We, workers and staff of the Kazan-Ekaterinburg military delivery section, declare that:

Russia did not overthrow that gang of courtier traitors for this—to submit to dictatorship by a Petrograd group of Bolshevik-leaning workers and soldiers which is trying to usurp power over all Russia. We railway workers shall not allow any local organization to assume the right to issue orders to the whole of Russia.

An army deputation asked the Prime Minister whether there was any truth to rumors that some new organization was intending to seize power. Prince Lvov answered that: "Before allowing any such seizure the Provisional Government would appeal to the wisdom of the people and lay down the authority and the responsibility for the country that it had assumed."

. . . And how is *Pravda* occupying itself? Its only task is to sow discord and mistrust. It will baulk at nothing, not even a gross untruth.

(Speech)

DEMAGOGY. There are people whose personal vanity and narcissism eclipse everything else in the world. It is said that Russia's fallen autocrat had these character traits. Mr. Lenin resembles him closely. He has overstepped the boundaries and become, morally speaking, a dead man. In traveling through Germany he spat on the soul of the Russian people among whom he wants to exert influence. It is no wonder that even the Bolsheviks are now turning away from him. Lenin cannot get over this: as a politician he is finished. For Russia he is morally unacceptable, and our advice to him is to go back to Germany. Lenin cannot deceive Russia, whatever "Communist" cloak he dresses himself up in.

(Russian Will)

STOCK EXCHANGE REOPENING! Holders of stocks and shares are invited to the Soleil Cinema, 48 Nevsky Prospect, for an organizational meeting.

Odessa, 23 April. A rally for deserters and men who had evaded the call-up was held in Aleksandrovsky Park. They decided to elect a special committee to handle the deserters' cases. Those present gave the commandant an ovation. "With the fall of the old regime we are elated to return to the ranks of the free army." But they set conditions: they would not return to their own units, and their families must be given rations.

GREETINGS TO THE PEOPLE FROM THE POLICE. Officials of the Elizavetgrad district police sent their "sincere congratulations on the new freedom" to the State Duma, the Provisional Government, and the Soviet of Workers' and Soldiers' Deputies. "We recognize of course that the revolution was for the benefit of the poor, from which most of us stem, and our heart is easy, knowing that our children will live better than we have. And we curse the ranks of the Petrograd police, who dared turn machine guns on hungry people . . ."

Simferopol . . . Disquiet regarding the concentration of old-regime adherents on the southern shore of Crimea. The question has been raised concerning the Romanovs and ex-grandees: in the interests of security, they should be distributed around the different corners of Russia.

. . . In many places on former royal lands near Alushta, the wildlife is being savagely annihilated.

INTIMATE THEATER—*FIRST NIGHT* . . . Unprecedented acts!

MAGNIFICENT APARTMENT HOUSE for sale.

For sale: splendid ARISTOCRAT'S APARTMENT.

Female cashier (Jewish) sought.

Nursery governess needed—Lutheran.

Presentable maid sought—for valeting work and serving at table, in Vladivostok. Send photographs with application.

FREEDOM LOAN. TO YOU, CITIZENS OF GREAT, FREE . . . WHO HOLD DEAR THE FUTURE OF OUR . . . WE MUST SPEND MANY BILLIONS. . . . COME, LEND MONEY TO THE STATE, PUT IT IN THE NEW LOAN, AND SAVE OUR FREEDOM AND OUR PATRIMONY FROM DESTRUCTION.

RUMORS OF A SEPARATE PEACE. Prominent public figures in America, Marshall, Morgenthau, Schiff, Straus, and Rosenwald, sent a telegram to Milyukov:

"American Jewry is alarmed by reports that certain elements are urging separate peace between Russia and the Central Powers. We are confident Russian Jewry are ready for the greatest sacrifices in support of the present democratic Government. . . . American Jewry holds itself ready to cooperate with its Russian brethren in this great movement."

London, 26 April. House of Commons. In response to a question as to whether the British government had made any kind of offer to the Russian government regarding the future residence of the former Tsar, the Under-Secretary of State for Foreign Affairs replied that the British government had made no offer of any kind.

The *Vossische Zeitung*: "Russia and its army are on the brink of total collapse. . . . It will soon be forced to conclude a peace treaty."

. . . Never till now has any revolution anywhere opened up such horizons, had such worldwide compass or taken place with so little friction. The revolution has unusual powers of self-defense and an almost supernatural capacity for healing its wounds . . .

(Stock Exchange Gazette)

. . . The time has come to establish labor conscription for all!

The **Donets basin**. In the Alekseevka and Prokhorov mines, at the insistence of the workers, the mine foremen and administrative staff are loading coal into the goods wagons with their own hands.

Nizhni Novgorod, 27 April. The local Soviet's *Izvestia* notes increasingly frequent cases of soldiers committing assaults and outrages and taking the law into their own hands, especially on railways and waterways, which are threatening to cause a total breakdown of the transport system.

Simbirsk. Telegram to the War Minister . . . using all goods and passenger trains . . . demanding immediate departure, holding up oncoming trains, not allowing coupling of supplies wagons which have now been waiting for weeks. Impossible to continue service . . .

Kiev, 27 April. Prisoners of war employed by businesses in town have gone on strike. Bakeries and bathhouses have stopped work and there are disruptions in the tramways and water supply. They are demanding an eight-hour working day and improvements in their situation.

Letter from the front . . . We feel cut off from the home front and any help from there. Loudmouths on the home front are trumpeting our heroism. But we fear our death will be the start of Russia's death.

(Russian Invalid)

Unauthorized action by peasant communities . . . Numerous reports of arrests and unauthorized actions, which interfere with seeding the land . . . the population must be warned that this is not permissible.

Disputes about equal rights for rural women. It is the most left-wing peasants who object to allowing women into the Constituent Assembly: women are illiterate, they say, and don't have their feet on the ground. When it was announced that prayers would no longer be said for the Tsar at mass, the women wept loudly. They must not be allowed to vote in the Constituent Assembly, for 99 percent of them would vote for the monarchy.

At an assembly of the Armenians of Rostov and Nakhichevan, in five minutes 2 million or so was subscribed to the Loan . . .

An announcement arrived at the Azov-Don Bank from Jacob Schiff, saying that he was subscribing 1 million rubles to the Freedom Loan. . . . H. Sliozberg drew up an appeal for Loan funds in ancient Hebrew and Yiddish.

. . . If I am not allowed to criticize the Jewish youth, then I will say this: I am the victim of coercion. The Okhrana had threatened me with expulsion. Even worse methods are being used under the new regime . . .

(R. Wilton, correspondent of *The Times*, in the *Stock Exchange Gazette)*

Jews' lack of rights in Finland . . . In an advanced, civilized country, which appears dedicated to the ideas of justice, an inhuman law has been introduced, banning Jews from entering . . .

POGROM THREAT. For almost the whole time since the second week of the revolution, information has been coming in from the regions about agitators stirring up pogroms—but we hear nothing about any measures being taken by the government. And yet, if a regime ever has the right to be intolerant and severe, then it should be in cases like this only. Pogrom activity must be crushed at inception. The Provisional Government must announce the most severe legal penalty for even the slightest display of pogromist agitation—and apply it right now!

(Stock Exchange Gazette)

. . . We must restrain ourselves from physical reprisals against the Leninists. We must not forget that violence is not to be tolerated, that the battle must be one of words. We are sure that it will indeed not come to violence, and that Bolshevism will die a natural death amid the massive enthusiasm elicited by the revolution.

(Speech)

BOGEYMEN. The Communists at *Pravda* are threatening us with retribution. But the Leninists have already begun to taste retribution, in the profound solitude where they have ended up. They have become the bugbear of all Russia, sullying the greatness of the Russian revolution. They frighten no one and perhaps we should not even pay any attention to the political demise of these bastard sons of the revolution.

(Russian Will)

Resolution from a group of sailors. We, representatives of the guard of honor of the 2nd Baltic Fleet crew that went to meet Mr. Lenin when he returned from abroad, declare that we had seen that ceremonial welcome as an act of gratitude to an outstanding figure, who had rendered services to the Russian revolutionary movement. Now that we know Mr. Lenin returned to Russia through the good offices of His Majesty the Emperor of Germany and King of Prussia, we are expressing our deep regret that we took part . . .

Civil liberty has revealed many conjugal ills, unnoticed until now. The necessity of freeing people from these oppressive bonds has increased.

. . . In various post and telegraph offices postmasters have, in recent weeks, been replaced by new, elected individuals. The Provisional Government commissar at the post and telegraph head office has asked the staff of his organization to refrain from these arbitrary dismissals, since they are contrary to the principles of freedom and inviolability of the person . . .

Jewel robbery. Last night there was a burglary at Fistul's, the jewellers. The burglars demolished a wall . . .

The EXTRAORDINARY COMMISSION OF INQUIRY is earnestly appealing to anyone who . . . discovered machine guns on rooftops during the days of the revolution. . . . No reports based on rumor alone please.

Coming soon: *SALE BY AUCTION* of entire contents of the **CUBAT restaurant** (Café de Paris, 16 Morskaya Street).

MERCEDES car for sale. . .

For sale: PURE-BLOOD ARABIAN stallion. Broken in.

STEEL SHUTTERS for sale.

Top quality *PICKLED CUCUMBERS* for sale, delivery included. One barrel minimum.

* * *

Victory's costly, as we know.
Help our soldiers smite the foe!
Loyal Russians, raise the cash—
You can do it in a flash.
Freedom Bonds yield 6 per cent—
You won't regret the money lent.
Just 3 billion! Lend a hand,
For our Holy Russian land!

DOCUMENTS—8

RESOLUTION OF THE PROVISIONAL GOVERNMENT

(Issued 27 April)

. . . The Provisional Government requests that all citizens who own land should continue to sow their fields and, at this difficult time, fulfill their duty to the liberated Homeland. Every unsown acre is an irrecoverable loss to our defense. . . . Entrust the populace itself with the job of protecting sowings and the equipment of the individual

sowers from possible violent acts, which must be considered as an attack not only on the interests of individuals but also on the interests of the state as a whole. The government has every right to count on the participation of all free and conscientious citizens in the guarding of sowings.

. . . But if the guard mounted by citizens were to prove powerless against acts of violence, the Government would consider it an obligation of the state to make good the losses suffered by farm-owners. For this reason any violence toward sowers will place a heavy burden on the resources of the state . . .

[2 0]

When Milyukov was invited to the Extraordinary Commission of Inquiry at the Winter Palace the day before yesterday, to give evidence in the case of that blockhead Stürmer (now in a cell in the Fortress), he had repeated, without the passion now, his earlier accusations: namely, that Stürmer was secretly sympathetic to Wilhelm, was working toward a separate peace, and was betraying our Allies' secrets. (Though it must be said that not one of the suspicions had as yet been confirmed.) And Pavel Nikolaevich had experienced a distinct sense of something very strange, for History had traveled a long way in these last five months.

His 14 November "storm signal" speech had now receded irrevocably into the distance, like a mountain peak. But Pavel Nikolaevich himself, having risen up the ladder of state to the stratospheric heights of intergovernmental affairs and now occupying the post he had dreamed of, in the building by Pevchesky Bridge, felt he was moving in the opposite direction, not rising but slipping and sliding downwards. That strange thing, which could not have been foreseen, was that just as, previously, everyone's favorite target had been the autocracy, now for some reason the target of everyone on the left was the leader of the People's Freedom party. Being the minister of a victorious revolution, of a liberal government—about which, it seemed, one could never shout "is it stupidity or treason?" as befitted Stürmer's pitiful government—he was not happy. And was he even really unrestricted in his actions? Alas and alack, no. From various quarters, harsh everyday reality was delivering frequent nasty little stings. And he had to protect his heart with an iron self-control.

The only places where that heart found repose, where it could soften again, were beneath the molded ceilings of the Ministry itself, at discussions with the Allies' ambassadors and at public appearances in friendly auditoria: at the Union of Towns congress in Moscow, at the Moscow Kadets' conference, and, most of all of course, at the Kadet congress—where Milyukov had been literally fêted and met with an ovation that would not die down. The whole hall had risen to its feet, calling him a courageous and unyielding leader—and he'd had to calm his admirers down and tell them they were exaggerating his importance. But, he said, the eyes of the whole world really are on our congress and, amidst dangers raging all round, our party stands as a true example of political prudence, an arbiter between classes and social strata. The speaker had understood this when he found himself in a post offering him a broader horizon. Not a single revolution has ever gone as smoothly as ours. Of course, no other revolution took place as late as ours. Ours was inevitable. We did not want this revolution, but now we must save Russia. And amid the impassioned unity of the congress Milyukov put aside emotions and associated himself with the resolution on the republic, and rejoiced at its wisdom—even though he had, throughout his life and as recently as the first week of the revolution, insisted unsuccessfully that without a monarch Russia faced destruction and disintegration.

However, the whole congress had taken not quite four days, and had been confined beneath the cupola of the Mikhailovsky Theater. But even along Petrograd's main thoroughfares the authority of the People's Freedom Party and its leader was not holding its ground at all well. And the roasting, the insults were not coming from the right, as was customary before. It all came from the left, the left, the left.

The socialists, who had once almost become allies of the Kadets, were now unbearable. They were ranting on that we mustn't entrust the nation's international tasks to functionaries, and we mustn't accept the "behind-the-scenes, anti-popular diplomacy of that insular, snobbish, caste"! They reproached Milyukov for "not democratizing" foreign policy. They hurled irresponsible accusations that the war was "continuing in the name of ideas uniting the Tsar (!?), Milyukov, Briand, and Lloyd George!" There's an impenetrable screen, they said! Give us more information! From now on, democracy (and by "the democracy" they had, strangely, begun to mean only anyone standing to the left of the Kadets . . .), the democracy itself must direct our foreign policy!

He wondered how the democracy was to do this *itself*? What about the delicate structure of the diplomatic network? And what use, then, were all the traditions, and the Foreign Ministry, and the minister himself?

But the most precipitate attacks the socialists had started making, and the most frequent, were sarcastic quips to the effect that the Foreign Ministry not only was not helping the revolutionary émigrés to return to their homeland as soon as possible, but was even hindering their return. This was reported absolutely hysterically in the socialist newspapers, and the well-known top hysteric, Zurabov, wrote that in our Copenhagen embassy he had been shown a telegram from Milyukov: "Kindly do not issue transit visas to any émigrés on international checklists." (This revelation was most unfortunate: the embassy had no right to show that telegram.)

To tell the truth, Milyukov had been really alarmed, this last week, to see that whole revolutionary émigré anthill, that swarm of locusts, in such a hurry to squirm its way, ever faster, across to Russia. They'd hung about, and hung about some more, in foreign countries but why, now, did they have to pour into Russia at top speed and lead her astray? It would be far better and calmer if we could organize ourselves without them here for the time being.

But a government created by the revolution could certainly not set up an obvious barrier to revolutionaries, nor allow so much as a shadow of suspicion of such a thing. So all he could do was give top secret instructions to consuls abroad and ask our Allies to do everything in their power to keep such individuals from going. But now the Copenhagen embassy had let the cat out of the bag and an exceedingly unpleasant situation had arisen: he had to wriggle out of that somehow and deny the story. But then came another major scandal: Trotsky, a well-known, venomous character, had left the United States by sea with a group of like-minded companions and been detained by the English authorities at the Canadian port of Halifax. England herself understood how dangerous this group's Germanophile leanings were, and Milyukov had also asked Buchanan to do all he could to stop their trip. But a rumpus kicked off concerning Zurabov as well as Trotsky's group (with *Pravda* on the attack), and Milyukov, with uncharacteristic indecision, first asked Buchanan to let Trotsky go, then asked him again to detain them, and then again to let them go. But this was top secret!

Publicly Milyukov himself, or on behalf of his Ministry, set up his defenses and refuted all accusations: no one had been detained anywhere and all gates were open wide to returning émigrés; urgent instructions had been given to offer them generous and courteous assistance, whatever their convictions. The minister was protesting particularly energetically, he said, against the detention of Trotsky's group, and passports were being issued to the émigrés without any impediment, even those who were unknown to us and we did not know whether they were even from Russia—the passports were being issued on the basis of assurances by émigré committees. So it was not the Provisional Government that was holding them all up but the danger of sea crossings and the impossibility of all of them being brought over at once, since the Germans had sunk some of the steamers on the Norway route. Also, there were strict regulations in force in the countries on the way. Milyukov hurried to exonerate the Allies as well: they were not responsible for any detentions, they were immediately fulfilling all requests from the Russian Ministry. No, the problem was that the Provisional Government had not immediately been informed (and it was true, Milyukov had only just heard of this at the Ministry) that apart from the list of "politically suspect" individuals, the Allies also had a "checklist of undesirable persons," suspected of intercourse with the enemy. Well, Zurabov, Trotsky, and Lenin had, by some error, found their way onto these lists. (Buchanan, indeed, had said that Trotsky was being held because he had, throughout the war, been speaking out in favor of Germany. But now he was happily allowed to pass.)

But Pavel Nikolaevich had been very naïve to think he could, by simply publishing the names of pacifists traveling across Germany, discredit them and curtail their political influence. They crossed Germany—and still arrived smelling of roses. Milyukov had always maintained that it was improper to accuse political opponents of plain corruptibility . . . But these people, Lenin, Trotsky, this was some totally new breed, simply beyond the bounds of all human norms, and he just could not think how to deal with them.

Fortunately, Lenin had come to grief immediately, at the Tauride Palace, the day after he arrived: he had defended pacifism so brazenly, so indelicately, that he had left the conference to hissing and catcalls. Even to the most red-hot socialists his speech had been stupid, insane. So Lenin was not at all dangerous—it was even good that he'd come and was demolishing his own case in full view of everyone. It was another inoculation against Zimmerwaldist utopianism.

But, despite all his excesses, he was giving a fillip to the Social Democrats' desire for peace as soon as possible. Now the Menshevik Executive Committee—and there was no ignoring the Mensheviks, for they were the most respectable of our socialists—had published a totally addled resolution, which was, essentially, parroting Zimmerwald: the most urgent task of the Russian revolution is the struggle for peace with no annexations or indemnities; we must prompt (read "force") the Provisional Government to renounce, officially and unconditionally, all plans for territorial conquests. It even said that we must draw up a collective declaration to that effect from all the governments of the Entente! And at the same time they themselves were announcing "to the proletariat of all warring countries" that they must apply concerted pressure on their governments. And these were serious Mensheviks? At the Liaison Commission Milyukov tried to persuade Chkheidze and Tsereteli that all this was utopian and absolutely impossible to realize: socialists in the West were free of such fantasies and stood firmly behind their nations.

He was sure of that! But it transpired that Western socialists were indeed subject to that same giddiness. On 21 April Albert Thomas had arrived (now he was a minister in France). The Russian revolution had put a special sparkle in Thomas's eyes and he had immediately started parroting everything the Soviet said. This had cut the ground from under Milyukov's feet: how was he to call for loyalty to the Allies more insistently than the French Munitions Minister did? At a reception at the Mariinsky Palace, he had tried to set Thomas right: "Despite the change of regime, we are keeping to the main aim of this war, the elimination of German imperialism. And the Franco-Russian alliance is identified with the strains of the Marseillaise. Thanks to democratization, Russia has become twice as strong and can withstand all the hardships of war." But here, in Milyukov's own milieu, that brazen Kerensky delivered a low blow: "*We*, the Russian democracy, are putting an end, once and for all, to all attempts to seize territories. *Our* enthusiasm flows not from the patriotic idea but from the brotherhood of nations, and just as we exert influence on our own bourgeois class—you must influence yours over there!" (And a further humiliation: it was Milyukov who had to translate these words from Russian . . .)

But Pavel Nikolaevich could never, in the job he had, lose his sense of the full depth of state traditions, at least the ones that dated back to the eighteenth century. He could not fail to feel at his back, at a minimum, Ostermann, Bestuzhev-Ryumin, Nikita Panin, Rumyantsev, and Gorchakov. After the Soviet's half-witted Manifesto of 27 March (which had, by the way, elicited a scandalous lack of response from across Europe) he, like those statesmen, could not keep silent and had to uphold the rational point of view. Besides, it had seemed to him then that the popular outburst was calming down, there was a change for the better in the garrison, the press was now bold enough to reproach the workers for shirking their work—so might the Foreign Minister also be allowed to speak up? And he chatted to journalists about freeing the Slav nations from Austria, about merging into Russia the Ukrainian lands controlled by Austria, and about the liquidation of Ottoman power in Europe, and said that control of Constantinople was the most important issue of the war, and demilitarization of the Straits would be damaging to Russia. That mastery of Tsargrad had been the goal of the Russian nation since time immemorial. And that the notorious formula "without annexations or indemnities" was a German formula and unacceptable to the Allies. Germany must atone for losses occasioned by its aggression.

But, as luck would have it, this appeared in the papers on 5 April, the day of the funeral for the martyrs of the revolution (and next to the account of our disastrous defeat on the Stokhod). And it was interpreted as a challenge to democracy, a lack of respect for the revolution. No one could have predicted the socialists' reaction—they lashed out with an absolute tempest! It spilled over into the government, and the timid Prince Lvov distanced himself from Milyukov, not for the first time, and Kerensky publicly contradicted him: this was Milyukov's personal opinion, he said, not the government's view, and this was not the first time in the past weeks that he had expressed his "personal opinion."

So what did that mean? Was he not allowed to say anything?

And the free press, frightened, did not defend Milyukov.

By now the socialists were not only hurling abuse but openly pushing to run things themselves, and those in the Soviet were at his throat, demanding that the government should publicly renounce any ambition to conquer territory. Tsereteli had now, fortunately, replaced that ruffian Nakhamkes in the Liaison Commission, and tried—such passion burning in those dark eyes—to persuade Milyukov to lose no time in sending a note to the Allies (Pavel Nikolaevich would know how to express himself diplomatically, Tsereteli was sure) and at the same time sending a solemn declaration to the army and the populace to the effect that, firstly, we were abandoning any imperialist aspirations and, secondly, committing ourselves to take steps toward concluding a general peace. The government would then, Tsereteli assured him, acquire tremendous moral force and "they will all, to a man, follow you." And this would effect a fantastic upturn in army morale and reveal the creative force of the Russian revolution.

Tsereteli could win you over by his tone of voice and his manner, such that you even doubted yourself. But no, Milyukov understood the whole situation very well—and he had immediately dismissed that "secondly" and was strongly challenging the "firstly." Such an appeal would produce nothing: it would only spoil our relationship with the Allies and with the mighty America, which was now coming into the war.

But—he had no backing. Even the ministers were, almost in unison, criticizing Pavel Nikolaevich, and he had to hold them back from impulsively giving their assent.

The tragedy was that this blind alley was not one you could maneuver yourself out of, no tight corner occurring accidentally, from which you only needed a bit of subtlety, some dexterity, to extricate yourself. This blind alley was one of principle, a barrier to all the concepts that Pavel Nikolaevich had always lived by, a barrier denying all meaning to his actions. It was also tragic that he knew he was absolutely right, and was aware of his opponents' incompetence. With the socialists' utopian, doctrinaire point of view and the infantile fantasies of that Tsereteli, no solid diplomacy was possible. Revolutionary disorders in Germany? Support from German Social Democracy? Totally groundless hopes—and you've already had time to satisfy yourself on that score. Austria, yes, Austria wants peace very much but would not dare conclude a peace agreement without permission from Germany. What fanatical narrow-mindedness, to suspect Russia's natural aspiration to ensure its security, to call it "imperialism"!

And the following day, with only the ministers present: why, he asked them, was the old government overthrown? Because it was incapable of bringing the war to a victorious conclusion. And are we now to repeat that mistake? In that case we'll be overthrown too. Are we now, when the troops are enthusiastic about the new regime—you can see for yourself how much support there is among delegations from the front, the spiritual bond forged between the government and the army—are we now suddenly to start retreating because some people are tired? We have no right to forget the goals and interests of the Russian nation! We need a definitive, long-lasting peace—and for that we need a decisive victory. We've already announced that the Russian nation has no aspiration to seize territory, to subjugate other nations—but we won't allow our own annihilation! What? The war has carried off millions of Russian lives—and now we're to return to the *status quo*? Unbelievable! No conquests, fine, but there has to be an organic restructuring of Europe. Annexations in Europe? The Allies don't want this either (they'll take Germany's African colonies), but we Russians have a particular need of the Straits. Besides, however you look at the theoretical possibility of changing the aims of the war, now is not the time to raise the question, when our military success in the struggle has not yet been conclusively established. Under these conditions we certainly must not, on the spur of the moment, change the aims we agreed with the Allies. As for a separate peace, it's frightening even to think of: it would delete Russia from the list of great powers—and would be disastrous for the revolution. No!! Russian democracy will not take that route! *Conditio sine qua non*: together with our Allies—on to the final victory!

But the ministers, weakened by pressure from the Soviet, wavered, and it became impossible to stand firm on every point. Some kind of announcement would have to be made. The "opposition seven," as Pavel Nikolaevich called them, now constituted more than half the government—and at their head was not even Prince Lvov, who had just docilely joined their ranks, but that loudmouth poseur Kerensky, whose very presence at governmental meetings inhibited people from speaking their mind openly. Once, arriving back from Kronstadt, he had lied shamelessly, even to ministers in a small meeting, saying that everything had calmed down there. Another time, by some unexplained process, he was proclaimed Prince Lvov's deputy as of 3 April and when, in mid-April, some ministers went to GHQ for a second time, the newspapers stressed that Kerensky "was asked" to take the chair during that period. He also developed the disgusting habit of pacing up and down the hall during government meetings, all keyed up, sometimes joining them, but then going off into the distance as if he was the most important person there and could just abandon meetings. And once he made a nasty scene, bawling at Milyukov, and then just made off. Unseen, below the surface, was an unfailing bond between him, Tereshchenko, Nekrasov, and Konovalov. They were joined, shortsightedly, by the other Lvov, the unstable one, and the faceless Godnev. Which, with the ever-obliging prince, made seven, a majority in the cabinet. And Guchkov was always ill or traveling, and would glumly sidestep any conflict within the cabinet. And Shingarev busied himself fanatically with agriculture and food supply. Manuilov was a nonentity: he was no support.

And Pavel Nikolaevich cursed himself: where had his eyes and his brain been when he was in sole charge of putting a government together? He could have taken more Kadets, and real Kadets, not traitors like Nekrasov. He could have given Nabokov, first of all, an important ministry, and Vinaver too. And how good the energetic Bublikov would have been now. And as Prime Minister, that fulminating patriot Rodzyanko would have been a hundred times better than the wishy-washy Lvov. Milyukov had not foreseen that immediate lurch to the left. What had he been afraid of then? He'd taken some silly arguments too seriously, given too much ground and skirted round things. His best quality was a skill for compromise and evasive action—but on that occasion it had done him a disservice.

But now, at least, it should serve to rescue him. He was not in a strong enough position to resist giving ground entirely, but he did remain rock solid in his decision as to the format for that new declaration. It would not be a diplomatic note to the Allies, but only an address to the citizens of Russia. (And, moreover, he would not draft a collective declaration for the Allies! He would never start passing on to the Allies the pressure he was under. That would be dishonorable.) And of course he would not be including that current, banal catchphrase "with no annexations or indemnities" that they were demanding. For if, gentlemen, we were to announce our "renunciation of annexations," this would not bring us one step nearer to peace, but would reveal our military weakness to both Germany and the Allies. Milyukov set about choosing his words for the 9 April declaration with great care, so as not to exclude his own honest understanding of the aims of our foreign policy and not to require any real changes in the course it was taking.

Then Nabokov kindly came to his aid: refine the way you express these "annexations and indemnities." Write it in a roundabout way, leaving a *reservatio mentalis*: enough space for the broadest and most subjective interpretation. And this kind of document, addressing the people, cannot be considered a diplomatic document. It is not *expressis verbis*, and will not tie us down during future peace talks. No one passes judgment on the victors. Who will remember this declaration? Look at President Wilson, who used to talk in exactly those terms, saying no one should be the victor in this war. But now that he's come into the war he's talking quite differently, and no one's reminding him.

And Pavel Nikolaevich announced in front of the ministers that he reserved the right, should this compromise document be interpreted in a biased manner, to interpret it according to his own understanding and explain any unclear expressions according to the orientation of his own policies and the national interests of Russia. He was very proud of some expressions that had been added especially skilfully (suggested by Kokoshkin): "The Russian people will not allow their homeland to emerge from this great conflict humiliated, with its life forces wasted," but also "in full observance of all the obligations we have assumed in relation to our Allies." And Kerensky unexpectedly added "the state is in danger" and "summon all your strength to save it," which made it even better. But even so he had to add, at the last minute, under pressure from the Soviet, "no forcible seizure of foreign territories" in lieu of a "no annexations" clause—and it became hard to interpret that in any equivocal sense. But the Liaison Commission thought even that was too equivocal, and were outraged by those "life forces, which must not be wasted," and by the "rights of the homeland," and threatened to launch a newspaper campaign against the Provisional Government the very next day. But then Nekrasov suggested that it would be better for them if they interpreted the declaration as a concession on the part of the government. And then they larded the text with condemnation of the old regime—and at last the socialists in the Soviet were satisfied.

However, when this Declaration of 9 April was published it was such a resounding success with the Russian public that Milyukov was embarrassed: surely he hadn't, without realizing, been too malleable, capitulated to the Soviet? The right-wing socialists' paper *The Day* also praised it. It was, they said, a move away from imperialism and toward the Soviet's manifesto of 27 March: these were truly democratic words. The Menshevik paper the *Workers' Gazette* was also full of praise. This was bad. The declaration was interpreted as an unequivocal renunciation of our claim on Constantinople. Then a cool wind blew in: the Allies were not happy. They disliked, were suspicious of "no mastery over other nations, no nation's patrimony to be taken from it, no seizure of foreign territories, no one to suffer humiliation." And then the German and Austrian press also received the declaration too kindly. That was a really bad sign. And then the turncoat *New Times*, which had been lying low, started attacking him on that same sensitive point: the declaration, psychologically speaking, tears up our agreement with the Allies and creates fertile moral ground for a separate peace.

Surely it didn't do that?? Where did they read that?

But yes, they had read it! And Paléologue and Buchanan reproached Milyukov cruelly: you have eight Allies and some of them have suffered more than you, and now a ninth, America, is coming in, and the whole war was initiated for a Slav cause. And *you* are the first to bow out? (Buchanan was demanding that we continue our action in Mesopotamia with an attack on Mosul.) Then it was the American Jewish bankers who sent a worried inquiry: surely there would be no separate peace?? And Milyukov sent a sincere response: "We are deeply moved by the kind words of the eminent American citizens of the Jewish faith . . . to ensure the triumph of great democratic principles. . . . As for the rumors of a separate peace, I can assure you that they are unfounded . . ."

But Milyukov was so badly wounded by all these reproaches, and in such close agreement with his critics, that he would rather have given up his ministry than renounce his principles and his determined pursuit of this war. And the previous week he himself, at the Kadet Conference in Moscow, had dropped his guard and, forfeiting all the hidden gains he had made from the 9 April declaration, revealed that the declaration certainly did not mean that the government was renouncing its obligations and rights as a member of the alliance, and the question of the Straits would be decided by the outcome of the war, and of course we would demand compensation from Germany for our expenditure on rebuilding regions that she has devastated.

It was diabolically difficult, this tacking between the sea of anarchism within our country and our firm obligations outside. Not looking like an imperialist while maintaining one's honest, Kadet nature. Not speaking out too much, or too little.

And then he suffered a blow from a quite unexpected source: from the president of the United States! How the Provisional Government had welcomed his entry into the war! What a splendid move! We're delighted! Congratulations! Free Russia considers itself particularly indebted to the United States! But now Wilson, having received Lord Balfour and Marshal Joffre in the States, and having declined to pass judgment on any political entities to be formed in the future, or on international borders, found it necessary to intervene on three of these: we must recognize the (as yet non-existent) Greek republic, with Venizelos at its head (not a bad idea, but it would mean deposing the Greek king); create a Jewish republic in Palestine (excellent idea, and far-sighted of him to say it now); and . . . about the Straits! Giving no thought to Russian interests (was it possible to take no account of Russia?) he said he had no opinion on the matter but he hoped that the Russians would renounce Constantinople! He had no opinion—but he did really. . . (This wouldn't have worried us if we had already been in action, trying to take those Straits. But we were not even getting ready to take them. We'd only just conceived the secret hope that Bulgaria would come over to the Allies—then we could have taken the Straits quickly.)

A real balancing act of superhuman proportions was called for. And now Milyukov, having achieved the post he had yearned for, saw himself stripped in some mysterious way of his previous authority and staying power. That pipsqueak Kerensky had appeared at all the meetings with foreign figures—with Albert Thomas, at Paléologue's luncheon, and at the celebration in honor of the American ambassador (and dragging his inseparable chum Tereshchenko, who spoke foreign languages, along with him everywhere—and they had already poked their noses in and told Buchanan that they were in agreement on the demilitarization of the Straits!). But that was not all: he had already, publicly, snatched the initiative in foreign affairs and publicly bragged in the Soviet that it was he who now really ran foreign policy and that the declaration was done under his influence (which of course it was, partially).

But who was not, by now, claiming to be the master of foreign policy? The Executive Committee of the Soviet also had its own foreign policy! It had set up its own Department of International Relations. What kind of effrontery was that?! It all but sent its own ambassadors to foreign countries. It did, anyway, send commissars from the Soviet into our embassies to check whether their "activity accorded with the new regime and the aims of democracy." If not, they would be "paralyzed." You didn't know whether to laugh or to marvel.

The Executive Committee hung over the ministers' heads like a great rock that leaned already and now threatened to come crashing down on them. The Provisional Government was accountable to the EC for its every move, even steps taken under pressure from the EC itself. But the EC was accountable for nothing. (One secret hope sustained Milyukov: that the EC would be riven by an internal split.) Already it was not only the Liaison Commission that was asking for reports from the government: there was also the EC trying to get its own commissar into every ministry. And at their Conference of Soviets in mid-April they—especially Nakhamkes—were brashly and openly discussing whether they should take power now or hold off for the time being. There you heard people saying that "the current ministers didn't want this revolution" and "don't trust any of them, not Guchkov, not Milyukov" and "Milyukov isn't firm enough in his feelings toward the House of Romanov" and "we cannot tolerate this government any longer": they lambasted this government just as, previously, the Tsar's had been lambasted, heedless of any conventional bounds of acceptability. And they even had the poor taste, the impudence to want to *summon* ministers to their conference. (And what would we have done if they *had* summoned us . . .?) This had strayed far from the "support insomuch-insofar" that Nakhamkes and Himmer had promised in the 14 March negotiations.

But you couldn't even say this aloud anywhere. At the Mariinsky Palace, before anxious delegations from the front, begging the government not to submit to any outside authority, Milyukov himself also had to confirm that the government was acting totally independently, that there was no second authority, that it acceded to the Soviet's wishes when it wanted to, but otherwise it refused.

A small episode, but so telling: On the day of the funeral for the martyrs of the revolution, Lvov, Milyukov, and some other ministers were on their way to the Field of Mars all together in one big, very grand limousine. But a militia patrol stopped them on the bridge across the Fontanka! And demanded to see a pass from the Soviet of Workers' Deputies. They did not have such a document, but they were the government, Prince Lvov himself was there. And they certainly recognized Lvov. But even so they would not let them through! And the government had to turn back and go to the nearest commissariat for a pass. But the commissariat turned out to be in the house on the Fontanka that had previously been that of the Minister of the Interior. And there they didn't immediately issue a pass but started telephoning to find Kerensky. And the ministers sat, helpless and humiliated, in a little hall and reflected that this had, of course, not so long before been Protopopov's house, from which they had tried so hard to evict him. And now they sat there—as if waiting for him to receive them. They would have shrugged it off and left—but they could not dare be absent from such an important revolutionary occasion. And they waited, and waited, until at last Kerensky drove up and took the government under his protection. And took them to the ceremony. (Which was, by the way, rather unpleasant, with awful, muddy weather. They took their hats off by the graves, standing on a temporary wooden footway, together with the EC. They could at least have kept quiet about this shameful episode, but stupid Manuilov immediately let out the whole story of their detention to the reporters surrounding them.)

The *cipher* department (where telegrams from diplomats were secretly decrypted) informed Milyukov that the Swiss embassy and some others were sending reports to their capitals . . . about the very likely fall of the Provisional Government! Well, how's that, for starters! No, things were not nearly that bad, but it was not pleasant to read.

And the Foreign Minister's situation was certainly not getting any better. Not to mention the fact that *Pravda* never tired of attacking him, they had started using another new technique: pieces purporting to be resolutions from factories, which the Soviet's *Izvestia* was then publishing on the editorials page. So the Triangle factory, if you please, had come to this resolution: "We propose that the Soviet of Deputies should demand, categorically, that the Provisional Government immediately publish, for all to see, all agreements with the Allies. The working class of Russia does not want to wage war on behalf of English and French capitalists' predatory aspirations. And the Provisional Government must tell the Allies to renounce annexations and indemnities. And it must take the initiative and begin peace negotiations." That was what it said. And all that, in those words, was written by workers? Were we supposed to believe that?

But the workers of the Old Parviainen plant were, it seemed, demanding even more: "The Provisional Government must be ousted!"

And *Izvestia* printed it, in the biggest type they had.

What was this new style? Why had this randomly assembled group set about giving directions to the government of our Great Russia?

And now, with the Foreign Minister's position so delicate, so precarious, Pavel Nikolaevich had opened the morning papers yesterday, the 26th—and could not believe his eyes. They all said: "We have been informed that the Provisional Government is at present preparing a note to be sent to the Allied powers in the coming days, which will explain in detail its conception of the aims and objectives of the war."

A stung Pavel Nikolaevich now leapt out of his chair, a first for him. Just who had taken this decision on his behalf? What kind of dirty trick was this? What kind of unprecedented political methods were these?

Now he remembered. At the Liaison Commission on the evening of the 24th, Chernov had appeared and was going on and on about his impressions of Europe, saying that no one there knew about our declaration of 9 April, so it would be good to repeat it in a note. In Europe, he said, it would be much appreciated. And Milyukov had snapped straight back at him that he himself was certainly no less knowledgeable about the mood in the West and that a note of this kind would provoke not sympathy but alarm among our Allies: it would give rise to rumors that Russia was getting ready to break the alliance. But Chernov's *People's Cause* had started stirring things up: a note, a note! It was an anonymous contributor.

But who had told them that? Someone in the government?

Pavel Nikolaevich sped off to the Mariinsky, to find out. Nabokov had already looked into it: it was Kerensky!

That swine! Barely containing himself for the duration of the meeting, at the end Milyukov asked, icily, who gave the press that communiqué.

Lvov? He knew nothing.

Kerensky, though looking a tiny bit embarrassed, responded insolently: he could not answer for the form in which the press had conveyed his words, but in the current circumstances, a communiqué of this kind had been necessary.

He was shameless! Just as icily (though seething inside), Pavel Nikolaevich said to Prince Lvov that he would immediately tender his resignation if Kerensky did not this minute issue a retraction. And a storm blew up. Even those of "the seven," the opposition, all distanced themselves from Kerensky, feeling his action had not been correct. And Kerensky, biting his lip, felt for the first time like the "hostage" he had been regularly, and proudly, proclaiming himself. And he used the telephone in Nabokov's office to call the telegraph agency with the retraction.

And today this, too, had been in all the newspapers.

But what would the Allies think? What would Russia think? You couldn't survive for long on the basis of one strange retraction like that.

And Pavel Nikolaevich noticed that the ministers had only condemned the form of Kerensky's interference in someone else's department. But really they wanted to give in and send the note, under pressure still from those "workers' resolutions."

So giving no ground at all had become impossible even for Milyukov. A note, some kind of note . . . something would have to be sent.

But he sensed that the timing was very bad! Yes, in the initial weeks the Allies had still thought we could solve our difficulties alone—now they were viewing us less indulgently. And although Milyukov was most certainly not a sensitive type, even so it pained him to think how disappointed in us the Allies would be!

DOCUMENTS—9

27 April
FROM FRENCH MINISTER THOMAS, WHILE IN PETROGRAD, TO THE FRENCH MINISTRY OF FOREIGN AFFAIRS

Telegram, encrypted

. . . Neither the fate of the war nor that of the Alliance seems to me to be endangered. . . . I beg you not to worry. . . . Everyone in contact with the revolutionary army assures me that a real improvement in the situation is gradually taking place. . . . Revolutionary patriotism can and must emerge. . . .

DOCUMENTS—10

27 April
FROM GERMAN STATE SECRETARY ZIMMERMANN TO GERMAN AMBASSADOR IN BERN ROMBERG

Encrypted

General Ludendorff agrees to allow the Russian émigrés, escorted until now via Stockholm, to pass through the lines of our Eastern Front, with a view to their carrying out peace-oriented propaganda directly inside the army. If people can be found who are prepared to take this on, we could try it.

[2 1]

At the session following the stormy Executive Committee meeting of 18 April, when it had almost broken off relations with the government over the oath and Platten, the scandalous minutes of that discussion were read, leading to a decision: from then on to produce the minutes in unattributed form, so as not to heap odium on individual comrades because of what they had said. It was, all in all, extremely embarrassing and undesirable to divulge details of what happened at the EC, and how. And none of this must be published, either in the soviets' publications, or the socialist newspapers. They had already, much against their will, published the full list of EC members, and even disclosed the real identities of those with pseudonyms. That was enough.

The left wing had suggested several times that Kerensky should be publicly disowned for his virtual betrayal of the EC. The majority of the EC disagreed, saying Kerensky's presence in the government was useful even so, and we had to take account of his popularity.

But then an even greater danger appeared, and was discussed as the first serious question. While we were caught up for a week in the hurly-burly of the All-Russian Conference of Soviets, an uncontrollable movement grew right on our doorstep at the Petrograd garrison. The battalions were now somehow communicating with each other (most probably via the Bolsheviks). Already having the Soldiers' section of the Soviet, which they thought was insufficient, they wanted to elect their own separate garrison bureau, like those already existing in several cities (bodies were being thrown together all over the place, chaotically, anywhere and anyhow), supposedly to decide specific military-technical matters. But this was an exceedingly dangerous proposal. The creation of another center outside the Soviet could certainly not be allowed: they could develop their own political program—and what then? The garrison would stop submitting to EC control. Revolutionary initiative must also be subject to limits. And whatever was Stankevich (who was so good at criticizing others) doing about it? Our Executive Commission of the Soldiers' section must forestall this initiative and persuade the garrison that the commission is sufficient representation—that it's already the garrison bureau they want.

But the soldiers' commission now announced that it was too small (about forty members), that they were overloaded with work relating to the country as a whole, and that, for them to do the work of a garrison bureau, they would need more elections throughout the garrison, to add at least one man per battalion—and they should all be included in the Executive Committee as well.

That was a pretty kettle of fish! The committee members already there were barely tolerable and now we were to add another sixteen? But we had to choose the lesser of two evils, otherwise we'd lose the garrison. So a resolution was passed to add those sixteen but not by means of new elections—there was no knowing who we'd end up with—but delegates from the existing battalion committees: they'd been broken in a bit by now.

Just recently, coming out of the Conference of Soviets, sixteen new members had been added, so that the EC could be considered All-Russian. (It was already expanding to the dimensions of a state: institutions, both governmental and provincial, were coming with requests, a motley crowd of strangers barging their way in to complain; clerks, officers, peasants with knapsacks, and weeping women.) Those newly elected sixteen were, it's true, embarrassed, sensing that their role was only temporary, until the Congress of Soviets, and they themselves said they did not want to take part in the constitutive work of the EC. This was good. Bogdanov had the idea of moving them all into the Intercity section. (The most intelligent, Gurevich-Ber, was entrusted with organizing regional congresses of soviets, each region comprising several provinces.)

But if there were further elections in the Soldiers' section, then we'd have to have further elections in the Workers', with another ten or so workers added. (Though they could be sent out on official business round the factories.) And by the time we'd also included into the EC all the members of the Social Democrat factions of the four Dumas, and the representatives of the district soviets, and the whole editorial department of *Izvestia* was attending the meetings, and representation of all the parties was increased by the recent arrivals, and the displaced members of the EC were also attending quite often—our ranks were now swollen to almost ninety people, and our sessions were becoming unmanageable and no discretion could be maintained: anything said confidentially here was retailed far and wide.

The way matters progressed at the Executive Committee was depending more and more on Tsereteli. The exhausted Chkheidze and ever-cheerful Skobelev were, although nominally heading the EC and the whole Soviet, becoming less and less significant after the inclusion of the arriving leaders, Gotz, Dan, Lieber, and then Chernov. The returning émigrés and exiles were inevitably crowding out the locals, the Petrograd members. (Meanwhile, Stankevich and Dan were wearing Steklov out with the reorganization of *Izvestia*, and Himmer, with Gorky's support, was enthusiastically readying his own newspaper, which was intended to eclipse all the revolutionary as well as the general run of Petrograd papers.)

Then the leadership of the EC had to attend the Minsk front-line congress, a gathering of uneducated soldiers of unknown political orientation. They might fall for monarchist propaganda: we had to take them in hand immediately and run the event as a socialist conference. The leading figures went off to Minsk for just three days, supposing that in their absence the other EC members would decide only minor matters in their daily meetings. And there were certainly some to decide. That tiresome Groman with the ever-snotty nose wanted to know what tactics we were going to employ for the elections to the Petrograd Food Supply Board. We could take all the seats but, he thought, we shouldn't, because then we'd have to assume all responsibility for the food supply in Petrograd—which was getting worse and worse. No one wanted to take on the chore of organizing the 1 May celebrations, with demonstrations, and they decided to give it to Sukhanov-Himmer, the worst possible candidate for the job. (But he contrived to find some enthusiasts to do it instead.) They spent a long time arguing about what slogan should appear on the EC's 1 May banner. The Socialist Revolutionaries were pressing for "In struggle we gain our rights," but the Social Democrats won the day, contending that "Proletarians of all countries, unite" was more international and generally applicable. They discussed Lurie's proposal that they should mark 1 May by ceasing military action for one day and the Soviet should appeal to our army and our adversary's not to fire the first shot on the day. Nice idea. But would it work technically? Would we be able to contact the Germans? How would they feel about it? And our military authorities would oppose it. And what if, on that day, there was a disaster on the front line, like the Stokhod setback? All the blame would be heaped on us and used against the revolutionary cause.

There were arguments too with the Interdistrict group: they were pushing to occupy Durnovo's dacha, now lying empty, but the EC didn't dare sanction this after the outcry in the bourgeois press about the Kshesinskaya mansion being seized. Then there were complaints from the Helsingfors Soviet about Guchkov, saying he was riding roughshod over the navy. And, from the Moscow Soviet, about Milyukov, saying he had, at the Moscow Kadet Conference, devalued the whole 9 April declaration by saying that there was nothing new in it, that the conditions for peace could not be brought about without the Allies and, of course, must include Armenia's and Galicia's incorporation into Russia. It's just as well that that vile creature blabs out everything he really thinks: we'll have to subdue him and nip this in the bud. There were two bones of contention with the Provisional Government, which had already dragged on for two months with no resolution: they were not allocating 10 million for the maintenance costs of the Soviet and were not, sincerely and definitively, abolishing the military oath of allegiance. And now some regiments were asking the EC what to do: who should we believe? And what were we all to do in fact, when three-quarters of the army had taken the oath? (We should never have gotten involved in that oath business.)

And then, a telegram from the front, from the 2nd Guards Division: our ranks are melting away, we're getting no reinforcements from Petrograd, and we want to know whether the Petrograd Soviet is still insisting that Petrograd troops not be deployed. The nondeployment of the Petrograd garrison, which in revolutionary mid-March had seemed so clearly right, was now becoming more and more open to attack. By this time we would have been happy to send them to the front, but the battalions all knew about their exemption and didn't want to go. (And telegrams were coming from provincial cities: their garrisons had decided, following Petrograd, not to go to the front either but to defend the revolution where they were.)

And at that same time a telegram turned up from the Moscow Soldiers' Soviet, which was even more alarming: certain military figures were holding negotiations with GHQ and Guchkov about convening a separate Military Congress, involving front and rear units but without the workers' deputies! So what was going on? Was it a split? And on an all-Russian scale now? Would there be not one Congress of Soviets but *two*? And what would be left of the single, unified will of the Soviets? Now there were no arguments among the EC: we have to stop them, nip it in the bud! This was the garrison bureau again, but ten times more dangerous.

We should have gone straight to the government. But almost the whole Liaison Commission was in Minsk. So we sent them a telegram there. That should be even better: at the Minsk congress they could pass a resolution against this Military Congress. That would have more authority. For the time being, the EC appealed to all the provincial soviets to oppose this initiative.

Steering the soviets was not easy. You had to keep a tight hold on the rudder. Resolutions started coming in from several front-line regiments in favor of a separate Military Congress and a separate All-Russian Soviet of Soldiers' Deputies, which would be amalgamated later on with the Soviet of Workers' and Peasants' Deputies. There it was. A cleverly arranged Black Hundreds–style plan was coming together. And a resolution arrived from the Dno garrison: we must hold new, *democratic*, elections for the Petrograd Soviet, to make it the *true* representative of the workers and soldiers. That meant stripping the revolutionary parties of their significance and influence.

Coinciding with these attacks—or was it all part of the same plan?—came Shulgin's provocative outburst (with a whiff of anti-Semitism) in his *Kievlyanin*, against Comrade Steklov. And at the same time Comrade Steklov's driver launched an attack on his passenger. Concerning the first of these, a resolution was passed to bring it to the attention of the Duma committee headed by Rodzyanko, and as for the second, they would carry out an investigation.

Right then, on that same day, everything piled up: rumors reached them that in the Volynian Battalion, the first into the revolution, the men were getting ready to arrest Comrade Lenin. And *that*—even the intention alone—could not be allowed: such ideas emerging from that corner could end up in pogroms against all revolutionary forces! It must be prevented! A delegation—Sukhanov, Bogdanov, and Vengerov—had to be sent to the Volynian Battalion immediately, to dispel those mendacious rumors about Lenin that were spreading among the soldiers. (Only Dan objected: before doing that the EC should take a position on something it had been avoiding: how should they view the fact that the émigrés had traveled through Germany?)

But the leading figures came back from Minsk, and every single one of these matters was displaced by the urgent need to reorganize the EC itself: from a select group of revolutionary leaders it had become an unruly coaching inn, full of all kinds of random deputies, where it was now impossible to speak openly or debate issues. And did we need these exhausting debates anyway? Dan produced a report proposing a reorganization: the full membership we now had would meet less frequently; minor, run-of-the-mill questions would be distributed among sections (there'd be eleven or thirteen of these); to settle matters of principle, we'd elect a new, small bureau, preferably consisting of party representatives only, and only via these could questions be passed for discussion by the entire EC. But wait a minute, we elected a bureau a month ago, at the end of March! Yes, but it has shown it can't function. And it doesn't include any of the active comrades who have just arrived back.

And then the opportunists started voicing their plan: not only should we get rid of the soldiers, the simple workers, the strangers to our group, but also our own left-wing members who were too quarrelsome, too exhausting—and assemble a bureau of like-minded people, kindred spirits. The left-wingers who had been running the EC in March but were now losing their hold on it, Sukhanov, Sokolovsky, Krotovsky, and all the Bolsheviks, one after the other objected vehemently: in that case let's have proportional representation of our Zimmerwaldist minority in this bureau! But Tsereteli, fearless and frank as usual, replied that having a minority in the bureau would only hinder its efficient functioning: in the EC its constant opposition and arguments on points of principle regarding every practical question didn't change anything but only brought work to a standstill. For the bureau we need to choose people who won't waste time splitting hairs, who can reach agreement easily and won't sacrifice our work in favor of partisan considerations. If you win over the majority in the EC, the bureau will be yours.

And there was more: they dismissed Kamenev's proposals that there should be at least one representative of each party in the bureau (so there would be one Bolshevik too). And they dismissed even more categorically the Bolsheviks' urgings to allow the EC members to be present at bureau meetings, with no voting rights and an obligation not to betray any information outside and not to use it for their own party ends.

This battle took up three days in a row, three whole sessions.

The Bolsheviks (eternal democrats) demanded that this bureau be presented to a plenary session of the Soviet for ratification—this was also refused.

In accordance with the new concept, the Liaison Commission would be abolished and negotiations with the government would now be handled by the bureau. This meant that the arrant extremist Himmer-Sukhanov, who, beforehand, had not wanted to join the bureau and be in proud isolation, was now excluded. But Steklov too, as if he had anticipated the same outcome, challenged the abolition of the Liaison Commission. One would have thought he had nothing to fear: as editor of *Izvestia* he should have been in the bureau. But the previous few days had seen the scandalous revelation of his petition as a loyal subject of the Sovereign to change his surname, Nakhamkes. And then Shulgin's article had turned up the heat. And now Tsereteli concluded that:

"For very particular reasons, the presidium group considers it impossible now to promote Comrade Steklov to this responsible post . . ."

Everyone understood why: the EC bureau did not want to compromise itself and become the target of acrimonious attacks. It was quite understandable, but Tsereteli had expressed it undiplomatically, too openly.

"But *what* reason?" demanded Himmer, incandescent, followed by Nakhamkes himself.

And Tsereteli had to explain the whole thing, aloud. Even then, it could still have been smoothed over, if the change hadn't been from a Jewish to a Russian surname. Tsereteli had not had anything anti-Jewish in mind, but the opposition immediately interpreted it as an anti-Semitic attack.

There was a great uproar. People rose in turn to speak, and then started shouting all at the same time that it was outrageous, shameful, an intolerable thing to do, nothing could top it! It was a total betrayal of the revolution, it was worse than Lenin traveling through Germany. Steklov insisted that it was a personal matter and had nothing to do with his public life. He referred to precedents: how many well-known European figures had also changed their Jewish names and chosen for themselves any name they wanted. It was a mere formality that the request had had to be addressed to the Tsar, but it never actually reached the Tsar himself, and there was no political motivation behind it. It could not besmirch twenty-eight years of revolutionary activity.

The noise, the fury, the quivering indignation were indescribable. Many were at a loss. The presidium announced that it considered it impossible to conduct a session to cries of "shame on you," and left. After the tall Tsereteli went little, old, adoring Chkheidze, and after them the sturdy, ever-cheerful Skobelev. (By now they regretted embarking on that trifling matter of the surname—they should never have touched it.)

The opportunists descended into disarray, even panic, and would have suffered a defeat if one of the deputies, a simple man from the Soldiers' section (a musician) had not made a fervent appeal to the old revolutionaries, our leaders and role models, to call an end to this quarrelling because we, the young people, are lost and don't know who to believe. And most of the delegates came to their senses. Dan proposed a motion of confidence in the presidium. The majority voted for, and the presidium members were informed of this and returned to the platform.

The bureau membership could not be finalized that day: there was yet another heated session on it, with stormy breaks in which the majority and minority went off for deliberations at opposite ends of the Tauride Palace, and the minority all ended up with the Bolsheviks, with Kamenev as chairman. Despite what had happened, some of the left turned their backs on

Steklov and crossed over to the majority. Toward the end of the session, they *invited* individual representatives of the minority to join the bureau, and they stepped up one by one to deliver a pointed refusal. Only Himmer, despairing of those Bolsheviks, eternal masters of the boycott, joined the bureau alone.

But even then the bureau didn't turn out the way it was supposed to and did not take the place of the EC, which continued to meet almost every day.

Still, in the course of those three stormy sessions a moment was found, when creating the sections, for a formal proposal that had developed out of a recent joke: to establish under the bureau its own counter-espionage section.

After much thought, the proposal was rejected.

[22]

(THE RULE OF THE PEOPLE IN THE COUNTRYSIDE: FRAGMENTS)

* * *

A village street deep in mud, it's raining, and not even the dogs are about. Fixed to the church railings is a notice, soaking wet, peeling off, from the Socialist Revolutionaries. The villagers are all in the school, they went to listen to the " 'lucionery."

He explains things like this: the main thing is to get rid of the rich landowners! You'll all get more land and there'll be plenty of bread. And in no time at all, you'll get an extra cow.

* * *

At a different meeting an SR came to a village and explained it differently: first they'll take everyone's land away, and then they'll give you all land for your own use. And a great row kicked off:

"If they do it your way we'll have a war in every village. I'll take my pitchfork to any drunk as thinks he's gonna take mine away! You pay me for my land first, then you can take it away. It's my sweat's watered that land!"

"That 'lution, that weren't cooked up so they could pick on ordinary folks!"

* * *

All they ask of people turning up in their villages is: make things a bit cheaper. Get the government to put reas'nable prices on metal, fabric, leather, paraffin, and stop the middle men from jacking up prices. And ask the government to check deferments that people in the fact'ries got—who's hidin' away there.

At other village meetings they proposed that someone should inventory all the grain, so that no one can hide so much as a single kernel. And make a list. And contribute grain and money to the new government, God bless 'em. And make boots and send them to the army for free.

* * *

And at their meetings they decide that: till we know the lay of the land no outsiders chopping wood in our forests. No more firewood for the city. No selling woodlots to anyone: it'll only go to outsiders.

In Petrograd province they don't allow any felling of timber at all—neither for heating the capital nor for the military.

But they've started chopping wood in the neighborhood for themselves, sometimes in the landowners' forests, sometimes the state's. Peasants from Serga township, in Perm province, have taken things into their own hands and started felling the Golitsyn family's timber, disarmed the forest guard, and sent their office staff packing. And peasants have also started felling the landowner's timber in Khvalynsk district.

And in Mozyr district they've started burning forests—because they belong to landowners.

* * *

Two villages in Khiletsk township, near Belozyorsk, demanded ten thousand rubles to permit a log drive for the Northern Railway on the river passing their villages. While they haggled with the lumbermen the water level suddenly dropped and the logs were left high and dry.

* * *

Peasants in many areas willingly took grain for the army—took it to the station, that is, not to the nearest city. But at the stations everything was in chaos and they didn't want to take the grain, there were no goods wagons, and they piled it all up under the open sky. Now the heaps grow and the grain rots. And the peasants can see it.

* * *

At some meetings, such as in Odoev district, Tula province, the resolutions were that from spring onwards, no landowners are to work the land. And inherited lands are to be confiscated outright, but purchased land is not to be touched. And zemstvo dues are no longer to be paid: it was the old regime that set the zemstvos up.

Soldiers would arrive, outsiders, just passing through, and the main thing they kept on about was: there ain't no laws no more, now we'll have laws the peasants'll fix for theirselves.

There seem to be a lot of them traveling round the place, all on leave.

* * *

For the whole of Easter week, people sat on the ledges round their houses, discussing the new law: seems like all the workers in the cities won't have to work no more. And we're gonna choose our own guv'nor.

The youngsters played cards all week.

* * *

Back in March they'd decided that: when it's time to start ploughing, we'll collar the landowners' lands, and then they can come talk to us about it.

"The time's come now, lads, that we got all the rights and the gentry got none. It's good times for us now!"

In Ryazhsk district, in Knyagininskoye: we'll do everything by the book. We won't touch the landowners. We'll just chase their workers away and take their cattle. Then they'll decide to clear off for theirselves.

In Elizavetgrad province the terrified landowners don't even sow their crops.

* * *

What were the organs of authority now? People everywhere were choosing their own now: people's power committees, public safety committees, provisional, executive, or administrative committees—whatever they were told to call them. They didn't usually choose schoolteachers for the committees: "teachers don't plough the land" and don't know our work, they go round in galoshes, they go their own way. But in some townships it was different, they did elect them, and priests too, and cooperative members, and the bosses of forestry businesses. But then city people started arriving and telling the committees to get rid of them, and to chuck out the individual farmers, too, and only keep the really poor peasant firebrands.

And in two shakes of a lamb's tail: we've naught but loudmouths and troublemakers on those c'mittees. And how can we get rid of 'em? We can't do a thing—or they might set light to the village. (And instead of our village constables we have their militia—another gang o' ruffians.) What can the committee do? Well everything: they make their own laws and they're the arm of the law. We plonked those bosses on top of us and now they've started arresting their own lot. That's the way it is.

* * *

The peasants of villages adjoining Krizhski monastery, near Sumy, took over the monastery lands and forests and put their cattle on them. And made the monks go out to work the communal lands.

* * *

In some of the provincial capitals they contrived, despite the near-impassability of roads in the spring, to convene peasants' congresses. Once there, they elected whoever they could—out of those who'd managed the journey—and then in each from the city members of cooperatives, zemstvos, the Union of Towns, and the Soviet of Workers' Deputies were added. The Minsk congress passed a resolution stipulating: no forcible assertion of rights to land before the Constituent Assembly, but landowners must not raise land rents or cut down their forests; all the land, including the peasants' allotments, will now become state property. At the Yaroslavl congress: we must continue the war until our liberty, equality, and fraternity are completely secure and German imperialism is crushed. At Voronezh it was: the war must be stopped as soon as possible, but without indemnities or seizure of territories, and for the time being we must stand firm, an indestructible barrier; the landowners must be stripped of their land with no compensation, but not before the Constituent Assembly; and we must ban the allotment of plots of communal land to individuals. At Kharkov: we must annul the Stolypin law allowing communal land to be parceled out. At Saratov (adhering to the SR program): private ownership of land in the Russian Republic is abolished forever; everyone is entitled only to land that can be worked with one's own hands following an established labor standard. At Samara: no one has any right to land except the man who works it; if a landowner does not sow crops this spring, his land and equipment will be given to the peasants of the township. At the Kherson congress the grain-growers were doubtful: even if all the land in Russia is handed over to provide for those without any land, will it be enough? The SR journalist Zak assured the congress that "there will be enough land for all, I did the calculation myself." The Chernigov congress accepted the whole SR program. At Tambov it was not just "Land and freedom" but "*All* the land and *unlimited* freedom." And at Tomsk they even ratified a constitution for the future Russia.

* * *

What'll happen now? The Tsar's been overthrown, so who will be the master? There's no way to know. Some sort o' K's and D's and S's and R's—where'd they all come from anyway?

And then these "Mensheviks," that means they're little guys.

No they ain't. They stand up for the little guys, for us.

* * *

The peasants were flummoxed by all these "parties": who can we believe? We're all in the dark . . . What're they all trying to do? Which one are we supposed to join? Then Vanya Nazhivin—a local lad—arrived from Moscow, educated now, and they asked him to explain.

"Which did you sign up with, then?"

"None of them."

"Well that takes the cake!"

And he started explaining each of the parties, what each was proclaiming, and what they were after.

"That's nothing to do with us. Tell us the important stuff."

"That's what I am telling you."

"No. What about the state forestland? Are we gonna get it?"

"But brothers—why should that land be yours? There are thirty thousand acres of building-quality pines over there. That's worth 50 million."

"Because it's next door to us."

"And what about the villages on the other side of the Klyazma? They don't have any forests there."

"That's their problem. Perhaps they have some treasure buried there. It's the luck of the draw. Long as they don't poke their noses in over here."

Nazhivin finished his explanation, saying the forest was remaining with the state.

"Ah. . . . Then what the devil is this whole rigmarole for?"

(From Nazhivin's writings)

* * *

With impassable roads, the villages are like little islands: some of them can't be reached even on foot. Yet deserters swarm in, and outsiders turn up, and everyone's yelling that we've got to parcel out the land now and chop the wood, ransack the estates, and loot the cooperative shops.

They explain it this way: "everything's yours now."

"That's right lads, we gotta knock the shopkeepers about. Now we got our liverty they gotta stop linin' their pockets."

In Simbirsk province, in the villages of Ubei and Tarkhany, many shops have been smashed and pillaged.

The disturbances nearly always begin with the arrival of deserters: guards are sent packing, timber cut, estates sacked. Armed deserters lead men of their own home village into the attack. In the district of Morshansk, in Tambov province, they've started ploughing the landowners' lands, including those of the provincial commissar, Yuri Vasilievich Davydov.

* * *

In Nizhni Novgorod province there has long been a deep-seated enmity between the peasants and the landowners. But even so, it's less marked now than in '05: the landowners' horses are no longer having their tongues cut out or their bellies ripped open. Of course, the age group that likes to fight is away at the front.

In Lukoyanov district, peasants have ransacked Filosofov's estate.

* * *

They even, when the landowner has already done the spring ploughing and his fields are ready to sow, take away his work force and the prisoners of war he employs (for no one would dare take the job against the will of the village assembly), and once he's failed to sow the crops: we'll do the sowing for our own benefit. (And they take away his cook too. Or else you better pay her more.)

And so, having got rid of his work force, they themselves fix either a low land rent or three times the usual daily wages, and only then will they start work.

In Tambov province they've started demanding that landowners sign a document renouncing any claim to their own land. Or else we'll arrest you.

In the Serdobsk district of Saratov province they made the landowners sign a similar document. And in Temnikov district too.

Many landowners in various provinces have taken to their heels and left their estates.

* * *

"Well, lads, let's hope they won't diddle us!"

"Diddle us? But you just help yourself. It's clear as day."

"Nut'n clear about it. We gotta look into it very careful. Now we ain't got no masters we gotta look out for ourselves, les' bad things happen."

"What we gotta look out for? It's all gonna be fair now: all the Russian land'll be shared out so it don't belong to no one."

* * *

The loudmouths are good at yelling, but what the peasants want is someone to explain: how will justice be done now? What will the village headman do? How will trade proceed? Who will look after the roads and bridges?

"While you're talking about one thing we can grasp it proper. But once you start talking about something else we lose the thread of that first thing. Us old peasants' can't follow it all."

"Look 'ere: 'universal, direct, equal, secret.'. . . Secret! But they're telling us straight: they're gonna press us all—only it'll be equal. We're never gonna get out from under it . . .

They say to arrange something called "arbitration chambers" between the peasants and the landowners.

"What's to arbitrate? Just take the land and sow it!"

"Sowshallism means they'll parcel out all the property and money and we'll get twenty thousand each."

"And those bourgies—who're they?"

"They're the ones that run the exchange."

"The timber exchange?"

* * *

In Gorbatov district, in Nizhni Novgorod province, some peasants came eighteen versts to see the steward:

"Give us the keys to the granary. You got grain there, and we got none left."

"I can't give you the keys, it ain't mine, that grain. You want it, you break the door down yourselves."

"What law says we can break doors down? We can't do that of our own accord."

And they went back to pestering him for the keys. He wouldn't budge.

Then one peasant yelled:

"Burn the gran'ry, lads! If we can't get it, they're not 'avin' it."

And they burned it. That grain went up smart-like.

But bread's sacred . . .

That peasant came to his senses:

"Tie me up, lads. It's all my fault."

But they wouldn't tie him up.

Then the guilty man trudged over to the new district committee. They said:

"You did wrong, yes. But these days we've got too many cases even without you. You go off home."

The guilty man thought and thought—and walked all the way to Nizhni Novgorod to have himself tried by the deputies there.

But he didn't find judgment there either.

* * *

Peasants started refusing to do their compulsory postal duty, and wouldn't take the mail round: what good is mail to us?

There were some places where they even threatened the post office managers: you gotta shut up shop!

In Penza province the peasants stopped fulfilling all the obligations they'd previously agreed to.

* * *

In Ryazan province it was mostly calm. But in Rannenburg district they really raised hell. (In this district some landowners had ruined their crops by not harvesting them. A peasant can't stomach the sight of that.) At landowner Oznobishina's place they parceled out all the land and started sowing. And they took twenty-seven horses away, paying her a seventh or eighth of their value. Landowner Vyacheslova was ordered to do the springtime sowing in three days, and three days later they seized the entire Trubetskoy estate.

Whole mobs of peasants took as their leader an old madman, "Polevoy, the playwright." (Before this, editors who refused to publish his articles would get a "death sentence" in a letter card from him.)

* * *

And how about a look at the nearby farmstead folk? At their assemblies they started passing resolutions to give their land lots "back to the commune." And not to let anyone go back to those lots from now on.

In the village of Udy, in Kharkov district, lot-holders agreed to go back to communal use of the land, if they were allowed to take in the winter harvest, sow the land already ploughed, and harvest the crop sown in spring. The commune said no.

In two districts of Nizhni Novgorod province fights broke out between commune members and lot-holders. In Semyonovsk district, in the village of Zakharovo, the commune members threw out the lot-holders, divided up their plots between them, and ploughed them.

* * *

After Bright Week, on 23 April, in the village of Stepnoi Kuchuk in Barnaul district they arrested five people suspected of robbery (but not caught in the act). They punched their eyes and teeth out and hung them from the ceiling and then let them fall. That went on for two days. They pronounced one of them innocent and the other four were taken to the township authorities.

In neighboring villages, soldiers returning from the front were gouging out robbers' eyes with wood splinters, smashing in their skulls with hammers, and cutting them into pieces. Children said farewell to fragments of their father amid a rabid crowd.

* * *

Then rumors started leaking in about a *monopoly*, but not of vodka, like before the war. It seemed the government itself was going to take our grain for half its value, and if anyone didn't give it willingly they'd take it and pay nothing at all.

The peasants were highly indignant. We don't trust our edicated people round here no more: they're tellin' us a load o' lies. And some of the peasants went to public meetings in town—people in town had been swindled too.

And as for the usual instructions from above—there were none of those.

* * *

A mad felling spree also began in the timber farms and people were grazing cattle there and killing the birds and beasts. **Everything's yours now!**

In Saratov province they took possession of a trial field of eighty acres and parceled it out.

In Ryazan province requisitions came for cattle to be slaughtered for the army. So instead of their own cattle the peasants handed over the landowners' pedigree specimens, without so much as a second thought.

* * *

But even so, if you cast your eye over the whole, immense expanse of Russian peasantry, there was still not very much unrest. It was rare for them to take over an entire township, and as for districts, Rannenburg was the only one. And many country areas were completely peaceful.

In many villages deserters were not welcome, so they went back to the front. Speakers would arrive and be listened to in silent contempt. And landowners were still respected.

* * *

Many peasants are dissatisfied, morose, and trust no one, seeing only deceit all around.

"So long as we got bosses we won't get liverty. We got rid of one lot, elected a new one, and soon they'll get fat and be just like the others."

"We've elected all kind o' bastards who'll hang round our necks. Before, we just had a headman and a clerk and they managed to do everything."

In the towns there's bourgies and factory workers too: they've fixed theirselves an eight-hour day, and they're fleecing the bosses and the people too. And us peasants have to break our backs working all day for those bastards.

* * *

Commotion in the countryside: Petersburg has said that 18 April is to become 1 May now. Where have those thirteen days gone then? And the saints whose memory falls on those days, do we just leave them out? How can we do that? In the almanac first May's a Monday, but the new one's a Tuesday. How will they fix that?

They say there's a new saint, and today's his day. Only they don't know whether to light an icon-lamp for him.

And there's a rumor: "Now Sundays will be every other week." "On the weeks in between—what comes after Saturday?"

* * *

Some outsider came to a village meeting:

"Now everyone'll be citizens, and we'll have civil marriages. No church weddings."

The women got all flustered:

"Civvy marriages? Silly marriages . . .? Filly . . .?"

"Does that mean whatever one you want, you take her, live with her as long as you want her, and when you're fed up, you chuck her out? What do you do with the kids?"

"Oh no, lads! With all the other stuff you can do as you please—but we're not turning our back on the Lord."

* * *

Comrades! Explain to the population, never tire of telling them, that it is absolutely necessary to put all their efforts into seeding the fields in time and to keep the agricultural equipment safe.

(Union of Employees of the Ministry of Agriculture)

* * *

[23]

So now simplicity and truth had disappeared from the relationship. In its place was convention.

Falsehood, even.

On his way home for lunch, or for the night, he could never predict Alina's mood when she met him. It was changeable, jagged as a saw-blade, and it changed two or three times a day: after a light-hearted interlude it would darken, brighten again, then darken. She hadn't been like this before. But he had to pretend he hadn't noticed, and not get irritated. Little by little it would smooth down. Before, in earlier times, they'd enjoyed a natural, easygoing, cheerful relationship, and a kind of ritual in the way they talked to each other, in their gestures, their kisses—so now too he must try to hold on to whatever remained of that, as if nothing was wrong. And those pet names he'd had for her—he must use them now, as well. That would be far more bearable than launching into any possible explanations. And if the custom was for Alina to extend both hands for kisses, to receive her husband's admiration and gratitude—and now she did sometimes extend them that way again—then he must not, out of embarrassment, out of courtesy, allow her to feel how tense he was, must not shrink from taking those hands and kissing them.

Whether in the dark moments or the brighter ones, it was all the same: he pitied her! He must do all he could to look after her and defer to her wishes as much as possible. She would reproach him: you have nasty aspects to your character! You clam up, you're so gloomy, you're impossible to live with! Georgi didn't argue: fine, I'll watch that. Indeed, who can really see everything about himself? Deferring to her was always worth it in the long run. Of course he would be deemed gloomy now. Anything to avoid arguing about it.

All in all, their life now was bearable. Only in the evenings did it become oppressive. If only there were no nights.

Every hour he spent at home reined him in and hobbled his progress. He must not lose any time! There were constant developments. He must do something!

But he could still not work out **what** to do. And with whom?

He would have liked to devote his energy to operational work. But that had tailed off completely. Officially they were supposed to be planning a possible attack on the Southwestern front, either in May or perhaps later. But no one had any faith in the plan and no one was taking it seriously or hurrying with it. No one was working on a response to a possible German attack either. Which in fact they were not expecting, anyway. Everything had melted away, nothing was clear. They were only totting up the figures for supplies, which arrived irregularly, and for extra manpower, which never arrived. Anyway, it was others doing that work, not Vorotyntsev.

However, there were several wall cabinets in his office, crammed full of the most important operational documents going back as far as '14. And seeing no other useful way to employ himself, on the very first evening after his arrival—and then every night when he was on duty and later, unembarrassed, during the days too, which had become so empty—Vorotyntsev threw himself into a tormented study of the secret history of past campaigns. The history he'd not been able to find out, or even guess at, from the regiment.

And all that war fired him up again now. He drank it all in, passionately, losing touch with reality, as if it were still possible to intervene. As if it were up to him to save something.

The war had been started on two independent fronts, as though in two separate wars, one against Austria and one against Germany. The dynamic campaign of '14 was also notable for the extreme stupidity on our side. As if we were intentionally confirming the low opinion the Germans already had of Russians. We made no use of our successes in Galicia to further our overall aims. Why did we dig into Austria like that, and with such a massive force? We were facing the Carpathians, wedged up absurdly tightly, with several armies squeezed together. Who was behind this maneuver? Was it Iudovich Ivanov, with Alekseev, or the obtuse Danilov from GHQ? It became clear now, from reading their correspondence: they were all in it together. The senseless compression of a front of four armies up against mountains. And what happened then could easily have been foreseen: there were insufficient troops in the Polish sector. And from that most inconvenient, elongated placing of troops, in September they were supposed to execute, with three armies, a massive lateral troop movement to the north, some even having to cross foothills, toward Warsaw. And on the San a sudden flood due to heavy rain severed bridges and we of course had not made provision for the use of lateral routes, either road or rail. Many corps made the whole journey, more than two hundred versts, on foot. But the roadways sometimes turned out to be log roads laid over bogs, which the Austrians had already used twice, and there'd been no time to repair them, and then there was more rain. And even the main roads were in ruts and the Russian columns were sinking into the mud, and the carts would get stuck at every step, to say nothing of the artillery. And we'd have to harness a dozen horses to each cannon—we killed them.

And where was the great plan in all this? Nothing but a great commotion. Vorotyntsev saw it now, in what he read. They could not reach Warsaw in time, and that carefree Sheideman—who'd taken over the 2nd Army after Samsonov—had surrendered the line of forts surrounding Warsaw without a fight. Then GHQ thought up a diversion, an attack from across the Vistula by the Southwestern army group. We built bridges, with great difficulty during the flood season, and then having failed at the first stage of the attack we destroyed those bridges ourselves.

He couldn't decide what, in this overview, sickened him more now: the hasty, yet nearly always tardy, instructions from GHQ or the panicky dispatches from that dummy Ivanov and his incessant calls for help, his constant failure to be ready by the appointed time, his total inadequacy over that whole autumn of battles. And then the Germans faltered, but the Austrians showed they were far from beaten. (After all, Ruzsky had let them go, unscathed, from near Lvov, and for that he'd been promoted to commander-in-chief of the army group.) And then, having barely completed our lateral move to the right in September, we sent many of those same corps, in response to Ivanov's yammering, on a lateral move to the left in October! Our armies were never in the right place. (Luckily the 12th Corps, which included Vorotyntsev's regiment, had remained on the left, in the 8th Army, and had not taken part in these lateral troop movements.)

And the Germans did not just falter, that October, but even started retreating from the Ivangorod area. But what a retreat it was! It was very orderly, and they managed to damage, irremediably, railway lines, roads, bridges, viaducts, and one in every three sections of railway track. They pulled down telegraph poles and even smashed the insulators and cut the wires. And GHQ had claimed this development as "our successful Ivangorod operation."

That autumn, the French had been the first to discover they did not have enough shells. And they came to a standstill, saying Russia must advance on the left bank of the Vistula, as if we did have enough shells . . . And we, of course, advanced, and on a broad front with ninety divisions, from the Bzura to Sandomir, and encountered little resistance. And now, with this bulge we had exposed our flank on the right to a concentration of German troops coming in from their own territory, from Thorn. We had, in effect, made the sleeve of East Prussia, which already hung over us, even longer. So could we expect an attack from the right? But Ruzsky not only was not expecting it, he even assured GHQ that the Germans were not gathering there, on our right. However, our friend Mackensen had in fact, via a dense and rapid network of German roads, assembled there six infantry corps and six cavalry divisions. Then he crushed the long-suffering 23rd Corps (which was well known to Vorotyntsev, being the corps in which he had rallied the men of the Estland Regiment in August to cover Neidenburg), and penetrated between the overstretched Rennenkampf and Sheideman lines, between the Vistula and the Warta, while those two commanders looked idly on. And he advanced that way for five whole days, while Ruzsky, his flank facing Mackensen, nonchalantly led his three armies westwards! And in five days he awoke to the fact that the Germans were already closing in on Lodz.

No! Vorotyntsev simply could not understand: if you're a commander or a commander-in-chief or a supreme commander, and you know your duty—which means you conduct reconnaissance and keep a constant eye on the map—how can you fail to foresee something like that? And not even see it when it's already happening? It was impossible to read the dispatches of those five days and not seethe with rage. What had, in the tumult of that November, with its wind and frosts with no snow for a cushion, seemed to the men executing the orders to be an incomprehensible vortex, now lay silently concealed in old documents, revealing the rancid incompetence of several generals. In the darkness of that November, no mere regimental commander could, despite everything, have imagined such a massive blunder on the part of his superiors: and he'd have had no free time to wonder about it, so busy was he trying to dig his men in, preserve their lives, and feed them. And it was quite beyond the wit of the commanders, judiciously settled in distant HQs, to imagine those battles in the autumn mud.

Pathetic GHQ! It was finding out so little, so late, had so little influence. Even Elizabeth, via mounted couriers from Petersburg, had given her weak field marshals on the Oder more intelligent and timely tactical advice. But

Nikolai Nikolaevich had such a spectacularly imposing appearance (along with Yanushkevich hanging on to Black Danilov's every word), and the Tsar was so magnanimous, so indulgent toward all his worthless senior officers. And how could it be that throughout the Great War, in the great Russian army, no real Supreme Commander had ever emerged, only puppets of the uncle or the nephew?

And that same Mackensen had again outflanked the ill-fated 2nd Army in the environs of Lodz, from the same side, the east and the south. And again that same Rennenkampf hadn't come to the rescue from the east in time: he was trailing along a few dozen versts behind. But it turned out, as Vorotyntsev now read, that in the very midst of the "layer cake" of armies that had formed near Lodz, Ruzsky had lost contact with the army and GHQ too was prepared for a general retreat. Only this time Pavel Adamovich Pleve (since deceased) was, with his 5th Army, also caught in this trap. This general, so short of stature, so ugly, so confident, so calm, he not only saved his own army but also rescued the 2nd, and would even have had the Germans surrounded, had Ruzsky's support not been so delayed.

Vorotyntsev had heard about those battles directly from Kostya Popov, who'd been a second lieutenant there and, later, in Vorotyntsev's own regiment. They'd been allocated a section on the Bzura, he said, near Brokhov. The area was as flat as a tabletop, and they'd been ordered to go on the attack from a thousand paces, avoiding two small marshes just before the German trenches. But in the exchange of fire the Germans lobbed ten shells for every one of ours. (At that time, after all, we faced harsher punishment for wasting shells than for losing men.) All the regimental commander could do was to put off our attacks till night, the deep, black autumn night, and send out two battalions (with him in one of them) to several lines. To make things worse, fog had set in and there was a covering of wet snow. Until that night, illumination rockets had been rarely used by the Germans, and our men had not even known of such wonders. But suddenly the Germans started sending up rocket after rocket, which picked out the advancing lines in the fog and snow. And bright darts from machine guns were raining down all round and the German trenches were shown up by flashes of gunfire. They were close now, but it was impossible to reach them. Some of the men were cut down, others threw themselves to the ground. The German fire was incessant, long-lasting, and very low, so that not only did our boys have to retreat, crawling, almost flat on the snow and mud, but at first even do it backwards, because they could not risk turning round as they crawled and exposing themselves for even a minute as a more prominent target. Popov was already lying right under a German machine gun, "like getting your head shaved with a blunt razor," and then crawled all the way back, across a whole field. The line in front of him, fifty or so men, were, as he watched, already rushing for the trench. And, illuminated by rockets, all fifty, to a man, were mown down in an instant; but with their bodies they shielded the second line. After that, all night they came crawling, one by one, across the field, and the whole field was shouting, wailing, "Help, brothers! Save me! Don't leave me!" And sobbing. But they couldn't even think about going to bring them in. And the snow continued to fall and covered them where they lay, like a shroud. Then it was day, and again they couldn't bring them back. Only during the following nights could they drag them into a mass grave.

And all **that** blood now—were we going to trample it in ourselves? Pour it out under pigs' trotters?

My God! What was going on? We had lost our minds.

And how many of these lost episodes, like that on the Bzura, took place during those years? How many such sectors? How many such regiments? Like when we occupied trenches after the Siberians, and on just a two-hundred-pace section of front, manned by a single company, we picked up their ninety corpses. When, digging a connecting trench, thinking it was a new position, we dug up bodies of either Germans or our own boys. When the German fire was such that a shell-hole embedded itself into another, and there was no point going by the usual calculation and hiding in there. It was that idea that had been drummed into us all, that we must hold the line *at all costs*, instead of combining firing with retreating and counter-attacking. Because we were frightened of losing a line, we just sat in bogs and pits and the enemy always took the best positions. Like when a battalion pulled itself out of a bog and made for the German ridge, so that the German barbed wire became its protection. And when, in March, the ground was still frozen and the lines couldn't dig in, the men would press close to the ground, like children to their mothers. But at midday the top layer would thaw and their greatcoats would be soaked. And by evening it would freeze again and the greatcoats become a muddy incrustation and injured men, in their death throes, would be encased in sludge.

And how much of that emanated back to GHQ? To the Supreme Commander?

And then there was the ill-fated expedition across the Carpathians, just before spring—a crazy plan dreamed up by Iudovich and Alekseev, with Nikolai Nikolaevich's approval, of course. Even from his regimental position in the trenches, Vorotyntsev was horrified. Now he read that, yes, the goal was to take Budapest and then Vienna. Now he could also read the sage advice of Joffre: in the mountains the Russians would need fewer shells . . .

Immediately after that came the bungle that allowed Mackensen to break through near Gorlitsa in May '15. It turned out, of course, that ever since March there had been reports from the front line of signs of preparation for a breakthrough: Austrian units had been supplemented with German ones, and we knew the numbers of those divisions, as well as that the German Guards were joining, with heavy artillery and several fleets of aircraft. And there were indications from Austrian defectors that the attack would be in late April. But at Radko's 3rd Army HQ, they didn't want to believe any of this, and the Army Group HQ was even calmer about it, certain that all the major action would be based on the Carpathians—and on our side we had done nothing at all to reinforce the sector. The Germans had managed to build a five-fold advantage in artillery, while our men had not even been given an instruction to remain in reserve positions in the event of artillery shelling.

And following that breakthrough came the Great Retreat on two fronts over a period of four months, with a norm per day of eight shells per artillery piece, and even fewer later on. It was a rare occurrence for any line to be held for two consecutive days. Otherwise, there was a battle every day, with a telling inequality of fire power, and a retreat every evening and a sleepless night. Each regiment had eight machine guns and not even enough rifles or cartridges. Sometimes we set up a defensive position, but somewhere, a little distance away, the invisible enemy would outflank us and we would be ordered to retreat. At other times we had no means of defense and would leave of our own accord. And so it went, endlessly. There were no fresh units to reinforce us, and sometimes there were not even any soldiers to carry the machine guns and the officers had to drag them. They were all so exhausted already, and the officers dreamed of sustaining a light injury and getting some rest.

And were we supposed to forget all that now, as if it had never happened? And forget all those comrades from the regiment?

Far afield—he was seeing it now in those reports —we'd sent four divisions to their deaths in the Novogeorgievsk mousetrap (all this to assuage public opinion, which was concerned that our strongholds were falling too easily). Even farther afield, we failed to support the Riga-Shavli sector and the Germans spilled in, all over Kurland, and could already, in '15, threaten Petrograd. And the lack of action by the Baltic Fleet . . . We always wanted to save it for something! (Having stagnated,it now dealt its blow—for the revolution.)

And how about '16, the Guards? In the army, everyone was saying that General Bezobrazov had sacrificed them all in the Stokhod marshes. But now, according to these documents, Vorotyntsev saw that Bezobrazov could not have stopped it: it was Brusilov's order, this irrational, nonsensical attack on Kovel, from the south, of all places—and on top of that, it was all to be taken care of in five days! It was Brusilov's order—but GHQ had approved it! For Brusilov it was a matter of completing the picture of his offensive. But what use was that Kovel for us? And did the throne really need to pamper the Guards for centuries if it was going to drown them for no good reason in the Stokhod marshes?

And the soldiers, those men who, in '14, had rushed to sign up within twenty-four hours and skipped the physical examination ("Fully fit, sir!")—those men knew nothing of how they were being led for those three years.

But throughout the whole series of blunder and disgrace they had a right to be angry!

They had that right, but even now they still had no inkling. All they felt was rage against imagined traitors, who were usually people with German names. And a blind hatred of the military salute and the officers' epaulettes.

On reflection, the astounding thing was not their current lack of discipline—which was being encouraged by Petrograd—but the confidence they still had in their new leaders, in the Provisional Government.

But this inert government failed to muster, direct, or make use of the force of the front against the Soviet gang on the home front (just as they had missed the massive turnaround on the part of the soldiers in early April). This strange government did not seem to know what it actually wanted. It had insulted our fighting men by rushing to issue a special decree exempting from criminal liability the "armchair hussars" from the Zemgor —some of whom had been involved in bribery and fraud during the war. Did that mean they were simply saving the skins of their like? Then, just four days ago, there'd been another decree: the deadline for deserters to present themselves was extended by five weeks—till 28 May!

Then why insist on continuing the war until final victory—"only by victory can we consolidate the new order"—and giving this kind of instruction to GHQ while, at the same time, themselves destroying the army? And what kind of naivety was this, constantly repeating that the ardor for combat would only increase thanks to the revolution? Did they really believe it? Because we had replaced "for Russia" with "for the revolution" . . .?

And that two-week Easter fraternization, the expression of the soldiers' true feelings, had immediately shown the arbitrary nature of the concept of "enemy," and the arbitrary nature of this war. The soldier was always looking forward to one thing, *making peace*, and never thought of borders, of changing regimes or politicians. A just yearning for peace to be concluded. And they were still waiting for the Provisional Government to conclude it. Peace. Nothing else.

Meanwhile Leonid Andreev churned out his article "It is not the war that has wearied us." Well of course it hasn't wearied you!

And the people's feeling was certainly right, if also blind and ignorant: if you're expanding your territory, you have to know where to draw the line, it can't go on forever, we're already spread wide and it's already hard to hold on to it. All of that "Pan-Slav mission" in the Balkans, Constantinople—it was all foolish nonsense. The Allies knew what they wanted out of this war. And we didn't. But even now they still weren't over-exerting themselves: the "great battle of the peoples for Soissons and Cambrai" came to nothing after a week or so.

It had already been clear last year that it was time to put an end to the war—although then we would have fought meekly to the end, given our customary obedience. But now, since the revolution, we were already in danger of a total rout.

A career soldier—and against the war? But war does not happen of its own accord. War is not an icon, not a shrine. War is only a means of keeping one's state safe. And if it's more useful to your state *not* to wage war, then you should not wage it. (But he could not say this quite as clearly to his headquarter colleagues . . .)

But an exit from the war was now more, ever more complex and dangerous than before. Before, we could have held the front securely and negotiated from a position of strength. But who would pay any attention to us now? Just a little push and we'd be down.

You could understand why the Germans weren't touching us now. But they wouldn't just contemplate our collapse for long: they'd come and take as much of the country as they wanted. To hold in reserve, for later bargaining. They really hit us hard on the Stokhod. Why not somewhere else?

It wouldn't be for some distant victory that we'd have to hold the front with our last ounce of strength, but so that we could exit the war without giving away any territory. Only, we couldn't *hold* it without some flexible offensives. But the soldiers were dead set against *advancing*! Not a step! We're off to enjoy that liverty! Come on, Vanya, let's parcel out the land!

We would have to simultaneously get out of both the war and the revolution. Some sort of extremely complex combined retreat.

And *who* could do that? Who has that strength, that capability?

But the greatest strategic challenges are those of getting out of a hopeless situation.

If that government won't dare disband the Soviet of Deputies, and together with the Soviet destroys the Army, then they must be got rid of together. There's no other option.

A good few officers would join, as long as the nucleus of the movement is created first. A strong alliance of military men.

But it must be created secretly. That'll be hard.

Who'd do it? Who would lead it?

Alekseev? No. No, he'd never dare.

Gurko! That is who could lead it, for sure! He's incisive, quick-witted, and he's tough!

Time to go and see him. And make the proposal, openly.

[24]

When the newspapers reappeared after the coup, General Gurko began to doubt the mental faculties of our English and French Allies. The Germans and Austrians were rejoicing over the Russian coup—and that was understandable—but so were the English and French. Why were they rejoicing? Were they in their right minds? Surely both sides in this war couldn't gain the advantage from one and the same event? One of them was making a grievous error. And once they realized what a parlous state we were in, the Allies (Gurko had formed his opinion of them from the Petrograd conference that winter) would feel free of their commitments to us and would even conclude a separate peace. And at our expense, since the Germans were not looking for acquisitions in the West: they would be perfectly happy with our lands.

Although Gurko had, from the very first minute of the Tsar's abdication, sensed in every fiber of his being that *all was lost*, he did not of course allow himself or his generals to lose heart and give up. That surge of "army democracy" had ushered in a new kind of war, within the army itself. So we had to develop new tactics, quickly. And do our utmost to prevent a split between the officers and men. Gurko made sure that all orders to the Special Army were posted openly in every town and village. He called on the men to *take their example from the Tsar*, who had abdicated the throne rather than incite civil strife. That was a lesson to us all: anything but civil strife! And he dismissed the "rumors of an election for superiors." That would be impossible, it would lead to a total breakdown of army command: only ill-intentioned individuals or enemy agents could be spreading ideas of that kind. Nowadays there was a fashion for soldiers' assemblies dressed up in the English name "meetings." Gurko ordered his generals and officers to steer people of moderation into running these assemblies, contrive to send their own sergeants, properly instructed, or intelligent soldiers, to intervene and propel the "meetings" in the direction needed. Once, leaving the cathedral after a memorial service for the martyrs of the revolution, Gurko himself addressed a crowd of soldiers. It was a great success. The Lutsk garrison committee adopted a resolution stipulating that no decision, of any assembly, would be considered valid until it had been ratified by the Army commander.

It was possible, despite everything, to organize something.

However, General Gurko did not have long to put his Special Army into order: Lechitsky, who'd been appointed to lead the Western Army Group, resigned the position toward the end of March. And the instruction came immediately: Gurko was to take command of the Western Army Group.

Again, as at GHQ the previous November, Gurko was overtaking generals senior to him in both rank and length of service. But it did not surprise him. For some reason he had a conviction, deep down, that he was to play a prominent part in saving Russia. Perhaps all this had been moving him in that direction.

But he calculated that, judging by the dates, his appointment had been signed at GHQ by Nikolai Nikolaevich who, since then, had been relieved of his command by Prince Lvov. And his response to Alekseev had been: no, the Provisional Government must ratify it. To get things done in the current volatile situation, he needed strong support. And he had already noticed, in the way the Provisional Government did things, a tendency to evade issues and remain silent.

The appointment by the Provisional Government came nine days later—and only then did Gurko say goodbye to the Special Army and leave for Minsk, where old Smirnov, commander of the 2nd Army, was temporarily running things in Evert's place. Smirnov was a tough old fellow but not one to run on the current shaky ground.

Because of that delay, our cruel early April defeat on the Stokhod did not occur on Gurko's watch. In Lutsk he'd been close to the encounter, to the left of it, but not in command. Not in command—but it worried him terribly. First in Lutsk, from rumors circulating among the staff, and then in Minsk too, he'd grasped the whole picture. We had taken that bridgehead on the left bank of the Stokhod, by the village of Chervishche, the previous autumn. It was on a front of ten versts, five versts in depth, but rains and frosts had then prevented us from broadening it. We had approximately a corps of troops based there, no fewer than the enemy facing them. The Stokhod was an abundant river and hard to cross, with the banks marshy. It was clear that they could not remain on that bridgehead when the river was in spate. They must either widen the bridgehead or leave it and move to the right bank. In early March Gurko himself, still at HQ, had asked Evert what precautions had been taken for the spring floods, and the 3rd Army commander, Lesch, had replied—and Evert confirmed—that they had set up an artillery barrage, the bridgehead condition was considered solid, and the enemy could not count on an easy success. This turned out not to be the case—far from it. But the main thing was that the revolution had started up then, and no one was thinking of tactics: the commanders' concerns and the spotters' attention turned to this internal upheaval, and the enemy had no disturbance for a month. The Germans brought up to the front line several thousand gas cylinders, heavy artillery, and an extra infantry division. And due to the delirium and the alarms of the revolution no one on our side noticed this, Lesch included. The Germans waited for a broad spate and at sunrise on 3 April they attacked the carefree bridgehead. Heavy artillery fired on our fortified lines, while the light batteries fired gas-shells on our reserves. Our artillery, from a distant location on the other bank, could respond only within its range and was unable to shift targets, having lost contact with the spotters on the bridgehead. The Germans sent over thirteen waves of gas attacks, shrouded the southern part of the bridgehead in toxic fumes and, from the north, broke through to cut off our crossings—and there were not many crossings anyway, as some had already been destroyed, some swept away, some inundated, and our soldiers, abandoned, panic-stricken, had to wade across the bridges with water up to their knees. On Heartshape Hill our men counter-attacked and were cut down with bayonets. Toward the end of the day Lesch gave the order to retreat, but the Germans had all the crossings covered with an artillery barrage. Only night brought the Germans to a halt and our men dragged themselves off under cover of darkness. In places where the thin ice on the marshes was still holding, the German artillery had smashed the crust and the retreating men, some of them injured, were engulfed. We lost more than twenty thousand men, up to two hundred officers and up to a hundred machine guns. Three divisions were put out of action, and only about fifty men from one of them reached the right bank alive.

That battle did, of course, remain local: the Germans had no strategic aim in mind and they did not cross the Stokhod. But judging by the thoroughness of the defeat and its ferocity, that rout was ominous. The first battle of the revolution.

And straight after that Gurko went to take over the front. And on the way there he had already decided to replace Lesch straight away, as a lesson to the others and to give them an immediate feel for the mettle of their new commander-in-chief. Evert had been dozing there for a year and a half and had allowed the army group to slide.

One of the first there to present himself to Gurko was Gorbatovsky, commander of the 10th Army. He proposed one remedy for the dreadful collapse they were suffering: to assemble, swiftly, a division composed solely of officers—it could be disguised as front-line training exercises—and take it to Petrograd and disband the Soviet of Deputies. Only it must be done straight away. Right now!

Gurko thought this was a bold idea. Perhaps it was for this that fate had handed him the Western Front? That would be the best move.

But first he had to look around, get to know the situation there, the people. Let's wait a bit.

Gorbatovsky left, dismayed. And some four days later Guchkov himself relieved him of his command, over Gurko's head and without even informing him.

Gurko was furious.

And very soon afterwards Guchkov came to Minsk.

They had last seen each other in Petrograd in late February, at the time of the Allies' conference. Gurko's brother, Vladimir, had arranged a dinner and there were other prominent Duma members as well. But then, before coming to power, Guchkov had been far more boisterous, much livelier than he was now, with those great bags under his eyes, listless gaze, and slow movements. Power had done him no favors. Then, they had all been wanting and expecting support from Gurko, as the de facto Supreme Commander: now Guchkov had come as the chief. But was he capable of leading an army at war? He was good at stirring up the public to gain support on questions of defense, but what kind of war leader was he?

Gurko welcomed him now with a storm of criticism: Guchkov's whole "purge" was only attracting careerists, and those who remained were beset with uncertainty and passivity, and Gurko would not stay so much as two more days if they were going to go over his head and remove his commanders.

But Guchkov already had his list for further "rejuvenation" prepared. And Gurko had not been there long enough to get to know many of his people and whether to defend them or let them go. Guchkov even refused to let Gurko bring his favorite chief of staff over from Lutsk.

And their relationship cooled even further.

But now was not the time for arguments with the government: the soviets of deputies were a persistent thorn in their side, and they had the Minsk Soviet right here, and neither the Minister of War nor the Army Group Commander could avoid going to introduce themselves. The Soviet, which included delegates from the social organizations, was in session in the theater. The presidium (lawyers and soldiers), seated on the stage, rose to greet the generals, each member shaking hands with them, while the hall applauded. It was one Posern, a minor zemstvo employee who had untidily put on a soldier's greatcoat and got himself the job of chairing all this. And before this strange gathering Guchkov introduced Gurko as chairman of the Association for the Military Power of Russia, which had been closed down by Sukhomlinov, and Gurko introduced Guchkov as a participant in the Boer War. Then they each made a speech, saying that we must intensify our struggle with the external enemy and put an end to the Easter fraternization, which had been initiated with the approval of the German command and was sapping our strength. It was not a local phenomenon: it was no coincidence that it was happening on all the fronts.

The hall applauded and there were cries of approbation. But that foolish role was abhorrent to Gurko. And then, for some reason, Guchkov dragged him off to a nurses' assembly as well, and he had to speak there too. This was not the way to begin as a commander-in-chief.

Guchkov traveled on, with his list of rejuvenations—and Gurko was left with all the shambles around him.

In Minsk he found a situation where it was not command directing events but events manipulating command. The senior military chiefs arrived to report, resigned to the fact that soldiers' assemblies had expressed *no confidence* in them. Regiments had already, three or four times, and a division once, refused to carry out combat missions. Everything that flowed into the army from the capitals—government resolutions, newspapers—was shouting about rights, always rights, and no one mentioned duty. And the uneducated, lowest stratum of the population had been seized by the seductive idea that life in our society consisted of rights, with no obligations. The main thing was that the fear of death had been allowed to appear and blossom, while all war depends on that fear being suppressed. Now the soldiers had one idea on their mind: we won't attack! (It was very opportune for all the cowards that the "peace without annexations" slogan had turned up just then.) And the principal right was not to fight at all. Because the front was standing quiet and there were no battles, the consequences of that had not emerged immediately. But Gurko understood that army morale was maintaining a fragile balance and could crash any moment now, within two weeks. And the command had to devise completely new measures, never conceived of before in any army manual.

And Gurko began by announcing to the Western Army Group: The Commander-in-Chief declares that all illegal acts committed during the days of the revolution are pardoned, but now wartime laws are coming into force and no infringement will go unpunished. (He sounded menacing, but how could he actually do as he threatened? How could he maintain his hold?) "Men! The enemy is threatening the heart of Russia. If the route to ultimate victory lies through freedom, then the route to ultimate freedom lies through victory." Another order said the elective principle was inadmissible on the front. If elections were introduced, it would not be the commanders who would take responsibility for operations but the subordinate ranks. Try sorting that out, then.

He had the idea of summoning each of the firebrands, especially the ensigns, to present themselves to him personally at the Minsk HQ, and anyone failing to attend would be tried for non-execution of an order. Unexpectedly, it worked! There was not one case of non-attendance. (Though sometimes they arrived with their armed detachment.) But Gurko could not undertake to win them all over individually. He embarked on a personal tour of the units. But the conditions were unusual. The commander-in-chief could not now brief the officers separately from the soldiers: it had to be together, otherwise it would be seen as a conspiracy. (So how could he assemble a division composed of officers?) And he'd have to suffer, too, seeing those red rags on the soldiers' chests and not daring to snatch them off. Once a brass band was holding aloft a red calico banner saying, "Long live the democratic republic," in Russian and Yiddish. Gurko went up to the nasty-looking character leading them and asked, "Well, what is the democratic republic?" But neither he nor any other band member could answer. And only a noncommissioned reconnaissance officer saved them: "It's all the freedoms we've now been given."

Some English and French socialists, brought here from Petrograd, wanted to accompany Gurko on one of these tours. He took them, even with a certain malicious glee: they would see more with their own eyes. But they contrived not to notice the chaos (preferring to see "democracy" instead!), and went back with rose-tinted hopes for the future. Complete idiots. Now he had to work on them separately, to convince them that the army was losing its capacity for combat.

But still it held up! Even at that stage it could still be maintained. At meetings Gurko would say, "The Constituent Assembly will decide everything, and in the army we have to avoid political conflict," and they would decide to await the Constituent Assembly. And the men of the 1st Siberian Corps were a sight for sore eyes as they welcomed their commander-in-chief, in strict military order, with not a single red rag on view, and the chairman of the corps committee greeted him publicly with a patriotic speech and called him "the soldiers' father," and the men applauded.

Even before Gurko arrived in Minsk, the Soviet of Workers' Deputies there had decided to convene a congress of soldiers' and officers' deputies from across the front, and he could not stop it now, or take control of it himself—he could easily come a cropper. So here again he had to adapt. A very red procession around town had been arranged, and the commander-in-chief (without any kind of red badge, of course) had to take his place at the head of the column with, on one side, the ever-present Posern in his crumpled greatcoat and, on the other, the massive Rodzyanko himself, who had turned up at this congress unexpectedly. And from the platform they had constructed on a city square he and the others had to address the *citizens* (of both genders) and then the same three moved off, standing in a truck (which followed the one carrying the band) and waving to the crowd, while flowers were thrown up to them. And then into the municipal theater, with its stuccoed balconies, painted pale pink like a lady's boudoir—but the seats were occupied by soldiers who had removed neither greatcoats nor fur caps and spat sunflower seed husks onto the floor, while their cigarette smoke wafted up to the high ceiling. From the balconies they sent down notes with their questions, on strings, and militiamen below untied them and took them to the presidium. And as for the broad-shouldered, towering figure of Rodzyanko—who, less than two months before, had come to Gurko's room in the Grand Europe Hotel and spent a long evening trying to persuade him to talk the Emperor into dismissing Protopopov and everything would be saved—his bass tones now rang out from the stage:

"The old government, which brought the country to the brink of ruin . . . The old regime's hopes for your front were to no avail . . ."

Was he alluding to that cock-and-bull story about Evert getting ready to open up the front to the enemy? He was a madman, and stupid. Though later he did say we must lay down our lives for freedom and victory.

After him came Rodichev, a Duma member, then a French colonel, then an English major, who said the Russian soldier was the best in the world . . . And: we need less politics in the army and more ardor in our combat.

And Gurko himself could not avoid speaking. Nor could he avoid adopting the now-prevalent tone, but he did quickly veer off the beaten track to address the hall on combat matters:

"I, the first commander-in-chief appointed by the revolution . . . The cornerstone is the closeness of officer and soldier . . . And, most importantly, we must nip this in the bud: the elective principle is not acceptable in the army."

They gave him an ovation. And he left.

Gurko had hoped, despite everything, that the congress would prattle itself out in two or three days. Not a chance! On the fifth day they were still prattling, and on the seventh, and even on the ninth—and it was the commander-in-chief who had to sign the order for the delegates' leave to be extended.

He himself, of course, did not attend those sessions, but they were reported to him. It swung first one way, then the other, like a pair of scales. "Down with the war" was rejected—they would not listen to that. And in the sections—they had sections too!—they rejected elections to the officer corps, though only for the front. In the rear it was allowed. And they wanted strict discipline, but only in the *narrow* area of service obligations. (Who in each battalion would decide what was and wasn't narrow?) But they would abolish punishments. Abolish deference to superiors. Abolish the officers' orderlies. When on day-leave, the right to spend the night away from barracks. The right to wear civilian clothes. And on the eighth day, from the stage, they even demanded that the term "officer" be abolished: all army ranks would now be "soldiers." And soldiers would play a part in putting together the command staff, so that the commander would be sure of his subordinates' loyalty. And personal power would be limited by the committees. The army must not have senior figures free of any control. There would be self-government "to defend the professional needs of soldiers"! And the soldiers' committees would periodically give their commanders an appraisal of their performance and those appraisals would follow them to their next appointment. And anyone who received an unfavorable appraisal from his men would always be relieved of his duties.

Moreover, the heavy Rodzyanko with his deep bass voice had left, as had the Duma members, having exerted no influence whatsoever on the congress, and all sorts of socialist leaders had outnumbered and eclipsed them. Here were well-known Petrograd figures, Chkheidze, Skobelev, and some real socialist rabble, and enormous delegations from the soviets of deputies of various cities: and they all spoke, spoke again, and the leaders spoke three times each and there was no one there to object.

By this time they were already discussing how to combat the enemy within at greater length than the enemy without. That Skobelev (who had the nerve to bear the name of a great general) accused the Petrograd officers of not supporting the revolution in the first days and said the Kronstadt officers who'd been killed had somehow deserved their fate, and then they'd cuddled up to the revolution, though even now some of them should be locked up, and the corps of generals was not up to scratch and must be purged, and the revolutionary army would promote its own great generals in their place . . .

And the revolution would disinfect the officers' brains.

You loudmouth! You venomous windbag! What are you pushing people into?!

That bastard will talk and then he'll be off. But you, you're here—now just try and command.

And they kept coming. One said we must bring back the International, another talked about class interests and said Putilov was in cahoots with Krupp, a third that we must bring all the Petrograd regiments to the front, a fourth that we must leave those who were useful to the revolution. And now a priest spoke from the stage and for some reason removed his pectoral cross and donated it, and people moved about the hall collecting donated crosses and medals, and the Minsk Soviet of Deputies maligned Evert, saying he was preparing an expedition to crack down (you've not seen anything like a crackdown yet!), and then they called Posern to the balcony of the Gentry Assembly to greet a reinforcement unit as it passed.

This whole madhouse was firmly oriented toward resolutions, and all these ravings could now be firmed up by the congress into decisions. But a resolution brought from Petrograd, that the war was of no use, did become transformed on the spot and became a call for discipline. But was there anything they didn't drone on about? The officers' allowance for accommodation and domestic staff had to be stopped (that idea came from the clerks) but the soldiers must continue to receive their standard front-line food allocation even on leave. And the wives of the "absentees" (deserters) should continue to receive their rations . . . And someone had put them up to soliciting the Provisional Government for ten million rubles to be assigned to the Petrograd Soviet (but what did that have to do with you soldiers?).

So, abandoning far more important matters, the commander-in-chief had no option but to go back and address them again. And, so that they'd pay attention and believe him, he had to repeat, just like the others, that the previous government had led us to the brink of the abyss, but now the army's military capacity was growing by the day. (You were sucked into such idiocies by this claptrap mill, constantly churning out its highflown nonsense.) And we have to show the Germans our strength, if only in small active operations, and at the first opportunity we must move onto the attack and sweep them out of our Homeland, not allow Russia to fall under the heel of our sworn enemy. And we cannot achieve that without attacking.

Dissent raged on that point, as he knew it would. Were they going to allow "capacity for active operations" in the resolution, or "capacity for attack"? They argued so much that they were dismissed for three hours to calm down. And now they voted for "active operations."

Then the congress rose—and applauded the commander-in-chief for five minutes, crying "hurrah."

It could still have gone one way or the other. And just a small nudge in either direction would do it.

Posern was shouting from the stage: crush the bourgies! Take control of the Provisional Government. But the older socialist Tsereteli, who was very sensible, proclaimed that a separate peace with Germany would mean the end of our democratic ideas, and after the congress he visited Army Group HQ and promised the general his support: we shouldn't lead an army into battle unless it is unquestioningly obedient. He asked Gurko how he was getting on with the social organizations. The general replied, not irritated but concerned: The revolution demands from all of us a capacity to adapt to unexpected situations. The new system, based on persuasion, is hard, but we have to resort to it—to avert the risk of something worse.

Before the congress dispersed, they instituted a permanent Army Group committee (with twice as many soldiers as officers), and from that they chose a "liaison commission" for dealings with Western Army Group command, and assured everyone that this would only increase the masses' confidence in the command, and "we shan't interfere."

This was hard to believe. But for the first few days the committee did not interfere. And when some units in the rear started looting nearby estates, the committee even helped smooth things down.

But what could the commander-in-chief himself do now?

In December he had firmly refused, on behalf of all Russia and all the Entente, to make peace with Germany. But what now? Surely the soldiers had not already changed course and decided not to fight?

Gurko had tolerated the Army Group congress. But immediately afterwards the Red Cross congress opened in Minsk. And Count Bennigsen came running to him with a complaint: they were making demands that would make fighting a war impossible.

And Gurko, furious, rushed over there, to the same theater. Now it was full, not of soldiers but of educated people, who were coming out with even greater idiocies, talking about the army medical service becoming totally independent of army command's direction and saying they would reorganize themselves on the basis of elective principles.

When the commander-in-chief appeared on the stage no one in the hall stood up and there were no words of welcome.

Gurko addressed them angrily, aggressively: being educated people you should be ashamed of yourselves for ruining the army and betraying Russia. The whole point of the Red Cross is to serve the army, not for the army to serve it. That if you don't adhere to service regulations, the army will manage without the Red Cross and you, its employees, will all be sent to the front.

He spoke and left, not waiting for a response. And an unimaginable hubbub arose in his wake.

But by the end of the day they had acknowledged that he was right and replaced their mutinous leadership.

So did his calling to be Russia's savior now consist of paltry activity like this?

Was he failing to espy some greater opportunity? Some more decisive step?

If so, what should it be?

[25]

Since he left, time seemed to have slowed down. It used to tear along—now it crawled.

But the whole time, even when Likonya was not thinking about him, really she was. He was a part of her.

And those March days, which had flowed past in a solid stream—later she separated them out, separated every meeting.

Because then she'd been fighting for breath.

Something else terrified her: *after* a new meeting, would she have no need to wait any more? Well then, let the new meeting come later: so the not waiting wouldn't come too soon.

She caught sight of an astoundingly beautiful woman—and wanted to be as beautiful, for him!

Letters. (He wrote!!) What joy, just to look, to see on the envelope those firm characters, in his hand. But fear too, each time a fear of opening it. What if . . .? What if she saw between the lines that he'd changed?

But just being called his "Twilight" was enough of a miracle. And if at the beginning of the letter he was "assailed by a warm emotion," that was already too much for her to take in.

Every letter was like a conversation in the dark, where the face was unseen.

She herself would have been happy to write every day. But she feared seeming forward.

I want to thank him!

Not thanking would be like not receiving.

[26]

(RULE OF THE PEOPLE IN MOSCOW: FRAGMENTS)

* * *

Despite the revolution, Easter was observed in Moscow with the usual ceremony, bells clanging from all the myriad churches, abundant light from candles and lampions, and people exchanging Easter greetings in the streets.

Trams bore the slogan "Proletarians of all countries, unite!"

Aleksandrovsky Garden, under the Kremlin wall, had always been so clean—but now, by mid-April, it was already strewn with sunflower seed husks.

There were lots on all the squares and streets as well.

* * *

Residents, even with ration cards, are taking their place in bread queues from three in the morning. Yeast has disappeared from sale. Militiamen with red cards go round the shops ordering price cuts.

There have been no sanitary inspections, and at the market bad meat and fish are being sold.

* * *

Public meetings, on the other hand, are subject to no checks, no limits. And in the warm days and nights Moscow becomes one big meeting. In squares, in gardens, on boulevards people—in little knots or anything up to great crowds—cannot get enough talking, debating. And if it dies down and disperses in one place, it will spring up somewhere else.

But most of all they meet at the Pushkin monument: the debates are constant, lasting deep into the night, by the meager light from street lamps. People cling so close to the statue's plinth that Pushkin appears to be sprouting flags and standing on the heads of the crowd. Soldiers, workers, working-class women, elegant ladies, shopkeepers, students. All the barracks send soldiers to listen and then report back. At the top is a speaker and, standing close, two more awaiting their turn. The main topic of debate is the eight-hour day. A soldier says:

"Here they are, demanding an eight-hour day, while we're doing twenty-six a day in the trenches. If you give him a high salary, who's got to pay for it? All of us, every pauper, every peasant, all the people of Russia, that's who. A pound of nails used to cost twelve kopecks, and now it's a ruble forty, how's that? And when they only work eight hours we'll have to pay even more."

And another:

"Let's change places. You can take our place at the front and we'll go to the factory. Only we'll work eighteen hours!"

And a worker:

"And what about the *bargie* that makes a fortune out of army orders? We're supposed to work for him for free? Why can't we look after ourselves a bit? Because we got to line the bargie's pockets?"

* * *

At another public meeting, on Skobelev Square, people are shouting from the plinth that the factories must be handed over to the workers. A howl from a woman in the crowd:

"Good Lord, what on earth's he talking about? They'd squander it all on drink!"

* * *

But the idea caught on and announcements were posted all over Moscow: the workers had brought in an eight-hour day, but have no plans to shorten their working hours to supply the army. They would work day and night for the army, if need be. And these unwelcome clashes with the soldiers were fomented by the factory owners.

In the Zemgor tarpaulin workshop, the workers put a sack over the boss's head and led him away, to get him out of their hair.

* * *

During the Easter period Moscow was seething with congresses: the regional teachers' congress, the Pirogov doctors' congress, and the cooperatives', the women's, and the Union of Towns congresses. And ministers came and spoke at all of them. And there was the congress of workers' organizations. And the Moscow region (six provinces) peasants' congress, which was run by intellectuals, some of them émigrés who'd just returned. They were discussing how, finally, they could create a Soviet of Peasants' Deputies.

The Moscow Old Believers' assembly called on the Old Believers of all Russia to support the Provisional Government, the grain monopoly, and the Freedom Loan, and to sell their grain.

An acute shortage of newsprint arose. The socialists started grabbing it, unauthorized, from the warehouses. Sometimes it came to blows.

* * *

Gangs of soldiers are still going round robbing apartments. Or, pretending to be militiamen, they carry out late-night "searches" of houses (Butyrsky commissariat). Twenty men broke into Shchennikov's shop in Haymarket Square.

In the village of Bogorodskoye they robbed the church of the Transfiguration: the thieves came down through the ceiling and made off with the tabernacle and implements used in church ceremony.

In the Presnya district, the Archangel Michael chapel was plundered.

* * *

There have been rumors around town that the notorious "14 March Battalion," formed of deserters and call-up dodgers, is going to stay in Moscow. The battalion committee deny this: "Valuing the new-won freedom of our homeland above all other blessings in this world . . . we have to get organized as quickly as possible, to arm, and go off to the front." But, they say, there are not enough officers and instructors.

The Siberian units at the front are complaining that in Moscow deserters are welcomed with open arms and even included in the Soviet of Soldiers' Deputies.

* * *

Every day at Bryansk station, soldiers burst into the carriages, throw the passengers and their belongings out, and take their places. Many people with reservations have to stay in Moscow. The station master has said he's powerless to stop it.

* * *

Near the Pushkin monument someone has put up a poster: "Don't forget he wrote *The Fisherman and the Goldfish*!"

* * *

The Moscow city governor's office has discontinued the registration of prostitutes—and the word itself has been eliminated, permanently. They have decided to close the dens of iniquity and houses of assignation. Yellow tickets are null and void and the compulsory medical examinations required by the administration are also abolished: the fight against venereal diseases will be founded on nothing but voluntary requests from patients.

* * *

There's a public meeting at the Gogol monument on Prechistensky Boulevard. The audience is extremely diverse, even including a covey of high school girls. There are speakers of various persuasions. A Bolshevik meets with no success. Then he bawls from the monument:

"Comrade soldiers! Don't listen to the bourgies, they're only trying to fuddle your brains. Join us, and all these tarts"—he indicates the high school girls—"will be yours!"

In the crowd a bestial roar issues from the soldiers' throats. The girls take fright. And that's put paid to the meeting.

[2 7]

There are some who get through a war and all that's left is a memory. Skirt the hill too high to scale, weather misfortune, and prevail—and in five years, maybe ten, that hateful war will wither away, clean as a whistle. But you who left an arm there, or a leg, or poisoned your insides permanently with those gases, or if your poor old eyes won't see the light of day again—that war will never leave you. You'll bite the dust before it does. It'll never leave you, the memory of that little farm garden where, blood pouring from your elbow, you last cradled your left forearm. Or the tall, luxuriant trees of that distant, foreign village Brusno-Novo, with some poplars taller, others smaller and rounder—for after that you'd never see anything again, your whole life long. That was the last thing and the image remains, fixed, while everything else around is a matter of conjecture.

And then you get shaken about in carts and trains, you writhe around, groaning, in hospital beds; and then you even spend time in an overcast Petersburg, which you'd never even dreamed of visiting; and for many months still they move you around, from hospital to hospital. And now, when it's time to go home, a limbless stump, or blind—you're not the same worker now, not the same husband, wondering how you're going to eke out the rest of your miserable existence—you hear a rumor that someone called Lenin has been transported here via Germany. He speaks our language and some of our people have joined him too. And they're calling for an end to the war and peace with the Germans. Without us winning the war—making peace just like that, with nothing to show for it. And these Petersburg types, who loiter in the streets with a cigarette hanging out of their mouth—that's all they're good for—have no intention of leaving for the front, none of them!

And that's the way it is. They've pulled a fast one on us. It's hard—more than flesh and blood can stand. We've been mutilated and beaten—and who was all that for? We've lost arms and legs—so you can just stroll about?

They spent the whole of St. Thomas Week conferring among themselves, with the help of numerous nurses and doctors. And on Sunday all the war invalids currently in Petersburg gathered together.

Some went to the Cathedral of Our Lady of Kazan for a war invalids' assembly—a massive crowd. There were speeches: we got into this war, so we need to finish it honorably, finish off the Germans for the sake of all those killed, all those gassed, and our own wounds. So they don't go attacking us a second time. Among those making the speeches was even a thirteen-year-old boy, uninjured thank heaven, who already had a St. George medal.

And then those who could walk, the less badly injured, set off on foot, in ranks as best they could, with nurses supporting some of them, while bandaged patients from all the various hospitals and the amputees already discharged were picked up from collecting points, taken by large wagonettes from the court stables, trucks and even private cars. And they all went to the Tauride Palace. In front of the crippled and bandaged ranks, the burned and blinded faces, walked three military bands, playing to raise the spirits of both invalids and spectators. And those, both walking in ranks and riding in wagonettes, who still had hands carried placards saying: "Glory to the fallen. Their death will not be in vain." And, "We'll fight for freedom till our dying breath!"—"Lenin and co.—back to Germany go!"—"Able-bodied men, relieve our ailing soldiers in the trenches!"—"Look at our wounds. They demand victory."—"Revise the pension laws." And, again, "Send Lenin back to Wilhelm!"—"Down with Lenin. He's a disgrace to Russia."

And they also managed to pick up from Finland Station the crippled prisoners of war who'd just arrived back, having dragged their mutilations and diseases through the niggardly German camps and suffered barbaric treatment there.

In the streets people doffed their hats as the procession passed. There were tears in their eyes. A woman in mourning dropped to her knees, weeping. On the corner of Liteiny Prospect came a ripple of applause for the men from a crowd of workers.

When they arrived at the Tauride, a smooth talker came out onto the portico, as was the custom, to welcome them. He was young-looking, flaxen-haired with a fat, well-fed face. This was Skobelev, a member of the Executive Committee.

"The nation that has successfully uprooted the rotten tree of Russian Tsarism will also take the country's destiny into its hands. The proletariat will not allow . . ."

Then, a disabled officer's voice from the foot of the steps:

"We've come to get clarification of Lenin's tactics and your opinion of them."

Skobelev:

"It's easy for me to discuss this with you, because I don't support Lenin's tactics. I've been opposing him for fourteen years. But let me tell you our opinion: every citizen of free Russia has the right to express his ideas. On your placards we read: Lenin go back to Germany, Down with Lenin. That's not right, comrades. We should be tolerant of his ideas. Everyone is free to say whatever he wants, and we have a good enough head on our shoulders to judge for ourselves."

A clamor began to spiral up from the crowd of disabled men.

"Down with . . .! Down with . . .! We won't listen to anyone defending Lenin!"

And that disabled officer mounted the steps toward Skobelev.

"So does that mean we fought for the well-being of people who now shout 'down with the war'? But we sacrificed our lives and we can't allow scoundrels and provocateurs who've sold out to Germany to hold sway in Russia. We gave our arms and legs—must we now look on while cowards shout 'down with the war'? No! Let them kill us first, the half-men we've become, and then it's over our dead bodies that you can conclude your peace with Germany."

"Hear! Hear! That's right!" shouted the invalids. The voices of some were also damaged. And the officer again:

"Yes, for freedom to win out we're ready to sacrifice what's left of our strength. But only victory over Germany will secure our freedom."

Skobelev tried again:

"We're saying that as well, that we should carry on fighting, until both sides renounce conquests, and behind that watchword stands the bayonet. And you, comrade officer, are profoundly mistaken when you say we'll sneak off and retreat. No, we'll stay by your side, dear comrades, till the end, or we'll die with you. But comrades, we must not forget free speech. Let the Leninists say whatever they want. We won't let them put any of it into action."

But dissenting voices were raised again and he made a swift exit.

Who could they talk to now? The invalids started pouring in, pushing into the palace itself—it was chilly outside, anyway.

Inside, the palace was as vast as a public square. There was a long hall with columns as far as the eye could see. They came to a stop there and clustered together. And the first to speak, from a raised platform, was a small, ginger-haired, elderly chap whose name they couldn't make out, who talked, not at all clearly, about the Soviet and the proletariat. But not a word about Lenin. After him came Gvozdev, who spoke in plainer terms:

"I'll give you an account, comrades, of the results of the Minsk Army Group congress. I've just got back from there."

They listened. There was a lot to digest. But there, nearer the front lines, the lads could see their problems more clearly. They could handle things for themselves there. But they couldn't see as far as Petersburg—they didn't know about Lenin.

"But what about Lenin?" shouted the veterans.

"As for Lenin, I have to tell you, comrades, that the way of fighting him that you propose is completely inadmissible. He must not be crushed or arrested. He's not a reactionary, not a counterrevolutionary. And of course we have to finish with the war, but it must be by reaching agreement with the German proletariat. And the slogan "war till victory" could anger their proletariat even more.

Then such a commotion broke out, such yelling, cries of "down with." Gvozdev wasn't allowed to finish—they sent him packing.

Now the veterans mounted the platform, some helped up by nurses. And they were of one mind: Down with Lenin! Get him off to Germany! The bosses here at the Tauride, they've been sitting here too long, overeating—they've never been to war. They'll never understand us.

"We're not saying Lenin has to be killed, but if he's a provocateur, a German spy, why can't you arrest him? And why is *he* arresting people around his mansion?"

"Well we'll arrest him ourselves, just us invalids! We'll find the strength, even if he does surround himself with machine guns and armored cars. We'll all go!"

While this was going on, some of the men had moved on farther, to have a look beyond the hall with the columns. They had found a large, white hall, with rows of seats in a semicircle on a raked floor. And the men began to fill the seats, from the front row all the way up to the back. And photographers appeared, taking pictures for the newspapers. The hall was soon jam-packed. Then a tall, dark, curly-haired man mounted the platform, ready perhaps to deliver a long speech. Only the invalids immediately started shouting about Lenin. Then, the speaker:

"I am hearing from among you, comrades, indignant cries, cries of 'down with Lenin,' and some of you are even demanding repressive measures against him. On behalf of the Executive Committee of the Soviet of Workers and Soldiers' Deputies, I must tell you that our point of view is quite contrary to that of Lenin. He is out of step with us."

"With the whole of Russia!" responded the hall.

"But in our opinion banning Lenin and his followers from expressing their ideas is not the right way to oppose him, for a free country must have free speech."

"Why should he be free," they shout, "when he's a German provocateur and spy?"

The dark man, from the podium:

"We can combat ideas without using force, just argumentation."

Fat chance! They shout. They do not listen to him. He doesn't try to finish his speech but leaves the platform and leaves the hall.

And taking his place, who's that, mounting the dais? It's our Rodzyanko, our warrior hero. The invalids applaud, and the nurses too, even before he reaches the podium.

". . . have come to greet you, you who did not begrudge your blood spilt fighting our enemy. I prostrate myself before you: I bow low before your sacred wounds. Free Russia will show its appreciation of your heroic achievements. . . . From now on the state's top priority will be its concern for you. Everything will be provided for you. The state will reward you for all your sacrifices. . . . But the enemy is not slumbering: it wants to snatch away the freedom that is so dear to us and bring back the old order. But we won't allow it! I am sure the great Russian people will triumph—and after our victory will come a time of brotherhood and equality. . . . We must, come what may, keep our mother Russia alive!"

The whole hall, all the disabled men, applauded and shouted their approval. Rodzyanko towered above them, breathless, happy. The Russian people had not forgotten him! The Russian people loved him!

One of the injured officers proposed three cheers for Russia's first citizen. There were many more than three.

The men stayed in the Tauride Palace for a good while longer, filling the whole building. And in the Duma Hall they held discussions and a resolution was adopted. Then the glib talkers also appeared: they weren't invalids, but they had the words that were needed and the cripples didn't.

Complete trust in the Provisional Government! (But the Soviet had the right of oversight.) Firm opposition to Lenin's propaganda, which was sowing the seeds of discord in the revolutionary army and setting one section of the democracy against the other. Lenin's passage through Germany was improper and damaging to the interests of the Russian people. The Soviet of Workers' Deputies must use all the means it can muster to neutralize his activities. Replace soldiers of old age with call-up dodgers from the revolutionary classes. And our salutations to those who remain in the trenches. And we must parcel out land to all those able to work it themselves. And, the final privileges the crippled men would be offered: their children would receive free education up to the age of fifteen. And, for the men themselves: their prosthetic limbs would be renewed at state expense throughout their lifetime, and they would have free transport back to their homes and for medical treatment.

That was all they asked for out of the mass of benefits promised by Rodzyanko.

. . . What the mutilated soldiers didn't know was that that very morning, after they'd left the Kazan Cathedral, people had turned up with black flags and spoken in support of Lenin. The crowd ripped up their black flags and dragged the Leninists off to the commissariat. But the militiamen there had refused to arrest them.

And now, after three in the afternoon, as the invalids left the Tauride Palace to take their places in the wagonettes and lorries, some soldiers and workers—goodness knows where they'd come from—descended on them and adeptly snatched the rolled-up banners and placards from their feeble hands, shouting:

"To hell with your army. It's in the pay of the bourgeoisie!"

They jumped into the trucks, and in place of "War till final victory" they set up placards they'd brought with them, reading "Down with war!" One cripple, then another, was dragged from the truck and thrown to the ground.

And there was no one there to intervene.

Then a soldier who'd climbed into the truck gave the men a lecture and told them they were sheep.

"Were you at the front, then?" they responded.

"I was." No way of knowing if that was true. "But I didn't want to lose my arms and legs like a fool."

Then one of the mutilated men answered, almost in tears:

"But it isn't just arms and legs—we're prepared to give our lives as well, for Russia's victory!"

But the Leninists didn't let him get any further. They persuaded the band to play a funeral march, to drown him out.

And they played for a good while.

And there, by the palace that housed both the Soviet and the Duma, there was no one to defend the invalids, not one strong, able-bodied man to face up to those louts, not from the palace commandant's service, not from the militia, not from among those who, that morning, had lined the streets to applaud the cripples.

The nurses went round trying to persuade the ruffians to let the men board their vehicles—they hadn't eaten since seven that morning.

The Leninists let them board, but still showered them with obscenities.

* * *

STRAIN, SINEWS, TILL THE FLESH FAILS

* * *

[28]

The ministers, after two whirlwind visits to GHQ in late March and early April, five of them each time, published their conclusion: discipline was firming up and no worrying symptoms had been observed among the troops. On the fronts, the crisis point of the revolutionary fever was now past. They hurried to inform the journalists as well. Nekrasov, strangely, told them the ministers had found at GHQ an organization in harmony with the unanimous wish of the people to overturn the old regime. (What did he have in mind? Alekseev himself knew no such organization.)

Soon after this, on Easter Monday, a telegram arrived at GHQ, addressed to General Alekseev, saying that the Provisional Government was appointing him Supreme Commander. And the telegram was expressly dated midnight on Easter night, the very moment of our Lord's Resurrection. Alekseev divined Prince Lvov's hand here: he had wanted, by this, to express to the general a particular confidence and warmth, as one Christian to another.

And, out of the whole telegram, it was that date that most touched Mikhail Vasilievich's heart: that blessing on his appointment promised help of some kind—help he was really counting on at this time of instability. The rest of the telegram did not seem to change his situation: he had already been performing the Supreme Commander's role for a month. Although Alekseev, like all military men, obviously wanted each new promotion he gained, every career advancement, he was not ambitious. (Even so, remaining chief of staff with Ruzsky or Brusilov appointed over him would not have been pleasant.)

However, within a month of the revolution, the situation had changed beyond recognition, to such an extent that General Alekseev did not receive, along with the job, the authority attaching to it previously. Before the revolution, not a single person or state institution had the right to give directives to the Supreme Commander or require him to account for his actions.

But at a certain juncture things had suddenly changed. GHQ had become subordinate to the War Minister and the government. No special decree had been issued, but now even the civil administration of the front-line areas had slipped silently out of GHQ's hands. And now the army group commanders-in-chief had realized this and were trying to establish relations with the ministries, bypassing GHQ. And just then the War Minister had launched his orgy of replacements of senior officers—and often finalized these changes during his trips, not with GHQ but with the army groups. And what a rush! What a muddle! Maybe there was an occasional great talent among those appointed, but hundreds more were promoted by pure chance—hundreds, because along with each general five staff officers were also transferred. Due to all these reshuffles, many commanders were plucked from their units, where they were known, loved, obeyed. And these, the best, commanders had to win influence all over again in new units and in the unusual circumstances of the revolution. But, worse still, the mass dismissal of senior officers undermined overall confidence in commanders and offered a justification for supervision by the committees and outrages from the men.

The short meetings in railway carriages when Guchkov passed through were not sufficient to contest this or put up any resistance, let alone challenge the decisions of the hopelessly inadequate Polivanov Commission. (Alekseev could only offer tacit encouragement to the commanders of divisions and regiments to cable Guchkov, protesting against this disintegration of the army.) Guchkov had even removed, without consulting Alekseev, the head of GHQ's "duty office," the department handling all the appointments and decorations. And, on top of that, GHQ had had the accusation of a counterrevolutionary conspiracy, betrayal by the Cossack staff officers, hanging over them for a month. The case was only closed the day before yesterday. All in all, the whole of the Provisional Government had stolen off into the shadows and avoided giving firm support to the officers.

What kind of Army could be maintained in those conditions?

GHQ had lost its power within the country, but to the Allies it appeared unchanged, all-powerful, and they kept pestering Alekseev through their military representatives, demanding to know when the Russian army would finally go on the attack. And he could not reveal to them either the true state of the Russian army or his own powerlessness. Since mid-April the French had gone on the offensive on the Aisne—not, fortunately, the major attack aiming to decide the war that they'd previously been threatening. (Alekseev had advised against this, while the Russians were in no position to support them.) Courtesy demanded that congratulations be sent to Commander-in-Chief Nivelle on the (thoroughly mediocre) successes of the French arms. Nivelle responded with his congratulations on Alekseev's appointment as Supreme Commander and hoped that "the Russian army will soon join its own efforts to our struggle." Alekseev could not, in reply, tell him how far off this was. Now he was tormented by the fact that he had, a month before, succumbed to the urgings of his commanders-in-chief and promised a Russian offensive in mid-May. Now it was finally clear how utterly impossible this would be. The English were worried: surely the Russians weren't going to let this perfect moment for a decisive attack on the Turkish forces in Mesopotamia slip through their fingers? And Alekseev had to give the excuse of problems equipping his forces (which really was difficult, across all those mountain ranges), and command Pavlov's cavalry corps to advance robustly on Mosul. (He had conferred with Yudenich on this: if they engaged the troops of the Caucasian Front, unspoiled as yet, in action as soon as possible, might it be possible to improve Army morale?) Just a few days before, he had extricated himself by telling the English commander-in-chief that the Russian troops would renew the action agreed with the Allies as soon as climatic conditions allowed. This had already been passed to the English newspapers, which were quoting it enthusiastically.

Lukomsky, who'd left to take over a corps, reported that a regimental commander had ignored army hierarchy and telegraphed the Tauride Palace direct, saying how grateful he and the regiment were to have been sent a Mining Institute student, a guardian of freedom. Some reinforcement companies had, it's true, set out from the reserves, but half the men had disappeared en route. The reserve battalions themselves had now, by and large, become exemplary schools of dissolution. In military districts in the rear, soviets of deputies had started demanding that soldiers be released into agriculture—and Guchkov had issued instructions on the subject. But they were not precise, not consistent: in some places it was those over forty years old, elsewhere those with injuries, in some places they had to wait for replacements, elsewhere not—and that added even more confusion. Ruzsky started firing old-timers thick and fast, without asking GHQ and with no thought of the wastage—and this put the other commanders-in-chief in a difficult position. And now, because food supply to the front was inadequate, GHQ itself was obliged to release into the rear all the non-Russians employed in auxiliary functions—and this set off a new wave of disquiet and envy among the rank and file. (And even then there was not enough meat on the front for every man to get his two pounds a day.)

Front-line forces were draining away into the rear, while all the rear injected in return was decay. In Petrograd, along with the Okhrana premises, the counter-intelligence offices were also ransacked on the quiet—and these were in private apartments. How had they become known? Some practiced hand had shown the way—and who could that have been but German intelligence? Alekseev was inclined to see a German hand in almost all our revolutionary events these days. What about Kronstadt? The killings there had seemed selective, based on lists of the top naval specialists—nothing like a settling of accounts by the sailors . . . And now reports were coming in from the Caucasus: Turkish agents were infiltrating the area and stirring up the Muslim population, perhaps fomenting an uprising. Fearing for counter-intelligence in Mogilev, where the Tsar's secret security service had just been scared off and disbanded, Alekseev was obliged to publish a special appeal from GHQ asking that citizens of Mogilev should not denounce the secret agents of the counter-intelligence department but instead help them—for there was no doubt that the enemy would now do their utmost to build a nest of spies in Mogilev. But the Main Military Court Administration sent an instruction from Petrograd to all the armies (bypassing GHQ) to halt investigation of all cases in progress. An army in action was left without military tribunals. Democracy was being used to make us defenseless.

And GHQ was indeed almost totally undefended now. The St. George Battalion was, finally, out of control and never obeyed orders. But Alekseev could not remove it and summon a unit of guards from the front, because the Petrograd Soviet had become so suspicious. Yet anyone who felt like it was turning up at Mogilev—unverified deputations, delegations, workers, soldiers, and sailors with strange kinds of "mandates" from soviets and executive committees. They were rushing around town and even poking their noses into GHQ—and no one dared stop them. Just try and restrain them and in a flash they'd go yelping to all the papers that GHQ is the center of counterrevolution, opposed to the revolution's achievements. The automobile detachment at GHQ would check the command staff's orders for cars: if a general was just going out for a drive, perhaps, or on personal business—then he must not be given a car. A fine state of affairs for staff officers!

And democracy was spreading even further: all the nationalities started demanding their own separate units. As if we could, while conducting a war, restructure the army! Previously, we'd shown weakness by supporting Latvian units, and then Polish ones. And now the others were demanding it, the Ukrainians loudest of all: a delegation, headed by a Kharkov lawyer with the rank of second lieutenant, arrived at GHQ. They asked for a corps, and straight away. They said Guchkov had already promised them one. Alekseev hemmed and hawed, and promised to make arrangements for the creation of two brigades. (But soon he heard that Brusilov had apparently, without asking permission, already started forming Ukrainian units. And now they were demanding that only Ukrainian units should be based in the whole of Ukraine and that Ukrainians from the whole of Russia should be sent only to Ukraine. They'd gone completely mad: what was left of the war now?)

But even so—no, no, the army hadn't yet disintegrated. But he had to hurry if he was going to save it. They needed an offensive now, a successful offensive of course: that would immediately reinvigorate it. But would it be practically possible, in its current state, to get the army into action? And even before that: would he dare broach the subject of attack out loud?

But neither must we allow the idea that we *won't* attack to gain ground: the enemy would move all its forces to the West. *Talking* about an offensive was necessary, in any case.

But what if we did move off, and revealed our weakness in the course of the offensive? That would be even worse.

Due to the unusual circumstances the army was now set on paths unfamiliar to the mind of a military leader. Something in the spirit and style of that mad time was required. And the minds of the generals were getting fuddled. Klembovsky suggested having the whole Army run by a triumvirate consisting of the Supreme Commander, a government commissar, and a soldier, the latter being elected. (Was high command now being totally sidelined?) Meanwhile, the fronts were suddenly, on their own initiative, holding congresses—perhaps that was indeed the right way out of this situation? But now the Minsk congress had been bubbling away for ten days—and what had been discussed? Everything that was beyond its competence: the attitude to take toward the Provisional Government, toward the Constituent Assembly, toward the democratic republic, the agrarian issue, the workers issue—and was that the job of men fighting at the front? Who were the chairmen of the congresses? For the Western Front congress it was a lawyer, Posern, the Romanian Front had been convened by a Socialist Revolutionary doctor, Lordkipanidze, the Caucasian by a Menshevik civilian, Gegechkori. And who headed all the major committees? Volunteers, students, doctors, lawyers, who only by chance wore a soldier's greatcoat. And Gruzinov was the same kind of civilian lieutenant colonel but he, having grabbed the Moscow Military District, had thought up another new idea: he would convene an all-Russian, purely military congress. And he sent two delegates to Alekseev at GHQ, to request permission to elect delegates to this congress from the whole of the army in the field, and they were already asking to be told the positions of all units and the numbers in them. And this put him in a quandary: perhaps this was the strong and solid body that was needed to oppose the Petrograd Soviet of Deputies? Alekseev could not decide—and he did not in fact have the right to decide, and sent them off to Guchkov. But Guchkov answered that he could not decide without first discussing it with Alekseev. And they would have carried on referring the delegates back and forth, but then Guchkov arrived at GHQ and they followed him here and obtained the approval of both Guchkov and Alekseev. And now they announced that the congress would meet in Moscow on 28 April. But then the Moscow Soviet of Soldiers' Deputies forbade it, showing that the Soviets feared the common voice of the Fronts and that such a congress would probably not have been a bad thing. But now it had collapsed.

But what did develop, perniciously, throughout the army, like boils, abscesses, were the committees. They were being transmitted like an epidemic, from unit to unit. It was impossible to stamp them out, but we'd been racking our brains for a month now over how to use them to benefit our combat capacity. In mid-April, coinciding precisely with Guchkov's visit, the unctuous, smooth-talking Lieutenant Colonel Verkhovsky arrived at GHQ from Sevastopol and animatedly described how the Sevastopol committees were, apparently, steering the spontaneous movement of the soldiers in a direction favorable to the state. And Guchkov had liked that and charged GHQ with working out a single set of regulations on committees. For if the contagion was spreading anyway, then the best thing was to steer it into fixed channels: to try to restrict the committees to housekeeping functions and increase the influence of officers in them. And then Alekseev signed a decree "about the transition to new forms of life" and charged Denikin, who had just been given the job of chief of staff to the Supreme Commander (another appointment made over Alekseev's head), with working up a judicious set of regulations on committees, making use of the Sevastopol experience, and reserving at least a third of the places for officers.

But this codification of very unusual material could not be dashed off in a day—it was two weeks' work for GHQ. Meanwhile the life of the committees, in the absence of a common set of rules, was developing uncontrollably, in whatever direction someone thought of taking it. The lowest-level committees were paralyzing the work of all military units. The division, corps, and army committees, which Alekseev himself, full of hope, had authorized, were now occupied almost exclusively with politics, the development of "revolutionary principles," and took it upon themselves to correct generals now out of their depth. Committees were being formed in every HQ and every greenhorn squad, as well as separate committees of paramedics, veterinarians, quartermaster clerks, radiotelegraph operators, noncombatant staff, and separate committees of Ukrainians, Poles, Muslims, and Georgians. We had to hurry with that single set of regulations! But Guchkov had contrived to give the same job to his Polivanov Commission, and four days ago the draft Polivanov Regulations had come down from Petrograd! And they were a total capitulation. But GHQ had prepared a set that was stronger, stricter, and it was already too late and pointless to renounce it: and how, in that tangle of divergent views, could they discuss it with the now-sick Guchkov? How many more days would pass without any kind of regulations? Alekseev ordered Denikin to complete the GHQ Regulations. And today, Sunday the 29th, he had signed them. Let Guchkov sort it out if he wants to.

He'd signed the document—with tears in his eyes. He was, supposedly, saving the army from something even worse, wasn't he? But what he'd signed, with his own hand, was the army's death warrant.

The chaos didn't end there. Yesterday's papers had announced another new measure to save the army, which had been adopted. Some random delegations that had happened to come together in Petrograd had hurriedly, without spending much time on it, ratified some sort of "commissariat manual" that someone had shoved into their hands at the Tauride Palace—and now it was already published. What was in it? We must create, in every army, on every front, and at GHQ(!), a commissariat of three men, one from the government, one from the Soviet of Deputies, and one from the army group or army committee. They will have the right to examine *all matters and all questions relating to the competence of the commanders-in-chief*! And all orders to the armies and the army groups must be counter-signed by the commissariat!

It was a madhouse! So they'd be in command instead of the generals? And at GHQ as well? And they'd be investigating the Supreme Commander too, would they? A month ago, Alekseev himself had asked Lvov to send a commissar to GHQ—but not on these conditions!

A madhouse! True, it was for the time being only a draft: it was to be passed to the Executive Committee of the Petrograd Soviet (why was it involved?)—for ratification within three days! It was a draft, but so peremptory, so forceful that, for an illiterate country: what, another new law already . . .?

Since the Tsar's departure, regular Sunday church attendances—the whole GHQ corps together—had somehow ceased of their own accord. Alekseev himself had gone one more time, during Lent, and then to the Easter midnight service. But that was all. Not because previously he had gone unwillingly, far from it, but now somehow it seemed irrelevant. Was it due to the worrying times? To the arrival of all this news at such inopportune moments? He had even, after the Emperor's departure, ordered that the Vladimir icon of the Mother of God be returned to the Cathedral of the Assumption in Moscow.

He'd not been to church this morning either. But that did not signal a leisurely Sunday—quite the contrary: now he could concentrate longer, from morning onwards, on his work, papers, and reflections, banking on there being fewer disturbances today.

He'd studied the mind-numbing plan for commissariats again.

And today he settled down to write a long letter to Guchkov, saying that the army's situation was worsening by the day and that the general was surprised at the irresponsibility of those who kept talking about the "magnificent state of the army." (This was also aimed at Guchkov himself.) He even wrote: **The Army is dying**.

There was now no other way to talk to those uncaring ministers in Petrograd.

Really he needed, urgently, to go to Petrograd himself and try one last time to explain things to the government: what were they doing?? It only needed one or two little shoves and Russia would be in the abyss.

And the command staff of all the fronts and armies felt similarly oppressed. Alekseev was ashamed to look his subordinates in the eye because he knew he could not protect them. He felt just as ashamed as if he'd been responsible for all this—although Petrograd had made the decisions.

Mikhail Vasilievich had, overall, become more touchy than ever, taking everything personally. For example, he read the papers, compared their reports, and discovered that, on the same day that the ministers had been so benevolent on their visit to GHQ, that murderous Steklov had continued to vilify and threaten at the Conference of Soviets in Petrograd. And the Mensheviks' *Workers' Gazette*, likewise, wrote that "GHQ is engaged in counterrevolutionary work." Then, suddenly, he saw in the papers that Colonel Sergievsky from GHQ had spoken at the Western Front congress: "During the days of the revolution the order to send troops to march on Petrograd was given by the ex-Tsar. But the majority of high command at GHQ was sympathetic to the liberation movement. And as soon as the Tsar left Mogilev GHQ broke with him and attempted to neutralize his orders. Only thanks to General Alekseev was bloodshed avoided. If it had not been for General Alekseev, it is also questionable whether the abdication would have been signed . . ."

And although there was nothing actually libellous there, the emphasis was perhaps a bit too crude. And although in the current political situation it seemed to be praising the Supreme Commander. . . for some reason Mikhail Vasilievich felt terribly uncomfortable about that item. And he was surprised that the worthy Colonel Sergievsky could express himself in such a terrible way. And he called him in, to explain himself.

But this was the first time, here, in the Supreme Commander's office, that Colonel Sergievsky had read all this! He swore that not only had he not said anything of the kind but he was not even at Minsk, which could be easily verified.

Astonishing.

Things became clearer the following day, in a different newspaper: these words had been spoken at the congress by Colonel Plyushchik-Plyushchevsky. Alekseev summoned him immediately. But Plyushchik-Plyushchevsky also assured Alekseev that he'd said nothing of the kind.

So it remained a mystery: where on earth had it come from?

But it was very unpleasant.

It was also very unpleasant to encounter the red-haired, podgy General Kislyakov at GHQ. He would have liked this Kislyakov to disappear, never to be seen again.

Alekseev had served there for a year and a half at the Emperor's right hand, reporting to him daily, almost never encountering any objections. And he had often thought to himself that the Emperor seemed to have nothing to do with any of this: he was not the one who'd studied these situations or reached the decisions.

Yet somehow, his presence had meant something. For many, Russia and the Tsar were one.

Today soldiers listened to the newspapers being read to them, with many inconsistencies between them, but all the papers would agree on one thing: Nikolai II was an enemy of the people, a fool, a criminal, and was assisting

Germany. A soldier might well scratch his head, perplexed: in that case, this war the Tsar started—what's it got to do with us?

* * *

YOU'LL CATCH ON, WHEN YOUR FOOTHOLD'S GONE

* * *

[2 9]

When, last month, they'd elected Klim Orlov from the Volynian Battalion to the Soviet of Deputies, the lads saw it like this: you're from Petersburg, you know your way around there, it'll be easier for you. They'd also made much of the fact that he'd been the first to shout "Enough blood!" to Lashkevich. And he'd also been among the four or five who'd fired into the yard at the officer's back as he fled . . . (Orlov himself was sure he was the one who'd downed him: he'd taken precise aim and Lashkevich had come crashing down on cue.) Anyway, who else could they elect? Everyone else had steered clear, ill at ease: why get into all that? They have to make speeches there, don't they?

But as for speeches, no, all month it had never once fallen to Klim to make a speech. Wouldn't be worth all the trouble, anyway: there are smooth talkers here, and there are muddle-heads, and some who don't get far with words and wave their arms about more. Nearly half the ones who speak aren't our kind, they're educated, bigwig types. But even just to sit there, you have to know what you're doing, and look right: after all, the State Duma still sat in these seats in February—try looking right in those. (And get there early. There aren't enough seats to go round. The others'll have to sit on the steps or just stand.) The Soldiers' section alternates with the Workers' section, we can't all squeeze in at the same time—for sessions together we started meeting in the Sea Cadet Corps, in a whopping great hall jam-packed with ordinary benches so all two thousand odd could fit, once they'd taken the model ships out.

Although he came from Petersburg and had been to listen to a student circle before, it still felt strange to Klim at first, as if he'd got dolled up in someone else's clothes. But then, attending sessions every other day, they gradually got used to it, got acquainted through offering each other tobacco. Between sessions they went into the hall with columns and discussed things there, and explained them to each other. There were some very brainy fellows. One soldier from the 176th Regiment, Matveev, wrote and wrote, noting down everything someone said. How did he manage? Klim happened to sit next to him once and was amazed at how fast he could move that pencil.

From him and from others Klim got some things straight: there is, at any one time, just one *item* up for discussion—and everyone, whether for the item or against it, has to talk about just that, not about what you yourself have figured out. But most of them stray from this path and talk about what's on their own mind. Sometimes they get corrected from the platform, sometimes not. That's why the meeting's so slow, stumbling along like a worn-out cow. And those on the platform bang on the table: "If we continue this discussion it'll take us three weeks!" Once they struggle through it, vote on the item, they throw you the next one straight away.

But you can shout out from your seat if you like what they say or, if you don't, "Get him off! Chuck him out! Clear off! Go on, go on! To hell with them!" And more than once Orlov had shouted too, with real feeling. And sometimes there'd be an uproar to match any fish market. One time, right there in the hall during a session, they started throwing leaflets—like pigeons fluttering around.

Another time people started walking between the rows, asking us: "What party d'you belong to, comrades? With what faction are you going to cock us? Me? None of them. At the moment I'm just looking. I'm fine as I am, a lance corporal in the Volynian Regiment. Before, I was a fitter at the Ludvig Nobel factory."

You pick up a load of new words here, only you have to keep your ears open: they really pelt us with words we've never heard before. Authority: that means they respect someone. Anarchy: they don't respect anyone. Counterrevolution. Indem-nities. Or they come out with: "Mars himself was for an offensive war against Russian Tsarism." Who's Mars? Then another delegate explained and I'm much obliged: Mars is the god of war and Wilhelm's going to put up a monument to him soon.

An *item* is all very well, but you only have to drop off for a moment, or not catch something—and there's no way you can follow what they're talking about.

The chairman says: we're allocating 150 thousand to publish newspapers that share our views. People must only believe our newspapers, not the bourgeois'.

Or they scold: soldiers all get two pounds of black bread and half a pound of white, so why are they making their way to shops and taking the workers' bread?

There's a good bit about the row with the workers:

"People are trying to undermine our authority and split the workers and the soldiers."

(Although Klim was a soldier now, here he was for the workers. He understood them.)

And they argued about the Stokhod, about who was to blame for us being routed, the soldiers or the generals.

"If we got rid of irresponsible ministers, we'll have to get rid of irresponsible generals. We've got to be constantly criticizing our generals. Not one of those bastards at HQ ever comes to the front line. They say, 'The revolution's to blame.' But we'll show them who's to blame."

Another time a fidgety type took a running jump onto the platform and kept wriggling around. But we could see he was a big cheese.

"Since I've been a member of the Provisional Government I have no time any more. But I feel drawn to you. I entered the government to be a judge and I shall judge and everyone is under my control. I won't stand for this slander, these rumors that I am indulgent toward the old government. Anyone who doesn't believe me must provide proof to the contrary. It was one of the old guard who killed Rasputin. We must work for the benefit of future generations."

Another time a fine gentleman came, well-groomed and handsome. That was Chernov. He'd just come back from abroad, you see, he'd been traveling round those parts for years. He knew everything:

"Abroad there's a campaign against the Soviet of Workers' Deputies. Over there you can sense the revolution moving from East to West. The workers of Western countries are oppressed by the nightmare of ex-poilation. Here we had a radiant dream. This time the land won't slip from the people's hand. But we must extend a helping hand to suffering Europe."

The soldiers who aren't from Petersburg like to talk about land. And leading figures from the soviets too, they explained what's going to happen. We'll take everything away from the big landowners without paying. But the owners of farmsteads will say that they paid for their land, and we'll have a real battle on our hands. But we mustn't seize the land ourselves, we'll wait for the Constituent Assembly, and until then the committees will parcel out the land and equipment at bargain prices.

But the subject that got the soldiers really boiling over more than anything else was army organization. Several whole sessions were devoted to it. First they discussed the Rights of the Soldier, and voted to publish them as a General Order. There was a lot of arguing over that. What the men wanted most was a way of controlling the quartermasters and procurement. At first they thought: let's put soldiers into every verification commission and give them the deciding vote. But then they thought it through. No. Giving yourself the deciding vote would mean taking responsibility for procurement, wouldn't it? And what if something wasn't available? How would we manage then? No, we'll only speak as observers, but so as to make sure things run smoothly. The longest debate was about the officers. Everyone was fired up about them.

"We need a complete reshuffle of the officers, otherwise we're done for. Our boys have just decided not to let officers anywhere near the machine guns!" (And there were cries of "Quite right! Bravo!")

"Officers are there to serve us, not the other way round!"

"Officers aren't the slightest bit cleverer than the men, specially at the moment."

"What are you doing?" came another voice from the platform. "All the good things are getting buried here! I propose we add in: all officers to be replaced."

"And in the regimental tribunal we won't have three of each, we'll have five soldiers and one officer."

"No. Listen, boys. What's fair is equal numbers."

"And should we give the committee the right to make arrests?"

"If someone shouts, 'Long live Nikolai,' we need to wring his neck. Why arrest him?"

"So will sergeants be elected too? And platoon commanders? No, let the bosses appoint them. There's no knowing who the young soldiers would elect."

"We've just got to do away with the discipline reg-lations."

"No, lads! We need discipline, but we've got to make the officers understand what discipline is. It's not about saluting."

"We hope the bad officers will be got rid of. But if we do it ourselves the enemy will take advantage of it."

Then a soldier with a big, fat face spoke. He was from the 1st Machine-gun Regiment, which had taken and held Petersburg:

"We don't obey Kornilov. Our decisions must be accepted, no questionings, we won't ask twice. We've told Kornilov to cancel all his orders immediately."

"Soldiers must grow from slaves into free citizens. They're entitled to discuss their rights. And now going to church isn't compulsory any more."

What soldier isn't affected by army rules! He's got to live under them. But there'd never been such a frenzy as when they started discussing whether the Petrograd garrison should move out to the front. Wasn't the danger out of the way now, after the revolution? So why not go to the front? But if the vote goes the wrong way, you, Klim, will have to go, leave your home town. Your family's here—but you'll be off.

Some colonels were allowed to speak first: they said the Semyonovsky and Pavlovsky Regiments had decided to send reinforcement companies immediately.

Well, they can send them if they like. But we'll stay here a while and see what happens. No surprise that officers want to reinforce the front.

Then they started pushing men forward who'd just arrived from the front.

"The Petrograd garrison'll be making a big mistake if it puts itself in a priliged position."

"You're wrong! It's not every military unit that can safeguard the revolution, only our tried and tested garrison."

"I beg you Guards, for the love of God, come and reinforce us. If you're assigned to us, don't hesitate."

And that plea really touched some of them.

"Perhaps we could keep two thousand from each battalion here and send the rest?"

Howls from the machine gunners:

"We're not sending anyone to the front and we'll keep back as many as we need!"

And today, Sunday, the workers and soldiers were all assembled together in the Sea Cadet Corps again and the first thing we discussed was sending reinforcement companies from Petrograd. That unkempt Sokolov, who we already knew, came up to the platform and started trying to persuade us. He said we'd always been against deploying them, and we'd made that commitment in front of the whole country. In bourgeois circles they say: why do you need so many troops here? And our answer is: we don't keep them here for military action but to give us authority. But now they're pointing out that there are big machine-gun regiments, one's got seventeen thousand men, and those kinds of regiments weren't set up for the Petrograd garrison but for the whole front. The heavy artillery division in Gatchina too. And we decided to agree, sometimes, to deployment. We'll work out a norm and send some of our troops—only, of course, as many as are necessary and only with permission from the Executive Committee.

They started jeering and yelling at him too.

They sent up to the platform some clerk, who'd been well-coached: counterrevolutionary armies, he said, hadn't been uncovered anywhere. If we don't send reinforcement companies now, then we'll end up on the black list of shirkers. And another reason we should send them is that every reinforcement company will carry our revolutionary spirit with it to the front.

You go then, and take your spirit, but don't try and rope other people in.

Then a soldier spoke: if there are fifteen hundred men in every unit but they're not armed, what kind of revlushry army we got? I say we leave 350 men in each unit, but arm them.

Yelling from all sides:

"That's no good! It's not enough!"

What did that mean? Four out of every five men had to march off to the front?

A determined soldier, from the platform:

"No! Never! The Petrograd garrison played a big role in the revolution and it should all stay here. Other towns can send reinforcements to the front. Otherwise it'd mean we had to go off and the police would stroll around here nice and peaceful wouldn't it? Better send the police off to the front."

Shouts:

"And where are we supposed to get that many policemen?"

"The front isn't a rubbish dump, we can't send the city police!"

Then someone from the sapper battalion: there are twenty-five sapper battalions in Russia, so why's it ours that has to deploy? We already told General Kornilov, and explained we're protecting Russia's freedom, and we're not going. We'll be strengthening the revolution here. Counterrevolution's taking a stronger hold and so's slander and what with the troops being sent off to work in agriculture I say we can't decide to send troops away from Petrograd now. We've got to say it's not acceptable.

"Ri-i-ight!" yelled Klim. And many others did too, and the hall was buzzing. The cries resounded under that massive, high ceiling.

But the bigwigs in the Soviet look after their own interests and know who to let speak: now here's a delegate from the front, from the 50th Division. He climbs onto the platform and takes his cap off.

"I bring you greetings from our division! I'm coming to ask you for help. Over there we're defending our bright, beautiful freedom. We've not left our trenches for ten months. There's only eighty men left in each company; where there was a battalion before, now there's only a company. But here, just in the reserve regiment, there are sixteen thousand: so we can ask you for help. Otherwise we could lose all the fortifications that cost us so dear."

The soldiers felt ashamed now, stopped shouting, and didn't know what to say. But a soldier from the 180th Regiment, here in Petrograd, asked permission to say a couple of words. And he called from his seat, in a jokey tone:

"What's this timid talk about? Things aren't so bad there. Is he from a second-rate supply train by any chance?"

The whole hall burst out laughing. But there were also shouts of:

"No attacks on the person!"

but they were laughing anyway. The last speaker might as well not have bothered. The next one was a Bolshevik:

"There was an agreement not to send anyone from here. Just let the government break the agreement once and after that they'll be doing it all the time. There are soldiers all over Russia but for some reason it's our troops that they all want to send to the front. And what they'll send us in exchange is policemen. And will you be free then? There's counterrevolution everywhere and our government is helping. We demand arms for the working class as well. And we won't let them deploy a single soldier!"

And now, if you ask every soldier in the hall again, three out of four will tell you not to send our men. But the bosses in the Soviet have some kind of mechanism—Klim had already caught on to this and noticed it several times, and others had too—pulling strings, somewhere unseen, and swaying the hall in whichever direction the Executive Committee wants. But they'd never seen that Committee together—just caught glimpses of two or three of them at a time, sitting high above the hall.

Today we'd already shouted and stamped our feet so much that we were thinking: nothing can make us give in; we're the masters here. But no.

Then they send another namby pamby up to speak, a "socialist revolutionary," and he says there's contradictions in the Bolshevik position:

"Counterrevolution isn't possible, because even if one company listens to an officer another one won't—they won't believe him. We're lying around on bunks and going to meetings when we should be going to the front. Perhaps they could give us some soft chairs as well? There are plenty of mama's boys in the battalions who should be sent to the front."

Well yes, perhaps we should send those.

And Sokolov again:

"Obviously we're not going to do anything to weaken ourselves. The Executive Committee is very careful. We'll draw up a directive, and you'll review it and only then adopt it. The garrison will stay, of course. Some individual detachments will be moved out, though—but only with the permission of the Executive Committee each time."

And somehow we voted to accept that, not really knowing how it happened. Anyway, when people raise their hands to vote here, no one counts them. You couldn't get between the rows to count, we're so squashed up.

No, you've just got to keep an eye on people, that's all. They said so themselves: don't ever trust the government, class interests will always win out. And suddenly they changed their tack: although the government is bourgeois, there's no reason not to trust them. And we had to ratify a loan to them.

So that's their new offer . . .

And they kept on about that loan, session after session: we had to ratify it. But they didn't put it to the vote. They said the report wasn't ready. Then the Bolsheviks started pushing, and they've got a real looker, Kollontai. She's got the gift of the gab and a good voice: we won't give any money for killing our German brothers in a war that the proletariat doesn't want! Let the moneybags give it, the capitalists and landowners, they can take the gold from the bourgeoisie! Those who need the loan can pay for it: we don't need it. Not a kopeck to Milyukov and co.! Not a kopeck to the 'perialists!

And that dame had been talking sense! And we shouted, "Good! That's right!" And if there'd been a vote there and then, the loan would've been defeated—she really fired us up. But no. That little old man, Chkheidze, made his way to the platform: we're not ready for the vote yet, it'll have to be postponed. So why start harping on about it? And people from parties spoke and all took a pass: not ready for a vote. Only the Bolsheviks were demanding a vote—and right now. And Zinoviev, a real live wire of theirs, said:

"And in the meantime, we've got to declare 1 May a day of mass fraternization on the front! And if there's any interference or misunderstandings, we'll say the officers were responsible!"

And today, after discussing the reinforcements question, when we were all exhausted, they trotted out that loan business again. It had really got under their skin. And Chkheidze came up again, but we couldn't hear half of what he said. But he didn't propose anything, didn't put anything to the vote and—we'd have to wait another three days, to hear the government's answer on a-neck-sations. Then we'd know whether the loan would contribute to the advance of the revolution or hold it back, and what steps that would mean for us. The Executive Committee decided we should wait the three days.

And now, after him, that good-looking Tsereteli spoke and he didn't say anything different: we must postpone this, as a matter of the greatest importance, for three days. This way we'll show what a close eye we're keeping on the government and the government will show how they listen to what we say. They didn't flinch at giving up territorial conquests. In a few days a note will go to the Allies, and that'll be a new victory for democracy.

Then, from the Bolsheviks: no, we have to say right now who's for the loan and who's against it. We Bolsheviks have always been against it. Supporting the loan is betraying the revolution. If they need money they should get it from the bourgeoisie's coffers: they've made fortunes during this war. We've got to be ahead of the government, not behind it. We need to know whether we have rule of the people or rule by Milyukov and Shingarev.

And that's right. What fool wants to give his money away?

And there were those others too, the anarchists. Their man said:

"The bourgeoisie have made money out of our blood. Not a kopeck for the war! People all round us are plotting counterrevolution. Sending reinforcement companies, and then the loan on top of that—that's oppression. No trust in the government, not for a minute! And no trust in any government, ever!"

We laughed.

We could laugh—but, surprise, surprise, the honchos still turned everything round again, the way they wanted it, and Tsereteli came up one more time:

"We're the advance guard of the revolution. We laid the first stone of the Inner National. If the government betrays us I shall be the first to go against it. Money? We'll get 99 percent of it from the pockets of the bourgeoisie, of course. But let's wait the three days, to see our victory."

The Bolsheviks started shouting again, attacking the loan. And one of the top leaders, the hulking Steklov, sounded a contrary voice: don't accept the loan, the bourgeoisie won't have to pay it, the people will. But his words sank without trace too, and the resolution was to wait three days.

We meet here, as if we're running the country. But they're conning us—better keep a closer eye on them. Now, for example, they've dreamed up a plan to elect the soldiers' Executive Commission all over again, going back to the units, bypassing us. But who's left there, to elect from? We know there's no one with any brains left—they're all here. They're stringing us along. We've got wind of their tricks. No, every commission now has got to be elected from among us.

Who's left in the battalion? Klim had teased Kirpichnikov and Markov even before: "Clueless country lads in the big city." Orlov was feeling more and more at home in the Soviet and saw this as his proper place, not suddenly marching off in a reinforcement company. He didn't even look in on his Volynian battalion that often. He was losing touch with it. He lodged at home, with his family, but he wouldn't even have wanted to go back to the Nobel factory. He had a different life now, and people were saying we'd be taking the revolution even further. We'd be needed.

He did go to his battalion—for battalion committee meetings. These days he was explaining to them how wrong they were to resent the workers. He did, of course, also look in on his training unit. Their training wasn't at all strict, and they would hang around in the yard or in town. And in Timofei Kirpichnikov's group he heard that the lads were going off to the Kshesinskaya place to arrest Lenin.

"Who gave you the right to do that?" said Klim, sounding a warning note.

"We got rid of Lashkevich," said Markov. "Who gave us the right to do that?"

"But what's Lenin done wrong?"

"He's working for the Germans. Everything he says is what the Germans want. They even gave him a lift to Russia."

"You're out of your mind, boys! What have the Germans got to do with it? He's our man, a fine fellow, and his Bolsheviks have got things clearer than everyone else."

"No," said Kirpichnikov morosely. "I left my blood behind, there, in Galicia. And now he says the Germans aren't our enemy? We should make friends?"

Klim started yelling at them. "What's wrong with you? You mustn't even think like that!"

But they didn't change their mind. And, on the quiet, they raised a detachment out of the various units. They planned to go at night, when there was no crowd, and nail him.

What was he to do? Klim couldn't stop them on his own. For the first time he went straight to the Executive Committee room. He thought he'd find Bogdanov there, or someone he'd recognize from the soldiers' soviet. He looked in: they were all strangers. So he said to two sharp-looking little chaps: it's like this, some of the Volynians want to arrest Lenin. Stop them!

They promised to do so. And thanked him.

[30'']

(FROM THE SOCIALIST PRESS, TO 30 APRIL)

Nervous Nellies were awaiting absolute collapse, but they have seen absolute orderliness, which is saving the country from ruin. Are the trains running? Yes, and even better than before. Are the soldiers performing their duties? Yes, and more conscientiously. . . . The time of the enthusiast is here. Our faith in the people was not misplaced . . .

(The People's Cause)

It has turned out that life without the Tsar is not harder, but incomparably easier. Soon even the most backward sections of our population will come to realize that.

. . . Iron hammer, beat your hardest!
Vault of heaven, blaze with blood!
Waves of horror will fling skywards
Spray from this relentless flood.
The nation's reckoning's at hand
For traitors to our Russian land!

(Izvestia)

. . . The Soviet is not creating any kind of dual power but, like a loyal sentry, standing guard over the interests of the working people. . . . We shall recognize the Provisional Government, as long as it takes account of the Soviet's opinion. The historical role of the Soviet is so considerable, its political significance so great that it does not need to be defended against those obnoxious accusations and ambiguous insinuations with which the hired gossip-mongers of the socialist press and the underground telltales of the bourgeois camp spatter its activities . . .

From the point of view of the participants themselves, the Kadet Congress is going splendidly. Sometimes it seems like the meeting of a mutual adoration society. From time to time *tableaux vivants* of general glorification form onstage as, to thunderous applause, the leaders are surrounded by groups of supporters and stand frozen in the poses of historical heroes. They had always tried to show that revolution was contrary to all laws, that the Russian republic was in the domain of Utopia, and that constitutional monarchy was the highest principle of political wisdom. And now, suddenly, they have to show that the revolution was legitimate! Never was such a rapid renunciation of a party's principles, such a sudden accommodation to changed circumstances . . .

(The People's Cause)

. . . In the officer corps of the Russian army, many have now donned red masks. Hurry up, GHQ, we want to see the back of you.

We must demand categorically that the Executive Committee of the Soviet transfer the ex-Tsar, and the ex-Tsaritsas, to the Peter and Paul Fortress.

Assembly of delegates from all the 12th Army fronts

Too many scruples. The secrets of the imperial palaces have only just been revealed—and now there are over-scrupulous types saying we must leave the Tsar and Tsaritsa in peace. No! No! Now, and for decades to come, we must expose this deception, lay Tsarism bare, castigate it with anger and laughter. Throw open, as wide as possible, the windows and doors of the imperial palace, be ruthless, tear off its roof, for all to see the criminality and shame, the vice and shamelessness! Let the people know everything, down to the merest detail, about both Rasputin and Vyrubova—lay Tsarism bare!

(The People's Cause)

Has the Provisional Government taken all the measures needed to suppress the Black Hundreds and the anti-Semitism that are raising their head here and there?

News of pogrom agitation retracted. State Duma member Friedman asks us to inform readers that his earlier reports of pogrom agitation in Podolsk province, which risked getting out of hand, did not correspond to the reality. No aggression toward Jews has been observed anywhere in Podolsk province.

Our government now has an advance guard of long-haired gendarmes, who are rallying the people to the Tsar. These are the priests. We must demand that the Provisional Government arrest the metropolitans who are influencing the benighted masses and organize supervision of the priests by the local committees.

Revolutionary revision of the text of liturgical books . . .

. . . a pathetic band of adherents to the old regime has, from its murky underground cells, been spreading rumors, claiming provocatively that our comrade workers are beginning to stray from the blood-soaked path that has led us to our desired freedom. No, comrade soldiers, that is a brazen lie: the workers are ready to work round the clock and die at their stations . . .

LABOR CONSCRIPTION. There are massive social groups that produce nothing: they have the means to lead a life of leisure. The application of labor conscription to these groups is absolutely necessary—and the sooner, the better.

(Izvestia)

. . . it is nobler to spill blood in the name of freedom on the barricades in Berlin streets than to annihilate, pointlessly, our brothers and neighbors . . .

We, machine gunners of the 1st Machine-gun Regiment, who have raised the red banner of freedom, send our fraternal greeting to you in your damp trenches. Wait for us. In dark times, we shall be with you to defend the freedom so dear to us, and may the terrible sound of the Russian machine gun make the enemy accept our honest proposal: peace without reducing peoples to slaves.

Hornstein, chairman of the regimental committee
Karpov, secretary

. . . But in the meantime we must, come what may, prise the grain out of the peasants' caches and stores, in the interests of that same freedom.

GREETINGS TO THE RELEASED POLITICAL PRISONERS. Suffering comrades! We beg you to apply your long-matured ideas to forging, as soon as possible, a state of well-being for the oppressed peoples of our free country . . .

. . . are demanding that the party leaders should stop hiding behind the anonymous signature "EC" . . .

. . . The Soviet of Workers' Deputies is the main headquarters of the revolution and the Provisional Government only its appointee. . . . Know, comrades, that our reserve regiment will, now and in the future, always support you in your efforts to monitor the Provisional Government more tightly. This is not the dual power that the bourgeoisie and the press, foaming at the mouth, are shouting about, but the reasonable, sobering voice of the laboring masses . . .

On 26 April, in the barracks of the Moscow Guards Battalion, a piece of news was going round: "Comrades! The coppers and minister-generals are being released from the Kresty and our guards there have been slaughtered." In ten to fifteen minutes our first detachments arrived by car and tram, followed by the whole battalion, in orderly ranks. It turned out we'd been tricked. But just let someone attempt a trial balloon like that again—he's sure to be crushed when he meets the gigantic force of our sons of liberty.

Private Polovinkin, Moscow Guards

In **Moscow**, public meetings held in the streets have recently taken on a counterrevolutionary character. It has been decided to send members of the Soviet of Workers' Deputies to all these meetings.

. . . We are receiving reports from Betovo township, Kozelsk district, that data are being collected all over the township on how many cows each inhabitant owns. It is proposed to requisition them, leaving one cow per five-person family. Grain is disappearing from circulation. Old peasants are naïvely appealing for advice: "Have we gotta be happy with the new order, or not?" And when someone answers: "Of course you have," they go off, relieved.

Investigations into the swindler going by the name of Captain Sosnovsky have not yet yielded any results. His assistant in the security section of the Ministry of Roads and Railways, Rogalsky, was involved in the murder of the actress Sezakh-Kulero and was sending telegrams to accomplices via the ministry's lines.

A group of **Moscow** citizens has petitioned for the hideous monument to Aleksandr III, by the church of Christ the Savior, to be demolished.

We, employees in the hotel trade—waiters, chambermaids, bootboys, bell-boys, messenger boys, kitchen maids, and doormen—must organize ourselves around our union and, by our joint efforts, throw off this feudal yoke.

The socialist group of deaf-mutes . . .

I APPEAL TO THE ROBBER who stole my suitcase and contents to return the copy of my war wound certification as well as my children's birth certificates. I am counting on his having retained enough of a conscience not to subject an officer, who has lost an arm in the war, to . . .

UNDER THE SIGN OF COLLECTIVIZATION . . . The rural areas of Russia are already widely applying the principles of collectivism. . . . Collectivization means turning peasant farming into a communal process, with the fields being cleared collectively, the agricultural machines being given over to collectives and the sowing and the autumn tillage being done collectively, as far as possible. . . . A democratically organized labor army, an army of constructive endeavor and creativity . . . Our epoch must proceed under the sign of collectivization . . .

(V. Chernov, *The People's Cause)*

The law on grain monopoly must not be understood as the forcible confiscation of grain: the law proposes that farmers should *freely* deliver their surplus grain to the government. And if they do not understand the state's need, and no voluntary delivery ensues, then requisitioning will come in, as a sanction. We live in a period of decisive measures.

People are thinking like old biddies: "There's a new government and no bread, and the queues are even longer." But it is not possible, in such a short time, to cure all the ills of three centuries of Romanov rule. The blabbering minions of the bourgeoisie must hold their over-active tongues . . .

(The People's Cause)

. . . Never in all its existence did England wage war out of moral, idealistic interests, but always with practical aims: to eliminate a strong opponent and conquer land. And even when her motto was "for freedom" it was for the freedom of the slave trade.

(The Day)

. . . the general assembly of the 2nd Artillery Depot . . . We must demand that Foreign Minister Milyukov stop giving his personal views, both in the press and in conversations with journalists, on the subject of his policy of conquests . . .

. . . if our demand that the poisoning of soldiers' minds against the workers be stopped is not met, we cannot guarantee that there will be no explosion of revenge against the bourgeois press . . .

(from a resolution of the Finland Reserve Battalion)

Our "persecution" does not threaten Lenin's physical safety. On the contrary, we defend his complete freedom of speech, in the hope that his political lunacy will finally become obvious to all.

(Unity)

. . . But there is no war of words either. *Izvestia* is turning a blind eye to the communists' campaign against the Soviet.

. . . of course the cries of "down with Lenin" from crippled soldiers and their demand that he be expelled are an unenlightened, regrettable occurrence. But *Pravda* must understand that an unenlightened, elemental force can also turn against its creators, so they had better not unleash it.

(The Workers' Gazette)

With Lenin's arrival in *Pravda*'s editorial office, we now have an organ that is openly and unequivocally defending the idea of civil war—a war against the Russian revolution, in other words. But we do not think that Leninism will succeed in changing the flow, so astonishing in its intellectual awareness, of the Russian revolution. Those anarchist firebrands are powerless.

(The Day)

We, workers at the Petrograd Metal Works, 7,000 in number, are supporting the resolution . . . to lock up the ex-Tsar Nikolai Romanov, his wife, and all his henchmen in the Peter and Paul fortress immediately . . .

Resolution. We, workers of the Old Parviainen plant, have resolved at the general assembly of 26 April, at which we were 2,500 in number: 1) To demand that the Provisional Government, which has only been a brake on the revolutionary cause, be deposed and its power given into the hands of the Soviet . . . 3) To demand that the Provisional Government publish immediately the secret military agreements concluded by the old government with the Allies; 4) To set up a Red Guard and arm all the common people . . . 6) To commandeer the presses of all the bourgeois newspapers conducting a slander campaign against the Soviet, and put them at the disposal of the workers' papers . . . 9) To requisition all food supplies for the broad masses; 10) To seize immediately all estates, all appanage, cabinet, and monastery lands . . .

(Izvestia)

. . . Even on the outskirts of Petrograd itself and in the Pskov and Novgorod districts, there is still a total lack of understanding of what has happened.

. . . and to think that a pedagogic fossil and Tsarist sluggard like this, and this kind of high-school headmistress, have still not been eliminated . . .

It is essential that we create house committees, which will keep an eye on landlords and, when necessary, institute criminal proceedings against them . . .

. . . not allow anyone's protégé into the militia.

The assembly of medics of the Orlov garrison considers it essential to abolish as soon as possible the compulsory physical examination of soldiers, since it is not compatible with the rights of free citizens. And the presence of nurses in military hospitals is undesirable.

Moscow. Recently, the "For Russia" society has been organizing large gatherings of Moscow's benighted elements.

. . . any deserters who do not return to their regiment by the deadline indicated will be dealt with as traitors to the Homeland.

The comrade soldier who took a bicycle from by the Military Commission entrance of the Tauride Palace is earnestly requested to return it.

Comrade N. Lenin has asked us to inform readers that no one invited him to the Grenadier Regiment rally, that he knew nothing of the meeting, and that he was very surprised that his name was put on the list of speakers without prior notification. At that time Comrade Lenin was addressing a rally of the Armored Division in the Mikhailovsky manège.

(Izvestia, 29 April)

WHAT THEY WANT. For some days now, rumors have been circulating all over Petrograd. . . . Some shady characters have been strolling about the streets, markets, bathhouses, and shops, collecting crowds and, anywhere and everywhere, inciting gullible people to arrest Comrade Lenin, give him a thrashing, sack the *Pravda* office, etc., etc. It goes without saying that all this rabble-rousing is with criminal intent. . . . Those old-regime swine, minions of the Black Hundreds, have started seeking a new opportunity for aggression. This shameless, abhorrent hounding of Comrade Lenin is necessary to those dark forces, so that they can start hounding all the socialists, and then the Soviet, and then perhaps they would succeed in bringing back the old order. We can agree or disagree with Lenin's views and dispute them most vehemently, but surely we cannot, here in a free country, allow the idea that instead of open debate we should resort to violence against a person who has devoted his whole life to serving the working class, to serving all who are oppressed and destitute. . . . For this reason, comrade workers and soldiers, we must act decisively and boldly to put an end to this shameless persecution.

(Izvestia, 30 April)

Boycott the bourgeois press! We, soldiers of the Izmailovsky Regiment, having discussed the question of the bourgeois press's unconscionable hounding of Comrade Lenin—a leader and veteran of the Soviet of Workers' Deputies and of *Pravda*, the defender of our proletarian and peasant interests—have voted overwhelmingly to boycott all the bourgeois papers. And we suggest that our comrade printers should not print them.

Followed by 9 signatures

30 April. The Executive Committee of the soldiers' deputies of the 12th Army declares that it has not authorized anyone to inspect how the Tsar is being guarded or to demand that the royal family be transferred to the Peter and Paul Fortress. The men who have spoken in the name of the 12th Army are impostors.

THE FIRST OF MAY. Just as the red flag has become the national flag of Russia, so 1 May is to become her national holiday. . . . Mankind's terrestrial and heavenly rulers, both of them cruel and despotic, demanded slavish obedience and blind faith. And in the holidays dedicated to the torments and suffering of mankind's redeemer was no vigor, no cheer, no rejoicing. But now a celebration of the brotherhood of all workers is born: 1 May!

The dam separating Russian and European workers has fallen. And we are bringing back the international 1 May holiday. Capitalists all over the world were already breathing a sigh of relief, hoping that the workers had, during the war, given up their 1 May celebrations. But now . . .

LET THE INTERNATIONAL ARISE!

[3 1]

Even from outside, Terenti Chernega's bellow resounded in the dugout:

"Tsyzh! What about some grub then?"

And here he was, bounding in. His shoulders seemed even broader, and he looked taller, as if the dugout had shrunk:

"Sanya, my boy!!" And he laughed his booming laugh.

Chernega embraced his friend—was it iron, that hulk crashing into Sanya's chest?—slammed his cap down on the table and flopped onto the block of wood that served as a chair.

"It's finished! Made it through all the sessions."

Sanya was happy. He'd been missing him.

"How long was it?"

"You won't believe it—nine days! We started on Friday and finished the following Saturday—nine days. They jawed on and on—they've really got the gift of the gab. How come we haven't seen them here before? If they'd all started talking at the same time they'd have drowned Wilhelm in spittle."

Chernega had been in Minsk for the congress of military delegates from the Western Front.

"Some of the socialists from the Soviet came in from Petersburg, four of them, two Russians and two Georgians—those four spoke three times each, and everyone applauded them. Idiots. Then there was a rumor that Kerensky had arrived, and they carried three of the Soviet men out, on their chairs, to meet him outside—but there was no sign of him. He hadn't come. We couldn't stop laughing. Well, then they kissed each other there, on the stage, a colonel and a Georgian, a sergeant and a colonel. They clapped that Chkheidze for fifteen minutes, but he couldn't string two words together—we didn't understand the half of it. On the podium he rolled his sleeves up and showed us how they punch the Provisional Government on the nose. And the hall roared."

"They punch the government on the nose?"

"Well, lead them by the nose then."

"Is that really how it is, Terenti?"

"Yes, seems like it. If not, they wouldn't have dared say so."

"Didn't you speak?"

"Yes I did! And how! I spoke on the first day. Then it came to fisticuffs. We were electing the congress chairman. All of us were for Sorokoletov, a gunner, he was on stage in his gear, you could see he was a real fighter. Only yesterday, he said, he'd been sitting in the observation tower, keeping his eyes peeled for the enemy and now he was here to do his duty as a citizen. But they wanted to foist some Jew on us, some Posern, who'd managed to struggle into a greatcoat, he was representing the Minsk Soviet, he said, a lawyer. Why aren't we commanded by our own men, front-line soldiers like us? We resented having to give in. You had to register with bits of cardboard like this"—he pulled a stiff little card, the color of tobacco, no. 220, out of his pocket—"and when they call you from the stage to speak they don't say Chernega, they say 220! No matter how much we argued, no matter how loud we yelled, and there were a lot more of us, they were stronger because—I'll tell you—someone, somewhere, even before the congress, had decided on Posern, that it would be Posern and that was that. And Sorokoletov, fine, he'd be the deputy. That's how it was, Sanya, my boy. That brought me up sharp, and now I'm thinking, no! We've really got to look into it, the cards are being passed under the table. I thought I had a ready tongue, but some of them there, phew! Fancy that, this one's laying into the government, and they'd arranged it all in advance. So we still need to fathom why they wanted us there."

"And why for nine days? Tell the whole story, in order. There's nowhere else we could hear about it." This was of great interest to Sanya and he also took a seat at the table.

The latter sighed like a blacksmith's bellows.

"That, brother," he mused, "is a tall order. It was a madhouse—no rhyme or reason to it. I never saw anything like it, only at horse-markets."

He stood up, pulled off his greatcoat, threw it up onto his bunk and sat down again.

"We had fifteen hundred delegates, and they billeted us all over the place, even in the military hospitals. Well anyway, we went to the station to meet that Gapemouth Rodzyanko. No other name for him. He just opened his broad mouth and stood gawking while everything passed by. The guard, the band, and that "Marseillaise"—sung by those who know it, while all we did was add a bit of voice—and then we started charging through the streets and General Gurko was there and that Posern was next to him. Gapemouth stopped to make a speech outside the theyetter, and he said I bring you greetings, with emotion too deep for words, from all the Russian lands, there'll be no going back to the old order, this great freedom—but then it started raining. Us deputies, we scooted into the theyetter of course but the crowd in the square listened to him for another half hour, and another one after him, Rodichev. Then they said the same thing again inside—that the old government had all but done us in, and now our fatherland was in danger and we had to knock those 'nointed sovrins—Wilhelm, Karl, Ferdinand, the sultan—with their divine rights off their pedestal. A lot of you won't get to see no new happy life, but you'll be happy to die for it. Why don't they go on and die. And then all that Sunday was like a holiday: there was no rain and everyone went out onto Cathedral Square. And the Jews walked separately, and sang their own songs and so did the Ukrainians. And everyone made speeches again. And tell me, what kind of a song is that "Marseillaise"—it's nothing to us, not a patch on our songs, like "Unharness Your Horses, Boys," but they sang it twenty times and the whole hall sang it, it would drive you nuts. And that's not the half of it! At one session they started giving up their George Crosses and medals as a contribution to the Soviet of Workers' Deputies! People came along the rows, collecting medals in their caps.

But Chernega's St. George Cross and two medals were there, on his round, bulging chest. He put his hand to them:

"I'm not one of those suckers."

Sanya wouldn't have given his away either. Crackpot idea.

"Yes, crackpot's the word. You should have heard what they were coming out with about the officers: we've not got enough victuals, they said, but the officers are sending our rations into the rear—what poppycock! They even wanted to abolish the officer grade completely. And one in four of them says officers have got to be elected! But the other three yell: shut your trap! And they want to cut the number of generals and use the money to increase the soldiers' pay. But how many soldiers would one general cover? They really went after our Smirnov, of course. Said he was a counterrevolutionary. But he led us for two years and we hadn't noticed. They're kicking a man when he's down. And they said every officer now has to run things so that every soldier has confidence in every order he gives. How about that?"

Chernega had been a sergeant and an officer—he knew what was what.

"And there was one who churned out the same old stuff, Skobelev from the Petersburg Soviet. He said that during the revolution the officers hid under their beds. And everyone clapped him, the fools. And in that hall, with fifteen hundred people, there were only about thirty officers. So then I pushed my way up to speak a second time: you're lying, I said, maybe you were hiding away, in Petersburg, but we were at our battle stations! And what do think happened then? Skobelev apologized, said he was sorry for giving that impression and he recognized the officers' readiness to make sacrifices."

Terenti thrust out his chest.

"But now of course, Sanya, my boy, the committees are senior to the officers. Now I'm on the corps committee, I'm senior to our brigade commander, that's for sure. And I can even challenge the corps commander."

"What about Gurko? Did he speak?"

"Gurko's a real man. We clapped him, our commander-in-chief! And he took a hard line: no elections for officers! In one regiment they'd elected their commander, and within a week they'd asked their corps commander how to get rid of the one they'd chosen. And Gurko told us how we must understand defense, too: it doesn't mean to stand stock still at your positions, the only way to defend yourself is by attacking, that's the only way to get the victory out of the enemy's hands. We applauded that. But when he left someone asked: if they order us to attack, how will we know it's approved by the democracy? Tsereteli replied: if anyone suspects someone has betrayed the revolutionary cause, he must refer it to the Soviet of Workers' Deputies for investigation and the traitors will be arrested and put under guard. And what did that mean? That we've got to start suspecting our officers again?"

Sanya had been watching Terenti and now, with a smile:

"Did you sign up with a party?"

"Nope, I told you: I'm keeping an eye out. Sizing it up. At times like this, you have to take a good look round. But in the theyetter, on the way into the big hall, you go through another hall, and there all the parties are shoving little books into your hand: read it, they say, read what we think. And there's nothing they haven't written about there: how the land's going to be organized all over Russia, five ways to choose from—it looks as if the land's their main worry. And the stuff they said about the government! We've got no government, Sanya, it's all just smoke, nothing you can rely on. And the things that Posern came out with! The Soviet was midwife to the government and we'll put pressure on it, lead it, control it, and we won't let it go back to imposing order and putting down unrest. And someone shouted from the hall:

surely we're not trying to bring in disorder? A lieutenant spoke: the government is elected by the people and the Soviet has no right to apply pressure. But from the hall, from two hundred voices: "Yes it does! Yes it does!" I can't tell you what it was like. And they sent a load of telegrams too—to that Kerensky, to Plekhanov, and some Brekho-Brekhovskaya woman."

"Anyway, what was the agenda? The order of the day?"

"Order? Don't ask me about order, Sanya. Even the water we drank was no good—murky, from the taps in the lavatory. Every speaker trotted out whatever was on his mind and then we went off into our different sections and bellowed at each other there, and then went back into the hall with everyone else. You'd be better off asking what decisions we came to."

"Did you come to any?"

"Oh, lots. Some that'll move us forward, others that won't. The main decisions were already taken, of course, that was no secret: they told us that in Petersburg they'd adopted things at a conference of the Soviets—and now let's vote to adopt them. But we did add in things we all agreed on: to re-examine immediately all the exemption certificates! And call up all those who were shirking military service somewhere! And send off to the front immediately all those already recruited, career soldiers, reservists, and militiamen as well."

"Why do we need all those?"

"To teach them a lesson!" answered Chernega, with a throaty laugh. "And all the gendarmes and policemen—off to the front with them! And that new militia of theirs—it mustn't accept men liable for military service—we don't want them hiding away there! And not another day's deferment for deserters, those wretches—off to the front with them! And in the rear units replace all the officers' orderlies and couriers with crippled and elderly soldiers, and send all the healthy youngsters off to the front! And all those who put on a show of getting registered in factories and mines—off to the front! And we've got to do a real clear-out of those Zemgors, Red Crosses, and War Industry committees, there's a lot of scum hiding away there—off to the front with them!" Chernega was exultant, baring large, even, flawless, white teeth. "And then, in the army supplies department, we've got to get rid of all those who aren't up to the job and put everyone under the control of our committees! They'll do an inventory of all our stocks so that no crumb goes anywhere but into the army's mouth! The-en . . . What else was there?" Now with less enthusiasm, Chernega remembered. "And there was a really bad decision: we've got to give the same rations to prisoners of war as we give Russian soldiers—have you ever heard of that before? Are the Germans feeding our men like that? No, they're starving them to death. Then . . . we approved an eight-hour day for the workers, as long as they work the full fourteen. The-en . . . The stuff that gang there crammed in—as if it was anything to do with us: take a broom to the priests and get rid of them, clean out the inspectors of schools, and purge their libraries of reactionary books—and replace them everywhere with revolutionary ones."

"What else was there?" Chernega was trying to furrow his brow, but that smooth forehead wouldn't go into folds.

"Ah yes! All our resolutions are to be translated into German and thrown over the barbed wire to the Germans. And this won't be our last congress, only the first, we'll be calling more now."

Tsyzh was already shuffling over to place all the settings, and a steaming mess tin, on the table.

"It's good to have you here," said Sanya. "You don't come and see us much these days—you're always in your committees!"

"And that'll carry on!" Chernega was already biting off a chunk of rye bread, his broad cheeks now bulged even more and he held a spoon. "Now I'm with the corps—so that's that! The committee's got to be on the spot to check everything, you see. But here they'll be replacing me with someone from another battery—haven't they sent him yet?"

An expression of pure satisfaction spread over Chernega's full lips and fleshy cheeks. He chewed, swallowed, and gave a little grunt.

"Ah, Tsyzh, your borsch! It's really something! Where d'you get your supplies? We'll have to start checking up on you as well."

And Chernega's merry little eyes flitted about, glad to be in his dugout.

"You'll sleep here, at least?"

"Tonight, yes. Tomorrow I'll check in at brigade HQ—and off I go to the corps."

Tsyzh went out, and Chernega said, seriously, scooping up borsch with his wooden spoon and gently blowing on it:

"Now's not the time for sleeping, Sanya. From now on we've got to be on our guard. People on all sides are taking advantage of our brothers."

He gulped his soup.

"Now we've really got to keep an eye on things: find out which is the most important string, the one leading us to the right end, and grab it. The government we've got now is dead wood—you only have to read their appeals about grain, all those polite requests—they've got no muscle, you can see it in everything they do."

And he ate, chomping appreciatively.

"Well what's the news in the battery? Is everyone still here?"

"Yes, still here. Oh no, they sent Barou away to military academy, to Petrograd."

"Right. And what about your leave?"

"I'll be off next week," smiled Sanya.

No matter how many times you repeat the word "leave," it still gives you a warm feeling all over.

"Going to Sablya?"

"No. Moscow this time, I decided."

And Moscow, for some reason, produced an even warmer effect on him. It was imminent. On its way.

"The lieutenant colonel's back, and now he'll let me go too. There's no shooting at the moment."

"He's back?" Chernega shook his head, moving effortlessly from joking to mourning. "Did he bury him? Where was his body all this time? How was it preserved?"

"He's not going to say, and it would be awkward to ask."

Lieutenant Anatoli Boyer had been killed in Helsingfors on 17 March and it was not until Holy Saturday, a month later, that he was buried, in Petersburg.

DOCUMENTS — 11

30 April
SCHLÜSSELBURG DISTRICT COMMISSAR SYTENKO TO PETROGRAD PROVINCE COMMISSAR YAKOVLEV

The Schlüsselburg district revolutionary people's committee hereby informs both the Petrograd Soviet of Workers' and Soldiers' Deputies and the Provisional Government that as of today, 30 April 1917, the committee considers the territory of Schlüsselburg district fully autonomous. All the internal life of Schlüsselburg district is organized solely by citizens of the district. External questions, relating to the interests of the citizens of the district but linked to the interests of citizens of all Russia, are decided solely by mutual, voluntary agreement between all the autonomous bodies comprising the territory of Russia. Neither the Petrograd Soviet nor the Provisional Government may, on any account, impose any kind of decree on the citizens of Schlüsselburg district without asking the citizens of the district for their agreement.

[32]

As the weeks of spring flowed away, another force was rolling in from South to North, golden, glorious, but now also formidable: Sowing time! The Sowing could not wait for all our arrangements to be in place—we had to turn our attention to it straight away. And behind that towered another hulk, the most terrible—Land Reform. And we'd been the ones who'd always promised this to the peasants as the most important of the reforms—so we couldn't renege on it now! But rumors of possible confiscation of land would mean the end of all sowing.

Russia, which before the war did not know where to export its excess grain, fortunately still, today, retained its old stocks, even in all the consumer provinces, and this softened the sting of the crisis from day to day. But, looking forward to the next few months, we had to hurry with introducing consumption quotas in all the major cities. Even in all the towns too? Even in rural areas? (And not to antagonize the city dwellers: the rural quotas must not be higher.) Would we need to extend the quotas to Siberia, Turkestan, the Transcaucasus? And what about sugar? It seemed inevitable that we'd have to bring in a sugar monopoly as well now, didn't it? And for tea? And tobacco, perhaps? And ration cards for meat?

The grain monopoly turned out to be immensely difficult to organize: Russia was totally unprepared for it. Announcing that all grain stocks are the property of the state was not enough: we had to *know* our stocks, and that meant we needed an *inventory*. And that meant that before the law could come into effect we had to create verification organs at every level. This role would fall, naturally, to the food supply committees of province, district, and township. But just how many members would be needed, even in a township food supply committee, to inventory at short notice *all* grain stocks held by *everyone* and determine the seed and fodder needs of each farmer (and each working horse and each colt), and assign the remainder to the state, with the owners keeping this grain safe until it's taken from them? And to weigh all the grain in every barn? Even in three months we couldn't get that done. Should we take people's statements on trust and only check suspicious cases? But will the peasants tell the truth when it comes to the thing they hold most dear? Anyway, for that kind of checking all the educated individuals in all the rural areas won't be enough. They'd done the calculation: the system of food supply committees and food supply boards across Russia will comprise roughly 180 thousand members—a massive new army of functionaries. And we'd have to maintain this army at the treasury's expense. And how much more will go on meetings and subsistence allowances? All in all—they'd done the calculation—it'll be 500 million rubles, won't it? On top of that, there was no way to avoid convening their all-Russian congress in May. And within the central food supply apparatus its own bureaucracy was growing rapidly. But life pressed on, and even while the monopoly was still only in preparation grain was already disappearing from sale everywhere. And how the objectors—and they were many—unsettled him. Some were trenchant: the whole project is "Shingarev's folly" and we shouldn't happily have committed ourselves on a question that was so poorly researched. (And they would not listen to Shingarev's explanations, that it was not he, personally, who had introduced the idea; it had developed within the social organizations.) Others found petty quibbles: with our fractured land ownership the monopoly cannot be implemented, or not soon, for everyone's grain is very different, some of it choked with chaff—so what coefficient could make them comparable? And where were the stocks to be kept and sorted? And how could we, in just weeks, replace a system that had come together over centuries? Compulsory requisitioning won't yield what the trader was able to extract: all the functionary knows is how to threaten. And will the population want to become dependent on food supply functionaries? And how to make the farmer sell next year's crop (he'll have to transport it too), which won't have been threshed? And how to make him do the following year's sowing as well, if he sees no benefit to himself because it'll be taken from him? And they'd warn him, saying forcible measures were almost certainly impossible now: the population would resist them since the quotas of grain and fodder set aside for the owners would be almost starvation level. And more dire warnings: in announcing the grain monopoly, they said, the government was also undertaking to feed the peasants in the case of a poor harvest. You're only leaving us enough "till the next harvest" but then, if it's a poor harvest, give us rations at state expense.

Ah. And they were right, too. It made Shingarev's head spin and at times he just despaired. And he began, unnoticed, to relax his stance little by little. He increased the quota set aside for the peasants—for the heavy labor they take on. (The socialists immediately went on the attack: you're depriving consumers in the cities. They have less meat and milk now, there's more in the countryside!) And in no time at all he started quietly raising the prices fixed for the grain taken by the state. Now they were a third higher than Rittikh's. There was only one, final, concession to Rittikh that Shingarev could not on any account make: payment for delivery of the grain to the station. That would infringe rent theory. No! Delivery would be unpaid. (But then, look how the number of horses in rural areas had decreased.)

But one thing leads to another. In mid-April, when announcing the monopoly, we published at the same time the government's promise to embark on establishing fixed prices now for iron, fabric, paraffin, and leather too. But it's one thing to embark on something, another to institute it fully. Shingarev soon realized that he was not strong enough to smash the industrialists' and banks' opposition in addition to the rest. No, he had to recognize that the monopoly would not be total: the state would take only grain ready for use, but would not concern itself with what it took to produce it.

In this whole, enormous task, Shingarev placed his most fervent hopes in the cooperative members—and he had managed to convene them for a congress in Moscow in mid-April, before the monopoly was announced. And how hard he had listened for every word of support! The cooperative congress not only voted for the law, but—what words he heard there! One peasant from Vladimir province said: "Yes, we *ask* the government to apply this law! As long as the enemy is on Russian soil . . . Tell them there, in Petrograd, that if we don't have enough young children, then our old hands are still strong enough to defend Russia. Those of us who have given the last of their sons will also give the last pound of their grain!" Yes, those were the words he heard! The very words Shingarev had always predicted! His ear had caught them several years in advance—and now they had resounded here! Shingarev, in the presidium, was barely able to hide his tears. And he replied to the congress: "Now I am calm. The mighty shoulders of the cooperative movement are supporting the load. The movement is small as yet, relative to our vastness, but in a few years we ourselves will be surprised at how it has grown."

Making speeches was, for all these weeks, a separate, uninterrupted current in his life. He was constantly being invited somewhere to make speeches, many in Petrograd and twice he went to Moscow, always for congresses. And there was no time at all to think about these speeches, to plan them, so he would deliver them impromptu, whatever poured out. After the Cooperative Congress he found himself at a concert in the Bolshoi Theater: "Let us kneel before the fallen heroes of our grey-clad Russian warrior host." From there straight to the train and, in Petrograd, from the train straight to the Kadet Congress, exuberant ovations—and wherever should he make a speech if not there? After that, he really had to go to the reopening of the Free Economic Society meetings—and that meant another speech. But what should he say? "The old regime strangled all manifestations of civil society. A rare joy has fallen to the lot of our generation, the joy of a return to cultural work . . . We have before us the prospect of correcting the innumerable follies of the old regime . . ." And then—off to Moscow again, for more congresses. Due to a major train crash, they had a five-hour wait near Klin and were late—but he did manage to get to the Pirogov congress in time for the closing session, to see his own people, his fellow-doctors, keepers of the sacred flame of the Russian intelligentsia—the most sublime, passionate words must be for them! "The old regime, rotten to the core . . . Comrades, tell everyone to abandon their life of luxury! Without grain, freedom will perish!" The next day he was off to the Congress of Towns, and the hall shook with applause. And: "I accept this applause, not for myself but for the Provisional Government. It is only now that we can live and work in complete unity with the people. The old regime collapsed because the people and the army had lost confidence in it."

It was at that same time that the Freedom Loan was launched, and all the ministers were charged with publicizing it whenever they addressed audiences. And so, combining it with the grain monopoly: "Should we print money? The presses are already printing it, day and night. But we must not avail ourselves of this sweet poison ad infinitum. The people must donate their savings and unneeded gold jewelery to the government." And (now back in Petrograd) he had to go on Sunday to the Gentry Assembly specially to speak in favor of the loan. "Here we heard the voice of a minister of free France, saying the Russian freedom was now as great as the French. Between the Great French and the Great Russian Revolutions there is indeed a striking resemblance. . . . The mistakes of an insane old regime must be corrected. Let us donate our savings to our country!"

And it was with real feeling that he signed and sent out all over Russia another appeal: "Let your hand grasp the plough more firmly, let it dig deeper into the moist earth, our mother earth. You are the compassionate heart of Russia: respond to the call of the Motherland. Agrarian unrest is inadmissible: you must not take the law into your own hands and cut down forests or burn the landowners' properties. That will only reduce our crops and be a step on the way to ruin."

Sowing the land this spring was becoming a matter of life and death. The sowing before winter had already been far less productive than usual, due to the high cost of labor. Now, due to disturbances in the countryside and, more widely, to threats being made, the big landowners were unwilling to do the spring sowing, and even began their retreat from rural areas. By now the middle-sized landowners were also wondering whether or not to sow. All over the South of the country, they were already missing the peak sowing period. And if the landowners didn't sow in spring, then by May the peasants would realize, and wouldn't sell their grain. And there'd be a famine. Shingarev's ministry was working constantly to lay in stocks, but it was the production that had to be saved. The land that the landowners were not now intending to sow had to be rented to the peasants in time. But what if a landowner refused? Force him to rent out his land? Take that step? (Force used against landowners wouldn't entail any dire consequences, after all.) And who would do that on the spot? The food supply committees, obviously. And how were we to provide a work force for our agriculture? Even the prisoners of war had by now started getting so out of hand that you had to offer them something advantageous, pay them no less than the average for their locality.

Meanwhile, threats from the peasants were increasing and the government, despite all the danger of worsening the social problems in rural areas, had to come to the aid of those landowners who were nevertheless intending to sow. But the government felt it was not possible to use military force against the peasants (and anyway, this was by now impossible for practical reasons). Their principle was to take an exclusively moral stance with the population. Somehow they had to explain things to everyone, in plain language. And now Shingarev resorted to an unprecedented measure: if the crops sown were spoiled, the government would reimburse the landowners for their losses. An unprecedented and massive burden for the government—but otherwise there would be no grain in Russia during that critical transitional period. And surely a free people would, after that, be ashamed to bankrupt their own treasury . . .?

The root of the agrarian unrest was not, of course, the sowing but the redistribution of land. The peasantry was racked with worry, awaiting that redistribution. The pressure was mounting: they could wait no longer, we had to defuse the situation! The land was so tempting, and there was no armed guard—how were the peasants to control themselves? But we must not allow a chaotic redistribution, before the Constituent Assembly. It was on this, the land policy, that the Kadets had always vacillated: all the parties of the left were demanding that the land be requisitioned, and without payment. But the Kadets would have liked to distribute only land belonging to appanage holders and monasteries. But private property? If we did take it, we should at least pay decent rates. The left wing of the party wanted total nationalization. But now, caught unawares by the revolution, they had not decided anything about the land at the March congress, and had put it off until May. But the Ministry of Agriculture must, at least, take a position. The battle had heated up over many years and it must be settled—but only, and specifically, in a way opposed to the Stolypin policy, opposing the farmsteads and the allotments. And the Ministry of Agriculture now stopped all the land-surveying and land-planning work being done in accordance with the Stolypin reform. (But that meant the remedial work also stopped on the swampy meadowlands of the Northwest, the saline soils beyond the Volga and the Siberian taiga.) But surely we weren't to oppose Stolypin to such an extent as to drive everyone, forcibly, into the commune? It's the peasant farmer who feeds us. Anyway, the allotment-holders wouldn't go. And dividing the land would require the breakup of large, technically advanced farm businesses, for the pieces to be put into hands less technically adept. And how about the land parcels with multi-field crop rotation? The cattle and poultry farms, the fruit- and vegetable-growing businesses, the sugar-beet farms, and both breeding and propagation nurseries—must we break all that up and parcel it out?

The revolution had indeed caught Russia unawares. Today even experts on agricultural matters are not embarrassed to admit publicly how little precise data they have on agriculture in Russia. The transfer of land to the people has turned out to be far from simple: such a reform could throw Russia back, far behind her present state, and sap the productive power of the land. At the moment insane agitation is fanning the flames in rural areas, and the reform is drifting in a fog. Before any reform we need an all-Russian land census: exactly how many peasants in each province need land and how much land can they be given? And the ravines are getting wider, not having been reinforced since the beginning of the war—how much land do they take up now? And what if a mass of the urban population also descends on the land? The quotas will be vastly reduced and there will certainly not be enough land. But now it's too late to try and persuade the peasants of this—they're fired up by our own agitation, especially those living near the appanage lands. But a census is a long process, and time is running short. And the option of moving away, far away—would they all want to do that? That, too, we should establish beforehand, take a poll.

For the time being—one more appeal from the Provisional Government to the population: this is the cherished dream of generations! But a great misfortune threatens our homeland, if the population of the rural areas will not wait until . . . It is a big mistake to think that every district and township can decide this question for itself. There would be a struggle between commune members and farmstead owners, village would rise up against village, township against township . . .

We had started by creating food supply committees (though not completing the job). Everywhere, "executive committees," varying in form and caliber, were springing up spontaneously, a new kind of local authority. But now, here and there, even more new committees were forming spontaneously: land committees. This was now the third parallel form of authority. (Pity we had not let the zemstvo take root at the lowest level, in townships!) But in the current situation, pressed for time, the government could not abolish them—it would be better to support and take charge of them. No one, including Shingarev himself, really understood exactly what the land committees would do or how they would differentiate themselves from the other authorities, what rights they would have, and what methods of action. But it was also impossible to stop the process.

Now disturbances had just broken out in Rannenburg district. The executive committee there had decided to seed the landed gentry's land forcibly, paying a low rent and not asking the owners' permission. Should he send in the army? But the government had already promised not to. So what did that mean? A telegram to the executive committee, saying it was unacceptable for them to take the law into their own hands and take decisions about the land in the absence of a law covering the whole country. The prosecutor had been sent from Ryazan to investigate the violence, but the Ryazan Soviet of Workers' Deputies had also set up its own "democratic commission of inquiry," topping the prosecutor.

And what ever kind of brain could grasp all that? There were dozens more questions every day. Here they needed a law to extend the fishing period this year in the Astrakhan basin . . . Here, to regulate the felling of forests by individuals . . .

And with all this back-breaking work he had to find the time to do almost everything himself, for the ministry officials seemed unlikely to understand all the intensity and the significance of what was happening well enough to give their efforts unstintingly. His hopes rested on Sasha Khrushchev alone, a friend of his youth. Shingarev had, thanks to Stolypin, secured Sasha's return from exile, and now he had summoned him to be his deputy.

Shingarev did not expect gratitude for all his labors—or, at any rate, not immediately. But today he had been shocked and hurt by a reproach from Prince Boris Vyazemsky, in a letter sent from Usman district. In mid-March he had come to see Shingarev and said such important things about the state of the rural areas and it seemed they had understood each other so well. But now:

"Andrei Ivanovich! I do not believe my eyes. Just when did you become a socialist? And your dreadful grain monopoly, and those omnipotent committees of ochlocrats—you are clearly installing socialism in Russia!"

Andrei Ivanovich stood there rubbing his forehead in an effort to understand. He could not believe his eyes either. Socialism? He was installing socialism? Never . . .

In the environs of Voronezh, spring was approaching, unstoppable. At his dear Grachevka as well. And although so many of the Russian lands were left orphaned this spring, unsown, the tiny spot on the map that was Grachevka whimpered its own particular lament: what about me? His father's land . . . But his father was already eighty. The duty of the eldest son. You do love all of Russia equally, of course—but Usman district is somehow more special. The year before last, they'd fixed up the house in Grachevka, which had fallen into disrepair.

And he and Fronya now came to a decision. There were, anyway, almost no lessons going on in the schools, there would be no exams, and students were allowed to leave—Fronya must take the children, they must all go to Grachevka and work the land.

"And the sowing, too?"

"No, you won't be able to manage the grain crop, you'll have to rent the land out again. But the vegetable garden and the orchard will be yours. It's not just the fresh air—there won't be enough food in Petersburg."

"But what about you? How will you manage?"

"There'll be just me."

"That's just it, you'll be alone! And by the time you get back to Monetnaya Street at night—nothing will have been done here."

"Good Lord! As a student I didn't have twenty-five kopecks to spend—and I didn't go hungry."

"Yes I know that. And you helped me too."

"I'll have dinner at my sister's on Sundays. And sometimes at Sasha Khrushchev's." (Shingarev had yielded his official, ministerial apartment on to Sasha.) "I'll manage. I'll have better things to think about than food. No, my heart will be at ease. I'll rest easy, honestly, Fronya."

He talked her round. And they started preparing for the journey. But getting tickets was also hard. There were thousands-strong queues and no tickets for travel before late May. He didn't want to ask Nekrasov, who had been so ill-disposed toward him in recent months, ever since they'd become fellow ministers. He'd even mocked Shingarev in public, saying that *now* there were freight trains (so where were they then?) but no grain to load them with. There was even a regulation, announced publicly, that officials in the Ministry of Transport were not allowed to show favoritism in the sale of tickets, and speculators would be imprisoned for up to four months. But needs must . . . and Shingarev found a useful connection and was able to get seats for his family in a second-class compartment.

And this evening he took them to the station with six suitcases—it needed two car journeys. He had been the one who organized everything but was now, suddenly, overcome by such melancholy, such misery, as if he'd never see them again. He tried to comfort himself:

"I might be taking another trip around the country and then I'll definitely come to Voronezh and spend a day with you. What a joy, to be in Grachevka! I'd love to do some digging in the vegetable garden with you."

His heart was heavy, but he didn't tell Fronya—though he saw the same thing in her pinched, strained eyes.

He kissed the children. And, after the second bell, kissed her dear face, every much-loved little wrinkle. It had been twenty-two years. Nearly their silver wedding.

[33]

It was a nasty business, that rally in the Grenadier Battalion manège. It simmered away for nearly twelve hours with fifty speakers, the best liberal and socialist tub-thumpers and even one revolutionary priest—but they kept on shouting "Where's Lenin? He lied to us!" We sent three Kronstadt sailors there to speak, but it wasn't enough. "Where's Lenin? We want to question him!" So we sent Dashkevich to explain that Lenin sent apologies but he was very busy in a session. "We want Lenin! He promised! That's why we're here! Lenin's a coward!" Plus insults, threats, and furious yelling. All the more reason not to appear in that melee: it would have been madness, and meant certain defeat. One of the Volynian contingent spoke: the German government has just given Lenin and his supporters a comfortable trip across Germany . . . And old Deutsch, showing no signs of pegging out yet: the German propaganda you hear from our prisoners of war is exactly the same as what Lenin's saying. Then his comrades had an idea: Vladimir Ilyich should get over to the Mikhailovsky manège straight away and address a half-squadron of the Armored Division, our neighbors in the Kshesinskaya house—which would mean he was "giving a speech somewhere else." Good idea. Off he went. But the Grenadier rally was still bubbling away till late into the night, still discussing—and cursing—Lenin.

In fact the campaign of harassment, fomenting animosity against the Bolsheviks, had turned out to be more serious, more long-lasting than we could have expected. Our Moscow comrades, for example, reported that people there were absolutely incandescent and whoever they were, wherever they met, they'd shout: "Arrest Lenin!" And they weren't from the parties: they were the most benighted types. And yesterday's demonstration by the war invalids was the most brazen, morbid propaganda stunt, dangerous because it used those stumps of men to illustrate a point and exploited the politically ignorant masses. And although only yesterday we organized a demonstration by the Kronstadt sailors and the 180th Regiment against the campaign, it didn't swing the balance.

It's quite clear that we have to be more flexible, more cautious. And we must hold back for a while on the slogan "an end to the war" and the one about the coup, and only use them extremely skilfully: we aren't in favor of brusque action, but persistent, patient clarification of the bourgeois deception. And when, yesterday, at the nearby Modern circus, our supporters held a big rally, they only included in the resolution the most incontrovertible watchwords: Confiscation of all the landowners' lands! An eight-hour day! A *war indemnity* to be paid by the capitalists! General armament of the working masses! No Petrograd troops to be sent to the front! And that was all.

It was now obvious that in the upper social classes, at bourgeois and socialist levels, the hounding had already abated, if not entirely disappeared. It could not have carried on anyway, among the incorrigible windbags (99 percent of all Russian politicians): as long as we firmly deny their accusations, they're easily persuaded to look the other way. Only yesterday, at the Kadet assembly, Milyukov had climbed down: we must not use force against Lenin! (This suited us very well!) Surely you don't want us to use the old regime's means in our struggle. And *Russian Will*, too, scared of its own print workers, has now lost its voice and fallen silent. (Lenin laughed at those Kadet assemblies, where they sounded off to thunderous applause, and that terrified newspaper. Shocking the bourgeoisie was a great revolutionary pleasure!) Tsereteli and Skobelev had changed their tune even more than the rest: no violence, they said, on any account—Lenin has a right to freedom of opinion. (This was certainly acceptable to us!) He was amused by Chernov's article about him yesterday, amused by this pompous SR pen-pusher, *explaining* Lenin to the public: Lenin is the victim of abnormal conditions, rushing along, not knowing where he's going. A maniacal mind. (Yes, yes, do explain.) Today Steklov's *Izvestia* also came out with a principled and trenchant article against the dishonest, abhorrent anti-Leninist campaign. (We must stop attacking Steklov; he's by no means the worst.) As well as that, we had a real stroke of luck. Yesterday's papers published two telegrams from Switzerland. One from Axelrod, Martov, Natanson, and Lunacharsky: "We can confirm that it is absolutely impossible to return to Russia via England." And from Mandelberg, Reichesberg, Kohn, and Balabanova: the solution is an exchange of émigrés for interned Germans. Well, gentlemen of *Russian Will*, are they all German spies too?

And so, within twelve days, the harassment campaign in the papers had dwindled and fallen away like a seed husk. Everything had been correctly foreseen.

But that was among an educated public. Russia's lower classes didn't dwell much on the printed word, and the hounding among them even increased during that period. In the streets they were tearing up *Pravda* and stamping on it. And it was in the lower strata of society that the real danger lay, a danger that could lead to outright pogroms. We couldn't carry on so unconcerned. And then came the hammer-blow: the Executive Commission of the soldiers' section of the Soviet resolved that propaganda expressing Leninist views was just as harmful as *counterrevolutionary propaganda from the right*!

An exceedingly dangerous attack! *That* was something we could not accept! They wanted to set the whole mass of soldiery against the Bolsheviks!

But even so, they added a reasonable caveat: no repressive measures could be taken against our propaganda as long as it remained only propaganda. That would be . . . acceptable. But would the masses, their minds now poisoned against us, take any notice of caveats?

And Lenin decided on a bold counter-attack. He really, really did not want to go and speak in public—but he was being forced into it. And today he went to the Tauride Palace, having sent word to get as many of his Bolsheviks as possible into the soldiers' Soviet, to call their comments from the hall. And without any warning to the leaders there he appeared in the White Hall, quietly climbed the steps to the presidium, passing the speaker, and announced to the bewildered chairman that he was Lenin and would like to make an unscheduled statement. The chairman's eyes nearly popped out of his head with surprise, and he immediately announced:

"Comrades! Lenin is in the hall!! And he would like to give his explanations regarding the Executive Commission's resolution. Do you want to hear what he has to say?"

"Lenin!" they shouted from the hall. "At last! Yes we do!" His supporters shouted and applauded with determined approval, but there were jeers from some of the others—and applause too, but theirs was ironic.

The chairman dismissed the scheduled speaker and motioned Lenin to the rostrum.

To that same Duma rostrum from which so many despicable parliamentary speeches had been made. And now Lenin had been transported from Switzerland to that rostrum as well.

There were seven or eight hundred people in the hall, and more in the gallery. But then, having heard cries that Lenin was there, even more started flooding in through several entrances. How was he to take mastery of such a crowd? Lenin maintained his composure. He could not make the gross error of using the same formulas here as he did among his people at the Kshesinskaya, but neither did he have a precise method for constructing a speech. It was clear to him that he must talk a lot, as much as possible. That would be the best way to convince the crowd.

"Comrades! I would like to give you my explanations regarding your Executive Commission resolution that said the propaganda of those you call 'the Pravda group' is as harmful as the counterrevolutionary propaganda of the right. That, comrades, is a very harsh accusation, and since I take full responsibility for the propaganda issued by those who share my views, I am taking the liberty of expressing my thoughts on its substance. What does the right wing want? Return to a monarchy. And the capitalists—they want the power in capitalist hands. But the aim of our propaganda is for all the power of the state to be transferred into the hands of no one but the Soviets of Workers', Soldiers', Peasants', and Farm Laborers' Deputies, which is, most certainly, the vast majority of the people! And we want to achieve this via patient clarification only."

He was trying to speak as peaceably as possible. With unbearable benevolence, even.

"From our side there has not been a single threat, direct or indirect, toward any individual. And we shall always act via clarification only, as long as no one exerts any violence on the masses. And however can you say of our propaganda that it is 'just as harmful as that of the right,' when the counterrevolutionaries want to saddle us, forcibly, with a Tsar again? There is a clear discrepancy, and the Soviet of Soldiers' Deputies cannot possibly share the views of its Executive Commission."

Lenin had been expecting a worse reception, expecting that, with his first words, they would start shouting "German spy," "traitor," and wouldn't let him speak, and it would be a fiasco—worse than if he'd not spoken at all. But actually his introduction had gone well. And now he had a winning topic, the topic that would pull on everyone's heartstrings—the land.

"Now, moving on, what are the essential differences of opinion between us? There are three main points. The first is land. We have always maintained that all the landowners' estates should become the property of the working people, and under Tsarism our party was cruelly persecuted for this opinion. But what, comrades, is counterrevolutionary in it? You may say that it is a truism and that other parties also had this in their program. But the difference is that today it is our party alone that advocates the *immediate* transfer of land to the people! And that is our watchword of the moment. The landowners have tens of millions of acres of land. And no amount of freedom can help the people as long as the land is not transferred to them. And if it is not taken away from the landowners immediately it will remain unsown. The immediate seizure of all land is the onward progress of a revolutionary people. And those who advise the peasants to wait for the Constituent Assembly" (now emphatic, now he was on the attack!) "are deceiving them."

Now came an error of a different kind from the first: he waited for the roar of approval from the hall full of soldiers—but it didn't come. In many parts they were smoking unhurriedly, and the heavy tobacco smoke rose, even reaching the rostrum. The hall started buzzing with conversation but it did not sound to Lenin like approval. Yet this was the part of his speech most likely to win approval. And it had not won it. He became flustered.

"How can it be? How is it that if the capitalists seize power from the Tsar it's a great and glorious revolution, but if the peasants take land from the landowners it's an unauthorized assertion of rights? Minister Shingarev has just sent a telegram to Rannenburg saying they must not dare take the law into their own hands and seize the land. Now does it look like freedom for the people when peasants—who are the vast majority of the population—don't have the right to take land, as had been decided, but must wait for the 'freely given' agreement of the landowners? What is democratic about three hundred peasants having to seek the agreement of one landowner? The landowners are never going to give land away of their own free will! *But who can stand in the way of the majority if it's close-knit and well armed?*"

No, it was not going down well. The voices were becoming more impatient.

"But we have never preached violence. The seizure of land should be founded on the strictest discipline. It is of course the Soviets of Peasants' and Farm Laborers' Deputies that will manage and allocate the land. It will be an organization of peasants without any control or supervision whatsoever from above, and without the landowners' hirelings. And the soldiers must help the peasants seize the land. If the peasants start taking land immediately, not waiting for an agreement with the landowners, not only will the cause of freedom have triumphed, but the soldiers will receive more bread and meat, because the production of both will increase. But you can't eat the land itself. Millions of households will have won nothing if they have no horses, equipment, or seeds—so these must also be requisitioned."

And still there was no roar of approval. Even so, it would be a shame to leave this subject: it was the most likely to win the day, the later topics less so. And Lenin started talking about Stolypin's criminal farmstead and allotment policy, which . . . The rich peasants were no more to be trusted than the capitalists.

People started shouting out from the audience:

"That's enough! Enough! This isn't a rally! Limit his speaking time!"

And the Bolsheviks shouted:

"We want to hear him!" and applauded, but they couldn't drown out the hostile cries.

Vladimir Stankevich, chairman of the Executive Commission, who had drawn up and seen through that resolution against Lenin, had been in the hall at the beginning of the session but then gone off to a distant wing of the palace and missed Lenin's arrival. Then someone had told him the sensational news that Lenin himself was in the hall, and he'd hurried back. (And he was not the only one. Other EC members, curious, also came.) But he didn't try to push his way to the presidium, and remained among the crowd in a gangway. He arrived when Lenin was saying that if we requisitioned the lands immediately the production of grain and meat would increase—and was seized by doubt: did this man lack intellectual capacity, or was he the worst kind of reckless demagogue?

His voice was flat, devoid of expression and, in addition, had a burr, and he used foreign words with no thought for his audience, and walked around by the rostrum, keyed up, even though there was no space to walk there. The figure he cut bore no comparison to the naturally handsome, captivating Tsereteli or the noble, stately Avksentiev.

Stankevich was reassured: that man could not entice the soldiers away.

And then they started shouting again: "That's enough! We've had enough!" came from many parts of the hall and Lenin faltered, though still appearing impassive, showing no change—but did that immobile Asiatic face with its sparse sandy beard ever change expression? The chairman, realizing his error, stood up and only now asked what proposals there were for limiting the speaker's time. They started shouting:

"Two minutes!"

"Five minutes!"

"Two hours!" (That was the Bolsheviks.)

A member of the Executive Commission, the military doctor Mentsikovsky, who'd been seated in a box close by, mounted the rostrum, pushing Lenin aside, and addressed the delegates with his customary energy.

"He's already been talking to us for twenty minutes about subjects that have been flogged to death, polemics against Stolypin and Shingarev. Later perhaps we'll hear polemics against Count Pahlen or Nikolai II? Who needs these truisms? I think Lenin could have formulated his statement more concisely and not taken up so much of our precious time."

The doctor, too, had failed to choose words better understood by the soldiers.

Then an army official spoke: Lenin's speech should not be subject to a limit. But such a clamor of dissent arose in the hall that we could only hear odd snatches of what he said. And he left the rostrum. But Lenin stayed. And amidst all this racket he even seemed to smile slightly. He was certainly sure of himself. Or was it an obtuse reaction?

Delegates were shouting from their seats in utter disorder and the chairman was shouting. Lenin bent his arms and wedged his thumbs under the armpits of his jacket, showing that he was ready to wait. People shouted, but no one came up to push him out. And in the ensuing calm the chairman announced that the speaker would be given half an hour. (From the beginning? Or from now?)

The hall agreed, but then the Bolsheviks started shouting, "Get that chairman off!" and those who'd got themselves one of the deputies' seats banged on their desks. Lenin raised his hand slightly, pretending to quieten his supporters.

And as if that uproar had never happened, without rancor, without emotion, he continued in the same flat, dull, even tones:

"Now, comrades, allow me to address the question of the Russian state order and its future forms of government. The kinds of republics that exist in other countries, republics with functionaries, police, and a standing army, are of no use to us. Neither do we need a Provisional Government composed entirely of capitalists. We do not need a government that tolerates the counterrevolutionary agitation of Guchkov and company in the army!"

The Minister of War conducting agitation in his own army!

"Does that mean, some may ask, that I am against power? Does it mean I'm an anarchist? My answer is no: that is calumny. We are not anarchists: we are in favor of power. And the power must be strong, but revolutionary! All power must be passed from the hands of the capitalist government into the hands of the Soviets of Workers', Soldiers', Peasants', and Farm Laborers' deputies. What, comrades, is counterrevolutionary in this? We are in favor of the kind of republic where, from top to bottom, there would be no police, no standing army, and no irremovable and privileged officialdom."

In other words, we must continue the disintegration happening now, under Lvov.

The soldiers listened, nonplussed: for them it was all a thick fog. No, Lenin would not succeed. But on the dais he was nowhere near as dogmatically bloodthirsty as he was in his newspaper and from the balcony of the mansion.

"The people must all, every single one, be armed, and the participation of women is indispensable, and there will be no 'oversight' or 'supervision' from above . . ."

(Lenin had no compunction about adding to the fog: there was no point in saying everything directly and clearly, it would not be appropriate here. Anyway, even he could not see to the end of this. After his appeal for the immediate seizure of land had met with no success, the necessity of continuing his unsuccessful speech here became burdensome. Even that half hour seemed a long time, and now he had to move on to the thorniest issue—the war. How to find a deft way through that?)

"People are slandering me, saying I support a separate peace. But all I am asserting is that the current war was initiated by Nikolai the Bloody and capitalists all over the world, and the new government is waging the same piratical war in the interests of those same capitalists. The working class does not want this war. Why does the Provisional Government refuse not only to terminate the secret, extortionate treaties but even to publish them? That means that the treaties concluded by the Tsar's gang remain in force—and are we to wage war for their sake? And yet there is a plan in them to divide China between France, England, and Russia."

Delegates started shouting:

"Where did you get that from?"

"You made that up!"

With that, the bomb went up: go and check it! Just try and check! Lenin, on a shock wave from the explosion, was speaking more confidently:

"The division of China! I know that for sure. And it's why they'll just spin the war out. We'll not succeed in ending the war while we have any capitalist government."

"And what do you suggest??"

"The war can only be stopped by a workers' revolution all over the world, and we are calling for this revolution. We never said the war could be stopped immediately, or even unilaterally, thrusting our bayonets into the ground while the other side is advancing. We didn't call on our soldiers to lay down their arms and go off home. The war can only be ended by a transfer of all state power into the hands of the class that genuinely has nothing to gain from safeguarding the capitalists' profits. Into the hands of the Soviet of Deputies. In 1915 we were already saying that if, during the war, the power was transferred to the workers, then we would strive to put an end to the war."

A piercing cry: "That's all very well, but **how**?"

Lenin didn't falter.

"One way of winding up the war is by systematic fraternization on the front. Russian and German workers and peasants in the grey soldier greatcoats can, by mutual agreement, make it impossible to continue the war any longer. And the fraternization has already begun! And not only on our front. We need to offer immediate, vigorous, all-round, unconditional assistance to the fraternization of soldiers *on all* the fronts. This kind of fraternization has already begun: let's help it along!"

Where had it begun? *How* could we help?? But he rushed on:

"Soon the majority will be on our side even in Germany."

"What if they're not?"

"In Germany Karl Liebknecht was promulgating our ideas and now he's doing hard labor. He is the sole representative of true socialism. The other socialists are, unfortunately, on Wilhelm's side."

"So then nothing will come of it??"

Lenin was confident on this too:

"If in Russia the power is in the hands of the Soviet of Deputies and in Germany there is no revolution to depose Wilhelm, in that case we shall point our rifles even more unswervingly at the enemies of our revolution! In that case we shall agree to a revolutionary war against the capitalists of any country! And it will culminate in a worldwide revolution, without stealing lands or suppressing peoples!"

And the Bolsheviks understood, from some sign he made, that he had finished and started applauding madly and stamping their feet, which set them very much apart from the rest of the hall.

And Lenin was already leaving the platform, but the chairman stopped him: notes had been passed up, with questions. "Why are you reinforcing Germany's unity?"

"Not only are we not helping to preserve Germany's unity—we're actually destroying it, by splitting up the German socialists. In Russia, yes, we're destroying the 'internal unity' of the workers and the capitalists. Let them put us in hard labor prisons, following in the footsteps of Nikolai II and capitalist England!"

"Why are you calling for civil war?"

"We're doing nothing of the kind," replied Lenin in astonishment. "I've not called for any civil war, but for patient clarification to the conscientious defensists."

"Did you peddle your views in Germany too? You should go and make your speeches in Germany."

"We published our views and sent them all over Germany."

"Why do you call retaking Kurland 'annexation'?"

"Because if we try to win Kurland back then the Germans will want to retake their colonies and the war will never actually end. Let each nation decide under what kind of state power it wants to live. Organize a Soviet of Workers' and Soldiers' Deputies in Kurland and let it decide what the people of Kurland want."

The delegates laughed.

Lenin cringed, and hurried off the platform. They were still reading out questions: "Why are you calling for the banks to be looted?" But he didn't come back to respond.

Stankevich thought that Lenin had won nothing, but he himself now wanted and needed to respond. But before he could get there the excitable Lieber, who had also appeared, rushed up to the rostrum. And this dark-bearded gnome, whom his supporters called the "Demosthenes of the Bund," started speaking rapidly and passionately—so unlike Lenin's tedious sermonizing:

"Comrade Lenin has not considered the sentiments of the united Russian democracy, and his group remains in the minority. It's not enough to talk about your wishes—you have to put the question in a way that will realize those wishes without the civil war that Lenin's propaganda would lead to. What is Lenin demanding? He says all the land must be put into the hands of the people. That's absolutely true, and other political parties are saying the same thing. But the Bolshevik leader is telling the peasants to go and seize that land straight away. That is what we object to, that propaganda, which we consider dangerous and harmful. He's even said, don't forget, that we must also seize the land of a significant number of peasant allotment-holders. Is that not a call for civil war? For the prosperous peasants will hold on to the land even more tightly than the major landowners. Calling for a battle in those conditions and overestimating our strength would be to repeat the misjudgment we made in '05. The terrible thing in this is that his demands don't correspond to the conditions of the time and the real possibilities. His slogan "Total expropriation of the bourgeoisie" is very nice, but doesn't that mean rushing into battle overestimating our strength? The bourgeoisie is still quite strong. And it's possible that a large section of the population would like to go back to the old order. We do not doubt Lenin's honesty, but his agitation is developing like an attack on the revolution. This is why the Executive Commission finds Lenin's agitation damaging."

Lenin listened to the beginning of this overweening impudence and then pushed his way to the exit, his face set in a sneer. We really, really must stop our attack on Steklov and transfer it to Lieber. Steklov wasn't yet lost to the revolution: he could even become one of us.

But overall his speech had been a success: we were no longer bogey men, anarchists, counterrevolutionaries, or proponents of a separate peace.

Well, the schedule for victory would probably be longer.

The Bolsheviks followed Lenin out. Some soldiers followed too, still asking questions: how did he feel about sending reinforcement companies off to the front . . .?

A hot topic.

"I'm not in the know on this matter, comrades, I can't say."

Quick—into the car.

DOCUMENTS—12

30 April
FROM GERMAN AMBASSADOR IN BERN ROMBERG TO IMPERIAL CHANCELLOR BETHMANN-HOLLWEG

Top secret

Mr. Platten, who accompanied Lenin and his supporters across Germany, visited me today to thank us, on behalf of the Russians, for the services we have rendered. Lenin was given a magnificent reception by his followers. We can safely say that three-quarters of the Petersburg workers support him. There is a greater problem in the propaganda circulating among the soldiers, who have formed the opinion that we are preparing to attack. Perhaps it will be enough to replace individual members of the Provisional Government, such as Milyukov and Guchkov, with socialists. In any case, there is a pressing need to increase the number supporting a peace, by means of some inflow from abroad. I therefore strongly recommend that those émigrés who are ready to depart should be given the same facilities as were Lenin and his comrades. It is all the more necessary to do this at top speed, since we fear that the Entente will start putting pressure on the Swiss government to prevent their departure.

The émigrés are sorely lacking in the means to produce propaganda. The funds collected for them have, mostly, ended up in the hands of the social patriots. I have given a trusted individual here the delicate task of ascertaining whether we could furnish them with this means without offending them.

[34]

Since Guchkov had returned, sick, from his trip to the south, there had not been a single day when he'd felt well. For the first three days he'd lain in bed and received colleagues at his bedside. Yesterday he felt better, got up, and received others too, from outside the Ministry. But not the military delegations that were arriving all the time, indefatigable, from the whole of the front. There was no way of stopping them—the entrance hall of the residence was jammed and the Moika Embankment in front was choked up with cars and people. He was already tired of those delegations, tired of listening to and talking about one and the same thing. This was clearly not good: the delegations were all proud to have come to the capital to show their devotion, but the Minister of War could not even summon the strength for a few kind words in reply.

There was already a timetable for today, all of it business, as if for someone in good health. But he had awoken this morning feeling worse, so weak, his heart ailing again. He lay in bed for a few hours more. But he had to fulfill his schedule. He got up.

And of course the navy was his responsibility too! How could he, just six weeks ago, have been so confident about taking on the Naval Ministry as well? Back then, it had seemed similar to the army, all of a piece. But—it was too much to manage. He'd had to appoint a strong admiral as his deputy in the navy ministry: he was to take charge of all practical matters. But Nepenin had been killed. Should he bring in Kolchak? But Kolchak was doing a splendid job at the Black Sea Fleet: he mustn't be moved. But otherwise . . . Guchkov could think of no other real candidate. He did not, of course, know the admirals very well. He'd appointed Kedrov, from the Gulf of Riga. But naval matters still kept finding their way to the minister. Here, right on his doorstep, that sly yet foolish Maksimov was demolishing the Baltic Fleet, and there were no hands to save it. If you fired him he'd send the fleet against Petrograd. (And we'd had to butter him up by increasing his yearly wages, even backdating them to the day of the coup.) It was not now commanders running the ships but committees. There'd been an orgy of officer dismissals, for "counter-revolutionary inclinations," for "lack of sympathy with the revolution"—and what were we to do with those officers, fired by their crews? You couldn't find jobs for them in HQs or in the ground forces either and, besides, committees had ballooned to vast numbers on land too, and they were also dismissing officers, expelling them. In Petrograd high-ranking naval officers and navy administrators were allowed to wear civilian clothes when off duty, so as not to excite the crowd unnecessarily: for some reason the naval officers' uniform infuriated them. Maksimov had reported to the ministry on a plan, which he considered very astute, to stop them tearing off the officers' epaulettes: to abolish epaulettes in the fleet entirely—they were too reminiscent of the old regime. Guchkov was indignant at first, but then he thought again: it wasn't such a bad idea, only they'd have to use a different argument, say that in the fleets of republican countries there were no epaulettes, only braids. So let us introduce them too. Navy HQ had worked out the details—who should have exactly which braids, how many of them, and with loops or not. And we'd make the center of the old cockade red. (This was just the time for Russia, fighting a war, to be occupied with changing the color of the uniform . . .) And today—he was barely out of bed—the first thing Guchkov did was to sign the order abolishing epaulettes in the navy.

And the second most urgent thing awaiting his signature was a decree renaming the battleships of the Baltic Fleet: so the *Emperor Nikolai I* would become the *Democracy* and the *Emperor Paul I* the *Republic*. . .

While Guchkov had been traveling south, here, in his absence, Kerensky had already proposed splitting up the War and Naval Ministries, and the ministers had "recognized this as desirable." And although Guchkov had flown into a rage when that little flibbertigibbet had, here too, stuck his nose into everything, he'd had to recognize with a sigh that, yes, he couldn't manage two ministries.

The War Ministry alone kept piling paperwork onto him—more than he could deal with. There were, for instance, things that had taken a long time to prepare, which not long ago had seemed vital for settling accounts with the old regime: today they were just relics, retained only to please the left. There was that business of helping the Extraordinary Commission of Inquiry by creating a further two special commissions, one for land forces and one for the navy, to look into abuses in procurement, armament, and support for our fighting power—in other words to unearth the "roots of Sukhomlinov-style management." And those commissions had to be given the right (in the spirit of democracy) to begin an investigation based on declarations made by certain individuals. (That'll bring out the informers.) And it wasn't long ago that Guchkov himself had been really excited about the war against the Sukhomlinov way of management. But now paperwork was trickling down to him by the force of inertia and he was signing it by inertia. (And now we have to include in all commissions of this kind—and this was unbearable!—representatives of the Soviet. What are they going to sniff out and find fault with?)

In life, Guchkov did not, generally, incline toward inertia, either in the way of inaction or indecision. But now he'd noticed, with concern, something strange: he was succumbing to such inertia—it'll run its course . . . just let it. No need to get involved unless it's absolutely unavoidable.

Now a measure was being developed that would reduce the generals' and senior officers' stipends: various allowances, "for fodder," "for rations," were to be cut. Well yes, that seemed fair, in the spirit of a democratic time. But at this high point of that democratic time we were hearing such demands as: while the members of all the soviets in the provincial and district capitals already numbered in the hundreds, and there was no limit imposed—they could elect as many as they wanted—now they all had to be excused military service! Or this: the national representatives of the clerks of the military court administration were demanding that the District Commander immediately arrest this or that officer as supporters of the old regime, and then set up an investigation. And the commander, having conferred with the minister, quietly let those officers retire, putting them out of harm's way. So *Izvestia* published a long, caviling letter asking why they'd been retired with a pension. Or: the committee of one of the riflery regiments was pointing out to the minister that he should not take on as his adjutant a particular captain because before the revolution he had worked for the right-wing newspaper *Russia*.

And what are we to do with the prisoners of war? They've become very brazen: they go on strike, they demand for themselves all the democratic freedoms—and the left-wingers support them, in the spirit of the International. But here was the right policy: when, in March, we took repressive measures as regards feeding the German officers we held, Germany responded immediately, saying they were prepared to allow our men imprisoned there to receive food products from Copenhagen. That's the way to handle it.

But whatever you set about doing—even if it's revealing military secrets in the newspapers, which are printing exactly which units are leaving for the front and the exact composition of the delegations from exactly which units—whatever you set about doing, it never seemed to be the main thing. The main thing was slipping away inexorably, and he couldn't manage to retrieve it.

Desertion!? That was probably the main thing. If every soldier who wants to can leave the front with impunity, what kind of war is that? What is a Minister of War to do?

Of course it was not really desertion at all. The peasant soldiers weren't running away from the war but taking leave en masse, so as to get home in time for the parceling out of land. More than anyone, it was the Provisional Government itself that was to blame. It didn't have a clear solution in mind for the land situation, so it didn't, in the very first days, make a precise announcement. There would have been no desertions then. But in the very first days—in the days that followed as well—there was no clarity. Everything was put off till the Constituent Assembly. And when Guchkov had published his appeal on the subject of desertion, he'd not been able to explain anything precisely. It was just "wait patiently," and something about the defense of the Motherland, of course. Cajolery, nothing more.

But then the authorities set a rumor running that anyone leaving the army would receive no land. And desertion immediately decreased. A good few deserters even returned to the front. So perhaps all was not lost.

But at the same time here, right under the minister's nose, his own Polivanov Commission was kneading and shaping (and backpedaling on) what would, inevitably, emerge: the Regulations on Committees and the Declaration on the Rights of the Soldier. The first army constitution in world history. And who'll be on those committees? Who in the army, apart from the officers, is literate? The clerks, the medics, and the Jewish soldiers. You can understand the Jews: they espoused this revolution to win rights for themselves. But as for the Russians, they're simply, ruthlessly destroying their state.

Then suddenly a telegram arrives from Novocherkassk, from the Don congress: Greetings to the Minister of War. We are ready to defend the Provisional Government against all attempts to limit its power!

And, for all these weeks, this was how Guchkov was being rocked between hoping and seeing his hopes dashed, between euphoria and despair. Only six weeks before he had seen himself, after a long wait, the intelligent, forceful leader of the Russian army and navy, surrounded by a galaxy of wisely chosen, decisive, brilliant officers. And now here he was, raised up over the army, a powerless, failing leader, unable to give any instruction without the Soviet of Workers' Deputies—and what workers did it have, for God's sake? It wasn't workers who ran things there.

And despite his distaste for them, despite swearing never again to have anything to do with that scum, he had invited their leaders to come, this very afternoon, to discuss things with him at the ministerial residence. And now he should, in view of the cardiac weakness that had returned, have canceled the meeting. But that would be awkward at this stage and, as a salve to his pride, he let it go ahead.

He never attended the late-night meetings between ministers and their "Liaison Commission." He knew this infuriated the Soviet, and that he was the one they wanted to see—for their complaints were directed at him. But he wouldn't let them see him. Guchkov could still feel the humiliation inflicted on him on 19 March, when he'd met their delegates here, at the residence. When he'd been traveling about, master of all the fronts, he had felt he'd left them behind forever, ascended to incomparable heights. But no, from those heights he had slid down helplessly on his backside across the ubiquitous slush, meeting them again for a second time. And he recognized, with shame, that they now seemed to be the masters—the already tyrannical masters—of Russia, and the ministers only their stewards, to be sent hither and thither.

The great, alert eyes and ears of the Soviet, that monster ("a fiend, horrendous, a hundred mouths barking"), had, it turned out, been following him from place to place, ever-vigilant, catching his every gesture, every word injudiciously uttered at those rallies on the way. At Kiev he had let slip that the Constituent Assembly would most likely not convene until after the war (which seemed obvious): and the Soviet published a rebuttal! (Do they believe that themselves, the fools?) In Jassy he'd said that the aim of the war was to crush Austria and Germany so that they would not, for the next twenty or thirty years, think of renewing their armed aggression. The objections were deafening: they branded him an imperialist! And they'd flown into a rage at their own All-Russian Conference two weeks ago, shouting: the Soviet's oversight must "hammer home its support for the desires of the revolutionary people"! The Provisional Government must be *summoned* to explain itself! And they very nearly did follow through with the summons. (And if they had, then our nonentities would have trudged over there . . .)

And whatever was the sense in meeting those bastards on equal terms?

But it couldn't be avoided.

Guchkov had invited the whole "Liaison Commission" plus a few members of the Military Commission to meet him today.

He'd put on a semi-military tunic for the meeting.

With some distaste, he had pictured the well-fed figure of Nakhamkes towering over them, so he was delighted to see that it was not Nakhamkes but an elegant, intelligent Georgian who towered; someone who'd not been with them previously—Tsereteli. Their chairman, Chkheidze, had not deigned to appear. Skobelev, that self-satisfied windbag, did come however. (Guchkov had begun, involuntarily, to distinguish their names and understand who was who.) The stupid, fusspot lawyer Sokolov was not with them. But neither was the sensible Gvozdev. In place of the previous, sullen navy lieutenant, we had the army lieutenant, Stankevich, also somewhat morose, but intelligent. Here too was that flea Himmer, who already seemed to be hopping, getting ready to jump in with questions and objections. And now there were two more—"soldier" members, Vengerov (there was a translator of Shakespeare with the same name: were they related?) and Binasik. Both were clerks, of course. (He remembered now, from reports: Vengerov had said at the Conference of Soviets that Guchkov's Order No. 114 was a mere *nothing*.)

The Military Commission representatives were on his side, but were not sufficiently influential to help in the dialogue to come.

And now these Soviet people had suddenly acquired total power over Russia. Why them? In recognition of what services?

But if there was any point in having this conversation, he had to talk to them *as if* they loved their country. He must talk to them openly, honestly: put yourselves in my position, try and see things from my vantage point. Is it possible to wage a war while allowing *that kind of* role for army committees, *those kinds of* speeches in the soviets, saying we won't advance, not one step?

The first one to jump in, of course, was Himmer, acting like the controller-general of the army and the government. But he even showed magnanimity: oh yes, it's an understandable mistake, confusing the political aims of the war—no seizure of territories—with the military-technical—moving a step forward from the trench. But yes, of course, it's incredibly hard to explain that difference to the uneducated masses, they can't assimilate these things.

But it's you, gentlemen, who put those nebulous aims into the minds of those uneducated masses. Now, somehow, we need to put that right.

But they didn't want to put it right.

"It's like this in all wars, gentlemen: everything goes smoothly until someone incautiously bandies the word 'peace' about. And everyone immediately starts pinning their hopes on peace, and the army is overtaken by paralysis. We must stop talking about peace out loud!"

But by now they couldn't stop. It was their sole form of political existence.

"We are for peace," announced little Himmer, crossing his legs to assume more gravity, but spoiling the effect by speaking too fast. "But we're also against our defenses being thrown into disarray. We'll make an ordered transition to peace."

Yes, of course you will.

But Tsereteli and Stankevich were serious as they looked at the minister. And they confirmed, perfectly sincerely, what Himmer had said.

"In that case, gentlemen," pleaded Guchkov, "why are you doing everything you can to destroy the army?"

Didn't they understand that?

"The democratic army will be even stronger and more dependable."

"But you know the Polivanov Commission is working. We've done everything we can to transform army life. What more do you want us to do?"

Uh-uh! A lot more, it transpired. All the initiative in this conversation had now moved over to Vengerov and Binasik. They had, it turned out, delivered the main speeches at the Conference of Soviets, about the rights and the everyday life of soldiers, and about army organizations. Everything, it turned out, had already been planned down to the last detail and already been passed unanimously by the delegates. Our army will, of course, be from now on not an army of career soldiers but a democratic army. The main thing for the soldiers will be to enjoy freedom of speech, publication, association, and assembly. The obligation to attend common prayers must be lifted immediately. And what about desertion of service or non-fulfillment of military orders? These must not be investigated by special military tribunals but by the ordinary civilian courts, based on common rights of man. And there must be no disciplinary punishments in the army, no soldiers sent to disciplinary units, for soldiers are citizens with full rights. And no set "hours" for leave from the barracks or lists of soldiers with leave-passes: if a soldier is not on detail he can go out in civilian clothes and spend the night outside. And the abandonment of the salute is not enough: the servile practice of the call to "Attention!" when a commanding officer comes in must also be abolished. As must the privileges of NCOs, sergeant-majors, and warrant officers. From now on all categories of soldier are equal!

He should have been more surprised that there still remained, in this madness, some small hints of sanity: officers at the front were not to be subjected to re-election. (But where there had already been elections for officers, the decisions would remain in force . . . And the men would retain the right to *recall* officers who were not to their liking.) And at the front, on a conditional and provisional basis, it was possible to retain orderlies (though only with the agreement of company committees).

And now on to the army committees. They must enjoy the rights of a *governmental authority* and make the decisions necessary for their unit. Yes, the army cannot be fit for combat if governed by dual powers, and *therefore* all the power must be in the hands of the committees.

Ah . . . he hadn't listened to Krymov in March. We should have got rid of them then, before they spread.

The anguished Guchkov looked at the fine features of Tsereteli and Stankevich and saw sympathy there. With those two, with others of the same kind in their group, an understanding would have been possible. But they were all, of course, subject to the unanimous decision of their Conference. And to resort to the extreme measure of *asking* them for help would also have been useless.

It was just as Guchkov had foreseen.

As a final argument, and this was not just rhetoric, he meant it seriously:

"Should I leave? I'm ready, gentlemen, to leave the minute you say so. I shall be happy to cede my job to you—as long as you undertake to save the Russian army! I'll be an adjutant, a pen-pusher for any other War Minister, I'll give him all my strength and my knowledge—but let him save the Russian army!"

And?

He looked at them all, each face in turn.

And—nothing.

They left. And Guchkov was taken ill again.

It's easy, thinking back after any landmark event, to make judgments as to the right course of action. It's only in the moment when something is actually happening that you're quite unable to discern the correct way.

He didn't have dinner—he couldn't eat a thing—and lay down for an hour and a half until the ministers' meeting that evening, to take place there at the residence. The ministers, of course, saw it as an imposition to have to meet there on account of his illness. He, the bravest of them all, the only fighter, had become a burden to them. He rarely attended their meetings in the Mariinsky Palace, and then there were his trips to the fronts when he sent Novitsky in his place. (What was the point of those trips? There, in the Council of Ministers, they were working out the penalty for resale of train tickets and seat reservations . . .) They also got in the habit of ignoring him, and took small decisions in the military area without seeking his agreement. They were still hoping that the moral force of the revolution would keep the flow of events within bounds. Laughable? But what else was there, actually, to hope for? Should we be uncompromising, resort to repressive measures? But there were no local authorities left for that, neither police nor obedient military units. And, while the Petrograd Soviet was gradually reorganizing itself into the All-Russian Soviet, the All-Russian Provisional Government was becoming more and more Petrograd-bound, hanging alone, with no support. Guchkov had advised them to convene the Duma again, urgently, to gain support from a legislative body. Shingarev had dismissed the idea. "You just don't know the Fourth Duma members. If you had to celebrate a thanksgiving service or a requiem you could convene the Duma, but it's not capable of legislative work." Lvov had even brought over some old draft laws that had foundered in the Duma, for the government itself to process. And Nekrasov was rushing round giving almost as many speeches as Kerensky (and at every appearance he would go to considerable lengths to declare to the crowd that there was no "dual power" hovering over them, to profess total confidence in the Soviet, which was the voice of the nation's conscience, that nothing could come between it and us, and that what kept the Provisional Government from acquiring autocratic power was that it willingly restricted itself by the oversight of the Soviet, thus forming the balanced opinion of the people).

So it ended up with Guchkov not even wanting to look at anyone in the government any more.

But today he could not avoid meeting them all, every last one of them: they had to discuss the text of the note going to the Allies.

And in that same, spacious ministerial office, with windows and a balcony overlooking the Moika, where at one time Sukhomlinov would sit, and where the Soviet deputies had just been sitting, now the ministers gathered and Guchkov extended his hand as they entered, for a weak handshake. He apologized for his informal attire. He semi-reclined in a comfortable armchair, and thought he'd like to remain silent throughout the meeting, sit it out with not a word: to hell with you and your note.

Milyukov took his seat, self-important in full formal attire.

But even before everyone was assembled the conversation came round to the subject of Lenin, and Guchkov couldn't contain himself (yes, he was ill, but this business had really got under his skin!). So are we going to cut Lenin down to size? We have to do something!

And the answer came in the dulcet tones of Lvov, the decision they had already come to, having thought it through: it was out of the question. Where Lenin was concerned, the government should not precipitate events, for that might give rise to conflicts or even, heaven forbid, a civil war. The government will continue to bide its time, preferring the initiative for action against Lenin to come from the people themselves, when they have perceived the lies in the Leninist propaganda.

Guchkov didn't bother arguing. He closed his eyes.

And he thought about Prince Lvov: what had become of his "Americanism," his administrative skills, his perceptiveness—qualities that had brought him to the forefront of the Union of Zemstvos? It had all been swamped by a benign fatalism—and even in meetings his gaze would often drift away into the distance and he would give a dreamy smile. All that was left of Lvov the zemstvo man was his way of not counting the millions of rubles of public money squandered. (While counting every kopeck of his own.)

Milyukov solemnly read out the note. Kerensky and company were demanding and highly critical, but Milyukov steadfastly defended his note. They haggled. Guchkov remained silent. And others did too. There was nothing so very new in that note.

Guchkov watched Milyukov through half-closed eyes and thought: an alien soul, rock-hard. This man certainly understands Russia's state interests, but from an exterior viewpoint, somehow. And he did not want to undertake anything together with Milyukov, even though the circumstances were driving them toward cooperation. The Soviet was abusing them both, and they had common enemies both inside and outside the government. But no sign of an alliance between them, nor even plain frankness, was emerging. They had long been strangers—the gulf could not be bridged. He was a Western professor. Guchkov didn't even want to have a drink with him.

But Russia had always boasted a multitude of dazzling talents—wherever had they all gone? However had the fighter Guchkov ended up among these bunglers and nonentities? In these six weeks he had dismissed 150 incompetent generals and other high-ranking figures and spent the whole time promoting talented men.

Yet there was no one around him. He was alone.

He had always, as far back as he could remember, seen life pulsating around him, a throng of people radiant with hope for a better future. But now it was as if he'd wandered into a lifeless salt-marsh. It struck terror into his heart: no one in sight, no one to call to. Would night overtake him here?

* * *

WE ARE BORN UNDER OPEN SKY,
BUT IT'S IN THE DARK WOODS THAT WE DIE.

* * *

[35]

(RULE OF THE PEOPLE ON THE RAILWAYS: FRAGMENTS)

* * *

Masses of soldiers, unwilling to travel in slow troop trains, storm passenger trains. Or make railway staff clear the way for the soldiers' own troop train, preventing any other movement on the line.

All the junction stations are choked up with deserters. (Many are hurrying for the "parceling out of the land.") They loaf about nibbling sunflower seeds and the platforms and floors of the station are covered with their husks. When a passenger train arrives, they force all the passengers off the train and make the station-master send it in the direction they want.

* * *

At Chernovodskaya Station, on the Transcaucasian Railroad, soldiers from troop train no. 13, unhappy at being overtaken by troop train no. 11, threatened the assistant station-master with reprisals unless he cabled a station farther down the line: hold train no. 11 until no. 13 passes.

At Glubokaya Station, they made station staff hold the passenger train bound for Batum and send their own train off first.

At Weymarn station, on the Baltic Railroad, a detachment of sailors clashed with the soldiers from a troop train over which of them should leave first. They came to blows and gave the station-master a beating too.

* * *

At 1 a.m. a troop train arrived at Velikoknyazheskaya station. The soldiers on the train, who were on leave, demanded that the speed of their train be increased by uncoupling twelve goods wagons loaded with unfilled bombs. The assistant station-master tried to remonstrate with them but they threatened to kill him and smash up the station. They wouldn't let anyone do any work for an hour, and the wagons had to be uncoupled.

* * *

The station-master at Simbirsk telegraphed Petrograd, the Military District, and the Soviet of Workers' Deputies: "Soldiers are traveling on all the goods trains and passenger trains. They insist on immediate departure, taking no account of goods trains coming in the opposite direction with food supplies. Goods wagons laden with food wait at stations for weeks but the soldiers won't let them be coupled on to continue their journey."

At Balashov Station, railway employees refused to work as long as soldiers were obstructing the proper movement of trains.

* * *

At Yaryzhenskaya Station soldiers dragged an engine driver out of his locomotive, and further violence was forestalled only by the intervention of people who'd seen it happen.

At Alatyr station soldiers used force to make an engine driver travel without his safety token into an occupied single-track section where a train was expected from the opposite direction.

Minister Nekrasov mentioned, in public, that such cases *occur sometimes* and it was pure chance that there had been no crashes.

* * *

No one is being allowed into a locked passenger carriage: "Official use only. State Duma Deputies." "We're not going to mollycoddle that lot! Break in, boys!" And they break the door down with their rifle butts.

Soldiers without tickets pile into passenger carriages, smash the glass, and climb in through the windows, not only into third- and second-class but even the plush first-class carriages. (The only ones they still have any respect for are the brown carriages bearing the inscription of the International Sleeping Car Company.) The velvet seats in a compartment with mirrored sliding doors are strewn with soldiers' greatcoats and sailors' black pea jackets. There's a strong smell of boots and the rich aroma of cigars is overpowered by the smoke from coarse tobacco. A lady in a silk dress grimaces fastidiously: hanging over her from the upper berth are enormous, rust-colored boots.

You'd think there was nowhere else to squeeze into, but at each stop another stream of people pushes in, through doors and windows, over shoulders and heads, some virtually hanging, others sliding under bench seats. They're blocking corridors, lavatories, brake-platforms. No one can get past. People are hanging on the running-boards and standing on the buffers—and somehow holding on when the train careers downhill.

Carriages are so over-full that springs collapse and axles break.

* * *

In a train traveling eastwards, at Tula it's already hard to get along the carriage corridors, at Penza there are soldiers traveling on the roofs of some carriages, and from Syzran all the roofs are covered with people. On the Aleksandrovsky Bridge crossing the Volga, they lay flat, but someone got knocked off and thrown onto the bridge deck.

* * *

The fast trains from Moscow to Rostov are packed with soldiers. Some spend their whole time riding the line, back and forth.

Soldiers sit on the roof as well. Near Likhaya Station a gust of wind dislodged one of them. As he fell he clutched at his neighbors and dragged them off too. Five of them tumbled onto the railway bed in a heap and all were fatally injured.

Two soldiers died in the same way near Voronezh.

* * *

At Yuriev Station, on the Northern Railroad, soldiers carried off to their own carriage all the food prepared in the 1st class buffet, together with cutlery and crockery. In third class they smashed up the furniture.

At Zhmerinka Station soldiers hacked four train robbers to pieces with their sabers.

* * *

Before the revolution, despite the war, passenger tickets were sold everywhere with no restrictions. Now, following orders from Nekrasov, the minister, ticket committees—consisting of the station master, traffic officer, and a representative from the social organizations committee—are being set up at all major stations to undertake overall supervision of the probity and orderliness of ticket sales. There are similar committees at sales points in town. People with an urgent need to travel apply to the ticket committee. Tickets are not sold to porters or commission agents. (Even so, a black market in tickets has sprung up everywhere.)

* * *

Navigation has reopened on the Volga and Oka. Soldiers are behaving as outrageously here as on the railways: they crowd out the accommodation in all classes, they send steamers in the direction that's convenient to them and requisition cargoes of food.

* * *

At the port of Vologda a group of fifty soldiers took control of a steamer that was supposed to go up the Sukhona toward Lake Kubenskoye. They prevented the loading of cargo and embarkation of passengers and ordered the ship down the Sukhona toward Totma. And from then on to Ustyug.

* * *

In March, peasants from several distant townships, some of them over a thousand versts away, brought 150 tons of grain over snowy roads to Golyshmanovo Station, near Omsk, "as a gift to the New Russia." It was temporarily stored in premises with a leaky roof, but still by the end of April no goods wagons had been found to take the grain off. And it got wet under the spring rain and started rotting.

* * *

At Taftimanovo Station soldiers in a train passing through disregarded the station-master's warning that the next stretch of line was occupied by a hospital train, and ordered him to let their train through. "The signal arm is down." Words incomprehensible to the soldiers.

At Arzamas a crowd of soldiers forced the station-master to allow a locomotive with a heated carriage—in which the soldiers installed themselves—onto an unfinished line. The railway bed, thoroughly soaked by the spring floods, subsided, and the carriage came off the rails and ended up crosswise on the line. The soldiers continued along the damaged line in the locomotive and then grabbed handcars for themselves and started bowling along on those.

* * *

On a station platform, by the train, stands an old man in bast-shoes and a hemp caftan, holding in his arms a heavy basket. He makes no attempt to push his way through that mayhem onto the train. But the soldiers climb onto the footplate and onto the roof via the hoop steps between the carriages. The old fellow:

"You monsters! Where are you making off to? You'll destroy Russia!"

The soldiers laugh down at him:

"There'll be enough Russia to go around, grandpa!"

* * *

At Gryazi Station, soldiers demanded that their train be re-equipped. While the work was under way, a refugee came up to them and complained about the priest in her locality, Father Bogoyavlensky: he was not giving out full rations, she said. The soldiers summoned the priest to the station and first abused him, then beat him unconscious. And he died.

* * *

At Stakelna Station a crowd of soldiers from a troop train waiting there attacked Shchavinsky, the station-master, and beat him cruelly for delaying their train for thirty minutes to let an oncoming train pass. Shchavinsky (in 1905 he'd led the strike at the Pskov railway hub) died from the beating.

* * *

At Tylovaya Station, on the Southeastern Railroad, a group of soldiers passing through would not allow a fire in a goods wagon full of hay to be put out, and arrested the railway employee leading the firefighting. They surrounded the station-master and didn't allow him to give instructions either, shouting, "Kill the railwaymen!"

* * *

AT LEAST WE'RE ALL IN THE SAME BOAT.

* * *

DOCUMENTS — 13

1 May
GERMAN GENERAL HEADQUARTERS TO MILITARY ATTACHE VON BISMARCK, BERN

His Excellency General Ludendorff suggests that only Russians not hostile to us should be allowed to travel through Germany.

1 May
ATTACHE VON BISMARCK TO GENERAL LUDENDORFF

Only Russians actively promoting peace are to be sent.

[36]

Suddenly on the 28th, Saturday, the whole of educated Petrograd was abuzz with rumors that Milyukov was leaving the government! It was so shocking and so unbelievable that not a single newspaper dared take up the story. But all the same, it was so very widespread that *New Times*, feeling its way into a new role under the new regime, published a firm rebuttal the following day. (With a suggestive disclaimer, however, saying that the Provisional Government would, in the very near future, be *dealing with the question of international relations*.)

You could have knocked Pavel Nikolaevich down with a feather! *New Times* supporting him?

And where had it come from? From Kerensky, of course. And his murky chums Tereshchenko and Nekrasov. And perhaps that blabber Vladimir Lvov. On the evening of 26th Milyukov had only threatened to resign. And by the morning of 28th all Petrograd was already talking about it. What good were those ministers, then? What good was that whole government?

In fact, for Pavel Nikolaevich the hardest part of being a minister was sitting through those wearying sessions of the Council of Ministers every day (if not every evening as well). He was forming such an interesting extension to his cabinet, creating economic and legal departments (and not removing any ministers from their posts, valuing as he did established tradition, and retaining Neratov as the driving force), as well as extremely important and substantive negotiations with the ambassadors, when—he had to tear himself away from all that and come here to endure those hours and hours. (And anyone doing serious work in his own ministry also attended with no enthusiasm.) Of course they were all, apart from Milyukov, occupied with domestic policy, but at the end of the war nimbleness and good sense would be required in foreign policy. If we didn't take the correct position in time, grasp it in time, stipulate what Russia's share was to be—then we wouldn't recover that lost ground even with the whole country putting in years of work.

They seemed to be working on supposedly important projects, in session all Saturday evening and that night—analyzing, delving into, ratifying point by point three laws of supposedly major significance: on the rules for municipal elections, the organization of the militia, and the establishment of regimental tribunals. But those tribunals were a stupid, demagogic measure that had been forced on them, and the municipal elections were showing no sign of happening before the end of the summer. Only the militia, in fact, was a burning issue, because the capital and the rest of the country were being rocked by burglaries and thuggery. But how could this militia manage, if the whole unified Provisional Government could do nothing more than issue an Appeal regarding each case, imploring, if not actually tearful? Printing presses were being seized and publications forced into closure? Well let the victims lodge a complaint with the tribunals. In the factories, not only the Russian but also the foreign technical staff were now being arrested? Make an appeal. And every one of these appeals must, insisted the gentle prince, be signed by every minister. And Nekrasov had conceived the idea of paying all the deputies of all the local soviets for the time spent in sessions, treating it as work time. And, for post and telegraph staff, "enhanced" and "extra enhanced" salaries (and this when the delivery of telegrams was atrocious). After this, Konovalov, Kerensky, and Shchepkin immediately started asking for 10 million here, 25 million there, for salary increases, one-off subsidies, and additional funds for a variety of purposes in their ministries. And they all got what they wanted, straight away. And ministers who hadn't asked for increases for their subordinates started feeling awkward in their presence.

So Milyukov also had to ask for increases. (Which he received.) Then, starting with Konovalov, but even Lvov joined in, a competition developed, to increase the number of a minister's deputies, all of them with fat salaries. Under the Tsar, ministers had each had two deputies, but now they'd started forming teams of three, four, and even five per minister. But in mid-April they'd had to discuss the fact that the State Duma, busy attacking the government, had not had time to ratify the budget for 1917. And how could they guess, now, how high spending might go? If they took last year's figure, then they'd far, far exceed it—that much was obvious.

But Milyukov sat through all that bickering, stony-faced and disdainful, not getting involved, not arguing. Firstly because he knew very well that Russia was exceedingly rich and it would take a long, long time to ruin her. Secondly because all this would be overridden by the army's successes and the diplomatic game being played on the green baize—as long as Pavel Nikolaevich was not prevented from conducting that game properly. And he didn't object, didn't challenge when two-fifths of all the government's decisions were about the creation of ever more new committees and interministerial commissions, stacked by now in two and even three layers. And when something was expected from the Ministry of Foreign Affairs, then Milyukov too would propose something: sending a mission to the United States on financial matters, or making representations to the Greek government that, according to the agreement of 1867, the Queen of the Hellenes' dowry must not be paid into the Treasury. (And that was not even the most trivial of matters: the minutes also recorded the fact that a certain "free artist" was giving the Provisional Government a small plot of land.)

Milyukov's colleagues had not grasped, not fully understood the extreme danger of the current imbalance—he alone had. A great, unexpected weight was starting to press down on the scales, on the side of disintegration. At its sessions, the government wasn't talking about it seriously yet, but Milyukov watched with near-horror how it grew and gained weight daily: it was the national break-up of the Empire.

Never mind Poland. Although her inordinate ambitions, to transform immediately from a subject kingdom into a great power by seizing a bit more Russian land, had always rankled with Milyukov, irritated him to such an extent that he struggled to keep a liberal expression on his face, he was readying himself to concede on the Polish question—it was inevitable. It was already impossible to stop at Polish autonomy, which had previously been in the Kadets' program: now the Allies' sympathy was adding to the pressure. But Finland? Finland had, it must be said, been both showered by the Tsars with privileges, such as had never been seen before in the history of states, and then also raised up into a much-loved monument by the whole of the Liberation and revolutionary movement. The Finns already enjoyed free industry and commerce all over Russia, while Russians had no such reciprocal arrangement in Finland: the Russian doctor, teacher, artisan there had lost the right to follow his trade and Russians had no right to work as civil servants. They had, in fact, even fewer rights than any foreigner, who was defended by his consulate. The Finnish currency was protected, they'd been absolved from Russian military service, the Russian police had no power to arrest or investigate people on Finnish territory—and the Finns were portraying all of that (and the Liberation movement had no choice but to support them) as the uncivilized Russian people exerting force on the freedom-loving, civilized Finns. Since the beginning of the war, young Finns had been joining the German army, blowing up our bridges and arms depots, and that too we saw, with some bitterness, as collaboration with our Liberation movement. But today?! Finland showed open disloyalty to the Russian revolution, and the Finnish press called on its Senate to take wider powers without reference to the Provisional Government. And while all over the world the Russian ruble was either staying strong or, after the revolution, strengthening, Finland was the first place where it started falling. But then, the most extreme act of defiance: Finland did not adopt Russia's law on equal rights for Jews and did not give Jews the right to reside there or give evidence in court, and they were still, today, expelling Jews. It was impossible to make them see reason.

But Ukraine? For decades the Russian Liberation movement had offered warm support to every Ukrainian protest, not delving into details or doing any investigations, for everything that rocked the autocracy had been considered useful. From mid-March, the Provisional Government had also approved teaching in the Ukrainian language and all measures to restore its culture, and had even begun to give way on the creation of separate Ukrainian regiments—even though that would mean the disintegration of the armed forces. But then things soon went overboard. The Kiev junior cadets' conference decided that all regiments on Ukrainian territory must consist exclusively of Ukrainians and that only Ukrainians could study at the Kiev military school—and that was right behind the Southwestern Front! We were already hearing at rallies: let's not wait for the Constituent Assembly, let's convene our own Ukrainian Constituent Assembly! And it wasn't the Provisional Government that dared to object to that, and it wasn't Brusilov, it was the Kiev Soviet of Workers' and Soldiers' Deputies: you stab us in the back like that? Our bayonets'll put a stop to that!! Even the Social Democrats didn't recognize the right of every nationality, every part of the state to organize itself separately. Grushevsky and Vinnichenko had backed away, apologizing. But just a few days later the Ukrainian demands had become even more ambitious: the territory of the future Ukraine would stretch from Grodno province and include the Kuban. At least they weren't, at that stage, demanding the Crimea. But when, ten days ago, the Ukrainian congress had opened in Kiev, they were already demanding the southern shore of the Crimea as well. Their congress vacillated as to whether to announce itself as the Constituent Assembly of Ukraine. They decided to set up Ukrainian legions all over Ukraine, and to demand that Ukraine be admitted to the future peace conference as a separate entity. And according to the rumors they had already sent delegates to the Don, the Kuban, and the Terek to begin the merging process. They were not yet saying directly that all they wanted was to secede, but Milyukov was no political greenhorn. When ever had that Ukrainian separatism had time to develop? The public had not even noticed. We'd been wholeheartedly supporting their cultural autonomy—and they'd turned out like this? And **such** a shake-up, in time of war, without waiting for the right moment??

And that wasn't the half of it! The Estonians, both the Irkutsk and the Trans-Baikal Buryats, the Moldavians, Latvians, Georgians, Lithuanians, Crimean Tatars, Khivans, and Bukharans were demanding autonomy. Only the Armenians, it seemed, had voted unanimously not to challenge us with nationalist slogans. The Chechens were planning a congress in Grozny jointly with the Cossacks—what would they announce there? The Kazan Tatars were insisting that separate Muslim regiments must be created. In Astrakhan a Central Kalmyk committee was formed. A Turkestan committee was formed, and a Transcaucasian, just behind the front, without asking permission. (GHQ and the government learned of it from the newspapers.) And they all wanted to get on with extending their territory immediately. The Lithuanians had mapped out their provinces, spilling over into the Poles'. The Zaysan Kirghiz wanted to move the Russians out of the steppes and take the land away from the settlers. The Georgian National Democrats were demanding that all newcomers be removed from Georgia. But the thing that shocked Milyukov more than anything, perhaps, was the fact that in Irkutsk they had already worked out a Siberian constitution, which was ready to go. The Siberians were, they said, a separate culture and their way of life was different from the Russians'. On economic matters they were in conflict with Russia, which was exploiting their wealth and their territory: immigration into Siberia must be stopped. It must be declared an autonomous province with its own legislation, and a separate executive authority must be created. The Russian government must be left with only war, peace, and treaties, and money, post, and telegraph.

The best minds of the Liberation movement had not foreseen anything like this resulting from the fall of the autocracy, Milyukov included.

However—finesse was required, and restraint. We must not express our indignation, publicly or in print: at a time like this, it would be seen as clamping down on freedom.

With his highly developed sense of a statesman, Milyukov understood that this process of disintegration could only be stopped now by a Russian victory in the war. Which was why loyalty to the Allies was now not just a duty of honor for Russia but a consideration in saving the state.

Unexpectedly, and unnoticed, the heavy mantle of an imperial heritage had descended onto the shoulders of the liberal professor, Milyukov.

But they understood nothing of this, the members of the government, the Executive Committee understood even less, and the socialist extremists, newly arrived from the West, less still. They were demanding, and expecting, from Milyukov: the note, the note! The note to the Allies about the aims of the war! And "the seven" ministers, so obliging, had already promised the EC such a note.

Motu proprio,[2] Milyukov would not on any account have sent such a thing. But now, clearly, he could not avoid it.

Milyukov, however, had never been a pushover: his ability to stand firm was beyond compare. Write a note now, new in crucial respects? No, that

2. On his own initiative (Lat.).

he refused to do. The most he would do was to send the Allies the declaration of 9 April (up to this point they hadn't needed to know about it) and, yes, with a note accompanying it. But even this kind of note could not be sent without a reason. Well, he could think up a reason, along these lines (which suited his aims): rumors have been circulating, which suggest that Russia is ready to conclude a separate peace, so we . . .

The ministers agreed.

But he'd need to hoodwink them too with this note, not to mention the Soviet. The Allies, on the other hand, must be assured of our determination, confident that we would wage war till total victory.

So he must start by rebutting the rumors of a separate peace. There will, of course, be no such thing. The proclamation of 9 April, enclosed herewith, shows clearly that the views of the Provisional Government are in entire agreement with those lofty ideas which have been constantly expressed by eminent statesmen in the Allied States, and given especially vivid expression by the president of the great republic across the Atlantic.

For the Allies, it was very clear: our view is no different from yours. But for the Soviet it was also clear, too much so. No, here it had to be counterbalanced by some democratic slogans: the liberating character of the war . . . amicable existence of nations . . . That would be acceptable to everyone and would worry no one.

And it would be useful to give the government under the old regime, incapable of grasping and sharing these ideas, another knock. But emancipated Russia can now speak in a language comprehensible to the leading democracies of our own time.

(But just try speaking that language . . .)

. . . And this is why Russia hastens to add her voice to those of her Allies.

The hint seems clear, doesn't it? Try and pick some holes in it.

No, it isn't explicit enough. Neither Buchanan nor Paléologue will be satisfied. London and Paris want to hear a precise undertaking that's incontrovertible and carries some weight. But how to express that, when confronted with the ugly, raging mug of the Soviet?

. . . Of course, the Provisional Government's declarations cannot afford the least excuse for the assumption that the revolution has entailed any slackening on the part of Russia in the common struggle of the Allies . . .

(That did seem to work! It's not our government, imperialist as it may be, but the people themselves who want victory!)

. . . The aspiration of the entire nation to carry the World War to a decisive victory has grown more powerful following the overthrow . . . And it is concentrated upon a task which touches all and is universally understood, of driving out the enemy who has invaded our country . . . The struggle is now understood by all . . .

A responsibility we all share. Excellent.

But this, alas, was not enough. Lloyd George and Clemenceau, and now Wilson too, were tormenting Milyukov pitilessly, looking daggers at him from their democratic heights: Not enough! We need it more precise! Are you staying true to your alliance obligations?

And all his reason, all his thinking was focused on them: Yes, of course! Can it be that you don't trust our democracy?

But his pen grew twenty pounds or so heavier—even with both hands he couldn't guide it, couldn't manage a vertical line.

. . . The Provisional Government, while safeguarding the rights of our country (that does tone it down, doesn't it?), will observe the obligations assumed toward our Allies . . .

Or do we need: observe *in every way* the . . .?

Somehow we have to finesse this situation, correct the unsatisfactory vagueness of the 9 April document with new promises, equally vague.

Both that day and the next, Pavel Nikolaevich was in torments over that note. And it wasn't, of course, his only worry. On Sunday, particularly, there was no peace, because it was on Sundays that all the public discussions took place, and he had to attend. In the afternoon he went to the Gentry Assembly, for a rally in support of the Freedom Loan—all the ministers had to. As it happened, the American ambassador was there too, so it was a good opportunity to tell him how pleased we were that the oldest democracy had joined the Entente Alliance . . . Ready to help us with both gold, of which it had accumulated a great deal, and locomotives. In the presence of help like this, Russia mustn't cover itself in shame.

There were so many speeches during those weeks, and each had to be concocted with some originality.

Then Tereshchenko regaled the magnificent hall with this news: Moscow commerce and industry had decided to give the loan 25 percent of its capital base.

This was barely credible: Moscow merchants waving away a quarter of all their wealth?

But that same afternoon, toward evening, he learned that a plenary session of the Soviet of Workers' Deputies had taken place at the Sea Cadet Corps, also discussing the loan. And they had decided not to support the loan for the time being, to put it off for a few days to see how the government behaved, in view of its promise to renounce all aspirations to territorial conquests within three days.

They were trying to wring out of us a renunciation of "annexations and indemnities." To force us into betraying the Allies.

So, while privately torturing himself over the composition of this note, and out loud trying to convince the public, and with the time approaching when he must debate the subject with his fellow-ministers, on Monday, yesterday, Milyukov had opened the papers—and gasped. He had completely forgotten that, one Sunday earlier, in the train leaving Moscow, he'd been careless enough to talk to the correspondent of the *Manchester Guardian*, which had published it last week. But it would have taken a long time for

Russia to learn of this had the *Stock Exchange Gazette* not had a London correspondent, and now this paper alone had taken an extract from it and printed, in a bold font:

RUSSIAN CONTROL OF THE STRAITS

There you are, trying to keep your balance while treading the finest of lines, and someone slings an eighty-pound sandbag at you.

Question: About the southern Slavs in Austria. Answer: Independence for the Slavs is the only satisfactory solution. Question: Can the declaration of 9 April have an influence on the future of Constantinople and the Straits? Answer: Russia must insist on its right to close the Straits to foreign warships passing through. And this would be possible if she could gain mastery of the Straits and the possibility of fortifying them. Question: But do you not think the United States would object to this solution? Answer: The way we interpret Wilson's declaration, the United States is not against Russia having mastery of the Straits . . . (Though it appears that Wilson was, in fact, against this.)

Alea jacta est![3] There was no point trying to maintain a balance now. The cards were on the table and he must have the courage to stand up for his convictions. So he'd write:

. . . continuing to cherish the firm conviction of the victorious issue of the present war in full accord with our Allies . . .

He had to come down on one side—and stick to it. It would be intolerable if relations with our Allies were allowed to waver. Intolerable if the share Russia would gain at the end of the war were reduced or weakened—especially now, when the war was nearing an end.

With indestructible resolve, Milyukov went to the closed-door meeting of the Provisional Government to discuss the note.

They organized it at the War Minister's, Guchkov's, residence. It was such an important matter that everyone had to attend, but Guchkov had not been seen at the Mariinsky Palace for over a week. So they all went to his place.

He emerged from his bedroom, unsteady on his feet. He greeted them, not with individual handshakes but a bow to the whole group, and let himself down into an armchair with a reclining back. His weak heart had been playing him up for a long time, and now it seemed he was the first of them to be brought down, injured.

Pavel Nikolaevich looked at that heavy, morose face with regret and with a deeply felt disapproval. Guchkov had never been a friend, never an ally. (When Milyukov had walked into the Third Duma after his American tour, the majority had immediately stood up and left, in protest against the liberal nature of his speeches there—and Guchkov had been among the first.) But

3. The die is cast (Lat.).

in these weeks, on these peaks they had inhabited, they could have joined forces. And, what's more, Guchkov was the only one here who properly understood the real significance of the Straits. How well they could have stood their ground together! They would have steered the government in a quite different direction. But not only had Guchkov not supported such an alliance: he was not even holding his own brief. That was the renowned duelist for you. His pessimism had weakened his will.

As Milyukov had expected, the battle—against "the seven" and for the minds of the others—was not easy. What they were attacking above all was his Straits policy, saying it was the detritus of outdated Slavophilism. (Milyukov a Slavophile?) He gave plentiful explanations, covering the matter in depth.

It's most unfair to confound my views on the Straits with those of the Slavophiles. It's not from chauvinist motives that I'm holding out for the Straits, and the question of Constantinople itself is for me secondary. (Though let's not forget that the Turks simply seized it—it was certainly not their property.) But we need a way out to the sea, to export goods from Russia's South. And we have to be sure the Black Sea can be easily defended. Demilitarized Straits (as Kerensky and Tereshchenko have already, publicly, agreed) would not guarantee this. Neutral Straits could easily be seized, and they'd be opened up to other countries' warships, which would mean we'd have to maintain permanent, sizeable forces in the Black Sea. Even the current Turkish mastery of the Straits is better than demilitarization. But today it's already Germany that's in Constantinople. So the way this question should really be put is: will the Straits be German or Russian? (And our seizure of the Straits must be accomplished *before* the peace conference, otherwise we won't get them.)

Then came a discussion of the "annexations and indemnities." The left-wing ministers had easily—and without giving it much thought—adopted that left-wing (in reality, German) slogan. Milyukov tried patiently to explain. To renounce "annexations" would be to renounce the restructuring of Central Europe and the Balkans. It would be easy for England to renounce it because she has no interests there and she'd hurry off to seize Mesopotamia and Palestine and not mind at all if Russia got nothing. What's the point of constantly chanting this slogan? To get Russia to release her Allies from the obligation to give us the Straits? Well that's a sacrifice they'll willingly make. Renunciation of "annexations" might accelerate the conclusion of a short-term peace, but it won't give Europe peace in the long run. And do you really think renunciation of Russia's rights will raise the spirits of our troops?

Kerensky (Milyukov had begun to find even his piercing voice unbearable) was insisting that if we didn't include "annexations and indemnities" in the note, we must at least have "self-determination for oppressed peoples." Milyukov saw his chance and agreed immediately. (That would be it: the restructuring of Central Europe, the liberation of the Western and

Southern Slavs, the Transylvanian Romanians, and, at the same time, the Alsatians and Armenians, and our adversaries would be reduced in size.) Kerensky's immature mind had not thought his idea through, not seen that the "self-determination of peoples" would demand exactly that: "annexations." How else could they free themselves? (This was a victory: "not to pursue the seizure of territories" left Milyukov more freedom of action.)

Kerensky picked holes in other expressions, suggested corrections—but for the worse, and even his supporters sensed it. Then he started talking total drivel: in this note, we must address not so much the governments as democratic public opinion in the Western countries. The ministers were embarrassed. Prince Lvov smiled foolishly. Somber Lvov froze foolishly. But Milyukov, the master of compromise, was not lost for words and found a splendid solution, combining this with what Albert Thomas had forced on him: "guarantees and sanctions which are indispensable for the prevention of sanguinary conflicts in the future." And he came out with: "leading democracies, inspired by identical desires, will find the means to obtain those guarantees and sanctions, which . . ."

That way he could keep Thomas (it was important to have him supporting the note) and satisfy Kerensky as well. And it seemed to suit everyone.

And Milyukov even assured the ministers: it may only be thanks to the war that everything is still holding firm here, otherwise it would have crumbled. (The ministers had, by mutual agreement, already launched the rumor, through several channels, that if we broke the alliance Japan would declare war on us and attack via Vladivostok.)

And, imperceptibly, the note turned out to be stronger than the Declaration. *Vivat* Milyukov!

But it was a historic moment, and the prudent Milyukov, foreseeing possible unpleasantness ahead, needed to hammer that triumph home: that means the full membership of the government is in total agreement with this document and takes responsibility for its contents?

Some said nothing, some nodded. Even Kerensky couldn't think of an objection.

Adopted.

It remained to fix a date for publication. The days had all started to drift, somehow. The Soviet had ruled that everyone had to work that Sunday, the 29th, while on the following Tuesday we would celebrate the international 1 May holiday—although this year they weren't celebrating it in the West, as they were taking the war seriously. No sense arguing with the Soviet. But perhaps it would be nice to date that note 1 May? But for that very reason there would be no newspapers on the 2nd. So it would be published on the 3rd, though it would leak out earlier, via the diplomats.

It would be even better that way!

By and large, Milyukov had stood his ground. He'd not offended the Allies and not broken up the Entente!

On the 1st, the weather was not at all festive: grey skies, a sharp, piercing wind, neither winter nor yet spring. A faint sun occasionally peeped through the clouds. Pavel Nikolaevich would have been interested to see that gathering of the people, but he felt some kind of constraint, unease in the face of large crowds; and he sensed danger too (and remembered the humiliation of being detained on the day of the funeral). No, that seething mass was no place for ministers, and for Pavel Nikolaevich in particular. He stayed at home. Anyway, he'd already been able, the previous day from his ministerial office at the Pevchesky Bridge, to admire the "Long live the International" banner stretched across the top of the Winter Palace. But today he was eagerly collecting reports by phone—he had asked everyone to call him. His wife, Anna Sergeevna, had gone to look, and she gave her account. His Kadet colleagues had also gone.

People were saying there were fewer people than on the day of the funeral, but even so more than half the capital had turned out on to the streets. No trams were running, no cabs, and all shops and restaurants were closed. Via all the bridges, all the streets, people were converging on the center (and thronging Basseinaya Street, under his windows). There was a multitude of red flags (not a single tricolor), which people on the bridges were barely managing to hold onto in the wind. But, surprisingly, there was perfect order: the columns were manouvering obediently, intersecting, giving way, walking in parallel lines without a single accident. The whole of Nevsky Prospect was a forest of red flags and placards, and at the corner of Sadovaya it was impossible to penetrate it. There were military bands all over the place, but no actual detachments of soldiers marching in organized configurations: they were strolling about in groups or alone. Platform trucks carrying speakers were making their way through the crowd. (But all those platforms were controlled by the Soviet, and not a single place was allotted to Kadet speakers . . .) Most of the platforms had gone to the Field of Mars, for this was the center for rallies and all the leaders of the Soviet were speaking there, and although Lenin was not there, plenty of Bolsheviks were. But everywhere else as well: someone only had to climb to some height and shout "comrades"—and there'd suddenly be a crowd and a meeting.

But what were the speakers talking about? What did they have to say about foreign policy?

On Mariinskaya Square, for example, anarcho-communists under a black flag with red lettering were shouting all kinds of rubbish: end the war right now, seize all the land, destroy all private property, don't trust the Provisional Government or any bourgies . . .

What rubbish. And elsewhere?

Just outside the Mariinsky Palace Steklov was speaking. And there were speeches from the balcony of the Astoria. And on Palace Square. Stop the war—that was heard all over the place, alas. But the crowd was asking *how* to stop it—the speakers couldn't answer that. Put your hopes in the brotherhood of peoples. The German people will wake up . . . People carried placards: "Publish the treaties with the Allies now!" (Oh o. . .) "Obukhov and Putilov works, take the cause of peace into your own hands!" (What asses . . .) Or else: "Bourgies into the trenches!" (That's a campaign starting . . .) A war invalid who'd been helped up on to a statue made a speech against fraternization with the Germans. An officer, on Palace Square: "We don't need other people's lands, but we do need the Straits. The question of the Dardanelles is more complex than it seems." (Bright fellow, that one.) A general would speak, now a soldier, now a woman in a red headscarf. At every location, most of the disputes centered on annexations and on the Leninists. The latter were going all out, rushing about the place in dozens of cars (very smart cars too—they'd stolen quantities of them), addressing crowds everywhere—but with no success. Many listeners were sharply critical of Lenin but well-disposed on other subjects.

It had turned out not to be so terrible. And it was a shame he hadn't heard it for himself.

And then more reports. These were colorful! Dozens of people in different national costumes, sailing along Nevsky Prospect on an enormous platform truck. Then an exotic parade of Muslims that impressed everyone: Tatars, Sarts, Tadzhiks, Muslim soldiers in turbans singing slow songs and holding red banners with a white half-moon, white stars, and inscriptions in Arabic. Everyone greeted them very warmly. On the Bund's banners the inscriptions were in Yiddish and their meetings were in Yiddish, as were their songs. The Ukrainians, Poles, Lithuanians, and Belorussians all marched in separate groups. All had their own choirs. (Yet again they were dividing themselves up by nationality. This was worrying.) The seamstresses carried the slogan "Value the labor of the needle." The Petrograd doormen's union had: "Do away with tips!" The amnestied prisoners: "Give us passports now!" Five- and six-year-old children: "Give us three years of free school, and a republic."

It was obviously not going to finish before evening. And for some reason Pavel Nikolaevich very much wanted to see it for himself. His official car was in the yard, ready to go. He put on a mid-season coat and a soft hat, and left. Should he cross Nevsky Prospect? No, he couldn't do that. And the Field of Mars was difficult for him—he'd have to go round it. He'd take Nadezhdinskaya, Kirochnaya, and Sergievskaya, and then follow the embankments.

No one had repaired the Petersburg roads after the snow, and they were full of potholes. Driving over them, one jolt could dislocate a joint. (Prince Obolensky, a Kadet, had just smashed the side window of his car when a pothole had launched his shoulder into it.) But today they'd drive slowly—you couldn't go fast anyway.

The singing was bad—we had no songs or hymns of our own. They were holding red flags and singing vulgar little German hussars' ditties. But twice he encountered placards reading "Down with Lenin," which pleased him.

And "Forward, sovereign nation—to glory in the world, for the ages!" But the trucks were crawling along, spattered with mud. On one stood a man dressed as a worker, holding a hammer, and another as a peasant with a sickle.

The Mars-Suvorov statue was hung with red flags and the Marble Palace and Pavlovsky barracks were garlanded with flowers. The whole of the Field of Mars was in menacing black and red, with a hundred thousand people and thousands of banners. They took a detour and avoided all that.

The Neva seemed to have frozen again, and again ice was clinging to the banks. But in the middle it was loose, floating downstream.

And the junior cadets. What slogans were they displaying? "In struggle we gain our rights" and "Proletarians of all countries, unite!" Well, well. So that's the kind of young officers that will lead us in war.

And at a rally, beneath a massive red and green flag: "Come and join us, comrades! That vile, Tsarist government persecuted free Esperantists, because we have equality and fraternity . . ."

Pavel Nikolaevich was in an open car but with his hat pulled down, looking out from under the brim. But on the English Embankment a crowd of soldiers coming in the opposite direction—unarmed, though—made his heart skip a beat: they recognized him!

They immediately blocked the road, stopping his car. There were hostile shouts:

"It's Milyukov! He's here! We've got him!"

But luckily the mood today was peaceable—this was no battle. And Pavel Nikolaevich was not, of course, easily frightened. He didn't start taking cover and excusing himself but instead stood up in the car to his full height, like an orator, as if that was what he'd been waiting for, and put his hat down on the seat, revealing his grey hair. His glasses sat securely over his ears. Fearlessly, he considered the angry soldiers, crossed his arms (he didn't like cheap gesticulating), and calmly addressed them:

"Comrades! The old regime could not, with its bureaucratic methods, unify the country. But today you see that unity in this festive national celebration. The first Provisional People's Government is working nonstop. But your support is essential. The enemy is near and is hoping to mount a major attack on revolutionary Petrograd. And I have received a secret telegram telling me that the German headquarters is counting less on the strength of its armies than on Russian freedom being drowned in a tide of anarchy. We earnestly call on all of you to unite around the Provisional Government . . ."

And he spoke along those lines for a while and the crowd quieted down. Two or three voices expressed approval. And they let the car through.

He'd got away with it. But it had been rash, taking that drive.

They turned off the Embankment and, unthinkingly, arrived in Theater Square, where there were also rallies taking place. Luckily, they'd stopped at the very edge of the square, behind people's backs. An extremely long banner stretched from the conservatoire to the Mariinsky Theater: "A hundred times blessed is the union of the sword and the lyre. One laurel wreathes them in fellowship." By the Glinka monument, from a platform draped in red calico an intellectual was addressing the workers, telling them what oppression the imperial theaters and all of Russian art had endured under the Tsar. But, not letting him finish, and cutting him off from the crowd, a truck with sailors and civilians on its platform squeezed in in front of him. And someone from the crowd, recognizing them, shouted:

"The German contingent's here!"

But a sharp little civilian, unembarrassed, immediately launched into a speech from the truck.

"I'm going to talk about the ministers. There are twelve ministers, like the twelve apostles. But there's a Judas among them."

Milyukov suddenly felt cold.

". . . The Kadets say we have no one to replace them? But we can elect twelve ministers from among the people . . ."

Milyukov was now so cold that he couldn't hear any more of the speech.

But the crowd started to get hostile and shout at the speaker.

He finished with:

"Well goodbye, you Black-Hundreds! We'll meet again!"

And the truck moved off, scattering the crowd.

* * *

We won't forget 'Seventeen,
Long live our freedom!
(from a song at the 1 May parade in Petrograd)

[37]

On 23 April, the fortieth day after Dmitri's death, they served a requiem at the Monastery and, keeping the burial till they were back at Lotaryovo, he and Lili left Petersburg that evening. They traveled by train, in an international carriage as far as Moscow, which was quite acceptable though packed, with people sitting in the corridor. The following day, in Moscow, they stayed at the Sheremetievs' house on Vozdvizhenka, where they chatted to their hearts' content: The whole of Russia is spreading, like dough when a kneading trough gets dropped upside down on the floor. And the new regime think their Appeals can pull it together again. That government hasn't taken so much as a ten-ruble fine from anyone—so who's going to take any notice? But if, now, it would show the first signs of strength, effective support would arrive from all over the country. But everyone's afraid to tell the truth, it's all flattery, burning incense to the masses, calls to "adore the peasant." Russia's learning freedom like a child learning the law of gravity by throwing itself out of a fifth-floor window: Let's take all the land! Grab all the money in the banks! Work less and get more! Not fight but embrace. It takes a forceful character to tell the people: I'm the one who knows what you need, not you! Everyone's started *speaking* against anarchy a lot—and that just shows their weakness. But armed gangs are openly giving the orders.

Then, from Moscow, they had to endure the full reality of current traveling conditions: the corridor was so full as to be impassable, and above their heads deserters were walking around on the roof. (Anyone seeing this must have understood that the war was finished.) Two conductors managed to squeeze the Vyazemsky couple plus Lili's maid into a two-person compartment and lock them in there—and for the whole journey people were trying to force an entry. Lili slept in the upper berth and Prince Boris and the maid half-sitting on the lower one. They'd never in their lives had to do that. At Gryazi they passed their luggage out of the window to their coachman—and would themselves have had to climb out of the window, had a large number of soldiers not also got out at Gryazi, so they could leave by the door—getting some nasty bruises in the process.

But how was one to *get out* of Gryazi now, to get back to Petersburg? Vyazemsky immediately, from the station, sent a telegram to his mother at 7 Fontanka: For funeral trip seek book private carriage both ways.

The train to Gryazi was very late, arriving at about five in the afternoon instead of midday. But once they were in the south, how warm it was! And it was astonishing weather, sometimes warm rain, but then it would immediately brighten, the sun dried everything out, and vivid rainbows burst onto the sky. There was no mud and the going was good. After the month in Petersburg, what a joy to breathe that moist, warm air offering a foretaste of summer and promising fruitfulness to the land he so loved. And what a joy to know that Lili, with no effort or pretense on her part, had fallen in love with the property and he could so freely discuss all his plans and worries with her.

But this year there were clouds on the horizon—and not just the meteorological kind. The closer they drew to the estate, the more worried Prince Boris became: what would he find there? They were already moving by twilight and could see nothing along the way. But against a background of grey sky the hexagonal front and square back towers were still visible, the windows were beginning to light up with electricity, and he could make out both the colonnade of the two upper balconies and the full length of the terrace below.

Home, at last! To listen immediately to what Nikifor Ivanovich had to tell him, while his fingers involuntarily sorted through to see what urgent letters there were. And look: a notification to come to Usman tomorrow for a meeting of the supervisory committee: "supervisory" because it oversaw the whole district, only it wasn't called that but, for some reason, "executive," as if it executed the will of some higher being.

The whole way home he'd waited, on edge: what would he hear from his steward? And, just in case, he'd pictured the worst, though he wouldn't have wanted to believe it. So now he was really surprised by Nikifor Ivanovich's account: the sowing was underway and would probably be completed with no problems. At first the local day-laborers hadn't taken part, as they were demanding two rubles fifty a day (and they'd threatened the girls with reprisals if they worked for any less than two). But then some Kaluga women came and applied for the work—and after that the locals came flooding back and now there was an excess of day labor and we were sending some of them back. The rates: a ruble and a half for the men, eighty kopecks for the women.

The sowing was under way! That was splendid. An hour in April—food for a year. If in mud I'm sown, a kingdom I'll own.

But the next morning he had no time to take a look at the fields or even the stud farm before speeding off, driving a pair, to Usman. There, more new impressions awaited him than he could have expected, even after Petersburg. What a mixture of new situations, faces, ideas, and information gleaned. At first it was interesting, but later dreadful, too. The supervisory committee comprised representatives of the town, the cooperatives, the zemstvo (here Prince Vyazemsky was the delegate of the district zemstvo assembly), zemstvo employees, teachers, soldiers of the 212th Regiment, workers, and peasants. (He was happy to see Tyurin here, from the Knyazhe-Baigora credit association, and a local man, Grigori Galitsky from Korobovka, both sensible men—the Prince had dealt with them at the time of the Duma elections.) Such a motley group had never before assembled in a single room—they had no idea how to talk to each other. But that might even turn out to be productive if things went well. In the committee the peasants followed the voice of reason and voted the same way as two-thirds of the committee. But the district commissar, Okhotnikov, a thoroughly well-meaning member of the gentry, turned out to be weak and could not impose the committee's authority in Usman and the district.

Ensign Moiseev of the local regiment, himself a lawyer from Nizhni Novgorod and openly Bolshevik, totally out-performed Okhotnikov in both organizational talent and rabid, rally-style oratory. He attacked the committee constantly for its bourgeois nature and created his own Soviet of Workers' and Soldiers' Deputies and a socialist club where he made utterly frenetic speeches. And, it turned out, he had managed, unchallenged, to launch the first agitators all over the district, ostensibly "to organize the masses," but they were in fact committing outrages and initiating searches and even arrests. When complaints about it came into Usman, Moiseev was asked to phone his agitators and tell them to stop. But, openly contemptuous of that request, he spoke over the phone in a way that only added fuel to the flames. Moiseev also started creating some kind of spurious "peasant union": his energy was boundless and no one in the district dared stop him.

(And by the way, why was this 212th Regiment based in Usman anyway, if it was supplying a division near Trapezund? Especially with the railways in the state they were!) One petit bourgeois in Usman was arrested just for saying "Well who is this Moiseev? He's here today but he'll be gone tomorrow," meaning that he was not a local man. Then that "he'll be gone tomorrow" was distorted, presented as an intention to kill Moiseev. But Moiseev, at a rally, feigned magnanimity, saying he forgave his killer.

Vyazemsky wondered whether he should make a complaint to Guchkov about Moiseev. Or, even better, find out via Burtsev whether Moiseev's past might harbor some political sin, judged by current standards. It would be a step fully in keeping with the spirit of the times, though repugnant to him.

Anyway, what kind of order could we hope to achieve, if revolutionary Petrograd was the first to destroy everything? According to a decree from Kerensky, eighty convicts from Usman prison had said they wanted to become soldiers and were dressed and shod in uniform and sent off to the front—and **all of them** had run off on the way. Eighty convicts, even dispersed over three districts, is quite a force!

Prince Vyazemsky spent two days in Usman: a good few matters still depended on the district marshal of the nobility, but he'd been absent for a month. And in these two days he'd had his fill of grim news. Voronezh was near Usman, Lipetsk district too, and communications were functioning well, unlike the vast, unwieldy stretches of Tambov province—and rumors were flowing in from multiple sources.

Everyone was saying the same thing—that a month ago had been far more peaceful, and the peasants had been ready to agree to all sorts of things; but now, whether due to the imminence of sowing time or the news now flowing out of Petrograd, they were demanding more—and taking it for themselves—and the process was quite advanced, unlike in Lotaryovo. In places they were felling state and private forests. They were demanding that no one from another village should be taken on for work, and that peasants from their own village must be paid no less than whatever fee they specify. And the way they understood what the government had announced—that every scrap of land must be sown—was that they would abandon their own land, leaving it untilled, and seize that of the landowners. If there was not enough seed for this seized land, it was: landowner, give us seed! Not enough equipment: give us your equipment! A township committee might leave a landowner with some of his own pasture—not to feed all his cows but only the cows needed to feed his own family. Or this: they would give him, in advance, the date by which he must mow his meadows this year, otherwise they would go to the peasants. And now some landowners' orchards had been left without their spring preparation, and vegetable gardens had been seeded with grass instead of the vegetables they'd been cultivating. And they even took the landowners' pedigree horses and used them for heavy work. (As a celebrated horse-breeder, he nearly had a heart attack when he heard that.) And they conducted searches on estates, ostensibly looking for weapons—and simply made off with whatever they could lay their hands on. And they were already talking about the grain reserves too. It seemed the only thing they weren't touching was the furniture.

There were landowners who were already selling off their own cattle and equipment, for whatever price they could get.

That, and similar, was what Prince Boris had feared when returning to the estate. But nothing, nothing of that kind had happened yet at Lotaryovo.

But if something did—where could he turn for protection?

A small estate owner from Voronezh arrived in Usman and told a story so piteous that he was close to tears. He was no high-born landowner! He just had a big farm. But it was properly run, with crop rotation, fodder grass cultivation, and a breeding nursery for pedigree horned cattle. One evening a crowd of peasants had turned up, about forty of them, and called for him. He came out onto the portico. (But what good is a portico when you can't expect protection or justice from anywhere in the district?) Until now he'd had excellent relations with his peasants. But now one man in the crowd spoke up. He was no ragamuffin, no: he was very prosperous. The farmer must divide up his land and give the commune thirty acres (which he had ploughed in the autumn!). And the village also needed pasture land, so he must let the villagers into his wood and also cut a route across all his fields for the village cattle to reach it. (That was goodbye to the crop rotation.) What was he to do? They had all the power. He agreed. (He'd noticed that they were somewhat shamefaced, at least, as they accepted his sacrifice, and they thanked him.) Two days later they'd looked into it and seen that the only way they could reach that wood was over their own, the village's, fields, which had been sown for the spring. The idea of the cattle route was dropped, and so was the wood, because they would be sorry to damage their own fields. But they still took the thirty acres.

Only one who runs his own farm can understand what it means to allow other people's cattle a route through. Or what if they come and grab the plant or breeding nurseries? It only takes an hour to devastate something that's taken years to get up and running.

We've lived with those peasants all our lives—did we not know them? They'd bared their teeth during the violence of '05, but those were isolated outbursts, where events had conspired to whip things up. But such a universal epidemic of spite and destruction . . .? Or had the peasantry simply lost its balance, without the habitual command structure and a bosses' will?

Would they never follow orders again? It was said that the people were like a drunkard now—they accepted no explanations of any kind.

But there was Lotaryovo, holding firm. And it was calm in the neighborhood.

We could probably get by somehow, couldn't we? Find a common language?

Aggression toward the allotment holders was even worse than that shown the landowners. Their land was being removed at the drop of a hat. Or they themselves would come to *surrender* their land. It's the way of the commune: might is right.

The ravings that all the peasants were coming out with now were, of course, about redistributing the land. Without them paying anything for it. And they wanted fifty acres each, in a single block, without them needing to resettle. And, seeing large estates nearby, how could they comprehend that that was only a small part of Russia? And that if the land was subdivided, between everyone in Russia, there would be barely five acres or even less than an acre per family, and no land available to rent. And the main thing they can't grasp is that it'll be necessary then to take land back from some peasants, too.

It was our garrulous, partisan political commentators, themselves understanding nothing of the issue, who'd been showering us for decades with cock-and-bull stories about the riches to be shared. These were the first agitators, even before Moiseev and his crowd. And now there are the current troublemakers with their red badges, their "down with the bloodsucking landowners." Everyone agreed: where no agitators had appeared it was still peaceful. The peasants' mood was changeable, but perhaps a path of reason could still be found. People had noticed that it was sailors from the Baltic Fleet and soldiers from the Northern Front who were especially vitriolic: "We'll do as we please, and anyone who's against us is a henchman of the old regime."

And they weren't slow to adapt "regime" to their own purposes: "*New regime, new machine*: the old one flattened us—now it's our turn!"

But surely we weren't going to give in without a fight, purely out of fear on that account? Prince Boris could not tolerate that. You had to fight, even when you couldn't hope to save more than some pathetic bits of wreckage.

Yes, sowing, with things in this state . . . it was a big risk.

Then right on time, on his second day in Usman, the newspapers arrived with news of a decision on the protection of crops sown. The Provisional Government was taking all the risk upon itself: it would reimburse all damage by cattle and deliberate wrecking. (This seemed to be the first worthwhile step they'd taken in two months in power.)

And Prince Boris dug his heels in: we'll stand our ground and not give in! He'd have to learn a new way of talking to the new peasants.

He arrived home late on Friday, exhausted. Everything at Lotaryovo was as calm as before, and sowing was still under way. (Now he would always, when having to absent himself, be concerned for his wife's safety.) And he recounted his impressions, at length, to Lili. Though so small, so fragile, how bravely she shared his determination to resist: they must not give in!

Sunday was the day appointed for the whole district to elect the village committees, Monday for the township committees. And then Tuesday for something out of the ordinary: uninformed, uncomprehending rural Russia was ordered to celebrate the international 1 May holiday.

A tactical initiative was called for: to go to the Korobovka assembly on Sunday. Boris attended the Sunday mass with Lili and then asked one of the peasants, then a second, then a third what time the assembly was scheduled for exactly. They all greeted him as they had before but then played dumb, saying they didn't know.

Oh well, that meant, that meant . . . They didn't want him there. So he shouldn't go. Yes, it was hard to get the upper hand. Pity. He'd missed a rare opportunity. They returned to Lotaryovo.

But at five that evening, or thereabouts, a peasant from Korobovka appeared unexpectedly, riding bareback: the assembly was gathered—and they were calling for the Prince.

He became worried. He took a light droshky. Did that mean they'd assembled and discussed inviting him and now they were all idling about, waiting impatiently? It was irrational—and typical.

The crowd stood opposite the new school, by the well. He drove up to them. They doffed their hats and there was a ragged chorus of "good-days," but the hats went straight back on, which, previously, they would not have done. Prince Boris spoke from the footboard of the droshky, trying to seem benevolent and calm, but sensing an unfamiliar relationship, something new:

"Good-day to you! I am happy to be invited here. I was already thinking that, with your freedom, you didn't want to know me any more."

Noisy protests were heard, but just for the sake of form.

"I came to help you with advice on a difficult process. I don't want to get in the way. I'll sit over there in the school and come out if you call. I would advise you not to run the assembly as in olden days, when anyone could speak at any time, but elect a chairman and ask him for permission to speak, one at a time."

He went off into the school and would occasionally glance at them, from afar, out of the window. What kind of new time was this? How to come to terms with it, find one's place in it?

Twice they summoned him for advice. How many committee members would be best? Should soldiers' wives be allowed to stand? Should the womenfolk be allowed to vote? (There were a few women at the assembly—that was also new.)

Then they summoned him a third time, to tell him the committee was elected, with eleven members (Korobovka had a population of 2,200) and they had appointed their old headman as the village commissar. Then the Prince invited just the elected men to join him in the school. They were the bosses now, and he would have to deal with them. They sat, and he made a sensible speech about the tasks of the committee, their responsibility to their electorate and to the authorities, and explained what the words "consolidation of the new order" meant. (And they understood everything! One of them later repeated to Father Leonid, accurately, the whole sense of his explanation.) They thanked him and asked him to come to the meetings from now on. Not a bad start, it seemed. The peasants' mood was actually ideal.

Yesterday, Monday, all the elected village committees convened in Knyazhe-Baigora to elect the township committee.

Many peasants had come just to watch. The chairman, who was the Velyaminovs' stove-man, could not handle the loudmouths, so Prince Boris sat next to him, quieted them down, listed those wanting to speak, and called them up. And he even started taking notes of the debates. All the most heated skirmishes were between peasants with personal accounts to settle, stemming from old resentments. The aspect of the peasant community was constantly changing: now enigmatic, menacingly rock-solid, now open and good-natured, with each individual absorbed into the generality—and then that generality would fragment into individuals again. The most aggression was against the township clerk and the management of the credit association, but everything turned out well: they elected the committee, and as township commissar (the peasants were already used to that powerful, incomprehensible word) they elected the Korobovka man Grigori Galitsky. Good—that would mean protection: Galitsky was one of those peasants with whom you could always come to a sensible understanding.

The Prince had barely reached home, well pleased, and told Lili all about it, when the township committee phoned him from Knyazhe-Baigora to invite the Prince on Tuesday to a solemn church service, which was how they had decided to celebrate 1 May. None of the Velyaminovs was on the estate. So today, in the early morning frost—the nights had become colder during that period—he had set off in the char-a-banc, without Lili. In the church everyone was looking round at him. After the mass there was a thanksgiving service, in the open air, everything very dignified, as before. And then? They shouldn't just disperse—wasn't something special needed, to celebrate this new situation? But what? No one knew. They started making speeches—meaningless, boring speeches—and the listeners were shifting from one foot to the other, dissatisfied. Prince Boris decided to have a try. Climbing onto a tree stump:

"I am your guest—I shan't make a speech. But let us give a rousing cheer for the mother who unites us into one harmonious family, without regard to classes or individuals. For free Russia—hurrah!"

And the crowd happily roared their "hurrah."

And then there was another cheer, for the valiant army. And that was all. They went their ways, satisfied, cheerful.

The Prince sped off home and had sat down to lunch with Lili, when suddenly the butler, Vanya, announced that someone from Korobovka was saying the committee had come and was calling for him. Calling him where?

Prince Boris put his napkin aside and went into the courtyard—no one there. He looked over toward the drying house—also empty. And suddenly he saw extreme fear in his servants' faces. He turned to follow their gaze and saw a crowd flocking past the stud farm toward the steward's house, mostly men but there were women too, and children—a thousand or so in all. But they didn't seem hostile and weren't carrying clubs. They held two red flags and two church banners. And, at the front of the throng, he could distinguish Galitsky, and someone from the village committee.

And the Prince suddenly guessed:

"Sima! Quickly, call the Princess and ask her to bring the camera."

Lili soon appeared with the camera, arriving at the very moment the crowd did. And they started taking photographs of them all, some with the Prince as well. Several times. The people were very pleased. He congratulated them on the special occasion (no one knew what the occasion was, though). And then? Would they go home now?

No, they were beginning to enjoy themselves. The Prince's own gardener, Fyodor, a Korobovka man, climbed onto a barrel and launched into a strange speech, along the lines of:

"We are happy that the red flag is making us into better people. We hope it carries on that way. Before, we would all have come bursting in willy-nilly, but now we stopped at the gates and asked permission—and the red flag did that. We must approach every person peaceably and, most of all, our Prince. His father did a lot for us, but even nobles had bosses, and they couldn't do more. And now our Prince isn't a boss anymore, and he's only working the land because our homeland needs grain and fodder. He's our educated, enlightened neighbor and may he continue to be, and always stay with us."

A thoroughly sensible speech. And it seemed to foresee all the dangers that were not yet spoken of aloud.

The Prince thanked them. And they held him aloft, shouting their approval.

Then they left. (It turned out they'd gone off to the hospital to express their approval of Dr. Shafran in the same way.)

So it had all turned out well, hadn't it? At least there would be no pogrom. As for everything else—they'd just have to rub along somehow.

But the whole Vyazemsky family, including Sophie and her children and Lidia with hers, had decided to come to Lotaryovo this summer. It was one thing to take risks on one's own account, but on theirs too? And the children's? And Asya was coming now, for Mitya's funeral, also bringing her children, and she'd certainly be staying a long time, by his tomb.

It was peaceful now, while it lasted, but he had to persuade them not to come. And he sat down to write the letters—to Mama and, via her, to his brother Vladimir at the front. If something started up here, no one could be sure of anything. No one must bring any children, not even Asya's for the funeral. If they needed to escape from here they couldn't count on getting away by train. With the Vorontsovs in Alupka, or indeed in any dacha in the Crimea, you won't be noticed, there are hundreds like you there. But here we're the center of attention, alone, our every step in full view. Just think about it: all the provincial governors went through terrible moments—but the Petersburg governor, Saburov, wasn't even taken to the Duma or stripped of his official apartment. Because in Petersburg there are hundreds like him.

But nowadays, with the current freedom, they couldn't send such a letter by post: the *comrades* might censor it. They decided to send their loyal pantry-man to Petrograd with the letter, straight away.

And he and Lili went off to Olshanka, to the steppe, the meadows, for a walk. The river Baigora takes its name from the Tatar word for "beautiful woman." It was all flowers in bloom, fragrance, bees buzzing, birds flitting. And walking like that in the peace of the steppe, under the same peaceful sky as before, it was hard to believe that in reality that wild revolution had taken place: today's insane Petrograd seemed barely credible. Or perhaps even today's Usman?

They made up a ditty: We've sown, yes we may have; but the reaping will depend on Moiseev.

And yet another danger was heading their way: the papers were demanding, ever more frequently, a complete re-examination of the army exemption lists. The district marshal of the nobility chaired, as one of his many roles, the mobilization commission. But a good few people here were relying on totally unjustified exemption certificates, issued as an indulgence thanks to their good connections. If you start purging those, the whole district will be your enemy.

No, it was not the same steppe, not the same meadow.

They turned back—and that evening they read aloud, together, Thiers's *History of the French Revolution*.

It was different.

And similar.

[38]

What a dirty trick! Some bastards are telephoning round the commissariats and saying Kerensky's given instructions for car 42-46 to be shot at on sight and no warning given. But that car's actually one that Aleksandr Fyodorovich has used several times. And his enemies noticed. And wanted to kill him this way!

And it was similar impostors, it seems, who concocted that demand—supposedly from the 12th Army—saying that holding the Tsar at Tsarskoye Selo represented a danger to the state so he must be transferred to the Peter and Paul Fortress. With his characteristic lightning reactions, Kerensky had rushed off to Tsarskoye Selo there and then, and put things right—all the newspapers are still talking about it. It turned out that no one from the 12th Army had sent any such demand: someone had launched it, anonymously, and then taken cover. (*Izvestia*, however, immediately published something purporting to be a resolution from the Metal Works—which also wanted Nikolai sent to the Fortress!)

Kerensky had, for years now, hungered after freedom for his homeland and he was, of course, a lawyer. But even so, it was only in these last few weeks that he'd realized that true freedom depended on the Ministry of Justice more than anything else. And what a driving force his ministry has been, in all the Provisional Government's work—and not only thanks to the minister's remarkable personality. If the grub is bad at a factory in Bryansk, and the Sarts working there slip away from their work, and those who don't get caught on the way make it to Petrograd, once there, they go to the Minister of Justice and no one else. The Ministry of Justice is like an immense empire all to itself, and it has to keep a vigilant eye on everything. The task of liquidating the committee for the struggle against German dominance has also, for some reason, fallen to Kerensky. And that of arresting the editor of the now-defunct right-wing paper *The Land*. And arresting his son, and organizing searches of the *Russian Readings* and *War Chronicles* editorial offices, because we'd be bound to seize some pogromist literature there that hadn't been destroyed yet. But now the Petrograd Duma complained to Kerensky that many people were apparently dissatisfied with his revolutionary tribunals (a worker, a soldier, and a judge). Many wanted to complain, they said, but there was nowhere to make their complaints: no body had been established to deal with appeals. (And it's true—when setting everything up, in the whirlwind of revolution Kerensky hadn't foreseen any appeals. One couldn't imagine that people might be dissatisfied with revolutionary justice too. And where, now, were they to go with appeals? These tribunals weren't part of any system. To the Senate?) And now lawyers all round are saying that we must, somehow, reconstruct the case files burned in the District Court fire. But why reconstruct even the many that were included in the amnesty? (Better call a conference.) Then should we only reconstruct the files that interested parties have applied for? But how would we reconstruct them? A real co-nun-drum.

And there were so many conundrums like that! He released from jail "all who want to spill their blood for the revolution." But large numbers of these jailbirds only made it from the prison as far as the recruiter and then ran off. Field hospitals on the front line refused to accept amnestied women criminals as nurses. He'd banned the use of fetters and punishment cells—you just have to appeal to the criminal's conscience—and now the warders couldn't cope, driven to despair by the lapse in prison discipline. What's more, the amnesty only applied to those held in prisons. Those the military authorities had exiled to Siberia for suspected espionage had been forgotten. But they'd been exiled without any real investigation and we couldn't keep them there (and as for reviewing the cases now—there's no one to do it and no time anyway). Which means they had to be released, all at the same time. And this problem: what are former Okhrana people to be tried for? They were serving police officers, so it's hard to find an article to apply to them. And provocateurs? They should, surely, be tried, but which article of the law to use? Someone had a good idea: to try both groups under article 102, for "membership in a criminal association" just as they'd tried all the revolutionaries. But just a few days ago the Maklakov Commission removed that article from the Criminal Code completely, as it was incompatible with the spirit of revolution. (Maklakov could have conferred with Kerensky beforehand. But he was hurt not to have been appointed Minister of Justice.)

And there were even bigger problems, bigger worries! (And Aleksandr Fyodorovich had to find the time to get all the gears turning, so that when he leaves the ministry, no one could stop them!) All over Russia, defense attorneys were appointed as prosecutors in both the appellate and district courts. That seed would become a healthy tree: the legal profession is our light and Russia's conscience. And he had, of course, to cleanse the ranks of the judges across the country most thoroughly. But the law on the books for the last fifty years, giving judges life tenure, was a problem. Shcheglovitov managed to find a way out of that situation, but only for some isolated cases. But now the challenge was to replace a large number of judges, and in a short time! The principle of tenure for judges had been very positive, but now was becoming an encumbrance. And with the highest judicial officials especially, including the senators, there was no need to mince words—or to feel sorry for them. Anyway, as it turned out, the overall revolutionary environment was a great help. It's a rare senator or judge in the Petrograd district who stands his ground if told to retire: they meekly resign, frightened, and already more than half in the ministry's First Department have been removed (and defense attorneys put in their place), and senators have been transferred into the "non-sitting" category (and defense attorneys put in their place). Kerensky spent that Sunday with his vice-ministers and they decided on a good number of important appointments to judicial positions. And an idea was born: yes, yes, we always demanded the principle of tenure for judges, as their guarantee against abuses by the administration. But that was necessary because the Tsarist administration was bad. But we shouldn't consider that tenure law as an end in itself, eternal: nothing could be worse than a bad judge who can't be removed! And it was in the Tsarist period that many bad judges were put in place and now it's imperative that we get rid of them, and quickly. Now, when the administration is democratic, we must abolish tenure for judges, even if only for a short time, and quickly rid ourselves of the bad elements among them. Then we could, if we wanted, bring back tenure.

And one good idea gives rise to another: could we go further, then? Might we be able to reinstate the system of exile as an administrative measure—long since banned at our own insistence—and get it back on track on new, revolutionary foundations? What a help that would be in the operation of justice! How much easier our work would be! Yes! We must get such a law onto the books, and bring exile itself out of the Ministry of the Interior and over to the Ministry of Justice.

Kerensky knew how accurate his assured, instantaneous decisions were—in fact, the more instantaneous, the more accurate. (This was the only thing helping him cope with receiving the intolerable queue of visitors: he took lightning-quick decisions and the visitors went off satisfied.)

Operational and ceremonial activities are coming thick and fast, often on the same day. Operational: what are we waiting for? Why aren't we taking another look at the Beilis affair? There could be some interesting finds regarding the reactionary diehards there. (Vice-Minister Zarudny had himself been a defense lawyer in the Beilis case, and his words there had even, in a sense, decided it. Now he'd order all the material over from the Kiev District Court and set his staff to work on it.) The ceremonial: we must compose a resounding circular to all the district court prosecutors. Aleksandr Fyodorovich already has the first phrases in his head, here they are, make a note: "There is no doubt that we are witnessing an alarming mood among the population—and it could lead to violent acts by particular groups. . . . And any civil strife would be a futile waste of the people's spiritual strength, which must all be focused on safeguarding the freedom we have won." I haven't got any further yet, please finish it up.

However, deep in the minister's heart is an unease he cannot shake off. Those "violent acts by particular groups"—what could we actually do about them?

And that terrible business with Pereverzev at Kronstadt is still dragging on, and there's no way for Aleksandr Fyodorovich to extricate himself with dignity. He thought it would quieten down, but it certainly isn't doing that. The yellow bourgeois press is gloating, fanning the flames, and the Kronstadters are angry too, sending menacing rebuttals to the Petrograd newspapers—and how is the Minister of Justice supposed to keep silent now? In Kronstadt it was *his* commission of inquiry that they sent packing, *his* prosecutor that they threatened to hoist on their bayonets and at whom they cocked their guns. And that insulted minister keeps quiet? Just who has the authority? But he can't criticize Kronstadt, either: that would immediately undermine him, dig the revolutionary soil from beneath his feet! (And some crazed voices are even heard saying that force must be used against Kronstadt.) The minister's situation has become unbearable and even shameful. The best Kerensky can come up with is: he'll prevail on Pereverzev to write, in the interests of the common cause and the authority of the Ministry of Justice, a letter to the newspapers saying that the Kronstadt incident was explained wrongly in the papers, that he himself committed an error by not explaining to that detachment of soldiers that he was not releasing their officer but only sending him to the Military Commission; and that Pereverzev himself sensed no threat of reprisals from the crowd and was subjected to no abuse and had a friendly chat with the Executive Committee; and that no resolution was carried sentencing Pereverzev to death, and that he went to that public meeting, not under arrest but voluntarily, to answer the people's questions. And the letter appeared today. That conflict, at least, Kerensky has successfully dodged for the time being.

But the scaremongers have been complaining to the Ministry of Justice the whole time that Lenin's actions run contrary to any idea of order and represent a danger for Russia, and measures must be taken immediately. But, excuse me. Even if we skate over the issue of rights, the rights of every human being including Lenin—just what has the Ministry of Justice got to do with this? Even at the Koussevitzky concert, where he'd have liked to forget his problems, the event organizer suddenly came out with a speech, saying it was Kerensky who would deal with the tendency that had penetrated Russia with the help of German imperialism and was transgressing the bounds of even "left-wing reason." Even the audience booed him and Kerensky gave him a rap over the knuckles: "The Provisional Government has the support of *all* the people and fears neither the far left nor the far right."

Where can he forget his problems, if not even at a concert? Some moments he wishes for such a place . . .

The Winter Palace . . .?

Oh, how he's grown to love the Winter Palace! There is something captivating in its majestic halls, passageways, and staircases, its separate station between the square and the Neva. Aleksandr Fyodorovich has gradually come to feel—and it's as if he felt this even earlier in his Petersburg life—that his career is inevitably destined to intersect with this palace and with the Emperor . . . And now it's happening. He's already had dealings with the Emperor, and as for the palace . . . if he becomes Prime Minister—and he will do, clearly, Lvov isn't the Prime Minister for revolutionary Russia—he'll move his residence and the government into this palace.

At the moment the Extraordinary Commission of Enquiry is working in the Winter Palace, so the Minister of Justice, busy as he is, has to drop in for visits. The entrance to the Commission is from the canal side, but Aleksandr Fyodorovich always drives to the main entrance and takes the long walk through, delighting in the palace halls. Doormen and lackeys in livery are at their stations everywhere, as before. The look of the palace and Aleksandr Fyodorovich's delight are spoiled only by the guards from the Preobrazhensky Regiment. They're not as undisciplined as others in Petrograd, and they aren't yet nibbling sunflower seeds in the palace and spitting out the husks, or blowing smoke into your face if you talk to them. But they rise from their chairs languidly, and it's not unusual to see them openly sleeping on duty.

To start with, fifteen investigators and some prosecutors were assigned to the Extraordinary Commission. But it soon became clear that was not enough. Nowhere near. Their numbers already doubled, more still are needed, because Kerensky has asked them to work quickly and give him results as soon as possible. So, with the office staff and typists, it's already 150 people. These are all housed in the "reserve" half of the palace, and the board meets in a beautiful, most imposing room. The role of the board is to decide who should be called to account, to draw up the conclusions of completed investigations, to ratify bail decisions, and to give procedural directives of a general nature. To help the board, there are also experts, professors, and senators. And, to facilitate the work, Commission members heard two lectures by Professor Tarle on the conditions and forms of the legal proceedings under which representatives of governments had been tried in the past at times of political upheaval, notably the kings during the Great French and the English Revolutions. And later, to be quite certain (these were, after all, jurists with roots in the Tsarist past), Kerensky also set up, attached to the Extraordinary Commission, a Supervisory Committee of six attorneys, who won't themselves carry out investigations but will observe, to ensure the procedure is correct. (Their caring heart and keen legal eye will miss nothing.) And the apparatus he set up functioned daily, with no Sundays, no holidays, from ten in the morning to seven in the evening. When they had to interrogate detainees in the Peter and Paul Fortress, they went over there, in cars and court equipages, with no fewer than three members of the board, plus office staff, typists, and curious members of the public.

And Kerensky was very, very pleased with the organization. How splendid it was, and how menacing. And he was especially happy with the chairman himself, Muravyov—the minister had made the right choice there! (Muravyov had accepted the post on condition that he be granted the rights of a vice-minister, which was duly done.) Muravyov was decisive, energetic, ruthless, and would repeat, with a significant change, the lofty phrase Aleksandr Fyodorovich himself had used in Moscow: "We need something of Marat about us!" And he proposed annulling the statute of limitation for *enemies of the people*. (Indeed, their crimes even before '05, even at the end of the nineteenth century could be revealed. He must give that some thought.)

And on the board a combat group formed around Muravyov (including the lawyer Sokolov). Its aim: to lay bare, decisively and swiftly, those hideous crimes! Yes, to satisfy the public's proper anger, we need victims! More criminalization! We have to bring deeds and actions under the Criminal Code.

But the investigators immediately started complaining about the vast scale of their work: they'd been used to starting from a concrete accusation, but now they had to rummage around in a sea of paper to try and find any such accusation. For information on Shcheglovitov, for example, they had to go through material from the whole ten years he'd been a minister. But several investigators had already been digging around for six weeks—and found nothing. (And Senator Zavadsky felt they had no reason whatsoever to keep him under arrest. Aleksandr Fyodorovich: "I'm holding him under the Marat standard!") Put primary efforts into revealing the greatest crimes: the clandestine German party at court that was working for a separate peace. But even there, strangely enough, six weeks of hunting through documents and interrogations hadn't revealed a single trace. They'd expected (and Kerensky himself had been sure of it) to collect overwhelming evidence on the Stürmer case—Milyukov must have had a good reason for the warning in his speech of 14 November, that "our secrets are being passed on to Russia's enemies." But all the archives of the Foreign Ministry, all the reports to the Tsar from his most loyal servant Stürmer, and all the top-secret documents were lying there, accessible to the Commission—and revealed no hint of treason. But the public was thirsting for results and the journalists had been asking Muravyov repeatedly, and he'd given them promises. Then, perhaps, use instead the Sukhomlinov case—which had already been investigated and the case closed, under the old regime. But the only thing revealed by all the established facts was Sukhomlinov's total carelessness and the government's dereliction of duty—but nothing in any way treasonable.

A few days before, they'd done another search of Golitsyn's house, he being the most recent Prime Minister, but found nothing. They'd arrested a doorman and a chauffeur but their interrogations had also been fruitless. Another strange thing was that not a single provocateur had been revealed among state functionaries. How could that be? Did no official ever help the police department? That's impossible! They probably knew them personally and the connection was never formalized on paper. How unfortunate. Beletsky was locked up in a half man-height black hole for not wanting to give evidence—to encourage him to change his mind. (Then the argument about the provocateurs started up again: what, exactly, should we accuse them of? Shouldn't we be trying them as "officials overstepping their authority"? Gruzenberg had suggested this, but Senator Zavadsky was indignant: how could officials be provocateurs? And if they were, then their *duty* was to carry out provocations, otherwise they'd be bordering on "dereliction of duty.") Well anyway, that fiendish police plot, shooting machine guns off roofs—at least we can prove that, can't we? In all the papers, from one issue to the next the Commission was on the front page appealing for witness statements about the rooftop shootings, but they only got rumors or feeble-minded nonsense. So the whole of Petrograd was sure that policemen were shooting from rooftops—but actually there was no shooting at all? It seemed that way. But then what charge could be leveled against the detailed police patrolmen? There were still, in late April, as many as three thousand of them.

Muravyov thought we wouldn't discover anything unless we focused all our efforts on the Emperor and Empress, started from the heart of the treachery! He was sure that during the days of the revolution the Tsar had intended to open our front up to the Germans. And then one newspaper published telegrams, unknown up to that point, from the Tsaritsa, clearly hinting at betrayal of both the state and her spouse! But they turned out to be fakes, made up by a telegraph operator. Muravyov dreamed of summoning the Tsar to an interrogation at the Commission. But now Aleksandr Fyodorovich, after his personal visits to Tsarskoye Selo, found he could not agree to that, nor even to a search of the Tsar's papers at the palace. Then via the palace commandant they sent the Tsar himself a demand to produce—for our investigations into the ministers—all the state papers and formal reports that remained with him. And the Tsar submitted everything, sorted and categorized into envelopes with explanatory dockets. (There were even fairly intimate documents, damaging to the Tsar himself.) Several investigators rushed in to study it all—and they too found nothing that contravened any law. Even within the Commission, one of the senators opposed Muravyov. According to Russian law, he said, the Emperor was not accountable to the courts for any of his actions, even if crimes were to be discovered. (Muravyov wondered whether they shouldn't, via the Kurlov case, accuse the Tsar of conniving in Stolypin's murder. But he could not carry the majority of the Commission with him.)

There was this legal impasse as well: despite everything, we could not try former ministers for serving the former government, when they were fulfilling their duties. Say, for example, we were to try them for obstructing the revolution from 8 March onwards—weren't they obliged to obstruct it? There's the paradox: how can we try them under laws that we ourselves, the revolution, have done away with? And if we were to try them from the point of view of the new authority—wouldn't that look like revenge? But if we can't declare them guilty of political crimes, crimes against the state, since no one has infringed any of the old laws, then—and now Muravyov took the Commission off in a quite different direction—in order to try them legally, we had to find criminal offences in their history!

But what the dickens . . . they didn't find any of those either. They'd got down to trifles: Gruzenberg suggested that General Ivanov had committed a crime on his way to Petrograd, by forcing two soldiers, who'd been behaving obstreperously as they approached, to kneel. And they wanted to try Frederiks for exempting one of his employees from military service. The Commission had strayed a long way from its path. Now (and Kerensky really wanted this) they started re-examining the whole story of the Lena goldfields shooting of 1912, in the hope of finding incriminating material on the responsible minister, Makarov. (But found none, alas.) At this point they brought the whole Batyushin Military Commission of Inquiry to trial, and it was the banker Rubinstein—previously arrested by that commission—who leveled the accusations this time.

And now a quarrel blew up within the Extraordinary Commission itself. The more right-wing members spoke up: by law, if the evidence is insufficient the proceedings should be terminated. In this case there was no evidence and all interrogations of ex-ministers had been for show, to create the appearance of activity and satisfy the public. Questions were being raised on side-issues quite unrelated to criminally punishable offences. And because the ministers and dignitaries could not be charged, and were only under suspicion, there were no grounds for holding them in prison, especially in the Peter and Paul Fortress and, what's more, for months on end with no charges brought. That showed a total disregard of legal procedure.

So what were they to do? Free Stürmer too?? Kerensky was outraged by that idea: that would make the worst possible impression on the public and discredit the Provisional Government, even destroy it. The public sees all the detainees as villains, and is on tenterhooks awaiting our conclusions. And we're dawdling!

And it was not just the Commission that had now grasped the situation. Nor just the wives of the detainees, who had literally besieged the Commission in the Winter Palace. Karabchevsky too, in recent times the lion of liberal lawyers, was also lodging a complaint, on Vyrubova's behalf but couching it in more general terms: keeping people locked up for months without bringing an accusation or even interrogating them is illegal. (Karabchevsky was given no reply.)

The old detachment of Peter and Paul prison guards had been sent off to the front and now the detainees were under the control of a new, revolutionary garrison from the 3rd Riflery Regiment, which recognized no authority, not even the Extraordinary Commission, and would allow no outsider a look-in. One Archil Chkhonia, an officer in a Caucasian Cossack uniform, was ruling the roost and calling himself the "fortress commandant," and his clerk was a high-school pupil. There was mud everywhere and they never took the prisoners out for exercise. And complaints were received, saying that they'd taken the detainees' own pillows, blankets, and linen away, thrown their mattresses out, stripped them of all their clothes, and given them in exchange badly washed, torn rags from the military hospital, and that they'd tried to take Vyrubova's crutch away, not believing she was crippled, and then felt around for the fracture in her hip bone, to make sure. And that, to make their job easier, they fed the prisoners only once a day and ate their food themselves, reducing the detainees' portions accordingly. And there were complaints that they beat some of the detainees, spat in their soup, and sprinkled sawdust, or even crushed glass, on their food. And that the soldiers guarding them held meetings to discuss whether it wouldn't be simpler to shoot them and drop them into the Neva. But there was no objective way of verifying those complaints, as the soldiers would not allow any superior officials to come and check. And as the Fortress had become like a public thoroughfare, soldiers from other regiments were now flocking in and the guards allowed the curious into the corridors of the Trubetskoy Bastion, to look through the peepholes at the Tsarist ex-ministers serving time. Others would laugh and, apparently, threaten them through the door, saying they'd come and finish them off soon. The prison supply system had collapsed and there were now no candles or kerosene, so when the electricity failed they sat in the dark.

But who would dare teach those revolutionary soldiers a lesson, rebuff them, let alone lay a finger on them? That could give rise to a colossal scandal throughout the capital and even bring the Minister of Justice down. And Muravyov was even more afraid of irritating the Peter and Paul guards and getting into arguments with them. When he went over there for interrogations he tried not to notice all that, and the habitually scared Tsarist grandees barely dared even complain. And in the Commission when Senator Zavadsky, supported by Rodichev, protested that the guards' extreme abuse of their power put the regime to shame, and that under the Tsar no prosecutor would have allowed behavior even remotely like this, Muravyov demanded that he take back his words, which denigrated the new order and glorified the old.

In those brief, fleeting moments when Kerensky had any chance at all of dealing with those problems, he understood Muravyov, but could also understand the position of the detainees, especially Vyrubova, whom Kerensky himself had arrested. How could he manage to replace that guards unit? In the meantime, they decided to appoint and send over a doctor, the celebrated Dr. Manukhin, with a left-wing past and who was also, in 1905, sentenced to the Fortress. And he's a friend of Gorky. He'll go round the cells prescribing medicines and a better diet and the guards would need to behave in front of him.

And what brief, fleeting moments they were! Where could Kerensky stop, what could he spend time on? Was justice his only responsibility? Yesterday, the day before the 1 May holiday, he had taken Albert Thomas to the Field of Mars to lay wreaths for the martyrs (escorted by a half-squadron from the Don Regiment, following their car). There was a large crowd. From the dais, Thomas had addressed them in the name of the French Republic: the struggle, begun by the Decembrists, has now borne magnificent fruit and Russia has now entered the circle of great democracies of the world. Then (Lvov and Tereshchenko had joined them) they inspected the Pavlovsky Battalion line, after which the soldiers paraded past the four guests in a ceremonial march-past, arms at the ready, accompanied by the band. (Kerensky sensed a military streak within himself, ah yes, something very military in his nature!)

And today, the whole day, the great international proletarian holiday (even the Extraordinary Commission had the day off), was nothing but rallies, speeches, flying from one thing to another the whole time. Evening found Kerensky at a concert and rally at the Ciniselli Circus (the box office takings went to the Breshko-Breshkovskaya publishing fund). And he stood straight, slim, elegant, young, loved by all, on a podium in the arena, under floodlights, many thousands of eyes on him, and the words came easily:

"Since the time of the Great French Revolution, no country has lived such great days as Russia is living now. Now only one task lies ahead of us: to consolidate our freedom. And for this we need iron discipline, a great deal of it. And no violence! The Provisional Government's strength lies only in the people's trust, and as long as I am in power it will use no other resource than the people's support. The Government is strong only as long as it breathes a shared breath with the people. Some ask: how do you govern the country? You don't even have any police. But, comrades, we have no need of police, because the people are with us!"

And suddenly he had a flash of inspiration and proposed that he would conduct the band, and the audience singing, in a rendition of the Marseillaise.

He conducted them, and it turned out magnificently, very heartfelt.

Then a soldier spoke:

"Citizens! Let us swear to respond without a moment's hesitation to the call of our minister-citizen Kerensky!"

And from all sides came:

"We swear!! We swear!!"

Then one of the band called out from their little balcony:

"Comrades! Aleksandr Fyodorovich is quite good at conducting the band. But he's even better at conducting the Russian revolution. Let's wish him the strength to remain in his responsible position for a long time yet!"

Applause. Wild applause.

Kerensky proposed that the whole circus should sing the International. And he conducted again.

* * *

Let's say no to hateful duy:
We won't swear that evil oath!

("Soldiers' Song" a leaflet handed out at the
1 May demonstration at Novgorod-Severski)

[39]

Manuilov was now firing professors by the dozen—professors who'd not been elected but appointed earlier, by the government. From Moscow University alone, thirty in one fell swoop, seventeen of them from the faculty of medicine. Whatever kind of teaching could be done now? Everything was paralyzed.

Yet there'd been some Duma members, the more intelligent among them, who'd warned that "we can't change horses midstream," change governments while we're at war, in other words. But now here they were, doing it on the fly—carrying out surgery as they ran.

Olda Orestovna had never lived such sickening times as these past two months of revolution. She'd read a great deal about European revolutions and could imagine this upending of all values, all concepts, the mixed feelings and, for thinking, sensitive people—the stream of humiliations and insults. Times when, as Taine writes, a random crowd in the street considers that its will is that of the people and is prepared for any infamy. But it's only when you see this repugnant scene on the street with your own eyes, the faces, the rubbish on the pavements and in the canals of our eternal city; when postmen give an ultimatum as to whether or not they'll deliver the post; and when that buffoon of a journalist Amfiteatrov calls on his readers not to spare our monuments and palaces, "the idols of the autocracy"—it's only then that you feel all the insanity of what they call the Great Revolution. What anguish you suffer from that impotence: could it be that we'll never live a normal life? Andozerskaya knew it would take decades for the revolution to settle. Her anguish at the impotence of a human being, with only one life to live, won out over her reflections as a historian on how it would all settle into our society.

But even more than the shame of her own humiliation, in her classes, in the street, and in front of her maid, Olda Orestovna suffered from the humiliation of all Russia. She was ashamed of the uncouth verbiage of the countless resolutions. Of the obvious abasement of the Provisional Government, for which she had no respect, what with the empty, panicky appeals it issued day after day. And she was ashamed of the power that that shady little gang, the Executive Committee, wielded over the whole of Russia. (They'd finally published the list—there were no well-known names there, and scandalously few Russian ones. That, at least, hadn't been the case in France.) And she was even ashamed of the Committee's powerlessness. Everything was so loathsome, so grotesquely cartoonish, that when Lenin suddenly appeared and started whistling like Nightingale the Brigand from the balcony of the Kshesinskaya mansion, ripping fig leaves off the Executive Committee, too, it was at least a whiff of something terrifyingly real. This was no cartoon: no grovelling in sight here. This was an undisguised naked dagger. Lenin's every idea was aimed straight at the death of Russia. But how many people there were who just laughed at him for getting so excited when he spoke that he seemed about to jump onto the balustrade.

No, Lenin wasn't the caricature. The Executive Committee was, proposing to fight him with words alone. How agreeable you've become—didn't you always fight with bombs, before?

It wasn't very far to the Kshesinskaya mansion, just along Kamennoostrovsky Prospect, and Olda Orestovna had been there twice, to stand among the curious crowd gathered outside, as if for a fairground attraction. Once she'd actually heard Lenin, a disappointing little figure with a speech defect and a colorless, shrill voice. Marat was no more attractive of course—but the real strength of his ideas was that they reached beyond the bounds of everyday reason and aimed to topple even the most unshakeable beliefs. At a time of total government inertia, with the administration in collapse, that lever could snap into action: ridicule was misplaced.

Today Olda Orestovna had gone to wander among the invented ceremonials of the "first of May holiday." All revolutions love spectacle and love to look at themselves. And picturesque sights were, of course, not in short supply. Dozens of trucks, hooting raucously, made their way through the great clusters of people and sometimes stopped. One of the speakers on duty on a truck would pay some compliments to the revolutionary people and the truck would move on. There was an unbelievable quantity of red flags. Now a banner depicting a cook, a maid, and a lackey, now waiters, marching with a banner saying "No more tips." Now postmen, telegraph operators, and tram drivers, all totally unreliable these days, in their own separate columns, now sappers, out of tune with the holiday mood, carrying a banner featuring St. George. And there were, unusually, a great many women in red headwear: simple pieces of red calico tied round their heads like headscarves, even whole columns of them, and the women in charge had red skirts too. There was teasing from the pavements: "Here come Malyavin's peasant girls!" But probably the most telling sight was at Bolshaya Konyushennaya Street: the whole street, jammed with thousands of concerned citizens queuing for rail tickets at the municipal ticket office, was barred to the parades and even to passers-by.

But there were things that pained Olda even more. A placard saying "A free church for a free people" and, following it, a priest leading two hundred or so schoolchildren straining their thin voices to chorus "Forswear the old world!" People were asking, from the pavement, "Father, what's a free church?" He would reply, firmly, "One with no Procurator and all posts elected. So Grigori Petrov could be elected bishop now." "But he's not a monk." "That's the point! We have to revise the canons in line with the people's understanding." And there were youngsters like this in several places, singing from the slips of paper they clutched: "March on the foe, hungry people." There were even six-year-olds. From the pavement: "You should be flogging them, not trailing them round the streets." A modern school pupil answered proudly, "I'm ten years old and I'm a citizen. You're fifty and a slave." And there was applause for the boy.

The streets looked peaceful, the revolution had now abated: the image of a joyful feast-day.

But it was terrifying.

And if you looked closely, there were most definitely faces showing no joy, strained faces, masks; for they dared not reveal themselves.

And how many people had not come out at all, not wanting to see any of it? (And how many had, like Olda, changed their clothes, put on something simpler. Wearing good clothes in the street made you feel uncomfortable.)

"Nikolai Romanov's got 36 billion in the bank . . ."

"You just need to tax bourgeois houses—you'll get billions that way."

"We'll impose a dictatorship on the capitalists . . ."

Armed workers were marching in ranks. Their slogan: "Arm the people—every one." Passers-by were astonished:

"Who else needs weapons? We've already armed 14 million of them."

"We must arm the proletariat."

"Against who?"

There was no answer. Peaceable parades, a spring holiday—but who was the enemy . . .?

Today, Olda Orestovna turned again toward the Kshesinskaya mansion, for we all have, lurking within us, a certain attraction to danger, explosions, venomous bites. The Leninists weren't bashful wherever they went, but least of all here. To an accompaniment of cheerful music, a column of sailors arrived with a splendid silk banner proclaiming: "RSDRP—Kronstadt committee." They set up the banner on the balcony—and a sailor explained at length that the bourgeois press had lied about Kronstadt and there'd been no bloody reprisals there and no separate republic.

"But we Kronstadters won't allow the cause of peace to be sabotaged by a few bourgies. We won't lay down our arms—for us Lenin is a sacred figure."

The audience wanted Lenin himself to speak. They were told he wasn't there, he was on the Field of Mars. "That's not true! We were on the Field of Mars—there's no Lenin there!"

And the next:

"It's not enough to say 'Down with the Provisional Government'! We've got to go and bring it down, and take the means of production into our own hands. As for Nikolai II—string him up from a lamppost!"

Whenever the objections from the street got too loud, the Bolshevik band played the Marseillaise and drowned them out. Then, from another Kronstadt sailor:

"Comrades! We are powerful. We want revenge for our blood spilt from 1861 to 1905. If necessary we'll hear the thunder of cannon in Petrograd again—and there'll be a lot more blood!"

Everything was being said so openly. Why had almost no one heard?

[4 0]

We change so much with the years that we don't recognize ourselves in old photographs, or in the ideas we once committed to paper. Yet that would be of no consequence, for everything develops and, in developing, changes. But what is painful in old age is remembering whole stretches of our life, whole stretches spent traveling in the wrong direction, wasted on the wrong thing—and painful now especially, when the time we have left is so precious, but we have no time now. When it is so necessary, so incomparably more necessary than ever before to have at least a little strength—and we have none.

Why was it so important back then to waste all that strength on the dispute with Mikhailovsky? Was he a real danger? Or to get so close to that petty, malevolent despot Lenin, both at the 2nd Party Congress and then after the *Liquidators*, and why had it seemed they would advance together for a good while? But now, in Russia's momentous, fateful days, has anyone shown himself more perfidious than that Lenin?

The human life is not long, but not that short either. And how many times in ours do we manage to change course and become a new person? His mother (a Belinsky, distantly related to the critic) had urged him toward religion, while what his father had demanded of all his thirteen children (from two marriages) was hard work! (He had a small estate of five hundred acres.) But when Georgi, oldest child of the second marriage, heard of his father's military exploits, he dismissed the idea of civilian life and began to dream of becoming a military commander. And at the age of nine he went to the Voronezh military high school and there devoured military books and was, incidentally, already getting into arguments with his religion teacher too. Then off to Petersburg, to the Konstantinovsky officer training school, and a period of passionate emulation of his older half-brother, Mitrofan, who was a graduate of the General Staff Academy, a brilliant officer and a pessimist and skeptic in the mold of Lermontov's Pechorin. (He later, mysteriously, committed suicide in St. Vladimir Park in Kiev.) But already by the time he was at the officer school, Georgi was now inclined toward democratic and revolutionary views. (When he went home, his mother was intending to sell some land, not to the peasants, at a lower price, but to a merchant. Georgi intervened: then I'll burn the merchant's grain and reveal what I've done to the authorities. They sold the land to the peasants.) And his desire to be a military commander faded away. When his training was finished he managed to get himself released from serving as an officer and at the age of seventeen entered the Mining Institute. Although having only a vague conception of the people, he thirsted to be among them. But he was very hesitant: how should he do it? He began by leading study groups with Petersburg workers. In December 1876 on the St. Nicholas day holiday some workers, but mostly younger students, organized a demonstration outside Our Lady of Kazan Cathedral—and there Plekhanov gave his first revolutionary speech, which has become celebrated in Russian history. And after that, to cries of "Long live Land and Freedom" they unfurled a red banner, which was also the first in Russian history. They even put to flight the policemen who'd turned up. After that day there were arrests, but Plekhanov escaped.

For three years he lived with forged documents. He tried, on the basis of a fake teaching qualification, to become a village schoolteacher. At a worker's funeral in Petersburg, together with a group of students he helped a worker who was speaking there avoid arrest. He sought out, wherever he could, events suitable for engaging in propaganda among the people. He even went to the Don, where the Cossacks were rebelling against the zemstvo that had been introduced there. He was detained several times by the police but always managed to get himself released. In the spring of 1878 he wrote the program for the Land and Freedom party: we must follow in the footsteps of Bolotnikov, Bulavin, Razin, and Pugachev, titans in the defense of the people's revolution. But two years later the ideas of Aleksandr Mikhailov appeared, opposing that program: work in a peasant environment is like filling the Danaids' leaky vessel—futile, endless. We should not pursue propaganda among the masses, but punish the government, throw it into disarray, and this way win freedom for the people. Tkachev too was calling for the outright seizure of power by the revolutionary minority, for a revolutionary dictatorship. So belief in the people's ability to achieve something by their own strength gradually declined. Populism's belief in the people was in fact eroding! Plekhanov objected to this. He agreed with partial terrorism—in the factories and the countryside, but only as a supplement to propaganda among the masses. And he left the Land and Freedom congress at Voronezh, to create the "Black Repartition." This soon went under, but from it grew the shoots of Russian social democracy. For those three years, Plekhanov was in the underground, and was even intending not to give himself up to the police without resorting to armed resistance (the occasion didn't arise, though). But in early 1880, when a mass passport check was expected in Petersburg, he went abroad with his wife Rosalia Markovna, a medical student.

It was probably a fatal error. When you leave, you think: it's just for a few months, just till after the blanket passport check, just a short danger period. What seems dangerous is only persecution by the Tsarist autocracy. But you don't know what an arid, draining, fruitless horror emigration is. You leave for a few months: if only someone could have whispered in your ear that it would be thirty-seven years! You immediately come down with tuberculosis (and permanent bronchitis). You have no money (your writing never earned any). Your wife feeds you (and she still needs to get her doctor's qualification). Of three daughters, one has died, two grow up virtually not knowing the Russian language. A shabby, faded coat, a threadbare suit, frayed trousers. You're expelled by the Swiss government (his wife stays in Geneva to work and Georgi Valentinovich crosses the border to a French village). Then France expels you too. You go to London. Then Switzerland lets you back in—and you stay for twenty-two years. (Even in '05 there was no way he could afford the journey to Russia.)

Thirty-seven years of poverty and just trying to survive. And what a long spiritual journey those very years. Following the murder of Aleksandr II, sympathy for the crushed People's Will party, and you must support them. Alliance with Tikhomirov. Then a split from Tikhomirov. The Emancipation of Labor group. Polemics and more polemics with the populists. And against the traitor Struve. Young, revolutionary Marxists come to the fore and they're not thinking along the same lines as you—polemics with them too. No sooner do they create a party than it splits in two. Then a fragile reunification.

And another split. Your brain has a vast stretch of decades ahead, and you have time to read, to work through other people's ideas and think up your own. Marx introduces the idea that beauty comes from productive activity alone, but that's too narrow. The soil that fosters beauty is incomparably broader: might it even be . . . biology, or race? Gorky writes *Mother*, adhering strictly to the tenets of proletarian literature. But it's so tendentious as to be worthless. Ropshin, on the other hand, almost manages to infect us with his renunciation of the revolution—but, speaking objectively, in art this is acceptable. And some force drags you deep into past centuries, the eighteenth, seventeenth, sixteenth for your *History of Social Thought in Russia*. You remain faithful to your revolutionary views, but your homeland's history bathes you in its own waters, different waters. And the Russian language of yesteryear teaches you to write differently from the way we write our brochures.

When you lived in your homeland you saw her as a battleground for ideas, for the liberation of the people. You needed to be deprived of her—for ten years, twenty, thirty—to see, with surprise, that you love her even as she is now, trampled down by the autocracy. In fact this feeling for your homeland probably kept you away from the terrorist activities of the People's Will party in your youth (though there was a time when he would train, stabbing a stool with a dagger, and he had admired the Chigirin conspiracy). He could not bring himself to join the defeatists during the war with Japan. But when the great European war began, and the German and French Social Democrats were supporting their governments no matter what they thought of them—what did that say about us? Were we more rejected? More cruelly orphaned? Plekhanov had, for so many years now, been calling via the International for Russia to be strangled by foreign isolation, not to be given loans, or anything else. But now he wrote to a Social Democrat Duma member: a vote against war loans would be a betrayal of Russia. Vote in favor. And he cautioned Russian workers against revolutionary activity during the war: it would be tantamount to treason. He'd discovered within himself a sense for limits—where the brink of death is for the homeland.

And that volte-face had not been at all easy: three-quarters of the Russian revolutionary émigrés had bared their teeth at Plekhanov, calling him a traitor to the International. How many grubby insults came his way from that coarse Lenin in Zurich and the venomous Trotsky in Paris—but why? Because Plekhanov and his group acknowledged the people's right to defend itself if attacked. Their sort of "internationalism" was simplistic wisdom, lacking in substance. (And for some reason Trotsky vilified only the Allies all the time, while forgiving Germany everything, even the sinking of the peaceful *Lusitania*.)

But when the February Revolution dawned, resplendent, how very much dearer his homeland became! And how much more worthy of protection.

And now was the year, the hour of his return! (By now he'd been thinking he wouldn't live to see it.) And what a roundabout route! From Italy to

Paris, Paris to London. On the North Sea not only was he was seasick but they all endured anxious hours fearing German U-boats, and donned lifebelts as a precaution. And how his agitation grew as the train neared Petersburg! Not only had Russia been returned to him, but she was free! On the other hand, though, Georgi Valentinovich understood that he himself had never, never been needed so much by Russia and the Russian working class as he was now, to explain to them the route to follow at this moment of the greatest and most devastating danger. From the pedestal of his unparalleled life, how he would command their attention! He might reconcile all the Social Democrats, or even all the socialists. Clearly he would have to join the Provisional Government. And head the Soviet of Workers' Deputies.

For a humble émigré, the welcome at the station was overwhelming. It was already close to midnight, but there were bands, and delegations from military units, factories, industrial plants, and the journalists' union. There was the assistant city governor (who passed on greetings from Kerensky, who could not come in person), all the top brass of the Soviet and the loyal Zasulich, who was already back. They managed to forge a way through the applauding crowd to the reception rooms, where Chkheidze gave a speech of welcome. But Georgi Valentinovich could only answer: "It is especially pleasing to me, the first to raise a red banner on Kazan Square forty years ago, to see these red banners. So very many of them! I would wish to die right now, except that I want to do some work for our dear homeland. Our soldiers are showing that they will not allow a return to the old regime. And I believe that. The bosses have succumbed, but the fatherland is still here." More speeches of welcome, and then they raised him aloft and carried him to the car. In the square outside Finland Station there was such a massive crowd that the car could barely move. But even that wasn't all—now they went to the House of the People, where the All-Russian Conference of Soviets was taking place and, to the thunder of even more applause, at ten to one in the morning, Plekhanov was led out onto the stage.

But by this time he could say nothing, nothing, not a word. Here were his fellow-countrymen, workers, soldiers, and socialists, ready to listen to him, without any impediment, on the soil of his homeland—but he was lost for breath. His strength had given out. The last sixty years, thirty-seven as an émigré, had drained him. It was now that he needed it, needed his strength—but now he could only bow to the hall in silence. And he could barely stand. He had to be supported.

Exhausted by the journey, he spent the next day in bed, in the care of Rosalia Markovna, and rested. And on the Sunday afternoon he set off for the Conference of Soviets, in the Tauride Palace. To say that his strength had returned would be an exaggeration, but he could speak. What singular emotion it provoked, the very thought of it: in Russia itself, a conference of true representatives of the working classes, open to all! And here, in the Duma hall, they rose to their feet and applauded him enthusiastically.

Thus had his first rally, at Kazan cathedral, been transformed! Now, again, he could hardly speak, not from exhaustion this time but from emotion:

"... the revolutionary generation, which struggled under the red flag for decades, not losing faith in the Russian people when all Russia prayed for the Tsar instead of supporting the revolution, ... We Social Democrats were a small group and people laughed at us, called us Utopians. But I say to you, in the words of Lassalle: 'We were few in number, but we snarled so well that everyone thought we were many.' I am an incorrigible supporter of Scientific Socialism and I said in Paris in 1889: 'The Russian revolutionary movement will triumph as a working class movement or it will never triumph.' Everyone was surprised: what a pathetic character, how can anyone believe in the Russian working class, and not the Russian intelligentsia. ... And now, when I have the inexpressible joy of standing in free Petrograd and addressing the Russian proletariat, I ask you, comrades, where is that utopia that people reproached us with? The old Tsarist regime, all eaten away, you could say, by moths and worms, the regime now covered in a shame previously unknown in Russia. ... When I stepped down from the train in Finland station, what music did I hear? The Marseillaise! The French ideas have taken root, over a hundred years later, at the other end of Europe ..."

Then he joked good-naturedly about the French and English socialists there and, linking hands with them, stood facing a torrent of applause from the proletarians and soldiers.

He addressed them with all the tact he could muster, so as not to exacerbate any differences of opinion there. But he did not skirt his newly formed belief—which had already occasioned him some heated disputes:

"People call me a social patriot. But what does that mean? A person who not only holds to certain socialist ideals but also loves his country. Yes, I love my country and have never felt it necessary to hide the fact."

No applause whatsoever. Silence descended on the hall, and whispers. And more whispers.

"I am sure that not one of you would stand up and say that that feeling must be torn from my heart. No, comrades, you'll not tear that feeling of love for long-suffering Russia from my heart! Given my origins, comrades, I could have been one of the oppressors, jubilant, sounding off, with blood-stained hands. But I crossed over to the camp of the oppressed, because I loved the suffering Russian masses."

And on to the central point of the present discord:

"There was a time when defense of Russia meant defense of the Tsar. That was a mistake, because the Tsar did not want to defend Russia—he ruined our national defense. But we must—and all the more now that we've had the revolution—use all possible means in our struggle with the external enemy, with the Hohenzollerns ..."

But once he was home he digested that mistrustful silence, and he felt there was something he'd not fully explained. And the next day, already suffering from a cold, he went again, to say a few words before the Conference closed: people in the West are worried that revolutionary Russia might bring more disorder to the running of the country. But no, Russian democracy is politically mature.

And now he fell really ill. The sudden transition from Italy's balmy climate to the terrible Petersburg weather took its toll. Now it was from his bed that he ran his *Unity* and watched the newly arrived Lenin's efforts to ruin things. Plekhanov, his group, and his newspaper had ended up far from the left wing now and somewhere in the center—in the most reasonable part of the center. From issue to issue of the paper, they explicated topics (and when Plekhanov had the strength he wrote articles himself, though he felt that even his pen had grown weak—he had lost his old grip). Regarding the war: it was brought about by the Austrian and German bourgeoisie—if they triumph, it will lead to the monarchy being reinstated here. The German people have not rebelled, and it is imperative for us to put an end to Prussian militarism. Even before, this war was already the peoples' cause, and now, since the revolution, it is all the more compellingly so, for we are defending our vital interests. On the substance of the revolution: the state of our society makes a transition to a socialist revolution impossible. The time for a split will come but it is not here yet. The revolution was carried out in unison, by all social classes. At the moment it is bourgeois in character, and it would be madness for the working class to seize power. That will become possible when it can bring along the majority of the country. But now the most sensible thing for the socialists to do would be to join the Provisional Government themselves.

This was his opinion, and he answered even more forthrightly when asked whether it was possible that he personally might join the Provisional Government: I have not received an invitation, but in principle I see no objection. On the way here, in France, I talked to Guesde and he sees none either.

And that was printed everywhere: Plekhanov's intention was clear. Days passed. His cold could not have been a stumbling block to the negotiations. But no one came with the invitation.

How strange.

But every word in *Unity* was a trenchant confrontation with Lenin and his anarchist nonsense about the collapse of Russia. His calls for fraternization with the Germans could rip the delicate young tree of our political freedom out by the roots. And now there was another strange thing: although none of the socialists shared Lenin's views, apart from *Unity* no one challenged him, exposed his full iniquity. They all held their tongues, evaded the question or somehow expressed themselves in a particularly mild, vague manner. And *Pravda*, with Lenin's unparalleled cheek, had itself gone onto the attack. No one had shown this to Georgi Valentinovich at the time, but to mark his arrival it had published a brash, scurrilous little rhyme that all but accused him of harboring police sympathies:

You are our great propagator
And our social democrator.
Your devoted friends' salute
Goes to you, Black Hundred brute.

(Later Kamenev falsely claimed, in public, that the editorial board was sorry: the rhyme's appearance had been "an oversight.")

Plekhanov did not of course urge people to do battle with Lenin by any means other than words. As for supporters of the old regime, they should be exiled to the North. To counter the rumors of rabble-rousing agitation in Bessarabia and in Kiev province, he and Chkheidze jointly published a call to put an end to the odious endeavors of the Black Hundreds. When dealing with potential pogrom organizers we must apply the law with the utmost rigor. We must counter the Leninists' anarchic sectarianism with the principles of scientific socialism. But actually counter it. And no one was doing that. Chernov was shortsightedly practicing his condescending irony toward the "bourgeois fears" that Lenin provoked.

Not until two weeks after Plekhanov's arrival did a representative of the government appear, Minister Nekrasov. But it was certainly not to invite him into the government—far from it. It was to head the commission for the bettering of material conditions for the railway workers!

For the first few minutes, this was unbearably hurtful to him. He had the feeling they were mocking him. But he took himself in hand and resigned himself to the situation. This would, at any rate, be a concrete role aiming to improve the lot of the proletariat, and even a leader in theoretical aspects should not disdain that: it was in a way a small part of that job as Minister of Labor that he'd been tipped for. He resigned himself—and agreed. And he went to the railwaymen's conference and spoke there.

He agreed to it because he had decided to transfer his sphere of activity to the Soviet of Workers' Deputies and join the Executive Committee. He let this be known. The Committee asked for a formal application from the Unity group, including Deutsch. This was duly provided.

But—this was monstrous! The Executive Committee members were his children; two-thirds of them studied from his books. And he alone could bring them long years of socialist experience. He could also explain to them the mood of present-day Western socialists. But now, by twenty-three votes against and twenty-two votes for, they rejected Unity, and only twenty-seven of them voted to invite Plekhanov personally. With only a consultative role.

Who, forty years ago, could have predicted such a fate for him?

Was it Bolshevik intrigues? No, it went wider: the EC members could not forgive him speaking so openly of his "social patriotism." But *who* were they actually? *Whose* delegates? Mythical groups? Or did they just come on their own initiative? Sukhanov, Steklov, Krotovsky, Lurie, and three dozen others like them—who did they represent? Just hangers-on at the helm . . .

So he had to spend forty years in exile, only to be rejected now by these youngsters? To languish so many years as an émigré, only to be left without the strength to play a part in leading events in his homeland?

This time he did not resign himself. He took offense and refused.

He hadn't the strength . . . He'd not conserved it. He'd expended too much in the past, maybe even on mistaken objectives, in useless debates.

Besides, his health had deteriorated considerably. The doctors advised him to move to Tsarskoye Selo. He'd have to go.

Today was the great holiday, the first openly celebrated First of May. Georgi Valentinovich was called on to speak at several meetings—in the Mariinsky Theater and the Ciniselli Circus. But he couldn't go. His strength had let him down on the very threshold of the future. Rosa went to the Unity rally to read his address. He also wrote a letter to a promising youth group, a collective of socialist students: "For the international proletariat, it is very important for as many people with higher education as possible to join their ranks. The socialist revolution requires a long journey of education. Nowadays people here are forgetting that, and calling instead for political power to be seized immediately . . ."

Would they grasp that? Would they understand?

Outside, the celebrations were under way, while Georgi Valentinovich lay prostrate in bed, looking at the ceiling. He, in fact, had taken part in the Paris socialist congress in 1889, when they had established the 1 May holiday. And now, when for the first time in his homeland it was being openly . . . Oh well . . . this sickness would probably not last long.

From time to time the sound of bands and revolutionary songs wafted in through his little top window. That Day raised the toilers above the prose of everyday hustle and bustle.

Friends dropped in, excited, spellbound, and told him about it. The Field of Mars was like a human ocean. Thousands of red flags, a dozen bands here and there, some playing the Marseillaise, others opera music. Trucks draped in red fabric were positioned at intervals in the procession, and public meetings held from them. Among the speakers, the soldier's greatcoat would alternate with the worker's jacket, the peasant's sheepskin coat, the Jew's long frock-coat, and the cassock. They talked endlessly, with expansive gestures. People listened intently, naïvely, without interrupting. Many speeches about parceling out the land. But there were also banners proclaiming "Down with the war."

"I've heard that Lenin's been to the Gunpowder district, calling for factories and industrial plants to be seized and workers to prepare for the dictatorship of the proletariat . . ."

He's mad! But who's going to bring him to heel?

"What happened outside Kazan Cathedral?"

"Soviet member Broido came down hard on the government: 'If we wanted to, we could overthrow this government in two hours and take the power into our own hands!' 'But aren't you afraid that two hours later you'll be overthrown as well?' 'No, we're the people—no one can overthrow us!'"

And this at Kazan square!

How are we ever to penetrate this turmoil in people's minds, make them understand that both our fatherland and socialism, both are in danger? Comrades! If we're really aspiring to freedom, what disagreements can there be among us?

* * *

YOU DON'T CRY OVER A HANDFUL—
EXCEPT WHEN IT'S HOLLOW

* * *

2–5 May

[41]

The Sevastopol miracle! That's what Petrograd was already calling Kolchak's success in the first weeks of the revolution. (The more successful weeks had been before mid-April. After that, the picture was not so rosy.) All Russia was collapsing, but Sevastopol seemed to remain untouched.

It had begun with that frank combined assembly of officers and sailors that Kolchak had dreamed up on an impulse, and then, on that joyful, amicable March night, meeting Duma delegate Tulyakov. He'd arrived late but had no airs and graces, and spouted the socialist mumbo-jumbo with great sincerity. This was the birth of the first revolutionary committee, headed by the sharp-witted volunteer Zorokhovich, from the fortress squad. (It later transpired that he was the son of a Simferopol businessman, and he would prove a great success in the first Sevastopol delegation to the capital.) And Kolchak, having consulted Lieutenant Colonel Verkhovsky, had realized he needed to act more rapidly than any of the possible usurpers from the ranks: he himself must be first to create sailors' committees on the ships, soldiers' in the detachments (two-thirds from the crews, one third officers). And out of those, a day later, a central military executive committee was formed, which had absolute confidence in Kolchak. And one of its first decisions was to ban all alcohol sales in Sevastopol and go after any clandestine dealing. Together with Verkhovsky he drew up new, democratic rules for life on the ships: then he issued an order investing them with legal force. And, best of all, every decision of the committees must be ratified by both the central committee and Kolchak—otherwise they would not be valid. And the Sevastopol Soviet accepted that!

This whole upheaval was completed in three or four days, without the battle-readiness of the fleet or the fortress being disrupted for a single hour. Ships immediately started putting to sea to maintain their blockade of the Anatolian shores, as if the revolution had never happened. And the Sevastopol military committee itself was quick to declare that Russia could look on its southern flank with a tranquil mind.

He had to exercise just as much skill, and fast, with the officers as with the men: he must overcome their caste mentality, their hidebound attitudes. He told them to frequent the mass of sailors as much as possible, not distance themselves. And he gave the fortress officers a dressing down because they couldn't stand "spending all their time with the louts." And now no enmity remained between officers and sailors, and all over Sevastopol they saluted each other, even with exquisite care, and courtesy was shown the officers. A soldier lit a cigarette in a tram, for example, and deliberately, brazenly, blew smoke into the face of a retired general. A sailor stopped the tram, using the conductor's bell: "You scoundrel, how dare you do that to a man who deserves your respect? Off this tram!" A few soldiers in the tram started protesting, but the sailor gestured out of the window to a navy patrol, and the soldier had to make a run for it.

In the streets of town, perfect order reigned, thanks to the patrols. And not a single red flag was raised in Sevastopol. The national flag was just flown the other way up, with the red stripe at the top.

But most extraordinary of all was the attitude of the Sevastopol workers, who proved even more conscientious than the crews. They announced that they would support Kolchak, and refused the eight-hour day, saying they would work as long as the fleet needed. Their own, separate, soviet was not merged with the fleet's, and relations with the admiral were of the best. And when, in April, the first breaths of "liquidate the war" wafted in and infected the sailors, representatives of the workers' soviet arrived, told the crews they should be ashamed of themselves and set about getting them back in line.

And how on earth had this miracle come about? Kolchak was confident that his main attraction was the personal charm he exercised over the fleet. He was a kind of banner, the fleet's standard. The sailors felt he was their leader and defender, in an immediate way, even bypassing all the officers. And no committee, no commission can take the place of this. Kolchak's every step, every movement, every word he spoke to the sailors was assured—and he always won. They both loved him and continued to fear him. The distance of the fleet from the capital, its isolation from the centers of revolt, also played a part, as did the fact that the Black Sea fleet was on year-round alert.

In response to German wireless and the proclamations dropped from an airplane, at the end of March Kolchak had addressed the fleet and the people of Sevastopol: "Enemy agents are doing their utmost to shatter the extraordinary order and tranquillity here. Treat this enemy initiative with calm disdain." And while, in the capital, the Soviet was haggling over the abolition of the oath of allegiance to the Provisional Government, on Kulikovo Field, on the outskirts of town, Kolchak assembled all the crews in the fleet, and the garrison, and himself pronounced the oath with a clear conscience, for all to hear. And they followed, in their tens of thousands.

To the admiral's mind, the restoration of the previous dynasty was clearly impossible by now, and it was barely imaginable that the people might elect another, as had happened during the Time of Troubles. Kolchak served neither one nor the other form of government: he served his country.

All the committees were patriotically inclined. The central military committee was led by an airman, Safonov (a name, coincidentally, close to

Kolchak's heart), the workers' Soviet by Vasiliev, and the Sevastopol Soviet by Kontorovich, newly returned from penal servitude and exile. Forty or so, with a greying beard, he was a Social Democrat, but reasonable. The admiral had transferred the Soviet from the modest anteroom of the fortress HQ into the palace, which had only just been built for the commander of the port. From its balcony, Kontorovich called for the men to keep the bloodless revolution unsullied: and they always responded with a cheer.

Now Kolchak was discovering that this, that, and other committee members were Socialist Revolutionaries. Some had only just joined, while others had been working for the party in secret while in the navy. For years they'd been trying to raise a mutiny, but now their speeches were frank and not the slightest bit seditious (the admiral and many officers would lend a sympathetic ear), and they set about maintaining order in the fleet. Well, well, well! There were good people even among the SRs. These men considered Kolchak a real democrat and willingly came to an agreement on all the directives. He was always invited to speak at their assemblies. (And he knew that if, at one of those assemblies, the battle alert sounded they would be at their stations instantly.)

And his speeches, his ardor proved convincing. Though he'd never aspired to a political role for himself.

And just how long could this calm, this isolated Sevastopol Miracle last?

But the route into Sevastopol from Russia was open, and some shady types, whom even the SRs considered enemies or German agents, had been coming in unnoticed. And there were no established methods or means of curbing these arrivals. Invisible, silent currents of thought began to form—currents hostile to the military executive committee. And the propaganda flowed, hidden, saying the officers were imperialists, serving the interests of the bourgeoisie, who only wanted the Bosphorus and the Dardanelles. In Balaclava someone was already saying that officers who favored continuing the war till victory should be thrown into the bay. One demand was heard, then another, for the removal or transfer of one or another officer—sometimes even with good reason. He had managed, for the time being, to calm things down in a commonsense way.

Hoping to explain all this clearly and firmly to the top brass, on 23 April Kolchak had made for Odessa, where Guchkov—an old, loyal friend of the fleet—was expected. But alas, Guchkov turned out to be not only overwhelmed with revolutionary ceremonials there—between which there was no time to slip in a serious hour-long discussion—he'd also arrived in Odessa with a heavy cold. He took Kolchak to a session of the Odessa Soviet, where he was hailed as the "first admiral to ally himself with the government of the people." (Nepenin, who was actually the first, was already forgotten.) And Kolchak, with an acquired ease, affirmed that he was a conscientious supporter of the democratic order, and that our smooth passage into new ways of living invited confidence that this process would carry on peacefully.

But they didn't manage to engage in serious conversation. Not even about some of Guchkov's methods, such as dismissing, by telegraph, the fleet's Chief of Staff, Pogulyaev (because he was an officer of His Majesty's suite). Kolchak himself had disagreed with the decision. (He had, at the time, sent a telegram: insufficient reason. Guchkov had insisted: the Petrograd Soviet has documents showing Pogulyaev in a bad light. Good God! Some Petrograd Soviet's word trumps the advice of the Admiral of the Black Sea fleet! We should really not be giving in to them like this. But he had to be dismissed.)

Kolchak told Guchkov in Odessa that he was very worried about the propaganda being spread by persons unknown, under the guise of free speech. Guchkov: things have gone so well in your fleet up to now that I'm confident you'll manage now too. Kolchak: but all the means I had of fighting this have now been removed by decrees from the government itself.

However, Guchkov was very, very sick, and barely taking things in. They agreed that Kolchak would come to Petrograd a week later.

But Petrograd was a long way off, and to be apart from the fleet for that many days, when so many matters depended on Kolchak being there in person . . . But he had to go, to get everything solved. Then he learned that Alekseev was on his way to the Northern Front and, it seemed, would continue on to Petrograd. So much the better: we'll all meet up. The papers were saying that Guchkov was already recovering and was working. Before leaving, Kolchak convened delegates from the ships and the garrison, to do some morale-boosting. He left Sevastopol on Monday in the small hours, and arrived in Petrograd early this morning, Wednesday 2 May, only to discover that Guchkov was not at all better and was dealing with things very slowly: he could only see Kolchak in the afternoon. But Alekseev, yes, he was expected tomorrow morning. Well that was something, anyway.

But on the way, at Orel, Kolchak had read news in a Petrograd paper of a monstrous directive from the Navy Minister: every officer in the fleet was to have his epaulettes removed! How on earth could they have taken such a reckless decision, without even consulting the fleet commander? Even when things were running smoothly and we weren't at war it would have caused quite a commotion. Whenever the uniform was changed, we'd always had a year of calm while the old ones were being worn out—but now, with things so finely balanced, how on earth could we drop such a weight onto the scales? And Kolchak learned of it in the worst possible place, in a train. He was helpless. He got flustered and was on the brink of turning back. But even if he rushed back to Sevastopol it would already be too late. And even if he'd been in place he couldn't have annulled the directive, just found some way to adapt to it. His role was pitiable. What state was Sevastopol in now, after this new blow? And what about the fleet's ground force units? They hadn't even been mentioned. No one had thought about them.

After Moscow, in a new issue of the paper, he'd read another piece of news: Admiral Kolchak was on his way to Petrograd, having been appointed to command the Baltic fleet! What on earth was going on? He didn't believe it—and he did believe it. That night his nerves were fraught and he didn't get a wink of sleep.

On arrival he went straight to the Admiralty: no, nothing of the kind had been said, it was a hoax. And the order to get rid of epaulettes? Having failed to prevent the Baltic fleet officers' epaulettes getting ripped off, Admiral Maksimov had extracted this undertaking from Guchkov. (In the ministry, there'd been such a panic that they were even prepared to swap uniforms for civilian clothes.) Was this how they stood up to danger? Saving their own situation by ruining others'? Kolchak knew Maksimov well, from the Baltic fleet: stupid, morally dubious if not actually corrupt. And now he seemed, in a grotesque way, to have emulated Kolchak's trajectory: from head of a mine-laying division to commander of a fleet. But thanks to a mutiny. And today it transpired that he was also to visit Guchkov this afternoon. That would be the last straw—having to share the meeting with Maksimov.

That he had to avoid. He must ask Guchkov to see him earlier. Even just an hour.

Because Guchkov was ill, the first half of the day was wasted. And that ruined Kolchak's other plans. He had been hoping, on this visit, to take a day out for a quick trip to Reval, to see Anna Vasilievna again (her maiden name had been Safonova—now she was married to someone else). But now he could see no way of finding the time. In the Admiralty he unexpectedly came across a painstakingly recorded register of the arrivals and departures of all naval officers (apparently because they'd been secretly leaving their ships). That constrained a side trip, too.

After lunch, Kolchak left the Admiralty for the minister's residence. And Guchkov received him from his bed . . . His face was old and sagging, the skin sallow, and his handshake terribly feeble. Not a good start.

Should Kolchak report that his fleet was in good cheer? Or first say how furious he was at the order to remove the epaulettes? But Guchkov launched the conversation, on a very different subject. Storm clouds were gathering over the Baltic fleet, he said, his voice weak, slow, gloomy, and they were expecting more killings. The officers were beside themselves with worry. Admiral Maksimov was largely to blame, with the repugnant, demagogic methods he'd adopted. Guchkov had now told him to stay in Helsingfors but today his chief of staff had arrived with a report bringing new demands from the sailors: they wanted the ships to be run not by commanders but by committees, all commanders should be elected, and other demands in a similar vein. And Guchkov could see no solution other than to appoint Kolchak as commander of the Baltic fleet.

So here it was. There's no smoke without fire.

Kolchak was in two minds, his feelings vacillating. Two minds because he had cut his teeth in the Baltic fleet and, as its passionate, impatient regenerator, matured with it. Kolchak's heart was still with that fleet. But how could he tear himself away from the Black Sea fleet now?

Vacillating because the worse things got in the Baltic fleet, the more dramatic, the more fragile they would become in the Black Sea. Perhaps it was a mirage? Could it hold? If the army couldn't hold its ground, it would be even harder for the navy to withstand the blows dealt it by the revolution. It was a vulnerable organism. A whole ship can founder through the action of a single rogue sailor.

He said he was willing: but I fear I shan't be able to change anything in the Baltic. And the Black Sea is by no means as successful as it appears. I'm not sure my prestige can keep things in check. It could finish up the same there as in the Baltic.

And it was so inopportune, with the minister exhausted, ill—but how could he not tell him this? What's corrupting both the fleet and the army is your system, Aleksandr Ivanych. Your orders. And now the order to remove the epaulettes.

It should have been said more forcefully than that! But Guchkov was ill. And an old defender of the fleet.

Guchkov lay motionless.

He would think a bit more whether to make the appointment.

In this situation, should he upset Guchkov with new anxieties? We've not had a single desertion, though requests for leave have, it's true, increased worryingly. It's almost a stampede. But the combat operations of the fleet never cease for so much as a day. Gunnery drill, training exercises, crew instruction. Torpedo boat and submarine patrols. We're tormenting the Turks nicely. Sometimes it's our hydroplanes making raids over the Bosphorus, or we'll send a torpedo boat to capture a schooner. In recent weeks our light warships have made a series of brilliant incursions on the Turkish coast. Near the Bosphorus our submarine sank a steamer carrying military supplies, two loaded schooners, and one barge. We destroyed the port armaments at Kerrasunde. The *Breslau* never comes out of the Bosphorus and the *Goeben* is under constant repair.

And all of that comes down to the fact—and this is the idea—that we absolutely have to take the Bosphorus! Up to now we saw the landing of troops as important and effective: now it's imperative. A successful operation on the Bosphorus would reinforce the Black Sea fleet and save the land troops from collapse. We must tell Alekseev that if the Turks know we're incapable of attacking on the Black Sea they'll shift their troops into Galicia—and attack him there! And the decision cannot be put off: only June or July will do for this job. But it'll take another two months after the order's received to prepare the transports. So we have to work quickly—before it's too late!

But in March Guchkov had ordered that no transports should be equipped for the second and third landing divisions: they were busy transporting ore and coal. Kolchak had immediately telegraphed back that the Romanians could provide their river flotilla for Black Sea use—it was in the Chilia branch of the Danube, not in use. That way we'd gain transports for two divisions. But the Romanians didn't want to help. While we were haggling with those skinflints, Kolchak received a directive from GHQ: take the fleet to support operations by the Romanian Front in the Lower Danube and near Dobrudzha. So, unable to find a solution for the land troops, they were—if you can believe it—going to set up a large operation against Braila. How could we pay out gold a coin at a time? What idiocy! No soaring ambition, no wholehearted feel for the glory of Russia! For the great Russian victory there was only one solution: to take Constantinople! Guchkov was even more exhausted, the light gone from his eyes.

"Aleksandr Vasilich, the operation on the Bosphorus is already, from the moral point of view, outdated. Revolutionary Russia does not want to conquer Constantinople."

"Not to conquer it! But to get it out of German hands! Otherwise, what was the point of maintaining the Black Sea fleet?!"

It was all in vain. Guchkov had lost all purpose.

Aides brought him papers—this was the kind of nonsense they were occupied with—about renaming ships of the Black Sea fleet, it being impossible to retain imperial names. In the Naval Ministry, they'd thought up: the *Aleksandr III* to become the *Free Russia*, the *Empress Catherine* the *Free Will*, the *Heir* the *Citizen*, the *Panteleimon* to become the *Potemkin* again, and the *Kagul* the *Ochakov*, as in Schmidt's time.

Kolchak had never, not in the terrible days on the Arctic Ocean, nor those testing hours at Port Arthur when he himself was so sick he could barely stand, allowed himself any concessions, forgiven himself the slightest lapse in spirit.

Nor made allowances for others.

Including Guchkov, now. He had no right to let himself go like this.

What could he expect from Alekseev now, as regards the Bosphorus? Kolchak was allowed to present his plan at the government session tomorrow. But if Guchkov had become this feeble, what about the others?

We were letting Russia's most brilliant intervention in this war slip through our bungling fingers—first under the Tsar and then under the revolution. None of them, not one, was keeping up with the new century—they were dawdling along as they had in the nineteenth.

Farewell, Great Russia!

(And what if the Black Sea fleet were really unable to hold out? If it collapsed in the wake of the Baltic . . .?)

Feeling battered, bruised, Kolchak trudged to the Hotel Bellevue, along a Nevsky Prospect still in the bright colors of flags from yesterday's mass demonstration. (And how had yesterday gone in Sevastopol?)

This was the state things had come to: the admiral of a fleet had to ask for an audience not with ministers but with socialists, to ask for support from people who'd been persecuted revolutionaries before. How times had changed! But the unusual nature of the times was also leading him into some unusual steps. People said Plekhanov was the most celebrated of all the Russian socialists and, at the same time, a sensible Russian patriot. A rare combination! He was in Petrograd. Kolchak must see him. And ask him to send some strong, persuasive agitators to Sevastopol to scare away those shady types who'd just arrived. And tomorrow, at the government meeting, he'd have to ask Kerensky for some equally persuasive SRs. If we can get them into the central military committee, we can sort everything out, even without the Provisional Government.

He walked as far as Karavannaya Street and his hotel. Again the evening and night had been wasted—and he couldn't get to Reval.

Or . . . should he go? Not give a hang about decorum or gossip? But tomorrow the government was meeting in the middle of the day. What if he couldn't get back in time?

What consideration should he have shown? He'd not considered that he was himself married, with a six-year-old son. (When he'd married Sofia Fyodorovna, had he thought much about what he was doing? He'd always been going off somewhere, in a terrible rush. He was engaged to be married before that first expedition with Toll and there was no time then. He'd married in a hurry before going to Port Arthur, and only had a few days before he left. It was like a dream. And he'd not returned till he was released from captivity, sick.)

Neither had he considered the fact that Anya was also married. She had a one-year-old son. He'd not considered the fact that she was twenty years younger than he was. He'd not given any thought to how it would look. When passion seizes you (not just passion for a woman—passion for the South or North Pole, or for Constantinople) and is cast into the form of an arrow, the arrow of decision—you don't see the limits of the possible. You'll do anything to achieve your goal.

Anya Safonova, daughter of a well-known pianist and conductor, was young, pretty, gay, the always-laughing center of their circle of naval officers, Essen's circle, when they met on dry land. And on dry land sailors meet to make merry. (And alongside Kolchak in Essen's HQ served Anya's husband, Timirev. He was her second cousin.) They'd spent the summer of 1915 in adjoining dachas on an island near Helsingfors. (When he was coming into Helsingfors and knew he would see her, that town had seemed to him the best in the world . . .) All the officers courted her, and at that time Kolchak's behavior still gave no reason to think he was any more besotted than the others. But they could never say as much as they wanted, sitting beside each other. "Will it ever be as good again as it is now? If only we might never be separated." But one evening—Helsingfors was kept darker now, with blue street lighting—they met in the street, in the rain, stopped for just two minutes and went their separate ways. But something special had happened. Kolchak felt it, though he didn't know what it was. (She'd said, later: "I thought, suddenly, that with *this one* I'd not be afraid of anything. What silly ideas we have sometimes.") Now she started reprimanding him if he'd been too attentive to another woman. And one evening at the club all the ladies were dressed in Russian national costume, and he asked her to have a photo taken and give it to him. And he hung it (with her knowledge) in his cabin, her picture alone. None of his wife, and not a single admiral.

Last July he'd been in Reval when his appointment to the Black Sea fleet had been announced. But time was short for handing over the mine-laying division and he could not even cross the bay. But suddenly she arrived in Reval (she'd learned)! And for three evenings—from evening till morning—they were together. They went for walks in the avenues of the Katharinenthal Park, which adjoined the naval officers' summer club, sat at a table, and could never manage to speak to their hearts' content. On the first evening, he asked her permission to write to her, and she agreed. He was leaving for the South, on a permanent basis; it was wartime—it seemed they could not see each other any more. And on the second evening she herself was the first to say she loved him. He replied, different suddenly, "I didn't tell you I loved you." Her response: "But I'm telling you. The whole time I'm wishing I could see you. I'm always thinking about you. And now it's turned out that I . . . love you." His: "And I . . . it's even greater than love." And they set off again, arm in arm, along the Katharinenthal's chestnut avenues. And then back to the club hall, where there was a crowd. (Her husband was at sea at that time and Sofia Fyodorovna in Helsingfors.) It was painful—and sweet. And nothing else.

In his very first days in Sevastopol he'd sent, special delivery, a giant of a sailor with a flimsy letter to Sofia Fyodorovna and a thick packet to Anya. (Everyone was sitting on the steps of the same terrace and the two were next to each other when they received the missives.) He'd never written letters like that, writing for a whole week at a stretch—he even wrote at GHQ, when the Emperor was there, on the train, and at sea too, while at the same time giving chase to the *Breslau*. He wrote to her of his duties, of what he'd found in the fleet and how he dreamed of seeing her. Later he wrote to both women by post and, when the opportunity arose, via someone at Naval HQ. And there was always one thin letter and one thick. And Anya would reply that she lived from letter to letter, as if in a dream, no longer thinking of anything else.

In the autumn Sofia Fyodorovna and their son Rostislav moved to Sevastopol. Anna Vasilievna's husband had been transferred to Reval and they were both there now.

For her name day, in February, he'd telegraphed an order for a basket of lilies of the valley, to be sent to her in Reval.

Anya herself was like these lilies of the valley. She was delicate, ethereal, and her tinkling laughter pulled at his heartstrings.

Fear—and fervor: was he going to break up two families? Rob two sons of fathers (for each must stay with his mother)? Lose Slavushka and accept her son?

And—it did not seem impossible!

Even on the surging waters of the revolution.

But to do that he would have to rush to Reval. Now!

Yet the Black Sea fleet was waiting for him. Balanced on a knife edge. Where a single day without the commander could bring catastrophe. And tomorrow morning Alekseev would be arriving. There'd be another battle for Constantinople.

But perhaps, when he saw those ephemeral ministers all together at the meeting—might he be able to convince them, all in one fell swoop? The arrow of the Bosphorus, already cast, was thrusting out from his chest.

DOCUMENTS—14

2 May

FROM GERMAN AMBASSADOR IN BERN ROMBERG TO THE GERMAN MINISTRY OF FOREIGN AFFAIRS

250 Russian émigrés are asking us to reduce the price of the ticket. They want a reduced aggregate figure for the whole of the special train.

2 May

FROM THE MINISTRY OF FOREIGN AFFAIRS TO AMBASSADOR ROMBERG

Please specify what proportion of the costs must be borne by the Ministry of Foreign Affairs.

[42]

Vorotyntsev wouldn't even have touched those newspapers if it weren't for the fact that now, when they were at their most loathsome—it was in those papers that the most important of these vile news items were to be found, and without them we could make no progress. Today, not understanding the politics was like wandering the battlefield knowing nothing about weapons. On this unfamiliar battlefield, he had to feel informed before acting.

One left-wing paper had scathingly called the officers "political babes in arms."

And they were right, of course.

Though it was actually the speechmakers in the government who were the real political babes in arms and, of course, the Petrograd journalists. However could they think that "the revolution is firing up combat morale"? They were destroying the country, while at the same time pushing mindlessly for the Army to carry on fighting.

Yesterday they announced the creation of "regimental tribunals" and now they're the ones who'll decide whether or not to punish a soldier for leaving his post, losing a weapon, or failing to obey an order. And now one regiment was already appealing in the papers for deserters *who had joined other units* at least to inform their regiment!

Was there still **time** left to save the Army?

His attempts to procure a travel assignment, in order to go and see Gurko in Minsk, had come to nothing. Anyway, there in Minsk that absurd Army Group congress of deputies had been raging on for a week and, judging from newspaper reports, Gurko had been involved at several points.

Ever since that terrible day in Moscow, that 14 March, it had seemed to Vorotyntsev that the Russian officer corps had suddenly changed, in a flash. It was as if, in that instant, they'd lost their sparkle, that daredevil exuberance, that fearless self-sacrifice. The most boisterous of them had turned chicken. He saw it in himself too, and so many others: it was confirmed over and over.

Most of all it was the sudden and unexpected aggression on the part of the men that had really demoralized the officers. Those soldiers of the past, obedient, always ready to serve—how they'd changed! That real intransigence, hatred even, toward officers who'd never seen it before, appeared monstrous: where had it come from? We'd been fighting side by side for over two years and death makes equals of us. So where did this come from? Realization had dawned too late: they see in us—and have done for centuries—gentlefolk! And that one thing they can never forgive us. Gentlefolk in military uniform—who are, what's more, making them carry on fighting. And not without reason, historical images—the new fashion— rose up in the officers' minds: masses all over France on the march in roaring hordes, bearing the heads of nobles on pikes . . . throwing aristocrats off a bridge into the Rhone . . . (But what kind of gentlefolk did we have here? The nobility had already been avoiding military service for decades, apart from the Guards—there weren't so many nobles among the officers. At Supreme Command and among the Army Group and Army commands the officers had no gentry background, almost without exception—there was not a single well-known, aristocratic family name among them. But, because of the past, no one forgave anyone anything now.)

And where there was no animosity on the soldiers' part—it was not always animosity—mistrust was everywhere and growing stronger by the week. And service as an officer was becoming utter torture. Now the officers were already so mistrustful of their own soldiers that they were fearful of going on the attack with them: the men might shoot them.

Vorotyntsev never missed an opportunity to talk to officers either passing through or arriving from their units. He wanted to hear their opinions of the situation, changing as it was from day to day.

And this did change his opinion: no, the whole officer corps had not been crushed, destroyed at one fell swoop, but it had been *split*. A single body of imperial army officers now, these last few months, no longer existed.

Some were already totally resigned to the new situation and prepared for a French-style republic. To an ill-educated soldier asking, "But however will we manage without the Tsar, your honor?" they would reply, "Don't worry. It'll all come right in the wash. At the moment we have the Provisional Government." We must not cut ourselves off from the soldiers and, as some officers were saying, not all the revolutionary acts were that bad. The revolution happened and came to an end. We officers did nothing to stop it—but now we had to get back to serving, to fighting! To save the army some were throwing themselves into committees. And then recoiling: they'd only destroy both the army and Russia! "No armies have ever had committees—what a pointless exercise"; "But Cromwell's army had a whole parliament, and even so he crushed the king!" (In other units there were no officers at all who wanted to join a committee, and they'd have the effrontery to elect to the committee whoever was on leave at the time, and couldn't then wriggle out of it.) Others, old-timers, shut themselves out irrevocably from that raging bedlam: if it all comes a cropper, so be it. Some lost heart, making the fevered transition from a fleeting state of excitation to a long-lasting melancholy. Others: our duty is above humiliations, above their slander, their affronts; the officer still has the right to die in battle, and no one can take that from him. And the dimmer ones: we must show the same authority we had before, undiminished, not changed in the slightest way. And they became fixated on war till victory—these were the officers the men hated most. (They were the first to be removed, yet among them were many loyal servicemen.) But among the new ensigns were some conceited ignoramuses who behaved loutishly, inconsiderately toward the men—and their undue familiarity developed into another layer of enmity toward our epaulettes. There were the crafty types, too, the scum who pushed their way to the top by obsequiousness toward the soldiers. They themselves were organizing rallies and were more dangerous than the soldiers in the committees.

But Vorotyntsev also came across officers who remained steady, were not hysterical, and were ready to lay down their life, not in battle but in the struggle against this new disaster. At least two out of every ten officers were of this caliber.

Only—**where** to start? And—**how**?

It seemed there were two or three such officers, ready for anything, at GHQ in the artillery administration and the engineering administration. But by and large the officers at GHQ now saw their salvation in the creation of the Officers' Union. Three days before, they'd sent out a proclamation calling for a congress. In it, humiliatingly, they'd demeaned themselves, justifying the officers' congress being held separately from the soldiers': not because, good God no, clearly not because officers have their separate or confidential interests, but because the revolutionary officer body didn't want to tear the revolutionary soldiers away from their worker comrades, with whom they'd be holding their own congress very soon now. But the officers' voice—the organizers promised this in advance—would be democratic. (In Petrograd they were also preparing an officers' congress, their own, also taking place in May, but there would not even be any front-line officers there—the rear units and revolutionary ensigns would dominate proceedings.)

Behind a desk at GHQ, with no unit to command, was no doubt the easiest position of all. Though there was, even there, a separate, "unified" committee (men and officers), in which of course the clerks and menial staff laid down the law. The committee had decided to relieve the Commandant of GHQ Support Services, a general, of his duties. And Alekseev and Denikin could do nothing to save him. The committee threatened to arrest him if he stayed, so the Commandant himself, terrified, asked permission to leave the job. The committee was interfering more and more in local appointments to GHQ jobs and the internal services (they abolished aircraft lookout posts—fly our way, German, come and bomb us), and they hung up their insulting resolutions all over the walls.

The normal GHQ security was insufficient now: sentries could no longer hold back the inquisitive, cocksure scum that was advancing on us. Strangers had already started appearing in the GHQ buildings. Were they committee members? Soviet members? Ugly mugs in uniform or civilian clothes were aimlessly wandering the corridors, either paying no attention to the GHQ brass or, on the contrary, pushing their way into offices, sitting themselves down without asking and coming out with absurd complaints, demands, or even plans for the conduct of the war. And you could not, of course, send those squirts packing—you'd immediately be branded "counter-revolutionary." The month-long detention of officers from the Cossack field ataman's staff gave many at GHQ a fright.

And the officers were gripped by such despondency at their own condition. Their own insignificance. Their own downfall.

Only yesterday Vorotyntsev had found himself in a particularly humiliating situation. Overjoyed as he was at successfully escaping the oath of allegiance to the Provisional Government—and he'd still not taken it—he was caught out yesterday. Although he read the papers, he had not noticed that that Tuesday, 1 May, an ordinary weekday, was also a great international proletarian holiday. Committee members had walked through their offices sending everyone they found, be they staff officers, even generals, out to the *demonstration*. And, in a ragged, disorganized column of demonstrators with red flags and placards, officers, men, and a band (sometimes it was the International, otherwise the Marseillaise), the top GHQ brass had trudged along to the rally as if beaten into it. Local prisoners of war, Germans and Austrians, joined the same column, fraternizing with Russian soldiers and, perhaps, even with officers. (What must the legations of the Allied powers have thought, as they watched from their windows? They had still not understood!) The rally was organized by a sergeant, with speeches designed for unsophisticated ears. And pilots turned somersaults, looping the loop below the clouds and throwing down red streamers.

And for the first few minutes, having been dragged into these murky proceedings, Vorotyntsev felt a humiliation such as he had never before known. But suddenly, after a few steps in this procession, he'd felt a kind of liberation from his body. The pathetic figure of a colonel shuffling along behind prisoners of war now seemed to be nothing to do with him: he was actually suspended somewhere in the air above, floating above this drunken cortege, and then effortlessly holding his position above this fairground sideshow, at a height about three times greater than his own. And he felt no revulsion, no hatred toward these lunatics. They were foolish, blind players, unwittingly acting out a senseless drama, for which they would all pay, as would we all—together with Russia. How ignominiously they were fettered, doomed to act against their own selves. They could not even stand up straight, but must play-act pathetically before offering up their own head.

And his consciousness had split in two so completely that he even lost track: what kind of procession was it, where was it, how did it end? His heart was so dark, so full of grief, that he'd not even noticed how it ended—yet he was already walking along a Mogilev street to his apartment.

And, as if that wasn't enough . . . this separate apartment he had, and this family life, were just not right for him at the moment.

Alina met him with:

"Have you thought about who to invite to your name day party?"

It was only then that he remembered: 6 May was approaching. St. George's day—St. George the Bringer of Victory.

"No—please let's not have a party."

It was as if Alina had been waiting for that. Her eyes dilated in fury. She'd caught him.

"What? You ruined my last name day party and now you want to cancel your own?"

"Please understand. I'm feeling wretched. And I'm busy."

"But the 6th is a Sunday!"

"I've got urgent work on."

"Oh yes? Don't you want anything to do with me now? You'd rather spend the day with *her*?"

No.

Not any more . . .

Ever since the Kiev train, he'd been strangely agitated, as if, in the turmoil of amorous passion that had consumed him, he too had taken part in the Overthrow.

He tried to banish the feeling—it would not go.

He was broken, helpless—due solely to that.

To act like a whole, undamaged person, you need to be whole inside. It's always that way.

Of course, there would be very few people he could talk to now as he had to Olda. She had become so keenly attuned to current events.

Just to imagine that conversation . . . She'd probably be saying that we restore the monarchy? And: who's to blame for letting it fall?

But it's too late now for us to apportion blame, who was wrong before and who was right, and who started this ball rolling. We all did it, we all ruined Russia together, all in our different ways.

Why try to find out now who ruined her? Better look for someone to save her.

By now it's not the form of government that must be saved, it's not one or another party—it's the living body of Russia itself.

So that we would have a place to live.

So that we would ourselves survive.

[43]

No. Alina felt it. In his heart he was not with her. Where were those old signs of attentiveness? The thoughtfulness? The compliments? All gone now. He was making no attempt to make his wife's life any easier.

In fact, did he even see her? Notice which blouse she was wearing, or which shoes? Not any more.

The guesthouse in November—what a cruel affront! A still-open wound! Since then Alina hadn't been in good health for a single day.

And since March? She couldn't believe a word he said. What utter torment, the thought of him corresponding secretly with *her*. She might even turn up in Mogilev—how could she find out, be sure?

What was it, basically, that had changed in him?

Black thoughts rise from the bottom of your heart, leaving your whole being deadened.

She had planted a little flower bed in front of their annex and put in some tobacco plants, to give off a pleasant scent on summer evenings. But she was all fingers and thumbs.

And she could read nothing. If she picked up Chekhov, her eyes would scan the lines, but only rarely did the sense penetrate. And she'd lose it immediately. And across all the pages she saw, in black, thick lines, dark lines, her own thoughts.

There was no saving her from her thoughts. When all her thoughts left her, then the pain left. But that didn't last long. If only she could rid herself of those thoughts. But she wasn't going to take sleeping pills during the day to do it.

That well-meant advice: be enigmatic with him, always gay, lighthearted—she hadn't acted on any of it . . . Could someone suffering as she did really take on those attributes? Her heart was brimming over with hurts. It was easier to speak out than to keep silent:

"No, ever since your first trip to Petersburg your attitude toward me is different. How can that possibly be my fault, and not yours? *Before* then, you saw in me—think back—things to feast your eyes on, to admire. But *afterwards* everything lost its shine."

"Why do you need me to admire you all the time?"

"Let's just say it's my weakness. But your admiration was the support I needed! Look at these old letters of yours, see how it suffused our relationship, enriched it! Let's read them together! You sang my praises in every key: my darling, my little star, my little Meadow Dewdrop . . . You are incomparable, you have no equal . . ." She recited them all by heart. "Your devotion was my support! What words, what feelings! Where are they now?"

She gave him a burning, penetrating look. He was disconcerted, mumbling feebly:

"But is this the time for a name day party? Who would we invite, in Mogilev?"

"Yes! I need company, I want some meaning to my life. I can't sit here, shut up like a prisoner!"

"Alina dear, things are very hard for me at the moment. Spare me this. Don't . . ."

"Do you think things are easy for *me*? They're a thousand times harder!"

Slowly, with some difficulty, he replied:

"If things are hard for you . . . if you're troubled by dark thoughts . . . Just think about the men, over a million of them, who've died at the front—and that means a million women widowed."

"It's easier for them. Their husbands died—they didn't fall out of love, weren't unfaithful."

"All I ever hear from you is 'my suffering,' 'what'll become of me,' 'What I want is . . .'"

Extraordinary. Did he really not understand?

"Yes! I do have dark times like that, when I lose all hope, when I can only think of myself. When there's such pain in my heart, how am I supposed to absorb other people's pain too?"

He didn't understand, because he himself hadn't been lacerated by the Beast of suffering!

"Good heavens, Alina dear—is there no way for us to live without torturing each other?"

"Live with it—it'll make you more sensitive to other people's torments!"

"But times are likely to get harder. What'll become of us all?"

It was always the same old wiles.

"Yes, and I want to be worthy! Worthy of the time to come and of my position! But for that I need to get well first! And you're not helping. You push me aside. You don't want me getting in your way."

He was perplexed: "But all the same . . . just compare the scale of events in our marital life with those dragging us all along by the scruff of the neck. And it's our duty . . ."

An exclamation of triumph from Alina: it was always so easy to get the better of him in their duels.

"Don't you talk to me about *duty*. Not about my duty to you or to Russia! When I *love* and am *loved*, then I'll do it, then I'll know my duty. But you, you always sacrificed me for the sake of your duty. In our life together I've never been able to show what I can do best. You've strangled my personality in the noose of your duty. You've destroyed me! Destroyed me!"

And she felt shrouded in darkness once more, in an even deeper gloom.

[44]

The French ambassador, Maurice Paléologue, had received an invitation to the event on 2 May at the Mikhailovsky Theater.

During these revolutionary weeks in Petrograd, the normal theater and the classical music concerts had become less important to people: there were even empty seats. But a new form had evolved, the "concert-meeting" where, as well as a concert, there were speeches by public figures: these tickets were selling like hot cakes, especially if Kerensky was expected to speak. The concert-meeting today, at the Mikhailovsky, was one such event. It was a benefit for released political exiles and Kerensky would obviously be taking part because the main organizer was his wife, Olga Lvovna.

Invitations of this kind arrived almost daily. And the French ambassador was already sick and tired of the endless revolutionary kerfuffle in the Russian capital, which seemed to have forgotten about the war. And he wouldn't have gone to this spectacle today had it not been for the fact—and this was the ninth day of his new situation, though the change had largely been kept from public knowledge—that Paléologue was no longer the real ambassador of the Great French Republic, nor even a totally independent person. It had all happened ten days earlier, when the French Minister of Armaments, Albert Thomas, had arrived in Petrograd. This was his second Petrograd visit since the start of the war and, meeting him late in the evening at Finland Station with a large entourage of officers and secretaries, Paléologue had no idea—his old heart had not even skipped a beat—*why* Thomas had come to Russia this time, what document he had brought with him. But twenty-four hours later Thomas had handed it to the ambassador. It was from the Ministry of Foreign Affairs: "The position you held vis-à-vis the former Emperor makes it hard for you to fulfill your duties vis-à-vis the current government. For the new situation a new man is needed," and a mandatory leave of absence was imposed. He would return to France and be replaced in Russia by Thomas. (Two days later this was reported in the newspapers as a short trip the ambassador was making to Paris for a meeting.)

Good Lord! Such featherbrains—and they're diplomats! "The position you held vis-à-vis the ex-Emperor"—it was that position that enabled us to have long, intimate conversations with the Tsar, which resulted in Russia's wholehearted, sincere loyalty to the alliance with France! And now, far from being grateful, they were actually criticizing him for that position? For spending so many years in the same place? For knowing this capital and all its circles so well, from those at court and around the Grand Dukes down to the left-leaning liberals? For having friends everywhere, and sympathizers and paid informants, so as to be told of every political tendency the moment it emerged? And for having the strength and tact to take part in the removal of Stürmer? And now . . .? (Why oh why hadn't he taken any notice? An article had already appeared in a Paris newspaper almost a month ago, saying that ambassador Paléologue had enjoyed such confidence on the part of the old regime that he himself could not have any confidence in the new one . . .)

Yes, your loyal Paléologue had been on good terms with the Tsar, but for that very reason he could now clearly see how our alliance with this country was crumbling. That none too bright socialist Thomas, beguiled by the revolutionary atmosphere, with his constant oohs and ahs of admiration, was sending Paris reassuring reports, while Paléologue had seen, with horror, how Russia, during the six weeks of revolution, disengaged irrevocably from the war and slid into anarchy. Yes, we still have to put all our efforts into holding it on course, but we must already look ahead and be prepared for the worst. And although Paléologue had been expressly forbidden from communicating with the ministry now, except via Thomas, fearing the foolish enthusiasm of that socialist blockhead, Paléologue now cabled his superiors: The new Russia is preparing to make unacceptable demands of its Allies. It is impossible for us to accept them, and unnecessary in view of America's entry into the war. Now we must be prepared for our alliance with Russia to be broken and gain some profit for ourselves from that break—at Russia's expense—without being sentimental about it. (In fact, it was already being said in France that, in terms of culture and development, the people of France and Russia were at different standards. Russia had certainly lost a large number of men, but all were from the ignorant masses, lacking political consciousness, while the front ranks of the French army included young men who had already proved themselves in art and science, talented, refined men, the cream, the flower of humanity. And from this point of view our losses were immeasurably more telling than the Russians'.) We must not feel we owe Russia anything. We must reconsider our promise on the Straits and secretly seek peace between France and Turkey.

This was Paléologue's thinking on France's behalf as the top Frenchman in Petrograd, but in reality, alas, he was now the second. And today he was compelled to accompany Thomas to that stupid concert, for Thomas was bursting to get there. To listen and to speak.

And here he was again, in that magnificent yellow auditorium (already the worse for wear at the hands of revolutionary audiences), a little corner of France in Russia, the habitual venue for French drama. Still the same dark yellow velvet curtain, but now without the state coat of arms. Still the two angelic ballerinas supporting the proscenium arch—and stretched between them was a banner reading "Long live free Russia!" In the royal box, directly opposite the stage, Paléologue and Thomas showed themselves at the balustrade and the whole hall applauded, and the orchestra, not in the pit today but on stage, launched into the Marseillaise. (In two other pairs of boxes, by the stage, sat freed political exiles. They'd already been applauded, beforehand.)

Then they moved on to Tchaikovsky's 4th Symphony. The audience, impatient for the meeting to start, clearly felt it was too long, and started fidgeting and muttering.

After that, the orchestra stayed on stage and Olga Kerenskaya led Milyukov on. There was no need of an introduction as the whole capital knew his portraits, and there was an immediate, vigorous ovation. (So the audience still had a sense of patriotism after all, if they applauded Milyukov like that.)

The Foreign Minister made a well-reasoned speech, paying tribute in separate paragraphs to England, France, Italy, and America, and after each paragraph the orchestra played that country's national anthem (the American one, apparently, for the first time in Petrograd), and the audience rose to its feet. (Paléologue would have liked to believe that it could all still hold, united and allied. But he knew, and it distressed him, that everything was crumbling, that these were perhaps the last weeks of the alliance—and his own last days in Petrograd, where he had felt so at home.)

Then the orchestra left, the music stands and chairs were moved out, and a woman singer, standing by the grand piano, sang two romances by Cui. After her, a man sang an "Anthem to Freedom" by someone called Pergament. Then out came a speaker. He was almost bald and the upper part of his skull seemed distended. This was Adzhemov, one of the Kadet leaders. With unexpected firmness he pronounced, out loud and with no hesitation, the odious name that was not mentioned in polite society:

"We must pay no attention to the propaganda of Lenin-Ulyanov. We already know the German socialists' response: they won't overthrow Wilhelm. And it would be treachery on our part toward our fallen, if we did not now continue the war till the end, if we lost the struggle for freedom, in which so much energy has been expended by our men, including some sitting in this hall. . ."

The male singer sang two romances by Glazunov—by this time the audience was very rude, not listening at all.

Then came a railwayman, representing their congress. All demands must be put on hold—now the only thing we have to do is continue the war till victory. We don't want to betray our fatherland and we don't want to hear about Lenin.

There was applause. But murmurings too. From one of the lower boxes a powerful male voice yelled:

"I've got some letters about fraternization with the Germans. Listen!"

He was a great big, hefty fellow with the hair of a Samson. Without a moment's hesitation, he climbed straight over the balustrade of his box and jumped down into an aisle in the stalls and mounted the stage. He was rather untidy and dishevelled.

"Who're you?" people shouted. "Where are you from? What's your name?"

Already on stage, he crossed his arms and told them, defiantly:

"I'm just back from Siberia. A labor camp. My name's Bernstein, Ilya."

Cries of respect:

"Ah, a political! Just what we needed . . . Give him the floor!"

And Olga Kerenskaya, who'd been in a quandary, now invited Samson to speak. He responded, unafraid:

"No, it was criminal, not political! But," he forestalled their response, and sternly, "my conscience is clear."

The audience liked that a lot.

There were cheers.

"Let him speak!"

Thomas, once the interpreter had filled him in, took Paléologue's hand, on the balustrade. He was beaming:

"What nobility of spirit! Peerless! What magnificence, what beauty! That's revolution for you!"

And on the stage, the ex-convict started reading a letter someone had received from the front, about the Germans fraternizing with our boys and not wanting to fight. But he was interrupted by applause, growing louder as the audience turned round. They had spotted, in the imperial box next to the Frenchmen, Kerensky, newly arrived and posing trim and tall at the balustrade, one hand slipped under the breast of his Austrian jacket.

They all started calling for him to come to the stage. He turned, in military manner, left the box and a minute later was on stage, next to the ex-convict.

He began speaking immediately. No, the Leninists did not worry him in the least. Now it's not words but actions that count, and everyone has the right to express an opinion. The government isn't afraid of anything!

And suddenly, after such a clear pronouncement:

"But the government is prepared to leave if it is not wanted."

What was this? Where would it go? Why? Who didn't want it?

Where had that idea come from? He'd expressed himself very strangely.

"We shall never use force to impose our convictions. But if we are to consolidate the freedoms we have won, we must not brand ourselves with the mark of treason in the eyes of world democracy, not cover ourselves with shame before our Allies!"

And that was all. Well done! What a fine fellow. A sea of applause. No, the Petrograd public wasn't lost yet.

Now Bernstein wanted to carry on reading the letter, but at this point the audience didn't want to listen. Kerensky intervened: Bernstein too should be allowed to say his piece. But Kerensky himself left.

They agreed. Bernstein read a second letter as well, and the audience started jeering. Then he made an indecent gesture and went off backstage.

Then, from the hall, a soldier started shouting, his voice sonorous as a cock's crow:

"I represent the Caucasian Front—forty-two thousand men! When are you going to stop your fun and games?! On our front we're fighting a war!"

He too was drowned out by enthusiastic applause.

From the stage, the singer Kuznetsova was announced, and she emerged wearing a magnificent, spangly gown, sang a Rachmaninov romance and then, in a passionate, heart-rending voice, an aria from *Tosca*. They listened properly to her. After that, a cellist.

Meanwhile, Kerenskaya herself had come to the diplomats' box, to lead Albert Thomas onto the stage. That had been prearranged. But as Thomas, bearded and with an over-sized head, followed her, beaming like an adolescent, he felt very emotional. He understood that he was taking part in major developments in world history, that he himself was history on the move. Now here he was, before the audience (his great paunch didn't seem quite proper for a socialist), there was thunderous applause, the interpreter interpreted, and the reporters' pencils raced each other across their notepads:

"*Citoyennes*!" (such French courtesy: no one here ever remembers the ladies) "*Citoyens!* Citizens of Russia! Like our revolutionary Russian comrades, we too came to this celebration full of enthusiasm, ardent fellow-feeling, and sadness. We in France learned of the first tremors of Russian freedom from political émigrés, exiled by the previous government. They opened our eyes to all the suffering, all the martyrdom necessary for the slow birth of today's freedom. This evening, among the memories jostling in my and my comrades' hearts, one stands out most vividly: the funeral procession in Paris, in which we marched together on that memorable day, accompanying the one who had been Grigori Gershuni, forming a long chain of friendship around him."

It was a construction of feeling, thought, and words that could only be appreciated in France. But how very convincing, that open, healthy face behind twinkling spectacles.

"Citizens! I come to you with these memories, and such joy at being able to speak to you about them openly, publicly. What a profound joy it is for us to join you in your great revolutionary movement! Yesterday my friends and I were assailed by extreme emotion as we mingled with that massive Russian throng, a throng possessed by a new faith and affirming its ideal and its revolutionary hopes."

The day before yesterday, he had laid flowers on the tombs of the martyrs—and made a speech. Yesterday he had observed from his motorcar that million-strong celebration of May Day—and made a speech. Revolution is an unending celebration of the heart.

"Citizens! There is now no place for reservations in the friendship between us Allies. French soldiers, be they republican or socialist, can now greet the young Russian revolution openly and with a free spirit!"

What a great big, empty-headed baby. Surely the French government can't have any confidence in him? Paléologue could only groan to himself.

However, both the laws of rhetoric and the crux of the matter required an antithesis here:

"But, citizens, at such a moment, when our hearts can beat in total unity, I would hate for any misunderstanding to come between us. Since the day of my arrival here I, a socialist minister in the French government, have been greatly surprised to discover from the Russian newspapers that people here consider the French government to be capitalist, a government of conquests and annexations. Citizens! Those who spread such ideas really do not know us."

(He had already explained in a separate interview that France was, of course, against seizure of territories. But Alsace-Lorraine must be French. And it would certainly not be right to allow Germany to keep its colonies.)

Consequently:

"Let's stipulate that the French government was, before, opposed to our party. It's also possible that, after the victory, the social struggle will start up again, with increased ferocity. But as long as the external enemy is not defeated, the workers and peasants of France will give their all to that combat!"

Applause.

"Citizens, one more word and I'm done. In the darkest moments of the war, when we already knew the unhappy result of the battle of Charleroi, when the enemy was just a few kilometres from Paris, all French hearts were pounding in the expectation of help from the East. We were awaiting Russian support, the promised cooperation. And, among the lakes of East Prussia, the heroic Russian soldier did not flinch from his duty. And, citizens, what awaits French democracy and worldwide democracy if, tomorrow, we say to the workers of France, 'you hailed Russian freedom, but it did not put all its energy into the struggle for liberation'? But that idea angers me and I, for one, totally reject it. Russian freedom must now become the dawn of freedom for all humanity."

Applause.

Right! The main points have been made, and accepted. But there's something else, something above all that: there's the air of the Great Revolution, hovering over Petrograd, that heartfelt connection, that historic kinship between us, which, today, you'd have to be blind not to notice:

"Just as, once, at the time of the Great French Revolution, our people wanted our new freedom to encompass the whole world—thus it is today. It is with this hope that I salute you here. And to those who disseminate these truths I bring the enthusiasm, devotion, and love of the citizens of France!"

[45]

What political figure (especially if he's a theoretician) has not dreamt of publishing his own newspaper? You'd gain a country-wide audience, for which neither your feeble voice nor the time you have for trips and public appearances would ever suffice. (And behind the barrier of newspaper pages you'd look a great deal more imposing, more powerful. You'd be no ordinary man, walking on two feet, but a whole front!) You'd cut through the dozens of muddled, warped, badly thought-out party policies with your own, new (and the only correct and decisive) word on the matter—especially on all the burning issues of the day—and within a few days you'll have brought enlightenment to tens of thousands (hundreds of thousands?) of readers.

On the subject of the war, literally four dozen opinions of all nuances, all deviations and deflections can be heard. But the only ray of light penetrating the situation and reaching the best possible solution—it's as if they're all blind, they don't see it! — is this: there can be only one possible attitude to the war. We must stop it as soon as possible! No, we do not call for the collapse of our army's fighting force; indeed democracy, a far-reaching democratization, would even strengthen it! But we must not use that dangerous word, worn to a thread by all the imperialists, "defense," for it's a radical contradiction of Zimmerwald! And an impossible demand to make of our liberated people, a program calculated to ruin the country. A true service to the Allies is proposing peace without annexations, that's what would immediately paralyze the German attack. But by threatening to split up Austria and expel the Turks from Europe we are depriving the German Social Democrats of the chance to fight for peace as we are doing.

We socialists are absolutely not proposing to break up the army, but simply to finish the war in an orderly fashion. And we're not proposing a separate peace: if we had to break with our imperialist Allies and Germany still didn't want peace, then Russia would declare a "separate war"! Yes! Yes! So there's no danger to our country if we now come out in favor of peace. Otherwise the army will not realize that it is spilling blood to protect freedom.

Your ideas jostle for space, so many of them that you don't always manage to voice them all, especially when your comrades from the EC are sitting next to you and are not, unfortunately, in total agreement with you, and they want to speak as well. And you heatedly repeat those indisputable arguments to yourself, and you can't always recall with certainty what you said out loud. The day before yesterday, for example, when Guchkov invited the Liaison Commission to his residence. Himmer thought he'd said:

"The War Minister is seeing the situation from the perspective of a continuation of the war, while our perspective is the conclusion as soon as possible of a general peace. The Soviet is doing everything possible to ensure that the army retains its capacity for combat. But it cannot sacrifice the interests of the revolution and democracy! When the soldiers see that our government aspires to peace as they do, and it's the enemy that is not laying down its arms, this is when the army will be reborn! This is when the Soviet can work directly on its combat capacity. Till then, we must just concentrate on broad democratization! If the army is falling apart, as you say it is, it's only because you're not democratizing the war sufficiently, either in your administration or your foreign policy." And (having touched on what was for him a tricky subject): "It's the Foreign Ministry that's ruining everything: the war aims have become obscure. But you must understand that no force can withstand the worldwide workers' movement of the current epoch!"

Russia's tragedy is that we, the working class and the peasant poor, are not yet ready to take power. If our dictatorship took hold too early, it would only provoke opposition from all strata of the bourgeoisie and would, in addition, given that the war is not yet at an end, lead to the ruin, the crumbling of the revolution. It would, therefore, be a fatal error (and this is something Lenin doesn't understand) to call on the masses to assume political power immediately. No, to bring the democratic revolution to completion, to consolidate the social gains of the worker and peasant masses, the Soviet's only task now is to push and push the bourgeois government along the path of the revolution. Push it, but also, therefore, tolerate it.

Tolerate the government—but did that mean tolerating Milyukov too?

This was what Himmer found hardest of all. He did understand the professorial air that had never left Milyukov (and always felt flattered by the personal conversations he had with him), and did not feel superior to him either in intellect or in the strength of his argumentation (making Milyukov one of the few such people in Russia), but felt, rather, only the penetrating clarity of his own socialist consciousness. Even so, Himmer was constantly assailed by the thought that Milyukov was the personification and the center of Russian imperialism. He had never believed any of Milyukov's reassurances—and had, alas, always been proved right! Sometimes he heard rumors about what Milyukov had said in personal conversations, sometimes newspaper interviews emerged, usually late, and they always contradicted what Milyukov had either, seemingly unwillingly, agreed to or else passed over in genteel silence in the Liaison Commission. Once, when receiving English and French socialists, he had explained that the declaration of 9 April, which had been wrung out of him, was false, and that "the Provisional Government has retained the main idea and goal of the war." Another time he'd cast caution to the winds when talking to journalists and said that "peace without annexation is a German formula that they are trying to palm off on the international socialists" and that we must fight on until the European part of Turkey is liquidated, Armenia is freed, and Galicia adjoined to Ukraine. This was where he blurted out what he sincerely thought! This was where he was attacking the revolution and our freedom! Milyukov was continuing the Tsarist war program but within the halo of the Russian revolution, which was so highly esteemed in Europe! And the revolution had to continue tolerating such a minister, who was not only the agent but, in essence, the creator of the autocracy's war program! He was forgetting that he was a minister only by the good graces of the Soviet, and that he could be deposed any time at the will of the Soviet!

Last week, Himmer had been unable to contain himself and had attacked Milyukov vigorously at the Liaison Commission. The issue was apparently minor (to the ministers it seemed totally insignificant), but it was in fact of fundamental significance: Fritz Platten had been refused an entry visa into Russia. And Himmer spoke most emphatically, opening out the question very broadly and defending the whole issue of Lenin's passage through Germany: Lenin is a Russian citizen enjoying full rights, to whom the Foreign Ministry had shown itself powerless to offer the possibility of a return to his homeland—so it's the Ministry's fault! And Platten rendered a service not to the German HQ but to Lenin himself. And if Lenin is a criminal, then why was he not arrested at the border and why is he free now? (Himmer was coming to admire Lenin more and more, and would have liked to have a real association with him. There was nothing dangerous about the embryos of Bolshevism—they could even guarantee the triumphant completion of the revolution.) The ministers, even Nekrasov, were dumbfounded, and brushed off the question, while the Soviet members kept silent, eyes downcast: our men had insufficient socialist logic in their thinking. And at the Liaison Commission Himmer had to accept the situation. But in the lobby, during a break, he made this threat to Milyukov: "Tomorrow, at the Executive Committee, I'll be giving a report on our meeting today. I'll be dealing with your refusal to allow Platten in, in the only way possible: I have to say that it was an infringement of the principle of political freedom in Russia. This is a precedent of enormous and fundamental significance. I have no doubt that the EC will react critically." But Milyukov, affecting equanimity, pretending not to even understand: how could this be an infringement of freedom, while wartime conditions prevail and we don't allow a suspect foreigner into the country?

No, it was impossible to come to an agreement with this imperialist brick wall—he'd have to blow it up.

He'd made the threat—but in actual fact no report on the Liaison Commission had ever been heard at the Executive Committee. Even without it, there had always been plenty of questions on the agenda, and in fact the Liaison Commission members themselves were loathe to tell tales, holding to the privilege of secrecy.

Himmer had, in any case, been cooling toward the EC ever since he'd ceased to be at its core, framing its policy, and the opportunist wing had gained the upper hand, crushing the internationalists. Now, in opposition, it was impossible to be as productive. It seemed better to throw himself into propaganda among the masses. He'd put his heart and soul into his new newspaper and these days it was there that he preferred to spend his evenings, till late into the night. Then, to add insult to injury, that week they'd elected him to the agrarian section of the EC . . . They foisted that repugnant portfolio on him because thanks to his articles on the economy he was considered an expert in agriculture. The last thing that Himmer had done for the EC was a week ago when, together with Bogdanov and Vengerov, he'd persuaded those ignorant Volynian soldiers, dispelled mendacious rumors about Lenin. Some scoundrels among them had been intending to arrest him!

No, the main thing now was the newspaper! Himmer had launched it thanks to an association with the name of Maksim Gorky (with money from Gorky, and other contributions that were arriving via him) and immediately put his efforts into making it a top-rank paper and, at the same time, the combat organ of the working class, and strictly internationalist. The masthead was designed in such intricate lettering as never seen on any other paper—you couldn't take your eyes off it: *The New Life*, *Новая жизнь*, with seven curving tails on the "ж," the "з" and the soft sign at the end. And the crossbar on the second "н" was like a thunderbolt striking from the side, like the badge of the signal engineers. The glory of the paper would not, of course, be Gorky's articles, for he'd dribble out his sentimental claptrap in each issue (between you and me he was more penguin than storm petrel), but, first of all, Himmer himself would find time to write pieces for each issue, some signed, some unsigned, some "from our correspondent." And now he had, thanks to his passionate persuasion and the various promises he'd made, already lured over almost the entire editorial team of *Izvestia*: Goldenberg, Tsiperovich, and even Steklov himself had left that hopeless, wishy-washy *Izvestia* hotchpotch to join him. Lurie and Uritsky would also contribute, of course, but literary figures were promising to collaborate as well: Aleksei Tolstoy, Prishvin, Gnedich, Brik. Big names! What a brilliant constellation! (Himmer was no political wet blanket—he understood the significance of Literature.) And the committee for military deferments had made a decision very helpful to newspaper workers. Previously, deferments had been allowed only to newspapers that were already appearing before the war (so that people would not set up new papers in order to dodge the call-up). Now, however, any newly created paper had that right, provided the print run was over thirty thousand. And that allowed him to take on an outstanding technical team. By an irony of fate, it would be printed at the works of that most reactionary *New Times*. The typesetting, on the other hand, would be done on the Petersburg Side, near Himmer's apartment, and he could easily reach it, even in the middle of the night.

The first issue of the paper had come out (partly by coincidence, partly by design) yesterday, the day of the First of May celebration, and they had really made a splash, to advertise its presence and get people talking: the first issue had a print run of a hundred thousand. The night before, Himmer had worn himself out and yesterday morning he had not at first even gone out to the festival that had been set up under his leadership. But then he thought again: he must drive around and see if people were reading his newspaper.

It was wondrous, divine! An unforgettable symphony! What mixed emotions, probably never to be repeated—he even forgot about the paper. Perhaps he dissolved into it all and ceased to exist. Or maybe he had brought everything under his control and was now riding like a conqueror around his possessions. He was intoxicated, his mind empty of thought. The words "Third International" displayed on the Mariinsky Palace! A Petersburg like this had never been described in Russian literature! It would be impossible to organize such a thing: it was above any organization! It was the joint inspiration of hundreds of thousands of people. And such was the atmosphere everywhere that here the slogan "War till final victory" looked like the work of the Black Hundreds.

Today, clearly, no newspapers had been published. But he still had to get the second high impact issue ready for tomorrow. Today Himmer had not shown his face at the Executive Committee, and done nothing but work on getting his issue of the paper out, beginning with a strong editorial on future moves favoring a peace. He spent all day and evening at the editorial office on Nevsky Prospect and was about to leave, to spend the night at the press on the Petersburg Side, but was still trying to coax a little additional paragraph out of his nibbled pen when, suddenly . . . Suddenly someone turned up with the note from the government to the Allies, for publication tomorrow. Was it brought to *The New Life* later than the other papers, as a deliberate slight, or did the others also get it at this time? The calm Bazarov opened the letter and read it out—and his hands even started shaking. As for Himmer, he flew into a rage and started reeling round the office and jumping up and down! What infamy! What base perfidy! He'd always anticipated, and rightly so, a dirty trick from Milyukov!

It was that note that they had been wringing out of Milyukov for two weeks already—thanks to both the arguments at the Liaison Commission and Kerensky's premature announcement in the press. That same note, but it *wasn't the same*, the sense was diametrically opposed! It was an open challenge to democracy! Outright mockery of the aspirations and interests of the Russian people! Criminal defiance! Blatant backsliding from the Soviet of Deputies' peace program! It was stunning evidence of the Provisional Government's ignoring the decisions of revolutionary democracy! The whole of that note favored the interests of Russian imperialism and English and French capital! All those lying slogans about the "liberating" aims of the war, which they'd used to poison the minds of the masses, were back again! The Allied governments weren't really the primary recipients of this note, nor were any of the Russian political leaders—it was Himmer himself, and Himmer alone, author of the Manifesto of 27 March! Yes, Himmer, who had been so vigilant, so alert for over a month, noting all Milyukov's bourgeois baseness and always, always expecting a really low blow from him. And here it was!!

If the government had sent such a note on its own initiative, we'd have said to hell with you, you pursue your bourgeois path if you like—but *as a response* to the EC's demands? A response??

Was it a misunderstanding? Naïvety? A brazen show of defiance? Conscious provocation of the people's anger? Of civil war, even? An unconcealed snub to democracy in gross forms never before seen?

So we were to understand it like this: Don't you start thinking, you Allies, that Russia is renouncing conquests! We only said that for the benefit of our illiterates. But we'll fight on with you, till outright victory, and we'll demand sanctions and guarantees! They're pushing ahead now, quite openly!

They've thrown down the gauntlet. We have to pick it up.

And another thing! The note isn't dated just any old date, but the date of the great celebration of the worldwide proletariat! Insult upon insult!

And just look, this is striking too: the note isn't diffuse, like all the pathetic, wheedling appeals from the Provisional Government. It's in short, clear words, and very specific! Which makes the challenge to democracy all the more brazen!

What were they to do?? It had been brought too late (and the government had kept it secret since yesterday, the cowards!), too late to replace the editorial, or any other front-page article. Everything was typeset now and it was already midnight. They couldn't disrupt their second issue, for then it wouldn't come out the next morning. (They'd created their newspaper just in time! Just in time to answer this blow!) Himmer and Bazarov threw themselves into measuring, counting, and telephoning the printing press. It was, it transpired, still possible to add a postscript of a few lines into the galley after Himmer's editorial (which now resonated in the voice of one deceived!) if they dictated it now, by phone. But Himmer was burning with rage. He'd lost all control and could not even formulate these few lines. But Bazarov saved the day by pulling together Himmer's ideas and writing them down: ". . . the battle-cries of Milyukov. . . his sacred promises to safeguard Nikolai II's secret agreements . . . service to the imperialists of the Alliance countries and the Habsburgs and Hohenzollerns . . . there is no place in the government of democratic Russia for one who champions the interests of international capital. We are sure that the Soviet of Workers' Deputies will not delay in taking the most drastic measures to prevent Milyukov doing any more damage."

"We are sure," although they were not now the least bit sure of this Tsereteli Executive Committee.

Himmer rushed to the phones and called, firstly, Chkheidze: this is where your constant opportunism has got us! Then Sokolov! Shekhter! Steklov! Kerensky! (This is what you've brought us to!) Why, he needed two or three phones at the same time, to call three different numbers at once! His small chest was bursting!

His head was spinning: it was true of course that he had to get Milyukov out of the government immediately and stop him doing any more damage, because everything he did was strengthening Wilhelm's position! But he shouldn't push too hard, or he might upend the whole Provisional Government as well. Himmer's previous idea still held good: the government should be answerable for everything and we should only push and prod them. We must not say that Russian democracy mistrusts the *whole* government. There's no need to transfer power into the hands of the proletariat yet! No need to go to the other extreme.

His brain was telling him this. But his revolutionary heart was aching to phone the Bolsheviks! Perhaps they don't know yet! Who should he phone? Shlyapnikov? But he's already been squeezed out and plays no real part. Kamenev? Too cautious—not what we need right now. But Krasikov, now . . . He's passionate. He'll report it immediately. Molotov? Too wishy-washy. Stuchka? He's stupid. Kollontai? Now she's a fighter, and clever. Or just phone anyone, but as soon as possible, and several of them! We'll get the ball rolling and they can take it from there.

Himmer would have given his eye teeth to speak to Lenin himself, but he didn't dare disturb him. Anyway, Lenin wouldn't have come to the phone.

And yes, Himmer remembered both his own theory and all the reasons for caution. And the time to seize power was not yet here. But he was carried away by the dizzying scale of Lenin's unpredictable ambitions! And he secretly wanted to give himself over to Lenin and whirl in that vortex—and take his chances.

[46]

It's intolerable, unendurable, unthinkable, and impossible that it might not be your opinion but someone else's that takes the majority of votes! And it isn't a pathetically inflated ego that makes you feel that. Not at all. It's because you alone have been concentrating on those issues for decades now: you see every objective in isolation as well as the whole system of objectives together. Only you have such keen, even perfect vision of situations! And from the situation comes the idea of our guiding watchword. What you can do, no one else can: you are like a law of nature. And this is why you suffer so, from every objection. They're always unreasonable.

But in the last fifteen years Lenin had, several times, overcome a hostile majority and finally won it over to his views. Your secret was your readiness to split the party, split it again and again, even if you ended up alone. To tread your solitary path, you need tremendous determination and absolute awareness such as very few others can attain. And everyone can see that you won't give way, for any reason, at any time, under any pretext—and that shatters the opposition. In any case, it would shatter those feeble-minded Petersburg Bolsheviks that Lenin found there, who'd been priding themselves on their underground work locally.

The more dangerous the divergence between the comrades' opinions became, the faster and more solidly he needed to weld them together, form them into an organization and gag them with resolutions. The last few days, outside the party the anti-Leninist campaign had been scoffing and sneering, and there'd been threats to arrest him, to kill him, and in the street people were tearing up *Pravda*. But Lenin, while fending off the external attacks (finding the time to write four to seven articles for each issue of *Pravda*, always unsigned: that made a stronger impression), also found time to set up the Bolsheviks' internal organization. Now, in a few sessions, they held a local Petrograd conference of the thirty-five people they had to consider the prime movers for the time being, and it didn't go badly: Lenin won. (He'd sent his confidants, Sasha Akselrod of the Azov-Don Bank, Zhenya Solovei of the Siberian Bank, Anton Slutsky, Kollontai and Lyudmila Stal, out to the urban districts to get themselves elected there, with Solovei and her husband actually creating the Rozhdestvensky district. And he'd squeezed some of those who'd arrived back with us—Zinoviev, Ravich, Kharitonov, and the reliable Sulimov, Krasin's assistant in his explosives work—into the presidium. And all the resolutions we needed were adopted.)

At first the local, Petersburg Bolsheviks did not feel any pressure from his arrival, his authority, his experience, or the glory of his name, and disputed many of his theses. This was not, they said, the moment to talk about changing the party's program or its name (perhaps he'd got over-excited: let's wait a bit on the name)—we must bring unity to our understanding of the moment (there it was—unity!). There were even some of our benighted Vyborg members who'd attempted to demonstrate that Lenin's theses were only significant in theory, not in practice. (But it's only practice that matters! Without it, why in pigs' name write the theses?) But the crafty Kalinin undertook to prove that there was nothing new whatsoever in the theses, for it had all, he said, been in the March manifesto that they and Shlyapnikov had drawn up: on the agrarian question they'd said the same, and the only new thing was that Soviets were the only form of government. (But that's the most important part! A direct path to proletarian power, an organizational structure ready formed. They should have seen that!) And they brought out the old principles they'd learned by rote: the bourgeois-democratic revolution is not complete and we must not transition to the proletarian revolution because the Russian proletariat is weak, an insignificant class, and it cannot win without the peasants; and don't keep going on about the Paris Commune—and no hope for a series of international revolutions. (Among his supporters, Lenin had used the term "Paris Commune" and *Pravda* had reported it. People had started accusing him of frightening the capitalists.) And in Russia, they said, it's too early to talk about socialism; and seizing power would be deserting the masses—Blanquism—and the Soviet was right to refuse power; Petrograd is not the whole of Russia, the power relations are different; the Russian proletariat cannot take power as that would provoke a counter-revolution and we aren't ready to fight in the streets yet; and the peasants fear the appearance of the proletariat on the scene. They even said we must not seize the land, because we wouldn't know how to handle it.

And he had to listen to all this balderdash on his home ground, in his own organization, in the Kshesinskaya mansion! What an iron will he'd need, vice-like, to keep a tight hold on, firstly, his supporters, then the proletariat, and then all the Russian masses. But his preparatory work had helped and many were now speaking out in favor of Lenin: The current Soviet is not voicing the same views as the majority of the proletariat. We have to try and develop the revolution further and confiscate the land. Dictatorship of the proletariat is possible (Goloshchokin, our long-standing member). Will the revolution continue into a second stage? It most certainly will. (Bogdatiev, a real fighter.) There is dual power because the proletariat, at the very beginning, seemed to fear taking power. Now it's more difficult, but we must not be frightened: power must be in our hands. The Provisional Government is of no use to anyone: we must create committees to express the will of the people. Just look at the peasants, who've overtaken us now and are already seizing land (the young Epstein-Yakovlev—he'll be a cadre too). Our revolution is launching the era of revolutions in the West (that was Safarov, who traveled back with us). Russia is moving toward an armed referendum, an armed plebiscite (Slutsky, finding just the right words). Until Lenin's arrival all the comrades were wandering in the dark and limiting themselves to preparation for the Constituent Assembly by parliamentary means. But Comrade Lenin has shed light on the situation. We must accept Lenin's watchwords and not fear the Commune! (Lyudmila Stal. Meanwhile, Koba Stalin sensibly kept quiet, though he was already breaking away from Kamenev.)

Lenin was hammering away, getting things into their heads (for it to sink in, he must repeat the same thing over and over, but in different ways). The revolutionaries' main mistake is looking back, to old revolutions. Now democracy in Russia is imperialistic. But it's impossible to find the truth in the Liaison Commission, oversight is impossible without authority. In Russia now, with the exception of the Bolsheviks, everyone supports revolutionary defensism, which represents the interests of the petite bourgeoisie and the prosperous peasantry who, like the capitalists, are extracting profits from weaker groups by violent means. Defensism is the peasants' transition to petit-bourgeois tactics: in defensism the lower and upper bourgeois strata have come together. And Chkheidze, Tsereteli, and Lieber are tagging along behind the bourgeoisie—they're dead, politically. We've always been against Chkheidze, for he is a dainty veil covering up chauvinism. "Revolutionary democracy" won't get us anywhere—it's just a phrase. (There of course, in the Tauride Palace, he had to express himself differently on the subject.)

The peasantry. Waiting until the Constituent Assembly to settle the land question would be a victory for the prosperous peasants, who have Kadet leanings. We must combine our demands to seize the land right now with propaganda about the creation of a Soviet of Farm Laborers' Deputies. What peasants need is not "rights" to land: they need Soviets of Farm Laborers' Deputies. We cannot confine ourselves to Soviets of Peasants' Deputies alone: we must immediately set up separate organizations for farm laborers and the poorest peasants. Land alone won't feed the peasantry: we must set up a Commune, to work it. A Commune is exactly what the peasants need. It would give them full self-government and a total absence of control from above. Nine-tenths of the peasantry will follow us if we can explain why we should have no police, no officials, and no army!

The crucial requirement in any political situation is the skill to explain the truth to the masses. Such freedom as we have in Russia now exists nowhere else in the world, and we must know how to make use of it. (Europe is one big military prison: capital governs it brutally.) Our soldiers are armed, but they've meekly allowed themselves to be deceived. The people have yielded the power to the bourgeoisie, through ignorance, inertia, and a habit of putting up with things. Only our party produces the watchwords that really move the revolution forward. And moving the revolution forward means taking power and implementing self-government. The replacement of the standing army by general armament of the people is an absolute must in our program. The army and the people must fuse: that will be a victory for freedom. **Everyone**, including the women, must be armed: this inclusive militia of men and women must be able to replace the officials to a certain extent. And the capitalists must open up their coffers and hand everything over to the people. It's a lie, a subterfuge, to claim that with a revolutionary army it's not necessary to arm the proletariat. The introduction of a workers' militia, paid for by the capitalists (without this it could not be formed) will have exceptional significance. The revolution cannot be guaranteed if this measure does not apply to everyone. There is no way out, except via the socialist revolution. As for the Constituent Assembly, no one is even planning to convene it: only those SR half-wits might demand it. There can be no other authority than the Soviets and that frightens the bourgeoisie. We must prepare the people, all of them, for the sole and absolute power of the Soviets: the Soviets' role is to oppose counterrevolution with organized violence!

This was how he got his way, by sheer force.

Even so, Lenin hadn't been sure he'd take the majority at the conference, so he told Zinoviev not to propose, for the time being, a resolution on the policy toward the Provisional Government.

But his opponent, Kamenev, started insisting (he was very sure of himself). So they moved on to discuss it point by point. And he had to concede point after point without a struggle: that the government was class-based; that it had got entangled with English and French capitalism; and that it was fulfilling the program it had announced only under pressure from the proletariat, and was conniving in the counterrevolutionary activities of the bourgeoisie and the landowners. (It's the weakness of any intermediate position: it's very hard to defend.) Kamenev made a long speech: we're avoiding giving a straight answer and the masses don't understand what we want. (We can't allow a *totally* straight answer to be given before the due time!) The watchword about toppling the Provisional Government is not organizing the revolution now but disorganizing it. (But at the moment we're not offering this kind of watchword in a *direct* form.) And since the Soviet is linked with the government, what are we to do? Topple that too? Of course, he immediately conceded, we'll gradually have to teach the masses that they will, later in the revolution, have to come out against the Provisional Government and take power. But we'll have to take into account the colossal role of the petite bourgeoisie, given how small, numerically, the proletariat is . . .

So he'd gone over to the Chkheidze-Tsereteli line! He'd altered the resolution, in favor of vigilant oversight of the Provisional Government's actions and against the watchword about overthrowing it—and he'd received six votes, Lenin twenty. Total defeat—the fate of all opportunists in the workers' movement!

Yesterday, the conference took a break for the 1 May celebrations. All the comrades were driven round to speak in the streets and at factories. Lenin went to the Gunpowder district (he didn't really want to—it was an open-air event, with thirty thousand people). His voice was not up to it. The idea of his speech was balanced: we must prepare for the dictatorship of the proletariat, prepare for the introduction of socialism—but without slogans bluntly advocating the overthrow of the government. And then—was it a coincidence, or had the Mensheviks arranged it deliberately?—that mad Lieber was put up to raise objections again. (Well, we'll tar and feather that Lieber—he won't be too pleased.) The SRs put up Chernov and Avksentiev. (The more Lenin got to know these two, puffed up, worthless, the more clearly he saw they were no leaders. People were saying that Chernov had announced in the Soviet that "each day increases our strength—we don't need to hurry." Well, well . . . And in *The People's Cause*: "Lenin did not even think of . . ." Lenin has thought of everything, and you, SR comrades, have not yet learned to think.)

Generally the mass celebration was not yet in our hands. Nowhere near. (And our mansion drew a pilgrimage of curious intellectuals and even bourgeois with their wives.)

Today the conference continued. There were reports on the position in the Soviet and the EC. The Petrograd proletariat hadn't elected the candidates they should have: now we have Gvozdev in the Executive Committee. And the soldiers are represented by nationalist elements. Chkheidze is conducting an appeasement policy, which ends up rendering our demands ineffective. The Executive Committee is being run by intellectuals who arrived there quite by chance, because new elections are not allowed. They're also trying to settle the most important matters within the bureau, where they accept no internationalists, so as to retain their majority. And it's amidst that muddle that we have to tease out a class policy from the petit bourgeois bog.

But the selection of delegates at the Bolshevik conference had been quite well calculated. So it was vote, vote, and off we go! The Petersburg Bolsheviks were now close-knit and not even the provincials would dare offer strong opposition. So off we go!

The conference broke up and the evening finished at the Kshesinskaya mansion. When suddenly . . . suddenly . . . we started getting phone calls from various supporters, in different localities, to tell us extraordinary news: the text of a scandalous note, from Milyukov to the Allies, had been delivered to the editorial offices of newspapers! It confirmed all Russia's commitments and promised to continue the war to the end! There was panic and confusion in the Executive Committee!

It was just as he'd thought! Lenin had even been expecting this kind of error from Milyukov! He was a nitpicker, with no imagination or daring. "Renounce conquests" is what he should have done—and the government would have been internally solid and would have seized the initiative while leaving the Allies stunned. But Milyukov had not grasped the whole situation or all the possibilities. He had confirmed the agreements—and he'd come a cropper!

They'd just brought a typed copy of the note over from *Pravda*. Lenin grabbed it with nervous joy, rapidly devouring it with his eyes. Yes! That's right! He was not really reading the text itself as much as seeing immediately how to respond to it: with a thundering resolution at the Central Committee. This was total confirmation that our party's position had been correct: the Provisional Government was imperialist through and through, all its promises were false and they could not be any different in the future!

This was a bomb exploding! And his thoughts left the now played-out Milyukov and immediately jumped ahead to the EC. What well-deserved ruin for Chkheidze, Tsereteli, and company! The politics of the Soviet leaders finally unmasked! Right, let's see what they do now. They'll be in a terrible state—there's nothing they can do about it. Swallow the pill? That would mean they must renounce any aspirations, ever, to an independent political role. Tomorrow Milyukov would be lording it over them. Should they try and dream up some kind of rotten middle ground? Now they've had their punishment!

Wha-a-t a stroke of luck! Just what we needed! How easy it'll be now, to mobilize the masses against Milyukov's note! This was what he'd come back a month earlier for! Having undermined his reputation by that journey, now he had to act as fast as possible, to make use of the time he'd gained! That note will definitively disperse the cloud of harassment hanging over us—and we can move straight out of our threatened position and counter-attack! We must strike soon! It was a once-in-a-lifetime chance of a double blow—to hit both the government and the EC!

Lenin's ever-active brain never slowed down as a result of any unexpected external factor: he would process any event that intruded, digest it, and carry on working.

He was burning, burning with impatience. But what to do? Start an uprising right now? Bu-u-ut—we're not ready yet. The success of our military wing, our *voyenka* has been patchy: in some regiments we have strong pockets, but others are very weak. We're ready for any risk, but not just for the sake of it. When Lenin went bathing, he was the first to step into cold water. But when at émigré gatherings there had been the whiff of a fight breaking out, he was always the first to leave. Advance bravely! But only on a target that is absolutely necessary.

The note was a stroke of luck, but it had come too early. He'd not been expecting to move so fast! He'd certainly, these last two weeks, been working strenuously to cobble together some troops, but events were overtaking them all the same. We did not yet have a Red Guard—it wasn't ready.

The stroke of luck had come too soon.

But mass demonstrations tomorrow would be essential. He had to stir up the factories where we were in the majority. And try to rouse the soldiers too.

There'd be no sleep for him tonight.

He sat down in the far corner and drafted the Central Committee resolution, his pencil racing across the page:

No changes in the composition of the government at the expense of the class struggle . . . no reshuffle of government posts, no resignation by Milyukov . . . The only way the petit bourgeois masses can save themselves is to go over to the proletariat side . . . Only the proletariat can smash the shackles of finance capital . . . The full power of the state—into the hands of the proletariat allied with the revolutionary soldiers . . .

From time to time Zinoviev phoned from the Tauride Palace with news of the turmoil at the Executive Committee.

Lenin would come to the phone—and had to hold his sides with laughter: what a madhouse! All mush instead of ideas! Endless muddle!

[47]

These days the Executive Committee did not sit in the evenings, only the bureau did. And even they didn't always stay late, and never with all twenty-four members. This evening in the EC only the leaders remained, and also some of the members were elsewhere in the Tauride Palace, in their commissions. Suddenly a packet from the government was brought in, addressed to Tsereteli. He opened it immediately—Chkheidze, Skobelev, and Dan were there—and, seeing that it was the note to the Allies, that very note, promised by the government and dragged out of them by the Soviet, began to read it aloud. While he was reading, Bramson came in, then Goldenberg, and they heard the second half.

Everything went smoothly at first and Tsereteli, who was entitled to consider that note his own, personal achievement, read contentedly, in a beautiful, resonant voice. The note confirmed the declaration of 9 April (wrung out of the government by Tsereteli), which was now being communicated to the Allies. It refuted the absurd rumors that Russia was getting ready to agree to a separate peace, and confirmed Russia's dedication to those "lofty ideas" of which the European statesmen and President Wilson had spoken. (He couldn't help but grimace there, because the ideas of revolutionary, democratic Russia were incomparably loftier than all theirs and it would have been more correct to refer to them.) Further on came a very veiled, complex sentence: on the one hand it talked about "self-determination for oppressed peoples," which all the socialists also advocated. But immediately after came "the liberating character of the war." The second phrase did not, overall, contradict the first if you read it with the socialist connotation. But spoken in the way it was repeated every day by the Allies—did it mean the war the English and French capitalists were fighting also had a liberating character?

Tsereteli hesitated, thought for a moment and read it again. The others were also now sitting up and taking notice. After two more, easy phrases, about the Provisional Government being imbued with the spirit of a free democracy, came the **hammer-blow**: the revolution in Russia has not entailed any slackening of her role in the common struggle of the Allies! And, for anyone who'd not yet understood: the aspiration (in Russia) of the entire nation to carry the world war to a decisive victory has grown more powerful!

Not only was there the "decisive victory" that we were all sick of, that odious slogan preaching war till final victory, but look *what kind* of war it was—not just our own, but a *world* war! And that war too was to be pursued till a decisive victory!? To the final victory of the English sepoys in Mesopotamia, of the Italians in Carinthia, and until the French crossed the Rhine? And the aspiration to that victory had even *grown more powerful* thanks to the revolution?? That was what hurt! They were insane! Milyukov had lost his mind! What had they written??

Tsereteli left off, not just stunned: his heart was constricted, racked by a painful shame, as a participant in that infamous document. He, loudest of all, had promised the plenary session of the Soviet, the All-Russian Conference (and squashed Nakhamkes on the subject) and the whole of Russia that they had come to an agreement with the government, that the latter would not now deviate from the chosen path, and that there'd be a "good note." And how on earth was he now going to announce this nightmare to the revolutionary people? They'll tear us all to pieces.

Chkheidze sat at the table with his head in his hands, eyes bulging.

Everyone was tense, faces contorted. They all understood.

Reading to the end, he was even more dismayed. It was oozing brazenness: "in every way observe the obligations assumed toward our Allies." But these were the obligations assumed by Nikolai II! And "a victorious issue of the war" again, and "in accord with our Allies" again and, the final nail in the coffin, the "*guarantees and sanctions*" that our democratic Allies needed to secure!

It was nothing like!! Nothing remotely like the agreement we'd talked them into: the whole sense of the socialist ideals of peace, of the Zimmerwaldist conceptions of peace and war, had been in that note! This one was a mockery, a slap in the face! Russian democracy, the first in the world, had already proclaimed its renunciation of imperialist objectives—and now it was being saddled with them again?

Tsereteli, distraught, ashamed, but also flushed with Georgian wrath, looked at his comrades. He was grievously wounded: earlier, he'd been so thrilled—prematurely, childishly!—by his success with that note. And the Soviet was already appealing to public opinion in Western countries, saying they *too* should put pressure on their governments, to achieve *the same* success countering imperialism. To suffer such ignominy now!

And they'd presented it to us—another taunt—as the fulfilment of our demands! Ours!

We had to stop it! Stop the note!

It was too late. They looked at the date: it had been sent, *by telegram*, to all the Russian ambassadors yesterday afternoon, 1 May, behind the backs of our jubilant people! While we'd all been rejoicing, diplomacy was rushing out that base cable.

But what about this morning? Why hadn't they let us know this morning? Why so much later, the evening of the 2nd? What villainy, already! They arranged it for a day when there were no newspapers and they could keep everyone in the dark for longer!

And don't even ask why they didn't show the note to the Soviet before they sent it.

Chkheidze, still fixed in the same pose, could only say, through gritted teeth:

"Milyukov is the evil spirit of the revolution."

But the others were shouting, cursing, angry and indignant.

Yes. If Milyukov had actually wanted to cause a split between the Soviet and the government, he could have found no better means.

This meant he was taking revenge for his defeat of 9 April!

Should they stop the newspapers printing it? They could, but it wouldn't be any use, wouldn't change anything. The note had gone.

Meanwhile, Lieber, Voitinsky, and the loyal Bogdanov had arrived and wanted it read to them. And the others also needed to hear it again. Tsereteli read it aloud once more and the buzz of indignation grew louder. Now Bogdanov read it out again. There was shouting, and not just from the left:

"It's a provocation!"

"A challenge!"

And if today Irakli Tsereteli had been that same fiery first-year student who, eleven years earlier, had flung down a challenge to Stolypin from the Duma platform in such anguished tones, he would now have been unable to contain his rage. He would, as leader of the EC and the Soviet, have triggered an explosion of infinite consequence and by the following morning a Russian revolution such as never before seen would already have been unleashed. But after his six years in the Aleksandrovskoye Central Jail and five years of exile in Siberia this was now a quite different Tsereteli, no longer a prey to blind anger. Now, during those rereadings, he was not seeking to emphasize the explosive parts but looking for mitigating, placatory elements, which could even, perhaps, justify this note.

And he found them. Yes, there were in it some very positive phrases as well.

In the overall interests of the revolution he had to behave more intelligently than that stupid, evil Milyukov.

And while they all started yelling and getting even more wrought up than before (except Chkheidze, who was still fixed in the same position—for since the death of his son he often fell into a kind of lethargy, and could stay that way for half an hour unless someone gave him a nudge), Tsereteli found a way to respond to the situation:

"Comrades! Firstly, let's not forget that the note is only an attachment to the declaration, and that declaration, approved by us all, has now gone to the Allies, with the note, and is now for the first time a diplomatic fact. To a great extent it neutralizes and overrides in a positive way the damaging nature of that note. And secondly, let us at least look at the expressions in the note individually, for the government cannot use the same language as our socialist Manifesto—diplomacy has its own language. And if we go through it, we'll see in the note a series of issues presented totally in the peaceable tones of democracy."

But world socialism hated that bourgeois diplomatic lexicon!

Bramson, usually so reserved and courteous, asked, with a nervy asperity, whether Tsereteli thought the government had deliberately couched the note in unacceptable terms, in order to distance itself from Soviet democracy.

Tsereteli, striving ever harder for moderation, replied that only one minister could have such an aim: Milyukov. The majority of the ministers, on the other hand, had in all their negotiations manifested a desire to accommodate their policies to ours.

"Then however do you explain such a note?"

"I think it was just extraordinary thoughtlessness on the part of the ministers."

And it was absolutely true. How else could it be explained, after such amicable meetings?

"But what good are puppets like that as ministers?"

"What's Kerensky thinking of?"

"Get Kerensky!!"

"Summon that Kerensky here!! Is he one of us or not? He's Nikolai Semyonovich's deputy, dammit, and he's never once been here!"

They were already standing or sitting at various telephones around the palace, summoning the rest of the EC members in for an extraordinary late-night session. Now a summons to Kerensky went out as well.

But an employee at the Ministry of Justice answered, saying Kerensky was ill and would not be able to come. Well get him to the phone, then! No, he has a bad throat and can't talk, even in a whisper.

Then they grasped it: when was it, exactly, that he'd fallen ill, given that he'd addressed the audience, loudly, an hour before at the Mikhailovsky Theater?

And immediately afterwards he'd suddenly been taken ill. Very ill.

He was lying, the bastard! It was a barefaced lie!

But there was no way of reaching him . . .

Meanwhile, new members were arriving, most of them left-wingers who were particularly excitable—Krotovsky, Lurie, Aleksandrovich, and all the Bolsheviks. This was their celebration, their triumph over Tsereteli's policies, and they were revelling in it, shouting and making demands. The discussion became extremely disorderly—they were mainly voicing their fury. How had the government dared not show them the note before they sent it?

At last, at midnight, Chkheidze opened the official session. Due to the late hour, fewer than half the EC members were there (and most of them from the left wing), but even that was enough. No session had ever been attended by all eighty or ninety members and only a third of that was considered a quorum.

The session progressed, with the reasonable right-wingers perplexed and hesitant, and the left yelling furiously, seeking to use the situation to get the Executive Committee back on their side and take the majority. They insisted that an extraordinary plenary session of the Soviet be held that very day! They shouted, quite rightly, that Milyukov was taunting the Soviet, that he had reverted to the position of the old Tsarist government (and you couldn't argue with that) and must be eliminated from the government within twenty-four hours! They accused the Liaison Commission of not having the courage to speak plainly to the government: why hadn't they demanded straight out that our government and the Allies should fall into line with the Soviet's Manifesto of 27 March?

Then Skobelev found a clever response, such as you wouldn't have expected from him.

"When the Soviet published its Manifesto, it was running on our Russian, broad-gauge track. But when the government addresses the European Allies diplomatically, it must adjust itself to their narrow-gauge track. In England and France you can't talk about a general peace as easily as we do here. Milyukov's note is not bad because of the diplomatic language, but because under the pretext of the language he is substituting our slogans with imperialist slogans."

Now Tsereteli realized that he should have started by telephoning Prince Lvov to get some explanations. But the chance had been missed—he couldn't phone after midnight.

The impetuous Krotovsky was quite frenetic: the time has passed for any more negotiations with this elitist government! To respond to the government's provocative act we must call on the masses! Now the people must appear on the scene and the whole world will see the will of the Russian revolution!

Even the Menshevik Bogdanov, usually businesslike, was beside himself with indignation and screamed, deranged:

"Yes! That note is aimed primarily at us, the majority on the Executive Committee! Face-to-face negotiations with the government no longer make any sense. We must appeal to the masses! Only their appearance will have any effect!"

Kamenev, however, maintaining an enviable calm, demonstrated in a scholarly fashion that the Bolsheviks, and only the Bolsheviks, had always been right: the current ministers are representatives of the bourgeoisie and cannot adopt any different policies, as is demonstrated by this piece of Mr. Milyukov's diplomatic handiwork. And as for appealing to the masses, the Bolsheviks have always been ready for this—not so as to change the bourgeois government's mind, that's impossible, but because street protests are the best school for re-educating the masses. (And Zinoviev was running out all the time, probably phoning Lenin's HQ.)

Chernov wasn't there to represent the SRs, only that crazy Aleksandrovich, who no one listened to normally. He was shouting: throw this government overboard! Get them out right now! We don't need their victory in the war! We had our victory on 12 March!

Stankevich came late but he did come, fortunately. He had already often found common ground with Tsereteli, and it was the same today. We mustn't lose our heads, he said. The declaration has, despite everything, been sent to the Allies and they are faced with the fact of our renunciation of annexations. This was no deception on the part of the government, but a misguided act by Milyukov, the well-known "master of the gaffe."

When their passions had been stirred up for two hours or so, they began to talk more: anyway, what should we do? What's our next step? They widened the topic out: the issue isn't just that note. It's that we're not exercising oversight properly. We have such power at our disposal, and we don't want to make use of it! People were critical: "oversight of the government" is, generally speaking, an outmoded measure and we need something different.

More and more reproaches were being leveled at the Liaison Commission, and Tsereteli, who'd now become its leading light, replied:

"In today's fevered atmosphere, it would not be hard to stir up the masses against the government. Some want to do that as a way of overthrowing the government, others as a means of persuasion. But if we unleash the energy of the people, can we keep it under control? Might that not trigger a full-blown civil war? The government itself needs the Soviet's support and will happily put the situation right without us calling on the masses."

But what should they demand of the government? Tsereteli was at a loss: he didn't know yet. He understood that he must not demand redress for the note in a form that belittled them: then they would resign and the Soviet would have to take power—but they weren't ready.

And they talked some more, and argued some more, while the hands on the clock passed three in the morning. Their brains were no longer taking things in and there was no point arguing. It was now impossible to find a solution and agree on it. They came to no decisions, deferred them, and would meet tomorrow, during the day. So when? Eleven? Twelve . . .?

[48]

It was nearly four in the morning when Stankevich got home from the late-night Executive Committee meeting. On the table was a note from Natasha. (They'd started leaving each other frequent notes now: he always got back late, and almost never saw their daughter, Lena.) It said Kerensky had phoned three times and wanted Stankevich to call him without fail as soon as he got back, no matter what time it was.

Oh yes? But hadn't he lost his voice?

Stankevich's head was splitting and he just wanted to sleep. But he made the call. The voice on the other end of the line was wide awake and agitated:

"Vladimir Benediktovich! Can you get over here immediately? I'll send a car."

"Have a heart, Aleksandr Fyodorovich! I haven't slept all night and today's going to be tough. I must get some sleep. Tell me over the phone."

"Absolutely impossible." The voice was categorical. "And it can't wait."

"Can't it really?"

"No. Quite impossible."

And he very nearly went. But he managed to convince Kerensky: nothing was decided at the night meeting and the day meeting won't start till eleven at the earliest. I'll drop in before that. And he collapsed into bed.

He liked Kerensky, liked his sincerity, his alert reactions, his straightforward demeanor. And during those mid-March days Stankevich had been surprised and delighted to sense in him the kind of man, of which every revolution has just one, who knows how to unlock everything with his miraculously intuited little key. Later, Kerensky's ways began to grate on Stankevich, his pose sometimes when speaking publicly, or his tone when discussing the front: those who'd fallen during three years on the front, he said, had by their deaths forged the triumph of a great new democracy. How easy it was to toss out phrases like that from Petersburg. They'd begun to touch a nerve with Stankevich. Nevertheless, Kerensky was the only one of our people—reasonable, moderate socialists—who was at the center of events and could still help us in important matters, and he must be protected from any loss of face. In the last few days Stankevich had made *Izvestia* publish Kerensky's speeches as well, which they'd never done before.

He slept for four hours and didn't even need any more. He doused his head with cold water and, skipping breakfast (and again not seeing his wife or daughter), went to Ekaterininskaya Street, to the Ministry of Justice.

The antechambers leading up to the minister's office were none too tidy—there were even cigarette ends around the place. Tired-looking messenger-boys had not yet taken their mattresses away—did they sleep outside the minister's door? (What was this? Not a new form of night guard for the minister?) But in the office was a vase of flowers, a large bouquet, absolutely fresh—roses, tulips, dahlias—and all of them red.

Kerensky, exercising his rights based on illness, wore a brightly colored, Turkestani dressing gown. He had clearly not had much sleep: his eyes were bloodshot. But his movements were as rapid as ever. They locked themselves in.

And he hid nothing, was absolutely open. And that candor always made a favorable impression. He was trapped! He was in a desperate situation! He'd simply not paid enough attention to keep track of all the craftily buried expressions in the Milyukov note. Maybe he'd been absent-minded, or in a hurry perhaps: it had seemed to him that the main thing was that the note should go—and he'd not expected such a dirty trick, even from Milyukov.

His voice was hoarse and staccato. He was grabbing aimlessly, at the newspaper, keys, and paper-knife on his desk. His face was feverish and haggard.

What he hadn't expected was the scale of the repercussions! So many phone calls—all night!! The officials on duty had to answer them. What indignation flooding in from all directions! And Milyukov would of course be flaunting the approval he'd extracted from the government! And everything would fall on Kerensky's shoulders! What's more, he was vice-chairman of the Soviet and his position lay right in the middle, between Scylla and Charybdis! So what happened last night at the Executive Committee? What? What?

Not only had Stankevich never seen him so helpless, but he couldn't even have imagined it. And that touchingly childish, close-cropped head, which had never progressed to a grown-up haircut.

Stankevich told him about the late-night Executive Committee. Kerensky didn't cheer up: he was in a tight spot! He'd be lucky to escape with his head: his ministerial post was certainly done for. (What would it have cost him to register a dissenting opinion one day before?) Today a whole storm would erupt, and today he'd be going nowhere—he was ill! He'd lost his voice! But he asked Vladimir Benediktovich to divert the debate, as far as he could, away from the fact that the ministers had given their agreement. What did the other ministers have to do with it? Milyukov alone had cooked it up! And drop in again later in the day to tell him what had happened: he'd die there if he was kept in the dark.

Stankevich was very sympathetic and promised to do what he could. And he'd come back again toward evening.

He left Kerensky, again in the plush ministerial car, thinking: yes, this crisis shows without a shadow of doubt that things can't go on as they have up to now. The fault is in the very structure of our revolutionary regime. It's impossible for the EC to do its own work using other people's hands. We must either give those elitists full governmental powers and stop getting in their way, or do away with the Provisional Government and take their place ourselves. Or else we could share power with them in a coalition, but openly and with full powers.

But the Executive Committee was so dizzy from this constant whirl that none of these three solutions would be acceptable—all would contravene one or other of their crazy theories.

And there was no fourth solution.

And no one yet knew how the Leninists would exploit all this turmoil.

[49]

On the way to Petrograd, General Alekseev stopped off at the Northern Front. From the train, a GHQ car took him to visit several corps HQs and he then spent some time in Pskov. He saw with his own eyes the absence of subordination, of training for the reserves, and of plain good order. Radko-Dmitriev, who not long before had been so fervently assuring everyone of the committees' triumphant role, was now reporting on the 43rd Corps: We can't be sure they'll do battle, they're all expecting a peace to be concluded any moment now. At the most insignificant enemy advance they're liable to abandon their positions without putting up a fight. As for the officers, the men seem to hold them captive. What did he see as the solution? To send the corps into the reserves and give them a long holiday.

An easy way out—exactly what the mutineers were after. That's where all these committees have got us. That hot-headed Radko, who'd bungled the disastrous Gorlitsa breakthrough in 1915, with all his honest dedication . . . But Dragomirov too, who from the very first day had demanded iron resistance to the committees, had also failed to save his 5th Army.

And anyway, how could they have managed a front that was five hundred versts long, when even Pskov itself, which had the army group HQ within it, was constantly being buffeted? Men of the massive Pskov garrison doing noncombatant work in the artillery parks, transports, bakeries, workshops, hospitals, and distribution points were loafing about, an idle rabble. And they held assemblies with delegates from Petrograd (you can imagine what a gift that was to the spies) and got rid of their superiors—while a prisoner-of-war camp just near the town, which housed twenty thousand, was now also beginning to stir.

And Ruzsky, clearly seized by impotence, clung to his last hope of support, Bonch-Bruevich, who knew how to talk to that unruly riffraff. (Alekseev blamed himself for not standing his ground in March and sending him the additional divisions he'd asked for as reinforcements—they'd just go to the dogs even faster now.) The general had been wrung dry, finished off. Where was his old aplomb? The high-flyer of not so long ago was unrecognizable. He'd been a towering figure at the time of the Emperor's abdication, but now he was saying, almost openly: is that what you meant by "revolution"? Thank you! If only I'd known!

And if only Alekseev too had foreseen all that! Gaining the upper hand over his long-standing rival did not afford him any pleasure now.

What can you say if, during his trip, a mob of soldiers climbs up onto the Supreme Commander's train, ignoring all the rules forbidding it? With the guards already firing salvos into the air, but the soldiers still clinging to the buffers and roofs? Could it be any worse?

On the morning of 3 May Alekseev was pulling into Petrograd for the first time since he'd been made Supreme Commander. And he grimaced, cringing in advance over the magnificent welcome that might await him: ministers, speakers representing progressive society, speeches, photographers, reporters. Mikhail Vasilievich was really not feeling up to that now—and not only because he was shy: he was arriving with concerns that were too grave for this, in a mood more in keeping with a funeral. But the most hideous thing of all would be if he were met at the station by someone from the Petrograd Soviet. He couldn't stand the sight of their ugly mugs.

But luckily the welcome was very low-key, with no ministers, no one from the Soviet, no speeches, nor even any reporters. Nor even Guchkov, probably because he was ill. He was represented by just one vice-minister; Alekseev had brought the other one with him. The taciturn Kornilov was waiting for him, with a guard of honor from the Semyonovsky Battalion and a band that struck up the now obligatory Marseillaise. There was nothing else left to play in Russia. The Semyonovsky colonel gave his report: his men were ready to defend their homeland and champion freedom till their last drop of blood. (If only . . .) The Supreme Commander responded and the men barked a loud "hurrah." In the square outside the station, a crowd was, in fact, now revealed, of close to a thousand people. The general was raised aloft—this was the current fashion—and carried back into the station. (Which was not too comfortable for his old bones.) There, Staff Sergeant Skomorokhov greeted him on behalf of the Semyonovsky Battalion committee. He went on and on, but at least the speech was patriotic. Pleased with that (and wanting to make a good impression on the committee), Alekseev placed his hand on Skomorokhov's shoulder strap and promoted him to warrant officer. After a couple more speakers addressed him in the name of the crowd, Alekseev could leave—and head straight for Guchkov's residence to get down to serious matters.

Serious matters . . . He was carrying a whole head-full of them around. Nothing in Russia today was more serious than the matter that had brought him to Petrograd. How can we save the Army and the Navy? And what objectives can we still set for them now? He'd not given up on the decision taken a month earlier to attack come what may, but neither had he done very much to advance the plan. The dream of a May offensive had come to nothing and now the question was whether we could manage it in June.

Now, five days ago, the Dvinsk garrison had suddenly passed a resolution: to consider dual power disastrous, to carry on waging war till victory, and to declare deserters criminals.

Everything is at a tipping point. Perhaps we can pull through after all.

But in the meantime the Allies' spring offensive has already petered out. What can we expect from them now?

He had to get it all off his chest, tell the government outright—and they must come to a clear, definitive decision.

But the first thing is to ask them, point blank, *what they're doing*. Do they understand where they're taking us?

[50]

Even Fyodor Linde himself did not know what role, exactly, he had been created for. He was torn apart by elemental urges—and held together by sound logic. His expansive, carefree nature had opened up vast areas to him: his thoughtfulness and methodical approach moved him to create a great philosophical system. At seven years of age he loved Schiller and also watched his father's chemistry experiments. (His father, a German part-apothecary, part-chemist, invented extraordinary formulas but took them with him to the grave, not having managed to pass them on to his son.) And he listened to his Polish mother's music. They lived on a tumbledown estate in Finland, near Mustamyaki, where steely, unruffled lakes, a mossy forest, and lonely northern winters gave plenty of scope for dreams. Fyodor, the oldest child, was sent for his schooling to Petersburg, to the exemplary German Peterschule: at twelve years old he was already engrossed in Kant and the boys often thumped him for his arrogance. It was true that he did not pay much attention to them: he was an outsider in his school and, indeed, in Petersburg. And to him that city, and the whole of Russian reality, were like a foreign, ghostly dream. Metaphysics, cognitive theory, cosmogony. Inner illumination, intellectual elation. The ideal had to be a blinding summit of perfection. The boy was soon seized by a thirst for power over minds and a profound certainty of his superiority over other people. He embarked early and enthusiastically on a grandiose philosophical structure, to which he devoted seventeen years of his life—with pauses during the '05 revolution. Its aim: to reconsider the whole edifice of world science and break with the old science. He created a new system of logic, for traditional logic, like simple human speech, was not capable of communicating the system of the logical world. This is why, in his work, hundreds of lines consisted of mathematical symbols alone (and some he had invented himself), with no words. He entered the mathematics faculty of Petersburg University, already expecting no warm response to his ideas. And so it was: not a single professor was sympathetic to his work. He managed to give a two-day-long account of his work to the Philosophical Society of Petersburg but, alas, getting this account typeset would have been extremely expensive, due to the unusual symbols. Linde wrote to Rockefeller, expecting that a patron of the arts would arrive bearing gold: for patrons of the arts, of course, throw money around left and right, with no understanding of the ideas they're supporting.

After his father's death, the family was short of money, but Fyodor was not good at navigating everyday life, and could do nothing to help, except produce fanciful plans from which even he would swiftly retreat when it came to putting them into action. His mother set about supporting them all by setting up on the estate a guesthouse for politically compromised individuals, only accepting guests through personal recommendation.

This brought new people into Fyodor Linde's field of vision. Marxism seduced him with the rigor of its method, empiriomonism with the turbulence of its ideas. But the factional disputes among the Social Democrats surprised him. He felt closer to the Bolsheviks but even though he'd turned out to be a born revolutionary—a thinker but also a rebel—he could not have become a member of any party. The reason was that his ecstasy would begin to wane the minute limitations were imposed on his individuality. Any collective is an averaging, a sameness of opinions. Linde could not reconcile himself to any organization—he could not become just a member of something. He felt he had the right to unbridled freedom and a totally autonomous spirit. He had his own brand of socialism: above universal anarchy came the absolute power of genius. And, perhaps, regulated miscegenation in order to generate, at last, individuals capable of being free.

Only in ecstasy could he satisfy his intense impatience, his combination of ascetic and voluptuary traits. If the fire in his temperament was love—then let it be real love! Revolution—then real revolution! His whole life long he strove to find love, but he could never incarnate it in any concrete form. Any liaison that formed would immediately lose its beauty and charm. It was always the virgin purity of the feeling, the sense of love not yet in bloom that moved Linde. He did not picture to himself any real woman, but the idea of a woman, a perfectly harmonious form. And, obsessively, he sought to meet that unattainable woman. He now grew very fond of poetry and declaiming, and he even danced, but if an assignation with a woman dragged on too long he got bored and broke off the relationship.

What he really discovered at university was the approaching revolution. The university's infinite corridor was an artery of revolution. From it students left for demonstrations and into prisons; there they dreamed of barricades in Petersburg and when, in '05, the gong had sounded for revolution the "academic legion" had formed there, to overthrow the hated autocracy. What it was, to feel he was there, on the spot, at the most fateful moment of the revolution! Revolutions are created by improvisation. Revolution is the explosion of unfettered freedom, and a personality that has taken fire in revolution can itself light up the whole world. Linde was captivated by the danger of this conspiratorial activity. He appeared once at a secret gathering in a semi-basement in Galernaya Street in the costume of a caballero with various weapons hanging all over his shoulders and sides, ready to engage there and then in mortal combat and keep on firing indiscriminately.

Alas, the revolution in Petersburg did not come to anything, and after the Manifesto of 30 October Linde's passion immediately cooled. But then he had to serve six months in the Kresty for firing a shot without due care. He was twenty-five years of age and his radiant imaginings had not been realized: he was faced instead with a measured evolution progressing at a snail's pace. At twenty-seven, having not yet graduated from university, he was expelled for nonpayment of fees. And that same year, 1908, the police discovered maximalist militants in his mother's guest house. They were staying there to rest after a successful expropriation that had caused a stir. They ran away, returning fire from across the Black River, but Fyodor and his younger brother were locked up for aiding and abetting the fugitives. They were sentenced to exile, but that was commuted to expulsion to Europe.

So now, like a new Childe Harold, Linde set off on his travels around Europe (his mother provided him with that contemptible commodity, money, without which you could not survive in Europe). In Switzerland he tried mountaineering. In Italy, amidst vineyards and olive groves, he settled down to finish his work on logic. In letters he mentioned the visitors who marvelled at his intelligence. But an amnesty marking three hundred years of Romanov rule was announced and now, no longer having the means to live abroad, Linde was obliged to return to Russia, with its fixed ideas and meager spirit.

Would that a tempest burst forth!
Spilling the cup of our woes!

But then came the worst thing: an explosion of barbarity in the shape of a European war, whereupon Linde was mobilized and assigned as a volunteer to the Finland Life Guards reserve battalion. Only thanks to his unquenchable intellect could he endure the deadly grind of military drill.

But he'd not yet completed his military training when the revolutionary events began in Petersburg. During the morning of 12 March, he was not in his barracks but happened to be in the Liteiny district—and now threw himself, with fiery eyes and fiery words, into "rousing" the men of the Preobrazhensky and Lithuanian Regiments. Then he turned to putting detachments together and spent all afternoon crisscrossing town, first on foot, then by truck, and only returned to his battalion late that evening. Shamefully, they had not joined in with the uprising that day. But Linde's evident revolutionary aura and his excited speeches bore fruit the following morning: he was elected to represent the battalion in the Soviet of Soldiers' Deputies and then, provisionally, as the soldiers' representative on the Executive Committee as well. For some days he was very active there, participating in drawing up Order No. 1 and speeding to Kronstadt by car as the inspired messenger of the Petrograd Soviet.

But alas and alack, those fiery colors and otherworldly music did not last very long: they faded from one day to the next. The revolution was losing its spirit. Everyday routine set in but, noisy and voluble as it was, Linde felt alienated from it. A catastrophic calm was developing: the revolution had adopted the poor expedient of creating management bodies, and Linde was in a deep depression. He felt he was superfluous to that Soviet, which was now so formalized: the soldiers' milieu bored him with its uniformity and it seemed (he wasn't quite sure) that he was no longer a member of the EC. Indifferent, bitter, he roamed around the Tauride and the Petersburg streets—for he'd not yet totally lost hope of a new, fantastical blossoming of the revolution.

But in the battalion they didn't know that he was no longer an EC member, and Linde would leave the barracks for the Tauride as often as he wanted. So also today, by a lucky chance, he'd turned up there early in the morning and heard about Milyukov's note. And the sting of that note galvanized him—it resounded like the gong launching a new revolution! And the general disarray in Soviet circles confirmed that insight. And instinctively—by an impulse of great Intuition, which is superior to the best-constructed Logic (he was astute enough at that moment not to confide in any EC members, for they'd certainly sink that whole, noble enterprise)—he rushed to his Finland Battalion and straight into the battalion committee, which was in its usual state of continuous session. They were deciding some boring, everyday business. It seemed to be about the nonreturn of soldiers who had absented themselves from the battalion, and whether they should now be classed as absconders and henchmen of the old order—or should the deadline for them to present themselves be extended again. Linde burst in, gave the chairman, Doroshevsky, a sign that he was going to say something and, still on his feet, began to speak.

"Comrades! The greatest hopes of the revolution have been trampled underfoot! That crafty Milyukov is deceiving Russia, taking advantage of our trust! Millions of people, of our brothers, have been slaughtered and mutilated in this satanic bloodbath, but the government still wants a 'final victory'—which is impossible! And it would do us no good! And to this end we must spill ever more rivers of blood? But what's even worse is that in this war it's not only people who are perishing, but the precious culture of Europe. If that crumbles . . ."—from time to time his voice cracked with emotion and he could not continue. "If European culture is destroyed, if our age-old ideals are eclipsed . . . No nation needs this war and it's time to put an end to it! That's enough blood! A river of it has already flowed for the sake of the capitalists' gold chest!"

But they didn't understand him: what was he talking about? So had they been sitting there at their meeting, and known nothing of Milyukov's note till now?? He took a copy of *The New Life* out of his greatcoat pocket, read out the commentary on the note and explained:

"That's our honest bourgeoisie for you, salesmen of naught but their own conscience! Milyukov didn't even want our revolution: in March he tried to rein back its elemental force! Milyukov always considered there were three enemies: Tsarist power, Germany, and the workers. Now that he has dealt with Tsarist power it only remains for him to crush Germany and the workers. And to do that the liberals have allied themselves with the 'black band.' When they began this slaughter, they didn't seek our agreement. And every day of this war sweeps away twenty-five thousand lives! This is the vilest of all wars known to history. The bourgeoisie want to sacrifice Russia and Europe on the altar of imperialism. We need to show them our power and our organization! Our battalion must, to a man, march bearing arms to the Mariinsky Palace, where the government sits, and set before them the will of our battalion! The government must stop the war immediately!!"

There were fifteen or so members on the committee. Three of them seemed ready to leave and start rousing the battalion. But the rest—including two officers—remained impassive, were not fired up. Even the words of Milyukov's abhorrent note hadn't made their blood boil. Their inclination was to wait a while, till the other battalions' opinions became clear. What? Wait even longer? Linde stood there (he still hadn't taken a seat) hurling rebukes: the Finland battalion was the only one in all Petersburg that did nothing on that great day, 12 March! They should be ashamed of themselves! And even more ashamed that, during those days, a Finland battalion second lieutenant had shot and killed a worker! And, lastly, it was just recently at our battalion assembly that we agreed a resolution to stop the world war and conclude a peace with no seizure of territories! And all this time Milyukov has been deceiving us! The government has betrayed us! Let's go and protest now, armed!

Pathetic, rational hearts! How much energy, how much fuel it takes to fire you up for decisive action! They started . . . a debate! People of little intelligence "stating their position"! Arguments from a philistine logic . . .

We must read the note again, they said, and puzzle it out . . . What about our loyalty to the Allies? Even our current inactivity at the front is treachery . . . Germany's stronger than us and they've seized our territory . . . A peace must be concluded that makes it possible for Russia to develop properly . . . But a demonstration against the government would undermine its authority, which is already not great.

Linde was wearing himself out in this bog, this dough! He was striding up and down the room, past those still seated, delivering monologues again, and then at last he did take a seat. It was nightmarish to think that he could not fire them up, that this once-in-a-lifetime revolutionary moment might slip through his fingers! It's not everyone whose nerves can endure time crawling like this, at a snail's pace—half an hour, another half-hour, another half-hour! So is everything lost? Will shame forever suffuse our faces?

But luckily there were, among those bourgeois in soldiers' greatcoats, some resolute hearts, and they supported Linde: we have to march on them, if our Executive Committee wants us to! (Then Linde saw what had happened. It was quite unintentional: he'd not lied to the committee when he said he'd come from the Executive Committee, but these men all thought he was a member. And he wasn't going to let the cat out of the bag now, of course!)

They voted. Equal votes for and against. And there were abstentions. They voted again: for, by one vote. They decided to split up and go to all the company committees, discuss the matter and hold votes there too.

How that sensitive heart must suffer, from this additional delay! Half the day was already gone. It would all come to nothing!

While waiting, he had the idea of getting some soldiers he knew to make placards saying "Down with Milyukov!"

Finally they brought together all the company committees and the battalion committee and the officers' committee, and Linde gave another fiery speech. Then there were gruelling, gruelling arguments. And they voted again.

And again they won, by two votes. Then Doroshevsky could not contain himself. He leapt to his feet and gave the order for the battalion to line up immediately—with their rifles! And all the officers, and the colonel, had to go with them!

At last! Victory! He'd taken flight! Commands resounded in the companies and the battalion moved into line, the right flank on the embankment side, the left on the Bolshoi Prospect side.

[51]

On 17 April, Bright Tuesday, General Kornilov had again posted this appeal around town: During the days of our great revolution, forty thousand rifles and thirty thousand revolvers were taken from the Petrograd artillery depot—more than enough to equip a whole corps. But the army in the field is in great need of arms. I appeal to the people of Petrograd with this earnest entreaty to return the weapons, so that we do not have to send unarmed men into battle as the previous government did.

And not a single damned piece was returned.

Several times he bade farewell to the machine-gun regiments: they should move out to Oranienbaum at least, and from there on to the front. As your commander, and as a Russian person, I salute you. You gave Russia her freedom: now you must secure that freedom with a victorious outcome to the war and not lay down your arms until then. Isn't that so, machine-gunners? "Yes sir!!" Cheers resounded across the square, with renditions of the Marseillaise. But as for the front—not a single company actually went. Although one did express opposition to Lenin.

And why would Petrograd soldiers go to the front? They got two and a half pounds of bread, and hot meals, and took other jobs on the side—some in the militia, some as yardmen or personal bodyguards, some manned stalls, others hawked goods around the streets—and they were free to attend the many rallies taking place. And even with this life they were deserting.

How was he to talk to them? If the commander of the Military District visited a battalion, not all the soldiers even deigned to come out of the barracks. In all his thirty-year military career, Kornilov had known nothing like this. For instance, he'd issued an order giving strict rules about the times when the men could leave their barracks, only allowing absence in accordance with lists drawn up in advance—but the Conference of Soviets annulled all that, without even asking! And even the cadets, who were, he'd thought, his last bastion of support, had published a sheepish denial in the Soviet's rag. No, they'd said, military schools had certainly not paraded before Kornilov: they'd wanted to go and salute the Tauride Palace and assemble for it on St. Isaac's Square, but the square was too small so they'd had to line up in Palace Square. And that was their "parade."

Petrograd was full to bursting thanks to a stream of delegations arriving from the front, with the result that there were now not enough hotels or furnished rooms. And Kornilov had to ask the army group commanders at least to stop allowing officers to come to Petrograd. What could those delegations absorb from the Petrograd Soviet and garrison? In exchange—it's hard to say which was worse—groups of agitators were leaving the garrison daily for the front, and not even informing him, let alone asking permission. The Soviet could get away with whatever it wanted.

But still they would write: "democratizing the army is not to the taste of all those generals and bureaucrats." And "we must protest most strongly against Kornilov's order disarming Petrograd's workers."

Blast you!

Well actually, all was not yet lost. Despite everything, Kornilov had administered the oath to his men, unit by unit, on Palace Square, even though the Soviet had "canceled" it. Despite everything, he had sent three heavy divisions off to the front, one armored brigade, and a dozen reinforcement companies (thanking the unit, each time, in his marching orders: he was happy to see their concerted efforts, which demonstrated their true understanding of comradeship). They had removed rebellious Kronstadt from the Naval Department and reattached it to the Military District, and Kornilov had taken a trip to their lair. It was not so bad: the crews paraded in front of the Naval Cathedral and there were even officers (those who weren't under arrest) bearing arms that had been returned to them—hurrah! And the sailors bore their commander aloft to his car. He also went to a plant, Tube Factory: why were they working so badly? Answer: we're ready to work fourteen hours a day . . .

Perhaps it was still possible to save the situation, if we could find the right measures and put them into action. He'd had the idea of promoting sergeants to warrant officers, twenty for each battalion—and they immediately restored order, never pausing even if it meant punching someone on the nose. He'd started visiting military hospitals and handing out St. George Crosses to invalids who were being discharged. He told the clerks of the General Staff—there were fifteen hundred of them in all, they'd become too committified and weren't doing any work—that our motherland demands that all healthy men go to the front: I'll replace clerks with women. That quieted them down.

In the Soviet they'd dreamed up another pretext: sending reinforcement companies would be dangerous, not only because of counterrevolutionary activity (it was already clear to everyone that there was none), but also because here, in Petrograd, there's the possibility of a German landing! So let the Petrograd garrison stay here till the end of the war, to defend the capital. And that riffraff would defend it . . .? The people who had taken to tackling strategic questions in place of the generals also gave General Kornilov an idea: what if we actually reconfigured all those rotten reserve battalions—which weren't, anyway, going to send any reinforcements—into ordinary regiments, advertised the landing threat, and sent them off to train for battle? They'd be a separate Maritime Front, including the Karelian Isthmus and the southern shore of the Gulf of Finland. There were, after all, here and in the surrounding areas, a quarter of a million reservists. And machine-gun regiments. And armored cars. And half our military equipment. He began readying this measure.

But Guchkov forbade it: there could be political complications.

And what about the complications arising from the removal of sailors' epaulettes? He hadn't thought about that. And immediately, that very day, Kornilov, fighting off this spreading fire, issued an order (one that looked very odd), saying that he had received no directive concerning the removal of epaulettes for ground forces (he could not say they were "to be retained" because you never knew whether they'd be abolished the following day) and therefore individuals taking it upon themselves to tear or cut off any epaulettes were liable to be arrested as *provocateurs*. (In his whole life Kornilov had never before heard the term, but now everyone was using it as an insult, worse than "traitor to the Homeland.")

The previous Sunday Kornilov had gone to Finland Station to meet a group of our men, crippled prisoners of war now returning from captivity. It made your heart bleed to hear and see what they'd endured. And what was the point of all their suffering? And how about his own 48th Division, surrounded and annihilated by Mackensen's breakthrough? Who among today's insolent mugs in the garrison remembers that?

Oh how he regretted being summoned out of the corps to this thrice-cursed Petrograd Military District. (He'd already, once, lost his temper and asked Guchkov to remove him from the District. He'd refused.)

The Provisional Government was a gaggle of useless squaws. What Kornilov found wearing was the ministers' constant, complex, secret calculations—they were never straightforward or direct. And Kornilov could not deal with people who weren't straightforward.

Salvation could only come from deep within the army. It was up to GHQ and, primarily, the Supreme Commander.

What kind of man was Alekseev? Kornilov had only seen him for a quarter of an hour, when he'd passed through GHQ on the way to Petrograd. He did not have the appearance of a fighting man. But a flicker of trust had immediately passed between them. Anyway, by virtue of the post he held Alekseev alone could now change the course of events.

And today Kornilov, full of hope, was meeting Alekseev at the station. He was longing to see in him now the leader he wanted. For a resolute Supreme Commander, a resolute commander of the capital's Military District would be a godsend, a force. And on receiving any momentous order whatsoever, even to arrest the whole Soviet—he'd accomplish it. (Or he'd try to accomplish it . . . What might hamper Kornilov was not the fact that he was the only strong general in Petrograd but his uncertainty as to how many loyal cadets and top-class detachments he could muster. Let's hope it's, well, more than three thousand. Ah, Krymov had been so right a month ago: that was certainly when we should have got rid of the Soviet. But how could he raise a hand against it without the government's agreement?)

He was full of hope as he awaited Alekseev, but he was, as always, impenetrable by even the most inquiring eye. It was the impenetrability of narrow, slanting eyes in a swarthy face where neither rosy cheeks nor pallor can give you away.

Once they were on their way from the station, they talked quietly in the back of the car. They continued the conversation at Guchkov's residence, until the minister was ready to receive Alekseev.

Kornilov told him how things were, flinging out the facts curtly. Corruption. Disgrace. Cossacks going the same way. And Kronstadt!!

He had no gift for conversation, for persuasion.

As for Alekseev—no, he was a peaceable little old man. His movements were gentle, rounded. We'll have to learn to work with the committees, he said.

"The committees are worse than the Soviets," Kornilov snapped back. "At least the Soviets are civilians, occupy civilian posts. The committees are military. They're in our midst. What kind of army is that?"

But all the same, he said, we have to show them more trust, forgive them a few excesses.

No, *this man* would not give him that order.

So who would??

[52]

General Alekseev had expected to have a long conversation with Guchkov early that morning and was counting on having his undivided attention—that was why he'd come. But they spoke for just ten minutes. Guchkov was both ill and busy with something. You'll explain it all at the government meeting this afternoon. Don't tone it down, no rose-colored spectacles, just tell them the plain truth. You and I can talk after that.

This was disappointing. Everything was going wrong. With the army disintegrating so spectacularly, there was a lot to discuss with the War Minister, behind closed doors! He couldn't describe it so frankly in the presence of other ministers.

But he had one stroke of luck: Kolchak was in Petrograd. And Alekseev invited him to meet during the free time before the Council of Ministers' meeting. What miracle had kept the Black Sea Fleet eager to win the war? Alekseev wanted to learn from Kolchak: just how were we to work with those committees? And why had Kolchak alone succeeded in this?

The last time they had seen each other was that winter, in Sevastopol, when Alekseev had been at death's door and undergoing treatment. But today the contrast between the one's health and the other's sickness was still enormous. Kolchak seemed to have an iron constitution, always ready to command, to go into action. He was perceptive, fast-moving, and never got lost in side-issues. And his elevated position had not given him lordly habits, the sloth that had ruined so many men. He had, on the other hand, one fault: he was too impetuous, too highly strung.

And now Kolchak—with his frank and penetrating air, his high forehead, and his aquiline nose, triangular like a sail—had come to see Alekseev. He'd lost weight since the winter.

The committees? Kolchak told him.

We had to cross a kind of threshold in our thinking, and allow things that we had until now, wrongly, deemed unacceptable.

All that made sense, and Alekseev would have been ready to follow this formula. But *how* to apply it? It wasn't turning out right anywhere. For some reason everything immediately fell apart.

Kolchak went into more detail.

When things had already succeeded, it seemed a very alluring prospect. But where was the key? Alekseev couldn't grasp it.

Not that Kolchak was blowing his own trumpet: truth to tell, in Sevastopol things are really not going that well. Order is holding, perhaps, based on what remnants of good sense are left. Take the SRs, for instance. There haven't been any clashes with them yet, but there could be. The memory of 1905 looms over us, menacing. They've already carried the coffins of its victims (or other people's coffins) around Sevastopol. Now the southern newspapers have started demanding that Admiral Kolchak personally find the remains of the executed Lieutenant Schmidt and send them to Odessa. And a delegation of sailors have already gone, unauthorized, to Berezan Island looking for the place where he was shot. What are all these worrying signs leading up to? An anonymous paragraph appeared in the Moscow paper, *Morning Russia*, saying that Lieutenant Schmidt had been abused during his arrest. Now, of course, we have freedom and everyone can tell whatever lies they want without revealing their own identity. Officers who witnessed the arrest have already issued a signed rebuttal of the claim—what will become of those officers? And then there are sailors from the mutinous *Potemkin* coming back from abroad and saying they want to join the fleet. Valuable reinforcements they'll be! And there was the *Catherine*, where they wanted to hoist a yellow and blue flag—because, you see, there were a lot of Ukrainians in the crew. And they held their assembly in the Sevastopol Circus under those same banners, called for autonomy for Ukraine—and all but demanded their own separate Ukrainian fleet. What's to be done with them? It's not in Sevastopol that the matter will be settled.

And what about navy epaulettes being removed? What a commotion that's causing. He'd just got a telegram from Sevastopol. What were they to do about the fleet's ground units? It was unclear. The officers had been ordered to go to the 1 May parade with epaulettes, but then there'd been a change of mind: no epaulettes. But this wasn't properly communicated. Some officers had, when they got to their HQs, hurried to tear them off themselves, but as for the others, it was soldiers in the street who ripped them off—unbelievable that such a thing could happen in Sevastopol—shouting, "So comes the counterrevolution! Seize them!"

There Alekseev could only nod agreement: it had been a gross blunder on Guchkov's part.

But this was not what Kolchak had come for. He'd come to bring his idea: what we need now, urgently, is some kind of major victory. But the land army isn't capable of a victory.

"But the fleet is! Let us take the Bosphorus!"

But Alekseev just sighed. It wasn't only that he had always been against this, and that we were not sufficiently mobile to get the preparations done within two months, but also now, in two hours, speaking of such a possibility to the ministers would, he thought, be quite beyond him. He wouldn't be able to get the words out.

[53]

The Executive Committee was to meet this afternoon, but with a different agenda: the convening of an international socialist conference in Stockholm, in which the EC wanted to take the leading role. Socialists from all over the world would gather and the entire International would say a resounding "no" to the war! And the worldwide slaughter would come to an end.

But the Western socialists we'd seen as yet in the flesh, those who'd come to Petrograd, had brought only disappointment and gloom. We'd rushed to talk to the visitors as comrades but by the end could not see any difference between them and our imperialists. The Westerners understood "self-determination of peoples" as applying only to peoples whose liberation would benefit the Allies—not to others. "Without annexations or indemnities" stuck in their craw—and to evade the issue they'd started finding fault, demanding that we, their Russian comrades, explain that slogan to them in detail. They would arrive at negotiations with interpreters, assistants, notebooks and take their seats with the self-important air of diplomats. Our Russian side (the commission members were Dan, Nakhamkes, Himmer, and Shekhter) was at a loss. The trouble was that no one in the EC or the central committees of the parties had ever seriously worked up this formula: what, exactly, should be considered an annexation, and what not? What did the EC feel about Alsace-Lorraine? Poland? Armenia? How far should self-determination extend and how should it be interpreted? What should be considered an indemnity and what reparation for damage? Our side could find no answers and equivocated. The other side: in general terms, we agree. But can you be more concrete? Then Thomas had appeared, with an attaché from the embassy, and tried to find out whether the Russian army was able to go on the attack right now and how many shells were being produced. It was unbearable! They were simply sucking the blood out of our revolution! And somewhere in those negotiations they'd got the idea that the Soviet recognized French rights to Alsace-Lorraine and immediately cabled Paris, and it was announced in the French press. And the EC's newly created department of international relations had had to cable Europe, over Skobelev's signature, refuting this cock-and-bull story.

They'd been indignant at those socialists, but then softened: they were victims of imperialism, tangled up in its nets.

And now—how ironic—instead of a conference on how to extend peace to Europe, the EC had assembled to discuss how to tear the lasso of Milyukov's war from its own neck.

They started off marking time at the same place where they'd fallen asleep the previous night: nothing had been decided and nothing understood. Almost the full complement of members were present and, in addition to all the intransigent left-wingers, there was the intransigent Himmer, making up, triply so now, for his absence the previous evening. He built up his argument, beginning by brandishing the All-Russian Conference resolution about its policy toward the Provisional Government: what are we arguing about? Our primary obligation is to carry out our resolutions! Have we already, in just three weeks, forgotten that? Here we have it, in black and white: we voted to "fend off Tsarist and bourgeois counterrevolutionary initiatives!"—but that's exactly what we have now! "Decisive steps toward preparing for a general peace without annexations or indemnities"—but where are these steps? They've got us in a stranglehold! "Support the government, *insofar as* it builds its foreign policy based on a renunciation of conquest." Has that been torn up now? Why are we hesitating? The moment has come for us to *repulse* the bourgeois government!

Some were furious

"They're not speaking in their own name but about 'the aspiration of the entire nation'! So they're speaking for all of us?"

"To a 'decisive victory'—and just what does that mean? Another ten years of war?"

Chernov—the EC was not yet totally accustomed to this imposing figure—did seem outraged, but in measured tones, and losing nothing of his dignified air:

"Fine, so we won't break our treaties with the Allies, but we mustn't wave the Tsarist originals in people's faces either. We must, tactfully, make the Allies understand that we have to take another look at the treaties anyway, because neither the new Russia nor the United States wants territorial conquest."

But most of the EC were opportunists and there were voices, though uncertain voices, defending the note, saying there were, despite everything, positive elements as well. And that the declaration had been sent along with the note, anyway.

As for Kerensky, he still couldn't be reached: he was ill! But a rumor had now emerged in the Tauride that Kerensky, Nekrasov, and Tereshchenko had voted *against* the note in the cabinet meeting—that at least gave grounds for hope. Then they remembered Kerensky's warning in recent days: if you push the government too hard *they'll resign*. And the cautious right-wingers, now with Dan and Gotz, tried to convince the group that the influence of soviet democracy had not reached all strata of society, that we did not have any democratic cadres already trained, and we could not now set up a new government: we couldn't manage the economy and the majority of the population didn't recognize us . . .

"They won't resign!" Himmer jumped up as if stung and even bounced up and down in the middle of the room. "They won't go until we throw them out! They'll stay in their armchairs and hold on until some real force comes and throws them out! They won't give up power—not for anything! They understand that that wouldn't derail the revolution; that by now there is nothing to fear from their departure—it's not as it was in the early days. But they'll resort to extreme measures to defend their class's cause. How pathetic, that theory of 'preserving the government'! Afraid of your own strength, you exaggerate the danger. If the government can't satisfy the revolution's minimum demands—peace, bread, and land—then *it must be crushed*!"

With his diminutive form and the break in his voice reducing it to a squeak, that did not sound so terrifying.

Then someone remembered:

"With things as they are, surely they're not expecting us to agree to the loan?"

They'd even forgotten that the loan was in our hands—we held all the levers.

Tsereteli, melancholy and embarrassed since the previous night, rose to his full height and gave his answer to the question of how on earth the Provisional Government could have sent that note without alerting the Soviet beforehand, without showing it to them. He told them he had, that morning, talked to members of the government and they'd been amazed that the Soviet was so angry: they couldn't even imagine that there was anything new in the note, anything that should have been cleared. They claimed they had understood "a victorious issue of the war" to mean the establishment of a democratic peace.

What kind of brain could accept that? Had the ministers become such hardened liars? Or were they blind?

But what had Tsereteli said in response?

That the common language of the imperialists should not be used when speaking of the democratic goals of the war. That the spirit of their agreement several weeks ago was not like that. But the ministers insisted they had not betrayed that spirit.

Then there was a message: a delegation from the 3rd Army had arrived and was asking for someone to come out to them: they were here to protest against the rumors that were causing dissension between the government and the Soviet.

Another trump card for Tsereteli and his group: well, comrades, just look how awkward it is when a conflict is revealed. We must stay reasonable. The best thing would be for us—our full complement—to have a meeting now, today, with the government, to explain our feelings and find out what could have caused them to . . .

"What is there to explain?" It was the acerbic Himmer who broke in again. "It was a clash of class interests, and differences of this kind are fundamentally irreconcilable! No explanations from the government will change the facts of the situation or revoke the essential demands of the revolution. The interests of capital have clashed with the interests of the people. That doesn't need any explaining: the stronger side must dictate the rules to the weaker! And now we must discuss what, exactly, we're going to dictate. But you want to substitute empty talk for revolutionary action! To drown the people's movement in a sea of behind-the-scenes deals! The people's arm is raised to deliver a heroic blow!" And he raised his own little fist. Everyone burst out laughing. "We have here treachery to the revolution and you're trying to interpret individual words. That's a chess move practiced by compromisers in all revolutions."

He was gasping for breath. Even he was now exhausted, and collapsed onto a chair. He'd certainly outdone all the Bolsheviks today! Because his March plan—to manipulate that powerless government—had been spurned.

However, calls were coming in on the Tauride phones from several factories and secretaries were running over here to report: the workers' committees were asking whether they all really needed to go to Mariinskaya Square.

What? Where did that idea come from? Stop it! Categoric cancelation!

"Was that you?" (to the Bolsheviks.) "Was it you?"

Kamenev's response, magnificently tranquil: if the majority of the Executive Committee decides to appeal to the working masses, the Bolsheviks can get that done immediately. But how could we do it without the Executive Committee?

But how, too, could such a thing occur in different corners of town in different factories at the same time? Someone must be running around lighting fuses.

Kamenev thought it was the political awareness of the masses that had increased. They had read the note in the newspapers and everywhere they were outraged. We should have more faith in the masses.

Of course. Increased awareness. If it had increased that much the revolution wouldn't have a care in the world.

And they started discussing again, one half-hour after another, and managed to decide nothing more than not to decide anything for the moment. But to have a meeting, the full complement of EC members with the whole government.

But when? Six o'clock had already been fixed for an extraordinary plenary of the whole Soviet, and *Izvestia* had announced it.

But what was the point of a Soviet session now? They didn't say it out loud but they thought it: why this session now? Last night, over-excited, they'd had the notifications printed, convening the meeting—but what good would it do now? They'd be rounding up two thousand people and making speeches—but the decision had already been taken: not to decide anything for the time being.

Stankevich summoned the courage to take the helm: we must stop the plenary session becoming a total waste of time. It should, rather, clarify the thinking of the deputies and steer the whole rickety Soviet ship through these squalls with a firm hand. The EC did not understand that it would be possible, at that plenary session, to speak even more forcefully.

Stankevich went up to Chkheidze—who sat bewildered, motionless in the chairman's place, his gaze wandering—bent over him and set about persuading him to entrust Stankevich with the first major speech of the session.

Chkheidze was only too pleased. He nodded, repeating "yes, yes . . ." By now he could understand next to nothing of this insane vortex.

Then people rushed in, not to report something quietly but, shouting from the doorway:

"The Finland Regiment has arrived in Mariinskaya Square, fully armed. And **taken up position**!"

How? What? Who? Who summoned them? Who sent them? The revolution? Or the counterrevolution?

"Who sent them, comrades? Who gave the order?"

No one had sent them. No one had given the order.

And the Bolsheviks were expressing genuine surprise—though mixed with delight.

Had the people taken up arms and come on their own initiative?

Were they going to arrest the government now? What would happen? What a scandal!

We've got to phone! Warn them! Run over there! Send someone!

Send someone to the square and talk the soldiers round. Who? Well, first Skobelev, of course, And the others can catch him up there.

The Executive Committee session had fallen apart without having taken any decisions.

The left-wing minority, the Bolsheviks, Krotovsky, Aleksandrovich, and Himmer, exchanged winks and moved off into a separate room.

A people's uprising? We must be on top of the situation, at the ready. If that opportunistic EC doesn't say the right thing, then we'll say it.

But according to Kamenev all this was a textbook scenario and inevitable: a class-bound, bourgeois government cannot pursue a policy that is not antipopulist. But a populist policy—we'll be the ones to pursue that, once we have proletarian power in Russia. But that time is not yet come.

And that was, of course, absolutely true.

But Himmer wanted something more. Making the simple point that the government was pursuing a policy of territorial conquest and that the people were no longer supporting it was not enough!

He wanted a revolutionary tempest of extraordinary force and beauty!!

[54]

Without traditions, without experience, and without staff it had not been easy to build a government—but even so, Vladimir Nabokov had built one over the last six weeks. There was none of the previous chaos, no unprepared sessions taking place for no good reason. A secretariat had been set up. The drawing up and circulation of documents and draft decisions was now proceeding normally. Several commissions of learned jurists were carefully preparing materials and coming to conclusions, especially on everything concerning the Constituent Assembly. Nabokov had even tried to discipline the ministers themselves, but there he'd had no success: he could not achieve fixed times for meetings. No matter what time they were set for they always began late and without all the members. And those who were always punctual were the dullest of them—Manuilov, Godnev, Shchepkin, and Prince Lvov himself. The others had taken to absenting themselves on trips and sending their vice-ministers. From the vice-ministers, Nabokov also formed, for questions of secondary importance and very minor bills, an efficient second cabinet, headed by Professor Grimm. The Judicial Conference was led by the brilliant Kokoshkin, who was indefatigable despite his physical frailty and now, during this period, his council had completed a "list of the most important questions" to consider when formulating the electoral law. Now it only remained to gather opinions on those questions and draft the actual law.

The government had churned out a good few laws by that time. Truth to tell, there had been almost nothing of major importance in the last month, except that just now, the day before yesterday, the decree on freedom of association and assembly had been published. (But such wide-ranging democracy had never been seen before—this was real freedom. You could create an association quite freely and it was almost impossible for anyone to close it as long as you stayed clear of the railway lines and didn't contravene any criminal laws.) Perhaps the amendments on the banning of strong alcoholic drink sales and restrictions on the sale of methylated spirits also counted as major laws. And the courageous refusal to grant the Finnish senate its brazen demand for an extension of rights. (They had come to this decision because Finland was refusing to grant full rights to Jews, which undermined its own position—otherwise it would have been impossible to refuse.) Apart from these it was a dull succession of insignificant laws that dragged on—but who, apart from the Provisional Government, could put these in place? The creation of courses to train new employees in prison administration; collective management of military hospitals; early graduation of foresters from the Forestry Institute; a law about the regulation of millet and buckwheat production; health resorts in the Caucasus and Crimea put into good order for the coming season; renaming the city of Romanov to Murman; the establishment of a pan-Russian contest for the construction in Petrograd of a monument to all the heroic fighters for Russia's freedom . . . You didn't know whether to laugh or cry. But who else could have been entrusted with this? And it was not all so unimportant either. The announcement, immediately after Easter, of the Freedom Loan, was a major decision. But then people immediately started worrying that it would not, in the end, be sufficiently successful (given the evasive behavior of the Soviet and the protests of many socialists) and started preparing a reform (another commission to be set up) of direct and indirect taxation: should there be a property tax? A tax on excess profits from industry? There was strong opposition to that from industrial circles, while at rallies people were demanding that the government "curb the appetites of the industrialists and traders!" So should there be government control of the economy? That would be the hardest thing to put into action. For the time being, at any rate, it was impossible to manage with the budget that the old government had drawn up for 1917. The government's rights would have to be boldly expanded and a new revolutionary budget worked out.

But how many matters there were that had got stuck in the mud, which they could not find the strength or the time to get moving—such as temporary arrangements for the land. They'd promised the rural areas to tackle, without delay, supplies of manufactured goods at fixed prices. But no one had any intention of getting down to that: it was something they'd never seen and they had no idea how to set about it.

Prince Lvov, Shchepkin, Manuilov, and Godnev would, overall, have been happy to remain not a government but a committee preparing for the Constituent Assembly: what do they want of us? We're provisional and we can't take on the building of a state. But life kept forcing them to. There were agonizing questions, which had been posed several times but had not received a decision. Could they, after all, introduce temporary measures for tighter security, with the right to make administrative arrests? But all the press, including the *Stock Exchange Gazette* and the Kadet paper, *Speech*, was against it. And now there was the threat of a sugar crisis. How could they manage till the next harvest? And smuggling had increased on the Finnish border, people weren't paying customs duty. How could we make them? Suddenly at the Minsk Army Group congress someone had pushed through a resolution on a question that had already faded from people's minds: an application to the Provisional Government to assign 10 million rubles to the Petrograd Soviet of Workers' Deputies for the organization of revolutionary work! Oh, not that again! They agonized for a long time over how people who had left the civil service because of the revolution were to live. The revolutionary decision was to pay them nothing, but that went against the whole concept of tradition and propriety: just where could these old men go? So they were, naturally, discharged in accordance with the old ways, allowing them to retain their ranks and pensions of no more than seven thousand rubles a year. But none of them, including Nabokov (he was cursing himself for this), had thought to ensure that this would not get into the papers. And there was a terrible, angry uproar and the whole socialist press lashed out at the government. So as to calm things down a bit they drew up, as a matter of urgency, a law raising the pensions of everyone in the country and removing those of compromised dignitaries entirely.

The Provisional Government issued almost as many benevolent appeals as they did laws and resolutions. At one time these were appearing almost daily. When they had not made up their mind to issue a categorical order, they appealed to people's better nature. These might address the Poles, or the Don province, or sometimes the whole population, about cooperating in sending deserters back into the army—and, in particular, frequent appeals went to the runaway soldiers themselves. And there were appeals to the workers of the coal mining enterprises in the Donets basin, to the workers of the South Russia metallurgical plants, to workers employed in specialized units at the front, asking them not to reduce digging operations or weapon or railway repair work. And the appeals to all citizens asking them to subscribe in great numbers to the Freedom Loan; and, also to the whole population, asking them to use the telegraph service less, since it was overloaded. And three days ago Prince Lvov had sent a circular out to provincial commissars about putting an end to violence relating to the land issue and the unacceptability of imprisoning people without legal authority—but there too it was not in the form of a mandatory law: the provincial commissars must appeal to the people's good sense. Prince Lvov's desire for peace, and the democratic spirit of the moment, meant the government was not inclined to give firm directives, which could not later be corrected: it was left to the independent decision of the people, who would find for themselves, in all areas, the best ways of organizing both the local authority and their way of life in that locality. The government was not to ban or interfere in anything: surely the people weren't pining for a return of autocratic methods?

Although Nabokov was, himself, also extremely liberal, he did not go to such ill-advised lengths! He was already suffering from the government's indecision. He hungered for some influence in strengthening it, but there he was restricted, not himself being a minister and having among them only one unwavering ally, Milyukov. Nabokov was experiencing at first hand the faster tempo of this revolutionary time: frantic work every day, phones ringing ceaselessly, visitors arriving hourly, and it was almost impossible to concentrate. And all of that was swept along in an over-excited, unreal consciousness, which had not calmed down since mid-March: did we really have a revolution? And how are we to bring the war to an end? And how can we hold on till the Constituent Assembly? But some ministers did not seem to feel that tempo.

More that anything, the ministers feared all conflicts, particularly any conflict with the Soviet. For the two weeks before Easter, delegations from the front had poured in and been received in the rotunda at the Mariinsky Palace. These delegates expressed their vigorous support for the government, saying the army was bewildered by dual power and needed one single authority, but the ministers replied, unctuously, that there was no dual power. Yet in fact pressure from the Soviet never let up. It was always felt by all the ministers, and at the late-night Liaison Commission sessions (which Nabokov always attended, though without the right to speak) they felt the full brunt of it. Nakhamkes would pull out of his pocket some crumpled, dirty, and maybe forged telegrams or letters from the front written in revolutionary jargon: the Bonapartism of this or that general, the counterrevolutionary leanings of some colonel or chief doctor. At these sessions, everything affronted Nabokov: even the very fact that the government was obliged to receive these instructions or reproaches night after night. But his taste was even more affronted by their unbearably plebeian behavior—all of them, Nakhamkes, Skobelev, Chkheidze, Himmer. (Only Tsereteli, unexpectedly, brought a whiff of aristocracy into the Soviet.)

Milyukov's position in the government had become more and more isolated, but Nabokov did not have the right to speak in his support. He could only offer encouragement during the breaks. Prince Lvov even stooped to currying favor with Kerensky—a repugnant sight. But what had become most striking, and deeply galling, was not even Milyukov's isolation. It was the Kadets: just how could that brilliant party, the flower of thinking Russia and the principal opponent of Tsarism, have failed to take all the government posts after Tsarism fell, failed to become a glittering array of ministers. Maklakov should have been there, Kokoshkin, Nabokov himself, and not with his current, restricted rights, Trubetskoy, Vinaver, Rodichev, and, in the second rank, Gessen, Nolde, Dolgorukov—sheer brilliance, of the kind Russia had always been expecting from the future free government. But where was it? How could the Kadet party willingly have handed the government over to some pale ragtag and bobtail bunch of hysterics, while the party itself was represented there by only the dazed Manuilov and the Kadet-rejecting Nekrasov? That was not only a failure by the party: a trusting Russia had been deceived, its age-long hopes dashed.

Nabokov's diagnosis was that this badly constituted government was in itself sick and in its current form it could not last. And there were, as well, Guchkov's almost incessant illnesses: today, because he was sick, they had again assembled not in the Mariinsky Palace but at his ministerial residence.

They'd gathered with a prepared agenda, but that had been pushed aside by the arrival of General Alekseev. The government was to hear his detailed report and take a decision regarding the army.

While members were still arriving, exchanges centered on a newly fashionable subject: Lenin. What that scoundrel was getting up to would have been inconceivable two weeks ago: he was just laughing at us, availing himself of all the freedoms that had been won without his help, to destroy Russia. No self-respecting Western democracy would have tolerated such provocation—he should certainly have been arrested: his actions far exceeded the bounds of political agitation. But no one, not even Milyukov, was proposing to do this on the part of the government: free speech was the sweetest and most delicate of the freedoms won by the revolution and it was impossible to take a position that might restrict it in the slightest bit. Especially when it had just promulgated a law on the total freedom of assemblies and associations. The ministers, led by Lvov, all inclined to the view that the government could only wait—only the people themselves could launch an initiative to take action against Lenin. Dissatisfaction with him was growing and some army units were even ready to arrest him.

That was all correct, of course, according to democratic principles, but if Nabokov could have done what he liked, he would probably have decided to have Lenin arrested, even if it caused ructions over at the Kshesinskaya mansion. Western experience shows us that even democracies must know how to show resolve.

Today Milyukov was not only imperturbable but also benignly triumphant: he was celebrating his success in saving a decent note without offering concessions and today it was published everywhere. Disgruntled comments had, it's true, already appeared in Himmer's *New Life* (that gnome had gotten himself a newspaper issuing thunderous invective) and the SR *People's Cause*—but it could not have been otherwise. Lvov had already heard from

Tsereteli that the Executive Committee was unhappy with something, but all that could easily be resolved. Shingarev arrived, as usual, overloaded with work, and deeply worried. He was here in body but his thoughts were elsewhere, immersed in business matters. And the main issue, squeezed out of today's agenda by Alekseev, had actually been the ratification of land committee regulations: now to be put off till tomorrow, the matter was certainly urgent, lest anarchy flare up and consume all of rural Russia. Tereshchenko was, as always, vivacious and self-satisfied. With his education, his foreign languages, his polish, his acquaintances (he'd claimed to be a friend of Blok's), he was confident that he belonged to the top echelons of society, if not quite the aristocracy, and he flitted about putting on airs and graces. But to Nabokov's refined taste (and Tereshchenko understood this) he was, with his not too bad English, the bits of knowledge he'd picked up, and his diamond cufflinks, just a plebeian with millions in the bank. Nekrasov, meanwhile, was the most secretive and hypocritical member of the government. In his whole life he'd hardly ever done any really constructive work or taken a sincere, principled stance. No, his stance had always been in readiness for something underhanded.

That show-off Kerensky had still not arrived. He was the only one now holding up the meeting, wasting his colleagues' time—but finally someone phoned: he was ill, he wouldn't be coming. Oh yes? And he couldn't have told us an hour ago? But Guchkov, in his semi-military tunic, was really ill: he moved, turned his head, spoke—slowly. The Minister of War and the Navy was the least dynamic of them now.

Now the meeting could begin, and Guchkov brought General Alekseev in. For some ministers this was the first time they had seen him, and for Nabokov too, although of course he knew Alekseev's face and even his modest figure from photos. No, even with the entrance of the Supreme Commander, no martial spirit was breathed into their meeting. His appearance, his movements, his handshake, and his voice were not at all those of a general in action but rather those of an army official, or even an official elsewhere: courtesy, restraint, words lacking resonance.

His documents were already set out on a small, separate table, from which he would make his report. (A table for secretaries had also been brought into Guchkov's spacious office, but for the time being there was no plan to have the meeting minuted, so the secretaries had been dismissed. In fact not very many items were minuted during government meetings. Following Nabokov's own proposal, neither debates nor votes by the ministers were committed to writing. It was a pity: much was lost to history. In the open sessions, of course, interesting debates were rare—all these were held in closed session, but there especially Nabokov had almost nothing recorded.)

Alekseev proposed to give an in-depth report and presented its outline: first, military equipment and food supplies, transport and industry in the front-line provinces, then the state of garrisons in the rear, reinforcements, horse stock, then the state of the army itself and, finally, strategic questions on which they needed to take decisions. It was clear that the report would take about an hour and a half and the subsequent discussion at least as long. The telephone on the War Minister's desk was switched off and his armchair brought from behind the desk closer to Alekseev's little table, into the circle of listeners. And Guchkov sat down immediately and leant back, making no secret of his tiredness.

It was immediately clear that some of the ministers were already bored. It was still rare for any of them to get a good night's sleep. They were all overloaded with their duties and public appearances, and they did not get enough fresh air.

Alekseev had not even managed to complete his description of military equipment supply—obviously the happiest point of his report, materiel supplies having mounted up till the day of the revolution (only in the past two months had the Petrograd factories fallen far short)—when the duty adjutant came in, saluted, and, excusing himself, reported that there was an urgent call from Mariinsky Palace for Prince Lvov or another of the ministers.

Prince Lvov smiled sweetly at Nabokov: he should go to the phone. Nabokov left the room quickly, not too upset at missing some of the report. But in the anteroom, on the phone, he heard the very worried voice of his colleague reporting that ten minutes ago the Finland Reserve Battalion had arrived in Mariinskaya Square with quantities of red flags and placards and they were now in position facing the palace. There were two thousand men, many of the soldiers were armed.

"Have they opened hostilities?" asked Nabokov quickly, having immediately sized up the possible danger. "No." "Have they stopped people coming into or leaving the palace?" "No." "And what's on the placards?" He'd go and read them from the window and report back.

Nabokov waited. This march in itself was not unusual. All sorts of demonstrations were allowed now; but why were they armed? If it was a parade, they'd be in Palace Square, outside Kornilov's HQ.

His colleague came back with the slogans: "Long live the Soviet of Workers' Deputies," "Down with imperialist policies," "Down with Milyukov," "Milyukov must go," and there were some more that he couldn't make out.

Nabokov asked him to carry on reading, observing, and reporting back.

What should he do? This was no harmless fun on the part of idle revolutionaries, it was already a scandal and a hostile act. Should he whisper the news to Lvov? But just what was Lvov? Why shouldn't the others know? It would interrupt Alekseev's report? But whatever strategic heights that report was leading up to, two thousand hostile soldiers under the walls of the government were closer.

Nabokov went into the meeting, apologized loudly to Lvov and Alekseev, and, still standing, told them what was going on—everything except the anti-Milyukov placards, which he didn't mention: he felt sorry for Milyukov and didn't want to expose him to the ministers' condemnation any sooner than necessary. On his own initiative he reported a substitute slogan: "Long live the democratic republic"—and later it transpired that he'd got that right.

The ministers seemed to wake up. They livened up and started talking, not expecting an authoritative answer from Prince Lvov. Guchkov frowned, moved as if to stand up and go—but changed his mind. Because Nabokov had not reported the "Down with Milyukov" placards, the demonstration did not actually appear that serious. Imperialist policy? So what? All in all, they could breathe a sigh of relief, happy that the government was not sitting in the Mariinsky and they would not have to leave and face the crowd: we'll sit it out here, working. And Prince Lvov asked Alekseev to continue.

But Nabokov knew the truth and by now had lost hope of it blowing over so easily. (Actually, though, there was a chance it might subside: there was no knowing what idea the battalion might take into their heads next.)

He went out into the anteroom and phoned his own secretariat. They told him: nothing new, they're still there. And they've added "No conquests."

It was just as he'd thought—that was left over from 1 May. Perhaps they'd simply enjoyed the walk the day before yesterday? And it was a sunny day, if a bit chilly.

But he had to warn Milyukov.

Then, on another phone, came a call for Shingarev from the Ministry of Agriculture, which was also in Mariinskaya Square. Nabokov did not call him out, but went himself instead. It was the same news.

Then Guchkov's staff received a call from the Military District HQ, reporting more or less the same thing. And General Kornilov was asking whether this was happening with the War Minister's knowledge. A colonel came over to report to the minister.

Then the phone rang again. It was Tsereteli calling from the Executive Committee asking for Prince Lvov.

Things were starting to swirl, like a Dostoevsky novel when everyone arrives inopportunely, and at the same time. Alekseev had arrived at the wrong moment and, with even more unfortunate timing, the Romanian Prime Minister, Brătianu, was arriving that evening and would need looking after.

And the Commander of the Black Sea fleet was in Petrograd! That, too, an urgent meeting . . .

[55]

From Nikolaevsky Bridge, across Annunciation Square and along Horse Guards Boulevard marched the Finland Reserve Battalion—without music but with its officers. The soldiers had slung rifles. The capital was already so accustomed to all sorts of processions—the day before yesterday the city town had been one solid procession—that passers-by paid no attention to this one, not even to the weapons. And the banners and placards swaying above the procession were also part of the natural order of things. The slogans "Long live the Soviet of Workers' and Soldiers' Deputies" and "No conquests" surprised no one. The only ones left openmouthed were those who also noticed:

"Down with Milyukov!"

That was the placard at the head of the column. At the end came:

"Milyukov must go!"

Down with Milyukov? Why? How could that be? Surely he wasn't old regime? What's happened??

Those galled by this, and some who were just curious, followed along on the sidewalks, after the column and as if dragged along by it.

Although sunny, it was certainly not warm. The soldiers were still in their winter hats and the townspeople in overcoats, some of them fur.

Where were they going? "Right turn!" The battalion turned into the square, past St. Isaac's Cathedral. They passed the empty, burned-out German Embassy, with its fresh slogan "Long live the German workers!," passed the Ministry of Agriculture and—"Left turn!"—extended their ranks all the way along the Mariinsky Palace, near it but not right up close. "Right!" And the battalion came to a standstill, strung out in front of the long, mauvish, three-story palace, the government's den—and facing it.

And now the bayonets, projecting above their shoulders, took on a menacing aspect.

But the battalion was taking no further action—they just stood there.

An excited public was gathering. "What's happening, citizens? Why are you here? What do you want?" The crowd, alarmed, was addressing not the browbeaten officers but the ranks, the soldiers themselves.

And, on the right flank, volunteer Linde in his baggy greatcoat loudly explained:

"As free citizens we have the right to demonstrate against any government decision that goes against the clearly expressed will of the people. The people want no conquests and Milyukov has no right to send a note like that!"

They asked the regular soldiers too. (But who was asking? Well-fed, pale-skinned types in bowler hats and expensive furs who had free time: people who weren't in the ranks, weren't at a factory workbench, weren't lugging sacks about and were free to hang around that square in the middle of a weekday. And what about those newfangled things they had on their heads—they don't wear ordinary hats like us. With those clothes you couldn't take their questions seriously: it's obvious they came buzzing round here because they were scared of the soldiers' bayonets. All this lot are on Milyukov's side.)

But even Linde himself could not think what to do next. Neither could the battalion committee, where the vote had, after all, been tight: they'd had to vote twice. And the officers had even less idea.

They'd thought, somehow, that someone from the government would come out to them. But no one came. Behind the second-floor windows faces appeared, looked out, and moved away.

But they were reassured by the long strip of red calico reading "Long live the International!" that was suspended across the façade from one columned protrusion to another and flapped in the wind from time to time.

And pigeons fluttered around and down onto the pavement.

There was no audience for a speech and no one to shout to. Linde had roused the battalion to action with such ardor. But now he was at a loss: the ministers weren't coming out. What could he do?

The genteel audience huddled together: how dreadful to imagine those soldiers breaking ranks now—might they dash into the palace? Even seize everyone in there!

But the battalion stood, silent, holding the placards with their slogans—though their arms had already gone to sleep and they passed them from one to another or even let them fall.

Forceful ideas were coruscating in Linde's brain: should they space out and surround the palace? Block the entrances? Or should they themselves go inside?

But even from the battalion committee there were objections: we came for a free citizens' protest march—it wouldn't be right to use force.

What could bring an end to the standing and waiting? Surely they wouldn't have to go back empty-handed?

They'd had their stroll—should they call it a day?

But then, from behind the battalion and to their left, from Morskaya Street, came a rumbling sound and another long column of soldiers came into view, also with bayonets at the ready. And the sharp-sighted could read even from here, on the front placard:

"Down with Milyukov!"

And not only that: this regiment had a band. It struck up a march.

The Finlanders cheered up no end: We're not alone! We were obviously right to come! Good thing we agreed.

Losing their stance but not breaking ranks, they turned their heads and stared, wide-eyed, in amazement. They sent a soldier to find out who the newcomers were and he returned, only just ahead of them: "it's the 180th Regiment!"

Now the 180th itself had arrived and was standing in line behind the Finlanders, facing the palace. The music died down.

Just you try not coming out to meet us! Just try to keep ignoring us!

Many of the Finlanders turned round. Voices were heard back and forth between the two regiments. Their placards were like ours, and there was one like the banner up on the palace: "Long live the International!" (Who's that then, International?)

And the genteel audience, now forming a denser circle around the soldiers, asked with increasing alarm:

"So what are you going to do?"

"Well . . . Wait for the Provisional Government."

The soldiers themselves didn't know and they all answered whatever they thought.

"Who sent you here?"

Some said: "The older soldiers summoned us."

Others: "We got an order."

Whose order? "Dunno."

"But where did you get those words on your placards from?"

"We got an order."

They stood and stood—but no one came out.

And no one gave any orders.

In the meantime, from behind them, beyond the Astoria, came more clattering of boots! And, moving into the square—was it another column of soldiers? Who were they? The Moscow Regiment! Real daredevils! And again, on their placards: "Down with Milyukov!" (That Milyukov's really done for.) "Down with Milyukov and Guchkov!" (So two of them to be sent packing, not one.) And in red letters, looking like flames: "Down with the war!!" The whole war!! It quite took your breath away.

The Moscow boys passed the royal monument, to be nearer the palace, and formed curved lines.

The soldiers were getting more and more sure: it had been right to come, all answering the same order.

But still no one important came out of the palace. Only employees appeared, errand boys.

During this time, all sorts of people had been attracted to the square: little kids, teenagers, students, functionaries, and various gentlemen with their ladies. Here and there conversations and arguments were joined. The ranks were not in such good order now, but even so the columns hadn't broken up.

Then a column of soldiers spilled out of Voznesensky Prospect and they came into the square as well. Who were they? The Kexholm Regiment. We waved to them and they waved back. Their placards were complicated: "War without mercy on the bloody Wilhelm and peace with the revolutionary people." "Forward to socialism under the banners of Zimmerwald." (Another German, that one.) "Long live a swift, just peace without annexations or indemnities!"

But these didn't even have time to get in position before loud music was heard from the right: a good band. (The music made everyone stand up straight.) They couldn't be seen yet—they were coming along the Moika. When they turned into the square, apart from the band there was only one company. But they were in black uniforms: a crew from the naval depot.

There weren't many of them, but they were very proud of themselves—sailors always are. They didn't go and stand behind the rest but pushed to the front, crosswise. The band fell silent.

Look round a bit, and . . . there must be more than ten thousand soldiers already in the square.

Plus the public, several thousand of them, watching from around the edges.

Who was in charge here? No one knew. He didn't make himself known.

In front of the 180th, a good-looking ensign was walking up and down, head high, looking very cheerful. "Now," he said, to encourage the men, "now they'll come."

But the ministers didn't come.

And no new battalions came either, although there was still space in the square, beyond the monument.

What were they to do now?

And a buzz of voices started telling them what to do: get that Milyukov here! And throw him out!

[56]

The calls started coming in thick and fast—the speed was terrifying—on all the phones in the War Minister's residence: another regiment had arrived in Mariinskaya Square. And they had those same slogans. And "Down with Milyukov and Guchkov" as well! They'd taken a menacing stance, and their number was increasing—they were more than ten thousand now!

The first street protest against the Provisional Government. This was serious.

Everything was in a muddle now and the Council of Ministers meeting was suspended. The ministers were going off to answer different phones and a phone was also plugged in where they were meeting.

Guchkov summoned General Kornilov, who appeared instantly. They went into another room.

They'd completely forgotten about the Supreme Commander and his papers laid out on the table, and it had slipped even the courteous Lvov's mind that they really must either go on with the discussion or reschedule it for another session. But how long would General Alekseev be able to cool his heels there, amidst all their hurrying and scurrying? His place was at GHQ. For a country at war, what issue was more important than the subject of his report? But now he just watched the ministers in silence, as if contemplating lunatics. He'd already guessed, back in Mogilev, that they were not coping well, but had not realized the extent of it.

Milyukov, who in general rarely blushed and never paled, was pale now. He too phoned his ministry.

Some of the ministers watched him with malicious glee or curiosity.

They had all thought, at first, that the Executive Committee had sent these units to the Mariinsky Palace. Prince Lvov had a long telephone conversation with Tsereteli, who assured him that no, no, they hadn't ordered this.

Then Lvov—his voice so weak that they didn't hear him at first—announced that the Executive Committee was insisting on a meeting with them to discuss Milyukov's note and hoped the good ministers would not object to this taking place this evening at nine o'clock in the Mariinsky Palace?

Yes, the disagreement had gone beyond the intimate scale that had seemed to contain it that morning. Without the Executive Committee, the government alone could not solve this.

They were not keen on going to the besieged Mariinsky now, but by this evening perhaps the crowds will have dispersed . . .

Guchkov and Kornilov came in, unnoticed at first. Kornilov stood like a statue, motionless, grim, gloomy. But as for the sick Guchkov, the lines in his face seemed to have filled out, his movements were crisper, and he looked healthier. He stopped in the center of the room, looked around—apart from the ministers, there was only Alekseev—and started speaking loudly and curtly. They immediately pricked up their ears, fell silent, and listened.

"Gentlemen! We cannot go on like this! Our behavior is pitiful. We can't remain a puppet with the Soviet pulling the strings, doing what they like with us. We'll never come to a proper agreement with them. According to General Kornilov we have about three and a half thousand strong, reliable troops. There are a hundred and fifty thousand in the rest of the garrison, but they are all undisciplined, with not a single strong unit. We can't crush them, but that isn't necessary. We can keep the government secure and adopt a different tone when we talk to the Soviet."

He wasn't saying everything yet: what new tone might this be? And how would this relationship with the Soviet be formed? Surely he wasn't thinking of applying force against the Soviet, too?

(Anyway, did he seriously believe what he said? Or was he expecting certain refusal?)

"Shall we give General Kornilov firm instructions now? And General Alekseev will draw the appropriate conclusions for GHQ."

The ministers remained silent.

All at sea.

But Milyukov sat there, sure of himself, scowling.

The polished Tereshchenko, who was already on his feet, now moved across the room, keyed up, as an actor crosses the stage to attract the audience's attention before his reply. He was, always, dressed as if for the stage at the very least. After Guchkov, and in the absence of Kerensky, he was the most determined person there. There was total silence as he said, not to Guchkov specifically:

"If blood is spilt, I shall be obliged to leave the government."

And this was the man Guchkov had just been about to include in his conspiracy? A fine accomplice he'd have made!

And it seemed they might all be thinking that way.

Except Milyukov? He spoke, tense, scowling fiercely:

"If we don't take this step, in a short while we could all find ourselves, *in corpore*, in the fortress. If we're not prepared for this step, then what value, actually, is there in our point of view?"

But Tereshchenko was also fired up and he replied proudly, still in the same declamatory pose:

"No! Even if armed men were to find their way into this room, we should not apply military force to defend ourselves! They are proposing amicable negotiations and there could be no better way than that."

And Nekrasov stood up, raging.

"We'd rather sacrifice our own lives than spill a single drop of others' blood!"

Ah, they might not all be against it . . . if someone else shored up the government for them. Anything rather than take the decision themselves and have the responsibility on their own shoulders!

Prince Lvov said, in the quietest of voices—so quiet was the room that he could be clearly heard—and with one of his most bewitching smiles:

"Oh, Aleksandr Ivanovich, why the drama? Why make relations worse? They just phoned me from the Soviet and they understand our position perfectly. That very nice Prince Tsereteli, and the others too . . . We'll meet this evening and jointly, amicably, we'll find a mutually acceptable solution. Everything will come right in the end . . ."

[57]

The sun was already far lower in the sky than at midday.

There was a plank-built stand on Mariinskaya Square, left from the festivities two days before, when it had been used for speeches. It was swathed in a tangle of red ribbons. No one had had time to dismantle it, and it came in useful now—for people to climb up onto and yell. The soldiers were turning round to see and the ranks developed kinks.

The leader of the Finland battalion, a volunteer, spoke first. Looking a bit rogue, lanky, not wearing his cap, he waved his long arms about and spoke breathlessly:

"The capitalists think nothing of our blood! Tens of millions of men snatched from the great thing that is life and sent off to kill each other! Dug into the ground, under the rain and snow, in filth, worn down by illnesses, eaten by parasites . . . Thousands of villages are being destroyed, dozens of towns, the fertile layer of the earth destroyed by landmines, and the whole earth polluted by rotting corpses. It's over two years now that we've been living this blood-drenched nightmare! And at the same time there are people not sitting in trenches but making crazy profits. And it's their interests that are being served by Mr. Milyukov, who wants to carry on with this damned war for all eternity . . ."

Then a student mounted the stand. His hair was dishevelled, his voice weak and the wind carried his words away:

". . . there is not and cannot be any greater crime than artificially prolonging a war! A peace treaty will serve the interests of world democracy . . ."

After him came a strapping sailor with a fine set of lungs:

"Surely we didn't molder in prisons for years, only to give up to the bourgeoisie everything we've won? I've just arrived from Helsingfors. Yesterday we had a sailors' congress and I'm here as its representative. We propose that the Foreign Minister should be censured for that note and dismissed!"

Shouts from around the square:

"Get him here! Get that Milyukov here!"

And suddenly, from the side, a car sporting a red flag forced a way into the square. From it two men immediately ran to mount the stand, as one might a lookout tower in case of fire. And one, flaxen-haired and plump-cheeked, began with panache and an easy confidence:

"Comrades! We salute the organized revolutionary army, which has come to the square to express its feelings! My name is Skobelev, member of the Executive Committee, here on behalf of the Soviet of Workers' and Soldiers' Deputies to thank the troops who are ready to support the Soviet's words with its bayonets! The Soviet is keeping vigilant guard over the interests of democracy. All night, the Executive Committee has been discussing the matter of the note and is still discussing it even now . . ."

There were cries of thanks. "Hurrah," as well.

"For the time being, the revolutionary army must stay calm and await the decision of its representatives. We are taking into consideration your frame of mind and the feelings you are expressing here, in the square. The Provisional Government, which came out of the very heart of the revolution, must also be respected. It does not exist 'by the grace of God' but by the will of the people! Now we appeal to you to refrain from separate, uncoordinated demonstrations and wait for our call. The Executive Committee itself will bring pressure to bear on the government!"

His place on the stand was promptly taken by the other figure from the car, swarthy, with long hair, almost like a girl's. His voice was weaker, and the wind was getting stronger, so not every word could be heard:

"Comrades! My name is Gotz, and I am a member of the Executive Committee! I salute . . . the revolutionary, conscientious . . . At the present time we cannot yet declare no confidence in the Provisional Government. . . But the Russian democracy does not want annexations . . . The Russian army must always be ready to defend freedom and must firmly repel all attacks from outside and from within . . . Our primary enemy is within, in the form of discord and controversy. And we must not tolerate them, comrades! Hurrah!"

At "Hurrah" his voice gave out completely, but those near him were happy to take up the refrain: no discord! And those further back took up from them just "Hurrah" and passed it on.

Those two climbed down, but now an ensign mounted the stand, his head thrown back, one of the leaders of the 180th, who'd brought them here. He took his cap off, revealing a straightforward, proud face. And resonantly, confidently, brandishing a fist to underline his words:

". . . The Provisional Government's imperialist, predatory, plundering note . . . Is our alliance with English and French bankers sacred? But who concluded that alliance? The Tsar, Rasputin, and the Tsar's gang of cronies! Soldiers! Up to now you've been defending the Tsar's shady treaties, which were kept hidden from you like a shameful disease. Milyukov, Guchkov, Tereshchenko, and Konovalov, capitalists, are in need of new markets. If it's necessary to do away with tens of millions more Russian men in order to pillage little nations, that won't stop our ministers. Fight the war because we want to pillage! That note from Milyukov is a provocation belched out by the old regime. It will help Wilhelm: if the Russians want to carry on fighting till the end, the Germans also have no option but to go on till the end! And what good is war to a soldier? It brings nothing but mutilations, death, and, for his family, hunger."

"What should we do, then?" came shouts from below. "Abandon the front?"

Ensign Lenartovich didn't let himself get distracted:

"We're not saying we should end the war immediately, no matter what the conditions. We are demanding renunciation of conquests! A start to peace talks!"

But the ensign couldn't finish: another large, open car arrived in front of the palace via the access ramp. In it were a general and two adjutants. As the general rose to get out, he was immediately recognized. All the battalions already knew his face: it was the Commander of the Military District, General Kornilov.

He got out of the car nimbly and speedily, casting a stern look at the ranks of the Finland battalion standing in front of him—and the soldiers, without any command, started turning round, turning their heads back to the way they'd originally been facing, and straightened their lines: you had to show respect for your Commander after all. Then among the ranks their own commands were heard: order arms, dress. Hundreds of rifle butts banged down onto the flagstones. Now no one was listening to the ensign on the podium. He stopped—and came down. And the 180th Regiment also came into line of its own accord.

General Kornilov began his review with the naval crew, then passed the length of the Finland, 180th, and Moscow battalions, and so on till he'd inspected them all. He was swarthy, lean, and agile. Golden sword-hilt. He walked past, his sharp eyes narrowed, surveying the scene and not uttering a single word of reproach, only from time to time a greeting—and the men replied with a chorus of "hurrah"s.

Then he mounted the stand and the strong wind lifted the skirts of his greatcoat to reveal the red lining. He did not shout, but his deep voice carried:

"The time is past, brothers, when you could not breathe a word about the things that were important to you. Now you are the armed people. This is your strength. But also your weakness. Your strength: you can back up any demand with bayonets. Your weakness: you are less disciplined than career soldiers. And I urge you to exercise strict discipline, for this will bring you unity. I'll tell you something about myself. My father was a Siberian Cossack and my mother a Buryat. I was born into a poor family and went to military school at the age of thirteen."

The square erupted into cries of "hurrah."

"I have had thirty-five years of military service and always kept away from politics. Do the same. My job and yours is that of a soldier. Staying calm and orderly. Only then can we serve our homeland. As the leader of the Petrograd garrison, I consider it my duty to bring your wishes to the attention of the Provisional Government. Today you showed your strength—now I am asking you to go back to your quarters."

And accompanied by lengthy cheering, sometimes in unison, sometimes exploding in bursts, he came down from the podium. He stood by his car on the palace access ramp.

The naval band struck up the Marseillaise, the band of the 180th struck up the "Marseillaise," and everywhere men were found who could give commands. They slung their rifles once more, turned around—and went off in their different directions.

Some went straight back to barracks. Others walked via Morskaya to Nevsky Prospect, happy now to march along the main streets. The people should see what fine fellows we are.

Linde, though, was running behind his battalion shouting, trying to persuade them not to leave.

[58]

General Alekseev would have been left with nothing to do during that time if no newspaper reporters had found their way to Guchkov's ministerial residence. Others had hurried to Mariinskaya Square, but these had come here: having the Supreme Commander in the capital was unprecedented. Guchkov gave Alekseev permission to hold a press conference and a room was allocated.

The first question, of course, was about the latest thing to cause a stir: how did the general feel about those troops leaving their barracks unauthorized?

Why should he get involved in that? He'd seen the ministers' disarray. With a sidelong look through his spectacles:

"I'm too remote from life here: I live in Mogilev. I can't say anything for certain."

Though you could see with half an eye what was really going on. But he continued:

"The army is suffering badly from all the events of recent months. The press should, with a sober voice, come to the army's aid. It should hammer home the fact that Russia needs victory. And then there's the Leninist propaganda, which is playing dangerous games with human passions. It ought to be stopped."

They'd be happy to help: they'd been thinking the same. But they'd been persecuted, called the *bourgeois* press—just try and answer that one! The workers and peasants had announced boycotts of the papers.

"Of course, God willing," (and God was the only hope now), "we'll get through this difficult period, fulfill our obligations to our Allies and win victory. The Russian people have common sense and honest, kind hearts . . ."

How was everything on the fronts? Especially the Northern Front?

In March, in raising the alarm about the Germans attacking Petrograd, we'd acted more correctly. But now Guchkov and the other ministers were demanding that the people be kept calm.

"Petrograd can be reassured regarding its future. We have sufficient forces. And they are looking after the capital. Petrograd is almost in a state of panic, but there's no good reason for that."

And something stirred him to say, more boldly:

"If we do have any fears for Petrograd, it's only because the ideas it radiates are not always healthy. Declarations that the war is over are causing disquiet in the army."

A question (to support the general): is there any fraternization?

"Yes, unfortunately. But that shameful practice is gradually being eliminated. The enemy are pinning their hopes—big hopes, but false—on the revolution and propaganda alone corrupting our army."

Could we expect more extensive battles in the near future?

"Yes. This summer general action will be launched both in the West and the East. Overall, 1917 will be a decisive year in the World War because the nations are so tired that any later than four to six months from now they'll barely be able to demonstrate combat capability."

Do the Allies believe in victory?

"They're unshakeable. But over here . . . ," he sighed. "Over here, unfortunately, the men are dreaming not of victory but of establishing a quiet, peaceful life. Even the United States entering the war has made no impression here."

Are there cells or nests in the army that the counterrevolution could rely on for support?

"No! From the generals to the soldiers, everyone is devoted to the new order. You should have seen the army's sincere, spontaneous joy"—the fib was involuntary—"as they welcomed the coup . . . By and large the present time is wonderful, but also troubled. We'll be hoping this temporary nightmare passes."

But perhaps he should have said it all—differently? Raised the alarm, said the Army was being utterly ruined?!

But he feared the Germans might get to hear.

He feared a conflict with the Soviet. And he didn't want to undermine the ministers.

[59]

(PETROGRAD STREETS: 3 MAY, LATE AFTERNOON)

* * *

Since midday rumors have been circulating in Petrograd, to the effect that regiments have mutinied, blockaded the Mariinsky Palace, and arrested the Provisional Government.

"Why aren't we doing anything, gentlemen? Shouldn't we come to the government's aid?!"

But—how?

* * *

Nevsky Prospect is getting animated now. Here and there excited groups have gathered. Like-minded types, they're not arguing but they're all indignant. Speakers mount any platforms they come across.

"What's going on, gentlemen? This isn't a Tsarist government, it's our revolutionary government!"

One ad hoc meeting merges into the next. We must . . . go. Where, though? And what would be the result?

Go? In which case we need to *carry* something. But what? Red flags, there are still lots of those around the place. And placards—there are some of those left from 1 May too. Although . . . they're about something different.

All the same, they set off on a march . . . At first uncertainly.

But people join them.

* * *

But a disorderly crowd of sixteen- and seventeen-year-olds is also marching, under the slogan "Down with Milyukov." A military doctor asks one of them:

"What should we do with the Provisional Government, then?"

"They can stay where they are."

* * *

Nevsky Prospect is gradually filling up with demonstrators supporting Milyukov and the Provisional Government. There are hundreds and hundreds of them already, people living in the center of town. They cross the Fontanka and the Moika on their way to Mariinskaya Square. To come to the government's aid!

The road traffic is slower now, but the trams fly past.

* * *

At the corner of Morskaya Street two marches intersect, the 180th Regiment, coming from Mariinskaya Square, and a civilian demonstration from the Moika Embankment—these wearing bowlers, student caps, and smart millinery. From the soldiers' ranks, cries of:

"Down with . . .!"

But the demonstrators coming from Nevsky Prospect don't lower their "Long live the Provisional Government" placard. Then the soldiers leave their line and rush at those clean-looking types, fists raised, throw punches here and there and slash the placard to pieces with their bayonets.

"It's an outrage! What lawlessness!" shout the pro-government marchers and the audience on the sidewalk.

And the soldiers come back with:

"Down with provocation!"

But they hurry back to their line and no scuffle ensues. The crowd of onlookers has grown and they're indignant. A tall officer voices the general *bewilderment* at soldiers allowing themselves to behave this way toward citizens who are expressing their opinion with the same freedom as they themselves enjoy.

* * *

After the end of the factories' day shift, workers' demonstrations make an appearance, even in the center of town. They march in their work clothes, carrying a few red flags and placards left over from 1 May: "Take a stand under the banner of Zimmerwald," "Life insurance for all at the government's expense." Several hundred march, singing revolutionary songs, to Znamenskaya Square, but don't stay long there, going off along Ligovka.

Following them come a crowd of women workers, four or five hundred of them, including teenagers, carrying "Down with Milyukov" and singing "Forswear the old world." They march rapidly along Nevsky Prospect to Znamenskaya Square, as if they just want to get this walk over with.

And coming in the other direction: "Full confidence in Milyukov!," and there are soldiers in that procession. The two pass without any friction.

* * *

At the beginning of Nevsky Prospect, Admiral Vesyolkin's car is stopped because he's mistaken for Milyukov in disguise. There are demands for him to be disarmed and arrested, but some sailors who know this admiral arrive in time. They're all taken to the Naval General Staff to be checked.

* * *

Opposed processions exchange cutting remarks but without any brawls. Also parading along Nevsky Prospect are some latecomers, small units from Izmailovsky and Petrograd battalions: "Publish the treaties with the Allies."

From the windows and balconies of Nevsky, people greet the pro-government demonstrations with vigorous waves.

* * *

All the way along, at every crossroads, the crowds are growing, listening impatiently to speakers and shouting either approval or condemnation. In some places a person in the street plays chairman and invites others, in turn, to speak. And they assail one another, gesticulating passionately. Now a lady starts arguing with a soldier from the guards. Then a worker in a black overcoat:

"We need to take that Milyukov down a peg or two."

A young lady in lace-up bootees gasps in horror.

And a student, who has climbed a lamp post:

"Milyukov says we have to fight on till victory—that means we'll be fighting forever."

A gentleman in a bowler, leaning against an advertising column:

"Russians are incapable of examining arguments critically. It's those who propose the most agreeable thing who win the argument. So what do they propose? Spare the enemy—who's stronger than us and has taken fifteen of our provinces!"

A front-line colonel, speaking from a flight of steps:

"We make no secret of the fact that we're tired, we've been separated from our families, we live in almost unbearable conditions. But the army is firmly against a shameful peace!"

He's lifted up with a cheer and borne aloft along Nevsky Prospect.

Curious foreigners, here and there along Nevsky, look on.

* * *

"We can't go on like this! Today they're shouting 'Down with Milyukov'—will it be 'Down with Kerensky' tomorrow?"

A beanpole of a soldier:

"You don't understand anything."

"Who does understand?"

A gentleman standing nearby:

"Russia always has to learn the hard way."

* * *

From the high steps of the City Duma, where speakers are appealing for confidence in the government, some students and officers shout "Let's go to the Foreign Ministry!" They hurriedly scrawl in chalk on red flags "Long live the Provisional Government!," "Down with Lenin!"—and leave. On the way more people join them, and by the time they arrive at the arch of the General Staff building they are about five thousand to emerge into Palace Square. Leading the march is a one-armed officer.

They turn to the right and stop, holding their flags. They wait to see whether Milyukov will appear. His deputy, Neratov, comes out onto a balcony:

"Russian freedom has always been dear to Milyukov and he'll never betray it!"

"We believe you! We believe you! Long live Milyukov!"

An ovation.

From there they decide to go on to the Mariinsky Palace. Perhaps they'll see Milyukov there.

Near the Astoria they encounter a hostile demonstration and there are some skirmishes. But militiamen jump out of a truck and pull them apart.

* * *

Some demonstrating workers have trudged along, out of habit, to the Tauride Palace, and found no one there.

Then Lieber comes out and makes an impassioned speech:

"Restraint, comrades! Overthrowing the government now would be absolutely pointless!"

* * *

Among the crowds all you can hear is either "hurrah" or "down with . . ."

"What about Kerensky! Let's go and find him and see what he says."

But he's nowhere to be seen, or heard.

A student from the Institute of Civil Engineers gallops along in the roadway, describing circles with his fist:

"Down with Lenin! Long live the Provisional Government! Long live freedom!"

* * *

From Clodt's horses, students try to convince demonstrators as they pass:

"Don't! Go home! A plenary session of the government is starting any minute now and everything will be decided then! We'll know the result tomorrow!"

[60]

Starting with that sleepless night and the alarming morning meeting with Kerensky, and then the increasing alarms during the day—today Stankevich had taken enough action and was satisfied. The main thing was that in recent hours he had essentially taken over the military power at the Tauride Palace. He'd assembled his Soldiers' Executive Commission (he was, after all, now the head of Petrograd soldiery) and swiftly passed a resolution and got it out by telephone to all military units: they must all return to barracks and not a single unit was to come out without an order from the EC. In so doing he had stopped the incipient mutiny, a repeat of February, in its tracks. Of course, thousands of soldiers were in the street even now, making a commotion under the great windows of the Sea Cadet Corps, and they'd already spilled out over the whole strip of land between the building and the bank of the Neva. But not a single unit, still less an armed unit, would leave its barracks. He had decided to take the helm—and taken it.

The Sea Cadet Corps was already used to the great crush with the Soviet there and the benches it had installed (the frigate model and the statue of Peter the Great having been removed). It was as if that spacious hall had never accommodated ranks of trim little sea cadets. Now two thousand men in dirty black jackets and slack soldiers' greatcoats were assembling there. This morning the announcement of this extraordinary session of the Soviet had appeared in *Izvestia*, in big, bold type. Anyway, the deputies could see and hear for themselves what was happening, and where, in the capital. And they were assembling with the newly acquired feeling of being masters of Petrograd, and the whole country—and of their own fate: what we ourselves decide now is how it will be. This idea had been instilled into them over the past two months.

But the EC members knew the Soviet had been convened in a panic, to no good purpose. It was impossible to cancel it now, but it couldn't take any decisions.

Chkheidze felt ashamed of the situation and dragged out his opening speech, trying to blur over the fact that they'd all been gathered here pointlessly. He began by telling the whole story of how the EC had been waiting for the government's next statement about annexations and indemnities, so as to decide whether or not to support the loan. And now the government had published the awaited document.

Outside the windows, the sun had still not quite set.

In the hall, silence reigned. Giving Chkheidze a rest, Bogdanov read out the note, demonstrating as usual his remarkable lung power. Chkheidze, on his last legs, rose again.

So, the Executive Committee sat all night but could not come to a firm decision. We agreed that "to a decisive victory" could be taken to mean whatever you wanted it to, and the renunciation of annexations and indemnities had been glossed over.

"Annexations and indemnities" had become such a well-worn phrase that no speakers ever explained them (or even defined them in the first place); but they had something repugnant about them, like worms and spiders, and the crowd had to understand that.

Now, this afternoon, the Executive Committee met again, and was again unable to come to a decision. And we convened the Soviet, to work out a common policy for our democracy. We want the Provisional Government to renounce the seizure of territories, without any fudging. We know the government also realizes how serious, how critical its own situation is. We shall tell them to send the Allies a new note, with a clear meaning. And, conscious of what is at stake at this crucial point, we decided to convene the Soviet and hear your decision. But let us not decide hastily, without carefully weighing up the situation. And we ask you to entrust the Executive Committee with the job of conducting the negotiations. This will take place at nine this evening.

"Where?"

"At the Mariinsky Palace."

Strident voices:

"They should come here, not the other way round!"

"What's wrong with them? Scared of us, are they?"

Uproar. Then Chkheidze, flustered:

"The results of our negotiations will be communicated to you all, in full. Tomorrow. Support us now and we'll take the definitive decision tomorrow. In view of the gravity of the situation, the Executive Committee wants to be in touch with you and we propose another meeting tomorrow"

"Why tomorrow?"

"Why not decide today, while we're all here?"

Thrown by that outcry, or losing his way in muddled thought, Chkheidze for some reason carried on talking, going off at a tangent, instead of finishing his introduction and sitting down:

". . . Now we're going to approach our comrades, the socialists of England and France, and ask them whether they're going to take any firm action to force their governments to renounce annexations and indemnities."

But from behind him someone tugged at his jacket—and he didn't elaborate. He sat down.

It seemed he had explained everything and for the time being they couldn't decide anything—so could they now stop discussing and go their separate ways? No such luck. Bogdanov already had a list of about fifty members wanting to speak.

But the first—he had already put his name down that morning—was Stankevich.

A clean-limbed, thin, severe lieutenant, his eyes narrowed (the university lecturer was unrecognizable since joining the army), he approached the platform for one more decisive skirmish. He wanted not only to give some meaning to this pointless session, not only to prevent the crowd from getting out of hand, but also to apply some pressure, publicly, to the SRs and the Social Democrats, who were bucking the quite obvious necessity of a coalition government. Stankevich had, it seemed, made a good plan for this speech.

He mounted the platform, smoothing his little moustache with two fingers, as officers frequently do. (And an officer speaking at the Soviet was rare, something noteworthy.) He stood a moment, waiting for total silence. Then, his voice resonant, commanding:

"Only yesterday, there was still unity between the government and the Soviet. But that unity has been dealt a blow. The Provisional Government has strayed from the path taken by the revolutionary people. In the note we read the old words about a victorious end to the war. Several members of the Provisional Government do not understand their duties as they should and even between them there is mutual misunderstanding." (This was the help he'd promised Kerensky.) "We have been told that the government was not expecting our censure. They thought they were, with that note, meeting the democracy's wishes . . ."

Boos and catcalls. (The Bolsheviks.) He had to be prepared for that, but also be more careful in maintaining a balance.

". . . But they were wrong. A mutual lack of understanding arose. But we must think about what to do now. What is the solution? We could simply overthrow the government and arrest its members."

Wild applause. (The Bolsheviks.) Had he gone too far in the other direction? But now he aimed for the most spectacular, well-planned oratorical twist. Of the original splendor of this hall, its upper section not yet stripped of fixtures, a large, round wall clock remained, and it was working.

". . . But that would be the conclusion of a primitive logic, and I attribute your applause to the fact that this reasoning is an over-simplification. Such measures are not the ones we would take. We are strong even without them. And this government is not the old one, which used machine guns to cling on to power. Just look!" And he raised a slim hand, to point. Everyone turned to follow it. "It is now five minutes to seven. And if we want to we can telephone now, from here, and at five minutes past seven the Provisional Government will cease to exist!!"

That made a big impression. And heads turned from the clock to the speaker and back again. Rapturous applause. (What pride, when the people become aware of their power!) But the speaker, in an icy, brusque voice, brought them down to earth:

"But why should we do that? A premature decision would only complicate things. When should we use force? Who should be shot? Because all the power is in your hands! And those of the masses standing behind you. There are various other solutions apart from violence. We won't hesitate for a moment to express no confidence in the Provisional Government if it doesn't satisfy our demands. But I caution you against making hasty decisions. This moment is too important for us to give way to our feelings."

This had really impressed the hall. Silence.

If only! If only we always had time to inform the masses about the domestic and international situation, about the true aims of the war . . . If only we could explain everything to the people, thoroughly! What is popular sovereignty? How do we conceive it? We say "democracy" but we understand it as the rule of educated people, like you and me, and none of us has any intention of submitting to the rule of the unwashed masses.

"Settling the issue of removing the government could be harder than you think. Now that the food, transport, and finance problems are so much more acute, it could be that we *need* the government to stay. At a time like this the burden of power is nothing to rejoice over—it weighs heavy. And taking power into your own hands would be premature and dangerous. After all, we didn't take this burden on in the first days of the revolution. So follow your leaders calmly. If they are not calling on you to seize power immediately, it's for good reason."

There was muttering and grumbling from the Bolsheviks. But as a whole the hall was firmly convinced.

"There's another solution, as well: we know the individual members of the Provisional Government who are standing in the way of unity with the democracy, and we could remove one of them, or several."

"Get rid of them all!!" came a roar from the little group of Bolsheviks near the rostrum.

But Stankevich raised a commanding hand for quiet. And the hall was with him again. Now he must say to the entire Soviet for the words that he also needed to ricochet to the socialists in the presidium:

"Democracy is getting stronger and we already feel that we'll be ready to share power soon and take over some of the ministerial jobs. And that is a sign of our maturity."

After two speeches like that, the presidium could not give the floor to anyone but a Bolshevik—and they were bursting to get onto the platform. But what was this? Where were all their well-known leaders? There was no self-sure Kamenev, no firebrand Kollontai, no strident Shlyapnikov. They put forward someone called Fyodorov: young, with a little moustache, the look of a worker but clever and nimble. Although unknown, he could reel everything off accurately, and all in accordance with the Bolshevik textbook:

"What a nerve, the bourgeois government suddenly deciding to implement Nikolai's old treaties with the Allies! The capitalists' government is unwilling and unable to finish the war and will never renounce annexations! Don't comfort yourselves with the illusion that we can come to some kind of agreement with them! Until such time as the democracy takes power into its own hands it will never see its demands met. Milyukov's note is a challenge to the whole of Russian democracy and a stab in the back for the world proletariat. The time has come for us to say to our imperialist bourgeoisie: get out of our way! It's either us or you!"

Applause. Some of the hall has gone over to the Bolsheviks. They slew round with every speech.

"Workers, soldiers, and farm laborers" (since Lenin's arrival, the farm laborers have replaced the peasants in all their speeches) "must recognize just how much force they have and *overthrow* the Provisional Government! Seize power, even if that will lead to civil war. Our watchword is 'the International'!"

The Bolsheviks chorus their loud and fervent support, and there are quite a few of them here, but even so the hall isn't shouting with them. The speaker, now even more shameless:

"You've nothing to fear! In any case, the civil war has already broken out. And it's only through that war that the people will gain their freedom!"

New and very frightening words. A barrage of hostile cries.

And when, outside, they bellow "hurrah" or "down with Milyukov," it's also heard inside. And those sitting nearest the windows can see, on the embankment, as dusk begins to fall, an ever denser crowd, from the very wall of the building to the granite embankment edge and stretching the whole length of the building. Several thousand people, flags, and placards, and they're shouting and brandishing their fists. They have speakers there too, addressing them from raised platforms. Perhaps they're all Bolshevik supporters? Now even the Soviet needs to watch out.

And onto the platform comes a good-looking, well-groomed man in the prime of life, with typical Russian features and thick, light-brown hair and little beard. His face has become familiar over the last two weeks: it's Chernov, and all the SRs here applaud loudly. He starts speaking with great relish, deliberation, and love of speech, as though not making a speech but enjoying a delightful meal, and a calming effect is communicated to the listeners:

"Comrades! The situation is so serious and so complex that the first thing I'll say to you is: calm. Stay calm and utterly determined. The next is: seriousness. Then: judicious forethought. Less excitability, comrades, and more sober discussion of issues. The situation is now graver than it was in those days of March. At that time we, together," (he'd been in Europe, though) "overthrew the autocracy—which was already rotten through and through, so we weren't constantly worrying that we might not succeed. And the situation was so clear: on one side was the government, on the other all the people. But now internecine strife has broken out between the victors—and there is nothing more dangerous for the revolution. The situation is unclear, reactionary elements have been lying low, but we all hear their viper's hiss—and what if civil war breaks out? The counterrevolution is not dead, it is waiting for civil war, so as to rise up against us, fully armed. We must be inspired by the gravity of the moment and not forget that it is pregnant with consequences. For this reason I am not going to propose to this meeting any premature decisions, but say instead: we'll see tomorrow what we should do. We have the right to be patient, for we are strong."

But only someone who didn't know Victor Mikhailovich Chernov would have thought he'd now said his piece. This was just the introduction. The whole speech was still to come. And off he went, and carried on, and on.

"The government must, of course, renounce all annexations and announce this to the whole world. We know that other countries' democracies will also start moving in the same direction." (A voice from the hall: "We don't see any sign of that!") "In the same direction—and they'll learn from our example. Or the Provisional Government will fulfill our demand to renounce conquests or return power to the authorities they received it from, the Soviet of Workers' and Soldiers' Deputies and the State Duma Committee." (Loud applause, but not from the whole hall.) "The struggle could be very difficult, and of decisive importance, but we must not be in a hurry to seize power as long as the prevailing conditions offer no guarantee that it can be retained. Do not put the Russian revolution in the situation of a pregnant woman who miscarries simply because she has been running so fast. Every day increases our strength: we do not need to hurry."

There was grumbling from the Bolsheviks. But Chernov was a champion in the composure stakes.

"The democracy will not take the power into its own hands until it realizes how strong it is. But when it does take power, it must be with the intention of never letting go. And history is leading us toward that goal! And that government will certainly work toward the nation's objectives. And I urge you to assume a calm that cannot be interpreted as a sign of weakness but, on the contrary, as a result of your confidence in your own strength."

And he went on, with an encouraging overview. We have nothing to fear from the future. If there was, at the start of the revolution, dissension between Petrograd and the front, now unity with the front is becoming ever closer. And every day is eradicating the difference between the mood in Petrograd and that in the provinces.

"Arm yourselves with patience, comrades! Not the patience of an enslaved Russia but the patience of people creating a new life! As for power—you'll get power, not by seizing it but through planned steps."

Chernov was even facilitating the presidium's job, somehow filling up the hours of that futile session. And he could have talked for a lot longer, but the list of speakers was now pressing. They started allowing speakers no longer than five minutes.

Then came another bellicose Bolshevik, with an incongruously tearful name, Plaksin. He said the Soviet of Workers' Deputies must take power immediately! (And roars from the Bolsheviks in the hall.)

In response to this an SR, Kaplan, tried some persuasion: we must not express our will through the wild yelling of a crowd, but by organization! The fate of the Russian and perhaps the worldwide proletariat hangs on what we decide here today. (Did he really think something was being decided here?) Let the Executive Committee meet the Provisional Government. Let them come to a considered decision!

And a Menshevik, Goltsman: the note is a provocation, but we trust the Executive Committee!

And a sailor from the Baltic Fleet, who wasn't on the list of speakers, not removing his beribboned cap:

"I'm here representing the troops who've rebelled against the Provisional Government. We demand that Milyukov be dismissed! And our own government—or else it's civil war!!"

And he read out a few confused phrases from a resolution that he said had been passed by the troops in Mariinskaya Square. There was no way to catch him out, to prove there'd been no such resolution—and the hall was being stirred up to an extent that the presidium had not foreseen: might this Soviet start taking decisions unasked? The commotion was unimaginable, with yelling from all sides of the argument.

"Give your name! Who are you?"

He didn't say.

But Stankevich had foreseen this and had briefed a soldier from the Executive Commission, who now spoke:

"Fine, we'll overthrow the government. But who'll replace it? Us? Our hands are already shaking, and they're going to be shaking a lot more. No, we mustn't build ourselves houses of cards that will be even easier to blow away than Nikolai II was. We must not play games of chance."

He was loudly applauded and the hall changed sides again. Success.

But now an anarchist came up to speak:

"Seize power immediately! Social revolution immediately! There are examples from history! We mustn't waste a minute!"

And a Bolshevik again:

"Today we can still fight Milyukov and his gang, but tomorrow their forces may increase!"

Then Broido was pushed forward to speak on behalf of the EC and pour some oil on the troubled waters: if we take the power into our hands, won't we cause a split in the democracy? Because not all the people are with us, some are against us, and other sections of the population are with us now but will they turn away from us if we rebel? And it's a lie that today military units wanted to occupy the palace and arrest the government. Nothing like that happened. If it had happened, it would have been a crime against the democracy.

Chkheidze, who was already not coping well with the Executive Committee, to say nothing of a Soviet of two thousand members (and on top of that he'd been called outside to address the crowd on the embankment), was trying in his now weak voice to give the hall instructions: now the Executive Committee must go to the meeting with the government. Forty more men are registered to speak—but we cannot discuss any more now. So go your separate ways around town, and exert your influence on the revolutionary masses: tell them to be ready for combat if it becomes necessary. But they can be sure that the EC will do everything necessary. Tomorrow we'll meet and discuss it.

The presidium stood up to leave and it was left to Skobelev to close the session. He had a good pair of lungs but the Bolsheviks were even louder:

"Continue the assembly!"

"We propose to elect Comrade Lenin chairman!"

He wasn't even there. But there was a new outburst of bellowing.

Skobelev:

"Calling for civil war is a crime against the people's freedom. I declare this meeting closed until tomorrow."

Cries of:

"No! Carry on!"

And, on top of that, there was still the din from the embankment. They weren't dispersing either.

The assembly was splitting into a multitude of little meetings. The Bolsheviks rushed onto the platform. Were they going to bring the little meetings back together now, and continue the Soviet session?

How easy it is to light a fire!

That same Kaplan, who spoke before, ran up again:

"What are you doing? You'll be deceiving Russia! Do you realize that if you announce your decision Russia will think it was the Soviet of Workers' Deputies who decided it?"

Some members did make for the door, not wanting to continue without the presidium.

"Our duty," said others, "is to go out into the street, to the revolutionary people!"

The Bolsheviks flew into a rage:

"Go off and haggle with them then!"

"Go and play the lackey!"

"Go and make plans with Milyukov to deceive the people!"

Some hurried out, others formed little groups, simmering away.

It was all a muddle.

[6 1]

The troops had left, but Mariinskaya Square did not quiet down. On the contrary. All the excited people who'd arrived while the troops were here had remained; and the rally, begun from the little stand set up in front of the palace for 1 May, continued unabated. There were several hundred listeners always thronging round it, and a motley assortment of speakers followed one another on the platform. For safety's sake they held on to the batten someone had nailed on as a guard rail. And fittingly, given that most of the arguing centered on the war, doves circled in front of the palace in the late-afternoon sun. And the birds, finding ever less peace and free space on the pavement, cooed in alarm and crowded near the palace entrance onto the edges of plaster vases, which had been damaged by the shooting in March.

Soldiers, now separated from the authority of their leaders and their placards, were all reflecting, sensibly: "Of course we mustn't abandon the war. We've always been for victory, and always will be."

But during the last few hours, not only in the neighborhood of the Mariinsky but all over town as well, people had heard about the troops' sally into the square, and groups from the far ends of town were pouring in. The regiments had left, but they were replaced by Petrograd residents of all ages and styles of dress: thousands were already flooding into the square. People couldn't hear from one edge to the other, and here and there little groups of like-minded people were getting together, and their own speakers emerged. Some stood on empty barrels they'd rolled along with them, or stools they'd brought, others on the coach-box of an open carriage provided by an uncomplaining cabman, while others, the more nimble, even climbed lamp posts.

And from group to group, and further across the square, behind the back of the light, graceful figure of Nikolai I, the only sounds that came rippling across were "hurrah" and "down with," "hurrah" and "down with," while even the fiercest arguments died down rapidly.

It was a peaceful, self-constituted gathering of the people, something unseen since time immemorial: in the frosts of early March, people had been running more, watching more, lighting fires and putting them out more, or hauling off people or stolen goods. Today the crowd had no conductor wielding his baton, no captain, no head—but there was one leader who constantly soared high in the minds of the whole population of revolutionary Russia: Kerensky of course! If only he could have appeared now and made a galvanizing speech! Everyone would have streamed off after him, unstoppable, in a harmonious tidal wave.

And in the section of the crowd nearest the palace they formed a delegation, consisting of an officer, a student, and two civilians. They would go to the palace, find out where Kerensky was, phone him, and ask him to come here—urgently! In fact it was surprising that he'd not yet appeared of his own accord.

Another two speakers took turns on the platform while beneath them people in the crowd debated with their neighbors. Actually, no military men there were speaking against the war, only against the ministers' secrets and in favor of clear objectives, while the civilians and the ladies all supported war till a final, decisive victory. By now the make-up of the crowd in the square was such that there were no real arguments and they were getting more and more supportive of the government. And they felt very sorry for Milyukov, who'd suffered such an unfair attack.

The deputation returned from the palace and the officer mounted the stage to announce: Kerensky is very ill, in bed, and cannot come to the rally. But he asks the citizens to remain calm and to trust the Provisional Government to stand guard over their freedom. Our dear minister sends his greetings to everyone here!

It was a big disappointment, but also a bit of charm coming from the dear minister.

This was not the first delegation to have gone into the palace on behalf of the crowd during the last few hours—they'd called for Milyukov, or Prince Lvov or any one of the ministers to come out. And how annoying: contrary to the general assumption that the Mariinsky Palace was where the government resided, not a single minister had appeared there all day.

At about six in the evening, a new column of soldiers emerged from Morskaya Street, with no band and unarmed. They were singing a chaotic Marseillaise, but then stopped. This turned out to be the Pavlovsky battalion, come late for the assembly. They were marching with almost no officers and in a rather undisciplined way. At the front of the line, the placards read "Down with Milyukov's predatory policy!" and "Long live peace with no annexations or indemnities!"

When they arrived, there was no room for them in the square, which was swamped. But even so, they found room to stand, side-on to the palace. And their ranks looked so un-military that members of the public happily pushed their way through and asked the soldiers why they'd come and why they didn't like Milyukov's note. Surely they didn't want to surrender Russia to the Germans? The Pavlovsky boys' answers were incoherent. Surrender to the Germans? Course not, no one wants that. What's in the note? There was not a single lucid answer. What are "annexations"? None of them knew.

Meanwhile, speaker followed speaker on the platform. A small man, about forty and almost a hunchback, climbed up. It was Aleksinsky, who'd been a member of the Second State Duma. He addressed himself primarily to the Pavlovsky men:

"I've just arrived from France. I saw the joy that seized the French democracy during the days of our coup. The workers were saying: 'Now we're reassured, your cause is in safe hands.' But what if they'd seen the picture in this square today? They couldn't have expected such a blow from Russian democracy. How could Russian soldiers march under such slogans? Shame on those who came and even greater shame on those who led them! But I hope that terrible nightmare will soon fade. We must think not only of ourselves but also of the world's future. The revolution must endow you with hearts of granite! I call on you to uphold the nation's honor! Now you sing the Marseillaise—but what right do you have to sing it if you mean to act against France?"

The civilian crowd was noisily applauding Aleksinsky throughout. But a Bolshevik appeared next, saying that Aleksinsky could not be trusted: he was published in bourgeois newspapers. This did not go down well and he was booed off.

The Pavlovsky battalion stood there for less than an hour, looking sullen and rather out-of-place. It was clear they'd missed the party. And their embarrassed leaders led the men back the same way they'd come, but without the Marseillaise.

In the square, people were saying that a detachment from a Jäger battalion was also approaching, from Demidov Lane, but some officer cadets with rifles had blocked the lane and wouldn't let them through.

An officer mounted the rostrum to speak.

"The bayonet power is on the revolutionary army's side! We are all on the Soviet of Workers' Deputies' side. The secret treaties concluded by Nikolai the Bloody must be made public!"

An officer! And he didn't choke on those words. He was dismissed with boos and catcalls.

A war invalid mounted the stand and made a heartfelt appeal for the defense of the motherland. He earned resounding applause and shouts of "hurrah."

Not a single military column was left, but there were plenty of soldiers in the crowd. They were all for the motherland.

All this was so rare in Russia: a crowd of many thousands, which no one had convened, a free rostrum and absolute freedom to say whatever you wanted, supporting whichever side you wanted.

But it was more than that: here, now, a custom from the March days was back again. Strangers were readily talking to each other like the best of friends, cordially—and how well they understood each other:

"They think free speech is the freedom to hound people!"

"Fanatical ideas! It's like an epidemic. Self-satisfied individuals scattering poisoned seeds among the masses—it smacks of civil strife!"

"Freedom was proclaimed and granted to everyone and everyone's getting drunk on it. And now we see indifference toward the fate of the Whole, of our motherland!"

"Ah, all that goes back to Aleksandr III, ladies and gentlemen. He was the culprit, the cause of all our misfortunes. He always put everything into reverse, and that went on for thirty-five years. We were never allowed to organize the people and that's why, as soon as the police force collapsed, we now find ourselves on the brink of anarchy."

Meanwhile the sun, inclining gently toward the north, was beginning to set, the long northern evening was coming to an end, and, though it was spring, it was cool. The wind was dropping.

But as for the ministers, they didn't appear, or offer any response. Wherever were they? The amiable crowd was waiting for someone to unify them and lead them—but that person did not materialize.

Then a new demonstration appeared, coming past St. Isaac's and toward the square. As it came nearer, you could make out the slogans: they were against the Provisional Government, for peace without annexations, and even "To socialism through Zimmerwald." And Mariinskaya Square met them with hostile cries.

They turned out to be workers from Vasilievsky Island, from the Siemens-Halske, Schuckert, and Cable factories. Despite the hostility they found themselves a place and stopped, not lowering their placards. But from the platform came:

". . . And they want to cast a gloom over our newborn freedom with their insane willfulness! That 'fraternization'—it's a shame and a disgrace! Who are they fraternizing with? With the people who are starving our soldiers in their concentration camps? Choking us with noxious gases? Renouncing their democratic ideals? Well, let them fraternize, but they should bear in mind that history will be their judge!"

Sensing an alien odor in all this, the leaders of the Vasilievsky Island men took them off, along Morskaya toward Nevsky Prospect.

And again this overflowing square was unanimous! What a miracle!

"We've had enough celebrating, ladies and gentlemen, enough eulogizing! Two months of it! Now we have to move on to taking power!"

"And on to the hard work!"

"At times like this, one moment of indecision is enough to forfeit power forever. It's better to make some errors in your actions than it is to hold back from acting at all!"

Yes, but—wherever were our ministers? The day was already at an end, dusk had fallen, the lamps had been lit—but no member of the government had been in the palace all day. In this, too, a sad symbol could be discerned.

But no! The crowd's inclination was not to disperse! It was rumored that an important meeting would be held in the palace at nine o'clock: the whole government and the leaders of the Soviet would be there. The tension among the crowd had so increased since midday, with nothing to relieve it, that now they wanted to wait for the ministers to arrive, and offer their warm support!

"If the counterrevolution was getting the better of our revolution, it wouldn't actually be so distressing: if our side wasn't strong enough, that would be unfortunate—but not shameful! But now the revolution is dying, shamefully, from its own internal disintegration!"

"It's only extreme left-wingers who have an uncompromising, iron will. On our side all we do is talk beautifully about ideals."

"Every country has its citizens and its men in the street. But here we have too many of the latter."

"Excuse me, but why this scoffing at the man in the street? The man in the street is the teacher, the doctor, the office worker, the accountant, the shopkeeper, and the peasant too. He's the whole nation."

Behind the palace, on the other side of the Moika, the moon was slowly rising. It was almost full.

While they waited, a stream of people made for the nearby Italian Embassy, to greet our Ally. There, the ambassador came out onto the balcony, greeted them with a bow and thanked them.

In the square the crowd grew and grew. Now it was so solidly pro-government that the minute anyone said anything hostile, there'd be an explosion of indignation from those standing nearby and he'd fall silent. And make himself scarce. As night fell there were fewer soldiers, and as for workers not a single one remained. It was the native Petersburgers living in the center of town who thronged, surged, and ruled the roost here now. The whole square, even beyond the Nikolai monument, was a vista of heads—if not twenty-five thousand, then certainly twenty.

Across the façade of the palace there hung still, remaining from 1 May, an enormous "Long live the International!"

The square is endless and it's all—us! And we're at one. And it's as if, in the course of this seemingly fruitless waiting, hour after hour after hour, our anxiety eases even more: a once-in-a-lifetime evening! Perhaps it's the turning point of the revolution! Either the government will be recognized or else anarchy will begin to spread across Russia. Perhaps these hours that we've spent standing here are the hours of a great patriotic drama. You whose hearts beat with love for Russia, do not leave! We must wait it out! We must exert our influence!

Ah, here they are! Here at last! They're arriving in cars, the crowds willingly parting to let them through. It's the ministers themselves! The first is Vladimir Lvov. Speech! We want a speech! He mounts the palace steps, burly, black-bearded:

"I promise you that the members of the Provisional Government, which came out of the State Duma, will be steadfast in fulfilling the nation's will."

The crowd was already fired up—it only needed a tiny spark! They lifted Lvov up—strapping fellow as he was—and bore him aloft, with cries of "hurrah," into the palace entrance hall.

Another car horn forging a way through the crowd—who was this one? The car drove up the ramp and out bounded the nimble Nekrasov (he'd developed some of Kerensky's ways), and commandingly, his voice audible many rows back:

"Today has been hard for us. We've heard calls for peace 'at all costs,' and those words pained us. The cherished aim of the Provisional Government is precisely that, to give the country peace. But peace after victory, and in no other circumstances. Allow us to hope that the country will understand that and support us." (But of course! That's why we're here. "Hurra-a-ah!") "The Provisional Government will, as a sacred duty, fulfill its obligations in their entirety, and transfer power only into the hands of those who express the will of *all* the people."

That was a hint! A hint that they wouldn't give in to the Soviet! That's the spirit!

"Hurra-a-ah!" And he too was lifted and carried up the steps and into the entrance hall.

Then the crowd nearly missed Shingarev, who was already on the steps, having come through the crowd on foot from his ministry. They demanded a speech from him too. He did not look at all inspired and his voice didn't carry far.

"We swore to retain power only until we had led the country to the Constituent Assembly. We took an oath to protect the people from internal and external enemies, and we do not want to hold on to power for a single hour longer than the people want."

Was there not, now, a note of weakness in that? Surely they couldn't give in?

"Citizens! If we have your support, the Provisional Government will complete its duty."

Bravo! Of course we'll support you! This is the whole of boundless Russia standing before you: surely you can see it? (Another, strange kind of phrase of his was lost on the audience: "but the government will not do anything that it is not within its rights to do.") "Hurra-a-ah!" And Shingarev too was lifted up and borne aloft.

No! The fatherland was not yet on the brink of destruction!

Then, to the sound of vigorous hooting, the giant figure of Rodzyanko in person, in a large open car, emerged from Morskaya. A roar of delight met him even before he was out of the car.

But the giant was unrecognizable. He no longer held his head as high, his shoulders weren't the same, and his height seemed diminished. He began, his voice almost a groan:

"Citizens! I feel all the weight of responsibility for the current situation, from which we, the Russian people, must find a worthy way out."

Oh. Does that mean things are bad?

"Tell me straight: do you want a separate peace?"

"No! No! Of course not!" The cries came, unstoppable.

Rodzyanko took heart.

"Do you want the Allies to turn away from us? The small, oppressed nations to curse us? The enemy is violating our sacred land—so why ever do you want the rear to impose its will on the people?"

Good Lord, that wasn't us! It hadn't been them, and those who did want that weren't in the square now! And no one had really been talking about "the rear," that was just an oblique way of talking about the Soviet. They'd understood that here! And Rodzyanko got carried away, his voice getting louder, more and more like a great church bell:

"To be free, we must be honest! Surely the Russian nation, in freeing itself from the yoke under which Tsarism held us all, did not think it would maintain its freedom by breaking the word it had given the Allies? Citizens! I beg you to trust this government, put in place by the State Duma . . ."

We do trust the government! It's our only hope!

". . . It's an honest government. And it will fulfill its duty in every respect. Long live the mighty, the free Russian people!!!"

"Hurra-a-a-ah!" The cries surged back and forth around the square. But what encouraged Rodzyanko most of all was an officer who bounded up the steps to stand next to him:

"Long live the Father of the Russian Revolution!" he shouted, in ringing tones. And that was the signal for twenty hands to lift that heavyweight Father in his turn, and carry him into the entrance hall.

Anyway, it was time: for now the car bringing Milyukov himself, bringing the glorious—or odious—hero of the day was arriving at last! People rushed to pick him up straight from his seat in the car and carry him up the steps, but he resisted—or, rather, was bristling, and walked there by himself. He wore a felt hat and forgot to take it off for his speech. He looked at the crowd rather ferociously, tensely, as if here too he expected to see not supporters but enemies. And he began speaking with difficulty, as if his throat was dry:

"I . . . saw the placards. But I am . . . defending the interests of the people. And I shan't leave until I have fulfilled my duty. Or . . . I die."

And he stood, fearlessly. He could have been torn apart. He was a target, provoking the common people with his soft overcoat, his very white muffler round his neck, his spectacles and soft hat.

But not only did not a single voice attack him or a single hostile hand reach for him, but he was enveloped in the sympathetic warmth and amicable hum that rose from the square. And the minister, now moving on to the attack:

"I am the Milyukov who, on 14 November, revealed the intrigues and treachery of the old Tsarist minister Stürmer! I am the Milyukov who took a stand against a separate peace! Surely I'm not to be branded a traitor to the Russian cause, the same stigma with which I branded my enemies?"

The crowd's response came—it was never in doubt. But the inertia of his constant readiness made him carry on, exposing himself to a terrible danger:

"Yes! We must end this war with a victory! I'm saying that again. And anyone who wants to can shout 'down with Milyukov' to my face."

But no one shouted any such abomination and only approval was heard. And he went on, becoming ever more determined:

"Shall I be alive then? Or dead? It's all the same to me. But it is not all the same to me if Russia covers itself in shame! Or if we fall prey to our enemies. That's why the old regime collapsed—because it failed to meet its obligations to the Allies. The Provisional Government and I will not allow Russia to be accused of treason. I shall do my duty and not leave my post willingly. Do you trust me?"

"Oh yes, we trust you! We trust you! We trust you! Long live Milyukov! Hurra-a-ah!"

Whereupon an officer—but a different officer—bounded nimbly up the steps and announced, in a piercing voice:

"Ladies and gentlemen! Milyukov sacrificed his only son for the good of Russia."

He'd remembered correctly, and not everyone knew that. Having lost his son in this war, Milyukov could have a preoccupation with victory!

"Hurrah! Hurrah! Hurra-a-ah!" and Milyukov too was now held aloft and carried. Then the members of the Soviet's Executive Committee started arriving in cars, several in each. No one recognized them—their photos didn't appear anywhere. But clearly they were not our ministers. They were met with a cold, hostile silence. No one was expecting speeches from them or rushing to bear them aloft into the palace. Above the palace the pale, yellowish moon was now high in the sky. People started leaving the square after some people had shouted: let's go to the English Embassy!

At a little distance from the entrance stood a French officer with two compatriots, a gentleman and a lady.

"That government," he said to them, "has turned out to be more *provisional* than we thought. It's history repeating itself. The same thing's happened here as in France—the people have knocked on the ministry window and announced: 'You no longer exist!'"

[6 2]

Such a disagreeable, completely unexpected conflict—and at such an inopportune moment!

For the past six weeks Prince Georgi Evgenievich had had occasion to meet only nice people, such as the unassuming, brave soldiers of army deputations, a delegation from the Russian theater association in Moscow bringing their new theater statutes, a Jewish delegation coming to thank him for their equal rights, and some old officials from his own ministry offering friendly advice to the new regime. And that same friendly climate pervaded the never-ending stream of telegrams that poured in. (And they came from all corners! There was one from Herzen's family living in Lausanne! When would they have ever heard of or remembered Prince Lvov up to then? But now he was replying to them.) Prince Lvov had definitely never met any of the repugnant monsters of the Tsarist regime who'd had all Russia—including him—in a stranglehold. And if, in some parts of our vast Russia, an impatient political creativity was seen and various types of new committees, new forms, were appearing and humming with activity, and if no one wanted to wait for the best lawyers in the land to work out impeccable new regulations for them, and if it had gone as far as disputes with landowners and the seizure of lands and thoroughly brazen nationalist demands for secession from Russia (invented problems, these—why hadn't they existed before?)—if all that was happening, it was due to a single cause: distance. The impossibility of meeting everyone personally, meeting their eyes with a kindly smile. As it happened, Prince Lvov was just then convening, for the day after tomorrow, a conference of provincial commissars from the central provinces, to overcome that incomprehension at a distance, when suddenly . . .

Despite the frequent, cordial meetings with representatives of the Soviet (who were, by and large, not bad people and some of them were really splendid), it was clear that there, too, something was being left unsaid, something not quite understood, and it had to do with that unfortunate note. It was extraordinary that they still, even now, blamed the government, even though they'd been in contact with us the whole time! So there has to be a meeting today! A meeting with the largest possible number of representatives, all the government, the whole dozen of us, and about forty will come from the Executive Committee. It might be a good idea if, so as to increase the number on our side, we invite Rodzyanko with his whole Duma Committee as well—we'll meet, come to an agreement, and everything will take its normal course again.

During these last six weeks, no one in the Mariinsky Palace had given any thought to Rodzyanko, his committee, or even the whole of the Duma. It was as if they'd never existed and had no role to play. But now it turned out that they were the very people we needed. How authoritative they'd look, at this joint meeting, like arbiters, especially Rodzyanko himself. And, via the newspapers, what an impression it would make on society.

Georgi Evgenievich phoned Mikhail Vladimirovich, who was very flattered and of course agreed.

The session was fixed for nine o'clock in the evening at the Mariinsky, but no one wanted to go over there, through that crowd, any earlier. All the organization was done by telephone, from the War Minister's residence. Then they brought the meeting with General Alekseev to some kind of conclusion, and following that the ministers conferred on what line they should follow at the evening meeting. Milyukov stood his ground, uncompromising on the content of his note, every word of it. He demanded, and was insistent on this, that all members of the government should hold to this line, because the whole government had approved the note, unanimously. And that was indeed the case—there was no getting away from it. How unfortunate! Could anyone have foreseen the trouble that would brew up as a result?

They were sure that by evening, as darkness fell, the throng would disperse—but it did quite the opposite! And the ministers had to get to the meeting through that excited crowd—though it turned out that by now the only people thronging the area round the Mariinsky Palace were friendly demonstrators.

For this large-scale meeting, they had readied a hall in the part of the palace where the now defunct State Council had sat. And, being unused to such meetings, they'd given no thought to the procedure. And a complicated incident arose. The press had spent the whole day languishing, rushing about, observing, agonizing, and now a great throng of correspondents from all the main papers of both capitals was in the Mariinsky Palace, standing in front of Prince Lvov and asking him to let them into the joint session in view of its importance. Well, openness is the sister of freedom, and the whole country would be all the better informed if he did. Lvov conferred with Tereshchenko and Nekrasov—and the press were invited to take their places in the hall.

The exultant correspondents made their way in, taking with them a team of shorthand writers, and took over a corner of the hall, setting out papers and sharpened pencils. They were ready before anyone else: the conference participants had not yet assembled.

While they were gathering, Skobelev suddenly came up to Lvov and declared, with a slight stammer, that the Executive Committee was firmly against the presence of the press. A fine kettle of fish! And how was it that the prince hadn't asked them beforehand? He hadn't imagined that they could be against openness. It was very awkward now, very awkward. But there was nothing for it—the prince went over to the press tables and said he was obliged to inform them that the Executive Committee was categorically opposed to their presence.

The correspondents were surprised—stunned, indignant—but they'd just have to comply, wouldn't they? And they filed out of the hall with their shorthand writers, the latter taking with them the pencils they'd got ready. The staff at the door were given strict instructions not to readmit them.

But the press corps immediately sent a collective letter requesting that Prince Lvov make the question of a press presence the first item for discussion.

Whatever was there to discuss? But he conferred again, this time with Chkheidze. Refused.

But even before they'd all assembled and the session had started came another request from the fast-working correspondents, this one addressed to Chkheidze:

"Nikolai Semyonovich! We journalists have, from the first days of the revolution, given sufficient proof of our attitude to the serious moments in the life of our homeland and have earned the right to be present at a session of such consequence. And the Provisional Government gave us that permission. To our great surprise, we were ordered out by the Soviet of Workers' and Soldiers' Deputies. We consider that a grievous error. We know how to do our duty."

The Soviet side was perplexed. They conferred. They went to Lvov again: the Provisional Government must join us and endorse this veto.

"But we don't have any objection to their presence," replied the prince, gently.

"But you're obliged to show solidarity with the Soviet and not shift the odium onto us. The situation is too critical—we can't have the press blabbing about it and distorting things in the bourgeois papers."

Now the ministers conferred: so as not to damage our relationship, must we give in?

Skobelev went and announced to the journalists: the veto is also on the part of the Provisional Government, because we cannot let everything said at this conference become public.

The journalists were not at all convinced by that: but we're certainly not planning to give away any confidential data. We agree not to report everything—we understand! The presidium can look through our reports and edit things out.

But no one liked the idea of having to spend all night working on this.

The session began.

But the correspondents in the Square Hall, with its upper and lower galleries and Pompeian décor, and those in the press room pined, languished, agonized, and sent notes into the meeting: if there are eighty people in there anyway, then journalists—who earned the right to be trusted during the days of the revolution—also have a civic duty to be there!

At last—it was already past midnight—a grim Guchkov came, dark bags under his eyes. He was taking personal responsibility for vetoing the press: he and Shingarev had been presenting confidential statistics.

[63]

(PETROGRAD STREETS, TOWARD NIGHTFALL)

* * *

Nevsky Prospect, evening, with light from street lamps and shop windows. A hundreds-strong crowd forges its way toward Znamenskaya Square, marching in the middle of the road and waving hats and caps. The crowd is civilian but there are a good few soldiers and officers too. And a placard: "Confidence in the Provisional Government!" They're greeted warmly from both sidewalks.

Cabs and trams are held up.

* * *

Two hundred or so high school students march along Nevsky with a silk banner: "Lenin and co., back to Germany go!" They got that from the war invalids' demonstration on Sunday. Cries of approval, laughter, and applause from the sidewalks.

* * *

Two names, "Lenin" and "Milyukov," are in the air. Lively debates, cries of indignation.

An ensign, who has a St. George cross:

"And what effect would Milyukov's departure have on the front—have you thought about that?"

"He's a bourgie, your Milyukov. You're all bourgies."

A new word like that, "bourgie"—you don't know how to respond.

"Do you remember how excited we all were after his speech at the State Duma?"

"Who's 'we'?"

A gentleman, southern type:

"To run a state, you need a statesman-like brain and a great deal of knowledge. And you mustn't try the Allies' patience—just think of the money we owe them. They'll start taking tough measures."

A group of mounted Cossacks approaches:
"We ask you to disperse. Government order."
A shout from a leather jacket: "What government's that?"
Wags in the crowd: "Lenin's!"
Everyone laughs.

* * *

On Znamenskaya Square there's a crowd several thousand strong. On the platform of a military truck, soldiers. One makes a speech calling for calm and order. He's applauded. But a student climbs up and makes a speech against Milyukov and the Provisional Government. The crowd doesn't want to listen:

"Down with the Leninists," they shout. "Down with the Bolsheviks!"

There's a constant succession of speakers on the pedestal of the Aleksandr III monument too.

"It's the capitalists who are making war, they're the only ones who'll benefit! The secret treaties must be published immediately!"

"What about everything the Germans have seized? Are they to keep it?"

"That's up to the inhabitants of those territories. On the front there's already fraternization with the Germans!"

"How can we fraternize with the Germans when they haven't got rid of Wilhelm? Does that mean we've got to fraternize with Wilhelm?"

"No! For them fraternization is the start of their revolution!"

A war invalid: "If it comes to that, we'll go, disabled soldiers and disabled officers—and we'll fight to the end."

But a sizeable demonstration from the Tube Factory pours in from Nevsky: "Forward to peace under the banner of Zimmerwald," "Down with Milyukov!"

They advance into the light of the street lamps. But they're met with hostile shouts. And there's no room for them in the square. They branch off along Ligovka.

* * *

Several demonstrations with Bolshevik slogans approach the Tauride Palace that evening. But there aren't even any lights on in the palace and no one comes out to the demonstrators. Their own speakers address them: we must topple the Provisional Government! They leave, crossing the Neva.

Late in the evening, a detachment of Volynians—the regiment that initiated the revolution—arrive at the Tauride Palace. "Long live the Provisional Government!" But here, where it used to hum with activity even at night, there's no one about. The Volynians march off to Mariinskaya Square.

* * *

Immediately across the Liteiny Bridge, in Nizhegorodskaya Street, a large rally has assembled—against the government and against the war. One speaker introduces himself: Margolin, member of the Soviet of Workers' Deputies. He speaks for a good while, about how the Provisional Government has deceived the people and not fulfilled its promises of 9 April. And how, at the Mikhailovsky Theater yesterday, he heard with his own ears Milyukov and Kerensky saying that we can only have peace with annexations and indemnities. Suddenly a loud voice from the crowd:

"My name is Zarudny. I'm a vice-minister to Kerensky. What you say is impossible. It's a provocation and a lie. And you are not Margolin!"

The crowd starts getting excited. They rush at the speaker—but he's vanished into thin air.

* * *

A demonstration, by workers only, emerges onto Nevsky Prospect and continues on for a while. At the head of the march are thirty or forty men with slung rifles. People observing from the sidewalks stand transfixed: these aren't soldiers with rifles but workers! That makes a big impression. They definitely won't give them up now without a fight.

* * *

On Nevsky a commotion is heard, shouts, coming in from Liteiny. Lit by the many street lamps here, a massive demonstration pours in. At the head is a large group of soldiers, and more soldiers form a cordon round the march. Their roars split the air:

"Long live the Provisional Government!"

"Down with Lenin!"

"Down with the Leninists!"

The trams have been brought to a halt and all the traffic stopped. They advance in their ranks, row after row—first-year and junior cadets, members of the intelligentsia, officers, women:

"Join us, comrades! For Milyukov!"

When the front of the march has turned onto Nevsky, the tail is somewhere far beyond Zhukovsky Street.

* * *

Along Nevsky Prospect there are debates at every crossroads.

"Why is it suddenly 'peace without indemnities'? Does that mean peoples who've lost everything are to be left destitute? Does that mean the Germans can hold on to the billions they stole from us?"

"Without annexations and indemnities—that means that *we* aren't demanding them any more. But what if someone demands them from *us*? Hadn't you thought of that?"

"That's not acceptable for the honor of the Russian people!"

"What do we care about your honor? What we want is peace!"

"You'll notice that all the extremist tendencies are led by doctrinaire émigrés."

But although the debates are impassioned, there are no scuffles.

* * *

Wherever more educated groups have formed, they all support the Provisional Government:

"Milyukov knows all the ins and outs of diplomacy! He's the most competent in foreign policy! What more do they want?"

"Milyukov and Guchkov were the most dangerous people for Tsarism! Are we going to chuck them overboard now?"

"Do we have to throw out the people who've spent their lives fighting the Sukhomlinovs and Protopopovs? People who paved the way for the overthrow? Tomorrow, will it be Chkheidze and Kerensky that we don't need anymore?"

"They're just annoyed that the revolution didn't bring them immediate prosperity, and lumping the blame onto the Foreign Ministry."

Militiamen do the rounds of the demonstrations, on foot and by car, asking the citizens to disperse.

They disperse. But ten steps farther on they get together again somewhere else.

* * *

On Nevsky Prospect—and everywhere else in the center of town—the bowlers, shiny buttons, ladies' millinery, student caps, and friendly soldiers increase in number from hour to hour—and the balance changes. Now the prevailing mood favors the government and continuing the war.

A gentleman in a top hat:

"Citizens! Now that we've toppled the old government in the name of victory—surely we won't shrink from advancing toward that victory?"

A lady with a sable muff:

"We didn't rid ourselves of the Nikolai II and Rasputin regime only to start a civil war now!"

Cars are seen here and there along Nevsky Prospect, with workers in them:

"Citizens, don't get excited. The Soviet of Workers' Deputies is calling for calm and restraint from everyone and securing the primacy of the people's will. A resolution will be published tomorrow."

But the Nevsky crowd is not thinning out—it even seems to be expanding, warming up.

* * *

Armed militiamen drive past slowly, asking the demonstrators to disperse and wait quietly for the Soviet's decisions.

At that moment some different militiamen emerge from Sadovaya, with a red banner: "Long live the social revolution!"

What a rumpus then.

* * *

About midnight, there's an ad hoc meeting in front of the Public Library. A cynical stranger is laying into the Provisional Government. At first the crowd listens calmly, then they start demanding his name.

"I'm a member of the Soviet of Workers' Deputies!"

"Your credentials."

He starts rummaging in his pockets—and doesn't find them. A clamor arises. The crowd starts advancing on him with threats. His pals screen him and he slips away.

* * *

After midnight there's a rumor that the Tsarskoye Selo regiments loyal to the government are marching on Petrograd.

* * *

Mounted soldiers gallop along the now emptying Nevsky, five of them, rifles slung slantwise across their backs:

"Down with Lenin! Do not trust him!"

[6 4]

In the square in front of the Mariinsky Palace, even after ten o'clock at night the crowd had not dispersed. Neither had it at eleven o'clock, nor even toward midnight. Not only had it not dispersed, it actually seemed to be growing. Everyone was held there by the knowledge that here in front of them, in the palace, right now . . .

And the crowd, becoming ever more united, thanks to standing there and chatting to the people nearby, waited: perhaps we'll get a chance this very night to get involved and exert some influence? *What* was happening there, in the palace? They could imagine endless permutations of the course and outcome of that so very important session.

"Russia will never forgive us if we can't save her at this moment of trial."

"We can only save her if we stay united. We must sacrifice the personal for the common good!"

"We must have faith!"

"Yes, faith is the only resource we have left, alas."

"The bloodless revolution seemed such a miracle! But here we are again with nothing to believe in but a miracle."

Lights were seen, enigmatic, in many of the palace windows, but few people knew the interior layout: just where could the meeting be happening now? What were they doing to our ministers in there? Were they trying to make them buckle, crush them?

"No, ladies and gentlemen, our revolution has the healthy instinct to put the country first! After all, the Executive Committee isn't calling for overthrowing the government. Good sense is already starting to prevail."

"'The power of the masses.' It sounds pretty, but it's a pipe dream. The masses cannot rule themselves without a minority leading the way, people who are used to thinking rationally and responsibly. That's why it's so important for the intelligentsia not to lose their heads now."

"And we mustn't forget, even in the most terrible times, that the excesses sparked off by freedom are also put right by freedom!"

From time to time scouts were sent in, to insinuate themselves into the meeting somehow, to discover something or ask someone, anyone, to come and address the crowd. But all they discovered was that even correspondents from the leading newspapers weren't allowed into the session!

What was it, what ever was it that they were deciding in there?? People's hearts were in their mouths.

No, we won't leave. Don't break up this gathering!

Just before midnight General Kornilov drove up to the palace and walked in, with a businesslike air. No one dared pick him up for the usual tribute and they did not ask him to make a speech but, as he made his way inside, the Petersburg crowd applauded enthusiastically and shouted their appreciation. Our general, our bringer of hope!

Today's noxious fumes must be dispelled without fail! This is where Russia's hopes lie.

No one knows what will save Russia, but she will be saved—by something strong, radiant, life-giving.

Soon after that, movement could be seen at the windows giving onto the second-floor balcony. Silhouettes were fumbling with something behind a glazed door. Was something going wrong in there? Then someone opened the next window along and a man, in overcoat and hat, squeezed out over the windowsill. Who was it? By the light of street lamps and reflections from the windows and the moon—

Nekrasov again! He jumped down onto the balcony, took off his hat and waved it in greeting, to attract attention. He was met by applause that reverberated around the square. And he spoke, inspired, his voice resonant, making sweeping gestures:

"Citizens! Minister of Foreign Affairs Milyukov" (wild applause and shouts of "hurrah, hurrah!" silence him for a moment) "is now giving his report on a question of the greatest importance to the state!"

What words these were! Even Nekrasov could not help his voice wavering: the crowd fell silent and waited.

"He cannot come out to you at this moment but he will come as soon as he finishes giving his report."

"Hurra-a-a-ah." That was even too deafening. Milyukov was becoming a symbol. But Nekrasov was not lost for words either:

"Citizens! Little groups of people cannot get the better of the Provisional Government! Those little groups are trying to present themselves as a large, organized movement, to pass themselves off as the voice of the people—yet they remain little groups. Your presence here proves they have no firm footing! The government is sure of the people's support and it will fulfill its duty."

What a commotion now! What exclamations, what applause! Yes, this is exactly what we believed in! What we hoped for! Russia will escape a bad outcome.

After Nekrasov, the crowd was more cheerful as they waited: our ministers aren't surrendering in there—they're even taking the upper hand!

And twenty minutes or so later they saw the high, glazed door onto the balcony, now clearly unbolted, open. And out through it came Milyukov, looking as imposing as usual, no hat on his large, grizzled head, bespectacled.

Finally the whole square saw him, including those who could not see him before, at the entrance, and their roar of approval knew no bounds, surging beyond the Moika, beyond the Astoria, and beyond St. Isaac's.

Whether it was thanks to the substantial height of the balcony, or to the success of his report, Milyukov seemed much calmer and freer than he had on the steps three hours earlier. And he gave a speech that was far more fluent, academic, and explicatory, even starting with a joke:

"Citizens! When, earlier today, I learned of the demonstrations and the placards proclaiming "down with Milyukov," I must confess I was frightened. But it wasn't for Milyukov that I was frightened, but for Russia: if that mood was shared by the majority, then just what was the situation in Russia? What would the ambassadors of the Allied powers say? They'd immediately have telegraphed their governments and told them Russia had betrayed its Allies and removed itself from their number."

He held his head high and, with increasing resolve:

"The Provisional Government cannot espouse that point of view. The Provisional Government and I, as Minister of Foreign Affairs, will do everything in our power to defend a position in which no one can accuse Russia of treachery. Russia will never agree to a separate peace—a shameful peace! As I said just now in the meeting, the ship of the Provisional Government is rigged, its sails unfurling. This ship can only advance when the wind blows, the wind of trust. And now I hope that you will furnish that wind."

A promising, joyous hum of voices around the square.

"We await your trust. With it, we can speed off on our way. And, with your trust behind us, we shall lead Russia onto the path of freedom and prosperity!"

Applause and exclamations:

"Long live . . . Long live . . ."

And hurra-a-a-a-a-a-a-ah . . .

And Milyukov swept off, every inch the victor.

Then the meeting continued, but the result was already clear.

The twenty-five thousand strong crowd began to dwindle. Groups of young people chorused the chant:

"Lenin and co., back to Germany go!!"

And in the now thinning crowd the cries resounded more frequently, and more noisily:

"Down with Lenin!"

"Arrest Lenin!"

But actually—who'd take that job on?

[65]

The meeting had been set up in a spacious hall deep inside the palace. The Executive Committee members were amazed as, in their shabby jackets, they filed through the magnificent Rotunda and then the no less splendid Square Hall, which also had colonnades on two levels. And past the delicate openwork balustrades everywhere, echoing the arabesques of the ornamentation, and across floors that were almost like mirrors—careful not to slip! Finally they arrived in the third hall. Here caryatids supported an enormous marble fireplace, on the walls all around were murals of stories from antiquity and everything was, again, interwoven with ornamentation. The cleanliness and orderliness of these halls flooded with electric light did, however, make it a strange little world, plucked out of the dirty, tumultuous revolutionary city and suspended above it, with an air of unreality. Yes, a government could, sitting there, certainly lose touch with reality. The millstones of Russian state policy had, after all, already been slowly turning in that palace for a century, and now life had overtaken them and they had seized up.

Eighty people in all had gathered to participate and there was not room for all of them at the big table, in the imposing armchairs of the State Council, so the rest sat on comfortable couches around the walls.

Everyone who'd been raised in status by the revolution, or not too drastically lowered, all Russia's new bosses—they were all here. The ministers sat at one part of the table—only Kerensky was missing. Chkheidze, Tsereteli, and Skobelev, the EC leaders, sat at another part. At one of the long sides of the table sat Rodzyanko—almost taking up two places—and the Duma Committee. Skinny little Himmer had to make do with a place on a distant couch, next to the boring, almost immobile Stalin.

The ministers had girded themselves for a robust defense. Earlier that day, at Guchkov's residence, they had already agreed: so as not to find themselves in the position of the accused immediately, they would begin this meeting not with the contentious diplomatic note but would first put it into the right framework: they must make the Soviet representatives understand the overall complexity and difficulty of running the Russian state. And Prince Lvov, opening the session, announced that each of these gentlemen, the ministers, would set out for the Executive Committee, within the limits of his own area of responsibility, the state of affairs in the country. Why this approach?

"The critical situation that has developed regarding the note is, gentlemen, only one particular case. Recently the government in general has been under suspicion, and we are sensing more and more often the Soviet's mistrust." Lvov's soft, somewhat honeyed tones conveyed an undeserved hurt. "Yet the government has done nothing to merit this: the Liaison Commission is our essential support and we always, on all issues, come to a joint decision together with the commission, and we carry it out. The 'insomuch-insofar' formula, in relation to your support, never troubled us. But now we feel no offer of support at all, and even an undermining of our authority. If this is the case, we do not think we are within our rights to bear the responsibilities we do. And we decided to invite you to explain your actions."

That was a misrepresentation of this session's history, wasn't it? It was the EC that had demanded it.

"We need to know," explained the prince humbly, "whether we are fit for our responsible role at the present time. If not, then for the good of the country we are ready to lay aside our authority and cede it to others."

What's that? What's he talking about? The ministers hadn't agreed on anything of the kind! What's he doing? Has he gone mad? Milyukov was outraged, but this was not the time to express objections aloud. How on earth could he? Why start by capitulating? Now, of all times, when the talk was about dismissing individual ministers, how could his counterproposal be resignation? Spineless!

Meanwhile, Guchkov had stepped up to the rostrum to speak first. This was nothing like the warrior, his health briefly restored, who earlier today had urged the ministers to resist the Soviet. He looked ill, old, and spoke gloomily—which did, though, chime with the subject he was addressing. His speech was wide-ranging, even touching on how the Tsarist government had led the army to disaster (his hobby horse, this). He gave an overall view of the situation on the fronts and the impressions he'd gleaned from his trips. At the beginning of his time as minister he'd felt optimistic. He'd entertained hopes that the Russian people, who had so magnificently managed the hard task of bringing down the old regime, would show enthusiasm and crush the external enemy too; that the same momentum would manifest itself in the Russian revolution as had appeared in the equivalent stages of the French. But in Russia, for some reason, the opposite had occurred. Guchkov had now lost his optimism. It had been extinguished by the facts. He had to say, openly, that on the psychological level the army's situation was giving rise to the gravest concerns. He would consider it criminal if, today, he did not inject some poison, a salutary dose of alarm, into the minds of those present. No, the situation was not hopeless, but it was extremely grave. And the most drastic measures were needed. The masses' understanding of the conversations about peace was simplistic: they thought we could achieve peace by immediately laying down our arms. Sitting here, in Petrograd, we had to be brave enough to imagine that the talk about a general peace had given rise to chaos and low spirits in the trenches.

The Soviet section of the listeners was outraged by these attacks. They exchanged looks: this was another offensive against their universal peace program! (Himmer was actually writhing in indignation!) Guchkov did, it's true, tone things down in his closing words, saying that neither he nor anyone else in the government intended any conquests: even our military situation alone meant we had to abandon that idea.

And—had the ministers still not finished? Shingarev now? What was wrong with them? The streets were seething and here they were holding academic lectures!

But, said Shingarev, the food issue is no less important than the state of the army. Thanks to doctrinaire social demands from extremist elements—and here he got really annoyed—our hope of regulating the food supply is becoming just a mirage. And the Leninists—he moved to a frontal attack—are, in their party's blind fanaticism, whipping up among the peasants a hunger for confiscating land. The Kshesinskaya palace is a nest generating venom. And as for grain—there won't be any.

Well, even if all that's true—we can't allow that tone to be used against the revolutionary democracy!

Then Shingarev softened his tone, now more conciliatory: both on the railways and in the barges there are already millions of poods of grain. We just have to wait for a few weeks, until the first results of navigation season. And we'll survive till the next harvest.

But when would they get round to that ill-starred note? When were we going to hear from Milyukov? He was sitting there among the ministers like a stuffed dummy. But it was the sugar millionaire who now approached the rostrum, his step light, sure of himself. He did not, though, begin with finance but went straight into the note, and his words were quite challenging.

Yesterday's note was no more than a rephrasing and development of the government declaration of 9 April, which was drawn up together with the Soviet. We do not understand—and consider unfounded—the mistrust the note has occasioned in Soviet circles. It's a sad disservice that the Soviet has done us! This mistrust could lead our Allies to break off all relations with us—but we're only managing to survive with their aid funding the means to fight the war. And responsibility for the consequences will fall on those who did not want to understand the gravity of this moment.

But **who** didn't want to? Was he saying the EC didn't want to? That the EC didn't understand the need to maneuver as smoothly as possible to get out of this dangerous conflict? This aggression on the ministers' part frightened Tsereteli. They were, basically, right—but that aggressive tone was riling the left wing of the EC and destroying all possibility of the agreement that had to be achieved, at all costs, here today.

In the area of finance, Tereshchenko was now saying that we are pursuing the most normal program, with the drafting of necessary laws already in hand; but this cannot be done quickly. We are already working on a significant extension of direct taxes on high incomes, plus a special war levy on incomes and capital. But while all that is being brought in, active support of the Freedom Loan is essential and we expect that from the Soviet.

For the Soviet group, this area was the shakiest ground.

Now a fourth minister came up! Again, it was not Milyukov, but Nekrasov this time. He spoke briefly, though, and didn't say anything to irritate the Soviet side. Instead, cheerfully: freight transport is being put right and passenger travel too.

To sum up: if, in the work of the whole government, there was one tranquil sector, which was not at odds with the Soviet's wishes, it was this one, Nekrasov's. Very pleasant minister, that Nekrasov.

Finally Chkheidze could not contain himself any longer (after the tension of this second day and a second night with no sleep, his brain was now beginning to fail) and he reminded the ministers that, since we're meeting to discuss the note, should we not hear what the Minister of Foreign Affairs has to say? The note contains propositions that are absolutely unacceptable to the Soviet of Workers' Deputies. It obscures the aims of the war and does not mention a renunciation of annexations and indemnities.

At which, Milyukov should have stood up. But what was he playing at? Could he not get up? Everyone looked at him and began to suspect that perhaps it wasn't strength that kept him frozen in that position, but weakness. Had he been laid low, overwhelmed?

He still didn't stand up, so to jog him into action Tsereteli took the floor: the Minister of Foreign Affairs has clearly not understood the psychology of the new, revolutionary Russia. He is using the methods of the old Tsarist government. In his department everything is continuing in the old way. Not even a single ambassador replaced, anywhere. But now we must, of necessity, address our Allies again, expressing ourselves with revolutionary precision.

There was nothing for it, Milyukov had to go up to the rostrum. But no one had ever before seen him, or heard him, so ill at ease.

The Allies will, naturally, concentrate their attention on the other document, that of 9 April, to which the note is only an attachment. And the Soviet was satisfied with that 9 April text. But in the West there are rumors that Russia is preparing for a separate peace. And it was to dispel those rumors that the formulas you now object to were added. Otherwise it would have been understood as confirmation of those rumors.

Mmm, this scenario was far-fetched, and everyone understood that. Even he knew it. A separate peace: he could perfectly well have forsworn it, straightforwardly.

But in the usual way of a speaker, especially when no one interrupts (which was what he'd feared) Milyukov started to recover. Such a sharp reaction to the note . . . People shouldn't be searching for a meaning that isn't there. And now came a long explanation, which got longer and longer and more convoluted, of certain facts, certain data, which actually confirm . . . And having summoned up fresh energy with all those detours, he was now firm: today's episode will make the most terrible impression on the Allies. Should we send a new note? Absolutely impossible. That would not only fly in the face of all diplomatic traditions and provoke a scandal, it would also outrage the Allies and leave them even more alarmed.

But had he been too firm? His position was, after all, that of the accused. And then, to create trust and even intimacy between him and his listeners, he proposed, infringing all the rules of diplomacy, to divulge here, now—and he was counting on the discretion of those present—the latest confidential diplomatic document he had received from the Allies. (Was he now destroying, as Stürmer had, the *most delicate fibers* of diplomacy?)

With that he won instant attention. But as he started reading . . . what was this? Some little-known, minor diplomat was informing him that the French Ministry of Foreign Affairs did not approve of the idea of a conference between the Allies to revise the objectives of the war.

How clumsy! What a clumsy oaf he was! He'd have done better never to have started all that fuss with the document. He'd only damaged himself.

Tsereteli and Stankevich, worried, exchanged looks. Milyukov was derailing the whole play for consensus.

Tsereteli leant over to Chkheidze and they whispered in Georgian for a moment. Meanwhile, Milyukov went back to his place, and no one else was given the floor. The meeting stopped short.

Prince Lvov froze. They could expect no mercy from the revolutionary Executive Committee—and the government would be crushed there and then!

But no. Chkheidze stood up and, tired, replied from where he was. In view of these facts and figures, the Soviet has agreed to meet the government halfway. The Executive Committee feels that in the current circumstances the departure of the Provisional Government is inadmissible. Strictly speaking, the difference of opinion has arisen only in respect of a foreign policy question. The government must immediately clarify the contents of the note to the citizens of Russia.

He sat down, and Tsereteli immediately rose and went to the rostrum. He took a very soft tone. The note is unsatisfactory, not in its entirety but in individual parts. "War till total victory" has within it the same sense it had in the old imperialist thinking, which we've now rejected. In your clarification, you must give a formulation that will enable the people to understand, clearly, that the Provisional Government does not adhere to the old, chauvinist tendencies. And that clarification must be sent to all the Allies, to the same addressees as before.

So there it was: sentence had been passed. It was extremely lenient to the government. Now, no matter how much longer they talked, it would stay that way. (Oh how Himmer despised those compromisers!)

On hearing this, Nekrasov walked past the armchairs and over to Tsereteli, bent down and quietly proposed that they, the two of them, should go and hammer out the text of those explanations right now. Why Tsereteli was understandable, but why Nekrasov—that was not. But everyone saw them leave the hall together. (A sordid, behind-the-scenes deal! And Stalin, sitting nearby, didn't move a muscle.)

It was already past midnight, the crowds in the streets had dispersed, of course, and perhaps the men at this meeting should have taken pity on their infirmities and gone off to bed too.

But before doing that both the ministers and the Soviet members looked over—in whose direction? To Rodzyanko, of course. The great arbiter, with bellows for lungs—was he not going to draw the conclusion and set his seal on it?

Alas, no. The cauldron that was his head, with its big ears, was not even rising above the armchair and his back was not held straight, but bent over, and he did not meet the expectant looks, casting his eyes down. But that's not possible, that he has nothing to say! He's never been lost for words. But now he was. Was he hurt? Crushed?

But who, of the Duma Committee, should speak now? That was why they were invited. Sitting next to Rodzyanko and quivering like a fiddle-string, almost bursting out of his chair and making signs to Prince Lvov, was young, if balding, Shulgin, sporting his pointed moustache. He was invited to speak. How easily he jumped up and walked over, not as might be expected at midnight, but in the style of his best ascents to the rostrum. Shulgin did, in fact, always mount the steps with a touch—slight as it might be—of scandal, to puncture the general ponderousness with some sharp dissonance:

"To Germany, a total renunciation of annexations and indemnities by all the Allies would be the most acceptable of all possible slogans: then she'd have no need to pay anything for the devastation she's caused. She would be released from the trap she stupidly got herself into. She'd be left with the power she had before the war, and Austria and Turkey would be in her hands. This is Wilhelm's dream. In, say, twenty-five years, or perhaps even sooner, Germany would start another war and attack, among others, Russia. No, gentlemen, we have to think of our future as well, not just the present."

But—who was he addressing that to? What crazy ideas: thinking Germany alone was guilty, Germany alone must be crushed, and even worrying about Germany attacking Russia again, in about 1942. That was old-fashioned thinking, trite and inimical to democracy.

Now, the complete antithesis of Shulgin, the jovial Chernov stepped up to speak, triumphant, self-assured, and generous with his indulgent smiles. He answered everything he needed to in one fell swoop, by talking about the international brotherhood of workers, the unifying power of internationalism, and his own impressions of the West, which were more recent than Milyukov's. He did not stint on the time he gave himself: he liked talking, and had arrived back in Russia so late that a lot had already been said without him. Now he was catching up. All the more reason for the courteous chairman not to impose a time limit. But at a certain point Chernov changed the subject and moved on to Milyukov, the accused at this evening's meeting. He must, said Chernov, embark on a radical reorganization of our diplomatic service and its overseas representatives, whose reactionary leanings had been so basely demonstrated in their efforts to stop the revolutionary émigrés' return. And the note? If they had really decided to renounce annexations and indemnities, then state this directly and categorically. Why express it so timidly? (Here he was, teaching Milyukov to show the pride proper to a great power.) Russia should speak with as powerful a voice as America, not like a poor relation. Pavel Nikolaevich? He was a very estimable man and a first-class statesman, and his participation in the Provisional Government was of course indispensable—but he could admirably display his talents in any other job, couldn't he? Minister for Education, for example?

Milyukov almost groaned out loud, so treacherously had this been prepared. It was as if he'd been poleaxed.

Now came another returned émigré, Zurabov, who had abused Milyukov in the press a few days before, calling him a hypocrite. Now he was going to speak—what form would the attack take now? Milyukov even half-closed his eyes behind his spectacles.

But, strangely, Zurabov dispensed with the personal attacks, and said something the other socialists here had not dared: if the Allies don't agree to renounce annexations and indemnities together with us, then we won't fight a war to defend their interests.

Even so, he didn't dare name openly the matter that nevertheless hung in the air above them, under the State Council chandelier: **separate peace**!

The next speaker would certainly have had no objection: it was the Bolshevik Kamenev. But he only set out his theoretical reckoning as to why any bourgeois government would pursue imperialist policies. But for democratic policies it was essential that the power should be in the hands of the corresponding class.

But it's you who are muddying the water! Cries came from the Soviet side: "Well you take power, then!"

But Kamenev replied that at the present time the Bolsheviks had no aspirations to overthrow the Provisional Government. As for a separate peace—they weren't proposing that either.

Finally, another glib speaker from the Duma, Adzhemov, managed to get the floor. He, too, was not mindful of the late hour or the time that he was taking up, his own and others'.

"The greatest weakness of the old regime was the suspicion that it favored a separate peace. And we were all calling it treachery. So surely now, when the people have prevailed, we . . ." (that includes you!) ". . . aren't going to put ourselves in the same position as the Tsar's underlings? With a bold move, we could put the Allies into the very same state of street unrest that the Provisional Government is now experiencing!" (That scared them!) "You'll say you didn't summon those troops—but they came to support **you**! Thanks to your actions, the government is now orphaned, abandoned!" (Oh, how he scared them!)

Was there already a paler sky outside the windows? The springtime sky of Petersburg . . .

And now came the final speaker, Himmer, exhausted from all his seething. He didn't have any great need to speak then—but he mustn't miss a chance. That whole meeting had been a farce. The majority of the EC, opportunists, had agreed on that vile compromise beforehand—and here, before our very eyes, they had betrayed everything. Nonetheless, even according to Himmer's own theory, the Provisional Government should not be overthrown for the time being. But his intransigent heart was pounding, and he was even annoyed with the Bolsheviks because they had not spoken trenchantly enough here—they, of all people! But what could Himmer do? Well, perhaps a gambit like this: From all the ministers' reports, it's clear that in every area things are collapsing. So, that being the case, how can you dream of continuing the war till total victory?

"And although you hear different opinions from the Executive Committee, the one I express is that of a very great proportion of the popular masses! The people have said clearly that they do not want to tolerate Milyukov's policies any longer and they do not trust a government like that . . ."

He appeared to be contradicting his own theory. It seemed he was being blown closer and closer to Leninist shores. But no one had noticed any of that yet, because they were all so utterly exhausted.

The meeting came to an end at half past three in the morning. At about three, they had all had a shock. First one anxious-looking messenger arrived and whispered his news, then another, and finally everyone got to hear: a military delegation had arrived from the Tsarskoye Selo garrison, representing its four riflery regiments(!) and various other units too. It turned out that the whole garrison had been on their feet all day since early morning and, finally, wanted to know what was happening. They were demanding explanations!

This was rather frightening. When they'd begun that meeting, and then let it go on longer and longer, in the square behind them was a dense crowd, sympathetic to the government and of no danger to the Soviet group. But the crowd had melted away and now, in that pre-dawn period when the palace was unguarded, now the People were knocking on the door with their rifle butts. There was no knowing what they might do. And who was sent out to talk to the delegation? The two healthiest and most indefatigable among them, Skobelev and Tereshchenko. And they explained to the delegation that it was now clear that there was nothing terrible in the note, only a few expressions that had given rise to doubts; but that kind of language was what they used in diplomatic communications. In fact, the government was not seeking annexations or indemnities. There was no serious cause for alarm: this would not mean catastrophe for the revolution. There was no reason to sever relations with the government.

The delegation marked time for a moment—and marched off to their truck, faith restored.

But as for the correspondents, not a single one had left—their papers wouldn't set the pages without their reports. Now they had to catch everyone as they left and question them: what did they think, what did they say at the meeting and what did the others say? Then they immediately descended on Skobelev and Tereshchenko, to see what they could dig up there.

Tereshchenko (knowing something and privately anticipating something that even Milyukov did not know, something that gave him a personal interest in keeping that note unassailable) answered them, triumphantly now:

"The whole Provisional Government is united in accepting the note. Any treachery toward our Allies would mean the end of Russia."

And they threw the journalists something else to chew on overnight, dictating a declaration from the Executive Committee: the Soviet of Workers' and Soldiers' Deputies did not organize today's demonstration by military units against the Provisional Government. That was a misunderstanding, put in train by certain persons who were not up to their job.

"Which persons?"

"We're looking into that."

[66]

For the previous morning, the 3rd, Lenin had drawn up a balanced, restrained resolution in the name of the party's Central Committee—and then waited to see how things would develop.

All the socialist newspapers had come out with an attack on Milyukov's note. But at the Executive Committee those Social Democrat halfwits hadn't managed to come to a decision all day. Typical!

They hadn't managed to stir up the factories all morning and even by midday they hadn't stopped work.

But what was quite amazing was that the regiments were beginning to march! That was tremendously significant! Such political receptiveness from the petit-bourgeois mass of the soldiery—no, we could never have expected that! That had made a tremendous impression on Lenin! What a success! The garrison already on our side!?

Over there on Mariinskaya Square, regiment after regiment was arriving, while here, at the Kshesinskaya mansion, Lenin was rushing about in an excess of revolutionary impatience. For the first time in his life he felt the wind of popular insurrection on him! It was outstripping us—and we hadn't organized it! And now it was already in full swing on the streets of the Russian capital! Had the civil war already started? What should we decide now, what slogan should we launch?? Before all the leaders of all the revolutions, from Spartacus to the Commune, Lenin was now responsible for making no errors and not losing the struggle.

A cool head (or perhaps it was just petit-bourgeois good sense?) told him that we didn't yet have organized forces, the Red Guard wasn't ready, the working class didn't have enough weapons . . . But his soaring, impatient revolutionary instinct (an infallible instinct!) was straining to take off into the clouds, itching for insurrection! This is the time to strike! That's what succeeds in a revolution—surprise attacks! Perhaps it would be possible, now, to topple the government??

But there weren't enough agitators! He'd sent Safarov to address the crowds in the center of town—and he'd been arrested in front of the Public Library and taken off to the militia.

If, for example, we could have persuaded the armored division to come out now onto Mariinskaya Square as well, and arrest the Provisional Government, the job would have been done! Then we would have moved on to instilling our proletarian will into the Soviet.

But the armored division didn't want to come out without instructions from the EC.

Meanwhile, the day was passing.

Only four regiments out of twenty had taken part in the march.

And those vile conciliators in the EC had already announced that they would be going to the Mariinsky Palace tonight, to arrange things with their capitalist colleagues. What drivellers! It was enough to vomit!

And with their same trite verbiage they'd dragged out the evening session of the Soviet, thus preventing it from coming to a revolutionary decision.

It was not only Lenin who was seething with anger, but all the other leading Bolsheviks too. They were descending from all corners of the capital and organizing ad hoc conferences here. And shouting:

"The Soviet must seize power from the Provisional Government!"

"Replace the whole government!"

Bogdatiev came hotfoot from the Petersburg Committee, which was in permanent session:

"They're holding rallies in the factories! Our immediate directive is 'down with the Provisional Government!' And the workers are organizing themselves to bring it down!"

Slutsky was hesitant: was this the right time to overthrow the government?

Akselrod, his jaw set firm: all power must pass to the Soviet.

To general laughter, Stal called on her comrades not to be more left-wing than Lenin himself.

Lenin was walking up and down, chuckling.

Sometimes you have to let a force of nature roll unimpeded.

Kollontai's eyes shone like stars:

"Vladimir Ilyich, let's have an insurrection!!"

These days she was doing trade union work with the laundresses, readying them for a massive strike. Again Lenin laughed the suggestion off:

"We're not going to join a socialist government either, Aleksandra Mikhailovna, at any rate. We'll criticize them from outside."

But, most definitely under her influence, he began to get particularly agitated, his voice gruff. Ultimately, even if we didn't succeed (which was the most likely outcome) it would still be a test of our capabilities! And a chance to look at the opposition's capabilities! Such ventures make the masses stronger! (But if we're beaten, will we have to hightail it . . .?)

By this time, night was upon us and everyone was asking what instructions were to be given to the agitators, out at their positions. Occupy the factories and plants? Go out onto the street armed?

Yes! Everyone—out to the plants and the regiments! Learn how to persuade! Learn how to agitate! Find crushing arguments! Incite as many military units as possible! Tomorrow, all detachments of workers are to be on the streets, armed! Explain to them that we're bearing arms for self-defense, but in the event of trouble—shoot! Don't write "down with Milyukov" on the banners—there's no point whatsoever in that, you'd be fooling yourselves—put "down with the Provisional Government!" The whole government is capitalist: it's a matter of class, not of individuals.

And off they dashed! Tearing off on foot and by car!

No sooner decided than acted on!

And Lenin, even more wrought up now, paced the second floor all night.

How sudden it was, how vast this enterprise!

It was one thing to give agitators a slogan orally or to write it on banners—it was obeying a force of nature, the will of the masses. But what would the Central Committee decide?

It was clear that a new CC resolution had to be prepared for the morning. Something more aggressive. But also very carefully formulated so that it could be tipped in one direction or the other depending on how events progressed. A Central Committee resolution was the official position of the party. You don't trifle with that.

. . . We are absolutely not threatening civil war. This is the mass of soldiers and workers replacing all the authorities. At a moment like this it is essential that we *submit to the will of the majority of the population*. And if it comes to violence, then it's the Provisional Government's responsibility! In order to ascertain the opinion of this majority of the population we must organize, immediately, a people's poll in every district of Petrograd, about their attitude to the note. And *about the desirability of one or another kind of Provisional Government!*

The Commune!! We'll organize a poll that will raise a real storm—and sweep away the Provisional Government! And there'll be a Commune!

. . . We must address the people, propagate our views and organize systematic polling in the plants and regiments . . .

It won't be a real vote, of course—who would arrange that, and how?—but a new and ingenious form of insurrection: insurrection during the polls!

And another idea for a line of attack:

. . . The reason the Guchkov-Milyukov government is trying to exacerbate the situation is that they know the workers' revolution in Germany **is already beginning**!

It was indeed possible, very, very possible, that it was already beginning. And Lenin's breast was bursting with excitement at that thought!

We must tell the masses the whole truth:

. . . By spreading rumors of irreparable devastation, the Provisional Government is browbeating the people into leaving the power in their hands . . . There is *no* other way out than to transfer the power to the revolutionary proletariat!

He'd told them frankly—but, at the same time, not so frankly. He'd told them—but hadn't revealed his mind.

. . . The policies of the current leaders of the Soviet are profoundly mistaken. Their attempts at conciliation with the Provisional Government are just adding pointless paperwork. That goes against the will of the majority of our revolutionary soldiers . . .

He made up his mind:

. . . at the front!

and

. . . in Petersburg.

And, as the finishing touch to this smokescreen:

. . . Hold another election for your delegates to the Soviet.

Meanwhile the Petersburg Committee sent a messenger over, saying they'd drawn up a leaflet and would have it printed by tomorrow morning, the 4th: "Overthrow the Provisional Government!"

Well, that's not the CC speaking. So give it a try.

The course of the revolution tomorrow will shed light on everything.

[6 7]

After the tragic deaths of 'tiger' Gershuni and Mikhail Gotz, although there was no post of chairman in the SR party and on paper there was no clear, formal leader, it turned out that no matter how you worked it out (removing Grandmother from the list, now too old and even a figure of fun, and that impresario of revolution, Mark Natanson—he was no leader), the party leader in all respects was Victor Chernov—who else? Even he himself could not have accounted for how this had happened over the years, but it did happen. He was the party's best theoretician, best philosopher, best writer. He had not, it's true, picked up the baton directly from the giants of the People's Will, the Zhelyabov group, but over the years he had associated with the transitional semi-giants, Semyon Rappoport, Rubanovich, and Yegor Lazarev. Standards of different generations cannot be exactly duplicated from one generation to the next. (Marx said something about this.)

And was he not duplicating in his own, individual, life the great destiny of the Russian people? He had grown up on the Volga, Russia's backbone. He was from an unsettled family of Old Believer "Runaways"—but are we not all, our whole people, runaways? His grandfather had been a serf, but decided to spare his son the lot of the peasant and sent him to the district's middle school. After school, he'd become junior assistant to the clerk of the district treasury and sat there doing nothing of consequence for forty years, working his way up to the post of district treasurer and receiving the order of St. Vladimir, which brought him personal ennoblement and the title of State Councillor, retired. Outside his work career, on the other hand, he had given free rein to his generous nature: he loved receiving guests and entertaining them lavishly; he was extremely successful at preference, whist, and billiards; he organized choirs and acted in amateur theatricals (he was of a very amorous disposition and was, in his passions, inclined to foolhardy behavior which, clearly, he handed down to Victor along with his good looks). He did not like the church and didn't even know the Lord's Prayer (and Victor didn't get to know much church ritual either). But he knew for sure that all the land must go over to the peasants: the landowners were only playing around with it. "I'm a peasant," he'd say, "and I'll die a peasant." And Victor felt the same. His high-born mother, who died young, had, in the backwoods where they lived, become engrossed in Pisarev's and Kurochkin's periodicals and also owned issues of Herzen's *The Bell*. Then Nekrasov's poems and the cult of the People edged out her misplaced patriotic enthusiasm (she wrote verses on the taking of Plevna, took the Treaty of Berlin as a personal affront, longed for Tsargrad to be returned to Slavdom). In his high school in Saratov, Victor discovered for himself Dobrolyubov, Buckle, and Mikhailovsky while, at the same time, legends were heard around town about socialists and nihilists roaming the eating-houses and marketplaces with daggers and bombs, to stir the people to insurrection. Even in Saratov there were intellectuals who handed down their smarts to the young (Balmashev senior was, alas, an alcoholic, but his little son, a future terrorist, had sat on Chernov's knee). At that time young people started leading a political life at a young age—and thirty-year-olds were regarded as old men.

Chernov was only able to study for a year in the law faculty of Moscow University, and with that his formal education came to an end: he was arrested and held for nine months in prison. Then, thanks to the intercession of the writer Mordovtsev, who pretended Chernov was his nephew, he was released to return to the region of his birth. In Tambov, Chernov carried on developing his populist aspirations and studying Marx a great deal, memorizing whole pages: he wanted to know Marx better than the Marxists, to know the whole arsenal of quotes off by heart, to support his arguments. (He had even experimented with this, making his case for the populist program with a selection of quotations exclusively from Marx, Engels, and Bebel.) He was feeling his way, coming closer and closer to the idea that would be the future basis of the SR: a mass populist movement founded on a close alliance between the peasants and the urban proletariat (with the proletariat in the vanguard and the peasants as the main force), combined with a People's Will kind of terrorism, in which terrorist acts would stand out like solo singers and the mass movement would gradually turn into a populist uprising. With the liberals, it would at first be "march separately, strike together" to deal with the autocracy, but after that victory the battle front would have to turn against the liberals.

Then, under the "coronation" manifesto, he was freed from surveillance. (By a lucky conjunction of circumstances he was never again sent to prison, nor into exile, nor put under surveillance.) And suddenly he felt an irresistible urge to go abroad! To immerse himself entirely in the disputes about ideas and theories that were going on there. And to absorb, to drink in the last word on international socialist thinking! What an attractive, promising prospect. And now he could combine that with something else: there, abroad, he could produce and publish literature for revolutionary propaganda in rural Russia! No sooner said than done. He did what was necessary to acquire a passport for traveling abroad and had the draft statutes for the future revolutionary peasant brotherhood inserted into the heel of his shoe. And in 1899 he left for Zurich, via Petersburg, taking with him his vision of the agrarian revolution that was imminent. In Geneva he became acquainted with Plekhanov—but there was a violent verbal skirmish. They did not get on. But the following year he was also in Paris and got to know the old People's Will members living out their days there: and he adopted their spirited tradition. Then back to Geneva. Mikhail Gotz became his best and closest comrade. Even calling them brothers would be an anemic term for such a meeting of minds. And so, between Geneva and Paris, the years passed. (The party's financial resources were always sufficient, and there was no need to earn a living until the 1914 war.) Countless storms blew up at gatherings of the Russian émigré colonies. He began to get published in Russia as well, in *Russian Wealth*, on philosophical subjects, though he still felt he must arm himself with a broader array of philosophical resources. But the main objective was to produce, abroad, literature for the rural population: this was why the Agrarian Socialist League was created. The resources needed for printing were found, but what kind of literature, exactly, should be written? How much should be produced? How could they get it over to Russia? And who there would distribute and explain it? The League had never had occasion to set up its own branches or agents in Russia.

In 1902 Chernov started wondering whether he should return to Russia to play a more active role. But he was roundly criticized by Gershuni: "People are expecting you to explain the party's future prospects, its program, its strategy, its tactics. You did study under Mikhailovsky, after all." And he stayed in Europe, to fill in gaps in theory, including terrorism theory. (To write about terrorism without, himself, having practiced it, was a difficult, awkward duty for an émigré to take on.) But Chernov's vocation was writing, and his pen never tired—to the extent that much of his writing was never published. He was also a connoisseur of poetry and wrote a little himself (experts were full of praise for his translations of Verhaeren), and a satirist too (he wrote humorous verses on topical subjects for his paper, *Revolutionary Russia,* the main SR organ). But most of all, of course, he was interested in the Europeanization of the populist movement (which was, alas, somewhat provincial): he would introduce some of the Western socialist tradition. He wanted to find theoretical foundations for an alliance between the workers and peasants, to write a set of instructions for work in rural areas. And he was already refining his "statutes for the peasant brotherhood," copying those of the Sicilian farm workers.

This was all the more crucial, given that the Combat Organization was acting independently, without the CC. At this time the SR party was blooming and there had been a series of thunderous actions, crowned by two brilliant attacks using a new dynamite technique, tearing to pieces von Pleve and Sergei Aleksandrovich, and the party was enjoying unparalleled prestige both in Russia and in the International (winning it a place there). In autumn 1904 Chernov represented his party at the Paris conference of all the left- and far left-wing parties (it was only the Social Democrats' attendance that Lenin thwarted), and there he saw his old acquaintance Milyukov. (Twenty years earlier Chernov, a student not yet trusting the power of his own writing, had asked the still-young university lecturer to rewrite, for the masses, a Tan-Bogoraz brochure. Once Milyukov had even chaired a debate between populists and Marxists, and seemed quite like one of their own—it's bizarre how people you know change over the decades!) In 1905, in the Manifesto of 30 October (was it a trap? were they deceiving the revolutionaries in order to arrest them later?), it became clear that Chernov couldn't stay there, abroad. And although the Gotz brothers tried to talk him out of it, saying that CC members had no right to risk their lives, he felt he had to go back. Could this really be the revolution?!

But he assessed the Petersburg situation as extremely insecure: the government is stronger than it thinks, and has just lost its way now. If we start trying to finish it off, it'll find courage in its desperation and this will be bad for us. No, we must be extremely careful in our attack. In Moscow he tried to prevent the strike and uprising, but in vain. (People were already reproaching the SRs with becoming more cautious than the Social Democrats—thus changing places with them.) Alas, the ideas of some of the SRs had proved fallacious. It was an illusion that the awakened peasant soul had been captured by the revolutionary movement and that now the peasantry, whole villages at a time, would immediately rush to join the Peasant Union. The SR slogans had not touched the aching heartstrings of the peasantry. And the troops were not moving toward insurrection. The antiquated foundations of the Russian state had not crumbled. So the entire membership of the SR Central Committee, not having come out of the underground, went abroad.

Then things went from bad to worse. After all their brilliant terrorist successes, History became a wicked stepmother to the SRs: the maximalists split off, then the Azef affair taught them a ghastly lesson and the practical organization crumbled. Even the leading SRs were overcome by a sense of moral catastrophe, an orgy of distress: if only they could run away and forget it all. It even turned out that there were no candidates to replace the leaders.

Those terrible years after 1908 and up to 1914—they would have liked to forget them. They had always been proud of their party's activism—but now the party itself **no longer existed**. There were only leaders, living abroad.

From the start of the war Chernov had, of course, renounced patriotism, stayed loyal to his internationalist principles and was among the few delegates attending Zimmerwald.

But they needn't have worried. Gershuni had been right when, still in Schlüsselburg fortress, he'd written: Russia in the twentieth century is destined to be what France has been since the end of the eighteenth—and, what's more, will escape the contemptible period of petit-bourgeois prosperity that has taken the capitals of Europe in its deadly stranglehold. And how cruelly mistaken Tikhomirov was, on the other hand, when he said our revolution would be Jacobin-Blanquist, that a pre-state would take shape underground beforehand, a kind of mafia, its sole aim to seize power. But the second revolution we'd been waiting for was now taking place! And in the most serene forms, the least bloody. And again now, for a second time, and again through Finland, Chernov returned home, to guide the revolution and reinvigorate the downcast, oh so downcast, SR ranks. Naturally he'd do that through their newspaper, *The People's Cause*. Tireless theoretical development was needed. Its cohort of writers was still there, luckily. But how were they to defend the local organizations? To get into the rural areas, the SRs' ancestral lands? To avoid giving up the proletariat to the Social Democrats? Or the army? The problems he had—it quite took your breath away. And as for leaders—the party was again without any. The older generation had not withstood the ravages of time. And you just had to look at the younger Gotz—he was so comical when he gave orders. Avksentiev had stopped developing and gone badly off course, drifting toward patriotism. The capricious, haughty Savinkov had split off a long time ago and in fact he'd never been one of us. Natanson was still stuck in Switzerland and he was, anyway, too old now. Grandmother was already beyond any kind of bounds for the age of a revolutionary and would ramble on endlessly. (We should have sent her off to America again—she's been good at raising money there.) But what do you find instead, when you get back? A thin specimen in the Khlestakov mould: Kerensky, passing himself off as an old SR. In his heart, you see, he was always one of us, only we'd never known or even seen him. But he behaves with such assurance, and the speed of changes in the SR ranks is now such that the new members immediately accept him as a veteran: for the party he is even becoming a dangerous figure, a conciliator and defensist. But he has attached himself to us, and disowning him would not be good for the party either: his speeches are tremendously successful. The appearance of figures like this is the price we have to pay for a revolution that's too successful, too lucky.

But what a historical irony: suddenly, at the moment when all hell broke loose among the popular masses, the most combative Russian party, renowned for its *acts* and its martyrs, having stood alone for sixteen years—and you can add another twenty years of People's Will tradition to that—turned out to be almost without any leaders and filling up with alien ranks. And Chernov felt he alone was shouldering responsibility for the destiny of not only the whole party but also the whole of Russian peasantry.

They took over a grand duke's house in Galernaya Street, with its own car and chauffeur. Naturally, Chernov immediately became deputy chairman of the Petrograd Soviet and was given a place on the Executive Committee, the solar plexus of the current revolution. But after our glorious, majestic revolutionary decades—how disappointing that there was none of this majesty to be seen around us. The Executive Committee! How grand it had sounded, that unseen, People's Will committee, before which Tsars and grandees had trembled! But when he entered he felt like a grounded eagle. They're a grey noncombatant herd, plus half a dozen eccentrics, low grade, fretting about minor issues like Lenin's extremism. There's a danger for you.

The first thing Chernov did was to explain—in a long article, written from the point of view of the history of our revolution—that the man in the street is always expecting the arrival of the Antichrist, and now Lenin has appeared. Speaking at the level of ideas is beyond them—so they talk about people. Some quick-tempered types were debating at the Kshesinskaya palace and—the phantom of civil war was immediately summoned up in the overheated imagination of the man in the street. Lenin can only be thanking his enemies for that free advertising. The bourgeoisie's hatred can bring him nothing but joy while we, his ideological opposition from within the socialist camp, must not show any irritation, for fear of ending up lumped together with the bourgeoisie. But actually Lenin is just a victim of the abnormal political conditions prevailing when that cursed autocracy hounded everyone into the underground, and no one knew who in his party had the most followers—though they all claimed they did. So the number of little anthills, each with its leader, increased, and overbearing characters with inflated pretensions appeared. Lenin, given his talents, is a major figure, but a figure pitilessly reduced in significance by the conditions of his time. And he has an imposing solidity: he seems to be entirely formed of a single block of granite, but round as a billiard ball—there's nothing to hook him with and he rolls along, unstoppable, not knowing himself where he's going. His brain follows a single track: I don't know where I'm going but I'm determined to get there. His whole being is imbued with his devotion to the revolutionary cause: he is undoubtedly not corrupt, but he does not understand the true interests of socialism. His one-sided, wilful ambition has blunted his moral sensibility somewhat. It simply did not occur to him, of course, that doing the necessary to obtain from Wilhelm the right to cross Germany was not far different from the shame of submitting a loyal petition to the Tsar. He has never been notable, anyway, for showing great tact: his opponents are always to blame—so crush them! He has enormous reserves of energy, but up to now he's been restricted to dealing with microscopic internal squabbles, and from that situation his insulting jargon grates like nails on a blackboard. He fences with a heavy beam which, due to its inertia, governs his movements. He upholds the truth, as a rope holds up a hanged man. But to me, fears that Lenin will destroy the new Russian life are risible, and it's risible when Lenin monopolizes the attention of whole newspapers. In Lenin it is just intoxication from the revolutionary air that speaks, and vertigo from the height to which events have elevated him. We do not need to fear Lenin's excesses: we, the socialists, will stop them spreading, and all the faster given that it will mean fewer ructions from terrified, chicken-hearted types getting in our way. So we must not fire up passions against the Bolsheviks, for they are our underground comrades. The simplest thing would be to involve them in a unified socialist government representing all parties, from Trudoviks to Bolsheviks.

The primary objective now, it seems, is to work out how to build up, quickly, a uniform network of soviets of peasants' deputies across the whole boundless expanse of Russia—and be sure we could rely on that third democratic force. Chernov was in effect now becoming the leader of the Russian laboring peasantry.

But in the Executive Committee of the Soviet of Workers' and Soldiers' Deputies he found too little Zimmerwald spirit—and started applying pressure on the presidium group. However, he now had doubts about his previous formula, according to which we should, immediately after victory over the autocracy, open a front against the liberals. On his return from abroad, Chernov had been in the Liaison Commission and the main initiator of the move to get Milyukov to send a note which would support European enthusiasm for Zimmerwald. But now that Milyukov had bungled the note, we had to think again, seriously, about whether to topple the whole Provisional Government.

As for Milyukov—he'd have to go, of course, be moved to another post.

The former timid student was deposing his former self-confident lecturer.

* * *

A FINE GAIT WON'T HELP A LAME CHICKEN.

* * *

[68]

General Alekseev was a habitual early riser. But one sleeps badly when away from home, and today he got up even earlier.

In Petersburg, though, people always got up late. And the boss, Guchkov, had spent all the previous night at a meeting—all the more reason for him to be sleeping now. But it was Guchkov that he needed to speak to most of all.

Yesterday had passed in a swirl of bad luck and turmoil. And his report to the government had been cut short. What unfortunate timing for his visit. And today, 4 May, at five this afternoon, he had to leave. But here, today, no one had time for the Supreme Commander. They were too busy with their infighting.

Should he go back to his forgotten army with nothing settled? And try to settle everything again via telegraph?

Alekseev got up quietly in the little room he'd been allocated and prayed to the East. He went to the communications room and made a call to Denikin on the direct line: he heard what was happening there and gave instructions.

But it was still early. Guchkov was ill as well: he might sleep for a good while.

Alekseev had one, incomplete, day left, but the Romanian Prime Minister, Brătianu, was also pushing for a meeting. As luck would have it, he'd turned up in Petrograd at this very same time. In fact, there was no reason for the Russian Supreme Commander to meet the Romanian Prime Minister: there were generals in Jassy for that, and the Provisional Government here. But now that they were both in Petrograd on the same day—it was impossible to avoid a courtesy visit. Romania was no real ally, it was our affliction and our ruin—but he could not avoid paying his respects. He knew the subject of the conversation in advance: Romania had joined the Entente powers (after two years of prevarication), oh not at all out of self-interest, no, but to fulfill ideals common to all mankind, to which the Romanian king was particularly dedicated. But the three and a half million Transylvanian Romanians must also be liberated and, as a matter of fact, the decrepit Austro-Hungarian monarchy eliminated—it's an anachronism, the whole of Europe is being contaminated by its decay. Next would come Romania's joy at the coup d'état in Russia, so helpful in bringing Russia and Romania closer (thank you)—but the Romanian authorities fear that the anarchist movement will sweep in, from the armies on the Romanian Front: just a few days ago there'd been unrest in Jassy itself, and people had taken the law into their own hands and freed revolutionaries from the prisons. So shouldn't something be done to tighten up the Russian armies on the Romanian Front and, at the same time, strengthen operational support for the Romanian army?

Even before it took place, he was irritated by this pointless conversation, of which he could neither change nor correct anything. Under the Emperor, Alekseev had done all he could to stop Romania, heaven forfend, from becoming our ally. But it did, anyway.

However, these vacant hours were too early even to visit Brătianu —he'd be asleep too. And Alekseev, listless, decided to go now to the Military District HQ and see Kornilov. After that it would be time to cross the square to the Winter Palace and see Brătianu. He phoned Kornilov to say he was coming—and set off.

Kornilov's appointment to the Petrograd Military District had not been appropriate for the recent, politics-ridden months—it had all been Rodzyanko's idea. It was a general-cum-politician that was needed, a diplomat with a statesman-like breadth of vision. But Kornilov could never reach that level: he was a division general and a man of combat. He didn't even seem to understand how complex the accursed politics were.

But the good thing about him was his imperturbability. (Alekseev didn't like highly strung generals.) Or perhaps it was just the inscrutability of his swarthy Asian features.

Kornilov felt he'd handled things quite well yesterday. And he was probably right. What else could he have done in the current situation? After all, he was the one who'd persuaded the regiments to disperse back to their barracks.

What kind of work was that for a general—conducting assemblies with the units under one's command?

It turned out that that night, when Alekseev was already in bed, Kornilov had gone over there, to the palace, for the conference.

Why?

Guchkov had summoned him and Kornilov had gone, thinking he was to receive firm orders of some kind and would go into action. But he had received no orders—perhaps they'd changed their mind in the last half hour? But then, in the entrance hall, he'd found himself among the correspondents and he'd had to answer their questions.

And what did he say?

He didn't have much choice: I believe the appearance today of military units in front of the Mariinsky Palace was the result of a misunderstanding created by irresponsible agitators. However, the overwhelming majority of the citizen-soldiers have shown complete understanding of the interests of the state and calmly remained in their barracks.

But on the square at midnight, twenty-five thousand people had been bellowing, acclaiming the Commander of the Military District. And with support like that—they weren't going to make a move? A strange government.

Yes . . .

If the government was in this state—where could our hopes lie?

In addition to everything Kornilov had reported to the Supreme Commander yesterday, there was also the so-called "workers' guard." Ever since the days of the revolution people had been stealing arms from the depots, and after that they'd managed to commandeer a great deal more from the city militia. One Botsvadze, a student from the Military Medical Academy and now a Vyborg side commissar, alone took nearly half their rifles. No one could understand how it was being done. Military District HQ had called on them to surrender those arms. They didn't surrender them. Why were they arming themselves? It was another army in the city—and no one knew who was in charge of it.

Bold, sharp eyes that caught on quickly. An intrepid brow. But he wasn't allowed to go into battle.

Even so, Kornilov was inclining toward that crazy plan, which had not been his idea . . . To save the Petrograd garrison from falling apart while it can't be sent to the front: to try to get it into shape here, on the spot, by military organization. To declare a state of emergency due to increased danger to Petrograd from a possible German landing after the ice has melted (and indeed, wouldn't the Germans just have to turn round, to get here?), and say that massed forces are concentrating for an attack on the Northern Front. (The day before, Alekseev had told the papers the exact opposite.) Perhaps a breath of danger, wafted over this rabble, and a regime of strict military exercises might even make soldiers of them? This is the draft order . . . Guchkov is against it, though . . .

. . . In order to form a new, powerful army . . . I hereby order that the Military District reserve units be re-formed into combat regiments and be started, without losing a minute, on the most intensive training for battle. These units are to remain in Petrograd but to be ready to meet and crush the enemy on its approach to the capital . . .

Might that work . . .?

It was not the most brilliant idea. (And we'd have to agree between us a single, unambiguous line on the danger to Petrograd.) But perhaps, perhaps . . . Anyway, what else could we come up with . . .? But where could we find armaments for these combat regiments? And what about a battle-ready officer corps?

Good, the Supreme Commander wasn't objecting to an order like this being sent out.

Alekseev looked out of the wide window, at the empty Palace Square. Red flags flew over the Winter Palace and the Admiralty.

The Army's life was following its course, destination unknown.

Seven million men were in the trenches—and no one cared.

[69]

Kolya Stanyukovich's relationship with his stepmother had broken down completely. Over the past few weeks her old SR friends had been inviting her to join such and such a group and "see Chernov," or go to such and such a house to "see Savinkov." And she would come home, overexcited by what she'd heard, exclaiming, "What leaders! What men!" And things had taken a sudden turn for the worse yesterday with her reaction to Milyukov's note, an SR-style "That scoundrel!"

But did people still care about the note? Much bigger things here happening in town! Yesterday, after classes, Kolya, with the two Saburovs and another ten or so fellow students, had tumbled out into the streets to defend the righteous cause, carrying an anti-Lenin placard and looking for a fight, but none came their way. Which made it all the more irritating to get home late and hear his stepmother's words. What was wrong with her? Had she lost her mind? Overthrow a government that's only just been formed? And now we had to "do as Chernov says!" But what about the front? And Kolya—even though he was always telling himself not to put relations with his stepmother under even more strain—was shouting now: "We'll come to regret it! That's a stab in the back for father!"

Today, again, no one had gone to school, but they were staying in touch by phone. Since the previous evening, the phones in every home had been busy—it was hard to get through. They were ringing and ringing, spreading rumors and more rumors: the government has already been arrested! No, Lenin's been arrested! Yes, troops have come in from Tsarskoye Selo to suppress the Petrograd troops' uprising! Everyone had slept badly—and, first thing in the morning, grabbed the phone again.

But Kolya and his friends were desperate for action. They wanted a fight!

What a radiant morning, the sun, pinkish, playing over the spires. We're always sitting through that in class, but now—what beauty, what freedom! And how strong we feel!

Oh, what deeds we'll do today! The fervor: *whose* cause will prevail? It must be *ours*!

On street corners along Nevsky there are little groups of excited, very respectable-looking locals. Glued to advertising columns and walls is something quite unheard of—an appeal from the Kadet Central Committee:

". . . Wilhelm is seizing our lands—and we are being asked to make peace with him as soon as possible? To sacrifice our friendship with the progressive democracies of the world? Surely free Russia cannot betray the noble peoples of the West? The CC calls on all who hold Russia dear to support, firmly and decisively, the Provisional . . . Citizens! Do not follow those who demand the dismissal . . . Such demands will lead to the collapse of the new order. The forces of reaction are lurking—waiting for discord to break out among the now free people, so they can raise their heads . . ."

A spry gentleman, his bowler pushed to the back of his head:

"There! We have leaders, we've not been forgotten!"

By one of the advertising columns, voices rise:

"And as for what people are demanding of the government, that it should put pressure on the Allies: the Allies aren't our subordinates—how can we make France give up Alsace? And if she doesn't give it up, what do we do then? Declare war on France? Or not give her any more loans? Or stop sending arms?"

Laughter.

"If we're so strong, why aren't we dictating the peace terms to Germany?"

A female student, keeping her hands in a little downy muff (how charming!):

"The Provisional Government can by all means announce that we're giving up our claim on Constantinople—but we mustn't betray our Allies!"

"The war is still far from finished and we're arguing about conditions in the peace treaty!"

The proclamations on the advertising columns, that "Citizens!"—that does raise the spirits, but for Kolya and his friends it's not enough: they want something even stronger! They want to make a real commotion!

They move on to the next column. Discussions here too. Dignified gentlemen:

"What about that 'down with Milyukov' slogan? If Milyukov goes, the whole Provisional Government will go—that's just elementary politics. And it'll be total anarchy!"

"Getting rid of Milyukov would be easy, but would they set about removing Grey, Asquith, Wilson? The 'Order No. 1' has no currency over there. And no one there has even heard their 'Manifesto to the Peoples.'"

"Who has heard it, anywhere? It was published in Germany—and what came of it? The Soviet of Workers' Deputies thinks it's possible to write a proclamation that brings the Allies to heel. Do they think a proclamation would arrive, signed 'Skobelev'—and the Americans would decide not to come into the war . . .?"

There's no one to argue with and the boys have no one to lash out at.

"What's this great storm about, anyway? What is there in that note that's new? That we're going to carry on fulfilling our obligations to the Allies? How could anyone disagree about that? We promised not to conclude a separate peace, so we mustn't! Agreements aren't binding on a regime, but on the state itself."

A tall, gaunt lady:

"But with just one day of these kinds of arguments Russia is already disgraced! We must not discuss such matters in front of the Germans!"

"Ladies and gentlemen! If there's conflict between the government and the Soviet, that's terrible! That's not possible for today's Russia! Harmony between them is now the foundation of our country's life."

"Who would dare touch the current government? It was put in place by the revolution itself! By order of the entire people!"

"It was probably Lenin who arranged all this!"

"Why doesn't someone bring him down a peg or two?"

"Actually, no one really understands it: what happened yesterday, exactly?"

The boys don't understand it either, although they were in the streets yesterday, out and about till late, and they thought they'd seen everything. But just what, exactly, is going on? How did it get started? Who lit the fuse?

No, the main thing is: what can we ourselves do? Today? And how can we predict where the most important events will happen? Where should we go?

From half-hour to half-hour excited groups, becoming ever larger, gather on Nevsky for miniature assemblies of thirty to fifty people. They move to surround whoever is speaking.

"We didn't overturn the Tsarist government because of the bread queues, but because it was failing to win the war! And now, when we're nearing total victory, we're suddenly supposed to abandon it and agree to a peace?"

An officer with a false, rubber leg (which pained Kolya—what if his father's leg got torn off like that?):

"When we need one last push, when the fate of our country hinges on another few weeks, perhaps—why do we have to hear that noxious call for 'immediate peace'?"

Kolya and his friends cross over, making for the City Duma. The dog-leg form of its external staircase is an open invitation to an assembly. About a hundred people have already gathered, and on the steps is an impassioned student with a radiant, open face. He takes off his cap, revealing hair combed back from his forehead, and addresses the crowd:

"March with the government! Otherwise our nation is finished! We gained our peace with so little effort, and we've grown used to it so quickly that it's gone to our heads. And now it's: give us immediate peace. Everyone has taken up the refrain 'Renounce annexations.' But that Zimmerwald formula is self-defeating. If you have 'peace without annexations' then you can't have 'self-determination of peoples.' With self-determination, Turkish Armenia would have the right to leave Turkey and join our Armenia, and Galicia to merge into the whole Ukraine. But then that would be 'annexations' away from Turkey and Austria! So we're supposed to leave the predators with all the territories they've seized? 'Without annexations' originated with the German Social Democrats. There that slogan is understood as: not one inch of German territory to be given up. So how can we restore Poland to what it was, at the expense of Russian territory alone, without any from Germany or Austria?"

Shouts of approval, and some applause too.

A civil servant in a uniform overcoat mounts the steps to join him. Mid-level administrators are usually docile and silent, but those here today want their voice heard too:

"So we're to abandon the 'little nations,' all those who put their trust in us? No, we have to end the war, not 'without annexations,' but in a way that there'll be no more bloodshed, ever again! And Germany will never come barging in here anymore!"

And the student, uplifted, takes over again:

"How we should feel about the war? The selfless American democracy is our example! If we abandoned the war now, we'd be regarded with such contempt by the free American people!"

Let's go, lads! Let's go further on! Somewhere, something's going to happen today . . . and we can prove useful!

[7 0]

Tereshchenko could not bear to watch, helpless, from the sidelines, while things went wrong.

That innocent act of sending the note to the Allies was growing into a dangerous political conflict. Even after that whole night, the government and the Soviet still did not fully understand each other. But when two institutions fail to reach an understanding, a private meeting between real doers can settle everything.

And although he had not retired till four in the morning, when it was already light, Tereshchenko jumped out of bed at nine with the vigor of a young man, and immediately realized that he must hurry to meet Tsereteli. Kerensky was out of action (being his friend, Tereshchenko knew this sickness was feigned), and his pride wouldn't have allowed him to negotiate with Tsereteli anyway. But Tereshchenko could easily continue Nekrasov's late-night attempt to finalize the document—the text was there.

And he rushed to phone Tsereteli, before the latter became immersed in the morass of his EC work. He caught him in time. They agreed that Tereshchenko should come round immediately. A ministerial car was already waiting at the front entrance.

Tsereteli was currently living in Skobelev's bachelor apartment. The latter had inherited considerable wealth (though it didn't compare with Tereshchenko's, and it didn't come from sugar but from flour: his father was a merchant miller in Baku), had contributed a substantial sum to the revolution, and had now become, to an absurd degree, a theater enthusiast. Now he'd be there too, sticking his oar in while they talked.

Among the laughable, insignificant riffraff of the Executive Committee (and you couldn't let them see what you thought of them) some serious figures did nevertheless tower above the rest. Such was the ever-attentive, ever-benign Tsereteli, the same kind of rapidly emerging star in the Soviet as Tereshchenko was in the government. Two months ago it wouldn't even have crossed anyone's mind that, to settle Russia's fate, these two would need to meet. But here they were.

Tsereteli's dark eyes, in that long, thin face, now seemed mistrustful (after Tereshchenko's defense of the note yesterday). But here was Tereshchenko assuring him that the whole story was nothing but a misunderstanding, and nothing untoward had been intended. Tsereteli nodded. He too was very keen to patch things up.

This was necessary for Russia's salvation but it was also, in particular, very necessary for Tereshchenko himself. Firstly, as Minister of Finance—for the whole fate of the Freedom Loan was hanging on this nasty little episode, and without the loan all Russia's finances would be on the verge of a rapid collapse. Secondly, and this was top secret for the time being, as a party who was more than just interested in the next moves Russian foreign policy would take.

The whole solution lay in producing the necessary, edited version of the "Clarification" in the government's name. This would not have been complicated if Tereshchenko hadn't feared Milyukov would dig his heels in and ruin the whole scheme.

Was it above all the "decisive victory" that had rubbed the Soviet up the wrong way? In that case we had to camouflage it with a long quote from the declaration of 9 April. Then we had to think up something about the "sanctions and guarantees." What he had thought of, partly last night with

Nekrasov, and then with Milyukov, was to add that these were not harmful measures: there would be an international tribunal, steps to limit armaments . . . Anything else? Well, yes: "etc."

But most unseemly of all was the idea of now sending that "Clarification" to the ambassadors of the allied powers like a diplomatic document. That would be extremely tactless—unbearably so!

They parted amicably, with Tereshchenko promising to get the document passed by a cabinet meeting as soon as possible, and then they'd immediately send it to the EC. And Tsereteli and Skobelev left for the EC: things would get busy there well before they did in the government.

But Tereshchenko would not have such an easy job. Milyukov would be offended from the very beginning, because the conciliatory document had been drawn up without him—and for this reason alone he'd find fault with every word. He was jealous because he hadn't been given complete control over the field of foreign policy. And jealous, not without good reason, of Tereshchenko because his English and French were better. And then there was the fact that what Milyukov, like any stubborn trader, feared most of all was selling too cheaply, giving in even a kopeck earlier, or for a kopeck more, than was absolutely unavoidable. What he lacked, actually, was an artist's flair, a sense of the whole picture, a knack for maneuvering: he was capricious, unwilling to take into account the fact that the Soviet had sprung up. He understood all politics as: take a firm stand and let nothing through. Essentially his note had been absolutely right and we could even, with a bit of flexibility, have made it both more loyal to the Allies and more demanding of them: we should also have received a good few bonuses from them—but the note had been ineptly expressed.

Buchanan had recently invited Kerensky and Tereshchenko, without their colleagues, to lunch at his residence—for he had recognized their growing power in the government. And they had easily found common ground: they all agreed that they'd expected a higher standard of political activity from Milyukov; that what he'd done in his six weeks in office had been disappointing and that he was unlikely to hold on as the master of foreign policy for much longer. And it was clear to all three of them (even before the note scandal) that Tereshchenko alone would be capable of replacing Milyukov.

But at this moment it was not so easy even to get the ministers assembled: some were still asleep, following that terrible night (Prince Lvov had only just woken up). Others, like Shingarev, were already at their ministries, but the latter was refusing to come to a meeting until three in the afternoon—his document on the land committees, which was to be ratified today, wasn't quite ready yet. Prince Lvov promised to try and convene a meeting for—well, let's say one o'clock.

No, with this weak-willed, senile government, you could only tear your hair out! They didn't understand the word "hurry."

Then Tereshchenko suggested to Lvov that he should assemble three or four ministers, with Milyukov, and decide the matter in camera.

But, from Pevchesky Bridge, Milyukov firmly rejected this: we must wean ourselves off these behind-the-scenes deals. A government decision can only be taken with all the members present.

[7 1]

Last Tuesday, designated for First of May celebrations (a blunder on the part of the Soviet leaders: their European mentors, it turned out, had not marked the day), the Public Library had, of course, been working. But the staff had still kept an eye on this half-a-million-strong procession from the windows, or when stepping out on to Nevsky Prospect: there was something terrible about it. The terrible thing was how organized it was, how, at the appointed time on the appointed day, half a million or even more Petersburg residents had paraded along the prescribed streets, in the prescribed direction, in the prescribed ranks—which was quite unnatural! And the singing! Exactly the same songs in a hundred or so different columns, and—the way they were singing! It was monotonous, as if under some compulsion, under a spell: the sound of a new paganism.

One of the library's wits, putting a twist on Kozma Prutkov, had quipped:

"Tell me this, if the color red didn't exist, how would you spot the friends of the people?"

The woman in charge of issuing the books:

"There's nothing funny about it. This is the very Acheron flowing—Vasili Alekseevich Maklakov was always threatening to stir it up. We already saw, in March, how turbulent it can be. But it wasn't flowing against us, and we were happy. But what if it starts flowing in our direction?"

And just a day later, that's what happened: on Thursday it started flowing against us. The library staff didn't see those regiments on Mariinskaya Square but, toward evening, processions started to flow past, under the very walls of the library. And they looked terrifying, with those brusque slogans, each one like a slap in the face: "Down with Milyukov!" and even "Down with the Provisional Government!"—especially terrifying when it was dark and they appeared under the streetlamps. And especially that column of workers marching with rifles. The faces had none of the sleepy good nature that they'd had at the May Day celebration, but were openly aggressive: what hostile looks they were giving the public of central Petersburg.

Going home after work, Vera had crossed Nevsky Prospect and approached one group deep in debate, then another (on the day of the revolution *he* had urged her above all not to linger on Nevsky . . .) and listened, both wounded and gladdened. Wounded by the hurtful suspicions, which either really had matured in these people's heads or else had been implanted from outside, but gladdened by how many members of the public were there, of the most simple, uneducated kind as well. Judging by their appearance they were shop-assistants, hawkers, minor employees, and, most importantly, there were simple soldiers, who answered the others' questions—soberly, clearly, their understanding unspoiled. "The soldiers are on our side!" It was not only Vera who discovered this yesterday evening, but all the respectable Nevsky Prospect types. Some soldiers, who had come out in their ranks onto Mariinskaya Square, were against us, but these, here, were all separate, free of their military formations, and all spoke reasonably in support of the government, of good order, and, although it was they who would have to go off and fight, they also supported a reasonable end to the war, not ending it halfway through and not in total collapse.

This was something new, for the Petersburg street and for all Russia's street: not meetings convened by someone, but spontaneous political debates with all social groups, including the common people, mixing. Petersburg, shackled, gloomy, had suddenly become a kind of Athens of the North. It had turned out, unexpectedly, that the Russian crowd felt the need to think about and discuss politics for themselves—and we'd heard a good few perceptive remarks, embellished with colorful folk sayings.

Vera herself had never once spoken up at these gatherings, trying instead to answer questions mentally and sometimes, she felt, more adroitly than those replying aloud.

On opening *Speech* this morning, she'd seen a long, emotional appeal to the country from the Kadet Central Committee—it seemed they'd been in session last night . . . And how can Russia, today, demand that the Allies change the terms of agreements already concluded? That would violate our solidarity with them at a time when what we need, more than anything, is their help. In doing this we would not spare ourselves the afflictions of war, but only stand alone before the greatest dangers. For it is already clear that our revolution has not led to a German one: instead the rapacious Hohenzollern monarchy is basing all its calculations on a rift between us and our Allies. Tsarism dreamed of a separate peace—but we, surely, do not?!

And there were more new twists and turns in their arguments, more exhortations. The appeal was too long, because of which, after reading it, Vera was more worried than when she'd got up this morning: the leaders were not so sure of things.

And there was another article in today's *Speech* that had also perplexed Vera: no politically aware citizen, it said, can stand alone, not belong to a party. If one is not in a party, it is impossible to do the political work of a free democracy. Let us change the formless mass of Russian society into a harmonious federation of political parties!

Something very dangerous must have happened: the central Kadet newspaper had never made such an appeal before. Although Vera had, for years, invested a good deal of effort into help of various kinds for the Kadet party, was in total sympathy with its program and had great respect for many of its leaders—nevertheless she had never felt the need to become an actual party member. She had seen it as a form of coercion, constraint. And in categorical formulations like this, broadening out to address the whole of Russian society. . .?

In Ekaterininskaya Street, high school students were handing out white, printed leaflets, proclamations, to passers-by. She took one. There, in large type:

"Citizens! Russia is living through terrible times . . .!"

Right, she'd read it when she got to the library. But as she walked in—there, immediately behind the plate-glass entrance door, the whole notice board was taken up by that same appeal, only now printed in really large type. Now it was not in the name of the Central Committee but the whole of the People's Freedom Party:

> Citizens! Russia is living through terrible times! The fate of our country, the fate of future generations, is being decided! The people have shown great wisdom in their loyalty to the Provisional Government. Let us rally around it; let us stop anarchy proliferating, for on its heels the Black Hundreds, now lying low, would arrive. . . . Milyukov, whose appearance in the government won us the trust of our Allies, has been declared an enemy of our fatherland! But those who say this know that Milyukov's departure would mean the departure of the whole Provisional Government—so where are they leading Russia?
>
> We are standing on the edge of an abyss. Citizens, go out into the street! Express your will, participate in public meetings, voice your approval of the government! Save the country from anarchy!

The barrier keeping us from that disaster felt very fragile . . .

The ferment was spreading from one part of the library to another. The feeling was: *let's go!* Why, actually, do we always give the street over to *them*, without putting up any opposition? When we're here on our home patch we speak freely, but why are we so reticent in the street? It's there, in the street, that everything is decided. Others were already marching yesterday—but what were *we* doing?

There were conversations in corridors, on the stairs, people passing on the mounting fervor:

"Indeed! We must stop brushing it aside with sarcastic little quips and go out onto Nevsky! And speak out loud against the anarchist propaganda!"

"Otherwise we're only encouraging those who . . ."

"If we have convictions, why are we keeping them secret? And if our convictions are trifling then we shouldn't be moaning that things are falling apart."

Volunteers were found to set up a ladder and take down the red strip, cut askew and with crooked lettering—"Long live international proletarian solidarity!"—that someone had hung across the façade facing the garden the previous evening. Someone was writing, on Whatman art paper "Trust

Milyukov," "Trust the Provisional Government." In the basement, library employees were cobbling together the panels to mount them on.

Someone brought into the entrance hall from outside a green, furled banner—the Kadet banner. Until now these had only been seen at the conference and at district committees. But now—was it going into the street?

We have to show people that there's more than just loudmouth Leninists in the capital. Once they get rebuffed, they'll disappear without a trace.

"You only have to breathe a word against them and they're shouting 'Bourgie! He's got to go!' "

" 'Bourgie'—that's the worst insult now, it's not 'copper' anymore."

" 'Bourgies' are the new doormats."

Peaceful librarians, educated library-users . . . "Street action": we used to think that was an inadmissible step for well-brought-up people, didn't we? But—the time has come!

And Vera was among those determined to go.

While waiting to leave, they read in *Izvestia* the Soviet's declaration that they weren't the ones responsible for yesterday's actions against members of the Provisional Government: "that was a misunderstanding, put in train by certain persons who were not up to their job." Ah, so that's what it was. But those persons were, all the same, playing about with other people's brains.

So who was it, then? The Bolsheviks? Although the revolution had prevailed, the Bolsheviks had not forthrightly revealed themselves. They still had their old, conspiratorial ways.

But *how* do demonstrations get started? Well, they made sure they were all convinced, then stopped all their work, got themselves ready, left two people on duty there, and:

"Ladies and Gentlemen! Please leave the building! By the main entrance, please."

They emerged in a cluster onto the sidewalk facing the Ekaterininsky Square garden. The cluster was timid at first. Then it grew bigger.

"Ladies and gentlemen! On to the roadway! Don't be shy."

How strange: *they* had always marched in the roadway, while we just watched from sidewalks. But now it'll be us walking in the road!

So what does that mean? That we're strong?

They grasped and raised high the two placards, one supported by a single pole, the other by two. The library's cataloguer led the way. He raised the green banner and unfurled it.

Yes! To demonstrate your convictions not in the sitting room but in the street you do, of course, need pluck.

All the staff were now out, together with the readers.

And passers-by joined them—out of curiosity, or fellow-feeling?

Now they were more than a hundred.

With two or three soldiers in high spirits.

"Ladies and gentlemen! We have the soldiers with us!"

And they moved off.

Again, on Nevsky, there were anthills! The same anthills as yesterday. Blocking the sidewalks. And spilling over into the roadway.

They turned left, past the Gostiny Dvor.

It was very, very strange to walk along Nevsky Prospect in the roadway. Cabbies restrained their horses and went round the marchers. Trams slowed down.

There was interest shown from all the sidewalks, thanks both to the never-seen green banner and to the novelty of people like that marching.

Cries of approval.

And they were joined by high school students, officers . . . Oh, what a lot of us there are now!

This was new to everyone. And marvelous.

On to Kazan Cathedral! That's where we'll speak. Wherever else?

[7 2]

(PETROGRAD STREETS: 4 MAY, AFTERNOON)

* * *

By now the whole of Nevsky Prospect is unusually animated, hectic. It's not now little knots of people but multitudes—or not far off—of the urbane public, something that never happens. And soldiers. No workers to be seen. All the trams trying to cross Nevsky are stuck in the crowd. They ring their bells and go slowly.

The intelligentsia have come onto the street! They don't yet know how to behave, where to march—they just want to show their civil convictions.

"Come with us, comrades! If you are for trust—then join us!"

Youngsters are climbing walls, bringing down the red flags from houses—there were many pinned up—and taking them off. Some people's flags already bear hastily scrawled legends.

Stuck on to corner walls and displayed in shop windows are the dramatic words of the People's Freedom Party appeal: "Go out into the street! Express your will!"

* * *

On the corner of Pushkin Street, a student standing on a crate shouts his objections:

"We're sick of these platitudes! The people are disgusted by this bourgeois sophistry!"

A high school teacher in uniform:

"What have the bourgeoisie got to do with this? It's not the bourgeoisie who are waging war: the war is to defend Russia's vital interests."

The student again:

"There's no good reason to trust the Provisional Government!"

From the sidewalk, a sailor with a deep voice:

"We trust the government completely. It's not let us down. Who can say it's betrayed us?"

Rising above the commotion: "Lenin and co."

The sailor goes up to the student:

"Take that tram driver—does he need much learning for that? Well, just you take his place and see how far you get!"

* * *

Near the Anichkov Palace, on the Fontanka side, is a large crowd. Among the ladies' hats and the bowlers there are also peaked caps and headscarves. Today there's been yelling, back and forth, about everything, but the local residents speak quietly. If someone shouts a rude comment it's likely to be a modern school pupil:

"We must reject the note and get the Allies to support the Soviet's manifesto!"

A lady, kid-gloved fingers interlaced on her chest:

"But we certainly can't make the Allies revise the treaties while we're fighting the war!"

"They must publish the secret treaties!"

"That's despicable! A secret treaty can only be published with the agreement of all parties."

A student:

"What's the point of fighting any longer when they're already fraternizing on the front?"

A tall, imposing gentleman in a good-quality coat:

"That's outrageous! First we were expecting the Germans to depose Wilhelm. They didn't depose him. Now we're putting our hopes in fraternization. Where did that dream come from, that the Germans wouldn't attack us? We're losing our minds."

The same lady, still with her hands on her chest:

"Be patient! America's just joined the war! It'll soon be over now."

The gentleman again:

"How could we alone declare peace?"

"Do you want victory?" retorted a female student, a fringe emerging from her little fur toque. "Do you need millions more cripples? Well, what we need is brotherhood between nations!"

A student, standing on a little mound of ice, addressing everyone:

"The Allies will seize territories no matter what. Then we'll have to fight them, won't we? No, someone's got to do the noble thing and refuse—from the very beginning."

The girl student, her fringe joggling about:

"We're happy to defend free Russia, but not the greedy appetites of the rich."

Two soldiers have rolled a barrel along with them. A wounded soldier, his arm in a sling, climbs onto it:

"Listen! How can you abandon everything like that? What did we spill our blood for? Why did I lie there, three months in a field hospital, no rest day or night? Our brothers are in the trenches, and there's no way we're going to listen to that lot egging us on! What about those who died, what'd they say? Who got us into this mess? Not us."

Shouts from the back of the crowd: "The Leninists!"

A student, standing on a mound of snow:

"What have the Leninists got to do with it? Look, I'm no Leninist. But the democracy must play the honorable role of mediator for peace. The secret treaties were concluded by the Tsarist government, and the democracy is not obliged to abide by their terms."

A sweet little high school girl taunts him:

"Are you against the war because you're scared to go to the front?"

A thick-set, grey-haired gentleman, firmly:

"Any democrat with principles must also be a champion of total victory!"

The same female student, irrepressible:

"Oh yes? Conquering Constantinople, annexing Armenia, taking back Poland—is that what the popular masses need? We've already won—by overthrowing the Tsar! And in doing that we've helped all the democracies in the world. Now Germany is fighting to survive and that's giving her the fearsome strength of desperation! It's dangerous, driving her to that . . ."

The thick-set gentleman isn't giving in:

"But the people have rejected utopian forms of peace and won't lay down their rifles! Until Germany renounces seizure of territories we shall stand up to her, unflinching!"

"But *where* are you standing up to her?"—that was a freelance artisan. "You go. Go and win the war yourself! Why d'you want other people to do it?"

Now a soldier with a thick beard, no rifle, has taken the injured man's place on the barrel:

"It's not 'cause the German's so glad we're free that he's not touched us these two months—it's 'cause we're gnawin' each other to death. He understands, that German, that if he went all out to finish us off we'd come to our senses pretty quick and pick up our guns. Now he's giving us a rest so we'll all be at each other's throats . . ."

They throng, they cluster . . . Who's to be believed?

* * *

From Nevsky, several dozen people rush off down Mikhailovskaya Street, shouting and cursing. They run, sending others flying, chasing someone—

but not knowing who. Some say they've spotted a German spy. Others: with bombs! Others: a provocateur!

They collar two youngsters—Leninists! They haul them off to the commissariat, where the two are taken in, but people from the crowd aren't allowed inside. They stand around for a while, then disperse.

* * *

In Mikhailovskaya Street, at the entrance to the Grand Europe Hotel, there's another large rally, attended by all kinds of people, from officers to cooks. And they're all citizens! A footman. A bank employee type.

Speakers follow each other on the steps but when one of them shouts "down with Milyukov," he's not allowed to finish:

"Get him off!"

But everyone listens attentively to a smooth-faced young soldier:

"Comrades! I've been wounded three times and I didn't want to go back to the war again. But now I'm going. It's only cowards who want to finish with the war. These here have no right to speak against the war: you'd do better asking those on the front—see what they have to say."

There are heated arguments everywhere, but no fisticuffs. The overall balance is in favor of the Provisional Government. And among the soldiers, too.

* * *

A large, organized Kadet demonstration of some three hundred people, with both green and tricolor banners, leaves from the Kadet club on the French Embankment. At the head of the march, moving slowly, is an open car. In it are Vinaver and some other Kadets, and at each stop they address the public around them. Behind them comes a truck with volunteers strewing the Kadet appeal leaflets about.

They march along Liteiny Prospect, then Nevsky. Then they go along Morskaya and turn off toward Mariinskaya Square. Along the way many soldiers, officers, and local residents join their procession: by the end there are several thousand of them.

In Morskaya Street the crowd lift up a French officer they meet coming in the opposite direction and ceremoniously deposit him in the Central Committee car. Vinaver greets him and the crowd shouts: *"Vive la France!"*

* * *

But here comes a very different kind of procession, a great throng forging a way along Nevsky: the front quarter of the column consists of sullen-looking workers, with rifles slung over their shoulders. And the other three-quarters are women workers and adolescents. Carrying: "Down with the Provisional Government." And shouting:

"Down with Milyukov! We won't let him suck our blood!"

"Let him die of his bourgeois lust!"

The response from the other procession, as they pass:

"It's not Milyukov who's sucking our blood, it's Wilhelm!"

And from the other side: "Long live Lenin!"

In reply: "Down with Lenin! Down with German spies!"

And they pass without touching.

But why the rifles? Just look around—all the soldiers on the streets are unarmed.

* * *

And there are other workers' demonstrations like this arriving via either Liteiny or Trinity Bridge.

They're hostile, sometimes avoiding each other as they approach head-on, sometimes marching in parallel in the same direction, exchanging insults.

The animosity is increasing. Faces are fevered, distorted:

"Long live the International!"

"Send the rabble-rousers to Germany—they'll be more use there . . ."

"Down with Milyukov!"

"Down with Lenin!"

"Down with the war! We don't want conquests!"

"We only trust the Provisional Government!"

The trams are moving more and more slowly, stuck in traffic jams. The taxicabs and carriages may as well stay off Nevsky altogether.

Now there are meetings on every corner—you can't pass.

"What pandemonium! Just what the Germans wanted."

"Wilhelm will be pleased . . ."

[73]

When the Executive Committee assembled after that all-night meeting, the leaders all had heavy heads from the lack of sleep, and not much energy left. (Even before today's session, there had been a joint session of the three populist factions. And the SRs had supported the Trudoviks and Peshekhonov's populist socialists, agreeing that the socialist democracy was not yet strong enough to fulfill the task of running the country alone, and a government of that kind would undermine Russia's credit in the eyes of bourgeois Europe. No, the time to break with the Kadets was not yet here.)

Tsereteli reported that Tereshchenko had come to see him this morning to finalize the conciliatory document drafted last night. And here it is. We're expecting an easy compromise, with no hitches. In the coming hours the Council of Ministers will ratify it. (It still remained to be established whether private contacts of this kind by Tsereteli with ministers were admissible: after all, he couldn't always know and be able to express the EC's opinion.)

The document might not be bad, and perhaps we could ratify it. After all it is, when all's said and done, the first step toward an international discussion of the renunciation of forcible conquest of land, isn't it? It's a great achievement for democracy. (Chernov: "for the workers' democracy.") The Bolsheviks, of course, did not agree: it was a defeat! But many EC members didn't understand it so well either: why do we have to be so courteous to the Allies? Why can't we put some pressure on them? We must, anyway, tell the Provisional Government again not to publish a single major political document without informing the EC in advance. And they must dismiss all the Tsar's ambassadors as soon as possible.

While they were waiting for the finalized document to arrive from the government, they started thinking that they'd have to take the Petrograd garrison more firmly in hand—they'd already begun, yesterday—so that there'd be no repeat of that wilfulness. Representatives of all the battalion committees must be summoned to the EC bureau tomorrow and firmly, definitively told that from now on not a single unit could go out onto the street without a direct order from the EC.

Chernov was looking around with an ironic smile: eighty of the ninety EC members here were revolutionaries fresh off the vine. No one had heard them or known them during the revolution and now they wanted to run everything. But since the noisiest of them were internationalist Zimmerwaldists, Chernov refrained from criticizing them, for he himself had been one of the original Zimmerwaldists, together with their Lenin.

But—what was that? Now the Bolsheviks were raising the issue of re-electing the bureau! We'd had elections a week ago—and we were supposed to run them again? Why? What for? They were just thirsting for power. So brazen.

Chernov, with his broad, tolerant, European views, found the convulsive atmosphere here alarming.

And the clamor went on and on. What confusion, with people jumping up and grabbing each other by the lapels: new elections or no new elections? And you could not get them to quiet down! All they could agree on was to put the whole question up for discussion again at one of the next sessions.

Then it occurred to them that restraining the Petrograd garrison would not be enough. They would have to restrain all those in the environs of Petrograd as well: Oranienbaum, Strelna, Gatchina, Krasnoye Selo, and, the most turbulent of all, Kronstadt. They had to draw up a radio-telegram for them all, to restrain them: they must send no troops into the capital without a written invitation from the Soviet! And dispatch the cable as soon as possible!

But didn't the local soviets and garrisons all over Russia have to be told too? That they must refrain from independent sorties and wait calmly for directions from the Petrograd Soviet?

But you can't draw up a radio-telegram with ninety people writing it. For that you'd need to appoint another commission. They appointed one.

They still had to call Linde in and give him a talking-to for his reckless action yesterday.

The government had still not sent its "Clarification." But then the phones started ringing. The calls were from all the industrial outskirts of town, and all told the same story: the workers of this, that, another, and yet another factory were stopping work by order of the EC! And going to demonstrate in the center of town!

"What order of the EC?" shouted Skobelev into the phone. "We didn't give any such order! We'll carry out an immediate investigation!"

But it was too late for investigations! The phones all around brought the same news: working Petersburg was in revolt!

Things were getting very uncomfortable here . . .

However, beyond the Neva and Narva Gates it was still calm.

But now they were coming from the Vyborg side and Vasilievsky Island—and they were **armed**!

Armed?! That's a provocation! Who's giving these orders? Comrades, no EC member . . .?

What's become of our authority??

More phone calls: from the Vyborg side and from Novaya Derevnya—there are major demonstrations approaching the center, and they're armed! And they're demanding that the government step down!!

But on Nevsky Prospect there are demonstrations in support of the government.

What to do? They mustn't be allowed to meet! We must stop the Vyborg workers.

Chkheidze himself would go, and Skobelev. They wouldn't dare disobey those two!

But Himmer bounded into the middle of the room:

"Comrades! The right to demonstrate is one of the subjective, public rights, applicable to all citizens, that we've now won! It must not be revoked or limited. You have no right to deprive the masses of the chance to be heard! Let the government first ban demonstrations by the bourgeoisie and the Nevsky Prospect public!"

That stopped them in their tracks. More discussions.

Twice Chernov, too, was called to the phone—it was factories where SR committees had been set up, asking what they should do.

"Try and stop it."

"Then we'd lose our authority. They've already decided, and they'll go anyway."

It was true. If the EC didn't acquiesce in the movement that had begun, we might be cutting ourselves off from the masses.

This was the moment of a historic decision by their leader.

"Then go and join them, and take the lead, with Zimmerwaldist slogans."

After all, the workers' actions testified to the strength and maturity of the populist movement. Which meant, didn't it, that the spirit of internationalism was strong among the masses?

And from the Moscow Gate they were reporting that . . .

It was scary.

Chkheidze, Skobelev, and Voitinsky, in an open car, met the head of the many-thousands-strong Vyborg column on the Field of Mars. Preceding each plant's marchers came an armed workers' militia. Someone had had the time to organize it magnificently and the placards were all prepared: "Down with the war!" "Down with the Provisional Government!" "All power to the Soviets!" "Make war on the war!"

In the back rows were women workers, some carrying tea kettles: they always took them into work and had now brought them here as well.

All three EC representatives stood up in the car.

The column paused.

Chkheidze greeted them on behalf of the Executive Committee. But he said there was no need for uncoordinated demonstrations now. The best thing at this point would be to go back to their factories and back to work. The government had already agreed to clarify the note in the sense that we wanted and therefore further demonstrations would be pointless.

And Voitinsky, fervent, eloquent:

"Comrades! We know you are ready, at any moment, to support us in our struggle. We know, without any demonstrations, that you are with us. We have also heard from dozens of garrisons of their desire to demonstrate. We have millions of bayonets! But for the time being they are not needed . . ."

From out of the crowd came the cries of its leaders: the workers themselves know what they need to do!

And they all thronged past, on toward Sadovaya.

As for the EC leaders, roundly defeated—what could they do now? Applaud?

[74]

Yuri Vladimirovich Lomonosov had not been in Petrograd yesterday, but loads of unconfirmed reports had reached Tsarskoye Selo by phone. He didn't think he'd be giving his lectures today, but went into town anyway, if only out of curiosity.

First he went to his institute (in the morning the cabs had been moving freely). Only a handful of students were there for lectures, the irredeemably placid ones. Even the railway engineers, the least revolutionary of all the students, had been carried off by the whirlwind! He canceled his lectures, had a brief chat with the excited professors, and set off by foot to Nevsky, to have a look. Today he was not, of course, in his Engineer-General uniform but a civilian overcoat and felt hat.

He had a quick look at the Kadet appeals that were stuck up everywhere. The intelligentsia had certainly become bolder—that was unexpected—but they are cowardly nonetheless. So as not to expose themselves to attack, it was "against the forces of reaction, the Black Hundreds, now lying low." Putting up a protective shield, just in case . . . A standard technique.

He needed to go to the bank—but with things in this state he'd never be able to get there. It was probably closed, anyway. His wife had given him an errand, some shopping. Fat chance.

The whole of Nevsky was deluged with words! All social classes, uniforms, and age groups were mixing, in a grand mix and in hundreds of little meetings. Only recently it had been hard to imagine, in the Russian people, a capacity for discussion. Now they couldn't stop. How did that happen?

Look at the square in front of Kazan Cathedral, Petersburg's favorite venue for public meetings. Students were expressing their rage there forty years ago and in the first year of the twentieth century too—and look how far things have gone since then! There's a sea of people here, stretching from the pavement of Nevsky Prospect into the embrace of the cathedral's curved colonnades—it looked like a quarter of Petersburg's residents. Here and there poles stick up above the crowd, red flags hanging from them. On both sides of the cathedral, by the Kutuzov and the Barclay de Tolly statues, a succession of vociferous orators mount little platforms. From the Kutuzov side:

"If we don't carry on with the war, Germany won't allow us into the world of justice! There's no other way into the Kingdom of Human Freedom!"

And a sharp taunt out of the crowd:

". . . or into Constantinople!"

And the first man, undaunted:

"What of it? The freedom to sail through the Straits is also justice! And if Stürmer and Protopopov didn't manage to drive Russia into the shameful impasse of a separate peace, surely Russia itself won't wander in voluntarily?"

Actually, though, this Russia could be driven anywhere you wanted.

"That's a lie about the separate peace! Who's suggesting that?"

And, from different parts of the crowd:

"Lenin! . . . Lenin!"

"And what about one side breaking the treaties? Isn't that a separate peace?"

A greenhorn volunteer soldier eagerly mounts the platform:

"But how can the victorious revolution even think of capitulating with a separate peace? Neither the Soviet of Workers' Deputies nor any party circles are proposing that—it's a lie! We are ready to end the war, under arms, in the name of our young freedom."

Freedom is a fire, young freedom is a flame—don't get your fingers burnt.

". . . It's a misleading slogan, that 'without indemnities.' It means we're to shift the burden of rebuilding the ruined nations onto the ruined peoples themselves! To take the burden of plundered Poland and Kurland from Germany's shoulders onto ours. Explain *that* to our workers and soldiers! The burden of a war we didn't win would weigh most heavily on the poor!"

And from the Barclay side:

"You say 'onward, to the brotherhood of nations.' But the German Social Democrats have been constantly telling us, all through the war, that they're fighting against Russian autocracy: so why shouldn't we, now, be at war with Wilhelm's autocracy? Now, when we don't have autocracy any more, who's preventing the German socialists from realizing their ideal and coming out of the war? You yourselves asked them—so why aren't they reorganizing Germany as a workers' republic? All that Zimmerwaldist verbiage is just hot air!"

Of course we wouldn't need to have these rallies or convince anyone of anything if we didn't have bunglers in the government instead of decisive individuals. We need to take the revolution by the scruff of the neck and direct its energy properly. (Working with Bublikov had been a waste of time for Lomonosov. It pained him deeply to have his hands torn from the enterprise on which his grip had been so firm. Such a gamble, such risks—only to remain in his previous position.)

Someone makes an announcement: now we have a speaker on behalf of the Soviet of Workers' Deputies, Comrade Lieber.

Yes, and your Soviet's not worth a straw either.

In civvies. Not tall. Lean. A small black beard, trimmed to a neat square. And in a staccato voice—he takes off immediately! He's obviously used to public speaking:

"Loud, bourgeois know-alls are flinging accusations at us, at the working class, saying we're not defending our homeland." He's almost jumping up and down: "But they provoked this war! They've been dragging it out endlessly—while they themselves, as they did before the revolution, just gorge on sweets in cake shops! The ruling classes are longing to take control of new markets to peddle their goods. And now the war is continuing in the name of ideas shared by the Tsar, Milyukov, Briand, and Lloyd George."

At the name Milyukov, there's muttering: no!!

But if we go into a bit more detail?

". . . Milyukov's note is a threat to the revolutionary movement that has already sprung up among the peoples of the Germanic coalition . . ."

There are shouts of "Where has it sprung up? When?"

Lieber carries on with his passionate address, occasionally throwing up an arm, constantly turning so as to be heard in every part of the square. But actually every part misses some of the speech, cannot catch it. Did you hear that? He's just as angry with Lenin as he is with Milyukov. Everything's getting muddled in people's minds: who's right, then—only the Soviet?

If only you in the Soviet were decisive people . . . But you're the same as the others—only good at wagging your tongues.

Behind them, more columns are marching along Nevsky, denser now. And shouting. But they . . . are they armed? Oho! This is just the beginning.

And from the Kutuzov side:

"Oh yes, of course Serbia and Belgium attacked first! Poor little Germany's only defending itself. It's not the Germans who've occupied our territory, it's us who are on German land! It was well worth throwing off the Tsar's power, so we could surrender to German militaristic junkerdom."

Just next to Yuri Vladimirovich an unkempt soldier in a dirty greatcoat elbows his way in to listen, picking his nose from time to time. You couldn't make it up if you tried.

From the Kutuzov side:

". . . 'War till the end' doesn't mean we must annihilate Germany and split up Austria-Hungary, but that we must put paid once and for all to the policy of territorial seizures—which you yourselves are railing against. What will you say when Petrograd's taken by the Germans? We aren't calling for annexations but for the defense of our hearth and home. German talk, the Myasoedov line, that's what Lenin's all about!"

And the nearer half of the square is shouting, yelling its support. And the officer, himself perhaps in the Petrograd service corps, finishes triumphantly:

"If we betray the allied democracies, they will not spare the traitors, and we'll become a German colony, and the Japanese and Americans will attack Amur province. The Allies will conclude a peace at our expense and Germany will say 'so be it,' give up Alsace-Lorraine, but will take our lands up to the Dnieper. And Turkey will take Crimea!"

Behind their backs, from Nevsky Prospect, marching feet are heard, and the marchers shouting their own words. More and more workers are surging along, formed into columns.

Riffraff.

But with rifles.

No. It's clear that this won't be the end of the matter. All this is very, very serious. We didn't see it coming.

It's in the nature of revolutions: they never stop halfway, but roll on, sometimes forwards, sometimes backwards, to the end, till they hit a brick wall.

Time would tell which direction Lomonosov himself should take.

[75]

Although Kirpichnikov now wore a George Cross on his chest, and although he and Misha Markov had become warrant officers, neither their training detachment nor the rest of the Volynian Battalion had become more orderly. Things were even worse, a lot worse: soldiers were absenting themselves and you couldn't ask why; they didn't want to do their training and you couldn't insist. And wafting in from all around, without anyone asking the front for their opinion, came that motto: stop the war! Why did this happen? New recruits—wimps never bombarded with shells—trying to be done with the war now?

One Colonel Pletnev, from the Ministry of War, came to the battalion to give a lecture. We must not shake the bloodstained German hand! Soldiers, do not take any notice of that paper, *Pravda*. Remember that the enemy is at the gates, and we shall stand firm by our noble Allies. And the whole rear must work honestly and not loaf about. He was right! The Volynians clapped. But just an hour later rabble-rousers from the Pavlovsky Regiment came running in: what, has someone been here poisoning the men's minds against the workers? No, where did you get that from? The next day there was an article in *Izvestia*: the Volynians have listened to a pogromist lecture by someone from the Black Hundreds! Whoever wrote that should have got his teeth knocked in, but it wasn't signed. Markov and Kirpichnikov took an indelible pencil and a sheet of paper—they'd write something too, conferring with a lieutenant on the battalion committee: we are protesting against anonymous threats against honorable people! We Volynians have been in the forefront of the revolution and proved . . . But all around us the place is teeming with German provocateurs and other vermin.

And what about the workers? They'd turned out to be real bastards: not only are they not sent off to war—well, all right—but they don't even want to do their job here! All the revolution means to them is: give us an eight-hour day! Our boys are there in damp trenches under fire, attacked with poisonous gases twenty-four hours a day, but this lot here, you can't give them more than eight hours' work, otherwise, you see, they won't have time for their politics.

If Timofei Kirpichnikov had known that before, he never would have made a revolution for them, and they'd just have to lump it!

Klim Orlov was one of those, only even worse. Why, did Timofei really know him? He'd spent two months in the training detachment. He'd dished out criticism of the top brass, a good fit for the times. But he'd not spent so much as a day on the front, even with that bullish mug of his. Here in Petersburg, he'd gotten himself an exemption, but no one knows how many mines he made. But when he'd been sent to represent the Volynian Battalion in the Soviet he'd started putting on airs. And he always thought whatever the big shots over there were saying was right. At first Timofei thought they were really laying down the law there in the Soviet, but then he found out: they were just herded in like sheep, to vote.

It would've been fine if he'd just sat there with his ears flapping, only Klim had decided he was the voice of the whole Volynian Battalion now—should've been a real soldier doing it. And when he came back to the battalion he'd even go barging into other people's business: Lenin's a good fellow, he'd say, don't you touch him. So you know better than anyone else, do you? Wilhelm sent us that loudmouth and he's ruining everything we've achieved—and he's a good fellow? He's free to spout the German line against us and we mustn't touch him?

Kirpichnikov discussed it with Markov, Brodnikov, and Ivan Ilyin. Some of the Volynians had, themselves, heard that weed speaking from his balcony over by Trinity Square, and the ones who could read saw it in the papers: the man's an enemy, plain and simple! How can we let him get away with all this destruction? What's the government thinking of? What a feeble government we've got, brothers.

There's unrest among the people, too.

Lenin had arrived on Bright Monday and in just a few days they'd spewed out such a lot of lies from that balcony that by the end of the week Timofei and the lads were already talking about going over and seizing Lenin, arresting him. Nothing complicated, they'd just go, fifteen or twenty of them, all with loaded rifles—that'd be enough. And they'd finish the job straight away, just shoot the rat. We shoot Germans, even innocent ones, so why feel sorry for this one? Even taking him alive would be no harder than taking an enemy soldier to make him cough up information. Surely launching the whole revolution can't have been easier than catching that Lenin would be now?

Klim certainly didn't quiet down—he went and complained to the heads of the Soviet: our boys are hatching a plot. And those bosses suddenly pricked up their ears and came themselves to visit the Volynian Battalion and even Kirpichnikov in his barracks. They were terrible fidgets but quick on the uptake, and they got to the point immediately. We are Comrades Bogdanov, Sukhanov, and Vengerov. You've got some wild ideas about going and arresting people, haven't you?

Well, says Kirpichnikov, the old ministers were arrested, weren't they? Well, the old ministers were, but our ministers—no one can arrest them. Comrade Lenin is our man, very much our man—he suffered a lot for the revolution. But why did he come back with the help of the Germans? He couldn't come any other way. And why's he always spouting just what the Germans want him to? Everyone's got the right to speak his mind, that's what free speech is for. So why don't you just let the Germans come here and speak their lot?

They didn't explain anything properly, those three, with all the gibberish they talked. But they categorically forbade touching Comrade Lenin or even thinking about it. We'd see that as a crime against the revolution and try you for it.

Timofei wasn't the slightest bit scared of their trial (these days the courts amounted to nothing), but he and Misha had a think. Right, say we arrest him—but which top brass do we take him to then? There are no real superiors these days, that's the trouble. The battalion commander—he's no leader now, no one listens to him. If we took him to the Soviet bosses they'd let him go immediately. And the government—who are they, where are they? And they're provisional, anyway; they'd let him go too. So why give ourselves the trouble?

Before, you could ask a good officer, but now the officers are all trying to keep their heads down.

Everything's gradually going downhill. There's no knowing where it'll end. You're ashamed, walking round Petersburg: outside bakers' or paraffin shops the queues are longer than before and when the women see soldiers, they shout insults from the queues: "You've sent Russia to the gutter!"

That week, Volynian Regiment delegates arrived from the front line: "Where's the help you're supposed to be sending? Give us reinforcements right now!" And a row brewed up and lasted all that day and half the next. "The Petrograd garrison shouldn't reward itself for the uprising by staying secure in the rear and deserting." To which the chairman—a sly type, he was—replied: "We'll be more help if we don't send reinforcements—they always melt away on the front, anyway. We'll give more radical help: we'll put an end to the war!"

Kirpichnikov just wanted to *go*, straight away, out of pure shame. He didn't know where to look. You couldn't hide behind the officers now. But they wouldn't let him go. He was needed here, for training. But Lance Corporal Ilyin went. Kanunnikov went. Somehow they managed to dispatch two reinforcement companies.

Then, once Sunday was over, there were great celebrations again on Tuesday. On Wednesday everyone was still in a daze but on Thursday, yesterday, the hurly-burly started up all over town. Timofei, Misha, and their little gang went out in the evening. On every corner people were giving speeches—you couldn't take it all in:

"Crowned barbarians have been keeping us in the dark, in total ignorance! Nikolai the Second kept us in a drunken daze for twenty-two years!"

"You can't have peace without strength! If our enemies understand that our strength is gone, they'll come to an agreement with the Allies and share up our land between them! And posterity will curse us."

". . . So then it wouldn't be those brigands who'd pay for the war, but Russian peasants?"

That was true enough.

"After your manifesto, Germany gave her answer on the Stokhod with asphyxiating gases! Fraternization? Why don't you tell your new German brothers that they must at least get rid of their gas cylinders?"

Good, that's right.

"It's not just every thinking citizen who wants to put an end to the war, but every soldier too. Attack? Not us!"

You wimp—have you ever gone on the attack?

". . . Got to get all those who are illegally hiding on the home front into the army . . ."

Now that's definitely right. There's so much to listen to that you get a buzzing in the head. And they talk so much, they take you round and round in circles and back again.

"Whoever's got the strength should seize power themselves, and run things better than the Provisional Government!"

"The soldiers didn't get it wrong when they elected seasoned revolutionaries to head the Soviet of Deputies and steer our ship . . ."

"Soldiers! For two and a half years you have risked your lives to defend our homeland. And if, now, we do not take some recompense for our sacrifices—how else can we pay tribute to those who died?"

Oh, that tugs at the heartstrings.

In the square, after nightfall, people were shouting: "Arrest Lenin!" But they weren't going to do it themselves. It was late when our Volynians walked back to barracks, talking: what if we charged over and arrested him anyway? Where could we get hold of a truck? But there was still the same problem: where do we take him then? They'll let him go anyway. Well, let's sleep on it.

And this morning they heard that there were even more people on Nevsky than yesterday, marching, shouting, arguing. After breakfast all the battalion's exercises were canceled and the lads spilled out again, to look and listen. Lunch was written off—we'll eat it this evening, we're in charge now.

Who are these marchers supporting? Most—by far—are against Lenin.

The lads went from group to group, listening. And wandered around Gostiny Dvor too—for no real reason, just to look at goods they'd never buy. And the big clock there showed three when they heard a great din coming from outside. They went out to look—it was coming from the Engineers Street end of Sadovaya. There was shouting and a band that sounded drunk, all banging out something for themselves, you couldn't tell what it was supposed to be. The first thing they saw was a truck bowling along Sadovaya with six machine guns pointing in all directions and not a single soldier manning them, just workers. Along the side facing Timofei and Mikhail they'd stuck a red strip that read, in white letters with streaks where the paint had run:

"Drop dead, capitalism! We'll get you with these machine guns!"

Well, well . . . Who are they threatening? The lads didn't understand. But the fellows at the machine guns didn't look very serious—just scowling as if getting ready for a scrap. And the genteel public crowded together to watch this amazing sight from all the sidewalks. No one shouted a response to those at the machine guns and no one stepped off the sidewalks to approach them, all were cautious.

The truck with the machine guns, not going fast, but even so outstripping any pedestrian, turned right into Nevsky and carried on in the same fashion toward the General Staff. Following after, lagging behind on Sadovaya, came the ones who'd been shouting and playing that discordant music. They were still about a thousand feet away and what you could see was a dark mass, at least a thousand people, charging along carrying red flags and placards, the small ones supported on a single pole, the others on two. At this distance you couldn't read them. And in front of them were ranks of workers with rifles and, along the sides of the column, a protective cordon, also armed. And, while they were still not near enough to read who this column was supporting, Kirpichnikov exploded with rage, turning to Markov and spitting on the ground:

"That's where they've gone, the state's rifles! While we don't have enough and HQ won't give us any. No one's got the right to carry them except soldiers."

On the sidewalks the elegantly dressed public were now more anxious. Some had sidled away, out of reach of any scuffles: people who wear good clothes have to watch out—the revolution's never going to teach them not to dress more plainly, or to smoke plain cigarettes. Others, the curious ones, still come to the edge of the curb to watch. And now there seem to be more of our grey greatcoats to be seen than before, and they step down into the roadway. An army doctor. A nurse.

It's closer now. The biggest placard is in front: "Down with the Provisional Government!," and the next has two workers shaking hands and "Long live the International!" Then, in a column four men abreast—they stay in line as best they can—about two hundred armed men. Some of the rifles slung on their shoulders are ours, some Austrian. There's workers of all ages, some real young. They've all got red armbands on their sleeves. After them, the band—you don't know what to make of it, they just crash their cymbals together very loud with every step. And then, like a herd of animals but in ranks, hand in hand, unarmed workers, women in headscarves, and more youngsters. Those in the flanking cordon barge right up to the sidewalk, scattering the onlookers, brandishing sabers, revolvers, rifles, or just unfixed bayonets—and one's got a kitchen knife.

The civilian bystanders have had a real fright, they shrink back and make themselves scarce. Some stand their ground, but still they don't move a muscle.

In the column there's not a single soldier.

"What are they doing with kitchen knives? They gonna start cutting people's throats?"

Standing nearest to the approaching march is a bearded militiaman:

"You lot don't know what you're doing!"

They hurl abuse at him, and make threatening gestures.

They march on. And further on "Down with Milyukov" can be seen, and "War on the war!" and a black banner with white lettering: "The machine gun and the sword . . ."—you can't read the rest, with that wind—and yet further on another armed column of a hundred or so and then another unarmed crowd with a protective cordon round them. How d'you like that! They didn't choose their places themselves, someone put them like that for a reason.

Suddenly it's obvious: they're marching to bring down the Provisional Government!

The front rank is close now, and the army doctor shouts out to them:

"Comrade soldiers! Those who hold our homeland dear, who want to save it from disgrace—forward! Don't let them through! Form a chain!"

And out he goes into the middle of the roadway. He's not a young one.

A volunteer cavalryman with a George Cross flies out after him:

"Come on lads! Come out here!"

And immediately twenty or thirty rush out to him, soldiers of different regiments, and some officers and officer cadets. And Timofei and Mikhail of course. And that nurse. (Markov never missed a beat—he'd already found out that her name was Zhenya.)

The officers and cadets have sabers or daggers, but the soldiers are all, every last one of them, unarmed—got tired of carrying our heavy rifles.

But even more soldiers run up from all sides, some from a long way off. Now there are about fifty of us. Standing across the whole roadway, in a sturdy chain. We won't let them through.

From the column of workers comes:

"Guchkov and Milyukov—to the fortress!"

"Long live peace and the brotherhood of peoples!"

With the soldiers there, the observers on the sidewalks have got bolder and they shout at the marching workers:

"It's a disgrace! Traitors! Renegades!"

And the column, to them:

"Bourgies! Provocateurs!"

From the sidewalk:

"Long live the Provisional Government!"

A worker from their protective cordon, brandishing his rifle:

"This'll be our answer to your government! We'll shoot the whole lot of you, all you bourgies."

A boy worker is randomly thrusting a Browning under people's noses.

A lady:

"You idlers! Soldiers on the front are spilling their blood and you're here on strike!"

A woman worker darts out of the ranks and snatches the lady's hat. The lady starts screaming.

The workers at the front of the column shout at the soldiers barring their way.

"Let us through!"

"We're not letting you through."

"Let us through or we'll shoot!"

"We're not letting you through! Put your weapons away and go home!"

"Are you in cahoots with the bourgies now? Who are you protecting?"

"We didn't serve our time in the trenches to allow this . . ."

"And we didn't win freedom for you not to!"

Observers offer explanations:

"We're against Milyukov too, but what's the Provisional Government got to do with it?"

What have they got against the government, actually? It's only just been set up—are we supposed to ditch it now?

The band has fallen silent but the crowd's roaring—roaring with a thousand voices—while the front ranks push forward, against the barrier of soldiers.

The soldiers hold on fast to one another and to the officers. They're from different regiments, don't know each other, and have no commander—but they hold together.

The marchers aren't roaring by now but howling, and brandishing revolvers and rifle-butts at us, as well as unsheathed sabers (but not slashing us).

Only, fifty men weren't going to hold out against the force of a thousand.

They overpower us and break through.

And barge on, the clashing brass cymbals keeping time nicely and the trumpets wailing.

And, like the rest, they turn right along Nevsky.

"Hey, Misha—how come we weren't too scared to fight the bosses this winter, and we weren't frightened of the military courts but now, against the workers—we're no match for them? And it's our own rifles they're using against us!"

The bystanders had retreated from the corner of Sadovaya, but on Nevsky Prospect, which was wide, they were further from the column, and shook their fists at the marchers menacingly from the sidewalks, shouting:

"Traitors! Provocateurs! Leninists!"

And the workers gave as good as they got:

"Bourgies! Spongers! Bastards! If you want to make war, go and do it yourselves!"

There was no answer to that from the sidewalks. They had no answer for that.

At the front and along the sides of the workers' column, those who were armed brandished their bayonets furiously, but those in the middle marched calmly, completing the distance as instructed, some of them simply waving their caps at the bystanders, meaning either "hurrah" or "down with"—you couldn't tell which. They didn't look happy as they marched past: they'd been working since early that morning and were weary by now. Their faces were haggard, covered with black dust or soot, and their clothes were dirty and greasy.

Timofei went up closer.

"What's your job?"

"We're from the New Lessner plant, on the Vyborg side."

"Where are the others from?"

"All the plants are here, marching behind us. And the bourgies won't stop us!"

At the end of the whole column came women and youngsters, really up in arms, shaking their fists. And the band was a long way away, so you could hear what they were saying:

"Down with the Provisional Government! Down with that scoundrel Milyukov! Down with the pot-bellied bourgies, those blood-suckers!"

Kirpichnikov was certainly angered by the workers demanding an eight-hour day all the time and not wanting to make any shells—but they didn't have a great life either, you could see that. That Lessner was sure to be one of those pot bellies.

At the back of the column came the real rabble now, dressed in tatters—not workers, more likely thieves. They were shouting loudest of all:

"Down with Milyukov! Down with the Provisional Government!"—and nothing else. Sometimes they bounded right up to the sidewalk and peppered whichever onlookers happened to be there with punches—but didn't touch any soldiers.

Then, all alone, a young fellow of about eighteen, trying to catch up with his group. He had a slung rifle too. Nurse Zhenya asked him:

"Which plant are you from?"

"Tube Factory."

"Where are you marching to?"

"General assembly."

"Why?"

"We're having a Eremeev night."

"What does that mean?"

"Beating people up right, left, and center, seizing banks and money. We've had enough of their bourgeois tricks!"

The whole procession had moved off toward Kazan Cathedral, but here groups were forming now, and those who'd retreated under archways or into doorways had left their hiding places and everyone was here, ranting away. A gentleman in a soft, grey hat, who was waving his dainty walking-stick and shouting so much that he was red in the face and running with sweat, called for everyone to form a column supporting the Provisional Government and follow those brigands. And a railway engineering student was calling for the same thing. People began to assemble on the roadway—a few civilians, a few cadets, and some soldiers—but all the onlookers only waved their handkerchiefs and hats from the sidewalks. No one wanted to join the march. The railway engineering student shouted:

"Hey, you, why are you dillydallying there? Are you scared? Join us and march for the government! Don't be afraid. Come on, quickly!"

Another student climbed up the wall of the Passage shopping arcade and took the big red flag that had hung there since the holiday. They stretched that flag out on the sidewalk, one of them brought chalk from a shop and they started writing across it: "Trust in the Provisional Government!"—but the chalk didn't write properly on the fabric and the words were barely visible, unlike the workers' slogans, which had been prepared in advance and painted on with brushes. They carried the flag in front of the little group and more people came to join them, and a few soldiers too. Kirpichnikov and Markov didn't know whether to go or not. None of their group was anywhere near. They were certainly disappointed that the workers wanted to overturn the government and that they'd broken through the soldiers' barrier. But since they'd seen, in the middle of that procession, those exhausted, besooted men, and women too, while the clean bystanders stood there, clinging to one another—why should we defend them? They're the people who go gorging themselves in restaurants at night and go about in carriages. They're not like us. What have they got to do with us?

But then a wounded officer shouted:

"Comrade soldiers and officers! Let's march with them! Military men should march, and be in the lead!"

And nurse Zhenya too:

"Let's go, lads!"

So they went. Suddenly there were several dozen more soldiers, then some civilians who'd got braver now.

Once they were marching, it was a shameful sight and a real trial for a soldier to plod along with them: they didn't form ranks but bunches, some thicker, some thinner. There was a flag in front and another at the back, also with "trust" but you could barely read it. In each of the two bunches there were about two hundred people.

And they walked for a while, past the Gostiny Dvor, to the City Duma, to the tower.

But the workers were already quite a lot farther on and you couldn't catch up with them straight away. People were saying: they've gone off to the palace where the government is. So we're going there too.

Kirpichnikov was among the first to hear, coming from behind them, beyond Eliseev's store, another loud din. They looked round—and it was a new dark mass rushing toward them, this one even bigger, about two thousand. These too had red flags, and a large placard held up on two poles with white lettering, but you couldn't read it from this distance. Some people started saying: they're supporting us, we should wait for them. Others said the opposite: quickly, let's get going, forward! They're against us.

It was clear to Kirpichnikov that they were the opposition. And there was an awful lot of them. The soldiers talked it over: no, we must go and face up to them and form another barrier and try and talk them out of the march. The most nimble among our crowd, the high school students, had already run there and back:

"Against! They're against!"

And those bystanders who'd assembled in a column to march after them now scattered in all directions and dropped the first flag, with the "trust" slogan, in the roadway. And as for the second flag, Kirpichnikov didn't notice what had happened to that, and he didn't notice whether anyone was carrying on in pursuit of the first column: by now all attention was focused on the second, and everyone was looking round to see how many of our lads, our grey greatcoats, there were. There were officers, too, but no more than two or three—and they'd been wounded. Officers were struck down during the March revolution, they weren't allowed to do anything. But there were officer cadets and thirty or forty soldiers, again from different regiments, without anyone in charge or anyone of senior rank, and without a single weapon—and a sailor from the Guards. These military men alone took their place across Nevsky Prospect. But Nevsky is a lot wider than Sadovaya and holding the marchers back would be harder. (The trams approaching from both directions had, one after another, come to a standstill.)

Now the slogans in the column approaching from behind could be clearly seen, in bold lettering: "Down with the Provisional Government!" There was no band, so you could hear the shouts more easily: "Down with Milyukov! Down with Guchkov! Down with the bourgies!"—and catcalls and abuse. And, as before, at the front was a detachment of workers with rifles, in quite orderly ranks (with red armbands on their sleeves again), and at the sides young lads were brandishing drawn revolvers and bayonets and further on, as far as the eye could see, was a dark column. But there was no time now to get a good look.

Standing by the curb, not part of the chain, was a hefty medical orderly, who shouted to the column:

"What are you doing? You're betraying Russia! You must listen to the government and the Soviet!"

A revolver was aimed at his face:

"We're gonna kill you! Come with us!"

"Kill me if you like, I'm not coming with you!"

"You'll soon see!"

And the bystanders shouted:

"Traitors! Leninists!"—but none of them left the sidewalk. Next to Markov was a soldier from a motor unit:

"But surely we can stop them, brothers, us front-line boys? Who ordered them to march? Let's stop them!"

But two officers, from the side:

"No brawling, comrades! Let them get past us, and then we'll arrange a demonstration in support of the government."

Yes, of course. After it's all been decided. Those weren't the kind of officers we had fighting the war.

"Stop, you traitors!"

And the medical orderly didn't quiet down:

"Why are you marching? Why don't you trust the government? We would march with you too if there was cause."

"It's not for you to know! Your bosses know!"

"Who do you want instead of Milyukov?"

"None of your business. You'll find out later."

"Ah, so you're not workers, you're Leninists!" cried the medical orderly. "That banner comes down, then!"

And he rushed at their flag.

But, despite everything, the column and the human barrier were now face to face and someone had to move. Our barrier was not solid enough—we couldn't stop them. But we could attack! And the two Volynians and the fellow from the motor unit exchanged glances and rushed forward. Charge, lads!

First of all, we had to snatch their rifles—they didn't even know how to hold them or how to shoot them, which way round. Kirpichnikov threw himself on a fellow with a moustache, grabbed his gun by the barrel and near the breech, gave it a twist, snatched it away and pushed him back with the butt.

"That's not your property! Don't be stealing!"

Other grey greatcoats also plunged in, and it started up quickly, you couldn't follow what was happening. Someone broke the flagshaft, someone trampled on the flag, and just nearby—a shot!

Timofei couldn't see who'd shot at who, but caught a brief glimpse of a fellow with light-brown hair aiming a revolver at him and, with the hand that was free of his rifle, punched the underside of his arm. The worker did fire, but into the air. Timofei grabbed the revolver and pulled it away from him.

And now, again from the workers—a shot! And another! There were six or seven shots and a soldier nearby, a Semyonovsky lad, fell, followed by another, farther off.

You scum! So that's the way it is! And the soldiers, enraged, roared at them, launched themselves for an attack, bulldozed into them, knocked some off their feet, smashed some in the face, sometimes even with rifle butts, snatched rifles from others—the soldiers were now carrying two each—and pressed forward.

And what madness broke out in the workers' column!

"They're shooting! They're killing people!"

The column was full of people who had never been under fire, and they even had women there. They broke through the barrier, darting off in different directions, some into shops, into a florist's, into building lobbies, and entryways, those with a rifle running off and shoving it somewhere, hurling it through a basement window: Me? I'm not armed.

Misha Markov had two rifles. The rifles were all loaded, that was the trouble. You stinkers, you shits! Who d'you think you're tangling with?

Right up to this moment they hadn't believed the workers would shoot.

Next to Timofei, the sailor had chambered a cartridge—Timofei placed his hand on the barrel of his rifle:

"No, wait! Let's try and sort this out."

Another nurse, a different one, was ripping up a flag the workers had lost.

The officers didn't have sabers any more—but here was one who did, and he leapt into the densest part of the column, where the demonstrators had stood their ground, and they tore off his epaulettes, took the saber, and blood poured from his face.

"Don't shoot, lads! We came out unarmed and must stay unarmed."

The skirmish came to an end—time for a breather. The young misses, the ladies, and the gentlemen who'd been on the sidewalks had taken to their heels. And those in the column who hadn't fled now moved back, closing up their ranks again, displaying their bayonets and their rage—but they didn't shoot. Two or three of them, prone in the roadway, were taking aim.

And hovering above the whole area was the sound of abuse: "Killers! Leninists!" And a woman and two soldiers were wounded.

And the Semyonovsky soldier . . . The Semyonovsky lad was dead.

Where did you wage war, little brother, on which battlefields? Did you ever think you'd meet your death here in Petersburg . . .?

But what can we do? There are such a lot of them. Now there's another detachment coming up behind.

Where is the might we once had, where are our ranks, our men? They've all faded away—we're no army now.

Someone shouts:

"Phone and get the Preobrazhensky Battalion here! They'll show them!"

But as for our Volynians—you couldn't get us assembled now.

From the sidewalk people called out to us:

"Just don't shoot, or there'll be heavy casualties!"

"We'll disarm them with our bare hands, those bastards, that scum!"

The public is coming back toward the street again and the insults get going!

"Killers! Traitors! German lackeys!"

An ambulance has approached from behind and is picking up the injured.

Those left in the column stand, hackles up, ready to defend themselves. But they stay silent, don't respond.

The same medical orderly as before:

"Lay down your rifles! And leave, calmly. Go wherever you like."

Markov:

"Don't carry any weapons! Why are you armed?"

They stay silent. A menacing silence.

No, Misha. There are more of them than us. They won't put them down.

We'd have to let them through.

Then the ordinary militia turn up, wearing white armbands. They ask the Leninists—beg them, even—to turn back toward Nikolaevsky Station: no one's going to trouble you.

No, they won't turn back.

Meanwhile, Gostiny Dvor—it's shut up tight, its shops closed.

The workers' militia stands, rifles at the ready. Rock-solid.

They're the strong ones. We had to let them through.

Our side shouted louder—but we let them through.

* * *

Whirlwind of the people's will
Ever more unbridled rage!
Fear not: these are the pangs of birth
Of a radiant new age.

(Vasily Nemirovich-Danchenko)

[76]

By the time the government finally assembled at Guchkov's ministerial residence, just after one o'clock, the events in the city were already alarming: unusually well-attended demonstrations, for and against, were clashing on Nevsky Prospect.

They assembled, yes—but without Kerensky. And Milyukov was so unhappy about this that he very nearly insisted on postponing the discussion till tomorrow. He wanted to be sure of apportioning some of the responsibility to Kerensky.

He was also unhappy with the proposed "Clarification." It conceded too much, it was too apologetic, and why had it been drawn up without him? Here, this word was not well placed, neither was that one. Now it would need several hours' thought. Pavel Nikolaevich would have to chew over every word. But the main thing was that there could be no question of ratifying that document without adding in the fact that the note had been the subject of careful and lengthy discussion by the full complement of the Provisional Government and accepted unanimously—the Minister of Foreign Affairs must not become the others' scapegoat.

And as for Guchkov, even on this occasion he left the meeting and went into his study. His surge of energy the day before had left him with none now, for exerting influence on the government. And now Alekseev was waiting for him. There were just a few hours left to fit in a meeting.

But it was at least good that the demonstrators had not found out that the government was in the War Minister's residence, and not charged over here along the Moika.

There was no talk of Kerensky out loud, but it seemed the ministers had all guessed the reason for his absence.

Nekrasov took the Kerensky role, in that he was now the one walking up and down the room expressing extreme indignation: what kind of a bloody schism is this? What irresponsibility (but not saying whose)! What unity we had during those March days! And how ever was it lost? (But not saying who it was who'd lost it.)

But Milyukov was dragging things out all the time, going off into a different room to think—thinking perhaps that he could somehow dispense with the "Clarification"?

But Prince Lvov was getting edgy because he had to receive Brătianu—it would be impolite to be late.

However, the ministers' meeting proceeded routinely, following an agenda listing the decisions prepared by the secretariat.

The Ministry of the Interior report was given by the diffident Shchepkin. It was time, he said, finally to legalize the dismissal of the provincial governors and vice-governors, the city governors and their assistants, who had been removed earlier by a simple order. We must recognize that they can never be returned to the posts they previously occupied, suggest that they apply to retire, set up pensions for them, and, for those who have no pension, a monthly maintenance allowance.

They had already got their fingers burned on these pensions and there'd been such a scandal. It would have been safer for the government not to allocate these people anything, but that would fly in the face of any concept of public service. And what, then, would be left of good order in our state? What fate would await today's civil servants?

Then—this was still Shchepkin—in a good few cities executive committees have arisen spontaneously and are demanding a maintenance allowance from the Treasury. It is impossible to satisfy all of them, so the proposal is to finance only the ones fulfilling duties given them by the government commissars, but not for maintaining their party propaganda and sociopolitical work, and not for the upkeep of party-, class-, or profession-based organizations.

"And what's more," Tereshchenko was quick to anticipate, "the state does not guarantee any loans already made by these organizations in the past few months."

His anticipation came from having already faced similar cases. For whatever you touched, wherever you cast your eye, all Russian society was like a crocodile with a thousand gaping gullets, just demanding money, money, and more money. Where was the Minister of Finance to find it, when even the Freedom Loan had now stalled, suspended thanks to that same, ever-present note.

But, occupying the post once held by the great, inventive Witte, he would have been deathly ashamed to drag every one of his problems with him into a government meeting. He could have deluged the place with problems of which he himself had despaired. (Many of them had already been discussed, anyway—fruitlessly.)

In recent weeks they had rashly increased, of their own accord, the salaries for village teachers, railwaymen, post and telegraph employees, and now soldiers too—where would he find the money to pay for everything? An irreparable breach had opened up in the Russian budget from the moment the Tsar had abolished the alcohol monopoly. Taxes had not been too assiduously collected either, the income tax being miniscule—they'd always relied on overseas loans. But after the revolution the police department responsible for tax-collecting had disappeared, along with the rest of the police force, so there was no one collecting it now and no alternative but to send out appeals to the population. Before the revolution, the Duma hadn't got round to ratifying the 1917 state budget, and now there was no Duma and no budget. The external state debt was 40 billion rubles—which cost two and a half billion a year in interest alone. Every day of the war was costing 50 million and since the start of the revolution they'd been issuing 30 million rubles–worth of bank notes a day, until the first days of the loan. And the ruble, which had in fact been rising thanks to the revolution, was now falling on the stock exchanges of the West. Subscription to the Freedom Loan had been launched to earsplitting publicity but, despite the honest support of the Moscow merchants and Jews all over the country, the results were as yet modest. Both friends and foes were keeping an eye on the fortunes of the loan: defeat for that initiative would be like a defeat in the war. (And there was another bungle: they hadn't managed to prepare the actual bonds by the time subscription was opened and for the time being they were handing out receipts, which many people didn't want to accept.) And the most irritating thing was the lack of support from the Soviet and most of the socialist newspapers. Instead, they were dishing up utopian proposals such as a property tax levied in a single payment, which verged on confiscation of property. The tax would be progressive, and anyone owning more than a million would give up 50 percent and then, they said, the workers would believe that the capitalists also loved their homeland. But if they carried out confiscations like this (not to mention the fact that Tereshchenko himself was not crazy enough to give all his wealth away) businesses would close, the economy of the whole country would collapse, and the workers themselves would suffer. Increasing the income tax and limiting profits from the war would be unavoidable but could not be worked out and seen through in a week. Russian finances could not be shored up without the participation of *all* the people. Great hope was invested in the prosperous peasantry. They had accumulated a great deal of money during the war—but democratic agitation was needed to help with this. For the time being they'd only managed to raise rail tariffs for goods and passengers.

Quite frankly, the Ministry of Finance had turned out to be nothing but trouble, and its affairs were in such chaos that Tereshchenko would be happy to be free of it and take a far more interesting job with greater freedom of movement.

But in the meantime, the meeting was proceeding. Manuilov had spent the last few days—since the teachers' congress where he'd had a good dressing down and lost his previous good name as a liberal—angry, irritated, and terrified by the specter of anarchy. Now he submitted for discussion the opening and financing of new high schools, middle schools, and modern schools, with students of both genders and teachers of both genders. They also had to ratify the personal maintenance allocation of fourteen thousand a year to his deputy, Grimm, and ten thousand each to the administrators of the school districts.

Konovalov asked for the leather monopoly to be ratified, for all skins to be put under government control, as had been done with grain, and for committees to be set up in all provinces to deal with leather matters, and with the right to requisition skins.

And Zarudny, from the Ministry of Justice, appealed for a pardon for three individuals convicted of robbery with violence: for the granting of pardons had also been transferred from the Tsar to the Provisional Government.

But all these were just preliminaries. Now Shingarev was ready, frowning gloomily, running with sweat, his eyes red from lack of sleep. He was to present his hour-long report for the ratification of the long-awaited land committee regulations, and an appeal to the population regarding this. And here the ministers were in for an even more detailed report—about the Main Land Committee and the provincial, district, and township committees, about representation of parties and organizations in the committees, about their objectives, plans for their congresses . . .

Milyukov was still not able to come to an agreement to the "Clarification."

Suddenly Nabokov was summoned and left the room, returning immediately, almost at a run, bringing with him:

"Gentlemen! General Kornilov, with an urgent announcement."

Saber at his side, still wearing his greatcoat, tensed for action, silent, his Asian face austere, he made a striking impression before even opening his mouth.

They were actually sitting there, going on and on, round in circles in their daily grind—on an extraordinary day! And could it be, could it really be that it wasn't over yet?

Prince Lvov, in a voice that was always weak but now even weaker, full of foreboding, invited the general to sit down.

But the general did not sit and did not even relax his unbending stance, his back and legs straight, his head bare.

"Prince! Ministers! Just now, in two places on Nevsky Prospect, local residents were shot at. There are deaths. I am requesting precise instructions: am I authorized to use military units to maintain order?"

He had not yet said where the shooting had taken place, who had been shooting, how many victims there were, or what he'd meant by "maintain order"—but all the ministers' eyebrows immediately shot up and they started backing away, some raising fingers, a hand, an arm, as if warding off a ghost or the devil. And in that tableau, that whole, spontaneous, silent scene, the general could already read his answer.

[77]

You couldn't even have dreamed up a more vexatious trip to Petrograd, he thought. And to crown all the failures—or was it a cruel joke?—it was today of all days that the *Stock Exchange Gazette* published a scandalous little article about the loss of the *Empress Maria*. It was scandalous because, thanks to Kolchak's efforts, that whole heartrending story had been kept out of the papers, and since October hardly anyone had known any details until now.

Since Toll perished in the Arctic Ocean and Makarov at Port Arthur, since Tsushima, Kolchak had suffered no greater affliction in his life than that of the *Maria*'s loss. He had loved that magnificent dreadnought as one might a living being. And that was how he had interred her. The whole funeral had lasted just over an hour. Amid black smoke and tongues of flame, Kolchak had instructed his men calmly and, after several explosions, given the order to open the Kingston valves and flood the magazines. Otherwise an explosion in the main powder-magazine might also have blown up the *Empress Catherine*—for she was moored beside the *Maria*. But it turned out that the *Maria's* mooring chain had, for some reason, not been properly attached and could not be freed quickly enough. Numb, distraught, Kolchak went down together with the ship, until the water almost reached the soles of his shoes. He scuttled her—and returned to his own ship, the *St. George*, in despair: it would have been better to risk that massive explosion and die in it himself.

For another month after that, he could talk of nothing but the loss of the *Maria*. But it was unbearable to him that newspaper hacks, feeling nothing for the situation, might rush to write "exposés" about it—all to the delight of Germany. At that time Kolchak did not allow the civilian legal authorities to pass on any reports of this or do any investigations of their own, and it was only three days later (as was now being, truthfully, reported) that the Ministry of Justice found out about it, from a coded telegram from the Prosecutor of the Simferopol District Court. Kolchak had acted on his own authority.

At that time the dreadnought had only been in service for six months. It was taking part in campaigns, when it suddenly became evident that some important electrotechnical works had been left unfinished—and there were no workers in that field either in Crimea or in Nikolaev (which was strange) and they had to bring forty-five men from the Putilov works in Petrograd. The *Maria* had only just returned from the Bulgarian shores when the works began.

How could a young commander's brain accommodate it all? He was busy with the fleet itself, with its combat duties, and on top of that he had administrative obligations for which he'd never been trained, and the fortress (with its inflated staffing) was also his responsibility, as was the town. How was he to keep an eye on everything or even find time to supervise and put in place all the personnel to keep an eye on it . . .? These workers lived on shore and were brought out every day in launches, to the barge moored to the *Maria*. There an officer should have checked all their documents but, as it turned out, he'd given the job to the bosun, the bosun had passed it on to a sailor, and the sailor—to no one. Then, on the *Maria* itself, discipline in respect of the bomb bunkers became lax, so that an unchecked person could have brought on an unchecked bundle and lobbed it into a ventilation hatch.

Within forty-eight hours he had arrested two engineers and some of the workers—two of whom then disappeared. (They were able to leave unhindered, and couldn't be found in Petrograd either.) Kolchak flew into a rage: Sevastopol must be slimmed down! Get rid of superfluous residents and superfluous institutions! (Those shady Greeks were still poking around everywhere in the vicinity of the ships.) We needed some new, stricter security measures, things we hadn't thought of. (Hardly any up to now had worked, anyway.) Some commission members were convinced that it had been done with malicious intent. Others said these were unforeseeable processes taking place in large masses of gunpowder hurriedly produced at a time of war, without sufficient quality control.

Kolchak had become obsessed by the idea that he himself had perhaps played a part in this event. He had taken some steps, unthinkingly: he wanted the sailors to like him, after the stiff Eberhardt—he wanted them to adore their commander! He'd stopped his sailors being incarcerated in the ground forces' guardhouse: now, guilty parties could be put onto their ships' tenders and from there onto their ships. (On the ships they might even be let off.) He allowed the sailors to smoke in some Sevastopol streets, only taking the cigarette out of their mouths when saluting an officer. (Could there be anything more absurd than that ban on the lower ranks smoking?) In late summer, when he'd only just taken over the fleet, seven drunken sailors had, one holiday day, created a rowdy scene in the market. The police and ground force patrols had arrested them and taken them away. But other sailors attacked the armed escort and freed the men. The head of the Sevastopol Gendarme Administration, General Redrov reported to the Police Department that the fortress was in a state of siege, and just look what . . . This report was sent on to the Navy Minister, Grigorovich, who took the matter up with Kolchak. Kolchak lost his temper, summoned Redrov, gave him a dressing down and forbade him to report anything, ever again: everything must be settled here, in Sevastopol. Redrov made another report, about this conversation. The Police Department asked Grigorovich for explanations and the latter, again, took it up with Kolchak. But Kolchak, by means of an order of the day to the whole fleet, dismissed Redrov and required him to leave town immediately. As it happened, at that time Protopopov had just taken over Internal Affairs, and didn't want to risk arguing with Kolchak—so the dismissal went through. (And was noted by the sailors.)

Perhaps Kolchak had succumbed to the general atmosphere, to blame the gendarmes. Social trends do drag you along with them, in spite of yourself. In this way he stifled the Gendarmes' oversight in Sevastopol.

This was exactly one month before the explosion on the *Maria* . . .

But it was this very popularity among the sailors that had enabled Kolchak to create the current, prized democracy of Sevastopol.

Only would it hold?

Was it, indeed, still holding now?

There, in Sevastopol, the apricot and peach trees had finished blooming and now there were roses and almond trees, the air was fragrant and the skies cloudless. As if there were no war and had been no revolution, the boulevards were packed with strollers dressed up to the nines, there were cinemas, and the summer theater on the Esplanade.

And it would be unthinkable to have Anya come down there.

And impossible to get to see her while he was up here.

He found an hour, out of the time he'd lost up here, for a visit to Plekhanov (Rodzyanko had advised him to go)—but that was not a success either. He was a dried-up little old man, pleasant and indeed at one time a famed revolutionary. But at sixty he was already finished. His health was very poor, he could barely sit up, and should have taken to his bed: you could already see in him the desiccation and yellowing of approaching death. His answer: "The Government is not controlling events. Nothing is going as we expected and there's little that isolated groups can do about it. But renouncing our claims to the Bosphorus and Dardanelles—that would mean living with foreign hands tight round our throat." All that was true. But he didn't say outright what Kolchak had understood from the conversation: that Plekhanov did not have any of those strong agitators to send to Sevastopol. He only had a few worn-out old men like himself. No young men had followed him.

Longevity is not always to be envied. You only need all those years if they have abundant strength and the capacity for action. But to pull oneself through decades without either . . . no—better to burn yourself out in battle.

And as for a visit to the Executive Committee's lair, Kolchak could not, despite the government's bowing and scraping to them, demean himself to that extent.

Now he sincerely felt himself ready to serve the new regime—it was, after all, our homeland today. But who would he be serving . . .?

Now we were seeing a second day of turbulence in Petrograd, an unprecedented pandemonium in this grim town. On his return from Plekhanov, he'd heard that armed workers had shot at unarmed soldiers at the corner of Sadovaya, only half an hour ago. Was it possible?!

But he went out onto his second-floor balcony, which overlooked Nevsky at the Karavannaya Street corner. From the other side of Fontanka another great procession of workers was streaming over Anichkov bridge and then passing under his feet. First in the column came glowering workers with rifles and, ahead of them, a placard reading "Red Guard." There were a few sailors, probably from Kronstadt, but not a single soldier. And there were shouts, with raised fists:

"Milyukov to the fortress!"

"Death to Guchkov!"

"Let's show the bourgies our strength!"

"Give the bourgies a thrashing!"

"Long live Germany!"

After that "Germany," Kolchak would happily have mown them down with a machine gun himself, there and then from the balcony.

In the sunshine everything was sharply delineated. There were red banners emblazoned in mosaic gold, and one black banner, which was ominous. As they came nearer you could see on it a skull and crossbones and "Long live the Commune!"

People on the sidewalks cursed at them, but then faltered, and started running off. There was a banging of shop shutters.

And so, sweeping Nevsky clear, they marched, victorious, past Ekaterininsky Square toward Gostiny Dvor and farther, with Kolchak keeping an eagle eye on them. And then he saw, there, by the City Duma, the flash of a raised saber and then—he heard shots. There must have been thirty or so.

Uproar. People scattered. In all directions, round corners, hundreds of people, a melee, and—was that someone left lying there?

Kolchak was now absolutely certain: the Provisional Government was not capable of running the state.

We needed a dictatorship.

Covering all of Russia.

But where could we get it from now?

[78]

Around midday Kolya was racked with hunger: he'd not had a proper breakfast at home and then, once he was out, he couldn't go back or pop to a friend's house—and it was hard to buy a roll anywhere now. But his stomach heated up a bit, burned a bit—and calmed down. It even cheered him up, which was how it should be today. Carefree!

On this day, full of people and sunshine, was there any part of Nevsky Prospect where Kolya and friends didn't spend a bit of time, didn't hang about, didn't have their fill of debate? But they didn't manage to see the shooting on Nevsky, not even the second shooting. When they heard it they ran over, so fast they could hardly catch their breath.

A sense of menace, absent that morning, had now blown in.

All Nevsky was seething. Two ambulances suddenly appeared. A student with no coat or cap was running along shouting, begging for another one: there were more people lying injured in the Volga-Kama Bank lobby. The trams were starting to move now but with difficulty, and with a loud ringing of bells because excited groups were forming, even on the tram tracks. The cabs were still blocked.

And everyone was immersed in animated conversation, some telling what they'd seen, others what they hadn't seen but had heard from reliable sources. It was the "workers' militia." No, they called themselves the "red guard." Or just, the Leninists. There's a body still lying in Mikhailovskaya Street. That was the Parviainen plant. Soldiers bravely disarmed that armed mob, with their bare hands. There were only five people injured but some civilians among them. No, there were fifteen or so. There was a woman with a saber wound to the head. Another student, sobbing hysterically:

"As if the pharaohs shooting us was not enough! Now we'll be shooting each other!"

"Armed men against unarmed crowds! Back to the old ways!"

With a cigar clamped between his teeth and the air of a wise teacher:

"Why didn't we use Lynch's law to settle accounts with them?"

People say bullets have hit upper floors as well. But now all the balconies are packed with curious observers.

A Georgian in a tall hat of fine, curly goat's fur:

"No one was killed."

"How can that be? People saw it!"

Some are saying the workers, not knowing how to shoot, ended up shooting their own comrades in the back.

Indignant cries:

"When the most fearsome people in demonstrations are Vinaver and some high school boys, who has the right to take up a gun?!"

"What about today's new militia? Why aren't they stopping it? Where are they hiding themselves?"

Now some soldiers have arrested a civilian. Looks like a worker. They search him for weapons.

A sailor, spitting on the ground:

"Petrograd's full of spyers! Like tadpoles in a pool here."

"Good to see that all the soldiers support the Provisional Government!"

"Get rid of Lenin! It's due to him that there's been shooting. Arrest him!"

But now those people are already out and darting about again:

"It was the dark forces that were shooting, to start quarrels between the workers and the soldiers! It was the bourgeoisie that was egging them on to shoot at an unarmed crowd!"

"Get rid of that lot! We've had enough! We don't want to hear any more from them!"

A soldier who'd lost a leg:

"I'm ready to give the provocateurs a thrashing with my crutch!"

Another sailor:

"They're the only troublemakers. They don't love their homeland—don't listen to them, chuck 'em out!"

People are saying that they weren't only from the Vyborg side, there were some from Polyustrovo and Vasilievsky Island. And they say lots were marching against their will . . . They'd asked the women: "Why that 'down with'?" "How should we know? We were working and they came up and said, 'Leave that, go to Nevsky!' And we did."

"Can't we use the numbers on the confiscated rifles to find out who fired the shots?"

"Unregistered—all swiped in the first days of the revolution."

Kolya and friends feel their arms and legs wanting to move off: where should they run to? Who should they look for? How could they help?

At the top of the Duma steps stand the mayor and his colleagues. They're powerless—they aren't running the town, are they? That's the very place, facing those steps, where the first shots were fired on 10 March. And today as well.

What'll become of the government? And of us all?

But the shooting has enveloped and united everyone. A soldier with more than one George Cross explains to the "bowlers" and the "millinery":

"I was wounded by the enemy five times and I can't accept it—our soldiers being shot, here, in Petersburg. The power must be firmly in the hands of the Provisional Government."

People have arrived from the Kshesinskaya palace, saying they'd seen the Leninists openly handing out five-ruble notes to hooligans and riffraff just to walk around town shouting, "Down with Milyukov" and "Down with the government."

The various rallies are mingling, flowing into one another. By now, it seems, everyone is out on the street—no one's working, anywhere. The shooting has shown everyone that something has to be done.

And it's this! People are taking the First of May banners down from walls and bringing out from Gostiny Dvor buckets of black varnish and white paint, and brushes. They spread the banners and placards out in the Gostiny Dvor arcades, and Kolya, whose penmanship is the best in his class, traces out: "Trust A. I. Guchkov and P. N. Milyukov!" and Dima Saburov writes, more simply, "Down with anarchy!" Other people have:

"No separate peace!," "Down with German militarism!," "Protect the Provisional Government!"

They let them dry a bit and then raise the inscribed banners, and a crowd gathers, to march beneath them. There's an understanding: now absolutely everyone has to march. There are shouts of:

"March to Kazan Cathedral. That's the appointed place!"

"March to Mariinskaya Square, that's the place!"

A column, already formed, arrives from the Znamenskaya Square direction. These are the employees of the office of the Nikolaevsky Railroad. And the Nevsky marchers step aside to let them through, shouting out to them:

"Long live Milyukov!"

"Down with Lenin, the Kaiser's hireling!"

The column's banners read: "Arrest Lenin and his henchmen!" And "Only harmony between the Provisional Government and the Soviet of Workers' Deputies will save our homeland."

No one's afraid now, they're all happy, confident of victory! And bit by bit they all move off. The crowd has grown—you can't see the end of it. The procession is massive and there are large crowds applauding from the sidewalks as well. And clapping and enthusiastic shouts and cheers from all the balconies.

"Get rid of Lenin and everything'll be fine!"

"Send him back to Germany!"

Approaching from the other direction—and willingly ushered through—is an open car. Standing in it is Aleksinsky, his back somewhat hunched, waving his hat and shouting his agreement with the marchers and his opposition to Lenin.

The crowd's delight is still mounting. Now, it seems, even if you started shooting you couldn't disperse them so easily.

"Hurra-a-ah! Follow us!"

"To Mariinsky Palace!"

[7 9]

That morning, after Alekseev left, Kornilov had about two hours to work in peace.

Peace? He'd never had a single peaceful day in that city ever since he was appointed. But—for two hours nothing new happened. And at the moment he was doing the work of the chief of staff he no longer had. (The Soviet wouldn't let him keep Rubets-Masalsky or appoint anyone else that he wanted.)

And how stupid, how cowardly the government was, not arresting that Leninist gang, everyone over there at the Kshesinskaya. All it took was a couple of trucks one night with armed detachments and two machine guns. That would have done the trick.

He did have some loyal detachments. And all the military schools could be relied on too. He could gather the forces. But the government was utterly spineless.

He sat working. Then people started reporting phone calls coming in from military units. Agitators were again inciting soldiers to go into the streets, into the center of town. And the only reason none of them had gone yet was that yesterday evening the Executive Committee had ordered units to stay in their barracks. But workers were pouring out of the factories. They were armed! And making for the center of town.

So it had come to that!

But even now he wouldn't have gone to the government yet if there hadn't been shooting and fatalities on Nevsky.

He burst into their meeting. They refused his request and advised him to ask the Executive Committee.

The Executive Committee? No one with an ounce of self-respect would go to them for help. That crew bore the greatest responsibility for the army's disintegration.

Was he the Commander or not, dammit? And what did he have to lose now, with the dog's life that was his job? He'd already, three weeks ago, asked Guchkov to transfer him to the front.

Did he really have to sit and wait till they came waving their stolen rifles under his windows?

All the military schools obeyed orders. But there was one: his own, much-loved Mikhailovsky Artillery School. Who to summon if not them? He gave orders to send a phoned telegram: the school was to send two of their batteries with all necessary combat equipment to Palace Square.

Just look out for our cannons, you urban scum.

Today Kornilov had decided to act for himself, not looking over his shoulder now. To remind everyone that there was, despite everything, a military power in this country and in this city.

Reports were coming in on the phones: workers were on the march, detachments with rifles in the lead. From the Vyborg side. And from Vasilievsky Island. And from the Moscow Gate.

Good, good. Come on in.

He sent another order, to the Grenadier Battalion (it wouldn't do any harm to have some loud stamping going past the Kshesinskaya mansion): they were to send a large company to Palace Square, with the necessary combat equipment.

However, for some reason the guns didn't arrive (he'd been keeping an eye on the square from his window). This snail's pace might be fine for taking your pots to market but . . . He had an aide telephone: why weren't they here?

The reply was muffled: the commander's order had arrived during a general assembly. All the cadets were there, with officers and soldiers from auxiliary services also present. It had not been possible to carry out the order without announcing it to the assembly. And now they were all discussing whether or not to send the batteries.

And this was *his* school!

Kornilov's neck was slender, and accustomed to a military collar—yet even so that collar began to pinch.

But now he'd started to move, he'd go on. There's nothing worse than stopping halfway.

And, finally—armored cars? (Khabalov's big mistake had been not using them in the March revolution.) He ordered the armored command to send two detachments to Palace Square immediately.

And now, in no fit state to do any work, he paced his office with a military gait. And every time he passed the window—had they arrived yet?

They had not.

Reports were being phoned into Military District HQ: crowds of armed and unarmed workers were crossing the bridges, making for the center.

So—it was even worse than March, then?

But does a general carry an ounce of weight if he isn't obeyed?

He paced up and down, beside himself with rage.

He remembered Krymov sitting there, talking to him. At that stage it hadn't been too late.

His adjutant: a delegation has arrived from the Mikhailovsky school.

"Really? Well, bring them in."

Two officers, two cadets, and two soldiers from the school's service staff. Without those two soldiers, would the others have spoken openly? But instead:

"We've been sent to find out whether the commander is acting with the agreement of the Soviet of Workers' and Soldiers' Deputies."

Ah, so that's how it is. (Well you can just go and . . .)

The Commander reminded the gentlemen officers and the gentlemen cadets that they may visit Military District HQ only when summoned, especially during teaching time. They had not been summoned. They could go.

The Grenadiers managed without a deputation. They telephoned: we cannot send a company, due to yesterday's order from the Soviet not to let any units out of barracks.

Ah, so this was how the order had turned out. Kornilov hadn't seen that coming yesterday: he'd thought it was for the best.

All he could do now was rush over to Guchkov. Alekseev would be there too, the whole of high command: you'd better give this some thought!

But his adjutant asked Kornilov to take the phone—there was a call.

He didn't ask any questions—just grabbed it and responded.

The *powers* were asking for Kornilov! Chkheidze from the Soviet of Workers' Deputies. Was it true that the general had summoned artillery and armored cars?

To hell with you and your gang. Why should a commander chat to that rabble? What kind of dirty, dishonorable job is this for a soldier—start with the arrest of the Tsaritsa and end up by toadying to that mob?

Now the Executive Committee wanted to explain to General Kornilov that mobilizing military units could make the situation very much more complicated. We're sending some delegates over to you. In the meantime, to observe the proprieties and for the sake of your reputation, we suggest that you yourself should cancel your orders.

Right! He'd never forgive them this humiliation.

And could he forgive the government . . .?

* * *

YOU CAN'T TIE A KNOT ONE-HANDED

* * *

[8 0]

Kostya Grimm and Vadim Andrusov also went to Mariinskaya Square.

"And how base," said Kostya, "those attacks on England and France. Who gave us the seeds of our revolution? What kind of ideological views would our revolutionaries have had, without the cultural heritage of Western Europe? All our revolutionary figures of the nineteenth century were, to a greater or lesser extent, nourished by Western enlightenment. It's a sad truth, but inescapable: Russia is no Messiah among peoples. It's a backward European country, but it is traveling the same route as the rest. Its destiny is closely linked to that of the rest of the world. Russia can't originate any effective initiative. If there's no social revolution after the war in Europe and America, we won't have one in Russia."

Yes, of course that was right. As Schliemann's grandson, Andrusov thought so with even greater conviction.

When, yesterday evening, a unit of the Pavlovsky Battalion had taken matters into their own hands and marched into Mariinskaya Square, neither of the two ensigns—and almost none of the officers—had come along to give the column a boost. That matchless joy of fusing with one's men, which Andrusov and Grimm had known on 13 March as they did the rounds of all the barracks crying "Get up everyone! The revolution's here!"—that joy had long since melted away, dwindled, leaving nothing. The soldiers were being carried off somewhere at a tangent, becoming ever more wayward under the influence of the committees and, now, against the young government.

But what a social barrier had risen up as well, against the insurrection!

And here, now, with every quarter-hour more people came flooding in through all seven entry points into the square, the first taking their place in front of the palace and later arrivals standing behind Nikolai I as well. And there were speakers in every group, all speaking in support of the government, order, and victory in the war. They were all sensible people. And there were very many soldiers out on their own—and they were all sensible. "The soldiers are with us!"

(If only . . .)

Someone standing close to the ensigns:

"Yes, it's getting harder and harder to argue with the peace slogans. Our argument can only be based on honor, on patriotism, while they're only moved by self-interest."

"Don't say that," came a thoughtful objection from a grey-haired gentleman. "This call for immediate peace is not just out of self-interest. You can divine the Russian soul in it. The people's hearts hear an age-old truth there."

Kostya and Vadim exchanged looks. Surely not? If so, we certainly won't be fighting the war till the end.

From the speakers' stand, a railway worker:

"Petrograd is going too far. In Moscow they don't agree—and neither do they on the front, nor in the country. I'm a delegate from the South-Western Railroad. Seventy thousand railway workers have sent me to tell you that we're ready to go without food, to go without sleep, to die! But nothing in the world could make us agree to a shameful peace."

That won him cheers.

And there were students too—on the government side! (When did students in Russia ever support the government?)

An officer:

"Where we are, in the Caucasus Army, we've only just heard about Lenin's dangerous propaganda here, and that he's totally free to spread it. The Caucasus Army is wondering why this dangerous propaganda hasn't been stopped yet. The Caucasus Army would rather die than allow a shameful peace! Down with Lenin!!"

A soldier with a shaggy, yellow beard:

"I got this bullet, see—went in under me eye and come out by my ear. I'd finish off this war myself, but for the life of me: tell me if you know how to do it."

There were already thousands there—getting more and more impatient for the ministers themselves to come out and speak. They sent a deputation into the palace. Where is it, for goodness' sake, our government? (Grimm kept quiet—he knew where they were.)

The pigeons, frightened away from the pavement, were now only frequenting the balcony above.

And there was still that same banner suspended right across the palace: "Long Live the International." And the German Embassy, behind it, with its solid grating, still looked out from the empty eye-sockets of its windows. But as for their "Long live the German workers" banner—someone had apparently taken that down during the night.

An English naval officer spoke, without an interpreter: fight alongside your Allies! The German fleet is blockaded in the Kiel canal. Every day brings us closer to victory.

A French lieutenant. A Serbian army captain. The wife of a Belgian officer: "Don't abandon us! Don't conclude a separate peace!"

Enthusiastic applause for them all.

Then two members of the Executive Committee arrived by car, Skobelev and Bogdanov. Standing up, they were trying to persuade the crowd to disperse and not create a disturbance: it's causing a division in our ranks, which is dangerous for our revolutionary aspirations.

The two ensigns objected:

"We're not creating any disturbance. Why should people supporting the government have to disperse?"

The Executive Committee will take measures to guard against excesses.

Well take your measures, then.

And they left.

But the crowd multiplied. There were already thousands and thousands of them and they were united. It was now getting cramped and you couldn't move very far. The groups were merging into each other.

Cars were now approaching the palace. The crowd made way, looked at them, asked one another—who's that? The passengers turned out to be the vice-ministers, gathering for their meeting. The crowd greeted them, but demanded speeches.

The Vice-ministers for War and Agriculture addressed the crowd. Then the elder Grimm, the professor who chaired the vice-ministers' cabinet and was himself Vice-minister of Education, also arrived. He spoke from the steps:

"Believe me, citizens, the Provisional Government will not, in these difficult days, allow the freedom we have struggled so hard to achieve to be torn apart. In coming to the square in your thousands, you have shown how dear your homeland is to you. To prevent the spread of clearly dangerous Leninist propaganda, go and talk to the less conscientious, the uneducated masses and explain to them that there is no room for violence in a free country!"

The son listened proudly to his father.

The crowd applauded, and cried out, "We trust you! We trust you!" But no one went off to start explaining. They themselves wanted to hear more.

And they stopped another one and demanded a speech. It was the Vice-minister of Justice, the lawyer with pitch-black sideburns, Zarudny:

"Citizens! We are not officials, we are people like you, citizens of Great Russia. And if we ever come to recognize that the Provisional Government has taken the wrong direction, we shall be the first to say so, loud and clear . . ."

Ladies and gentlemen! Russia has, at last, an honest government. At last we have a free Russia!

". . . Fortunately, we see no such mistaken path. But while passions are running so high, our work of setting up the new order is being hampered. Unfortunately dark forces clearly remain. Civil unrest is useful to them, and they are stirring it up . . ."

Was it the inextirpable Rasputin-Protopopov spy network?

The vice-ministers went on in.

The crowd was getting ever denser, though they themselves did not know what they were waiting for. They had now even climbed the massive columns on both sides of the palace. And then . . .

. . . Then a terrible rumor reached the edge of the crowd and spread like wildfire: there's been a bloody confrontation on Nevsky. Was that possible . . .?

Yes, there's been shooting! Killings!!

Who was shooting? Who's dead? How many?

Who attacked who?

Should we rush over there? (And are we ourselves safe, here?)

Now a witness—he looked like a shop-assistant—mounted the stand and told everyone: a group of workers, armed with rifles, had shot at government supporters.

The crowd began to roar with rage.

They shouted out all sorts of things they thought should be done now.

Then a truck packed with soldiers approached from Morskaya Street. The crowd made way and it drove into the center of the square. A civilian in an overcoat came to the tailboard. His sleeve was bloodied and not even bandaged:

"Look, they got me. Point-blank."

What pandemonium then!

"It's a disgrace!"

"Arrest them!"

A soldier from the truck:

"It was the dark forces that were shooting, and they had German help. They just hid behind workers' jackets and soldiers' greatcoats."

But things were no clearer. A sailor from a Guards crew:

"The ones who were shooting called themselves Leninists. Let's get a deputation together and the witnesses can go with them and inform the Provisional Government."

A delegation willingly formed and the fellow with the bloodied sleeve and two soldier witnesses joined them.

Soon that same very dark-haired Zarudny appeared on the palace balcony, scaring the pigeons away. You could hear him from a long way off, only you had to half-close your eyes to see him against the sun.

". . . We have decided to take the most stringent measures. I shall form a special commission of inquiry immediately which will, I'm sure, be sanctioned by Minister of Justice Kerensky. And it will set to work straight away, identifying the guilty parties. In a few minutes, representatives of the investigating authority and the prosecutorial inspectorate will be here. I'd be very grateful if the witnesses would remain here and give their testimony."

Cheers broke out all over the square.

No, we won't yield! We're Russian society. They won't take us by force!

The government hasn't been idle! Our citizens haven't been left to the whim of fate. The guilty will all be punished.

Across the whole of Mariinskaya Square cries were heard:

"They're starting a civil war!"

"That's what they've been preaching the whole time!"

"Give us the chance to disarm the dark forces!"

"Lenin must be arrested!"

They'd forgotten that it wasn't the ministers themselves who stood before them.

Zarudny:

"We'll communicate your wish to Kerensky."

Grimm came to his aid:

". . . The most energetic measures will be taken in our struggle against the perpetrators of violence . . . In a country where the death penalty has been abolished, there can be no place for anyone stirring up brother against brother."

Well done, father!

Delighted applause from the crowd.

This went on for a long time and the buzz continued even when the balcony was empty. They had the idea of drawing up a resolution, and someone collected people's opinions while someone else wrote them down. Then they announced them three times to the crowd, each time facing a different part of the square:

". . . The citizens ask the government to stand up for the law and for citizens' personal security . . ."

They took this into the palace, but demanded that it be given, without fail, to Kerensky himself.

In the meantime, whole columns of demonstrators were pouring into the square from Morskaya. Their placards read: "Complete trust in Citizen Milyukov!" and "Long live Guchkov!"

Goodness, all Petrograd was here! And all Petrograd was united!

Who's doing the shooting, then . . .? Who's stirring things up?

Demonstrations were arriving—but here people were saying an even bigger event was about to begin outside Kazan Cathedral.

An excited crowd formed a column and streamed off in that direction.

[8 1]

(PETROGRAD STREETS: 4 MAY)

* * *

On the prominent external stone staircase of the City Duma hangs the slogan "Lenin and co: back to Germany go!"

On Nevsky Prospect Lenin's name is heard constantly. The government must order his arrest!

"He came back to stir up unrest in the army!"

"The Leninists are protesting against war on the front—so why are they stirring one up inside this country?"

"And when we sign the peace—then they'll organize a real war for us!"

"They'll do nothing of the kind! The Leninists certainly don't want civil war! They don't even want to take power: they know they couldn't handle it."

An old fellow, about seventy:

"I've got four sons at the front, but what I say is: fight on till victory!"

* * *

Five injured soldiers, St. George Cross holders, in an open car hold a placard with "Trust the Provisional Government!" They get a noisy welcome.

Near Nadezhdinskaya Street they encounter a crowd five or six hundred strong, some of them armed: "Only trust the Soviet of Workers' and Soldiers' Deputies!"

The soldiers in the car shout out to them:

"Hey you, heroes of the rear! Give those weapons over to the front—they need them there! It's shameful to parade around here with weapons!"

The column falters.

* * *

Two opposing demonstrations march along Nevsky side by side. They don't snatch each other's placards, but do exchange insults:

"It's the bourgie-ua-sie marching. With the easy life they have! They should try working their fingers to the bone like us."

"You're parading, with your 'down with the government'—you think you're bringing peace any nearer? You're leading us straight into civil war!"

"And a bayonet in the gullet for Guchkov and Milyukov!"

* * *

"All power to the Soviet!" "Only trust the Soviet!"

At the corner of Liteiny and Nevsky, a little group of workers and soldiers pounce on a car and snatch a placard reading "Complete trust in the Provisional Government."

At Fontanka, the opposite: people are tearing up Leninist placards and throwing them into the water.

But a student shouts:

"Milyukov and Shingarev are the biggest landowners!"

* * *

A railway engineering student, Balykov, goes up to a column of Leninists and asks them to explain why they're armed. The Leninists fall on him, and he gets a gun butt in the head and a serious beating, until soldiers come to his rescue.

Volunteer Ginsburg, also a student, crosses Nevsky, cutting a corner to reach a different column of Leninists on Sadovaya. He shouts, sternly:

"Russia's fate won't be decided in the street! You can only come out onto the street when called out by deputies, otherwise you're not true citizens! Those criminal placards must go! You'll only get onto Nevsky over my dead body!"

Some gun-barrels are aimed at him, but don't shoot. An elderly peasant embraces Ginsburg and kisses him.

At the end of the column are all sorts of riffraff, and dishevelled women in headscarves. Someone asks one of them what she wants to achieve and she replies:

"To distruct the old guv'ment and Nikolai the Second."

Everyone laughs at her:

"The old government's been gone a long time now."

* * *

A crowd ten thousand or so strong— with "The Provisional Government is how we save our motherland," "Long live Citizen Milyukov" and "Long live the Allies"—has arrived at Kazan Cathedral. People say Rodzyanko and General Alekseev are to speak there.

A sea of heads. Hands hold up a large portrait of Kerensky. They wait.

But neither Rodzyanko nor Alekseev comes. A student shouts from a truck:

"People have turned up here with kerosene, to set fire to our homeland. One of them's brought a whole barrel from Germany."

An officer holding a red rose waves it to attract attention:

"This is a red-letter day. Again we can feel the Russian people united by love of the motherland. People who claim they are defending freedom have fired on the Volynian soldiers who gave us that freedom. Impure mouths must not proclaim words of peace! Fresh and joyous as this flower, the soul of the Russian people . . . But peace is impossible without victory."

A disabled soldier from a German prisoner of war camp speaks about the torments our men suffered there.

"Lenin and his supporters traveled across Germany, soaked in Russian blood!"

Soldiers shout up to him:

"Down with Lenin! Shoot the Leninists!"

Someone acting as a chairman tries to persuade people to react with words alone.

"But they're shooting!"

The truck moves off. The rally continues from little speakers' stands. A civilian intellectual:

"I have no party affiliation. Just now, on the Field of Mars, I heard calls to thrash the intelligentsia! And they say they're fighting for their principles? Surely you have to give Milyukov his due as a political figure?" (Cries of "Long live Milyukov!")

An army doctor:

"I'm going back to the front—and what picture am I to paint of the situation here? Don't deal us a treacherous blow from the rear! The army has to know it can confidently stand with its back to you. A small group of dullards is trying to split apart the talented power that leads us. The Provisional Government must join with the Soviet on a common platform of love for our homeland."

They raise him aloft.

A delegate from the other rally, from Mariinskaya Square, mounts the stand. Over there, Zarudny has promised that all legal measures will be taken against those who've been shooting. And the prosecutors have already launched a murder investigation.

Let's go over there! That's the main rally. That's where the government is, and ministers will address the crowd there!

The vast crowd starts getting entangled and turning round—to go to Mariinskaya Square!

* * *

More and more motor vehicles have appeared, both cars and trucks. They drive along one block at a time, stop and give speeches from their vehicles.

"Recent events have shown that some elements among us are trying to stir up a civil war. But our people's common sense will keep them from responding to these calls."

A piercing voice from the crowd:

"In '05 you Kadets were yourselves calling the people to seize power! Why don't you like the idea now?"

On the squares where there are rallies, Red Cross ambulances, both horse-drawn and motor-powered, are standing by. Others move along slowly, keeping pace with the marches.

* * *

Toward five o'clock the workers' columns have finished their march and left—and Nevsky fills up with a motley crowd. They are elated and confident that the pro-government, pro-Milyukov side will prevail!

"Look! It's not capital demonstrating in support of the government—it's the people!"

"We've suffered penal servitude, we've gone to the gallows, and now we, the intelligentsia—now we're 'the bourgeoisie'?"

"But who isn't 'the bourgeoisie'? What about the peasants—aren't they 'the bourgeoisie'? The majority of the Russian population is! How absurd, the pretensions of the 'proletariat,' those three percent or so, claiming the right to some kind of dictatorship . . ."

A column of children from the most junior school classes marches under a placard: "Long live the Provisional Government!" From the sidewalks they get an enthusiastic welcome, and people wave their handkerchiefs.

Tereshchenko drives past in an open car. The Nevsky crowd recognizes him and greets him noisily.

* * *

From the Admiralty side, olive-green military trucks are constantly pushing a way in and trundling along Nevsky, full—in the triumphant style of the March processions—of soldiers and civilians. But they are unarmed and they wave to the crowd with their hats, high-school caps, and round sailors' caps, baring their close-cropped heads. Above the cabs of trucks fly banners: "Support the Provisional Government!" and "Work here means victory there!"

They are greeted with a roar, and people on the sidewalks respond, waving handkerchiefs and hats.

From one of the trucks they scatter copies of the Kadet appeal. From another, as a reminder, leaflets with Wilhelm's speech to his Guards, calling for total destruction of Russia. People are picking them up and reading them out loud. When the trucks stop for speeches, people in the crowd try to climb on board, too.

Wounded soldiers recovering at Sergei Aleksandrovich's palace and other military hospitals are also here, waving.

It seems all Petrograd is for the government! Is anyone still against them?

And Kolya and his two friends are happy—they've found transport in the back of a truck.

Inscriptions in charcoal and chalk have already appeared on trams as well: "Down with Lenin!" "Wilhelm! Take your Lenin back!" And each such tram that passes is greeted with applause by the Nevsky Prospect public.

* * *

In one truck is a soldier with expensive flowers in his hands. The crowd applauds him.

In another are more St. George Cross holders. An officer is on his feet, has taken the little white-enamelled cross from his chest and, arm outstretched, holds it in front of him. Applause from the crowd.

From the trucks leaflets are scattered: "Set aside private interests! Unite to defend Russia!"

The roadways are the routes of the revolution. Those who master the roads lead the revolution.

* * *

Then, a rumor is heard on Nevsky: six motorcars with armed men have gone to arrest Lenin.

The curious swarm off toward Trinity Bridge.

[8 2]

The Executive Committee session dragged on and on. It was draining. The Provisional Government hadn't delivered the text of the Clarification that had been coaxed out of them . . . still not delivered it . . . and even now hadn't . . . And that was despite the majority of the EC having agreed to it a good while before: just send it over, they'd said.

In the meantime someone had been stirring up the factories . . . No one here dared say it was the Bolsheviks—even though their leaders were not here today. No one dared say it was the Bolsheviks, because it was not strictly proven . . . But the plants were marching and marching, in armed columns, into the center of town, and Chkheidze's and Skobelev's missions had not made an iota of difference. But in the center the petits bourgeois were throwing aside all restraint in their defense of the government, and clashes could easily be expected. And clashes there were, with shooting and fatalities.

There were not many killed—but what a clear sign that events were out of control! The most dangerous element was that it was armed workers shooting at unarmed soldiers! What might develop from that? We'd only just managed to soothe the soldiers' animosity toward the workers on account of the eight-hour day—but what would happen now? Some EC members were sent to various positions on Nevsky in an effort to calm things down.

They weren't saying it aloud, but—how alarming and how unexpected, the little Leninist group giving orders to the masses, over the head of the Executive Committee! And the masses were armed!

Probably someone—not Tsereteli, who was powerless without the Provisional Government's Clarification, on which he'd staked everything; and not the diplomat Chernov, of course; still less Gotz, who was now in secondary roles; and not the reticent Dan; but maybe Stankevich, or the hot-tempered Lieber—one of them would, any minute now, blast the Bolsheviks point blank. (They'd got Lieber so riled up that it seemed you could wake him up in the middle of the night and he'd be ready there and then to resume a furious anti-Lenin speech.) Blast them and then—there'd be an explosion? A break-up? A schism in the Executive Committee? And the total collapse of the revolution?—

But then someone came running in to report that the Mikhailovsky Artillery School had received an order from General Kornilov to send two gun batteries to Palace Square! But the Mikhailovsky cadets would not go without the EC's agreement.

A stab in the back?! What a traitor—a real General Galliffet!

And it was the same with the armored cars that Kornilov had summoned.

And the menacing shadow of Counterrevolution, of sinister counterrevolution, which has always destroyed all revolutions, loomed over the troubled meeting. This is where our main danger has always come from—the right! The right! And we mustn't forget it.

The EC instantly closed ranks, including the Bolsheviks: we have to stay united! As for Kornilov, we won't confront him face to face but give Chkheidze the task of phoning him right now and telling him that no summons to troops is permitted, for any purpose. And then a commission must be sent over there as well. (And permanent commissars must be stationed there, finally, to ensure this doesn't happen again!)

And why did the Mikhailovsky students and the armored cars not go? That was thanks to the providential step taken yesterday by Stankevich's soldiers' commission, forbidding regiments to demonstrate against the government without permission, and telling them to wait for an order from the EC before leaving their barracks.

That had been a godsend. It had saved us! But now that measure had to be developed and strengthened, so that soldiers didn't take it into their heads to go out and settle accounts with the workers.

And they set to work, feverishly, on another new appeal, to the whole population . . . Citizens, at this moment, when the fate of our country is being decided and every incautious step is a threat to . . . For the sake of the revolution's salvation . . . Trust that the Soviet will find the ways . . . Remain calm . . .

But the most important thing is that the soldiers are not to leave their barracks, armed, unless called out by the Executive Committee.

Comrades! This isn't specific enough! What if there's a bogus phone call? Or if another Linde appears?

All right, let's say that every instruction to a military unit to go out into the street must be done on a special Executive Committee form. And validated with a stamp.

Nonsense! Anyone here who feels like it can stamp one of our forms.

All right, let's say it's also got to be signed by at least two EC members.

But we have ninety members. You could always find two who would . . .

All right, not just any two, but two of a specific group, a group of seven, for example. Now, who? Chkheidze, Skobelev, Bogdanov, Lieber . . . And from the enlisted men Binasik and from the upper ranks Filippovsky . . .

Everyone laughed: seven dictators, then.

Revolutions love coming up with antics like this. Later they go down in history: "The Seven Dictators."

And another addition: every instruction must be verified by phoning us here.

And the workers? You couldn't give them orders like that (and the Bolsheviks wouldn't let you) . . . Comrade workers and militiamen! The purpose of your weapons is only to defend the revolution. You do not need them at demonstrations or assemblies, where they become a threat to the cause of freedom. When you are going to an assembly, do not take a weapon . . .

Oh, and a little something from the literature section . . . No acts of violence by one citizen against another can be permitted in a free Russia . . . Anyone stirring up trouble is an enemy of the people!

Now to get the order typed, reproduced, distributed, and telephoned to every barracks as soon as possible. And post them all over town as soon as they're ready.

But what's the government up to? It's almost time for us to leave for the Soviet—and we still don't have the Clarification!

Ah, finally! Here it is at last. Tsereteli, biting his nails, opens the packet and reads it anxiously. No dirty tricks? No changes to what we agreed?

Well, no glaring misrepresentations. In fact, half the Clarification is a quote from the Declaration of 9 April. And they're back-pedaling on the "sanctions and guarantees" now.

Tsereteli, his voice firmer, reads it aloud.

They're all too tired to argue. And they wouldn't be able to change each other's minds anyway. They go straight to a vote. The Trudoviks, populist socialists, SRs, and defensist Mensheviks: thirty-four votes, for. The Bolsheviks, internationalist Mensheviks, and unattached members: nineteen, against.

Adopted. We'll propose that the Soviet accept the government's Clarification as satisfactory.

And get over there, to the meeting of the Soviet at the Sea Cadet Corps, at top speed.

[83]

(PETROGRAD STREETS: 4 MAY, TOWARD EVENING)

* * *

A rumor circulates on Nevsky: Moscow is angry and threatening punitive measures against Petersburg—they are going to cut off food supplies.

And another rumor: Lenin had issued an order for the Kronstadt garrison to be summoned to Petrograd immediately.

And this piece of news: the Executive Committee had approved the Provisional Government's explanation.

Cries of "hurrah."

* * *

And from Trinity Bridge came the rumor that a crowd carrying anti-Lenin placards had set off toward the Kshesinskaya house, but never arrived. On the way, they were warned that they'd be shot at, as they had been on Nevsky, and a good few of them dropped out. But some did nevertheless cross the bridge, and were met by armed men, who ripped up their placards and gave them a thrashing.

* * *

Near Politseisky Bridge, Skobelev was standing in a car, making a speech:

"The Executive Committee will not permit extreme behavior or slogans such as 'arrest the spy Lenin!' Only the old regime relied on the force of bayonets. But the new regime will act through the power of the word and of persuasion."

And then, just by him, some people stopped a car bearing the slogan "Trust the Provisional Government" and would not let it through. But Skobelev appeared not to notice, didn't intervene and continued on his way.

* * *

There were rallies outside all the embassies too—the French, Italian, and English. Buchanan addressed demonstrators from a balcony several times: Britain is not waging war for the sake of conquests—our only objective is the triumph of high principles and justice. Support the Provisional Government!

And just then, in front of Buchanan, a little group of sailors and workers broke up the demonstration, beat up the demonstrators, and tore their anti-Lenin placard to pieces.

* * *

The war veterans were taken from the rally outside Kazan Cathedral to their hospital on Kamennoostrovsky Prospect. They took the sensible advice they'd been given, and rolled up their "Long live the Provisional Government" banner before they came to Trinity Bridge, so as not to provoke the Leninists. But even so they were recognized, rifles were aimed, and the occupants of "Lenin's palace" started shooting at them. No one was injured, but the truck had to stop and the Leninists ran over and started dragging the invalids out. They assaulted Feliks Volchak, who had lost both legs in the war, and dragged Vasili Moskalenko, who had lost his right leg, over to the Kshesinskaya mansion. There they threatened him with revolvers and interrogated him: who had paid them to support the Provisional Government? "Let's execute him!" they shouted. But they just released him with a threat: don't let us see you round here again or you'll lose the other leg. And they seized another two one-legged invalids, Vasili Romanov and Leonard Duda, and took them to the Vyborg side and locked them up there till night fell. Then they drew up a charge sheet and promised they'd be tried two days later.

* * *

Many demonstrators had left Nevsky, feeling they'd won a victory. But workers were still approaching from side streets and still arriving on Nevsky, for that was the only place where you could *prove* something. They were all the same, with anti-government placards—and again Nevsky met them with: "Traitors! Provocateurs! You sold out to Germany!" And the workers retaliated: "Bourgies, provocateurs, skulking in your burrows—and now you've crawled out again!" On the corner of Pushkin Street students and high school pupils snatched the flags and tore up the placards of the Cotton-Mill and Thread Factory workers.

"Where's our freedom?" shouted the women in response. "We've got the same right as you!"

On Znamenskaya Square, trucks full of soldiers, war invalids, and students barred the approach of yet another column of Leninists—no one bearing arms was allowed through.

And there were black, anarchists' flags as well: "Take lands and factories with no compensation." Officer cadets from the Konstantinovsky Artillery School attacked one such column by the City Duma.

But on the Field of Mars a truck with a placard proclaiming trust in the government was smashed up.

* * *

Streets were filling up again, and skirmishes were in the offing. One decently dressed gentleman wearing a sportsman's cap and pince-nez let slip an incautious word that earned him a punch in the face from the column. He would have been beaten some more, but soldiers and women came to his aid.

A gaunt Englishman, a military man with a slight limp and walking with a stick, followed after the column shouting an English-accented "Provocateurs! Traitors!"

* * *

As dusk turned to night, on the corner of Morskaya and Nevsky shots were fired into the air and the crowd recoiled. And shouted, furiously:

"Stop the shooting! You've sold out to Germany!"

"Let them shoot! We'll die for our freedom, if it comes to it!"

With nightfall came a certain jumpiness: the valves of a car in need of fixing caused it to backfire—and the crowd scattered in all directions, screaming that they were being shot at.

* * *

Some people, left from the workers' demonstrations that evening, stayed on Nevsky and walked up and down, milled about and tried to convince soldiers with their propaganda. It was vicious:

"All those bourgie gentleman types hanging around doing nothing, you need to get them and shoot them all."

After eight and nine in the evening, large groups of unarmed volunteers, officer cadets, and soldiers walked up and down Nevsky, calming the public and suggesting, in the name of the Soviet, that they should leave Nevsky clear, not gather in large crowds, not demonstrate either for or against, and not get excited. They joined hands to form chains and gently pushed the public back from Nevsky into the side streets. Many of the marchers rolled up their flags, put away their placards and dispersed.

The evening was clear now, and cool. The stars could be seen and now the moon was rising.

[8 4]

Since Lenin arrived, the situation among the Petersburg Bolsheviks has been desperately complicated. Only a minority accept his program and even they have reservations. Even those who accept his watchwords don't want to submit to the authority of émigrés: "We're Petersburgers," we were here, on the spot, at our posts. Our émigré group is too small. But Kollontai was amazed to see that, despite this unfavorable balance, and even without having asserted control over the Central Committee, Lenin had boldly organized and, in the last few days, triumphantly led a party conference of the Petersburg Bolsheviks. Not only that: he's already ventured to convene an all-Russian conference for the day after tomorrow as well (to confirm the CC and take over the party apparatus as soon as possible!). Kollontai will be there, representing Petrograd again, Shaya Goloshchokin is to be seen as representing the Bureau of the Central Committee, and some loyal members have managed to dash off to the regions and return as elected delegates. Klim Voroshilov succeeded in Lugansk but Sima Hopner got stuck in Ekaterinoslav, and Max Saveliev was defeated in Kiev by Pyatakov and Bosch (but Lenin decided to give him a place at the conference anyway).

Aleksandra Mikhailovna admired Lenin's tactics, high-risk and brilliant, especially in comparison with those of the EC and the government. Two weeks ago he'd been utterly alone, rejected, ridiculed. Now he was already beginning to take the party with him.

And, chiming with this singular moment in history, Aleksandra Mikhailovna sensed in herself a rare blossoming, good health, a mobilization of her mental forces and political understanding (almost equalling Lenin's, and she had been his worthy partner during the outrageous speech at the Tauride Palace), and a hunger for public speaking. Along with that came the sense of total personal freedom at the age of forty-five (for she was now no longer with Sanya Shlyapnikov). "Forty years old and her tale is told," went the old saying, "but at forty-five her charms revive." Several of her comrades had trouble maintaining their party sang-froid in her presence.

What Sanya had successfully accomplished by early April was the arming of a workers' guard. (Then he'd ended up under a tram—though, luckily, not badly injured.) As her final tribute to him, Kollontai is to give a lecture at the university the day after tomorrow, "The Self-Defense of the Working Class."

For the moment, this self-defense has just begun on the streets. But it isn't enough to ensure victory, and has met with antipathy and anger. Be careful! And today Lenin has given Aleksandra Mikhailovna a most urgent task:

Save the situation! Go to the Soviet plenum and take leadership of the Bolsheviks—Kamenev is too academic and no fighter; squeeze him out, and the Petersburg group and Fyodorov—and be the main speaker representing us. Yesterday the Soviet showed it has enormous power, and today that is where the course of events is determined. We're a tiny minority, but you'll have to make an enormous effort and take the Soviet along with you. Reject categorically all accusations that we were responsible for the shooting! The Executive Committee is, of course, incorrigibly opportunist, and for the moment we can't seize the power there. But for the masses there's no EC, no one understands the structure—there's just the Soviet. Get control there and all the power will be ours. You're a born fighter and you'll enchant them. If you can't turn the Soviet round, no one can. As for tactics—you'll see what's best when you're there. And if it doesn't work, you must just disrupt the assembly. Don't let them vote us down.

At five o'clock we sent our people to reserve benches, so that the Bolsheviks could sit together: we'd be more united that way, more solid, noisier, we could quickly pass on decisions and react instantaneously. A minority, if it's close-knit, can slash a majority and march straight through it.

At six o'clock, the time fixed for the meeting, Kollontai also arrived, and took her seat (under her jacket, she wore a scarlet blouse with lapels that sparkled). But the presidium (which includes Kamenev) still isn't here. That means the EC, poor, timid puppets, have been bargaining with the bourgeois government all day.

Fyodorov is not happy that he's been left out, and the other Petersburgers grumble a bit. But Lenin has already tamed them.

More than half the hall is in soldiers' greatcoats. That's bad. That grey mass of peasantry is smothering the working class.

But—she couldn't fail to conquer a male crowd.

She fidgets, impatient: when will it get started? Hurry up with it! The big clock in the hall already shows seven—and the leaders are still not here, they're still haggling.

On the embankment, under the windows of the Sea Cadet Corps, the crowd is getting agitated. Several of the factory columns have come together here. (Thanks to a bit of work on our part.) We still have the same menacing slogans. The EC members will have to forge a way through all that noise and even give some explanations out there. Everything will have an effect on their nerves. Everything must be used to our advantage.

The two thousand deputies—the masters of Russia!—were not shouting, not calling for their leaders to hurry up, not stamping their feet. They were meekly overcrowding the hall, waiting to be led. The masses . . .

You can't say this aloud anywhere, but we do need to add a small correction to class theory and the dictatorship of the proletariat—on the subject of powerful personalities. Without a group of powerful personalities, no dictatorship of the proletariat will achieve anything. And the worry is that currently, in the Bolshevik leadership, there are two and a half powerful personalities—and that's it. All the rest here in Petrograd are grey and faceless.

Well, Trotsky's about to arrive, of course, and he's a fiery type, a real personality! But will he join us? And there's Parvus, that goes without saying—but he's a German now. Well yes, Bukharin and Radek, perhaps, when they arrive. And Rakovsky's already in Odessa. And perhaps we could make something of Nogin. But no one else. It's all administrators—terrifying! It's a bit thin for all of Russia, isn't it . . .?

And here they are—the EC top brass. Kamenev is on his way over. Now he'll tell us what happened. And that lanky Tsereteli and little Chkheidze—they're inseparable, a real Long and Short—go up to the presidium, along with that Molokan blockhead Skobelev, and all the rest of the conciliatory riffraff. Satisfied faces. (Kamenev reports: the lackeys were haggling. Tsereteli had already done a deal with the government, this morning. I don't know why they didn't send their corrections all day. The EC leaders want to mislead the Soviet, talk about their "great victory" over the government, whose boots they are actually licking.)

The meeting started—at twenty past seven.

First to speak was Chkheidze, in a weak voice, dragging along the millstone of chairmanship duties now quite beyond him. At the meeting with the ministers it had become clear that the Provisional Government was putting into its note the same content as we had in our declaration of 27 March.

That's shameless!

Now we've received the clarification we needed, and Comrade Tsereteli will read it out.

And the socialist prince mounts the platform. Only just back from Siberia, and he's lost no time getting himself to the top of the whole Soviet. He's dangerous, with his pleasant appearance and voice, and he speaks and thinks clearly. He gives the impression of sincerity. (And sincere he is—sincerely misguided.) But he's not too dangerous. Lenin doesn't see him as a leader: he doesn't have a fighter's tenacity. In a life or death struggle, he won't hold his ground.

And now he speaks: the question of a peace must be addressed on an international scale—it cannot be decided by the Russian democracy alone. (We know that, and we agree.) We were expecting our renunciation of annexations to call into existence a reciprocal movement in worldwide democracy. When the Provisional Government's note was promulgated, we read with alarm the words "stuggle to a decisive victory," that well-known formula of imperialist policy, which means never-ending war. Every unclear phrase is a blow leveled at our democracy. The Provisional Government's reply was that it was only a matter of unfortunate formulation. (Those elitist bastards!) Then we demanded that they publish a clarification, dotting all the "i"s. (And what have the deputies understood of these "i"s, Prince? And how many need dotting?) And now, today, the government has sent us the clarification, which will also be communicated to the foreign powers' ambassadors.

It's the evasive babble of a terrified government trying to extricate itself; a little bit of paper saying nothing. Now we should carry on frightening them some more, but Tsereteli, of course, is in a hurry to proclaim the "clarification" a Soviet success.

And now, he says, the conflict that *could have arisen* has been averted. (And what about our columns? He says not a word. Noted.) So the government has not broken with the democracy and has proved that it deserves our support. If the Provisional Government were acting under the influence of the bourgeoisie, then we should take the power into our own hands—even though we are not yet sufficiently mature to take that on. But we have no further grounds to suspect the government. It is with the people. And now—this Clarification is the beginning of an international discussion about renouncing the seizure of territories. When other governments follow this path of ours, we shall be closer to a peace. The Provisional Government will remain in power and we, by giving it our support, will be able to transmit our influence, inspiring the proletariat of other countries. (What nonsense! We had to listen to a great many such refined, bourgeois yes-men in Europe! And now we've got them here too.) And here is a resolution, for our meeting. And he reads it out. (And it's the same evasiveness in different words. Having suffered a shameful defeat, they're portraying it as a victory.) We warmly welcome the rallies and demonstrations of the proletariat (which they themselves had tried so very hard to stop). The Western governments are now forced to take a position, face to face with their democracies . . . (And pigs might fly!) And finally, speaking on his own behalf: we have achieved a great conquest with this. And he congratulates the Soviet on its victory.

And what an ovation! What an ovation! The poor, deceived masses . . . Yes, it'll be an all-out battle that we wage today.

The presidium is clearly scared stiff.

The conciliators send Stankevich up as the second speaker. It seems that this pair is already well broken in. Stankevich does not seek to charm his listener, but his military appearance and stern, simple phrases make him, in a way, even more dangerous.

He had, you see, already said yesterday that this was all a misunderstanding. The incident is all over, but it has shown that we are unstable: because the government did not find the right words, we lost two precious days' work. We, members of the EC, thought the workers paid attention to the bodies representing them, but the regiments and the workers appeared on the streets without consulting us. (Ah. What a pitiful position! And the further it goes, the more you'll lose your grip.) But we'll be able to lead you to victory, when the whole of our democracy is in harmony and unified—so listen to us. The slogan "Down with the Provisional Government" appeared without our permission. (But he's not saying *who* gave rise to it!) We can use force, but only when we have an organization. (Well that's true.) And how can we overthrow the government if we're only Petrograd? We need firmer authority, yes, and tomorrow's slogan will be: Socialists to enter the government. (Starting with Millerand, you'll all end up on that path—you won't be able to think up a more intelligent way.)

Then the SR Shapiro jumped up, a rather bold fellow, and spoke in a quite different vein from the presidium. If the government had been ours it would already, on 27 March, have approached the foreign powers with our Manifesto. But since it did not approach them, it means it is not on our side. Even though the revolution that promoted them, they are from the franchised class. The government is leading our cause toward counterrevolution. Guchkov has only dismissed sixty generals—but there are fifteen hundred of them. And Chernov has been calling for calm. (A dig at Chernov, too, well done!) But if it looks as if we're trailing along behind the government, many of our people will abandon us. Revolutionary action is essential—and it cannot be put off! One example: the front has decided that Nikolai II must be transferred to the fortress—he was a criminal Tsar. So why is he still in his palace? The people want to know what they are fighting for and who the real enemy is. (Fine fellows, SRs like that, we must support the extremists among them. Otherwise, any cabby nowadays can sign up and call himself an SR.) Most people know that this war is for the sake of the industrialists and that Germany is not Russia's enemy. We need a reshuffle of the ministers, especially Milyukov and Guchkov. The sooner we get rid of them, the better!

Clearly there'd been a misunderstanding in the presidium. They were leaning over and whispering to each other. Shapiro had probably managed by some fluke to register to speak, and they'd thought he was representing the whole SR faction. Now they sent up a genuine SR representative. This one was smoothed down—no irregularities: although the SR party does support revolutionary methods, the population must not lose their heads. Maintaining calm is the first priority—seizing power now would be premature. The Soviet must initiate relationships with the socialists of other countries so that they too, in their countries, will renounce annexations and indemnities.

And now it was the Bolsheviks' turn. Kollontai decided to let Kamenev speak first, and whispered some last points to him, and told him not to try to justify the shooting, don't even mention it. That way it might fizzle out on its own. She herself intended to make a thunderous development by speaking later, just before the end—the crucial moment.

Kamenev begins correctly, but in too tranquil a tone—that's not the way to capture the masses:

"I do not think the note, and everything that has played out around it, can be settled by publishing a new document intended to dull the vigilance of the revolutionaries. The government has challenged the democracy and I want to know: how did it dare?"

It was all true, but there was no fire, no élan—and without any fire even correct ideas can't persuade listeners. No, the hall was not won over. Tsereteli's lilting tones and Stankevich's commanding precision were more persuasive than Lev Borisovich's sybaritic demeanor:

"The government's class-based psychology has shown itself, but the responsibility for this lies with us as well, since we allowed such a note to appear. What effect has this had abroad? We like to say, here, 'we can overturn the government with a telephone call.' But you're getting intoxicated with your own strength, while not taking any action. What if the Provisional Government announces that it will honor the Tsarist treaties? Settling our nerves on the basis of an explanatory document is a sign of our weakness. It means we are losing the revolution. We have no good reason to trust the Provisional Government and it must be overthrown. But that is impossible as long as it's protected by the EC."

That was, true, of course, but it was lukewarm and theoretical—it only sullied a magnificent concept. No, Lev Borisovich will never become a fighter—he's an aesthete, an analyst. He adopts hard-hitting Bolshevik tactics only reluctantly, as if he himself were ashamed of the intransigence of his position.

"The only government that could save the revolution is one capable of giving us peace now." And, anticipating an outcry and the usual accusations leveled at the Bolsheviks: "It would not, of course, be a separate peace, no. We can only put an end to the war when we ignite the worldwide revolution."

Then came someone from the Menshevik faction—you might as well not even listen to that one: there's nothing in the world more wishy-washy, more feeble than Menshevism.

They align themselves, of course, with the EC's resolution. The Bolsheviks' policies are, of course, disastrous. Seizing power is easy but it's hard to keep hold of it. (Oh, give it to us, give us the power! We'll show you how to keep hold!) Given the heavy burden of our Tsarist legacy, if the Provisional Government gives up the struggle—could we really manage any better? The proletariat must not take power now, only to fail dismally tomorrow. At the moment, we can't solve the social problems. We have to get ourselves better organized, so as to give a good account of ourselves at the Constituent Assembly . . .

What mediocrities! That's all your dried-up, doctrine-ridden little brains can come up with. Just look out of the window! Look at the embankment—there's a storm brewing out there! It's our masses! It's our placards they're waving. Read them, before the light goes.

(Chkheidze had already gone out to try and calm them down. They'd lifted him onto the roof of a car and he'd thanked the workers for their proletarian vigilance and tried to persuade them to wait patiently until tomorrow, when the Clarification would appear in the newspapers—pathetic old fool. A Bolshevik, just arrived, came to tell Kollontai about this, passing the message along the row.)

And another Menshevik. This chicken-liver was full of admiration at the way the Executive Committee had managed to find the way out of a hopeless situation.

Naturally, after each conciliatory address the whole Bolshevik sector in concert raised such a row, such stamping of feet, such catcalls, that it drowned out the whole assembly. And each speaker would, even before starting, cast a nervous glance over to their side of the hall.

But now the handsome fellow with the golden-brown beard, Chernov, stepped up to speak. With this one, you had to be more careful, to avoid getting into conflict with the whole SR party. Kollontai gave her men a sign—no noise for the moment.

But Chernov showed no appreciation of the Bolsheviks' silence and launched into a mocking dissection of Kamenev's speech: we had to show that the revolutionary democracy is strong, that we can apply pressure to the government—and we showed that. (*We*, not you!) If we cannot tolerate the government any more—then what can we do? And what are we to do if the government hands in its notice? (The whole Bolshevik section, to a man, burst out laughing and very nearly threw the speaker off course.) Today Comrade Kamenev is proposing to overthrow the Provisional Government, but three days ago this same Kamenev was saying (because he's always trying to argue with Lenin and thus hands over his trump cards) that the slogan about overthrowing the Provisional Government could slow down our long-term project, which is key to the fundamental task of his own party. What, exactly, does Comrade Kamenev want?

And the hall takes its revenge on the Bolsheviks by applauding wildly. Kollontai purses her lips—soon it'll be time for her to fly into a rage and put everything to rights.

"In proposing to overthrow the Provisional Government, Comrade Kamenev has not offered any positive measures. He is suggesting to others that they should constitute a government, while he himself will only criticize. Our country is, he says, on the brink of destruction, but he himself does not want to set off down any route. He is Ivan Tsarevich at the fork: not sure which of three roads to take."

Laughter and applause. The regulation ten minutes were exceeded a while ago, and now it's over twenty, but no one so much as extends a hand to stop Chernov. He likes speaking, oh how he likes delving slowly, slowly, into all the details. But this would certainly not be a plus for a revolutionary leader. He'd never be able to keep up with the speed of events, let alone run them.

"But, comrades, this moment is crucial, and if you do not, for the time being, feel strong enough to take power, then do not take it!"

Philistine wisdom. But the hall burst into cries of approval. The poor, feeble-minded comrades were convinced.

"As long as there are disagreements and fundamental differences of opinion, I do not advise you to seize power, only to see it slip through your fingers tomorrow—and I warn you of the dangers of such slogans."

Now that's where you're such a featherbrain. Reasoning like that, you'll never take power. Kollontai, admiring Lenin's sweeping tactics, had already adopted them: take power—always! Strive every minute of the day to take it! Take power even when it seems utterly impossible!

The waiting is insufferable, especially when the next speaker is you. Your first experience, your first major speech of the kind. Concentrate hard! Nerves of steel! No one's said a word about the shooting—all the more reason to go on the attack! Looks as if he's finished, said everything he needs to? But no, he can't stop himself.

There's more, and more: how, for the SR party, the peasants' interests are the top priority, and how . . . And can we really, hand on heart . . .

At last, and without anyone making him stop, he's run dry. And the crowd, which has not been spoilt for speeches, applauds him. (But not a single Bolshevik, of course.) Then Chkheidze suddenly plays an underhand trick: he proposes to curtail debate! He's tolerated half an hour of unbearable twaddle—and now he's going to stop debate?

With the banging of every bench-leg, the stamping of every foot, the air in every gullet, a hurricane of indignation rises from the Bolshevik section. And piercing whistles, as if between brigands. Wha-a-at? No-o-o!! The majority can, the minority can't?? That's disgraceful! A dictatorship! Provocateurs! Get rid of them!

"Let's get out of here! We're going!"

Those who'd taken off their jackets are putting them back on. We're leaving this shameful gang! Provocateurs! Dictators! They're suppressing freedom of opinion!

What joy there is in any fight!

We're less than a quarter of the hall and we've made enough noise for four halls this size.

The presidium gives in, and Kollontai mounts the platform. (The soldiers gape at the sight of such a beauty!)

Has she missed the chance? Is it impossible? But she has to turn the hall round! She raises her lovely features, tosses her curls back, and, with all the resonance of her beautiful voice:

"I call on the Soviet of Workers' and Soldiers' Deputies to join battle, an irreconcilable battle, with the Provisional Government. For that government is going hand in hand with the English and French bourgeoisie!"

A shrill voice interrupts, playing on her nerves:

"But not the German . . ."

On we go! Stick to your line: "Attempts at conciliation with the Provisional Government, all the papers back and forth, are pointless heel-dragging! And that brings with it the danger that the Soviet will stray from the will of our revolutionary soldiers on the front! And those in Petersburg! And our brothers abroad!"

Each phrase must be like a slogan! A gunshot! A call to come to their senses! They must follow their feelings, after all! Both the feeling of feasting their eyes on an irresistible speaker and a feeling for the grandeur of the International:

"Be careful! Don't accept a compromise resolution! Even if it's defended by well-known individuals, it is a lie! Think about Karl Liebknecht, in prison in Germany! You have extended the hand of peace to the peoples—but you yourselves are keeping your imperialist government? We must prepare ourselves for the moment when power will come over to us, to the Soviet of Workers' and Soldiers' Deputies! And only then will we have peace!"

They're listening! This is bold and direct, not the evasiveness of the conciliators.

Well yes, they are listening, but there's also some muttering around the hall. Suddenly you have the feeling that their enchantment has trickled away without achieving its full effect.

So you need to o-ver-whelm them with a torrent of proposals: to organize an immediate vote among the whole population of Petrograd, in all urban districts and environs! What do they think of the note? What party do they support? What government do they want? In the plants! In regiments! In the street! Hold peaceful discussions and public meetings everywhere! Total freedom of discussion! (And throw the capital into chaos for a few days.)

She saw out of the corner of her eye that Voitinsky and Dan were pushing their way through to the presidium. She attached no importance to that (they wouldn't take the floor away). Then she lost them from view, they'd disappeared behind her back and she hadn't seen them mount the platform and whisper to Chkheidze and Tsereteli. Suddenly Chkheidze summoned up enough of a voice to interrupt Kollontai. That voice sounded so different, so sick, as if he'd lost his son not a month ago, but this very minute:

"Comrades! An urgent and tragic message. Please keep calm."

He'd cut her off. And, given the tone of his voice, she was at a loss how to object. The hall was suddenly silent as the grave. Voitinsky (the sight of him touched her heart—he'd been with Sanya in the accident) immediately took over, from the presidium desk, explaining that they'd just been to the *Izvestia* printing works and had themselves witnessed, on the corner of Sadovaya and Nevsky, many rounds of shooting! A crowd of unarmed soldiers and citizens was attacked by another crowd, this one armed, who opened fire, quite indiscriminately. Everyone scattered or fallen to the ground and suddenly the place was empty. Two dead soldiers and several other casualties remained, while the armed group went back in the direction they'd come from, along Sadovaya.

"Who were they? Who were they?" The voices from the hall were strident. (Kollontai's heart sank: ours again, Shlyapnikov's guard. What bad luck! Now we're in real trouble.)

But Voitinsky—for every socialist does, after all, have a socialist conscience that respects certain limits—continues:

"I know who they were and where they come from. But for the moment I consider it premature to name them."

"It was the Bolsheviks!" come yells from the hall.

"Get rid of that bastard!" comes the instant chorus, at the top of their voices, from our group—they never let you down. "He's insulting our whole party!" And some even start fighting their way through toward that voice to punch the culprit in the face.

The noise of shouts and swearing comes and goes across the hall. It seems there could be an exchange of fire right here, any minute now. Chkheidze is constantly ringing his little bell but only the people nearby can hear it.

What now? How to save the situation? The hall's in a rage—against us. And we were the ones who spoilt everything. The left hand doesn't know what the right hand is doing. And our active forces are out there on the street, while there aren't enough of us in here.

Kollontai couldn't think what to say. What could you say, anyway, in this uproar?

The storm continued furiously under the high ceiling of the hall. By now it was not the little bell but the raised hands of several presidium members that told delegates to listen to Dan.

Thickset, cold, round-faced (and he was one of the most incorrigible, brazen conciliators), perplexed and surly (that's his manner, which means he'll never be a leader of the people), he continued the report: After the hubbub, a crowd formed around the victims again and we heard loud accusations against the workers. The wounded soldiers were surrounded by soldiers who were also accusing the workers of the shootings. That was very dangerous. We need to take all possible measures against counterrevolution. (And even he, despite everything, did not dare say it was the workers' guard who'd shot them. The limit set by his conscience. Things weren't that bad yet.) And there was resounding criticism of the Soviet itself! Something, somehow, has to be done . . .

And now the turbulence started up again around the hall and no one could listen anymore.

What was Aleksandra Kollontai to do? Her speech had been disrupted. She had to remove herself quietly (but not lowering her eyes—not with those scarlet lapels!), and go down to join her group and look for a solution. Unprecedented! A Bolshevik who hasn't finished her speech leaving the rostrum voluntarily . . .

In the presidium they're conferring, conferring some more, writing something. Then Tsereteli stands up to his full, and considerable, height and raises his hand. And he stands like that. It's extraordinary, the influence he has: they've fallen silent and are ready to listen.

But he himself isn't going to speak. He's quieted the hall for Chkheidze, who gives the floor to Skobelev. Skobelev comes to the now-vacant rostrum and begins to read out a draft resolution, in a voice appropriate for decrees:

". . . Demonstrations, rallies, and public meetings on the streets are to be stopped for two days. Anyone calling for an armed demonstration, allowing shots to be fired in the street, is to be considered a traitor to the revolutionary cause . . ."

The Soviet is being turned against the Bolsheviks! Her mind races: how to stop this? How to counter this move?

Skobelev, on his own behalf:

"Those who opened fire are traitors, enemies of the people's freedom. They are a dark force, against which we must all fight"—he hesitated—". . . using legal means."

Aha! So that's it! Now we can . . .

". . . They are trying to foment civil war, and that could sweep away everything the people have won."

And during a pause Dan, exercising his rights as a witness, adds:

"No one wants to believe that workers could have shot at soldiers. The hand of some provocateur was at work here. This smacks of counterrevolution, which is why we need to take firm measures."

That was it! Kollontai came alive—and from her seat, at the top of her voice:

"Declare as traitors those who are hounding Comrade Lenin!!"

Skobelev started muttering:

"We can't adopt a resolution like that, but we are against any stirring up of people's passions. We must get the Executive Committee to stop all hounding of any kind."

More proposals erupt from the hall:

"Shut down all the bourgeois newspapers for a few days! Stop their propaganda!"

"Condemn Lenin's policies!"

A great roar from our people. Proposal refused.

Amidst that uproar they take a vote on their conciliatory resolution on the subject of the note and get the majority they need.

So they have outvoted us after all. That's scandalous.

The Bolshevik group hammer on the floor with the legs of their benches, and stamp their feet: let us read out our Bolshevik resolution!

Permission refused.

Through the noise and the chaos, the presidium is insisting that all members of the Soviet must now disperse and exert the most vigorous influence on their comrades to stop the bloodshed. They must all leave their weapons in the barracks and at the plants. Go out into the streets now, in pairs, a soldier and a worker together, so the people can see we're not enemies. And explain to them the sense of the Soviet's resolution.

But we're staying here! (The order is given.) We're going on the attack!

Chkheidze puts his hands together above his head, almost as if in prayer. He can't be heard, but you can guess what he's saying: just don't let there be clashes between the workers and soldiers! If there are, we're finished.

The Bolshevik voices become one:

"We're not going anywhere! We're continuing the assembly! Declare Comrade Lenin chairman!"

[85]

When you're milling about in a great throng, especially if you're at the back, it takes a while to find out what's happening. The thousands-strong crowd was still out and about on Mariinskaya Square when the light had already faded and even the street lights were turned on. And then we heard that our ministers would be meeting at the War Minister's residence, on the Moika.

Then began a slow eddy, a circling movement, and a portion of the crowd flowed off in that direction. On the corner of Gorokhovaya Street another great mass had gathered, with flags, waiting for Milyukov to come past any minute now.

For some, their enthusiasm caused them to wait even longer, while it made others move off toward the War Minister's residence.

As for our opponents, our enemies, the Leninists, not a single one—not even isolated agitators—remained now. Everywhere there was only victorious common sense.

They streamed off to the minister's residence, but when they arrived they could barely squeeze into the space outside. They started calling, demanding, requesting—and a door opened. Out onto the pavement, accompanied by two adjutants and wearing a tunic without epaulettes, came the squat, even square-ish figure, so well known to all Russia, of Guchkov. There was a loud "hurrah," which meant he could not avoid giving a speech.

His voice wasn't strong now, but the Moika Embankment was not very wide and those who had squeezed their way through to the house could hear. The War Minister asked them to maintain their support for the Provisional Government. And to rebuff those wanting to add to the horrors of these three years of war the horrors of a war at home as well. We must put all our efforts into ensuring that we do not ourselves spill any precious Russian blood, of which so much has already been spilt by the Germans.

Those nearby heard him and cried "hurrah," lifted the minister and bore him aloft into the residence. But those standing to the side, along the Moika, started asking, shouting, for the minister to come out onto the balcony and speak again, from there.

And he did appear, and said, sterner now:

"Dear friends! A new fratricidal horror has been engineered by a handful of people who do not hold Russia's future dear. I am, in fact, sure that those people are in the pay of the Germans. And an unenlightened, ignorant crowd followed them. Never in all its history has Russia lived through such a terrible time, even perhaps in the Time of Troubles. A curse on these people! I call on you to be united. Let us swear that we shall not allow our freedom to be trampled underfoot." (From the crowd: "We swear! We swear!") "Let us swear to support our brothers, suffering in the trenches. I believe that this disorder will pass—indeed it has already finished—and Russia will be great again!"

"Yes! Quite right! Hurrah! We swear!" they cried, approvingly and for a good while, even after he'd left the balcony. And they shouted their opposition to Lenin, with no one there taking up the cudgels on Lenin's behalf.

Out onto the balcony after Guchkov came a bandaged soldier with a brand new St. George Cross on his chest. The crowd pricked up their ears. He declared, not at all shy:

"I'm in a motorized detachment. This afternoon, when I saw that gang of Leninist bandits interfering with our lives, and their flags saying 'Down with the war,' and they were shouting 'Down with the war' too—and to me 'Down with the war' is 'Down with Russia'—me and my comrades started protesting and grabbing those flags off them and breaking the staffs. And they shot at us and I was wounded. And now Minister Guchkov has just awarded me the George Cross."

Great rejoicing in the crowd.

"What's your name?"

"Me? Gilevich!"

"Long live Gilevich! Our thanks to Gilevich!"

Now the other ministers began to arrive: that prediction had been correct. The first was Prince Lvov, and he was met with deafening assurances of trust from the crowd. And standing in front of the door he replied, but in such a weak voice that his words had to be passed back, row by row.

He was, he said, grateful for their support. Without that support the government could not survive. And it is good that you are all fighting anarchy—but fight it with words, words alone. The Provisional Government will safeguard your freedom: we are ready to die for you all. The Russian people's sense of honor will help the government find its path toward the right way of life and stand up to the handful of troublemakers.

Even before the prince was allowed to leave with the crowd's gratitude, an enormous car delivered the chubby Konovalov. The people shouted "hurrah" and were favored with a speech from him too.

"Citizens! Our fundamental duty is to live up to the demands placed on us by history. A few months ago the Russian people were slaves. Now they are free, and their will is to be expressed at the Constituent Assembly."

Hurra-a-ah! Then they caught Tereshchenko, sporting a snow-white dickey and black bow tie, on his way in:

"The trust we encounter from the Petrograd population and the support shown us at this difficult time by the Soviet of Workers' Deputies . . ."

Hurra-a-ah! And here's Nekrasov, too. Animated, his voice resonant:

"Citizens and soldiers! I bring you our profound gratitude for your trust. We do not attribute it to ourselves, but to the great Russian people's wholesome conception of a state that shall win out over anarchy."

At last the hero of the day, Milyukov, also arrived. He had his car stop some way away, wanting to pass by the crowd discreetly, on foot—fat chance! They demanded a speech, and from the balcony. So now his dignified, grey-haired, bespectacled figure appeared on the balcony. And, through the trees, the moon illuminated the scene. A speech began to flow, as if specially prepared for the occasion:

"Citizens, in your greeting I find new strength to carry out my responsibilities. Tell me where I have gone wrong and I shall sincerely repent of my error before you. Was I mistaken when I said that Russia would not conclude a separate peace?" ("No, no!") "Was I mistaken when I told our Allies that Russia demanded the liberation of oppressed nationalities?" ("No, no!") "Did I have the right—since we wanted no annexations—to say that we would not allow the enemy to seize any territory of ours?" ("Yes, yes!") "Do you agree that we have to make this war the final war?" ("Yes! We agree!") "If you agree—well, this is exactly what we said in our note, which was unanimously adopted by the whole Provisional Government! Citizens! I am the first servant of the people, and the first to submit, willingly, to the people's will. And if the people willed another path, I would consider it my duty to divest myself of the burden of power. When treachery appears out of dark corners, the free will of the Russian people is especially dear to us. We are supported not by the force of bayonets, but by your confidence. But if you came here today to defend this government, I can say to you: yes, Russian citizens, you have deserved the freedom you won, since you are so able to defend it! We shall meet again in the good, radiant days of victory over our enemies. I would not have dared say that to you, had I not known that it will indeed be thus!"

The ovation filled the air for a good while, as Milyukov took his bows and finally went inside: the government session was set to begin.

Those who knew that Kerensky had, unfortunately, on these most fateful of days, been taken ill understood that there was no one left to wait for now, and started moving off. But those who did not know waited, quite understandably, for Kerensky.

And believe it or not, their hopes were not disappointed! A loud car horn was suddenly heard, coming from the Nevsky side, and—the crowd readily made way—under the embankment street lamps they caught sight of their idol.

What a stir that caused! What applause! How they sang his praises! They wanted a speech!

But Kerensky was pale, delicate: clearly the poor fellow's legs could barely support him. He still had one arm in a sling but with his free hand, turning to right and left, he pointed to his throat, indicating that he could not, alas, speak. And an adjutant explained that Citizen Minister Kerensky had been seriously ill yesterday, had not gone out at all, but had come now, sick, to this emergency session, although his doctors had forbidden him to speak.

Alas, alas. With cries of "Long live Kerensky!" and "Long live the Provisional Government!" the crowd began to disperse.

Inside, Kerensky had not been expected. Sidelong looks were given, glances exchanged.

The government members began the meeting embarrassed, now endowing the looks they gave with an excessive, insincere cheerfulness.

Nabokov handled their issues efficiently, looking stern and worried. There were routine questions, for which he had already prepared conclusions. And there were questions that weren't on the agenda. And they could also discuss today's events.

Or not discuss them. For the whole of that day (and the day before) the government had not involved itself at all in the unrest on the streets, leaving the Executive Committee to pick up the pieces. It had not even done anything to ensure its own preservation: things would take their course.

And now they were exchanging looks, in barely concealed amazement that they had managed to survive those two days and come out unscathed. And now they were in session.

And the anarchy had been put down.

Milyukov was puffed up with pride over his victory. Now we must decree that no minister would even have the right to resign his post out of political considerations.

But Guchkov, gloomy, lowered his head, chin touching his chest. He was ashamed of these two days. And of his own role.

And he was stunned by Kornilov's lack of success, mindful that he himself had done nothing to help.

But he could say nothing more about all that to these ministers.

[86]

Although the "Red Guard" had not managed all day to gain the upper hand on Nevsky—and had, in fact, lost more and more support in the afternoon, after the shooting—the Bolsheviks (and the Interdistrict group) wanted the factories that were following their orders to continue their march on the city's main thoroughfare, even as night fell, to stop the bourgeoisie celebrating in peace.

So they carried on marching all evening, keeping the same formation, with an armed column in front and also, sometimes, at the rear. Now bolder, the throng of observers on Nevsky was not as scared of the rifles as they had been, but were nevertheless on their guard. Even after the shooting in the afternoon there had been no reaction, with no armed soldiers seen anywhere.

The workers' militia, the Red Guards, though putting a brave face on it, with loaded rifles slung over their shoulders, had neither the soldier's confidence in using them—some had still never fired a single shot—nor the nonchalance needed to actually shoot at live people. They marched with rifles but were themselves rather afraid of them.

So, by mutual consent, everything went off fine, with no skirmishes all evening, but some very sharp exchanges:

"You Leninists! Down with Lenin!"

"Down with the bourgies! Long live Lenin!"

"He's in Germany's pay!"

"You've got fat through the sweat of our brow!"

"Death to the bourgies!"

Patrols of both the unarmed, peace-keeping soldiers and the city militia, which was now back on the streets, had already put in some work, calming people down and getting the public to move on. On Nevsky there were already far fewer people about. By ten o'clock it seemed no one else would come, that it was all over. Clusters of residents of this central district remained, still expressing their indignation and celebrating their victory.

But then, from the Admiralty side, another long column appeared on Nevsky: when passing under street lights—and there was moonlight anyway—it was clearly visible. Armed and unarmed marchers alternated in the same way as the others. These were from various different plants, as they explained:

"We're from the Nobel. Taking a walk!"

"We're from all districts. We're interdistrict."

There were also workers from the Aivaz and Ekwall. They carried the slogans: "Down with the Milyukovs and Guchkovs!," "All working people, arm yourselves!," and "Make war on the war!"

Marching in the armed contingent at the front were seventy or eighty men with rifles, drawn revolvers, and unsheathed sabers. This time there were also a few armed soldiers among them.

And all the way along Nevsky the same exchanges arose between them and the bystanders: "Down with the Leninists!," "Stop the bourgeois harassment," and sometimes from the column there were half-hearted cries of "hurrah" and some of them started up a revolutionary song. But it was already clear that, unlike the first columns, who'd marched earlier in the day, these were arriving too late, too tired, despite their unsheathed sabers.

Just before the intersection with Sadovaya, some peacekeeping soldiers, under the command of an officer cadet from the engineering academy, formed a chain and barred the column's way. They asked the marchers, on behalf of the Soviet, to remain orderly, fold up their anti-government and anti-war placards, and disperse. Those at the head of the column replied that they were already about to turn off, onto Sadovaya, to cross the bridge and go home.

"We'll stay orderly, but if anyone touches us we'll open fire."

Then the soldiers lined the route, clearing the way, and the demonstration turned into Sadovaya.

But a tramcar was making its way along Sadovaya toward them. From the workers came cries of:

"Don't let the tram through! They're all bourgies in it! They'll have to get out!"

The tram driver wanted to continue slowly on, trying, through his window, to persuade them to let him through. But the frightened passengers started jumping out of the tram in a panic.

At this stage, about two thirds of the workers' column had rounded the corner, but it was over-extended: those at the front were already approaching Engineers Street, while the tail was only now turning into Sadovaya from Nevsky. Here, on the corner, a crowd of passers-by and soldiers had gathered and were shouting, pushing up close to the column. Then they started wrenching the column's final placard away from them. The tail of the column was rather sparse, while the sidewalk was full of people.

"Comrades, don't let them! The bourgies are robbing us!"

"They're stealing our banner! Let's get even!"

Then some of the workers from the tail section ran to catch up with their comrades and get them back, to help out. The engineering student officer ran after them and tried to persuade the workers who'd gone ahead that they should not all return, but send back just a little assistance, and now he and his men were going to get the whole tail through safely.

But it was already too late for persuasion. Armed men ran back from the main column, unslinging their rifles. In front ran a young man of thirty or so, with a dark moustache and a red armband—though he was not even a worker, for he wore not a cap but a soft, black hat with a brim, and had the look of someone rather educated. That look would stick in the witnesses' minds. And when he saw that the chain formed by the soldiers was preventing the column from running back, he raised his hand and fired his revolver, as a signal.

And the workers, clicking their safety-catches off as they ran, aimed an uncoordinated salvo of rifle fire at the soldiers and, more generally, down Sadovaya in the direction of Nevsky, firing at random.

And one soldier from the chain trying to dissuade the workers, one Garkulya, who wore the uniform of an automobile unit, fell dead and someone else nearby was injured. A nurse immediately appeared by them—that same Zhenya Shelyakhovskaya, who had already, that afternoon, found herself in a scuffle and shooting on that same crossroads.

After the shooting—no one was fighting over placards now, they'd all given that up—panic broke out among the whole mass of people, both the Nevsky public and the workers, and everyone was mixed up together. Some dashed into a coffee house or the Majestic cinema, others dropped to the sidewalk or the roadway, a third group were, stupidly, raising their hands. Some ran farther, to the Gostiny Dvor, while others hurtled off toward the rounded form of the Public Library, and together with them went armed workers, still shooting from there, in a hit-or-miss fashion: even they didn't know who they were shooting at, or why—it was just their unfamiliarity with weapons.

By this time there were no salvos, no orders being followed—only disorderly, unremitting shooting, forty or so shots. The community governor and head of the city militia, Yurevich, also happened to be there under fire, during those five minutes of panic, and scurried off with his adjutant. And, passing by in their car, Executive Committee members Dan, Steklov, and Voitinsky barely escaped also getting caught up in it.

A tramcar escaped the shooting by crossing Nevsky toward the Corps of Pages.

They carried on firing like this until the workers realized that they were the only ones—no one else was shooting. Then they began to move off.

The battlefield was left in the workers' hands but they themselves were in a hurry to get away—and in such disorder that they were now not only taking the Sadovaya route but also, depending where they happened to be, taking Nevsky toward Znamenskaya Square.

Did they think the guilty parties would be arrested? There was no one to arrest them.

Zhenya Shelyakhovskaya stopped French minister Thomas's car, which was passing by, empty, and took one wounded soldier to the Nikolaevsky Military School, where he served.

Twenty minutes later Red Cross motor ambulances also arrived to pick up the wounded. There were six, of whom four were soldiers, one of whom took a bullet to his head. Three soldiers were killed—as well as Garkulya there was one from the Izmailovsky Regiment and one who'd come as a delegate from the front. And one worker had been killed, but by a bullet from behind—fired by his own people. The bodies were carried into the Majestic.

The bystanders who had run off in all directions slowly returned to the crossroads, bellowing angrily, the women crying. Irate officers tried to convince each other:

"Why are we just looking on? We've got to tackle those Leninists!"

Small groups were gathering by the street lamps, where it was lighter:

"What the devil . . .! No one has the right to shoot!"

"How can they shoot at their brothers?"

"How can they shoot now, when we have freedom?"

"Why are they goading our soldiers?"

"Bring them to their senses. Tell them it can't be allowed!"

They remained in a state of ferment for a good while.

An hour later patrols representing the Soviet of Workers' Deputies were vigorously calling for everyone to disperse. All demonstrations were banned for the next two days.

The public complied.

It was still nighttime but with springtime's early white light, the Soviet's appeal was being posted in the streets.

As was the City Duma's, for ". . . peaceful and organized participation in the political life of our homeland . . ."

Late that night a rumor was heard around town that Lenin had left Petrograd.

* * *

WHEN THINGS GO TO POT, TO HELL WITH THE LOT!

* * *

[8 7]

What a botch-up! Not enough manpower to take the center.

But we do seem to be finding a way out.

Yesterday, when the whole town was in an uproar, around the Kshesinskaya mansion it was quiet all day. But toward six in the evening an enormous crowd, ten thousand or so—unarmed, though—suddenly arrived. There were soldiers, petits bourgeois, intellectuals, all mixed up together, with red flags but slogans proclaiming trust for the government and against us and shouting, right near us, "Arrest the spy, Lenin!" It was a rather frightening moment and Lenin really did think he might have to pay the price for the proletarian cause. But then our men, armed, came over Trinity Bridge to the rescue and started tearing up their banners and flags, breaking up the crowd and driving them off with their rifle-butts. (Lenin had previously given strict instructions: near the mansion, no shooting at anyone except in a real emergency. But there had been some infringements.) And the crowd was sent packing. But just then an armed military unit was marching past, along Kamennoostrovsky Prospect, and the people we'd chased off ran to ask for their protection. It was another really dangerous moment: should we hurry and leave the Kshesinskaya mansion while, to one side of us, Kronverksky still lay open? It would be the height of stupidity to risk our lives at the very beginning of the struggle. But no, we sat it out. The military unit hesitated and our good, new young ensign helped us manage without any shooting.

Farther away, on Trinity Square, someone had started knocking together a stand. There was a rumor that Aleksinsky and some other stinking social patriot were to speak. But we told our people not to smash it up. The speakers didn't turn up anyway.

There was also a rumor that Kornilov had sent a thousand grenadiers over here, to put down the rebellion. But they never arrived.

And on top of that, there was the disgraceful provocation at the telephone exchange yesterday: apparently the young ladies had taken it upon themselves to disconnect the Kshesinskaya telephones—a low, mean form of harassment, cutting us off entirely and leaving us without any means of communication at the most dangerous moment! So all night the phones were mute—a state of siege! But Lenin gave the order not to react, to wait for things to blow over.

That night could have been critical, dangerously so, and Lenin, not sleeping (his head ached and ached and no powders were helping), paced about constructing plans, promising himself never again to commit such an elementary blunder as he had yesterday, and to stop the adventurers in time. But the night was also calm. Our people had set up active defense measures, with armed workers stationed at various points and patrolling the square and Kamennoostrovsky Prospect, trying to persuade the groups that had formed there to disperse.

The maneuver he came up with was as follows: today, 5 May, first thing in the morning—regardless of measures taken by the government, Kornilov and the Soviet, and the expected howls from the press—first thing, we must send our new, third Central Committee resolution out as rapidly as possible to all the editorial offices. This will neutralize our resolution of yesterday (which is in today's *Pravda*—what a brouhaha!) and thereby curb the mounting passions. In a crisis every half-hour counts, sometimes every minute. You have to grasp changes in a situation rapidly and manage, unnoticed, either to cross a front or give it a new orientation. So, first thing in the morning, having shown the new text to Zinoviev only, not waiting for the others, he hastily sent messengers out to the newspapers with this new, third Central Committee resolution (dated the *morning* of 5 May), even though it would only appear tomorrow. But everyone must know about it today.

So here we are. We're complying absolutely with the EC's decree about a two-day ban on public meetings! (The balance of power between us and the bourgeois mass is now such that this works in our favor.) The slogan "Down with the Provisional Government" is wrong now, because without a solid majority of the people on the side of the revolutionary proletariat it's either mere words or else, objectively speaking, it amounts to initiatives of an adventurist nature. (This is what we'll call it, as a way of distancing ourselves.)

Even when morning dawned we suffered no outrages here. By the *Vigilant* monument a crowd of about two hundred had gathered and we thought they were going to come over here and attack us (while the petits bourgeois thought it was Leninists gathering there). But it actually turned out that some Chinese fellow was giving a presentation.

Curious types approached the mansion—and they were scared too—but there were no incidents. And Lenin gave the instruction: no speeches from the balcony today.

Now, satisfied that the tension had eased, we sent Bogdatiev and another two of our people to the telephone exchange to make a bit of a scene. Bogdatiev knows how to stand his ground. There they presented their Central Committee identification and demanded, with threats, the names of the operators: we'll be taking stringent measures against strikes of this kind. The manager of the telephone exchange immediately took fright: the management knows nothing about it, it's the operators' own initiative. "Give us the names of the guilty parties!" We can't ascertain who they were right now—come and acquaint yourselves with their operations. Our comrades moved on into the control room—where those tarts set up a terrible racket, with catcalls: "Get out of here! Down with the Leninists! Kick 'em out!" And suddenly—summoned by someone as a provocation—a detail of fifty soldiers arrived. "Who's to be arrested here?" asked their officer. They wanted to arrest Bogdatiev's group—what effrontery! But the manager of the telephone exchange assured them that they didn't need to arrest anyone, that they'd sort this out themselves. The soldiers left, Bogdatiev went to the Municipal Board and the board gave the ladies a good roasting: they must carry out their professional duties without political bias.

Someone brought in all the morning papers. They showed clearly that the government was in no state to take any action. All the bourgeois press had, of course, taken fright: none had dared accuse the Leninists of the shooting. They were all indignant, screaming—but it was unclear against whom they were directing their indignation. (They understood that their employees also risked getting their teeth knocked in. And that the typesetters would stop compositing their papers.) And Kornilov, having been blocked by the Soviet yesterday, was nowhere to be seen.

The *Workers' Gazette* and *The People's Cause* (with deft handling these could also be useful) were definitely very angry, but it was all against the government and against the Kadets, who had stirred up violent inclinations. The Mensheviks' Organizing Committee published its resolution on the crisis and it, all the more so, avoided naming the Bolsheviks. *Izvestia* frightened itself with its headline, set in massive type: "Shootings by provocateurs"—but sensibly made no concrete accusations against anyone: "There will be a meticulous investigation, with the participation of the EC."

And so the most critical moment has passed.

The critical moment is past—but the crisis, perhaps, is not over yet. In tomorrow's *Pravda* we'll have to say: the overwhelming majority of the workers in the demonstration, who carried placards declaring "Down with the Provisional Government," understood that slogan only in the sense of bringing down the government when they, the workers, have won over the majority of the people. Do not let yourselves be led astray by isolated individuals who are inclined to hurry, who cry "Down with the Provisional Government" before the majority is solidly united. We are not in any respect Blanquists: we do not support plotting! Nothing could be more absurd than the tale that we were "firing up" a civil war when we declared, in the clearest and most formal manner, that patient *clarification* is our main focus. As long as the capitalists do not move to exercise violence against the Soviets, until that time our party will preach **total renunciation of violence**!

In the meantime, the leaders of this Soviet are disgusting, behaving so stupidly. Their fault is not so much that they haven't seized power, but that now they're putting on an act, pretending they've "defeated the government." They have, in effect, supported the imperialist note and today—the swine—they're going to reward the Kadets by voting for the loan too. Now that will be a total, absolute betrayal of socialism! Kollontai, furious, told him about yesterday's nasty spectacle at the Soviet, which she hadn't managed to turn around. (And her opinion of Chernov: judging by his speech, he's wishy-washy—he'll never make up his mind. That's excellent! A strong SR leader would be far more dangerous for us in a petit-bourgeois country than any Menshevik. That verbose Chernov houses nothing but pretty phrases. He's never done and never will do anything. He and Lenin might both appear to have spent their whole life as émigré journalists and done nothing but write. But what a difference: Lenin, through his writings, organized the physical structure of his party.)

Yes, there'd been some hours yesterday, toward nightfall, when it seemed we'd lost. But today you already have to acknowledge that that was not the case. We couldn't win, because we didn't manage to mobilize our forces. We'd overestimated the success of 3 May and not done enough organization for the 4 May demonstrations. Which means there are still some skills we don't have. Beyond the Neva and Narva Gates we didn't rouse anyone into action. Only a hundred and fifty bayonets arrived from Kronstadt, and they came late. That will never get the job done—they only came in useful for agitation around the barracks. That shameful episode on the Ekaterininsky Canal alone, when the workers gave up their rifles to soldiers—that really showed the essentially petit-bourgeois nature of our soldiers. It was rash of us to expect they'd be capable of a revolutionary surge. (And look how many threats to Lenin have come from their ranks!) And it was tragic, that delay on the part of the Helsingfors Soviet! Their telegram to the Petrograd Soviet, saying they were ready to topple the Provisional Government the minute we asked, only came today. If only we'd known that a day earlier! That was a very, very big mistake we made, not coordinating with the Helsingfors Soviet during that period.

In Petrograd we didn't win, that's true. But we didn't lose either. On the contrary—during these days we've come to know our strength and our capacity for moving the masses. Now, in the Soviet, they're yelling that "the Bolsheviks aren't in any state to take power into their own hands." But we are, almost! With allies like Kronstadt, Helsingfors . . .

Organization, organization, and, again, organization of the proletariat! And our top priority—the Red Guard! This time it turned out that it wasn't ready. We missed our chance. We've got to speed up! (This wasn't discussed at the Petrograd conference and we won't bring it up at the All-Russian conference: no blabbing, we'll just do the job at top speed.)

And now our most serious blunder has come to light: we failed totally to organize propaganda and agitation among urban domestics and odd-job men. And it was, to a significant extent, these people that the bourgeoisie relied on for support yesterday. Take their domestics away from them! That's the current watchword. Pay particular attention to household workers!

Street demonstrations are banned, but everywhere we must adopt and distribute resolutions that benefit us! Intensify the resolutions war!

The whole issue of today's crisis is that the agreement between the Soviet and the Provisional Government has turned out to be nothing but empty words. The leaders of the Soviet have reached a compromise and given up all the stands they'd taken. It would be possible to "patch up" this crisis, but no good would come of it, only harm. All our efforts must go into nurturing, educating, and uniting the slow learners in every plant, every section of town! A repeat of similar crises is inevitable. (Soon—we'll be repeating them very soon.) Will the great masses accept that "the matter is closed"? Time will tell. The lesson is clear, comrade workers! After the first crisis, more will follow. Our task is to refuse to participate in the game that is dual power. There is no way out except the worldwide workers' revolution! Such a revolution is clearly rising up in Russia, Germany, and a series of other countries. The proletariat is opening the way to a radiant future for all working people!

But now, at the conference, we can't be sure far-left Bolsheviks won't launch an attack. We have to anticipate that too. Comrades, some of you might have the idea that we've renounced our former beliefs: we used to speak in favor of turning the imperialist war into a civil war, but now we're talking about clarifications for the masses. But the reason, comrades, is that now is a transitional period: the armed force is with the soldiers but Milyukov and Guchkov have not yet applied any force. So now we have peaceful, patient, class-based propaganda. Now all struggles, except political education and nurturing, could damage us. To shout about violence now would be pointless. Our current task is not to bring down the Provisional Government—which is sustained by the loyalty of the petite-bourgeoisie and a section of the working masses—but to organize and to clarify our class-based tasks. If we talk about civil war before people understand why it is necessary, then we'll lapse into Blanquism. We are *for* civil war, of course we are! That's our central tenet! But only when it's waged by a politically aware class. For the moment we are renouncing that watchword.

But only for the moment.

The arguments were ripening in his mind even before he saw an occasion to articulate them in public.

But that's better than when ideas, if not spoken in time, later burn themselves out, painfully, in your breast.

DOCUMENTS — 15

5 May

GERMAN CHARGÉ D'AFFAIRES IN BERN TO THE MINISTRY OF FOREIGN AFFAIRS, BERLIN

The Émigré Committee in Zurich is asking us to guarantee that another train with 150 to 200 émigrés will be dispatched within a month. Such a guarantee would make it easier to select particularly suitable émigrés for the next train, enabling us to persuade others to travel later.

A reliable, trusted figure (a socialist) strongly advises us to allow the most important émigrés to pass through Germany before the return of Grimm, who might obstruct their departure. At one time Grimm did, out of fear of the Entente, try to block the departure of Lenin's group. Might it be possible to hold Grimm back in Stockholm?

[8 8]

The future historian, drawing on the bare facts, will simply throw up his hands in disbelief. After the stunningly smooth course of the first period of the Russian revolution—the only such time in history when, through a surge of enthusiasm on the part of a whole nation, a collapse of the state apparatus was averted—where did this tornado of 3 and 4 May come from? But seen in the light of psychological analysis everything becomes clear. Certain persons of limited *mentalité*, with an impaired facility for logic and even for elementary, everyday morality, people whose approach to facts shunned all criteria of good faith and truthfulness—these individuals launched slogans that were not properly thought through but were seductive, inviting the vague hope of an end to the slaughter. One such was the renunciation of annexations and indemnities. It was an equivocal slogan, either a fetish of faith in democracy or a bit of cheap phraseology to the effect that the war was being waged by capitalists. And something very predictable happened: those demagogues won over the ignorant masses, who were all weary and disillusioned—and their hounding of the "imperialists" delivered results in the form of two days with an absence of authority in the capital. Naturally, the Leninists immediately took advantage of this situation. But all the socialists in the Soviet, those defeatists-turned-defensists, also felt it necessary, for their purposes, to shout about "Milyukov's imperialist policies." To maintain their prestige among the masses they had to pursue a continuous "struggle" against the "bourgeois government." Among broad swathes of society there is no understanding of the mechanism of state or of international relations. That makes seditious propaganda easier and the government's position harder. (They should have thought about the impression this was making on our Allies and the delight they were giving our enemies. From the very first days Hindenburg was trumpeting the hopes he had of our revolution.)

The specter of anarchy had begun to hover over Petrograd. That's how far things went!

But those same days of absent authority did show that there were no grounds for hounding the government, that the Provisional Government's moral base rested, granite-firm, on the confidence of the population—that of Petersburg, at least. The whole of Petrograd came out onto the street to proclaim, loudly and solemnly, their trust in the Provisional Government. In their case no one was "taken off" work, as they were in the plants: each demonstrator joined the march out of personal conviction, to put an end to that disgusting mayhem. The Leninists' murderous excesses had exhausted the people's patience—and dealt an irremediable blow to their own treacherous, anti-national propaganda. The specter of internecine war faded and the masses unexpectedly demonstrated their feeling for the interests of the state. And since those days, since that absence of authority, the way has opened up toward a radiant future.

What a convincing, and irrefutable, victory. Your heart could burst with joy.

Faced with trials of this kind a political figure must be, above all, a man ready to expose himself to the wrath of public opinion. And Pavel Nikolaevich had, during all those days, been such a man. Even while composing the note he had been rock-firm with Kerensky, made him agree to the text, and no one in the government had dared argue after that. Pavel Nikolaevich had already been celebrating his triumph all day on 2 May, when the note, before even being announced in the Russian papers, had already been sent via diplomatic channels and was now irrevocable. A fitting way to stand one's ground. (That day was only spoiled somewhat by an unpleasant episode, when his car was stopped on the corner of Basseinaya Street and Liteiny Prospect: for some reason the license plate seemed suspicious to the militia, who thought it might be one of those "black motorcars" of recent legend. They arrested Pavel Nikolaevich and his driver and took them to the subdistrict commissariat. It was humiliating for the Minister of Foreign Affairs not to be recognized, especially just a few steps from his own home! The old police would never have allowed such boorish behavior. He'd suggested they should pop into the *Speech* office, which was nearby, and they could identify him. But no, it had to be the commissariat. They did recognize him there, it's true, and set him free with their apologies.) That same evening Milyukov received an enthusiastic welcome at the Mikhailovsky Theater. And on 3 May Pavel Nikolaevich spent another half-day celebrating his victory—never suspecting that his enemies had hatched a plot to unleash the Acheron against him.

The Acheron!! It had before been launched against the moth-eaten stuffed dummies of the old regime. But who was the target now? A revolutionary minister? Now we've seen everything.

Truth to tell, this tremendous resentment was such a surprise to Pavel Nikolaevich that for the first few hours he was, seriously, struck dumb: suddenly the ever-friendly Petersburg pavements were burning beneath his feet—and, for some reason, his feet alone! Intransigent, full of hate, of fury—what slogan were people displaying? Down with Milyukov—specifically and only Milyukov!

What a tragic misunderstanding on the part of his fellow-countrymen! One that is, incidentally, the lot of all great men, starting with Socrates. The crowd cannot stomach people with lofty, principled convictions.

To wait twenty years for this post, only—having barely begun his illustrious career—to resign?

But why be angry with the foolish crowd? They were egged on, those vile placards thrust into their hands. But what astounded him was the undeserved hatred on the part of the socialists, for whom Milyukov had done so much in earlier years, affording them so much protection from Tsarism. And as for that note, the socialists had demanded it, wanted it, it was on their insistence that he'd written it—and they'd lashed out against it? And now he had to listen to all these recriminations from that same socialist wing? Himmer's *New Life*, which had only just appeared on the scene, had taunted him savagely: "Milyukov of the Dardanelles has thrown down the gauntlet, a challenge to the whole of our democracy and our whole people"! It's an uncomfortable feeling when the "whole people" is being set against you, personally. Chernov's *The People's Cause* went further, already outlining a future government ranging "from Trudoviks to Bolsheviks." And Chernov, with his sweet little smile and his clowning, had already suggested to Milyukov, at the nighttime session in the Mariinsky Palace, that he should move over to the Ministry of Education. And even the sensible, moderate Trudovik paper *The Day* accused Milyukov of using ambiguous phraseology in the note. (There is ambiguity there, of course—you haven't got to the bottom of it yet. But it was lucky that everyone jumped on the note and seemed not to notice the *Manchester Guardian* interview. It's crowd psychology—wherever the first one rushes in . . . But the interview was a far more delicate matter, more dangerous. You couldn't defend it so easily.) The note wouldn't have been open to attack if he hadn't listened to Thomas and put in his "sanctions and guarantees." They were the root of all the trouble.

But even if everyone else's brain fogs up, let mine stay clear! Why did we even have a revolution, if not to finish the war with a successful outcome? Our glorious revolution has now been spoiled by people saying the war is at odds with it! Now, when the Americans are bringing in heretofore unseen compulsory military service, when in a year's time 2 million men will have been called up—now we're to give up? And what naïvety. No one in the world will believe that a warring power is renouncing compensatory land acquisitions! We mustn't look like half-wits. The war would have followed a normal course if those Zimmerwaldists hadn't turned up—nothing would have happened. Even Nabokov had a mental aberration. He said at that time that war weariness was one of the causes of the revolution and that now it could have a pernicious effect. But no, no. The war wasn't the cause, that's all nonsense! We mustn't take any notice of self-seeking interests. In fact it's only thanks to the continuing war that the country remains united.

But the struggles with the Zimmerwaldists get harder by the day: from their mountain village in Switzerland they've shown extraordinary tenacity in getting themselves transported to Russia and already managing to proliferate in Guchkov's army. And they're already unstoppable in Milyukov's own domain: they've launched a sort of foreign ministry of their own in the Soviet, a showcase for the West to view revolutionary Russia. And they're sending abroad, at the state's expense, both telegrams contesting government policy and messengers who bustle around in Stockholm. This "EC department of international relations" had already begun to stick in Milyukov's craw. It was simply an insult to the Minister of Foreign Affairs.

But we could have put up firm resistance to anything at all if the Provisional Government had remained unified, fearless. But apart from Milyukov there were no reliable ministers left: they'd acted despicably, allowing a poisonous legend to develop, according to which the government had nothing to do with all this and it was Milyukov, their *bête noire*, who was doggedly pursuing his own, independent line—and all the demonstrations began to turn against Milyukov personally.

But just then, when the whole attack was concentrated on Milyukov, his character—the adamantine character of his favorite hero, Turgenev's Bazarov—became even more obstinate, telling everyone they'd come to grief! The Acheron was raging, but Milyukov was beating it back fearlessly, facing it head-on from the palace steps, from the palace balcony: "Seeing those placards I did not fear for Milyukov, I feared for Russia!" A figure of solid willpower! The crowds were marching—and Milyukov really was ready: they could lynch him—he still wouldn't give way on what he considered right. He was of course buoyed up in this firmness by his sensing the Western Allies behind him, and his honor in front of them. (Although Buchanan had developed an equivocal attitude. Paléologue was loyal, but he had his own tragedy: he was being called back to Paris.)

And so he stood his ground. After a storm like that! And he only had to give such modest clarifications, totally insignificant. And everything had turned out fine.

Today he received the Japanese ambassador and told him that these disturbances had marked the culmination of our difficulties and now everything would go better. He also saw Albert Thomas and (although Thomas was at fault on many issues and insincere in the act he was putting on with the Soviet) said to him ceremoniously:

"*J'ai trop vaincu*! I've won *too great* a victory!"

What a victory! And the Kadet party and the government had only become stronger through this crisis. And the right course now was to continue the battle!

But who understood that? Even the Kadet Central Committee didn't understand. Its appeal yesterday to the masses had, after all, given rise to a great popular movement! It had broken the force of the Leninist detachments! Today we should have developed this action so as to finish the enemy off! A powerful new appeal by the CC had been readied, and it was to appear in *Speech* today—it had already been typeset overnight. But then, yesterday evening, the Executive Committee had issued its appeal: no demonstrations and everyone to keep mum. And the Kadet CC members vacillated and Milyukov, with all the strength of his conviction, could not give them the boldness they needed: they felt they shouldn't anger the Soviet. And they withdrew the combative appeal from *Speech*, replacing it with a conciliatory editorial.

Faint hearts. That's not how history's made!

Pavel Nikolaevich was touched by what one of the Kadets' local activist groups had said: "Your presence in the government serves as our guarantee of Russia's accession to the circle of civilized nations. If you had been forced to leave, it would have proved the absence of any sense of nationhood among the people." And there were a good few other resolutions of a similar nature.

And who most surely did not understand the situation was the government, which had lost its nerve. It didn't realize that it had in Petrograd more supporters than opponents, that it was in control of the situation. They didn't appreciate their triumph, with the loan now supported by the Executive Committee and the Soviet voting on it today. But despite this, at today's meeting Milyukov had found the government in a state of panic, saying that we must seek a coalition with the socialists, that we couldn't manage alone.

They assembled at the Mariinsky, without Guchkov. (And without any crowds in the square outside.) As for the meeting itself, it was barely a meeting at all, just minor issues such as a supervisory committee to keep an eye on the Trubetskoy Bastion. Otherwise they just sat chatting, exchanging views. And Milyukov, filled with triumph, gave one of his best speeches, which, alas, was not recorded. He tried to communicate to them his courage, his understanding of the situation: do not accept that label, "bourgeois government"—we are the government of all our people, and we're preparing the country for the Constituent Assembly—you saw with your own eyes the people's support. However could the defeatist idea of a coalition with the socialists, *ab initio vitiosa*,[4] gain ground? Why, when we have won the battle?

Prince Lvov, preoccupied, hurried to get off to his ministry, to a conference of provincial commissars, which he used as a cover. And the exhausted Shingarev was also looking for a way to get back to his current work. Tereshchenko and Nekrasov looked as they always did, roguish and conspiratorial. Kerensky carried on pretending that his voice was not yet fully functional, just turning his nose up at Milyukov's speech—clearly, he'd already thought up another dirty trick.

They were told that delegations from the front, from the 9th Army, the 1st Guards Division, and the Orenburg Cossacks, had arrived in the entrance hall—they'd waited in Petersburg all through these turbulent days. And it was Milyukov, the most energetic and sure of himself, who went out to them.

"You have seen here people who have lost their way, demonstrating against the government of the people. The old regime used physical force in such cases—we'll never do that . . . What we understand by the phrase "a victorious issue of the war" is not making slaves of other peoples but nipping in the bud any possibility of such wars starting up in the future—rendering the predatory nation harmless and including it in a peaceful family of nations."

[8 9]

Shulgin's behavior, both political and personal, featured impressionist traits of which he could not rid himself. He knew that. He visualized the decisions to be taken and conducted himself more like an artist than a politician. In March, having played a part in both the abdications, elegance dictated not to get into a tussle for a ministerial portfolio. To stand proudly aside. And not to give up his *Kievlyanin*, or abandon his Southwest region: Shulgin saw Kiev and its environs as Russia's heart, where still, perhaps, our future would settle into its most stable form.

But political figures cannot let themselves lapse into somnolence or fantasies, even for just a week, or they immediately lose control of events. It was just such a lapse that the whole State Duma Committee had suffered after the two abdications: they'd been counting on events having received such a surge of energy that the revolution would take the right course, of its own accord. But it was only the self-absorbed Rodzyanko who was still, even today, trying not to notice the results of that lapse. Of the whole Tauride Palace, the Duma Committee now had only the Duma library and a tiny room next to it. The Soviet had overflowed into the rest. The Committee of

4. perverse from the start

twelve prominent members—formed to great acclaim during the days of the Revolution—immediately lost six of them when the Provisional Government was set up. For completeness' sake, they were replaced by another six, but of them only Maklakov and Efremov were prominent figures, the other four just filling chairs. And, what's more, Maklakov only rarely attended meetings. Others missed them too. The Committee had not, actually, been annulled but it showed no sign of life to the outside world. At their meetings they discussed things that even the kids in the street already knew. And still there were, around town, trams covered with banners appealing for donations to the "martyrs of the revolution" (though today it was no longer entirely clear who this referred to)—but even that was signed: "Committee empanelled by the State Duma," which was not us anymore but someone else. Of course the Committee still, since the first day, fervently supported the Freedom Loan. And innumerable messages of commendation for the Committee were still arriving from all over the country. And the Committee was still charged, by the government directly, with assembling Duma members to form a council for church affairs: the authority of the Duma would help Vladimir Lvov to carry out shuffles in the governing body of the church.

And now Duma delegates were sent to the fronts with the instruction to act in total harmony with the Soviet of Workers' Deputies representatives who were going with them. (And for the whole trip they treated the Duma members as if they were under police escort.)

It was not for nothing that that artful dodger Nekrasov—who had managed, not so long ago and thanks to all his intrigues, to become Vice-president of the Duma—now sent a letter resigning that title. (He didn't want to look ridiculous.) Maklakov was clearly demoralized. He kept out of the way as much as possible, sought an independent role for himself, sat on the commission for revising the Criminal Code (while criminals were just being turned out on the streets in droves: do go on thieving!), and sometimes went to Moscow to make speeches.

But Rodzyanko was clutching hungrily at any honors still available that could show his special position: he rolled up to the Minsk congress to trumpet his praise for the freedom that had been won; and now today he was *receiving* Brătianu in what had been his own, sumptuous office (he'd asked the Executive Committee to vacate it for a few hours). And this was how his life lurched along: he was sincerely moved (for the benefit of the newspaper) by Prince Lvov's profound trust in the great heart of the Russian people, which was the fountainhead of justice, truth, and freedom. But when it came down to practical things such as getting a train or an escort allocated to him, he would turn not to the government but to the Executive Committee. He had become utterly sluggish, weak-willed, and dispirited.

Some Duma members were exasperated by Rodzyanko's inaction: for the last two months he had not been able, or even wanted, to get a Duma session convened, something which in earlier times had been the most desired and the most talked-about of acts and the cause of so many battles with the Tsar. Rodzyanko, who was himself languishing, used the pretext that convening the Duma would be impossible in these anarchic conditions: there would be open conflict with the Soviet in conditions unfavorable to us. We'd now got to such a low state that an expression was doing the rounds: convening a Duma session was like "galvanizing a political corpse."

Shulgin was feeling more and more alone, lost, in the Duma Committee. Humiliated, too. It was painful for him to walk around the Tauride Palace, over those floors now covered in spit that would take forever to clean off, around the deserted ministerial wing, now bearing the eternal stamp of a prison—and, especially, to go into the Duma hall, which had known ten years of a constitutional Russia and so many brilliant rhetorical battles. But now—not even to mention the Tsar's portrait yanked out of its frame and the traces of cigarettes stubbed out on the white walls—the speaker's rostrum and the presidium platform were covered with idiotic red calico, and during the Soviet mob's assemblies a solid cloud of tobacco smoke hung over the hall, while people shouted, as the spirit took them, from their seats, responding to the incoherent speeches of simpletons or the tortuous verbal gymnastics of the leading "revolutionary democrats."

Horrified, he asked himself: whose hands is Russia in?? To be in their hands, that bellowing mob stinking of tobacco, would be a nightmare. No matter how beautifully you kindle ideas of freedom, still no majority is capable of leading itself. And anyway, it wasn't that crowd doing the leading—actually it was the brazen, grasping types in the Executive Committee who were manipulating everything. Shulgin didn't know and didn't want to know about their internal skulduggery, but the biggest of them, the butcher-like form of Nakhamkes, could always be distinguished at their head. (And Shulgin had given free rein to his caustic turn of phrase in April, squeezing into his *Kievlyanin* an article about him which had, apparently, cut him to the quick. The EC had complained to . . . Rodzyanko.)

Oh, where had those weeks of March and April gone! The whole of the pre-revolution Duma (with its Progressive bloc and with Shulgin in that bloc) had strayed off course. And the whole post-revolution Duma, along with its now pointless committee, had understood nothing, had spent two months fighting the counterrevolution myth—and entered into a shameful compromise with the dregs of society.

Yet if you're still young, full of strength, with sound mind, how can you renounce any ambition to steer events?

But events had rolled along of their own accord, into a dead end. As it happened, the date finally fixed to start disinfecting the whole of the Tauride and eliminating the filth that had accumulated over these seven weeks was 3 May: the Soviet would have to squeeze up while the two halves of the palace were closed off in turn. And it was on that very day that the Duma Committee members read, early that morning, Milyukov's sensible note and were celebrating the fact that it seemed the government had started speaking the language of firm authority, that the government was standing, with due dignity, on its own two feet. But then, immediately afterwards, terrible rumors reached them: rebellious regiments had stormed the Mariinsky Palace! The whole Provisional Government had been arrested! And once or twice a worker-soldier deputy (or whatever the hell they're called) had come right into the Tauride, obstructing all the disinfection, and read out the note from that same rostrum from which, six months before, Milyukov had so confidently delivered his "storm signal" speech on 14 November to the applause of the spotlessly clean Duma members, in their frock coats and ties. Now it was rabble yelling from their seats "Down with Milyukov! Give him the sack!"

The Duma Committee had gathered in the tiny room off the library, where they sat, determinedly, in conference—but they were putting on record the contradictory rumors they'd heard rather than anything else. They couldn't take any decisions. Rodzyanko was phoning Prince Lvov all the time but getting neither reassurance nor instructions from the other end. Finally it was decided to hold a joint session that evening. For this once, at this difficult moment, they had to include the forgotten Duma Committee!

And Shulgin had darted into that little opening. To speak his mind, at least to that meeting, even if his words wouldn't reach all Russia.

But he'd moved no one. And his words had not reached any target.

Meanwhile, yesterday's events had involved many tens of thousands. Workers had shot at soldiers three times! How hard would it now be to stir up the soldiers and sweep away this monster? But we did nothing of the kind! No determined ministers soared above the crowds—they were all hiding away somewhere, letting these hours slip through their fingers, hours when they could not only have crushed Lenin but perhaps curtailed the Soviet's activities too. The Kadets remained Kadets, all their effervescence dissipating into the air, to no effect. And that cowardly City Duma—which had shouted so loudly against the old government on 10 March, when the first corpses lay just by their steps—did not, now, when more corpses lay by those same steps, seek to stigmatize the guilty party, but made a "conciliatory" address to citizens: "differences of opinion spill over into conflicts that favor only counterrevolution . . ." Give it a good kicking. No danger in that, it's already dead.

And so the metronome of the revolution beat out the time. The hours for arresting Lenin had been missed—and the faint hearts in the government had rejoiced at the fraudulent reassurance issued by an Executive Committee scared by the appearance of masses endowed with common sense. They'd put a revolutionary muzzle on the more politically conscientious section of the population: since it's turned out that there are more of you than there are of us, and since you're not fooled by our red ravings, then be so kind as to be silent! When the masses with some common sense gained the upper hand, that's when they'd started chasing everyone home.

And the Kadets, having missed yesterday's unparalleled opportunity, were now celebrating their victory, not seeing that they'd been the losers that day.

And this marked the end of the first recurring paroxysm of the revolution. Judging by the French revolution, they'd be repeating from now on—and becoming more acute.

Today's newspapers were asking whether or not it was true that the soldiers were killed with exploding bullets—which are not used in the Russian army—and if so where did they come from?

There was no attempt to find the answer. Prosecutor Pereverzev, who had announced yesterday, loud and clear, that he was launching an investigation, was today already wriggling out of it: "For the time being it is still difficult to say anything about the culprits of the bloodshed. In one place the shooting by armed workers began only after *someone* fired a shot into the air."

The really despicable thing in all today's papers was that no one said the shooting was due to Lenin—they only celebrated the Executive Committee's "tact," and said that "fortunately" the crowd had not marched on the Kshesinskaya mansion.

But even more despicable was the fact that all the socialist papers were now laughing at the Kadets and cursing them for the one bold and correct step they'd taken—for yesterday's appeal to the citizens to come out and demonstrate in favor of the government. The remarkable patriotism shown yesterday by the soldiers, the students, the educated public, and the Petrograd man in the street was vilified by the socialists as the appearance of the *cultured rabble, the cultured mob*. And, they said, it turned out that it was actually the Kadets who had stirred up anarchy and civil war—not the Leninists at all!

Shameless! You felt offended on the Kadets' behalf, even if you weren't one of them. In full view of everyone, the Leninists had corrupted the army and Russia, they'd spread treacherous propaganda—and the Executive Committee hadn't dared put them in their place. Finally an indignant populace had taken to the streets—so everything was their fault, not that of the real incendiary, Lenin! It was the Kadet party who had "organized the outrages," who were "defenders of the counterrevolutionary classes"—all the socialists had taken on Bolshevik tones.

It was certainly not the Kadet party that Shulgin wanted to find himself defending now: along the political path he'd taken, it had been the constant caustic interlocutor on his left, with its own excellent speakers, who would talk their way out of trouble. But in the course of those two days it had become clear to him that the conflict was far from settled: the government, undermined, was tottering on the brink of destruction, but there was now, alas, no other potential government in Russia. So the only choice left was to support *this* one, so as not to end up with something even worse.

And Shulgin now—with compelling urgency—put his conclusions, which had long been clear to everyone with any common sense, before the Duma Committee as soon as they arrived—giving them no time to settle down and start daydreaming again.

The Provisional Government is hanging in mid-air, with nothing above or below it, in a void, in the position of one which has seized power or even usurped the rightful power. It can no longer exist without a consultative body, where it could exchange views with representatives of various political tendencies. The normal body for this would be a parliament. But the Duma has not sat, ever since the revolution, so we don't have that kind of forum anymore. The Soviet of Workers' Deputies? But it represents only the lowest social strata of Petrograd and does not reflect the mood of the whole country (all the rest of the country was "bourgeois," and not represented anywhere). And besides, the details of their sessions don't get into the papers—and those of the unelected Executive Committee are kept absolutely secret. And representatives of the Provisional Government don't speak at the Soviet's meetings either: that isn't their audience. But if a consultative body had existed now, no misunderstandings or conflicts would have arisen, as they have in recent days. The government could have relied on public support. It would have been possible to convene this parliament-style body, even if only in cases where the Provisional Government wanted to provide explanations to various political tendencies and listen to their opinions . . . (What a humiliation for the previous, proud Duma! The Tsarist government would never have dared not to convene us!) It could be constituted of equal numbers of Duma and Executive Committee members. And representatives of the press should be allowed in, so that reports could be published (as they had in the State Duma—oh, happy days!).

His listeners were interested. They discussed it. There were objections that the creation of this kind of pseudo-parliament would make the country think the Constituent Assembly would not be assembling at all soon. (Which it wouldn't be.) Also, that the Provisional Government would be bombarded with inquiries—which would make their position even more difficult. (How had the Tsarist government floundered under our inquiries? That hadn't bothered us.)

There were also some who supported Shulgin, the bolder ones: the State Duma should not stay completely silent, especially with events like these going on. For Russian public opinion to be voiced correctly, it is imperative that not only the Soviet of Workers' Deputies be heard!

(The Provisional Government should latch onto a project like this with both hands! After all, we're going to save them from the Soviet! They can't survive in the current conditions!)

They livened up, and while waiting to get down to the real business they called a private meeting of the Duma members for later today. Whoever could come would come . . .

But that, of course, fell far short of what was needed.

The government did not react to Shulgin's proposal. And, needless to say, the Executive Committee ignored it.

But then Vinaver pressed his own item: he was pushing for a celebration in honor of his much-loved First Duma. On 10 May it would be exactly eleven years since it was convened. (That presented them with a sizeable task: would they have to evacuate and clean the White Hall? And, what's more, they'd have to ask permission from the Executive Committee.)

That was not a serious substitute—it only diverted attention away from Shulgin's idea. But perhaps . . . Perhaps that substitute could also offer a way? You never can tell!

Lvov started procrastinating on this project too.

And Shulgin could already imagine the speech he would have to give there. He felt roused to action.

[9 0]

Steklov's authority had been undermined and things were going steadily downhill. He was now being given the most insignificant jobs: to go and investigate an explosion in a Gunpowder district factory; open a soldiers' club beyond the Narva Gate; go to a concert-meeting at the Mikhailovsky Theater—it was a plain lie, tell him that Chkheidze and Skobelev would be there too: they weren't—and he just hung around like an idiot, doing nothing. And just then Dan joined the editorial team of *Izvestia*, and Steklov's hands were tied: he was not to express his singular, nuanced party opinions. But what had actually appeared in *Izvestia* up to now, other than his own line, his trenchant headlines, the sharp blows he delivered?—you could always recognize the writing, even without a signature. He'd also lost his membership in the Liaison Commission and not been elected to the EC bureau. But he could still have recovered from being edged out like that if it hadn't been for that dreadful fiasco over his name. Some swine had, in an idle moment, been going through the government office archives and somehow dug up his petition to the Tsar to change his name from Ovshi Moiseevich Nakhamkes to Yuri Mikhailovich Steklov. And instead of snuffing the story out, or bringing the document to Steklov himself, he'd started showing it around, and it had leaked to the bourgeois press. And now it was being spread everywhere. But any approach to the Tsar, with its "I fall down at Your feet" formula, had long been considered—and not just by revolutionaries but in society as well—the very worst, most shameful thing, worse than forgery, theft, or the seduction of minors. Such a revelation would finish off any political career: people didn't usually pick themselves up after that.

Revolution is more complicated than chess: there is no defined set of possible moves for each figure, from which you can choose. Here you have an indeterminate quantity of them, they are totally unexpected, and from the most varied of figures—such that you need really brilliant intuition to discern and select every day's possibilities and decide on the best moves. And now Lenin (while in emigration Steklov had underestimated him) most definitely had that intuition. Here he is, arriving a month late for the revolution, all the places taken, all the programs up and running—and announces his own program, shocking and absolutely unacceptable to everyone. They all recoil, yet two and a half weeks later he brings the Petrograd workers out onto the street, against the government and, yes, in effect against the Soviet as well. (Today, 5 May, at the meeting of the garrison's battalion committees, two representatives from the armored division indiscreetly let slip that they'd recently been asked to send armored cars to arrest the Provincial Government and for firing in the streets! And the armored division was *asking to be forgiven for the blood spilt on Nevsky Prospect.*)

It was indiscreet because it was no secret that the armored division had previously been stationed at the Kshesinskaya mansion, and they hadn't lost their connection with the Bolsheviks.

But luckily Steklov's ideological closeness to the Bolshevik position had, over recent months, helped him take the right steps in relation to them. Not only had he always voted with them, but he'd also expressed consistently favorable opinions of them in *Izvestia*, had been in time to accompany the Bolsheviks' rapid creation of a workers' militia with an approving article, and also been sympathetic to other steps they'd taken. At first he'd made the mistake of saying Lenin had lost contact with the Russian reality, and speaking against him on his first appearance at the Tauride Palace—this was a time when everyone was speaking against him—but the very next day (with no hard feelings against Lenin for calling him a "social lackey") he'd made no bones about offsetting his error with an article in *Izvestia* sympathetic to Lenin's passage through Germany, defending him against the slander of dishonorable and repugnant dark forces and even—although it was the Soviet's organ—refusing to publish the soldiers' Executive Commission resolution against Lenin, which would have been dangerous for him. And for the same reason he made no mention at all in *Izvestia* of the war invalids' demonstration. Oh, he could do Lenin a lot of good, back him up in so many ways. With every passing day, Lenin was making speeches that were ever more explicitly against the Soviet itself. And here the Soviet's organ was defending not the Soviet but Lenin. Amazed by the latter's incisive, rapid, and strong grip, Steklov now showed that he was in every possible way Lenin's ally. The *Izvestia* platform was already burning beneath his feet, but he carried on delivering articles that were imbued with Lenin's way of thinking and even an editorial supporting Lenin on the day of his second difficult appearance at the Tauride Palace. As he left *Izvestia*, he wanted to give the door a good slam! He had, anyway, already broken his ties irrevocably with the jubilant traitors, Tsereteli's majority.

The crisis of 3 and 4 May had given Steklov a chance to vent great quantities of spleen on Milyukov, in two issues. One on his disgusting, imperialist essence (and the deal he'd obviously done with General Alekseev during his visit at this fateful time: one raven calling in another for the kill); and one on the bourgeois hypocrisy of the (cleverly directed) pro-government demonstrators, hiding their hunger for Constantinople and Armenia from the soldiers. He also addressed the crowd outside the Sea Cadet Corps: "In about two or three weeks we'd have been able to conclude a peace with Germany—and the capitalists like Milyukov, rolling in money, took fright at that." And, as a smokescreen to shield Lenin: "The scheming of the Black Hundreds, who already, yesterday, tried to create uproar in the streets . . . We are warning those individuals, who will not be tolerated in a free state . . .!"

Although—going the whole way into the Lenin camp would mean submitting to Lenin's stifling discipline.

And besides, Steklov did have one foothold left: international support. His name was known in Stockholm through socialist channels. And when Kolyshko had arrived from Stockholm (he'd been Witte's secretary at one time, was a well-known journalist, and now had a German wife in Stockholm, where he had contacts with important Germans and with Parvus's circle)—when he arrived he'd brought with him, from the Germans, a plan for a truce with Germany. It was addressed to the two most distinguished socialists in Russia—Kerensky and Steklov!

Well now there is a document for you! Steklov could not stoop to ask Kerensky what he'd done with that document, but most probably he'd done nothing with it, because since he'd become a minister he'd got stuck in the mire of defensism. So now history had entrusted Steklov with the job: he himself would take on the grandiose, momentous step that would decide the fate of Europe. And there and then he charged Kolyshko, as he was leaving for Stockholm, with communicating his agreement: let them send some German Social Democrats straight to the Dvinsk section of the front to negotiate with us.

But for all that to be done via Stockholm and Copenhagen, the route was too circuitous. We had to talk more directly and more speedily. Just then an acquaintance of Steklov's arrived from the Northern Front. He came often and was an absolutely reliable sergeant, who was serving as a clerk in Riga and spoke German. And Steklov gave him instructions: do some fraternization and try to get a German officer of no lower position than regimental HQ to come, and get him to pass up through his command structure the message: there is, in the Executive Committee, one Steklov, a prominent figure and Chkheidze's first deputy, who is very influential and ready for peace negotiations. He could also discuss the ceding of territory and payment for the excessive number of Russian prisoners. And Steklov is prepared to come to the front at a moment's notice, to talk to German parliamentarians. Without Steklov such negotiations will fail. And, he told the sergeant, if they bite, I can come from Petrograd, summon me straight away!

To bestow on Russia the gift of immediate peace! That would be a step in line with his stature! And Russia would not forget it.

Neither would the International.

If he didn't do it, he'd carry on slipping down, lower and lower, and soon there'd be not a single foothold left.

He'd not yet made the decision to go, as a last resort, cap in hand to the Kshesinskaya mansion—but he was already resigned to the fact that he'd probably have to.

* * *

*IF YOUR RIDE ATOP THE WHEEL—
LOOK AT THE GROUND BELOW*

* * *

[91]

On Tuesday, for the new First of May holiday, the weather in Moscow had still been terrible: darkly overcast since early morning, sleet, cold all day, and a leaden sky with occasional swirls of wet snow, fine cold drizzle, or else something more like hail. And Ksenia had been assailed by an oppressive melancholy, exacerbated by those marching columns and ranks making such an effort to look happy. And she had her own particular melancholy weighing on her heart: for this was her fourth spring in Moscow and none of her hopes had been realized. She had just one little year left and she'd have to return to her Kuban backwood with nothing. It was a bitter feeling, such helplessness. Life was slipping away. (While Zhenya, in Rostov, had already had her second baby. And it was a boy!)

But from Thursday there was warmth in the air—and in the Golitsyn Courses' sector of the Petrovsko-Razumovskaya Academy the fields couldn't wait—and many skills were now demanded of fourth-year students. But so much study time had been lost on account of the revolution. So every day, first thing in the morning, they made their way there on the little local train they called "the steamer."

But Ksenia was now reconciled to her lot as an agronomist and found considerable pleasure in trying to understand and steer the life of plants. And there was her father—he was expecting her help in this area.

So today as well, Saturday—and it was even warmer—Ksenia worked all day on the plot with the other students. And while she was bent over she didn't notice, but going home that evening, at past six o'clock—what backache! And her legs could barely carry her. She'd go straight to bed now—and not move a muscle!

But the phone rang: an impromptu party at her friend's place. Come over, and make it snappy.

"Oh, I can't—I can hardly walk. No, I won't come."

She sat down to finish her dinner. And suddenly felt an urge: how could she not go? Why stay cooped up here on her own?

And she phoned back straight away:

"I'm coming! I'll hurry over!"

And what about those legs? It was as if they'd never been tired. Her back? Straight, young. A spark had kindled inside her—and everything was cured at once. She put on a cream blouse with puffed sleeves and a full, chocolate-colored cloche skirt—they'd only appeared this winter, not many people had them.

Now she had to rush across town, to Chistye Prudy. She managed to find a cab.

Since the revolution Moscow was without its orgy of lighting from the *cafés chantants*, without raucous laughter issuing from cars and sleighs, without unbridled chases, sleigh-bells tinkling, and without the open debauchery there'd been last year. The public had taken fright and pulled themselves together. Instead, you could expect any kind of brazen behavior. Today, in the middle of the day, a Red Cross ambulance had arrived at Petrovsko-Razumovskoye with, sitting next to the driver, a male passenger who was drunk. Inside were several women, cursing at the top of their voices. Students had come bounding up to ask for their papers, and the drunk had pulled a revolver on them.

She arrived at the party late—the others were already there, more than a dozen students, both girls and young men, and she knew almost all of them. They young men weren't all in uniform—since the revolution they'd begun to ignore that rule. She was late, and the unrestrained hubbub and laughter were already loud—but look, here was someone unfamiliar, a young officer with abundant golden-brown hair and a thoughtful face. And he glowed, but not from excitement. He had some kind of steady light radiating from within. And his look made Ksenia quiver inside, even before they were introduced. He was Second Lieutenant Lazhenitsyn, on leave (and before, he'd been a student at the university, studied with Boris here). And that radiant look, which was not even addressed to her, made her quiver so inside. The look in her direction only came later.

And when they were being introduced his slightly sad eyes seemed to shift a tad—toward surprise.

And from that moment a fountain of elation began to gush in Ksenia's breast! It was that first, intent meeting of their eyes that did it, that changing, that variation in his eyes. But what had happened? Something had happened! (Even—oh my goodness, could it be that very thing that had to, just had to happen one day!)

It was only later that she also noticed his St. George Cross.

Everyone was chatting animatedly, the conversations covering all sorts of subjects, people interrupting each other and moving between groups. They were in no hurry to get to the modest supper of black bread sandwiches, and no one was expecting any alcoholic drinks. And in the course of moving between groups the Second Lieutenant seized his opportunity and sat down next to Ksenia. And she lost her carefree ways, her constant motion: she just sat and sat on that chair, never moving off even if someone called.

In the group were perhaps seven young ladies—but he did not leave her side.

Amidst the general hubbub they chatted, not feeling at all shy. Firstly, it transpired that they were almost neighbors: he lived near Nagutskaya station, and how often he'd passed through Kubanskaya station—and you can see our house for just a moment from the train as you pass. Close neighbors meant fellow steppe-dwellers. (And that meant peasants . . .) And suddenly her Pecheneg Kuban backwood was nothing to be ashamed of, not something you never mentioned. The Stavropol steppe had suddenly, generously, brought them together, separating them from the Moscow group. Sanya began to tell her how he worked on his father's farm and Ksenia felt ashamed that she herself hadn't—she'd been waited on hand and foot—but now she would, she'd start working! And had chosen agronomy—he strongly approved. He'd understood, from phrases she'd let drop, that her family was prosperous—and that too he accepted without criticism.

And now, somehow, Ksenia's brain was assimilating so much, and so clearly—she heard every word and understood everything in detail, she answered rationally, correctly—while in her breast that fountain of joy, unbridled joy, that had opened up was still gushing! And why? It was a simple conversation, and it had been a simple handshake when they were introduced (but the hand feels everything, and her hand felt it was still nestling in his!) Nothing had happened yet, but there was already happiness in the fact that they'd met—and that could never be taken away, never!

But the most surprising thing was that given the chance nature of this meeting Ksenia felt more at ease than she ever had before. It was a simple, not frightening, seemingly long-familiar feeling of closeness to him. What a wonderful state to be in!

Suddenly, though: a terrible fear. Might he now, somehow, show himself in a less good light? Would it all come to nothing?

But no! No! With every word, he—no! That couldn't happen!

To think that the year before the war they'd both been studying here in Moscow—and never met!

Now he's talking about the front, his voice somewhat muted. Not hurrying. His moustache is golden, the color of wheat, and not large. Lips without a trace of hardness. Soft, golden hair—and what thick hair—lying neatly groomed above a high, smooth forehead.

They'd forgotten everything, separated themselves from the group so completely that the others were already directing jokes at them. Quite right too: Ksenia could not tell you who was here now—she'd not even found time to register their presence! She had to tear herself away, alas.

But even at a distance, whatever they were doing—playing charades, musical chairs, drinking tea and eating sandwiches, dancing in couples to the piano—Ksenia always saw and felt him from afar. And she knew for sure that he too was occupied with her alone and, like her, had not looked at the others as much as he should have.

He wouldn't dance—he said he'd got out of practice on the front. But Ksenia was charged with such a wild gaiety, ever more explosive, that an idea came to her. And she announced that she'd now perform a dance solo—though not in costume.

Everyone applauded and took their seats. Ksenia and the student who played the piano looked over the scores for a csardas and found one. And off she went, dancing for all she was worth! Oh my goodness, dancing was the best ever idea! A direct means of expressing beauty! (And Sanya was standing by the doorpost, never taking his eyes off her.) How easy it is! You know the dance, you've learned it very well, the same movements, hand-clapping, and stamping—only the cloche skirt was too full—and the same torrid rhythm as always. But—no, it wasn't! It was a special, once-in-a-lifetime dance. By this time she had sensed in him a certain slowness, a caution—but with that dance she meant to explode all that and get everything spinning. Please, please let him feel it! And even while gyrating wildly she was able to catch a glimpse and note that he'd moved forward.

Toward the Future!

Our future . . .?

By now she'd completely forgotten how exhausted she'd been and how her legs couldn't carry her to the party. What luck that she'd put on a spurt and got there!

And all evening she'd never noticed the time—how could it be eleven o'clock? People were already leaving.

She had no doubts: of course he'd see her home.

And of course he did.

The party had whirled along like a dream: had she paid attention to everyone? Had she said goodbye to them all?

They went by cab, along Pokrovka Street, across Varvarinskaya Square and along the Moscow River and Sofia Embankments—and all of these would, from now on, be the first places in Moscow that they'd shared. And when the cab made a turn the full moon, high in the sky, lit them generously, now from the left, now, welcoming, from ahead, and now from the left again; sometimes it was hidden behind high buildings close by and sometimes it lit them from across the river—and all this remained as a single, fluid, happy memory of floating along under the moon, with the first little leaves appearing on the trees. And for the whole time his face was clearly visible, with its special purity of expression, and in his slow speech was a determined striving for purity: there was not a trace of coarseness in him.

And even with all her excitement Ksenia understood their conversation precisely (she could even repeat it all now, word for word)—and at the same time she could feel a sudden and forgotten sense of liberation: the way you are, with all your Kuban simplicity, is good—no need for play-acting or pretence.

It was not cold, even at night, and the puddles weren't freezing.

They alighted at the gate and stood for a moment in the half-shadow. He suggested straight away that they should meet tomorrow and of course Ksenia agreed, not even trying to remember what she'd planned for tomorrow.

And he squeezed her hand in both his, as if to express his feelings—and to hold on to her.

But now she couldn't stay out any later, or her landladies would be angry.

First thing, at the mirror: how did I look today? How did my face look to him? My eyes? Were they shining like this?

But what joy! She felt light as a feather! And whatever she looked at in the room—how it glowed.

His one fault: Isaaki Filippovich—not a beautiful name at all.

But Tomchak wasn't great either.

He was an Orthodox believer, and serious about it. (And of course we'll get married in church.)

How many love stories she'd read. And how many cruel mistakes they told of, freaks of fate, misunderstandings that defied explanation. Take Hamsun: in his books love is always fretful, agonizing, always a battle between a man and a woman, the hunter and the hunted, one trying to snare the other, who runs away. And if the second has a change of heart and the love is mutual—then the first immediately cools. Could it be that happy, mutual love doesn't exist, anywhere on Earth?

But it's not like that! That would be impossible—monstrous! Ksenia foresaw, with every fiber of her body, a different love: having fallen in love, you do not struggle.

Anyway, Hamsun says that too: "Love is a golden luminescence in the blood." Yes!!

What utter joy!

Maps

Russia, March 1917
state borders
internal borders
main railway tracks
Austrian-German and Turkish front in March 1917
Mogilev
General Headquarters (GHQ)
Minsk
Army Group headquarters
Sweden
Grand Duchy of Finland
Gulf of Bothnia
Murman Coast
Port Romanov
Kola
Kandalaksha
Tornio
White Sea
Kem
Arkhangelsk
Pomors
Pechora
Northern Dvina
Petrozavodsk
Lake Onega
Kotlas
Abo
Aland Islands
Vyborg
Lake Ladoga
Helsingfors
Sveaborg
Kronstadt
Petrograd
Baltic Sea
Reval
Estland
Tsarskoye Selo
Nizhni Tagil
Chudovo
Ustyuzhna
Vologda
Vyatka
Perm
Pernov
Derpt
Livonia
Luga
Vesyegonsk
Borovichi
Novgorod
Ekaterinburg
Vindava
Staraya Russa
Bologoye
Bezhetsk
Rybinsk
Kostroma
Pskov
Dno
Libau
Kurland
Riga
Velikaya
Rakhlitsy
Ostashkov
Volochok
Yaroslavl
Novorzhev
Ivanovo
Mitava
Torzhok
Tver
Kashin
Chelyabinsk
Rezhitsa
Vyazniki
Makarievo
Volga
Yelabuga
Menzelinsk
Kovno Province
Dvinsk
Velikie Luki
Dmitrov
Vladimir
Zlatoust
Rzhev
Moscow
Nizhni Novgorod
Kazan
Neman
Kovno
Polotsk
Western Dvina
Moscow River
Klyazma
Kama
Ufa
East Prussia
Sventiany
Oka
Vilna
Podsvilye
Vitebsk
Vyazma
Arzamas
Podolsk

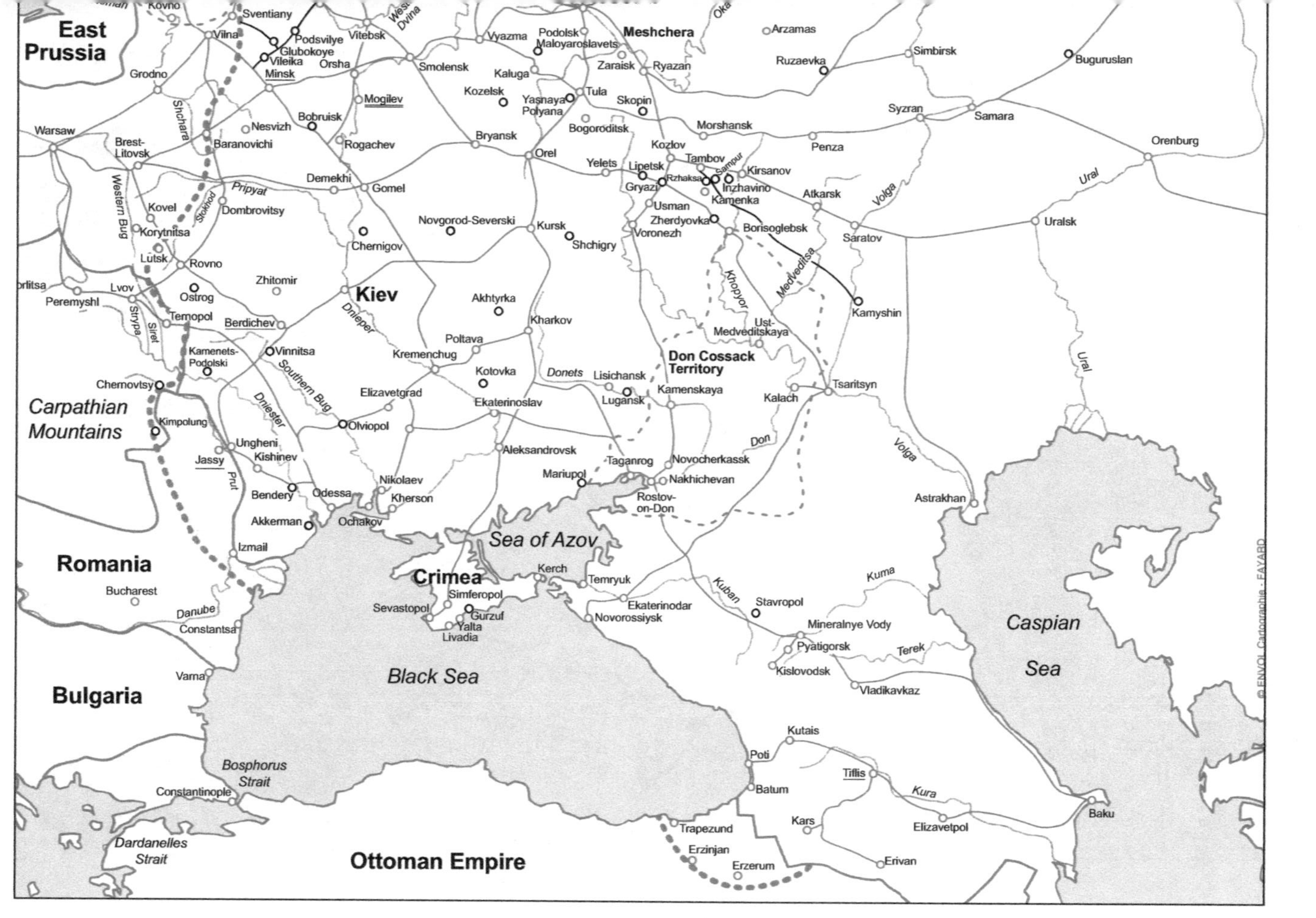
East Prussia
Kovno
Sventiany
Vilna
Podsvilye
Glubokoye
Vileika
Vitebsk
West. Dvina
Orsha
Minsk
Grodno
Shchara
Warsaw
Brest-Litovsk
Baranovichi
Nesvizh
Bobruisk
Mogilev
Rogachev
Smolensk
Vyazma
Podolsk
Maloyaroslavets
Meshchera
Oka
Kaluga
Kozelsk
Yasnaya Polyana
Tula
Zaraisk
Ryazan
Skopin
Bogoroditsk
Bryansk
Orel
Yelets
Lipetsk
Kozlov
Tambov
Sampur
Rzhaksa
Kirsanov
Inzhavino
Kamenka
Gryazi
Usman
Zherdyovka
Voronezh
Borisoglebsk
Morshansk
Penza
Atkarsk
Saratov
Arzamas
Ruzaevka
Simbirsk
Syzran
Samara
Buguruslan
Orenburg
Ural
Uralsk
Volga
Western Bug
Kovel
Stokhod
Pripyat
Dombrovitsy
Demekhi
Gomel
Korytnitsa
Lutsk
Rovno
Novgorod-Severski
Chernigov
Kursk
Shchigry
Medveditsa
Khopyor
Kamyshin
Lvov
Peremyshl
Ostrog
Zhitomir
Kiev
Dnieper
Akhtyrka
Kharkov
Strypa
Siret
Ternopol
Berdichev
Kamenets-Podolski
Vinnitsa
Southern Bug
Poltava
Kremenchug
Kotovka
Donets
Lisichansk
Lugansk
Don Cossack Territory
Ust-Medveditskaya
Kamenskaya
Kalach
Tsaritsyn
Chernovtsy
Carpathian Mountains
Kimpolung
Dniester
Elizavetgrad
Ekaterinoslav
Olviopol
Ungheni
Jassy
Kishinev
Prut
Aleksandrovsk
Taganrog
Novocherkassk
Don
Mariupol
Nakhichevan
Rostov-on-Don
Astrakhan
Bendery
Odessa
Nikolaev
Kherson
Akkerman
Ochakov
Izmail
Sea of Azov
Romania
Bucharest
Crimea
Kerch
Temryuk
Simferopol
Sevastopol
Gurzuf
Yalta
Livadia
Ekaterinodar
Novorossiysk
Kuban
Stavropol
Kuma
Mineralnye Vody
Pyatigorsk
Terek
Kislovodsk
Vladikavkaz
Caspian Sea
Danube
Constantsa
Varna
Bulgaria
Black Sea
Kutais
Poti
Tiflis
Batum
Kura
Baku
Kars
Elizavetpol
Bosphorus Strait
Constantinople
Dardanelles Strait
Trapezund
Erzinjan
Erzerum
Erivan
Ottoman Empire
© ENVOL Cartographie - FAYARD

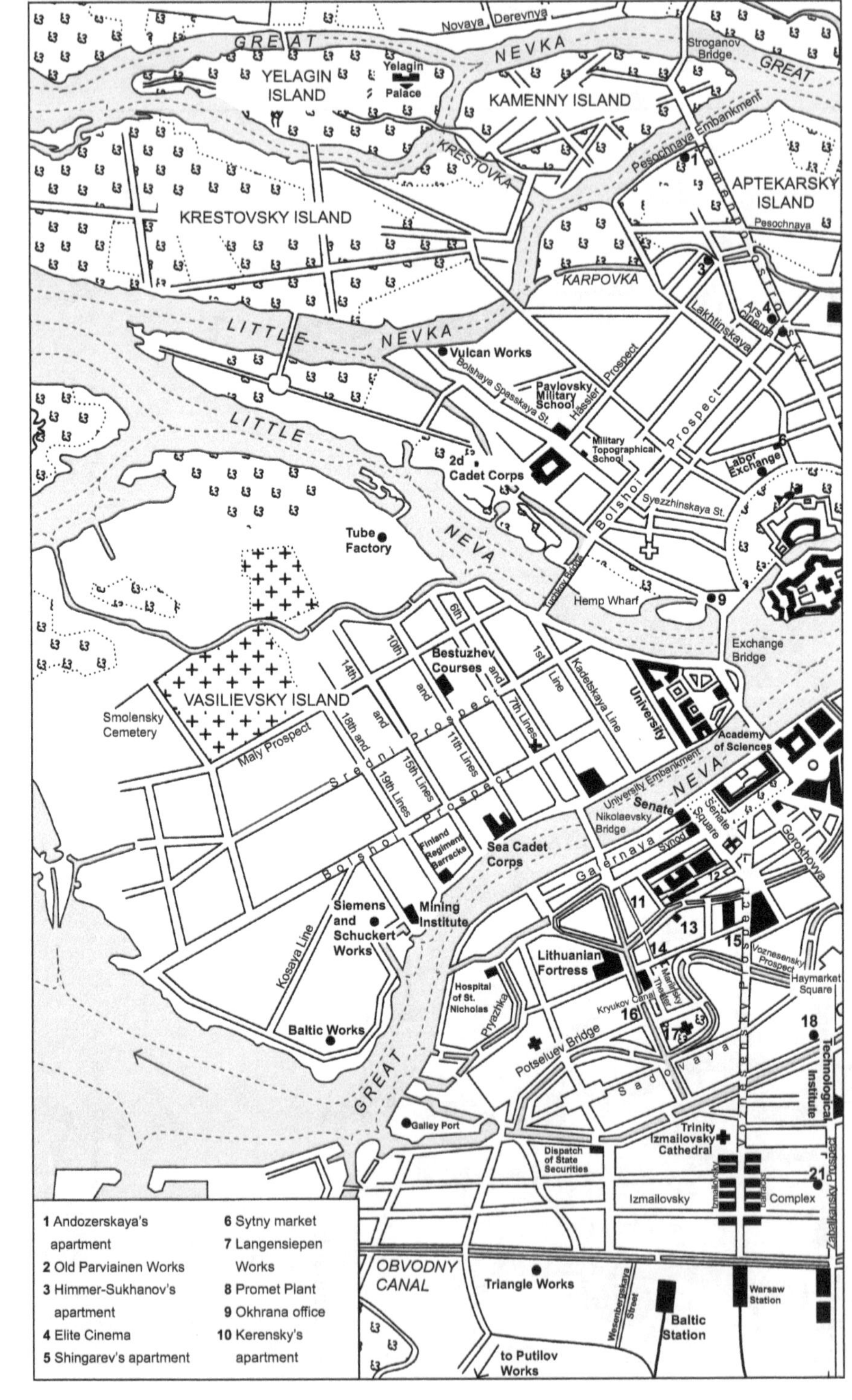

GREAT NEVKA
Novaya Derevnya
Stroganov Bridge
YELAGIN ISLAND
Yelagin Palace
KAMENNY ISLAND
Pesochnaya Embankment
KRESTOVKA
APTEKARSKY ISLAND
Pesochnaya
KRESTOVSKY ISLAND
Kamennoostrovsky
KARPOVKA
Lakhtinskaya
Ars Cinema
LITTLE NEVKA
Vulcan Works
Bolshaya Spasskaya St.
Pavlovsky Military School
Hassler Prospect
Military Topographical School
Bolshoi Prospect
Labor Exchange
LITTLE NEVA
2d Cadet Corps
Syezzhinskaya St.
Tube Factory
Tuchkov Bridge
Hemp Wharf
Exchange Bridge
Bestuzhev Courses
6th
10th
1st Line
Kadetskaya Line
University
14th and 15th Lines
18th and 19th Lines
7th and 11th Lines
VASILIEVSKY ISLAND
Smolensky Cemetery
Maly Prospect
Sredni Prospect
Academy of Sciences
University Embankment
NEVA
Senate
Senate Square
Nikolaevsky Bridge
Synod
Gorokhovaya
Finland Regiment Barracks
Sea Cadet Corps
Galernaya
Bolshoi Prospect
Siemens and Schuckert Works
Mining Institute
Kosaya Line
Lithuanian Fortress
Voznesensky Prospect
Haymarket Square
Hospital of St. Nicholas
Kryukov Canal
Mariinsky Theater
Pryazhka
Baltic Works
Potseluev Bridge
Sadovaya
Technological Institute
GREAT
Galley Port
Trinity Izmailovsky Cathedral
Dispatch of State Securities
Izmailovsky Complex
Zabalkansky Prospect
OBVODNY CANAL
Triangle Works
Wesenbergskaya Street
Warsaw Station
Baltic Station
to Putilov Works
1 Andozerskaya's apartment
2 Old Parviainen Works
3 Himmer-Sukhanov's apartment
4 Elite Cinema
5 Shingarev's apartment
6 Sytny market
7 Langensiepen Works
8 Promet Plant
9 Okhrana office
10 Kerensky's apartment

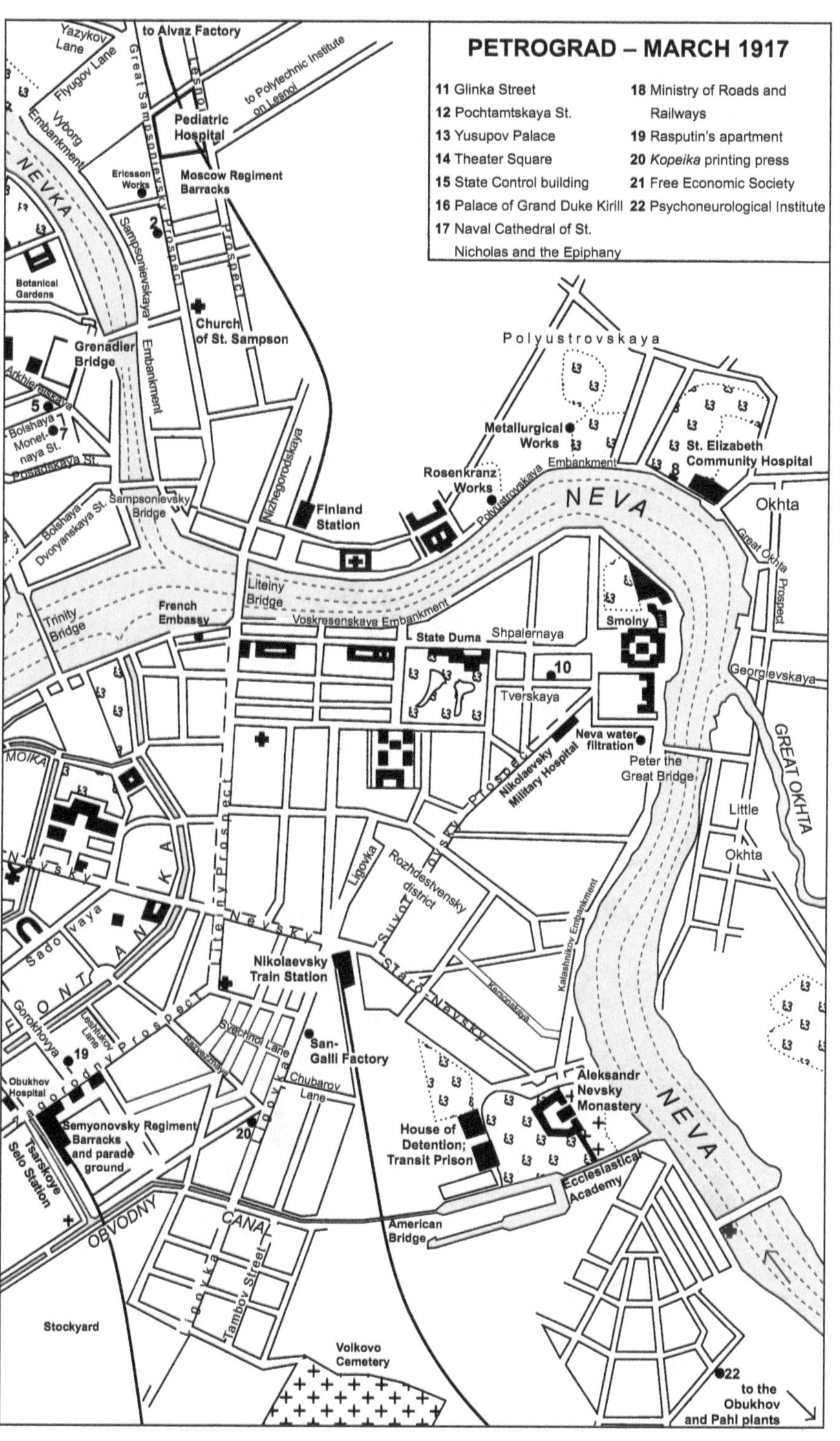
PETROGRAD – MARCH 1917
11 Glinka Street
12 Pochtamtskaya St.
13 Yusupov Palace
14 Theater Square
15 State Control building
16 Palace of Grand Duke Kirill
17 Naval Cathedral of St. Nicholas and the Epiphany
18 Ministry of Roads and Railways
19 Rasputin's apartment
20 *Kopeika* printing press
21 Free Economic Society
22 Psychoneurological Institute
to Aivaz Factory
to Polytechnic Institute on Lesnoi
Pediatric Hospital
Moscow Regiment Barracks
Ericsson Works
Church of St. Sampson
Botanical Gardens
Grenadier Bridge
Finland Station
Polyustrovskaya
Metallurgical Works
Rosenkranz Works
St. Elizabeth Community Hospital
Okhta
NEVA
NEVKA
Sampsonievsky Bridge
Liteiny Bridge
Trinity Bridge
French Embassy
Voskresenskaya Embankment
State Duma
Shpalernaya
Tverskaya
Smolny
Georgievskaya
Neva water filtration
Peter the Great Bridge
Nikolaevsky Military Hospital
GREAT OKHTA
Little Okhta
Rozhdestvensky district
Nikolaevsky Train Station
San-Galli Factory
Aleksandr Nevsky Monastery
House of Detention; Transit Prison
Ecclesiastical Academy
American Bridge
Semyonovsky Regiment Barracks and parade ground
Obukhov Hospital
Tsarskoye Selo Station
OBVODNY CANAL
Stockyard
Volkovo Cemetery
to the Obukhov and Pahl plants

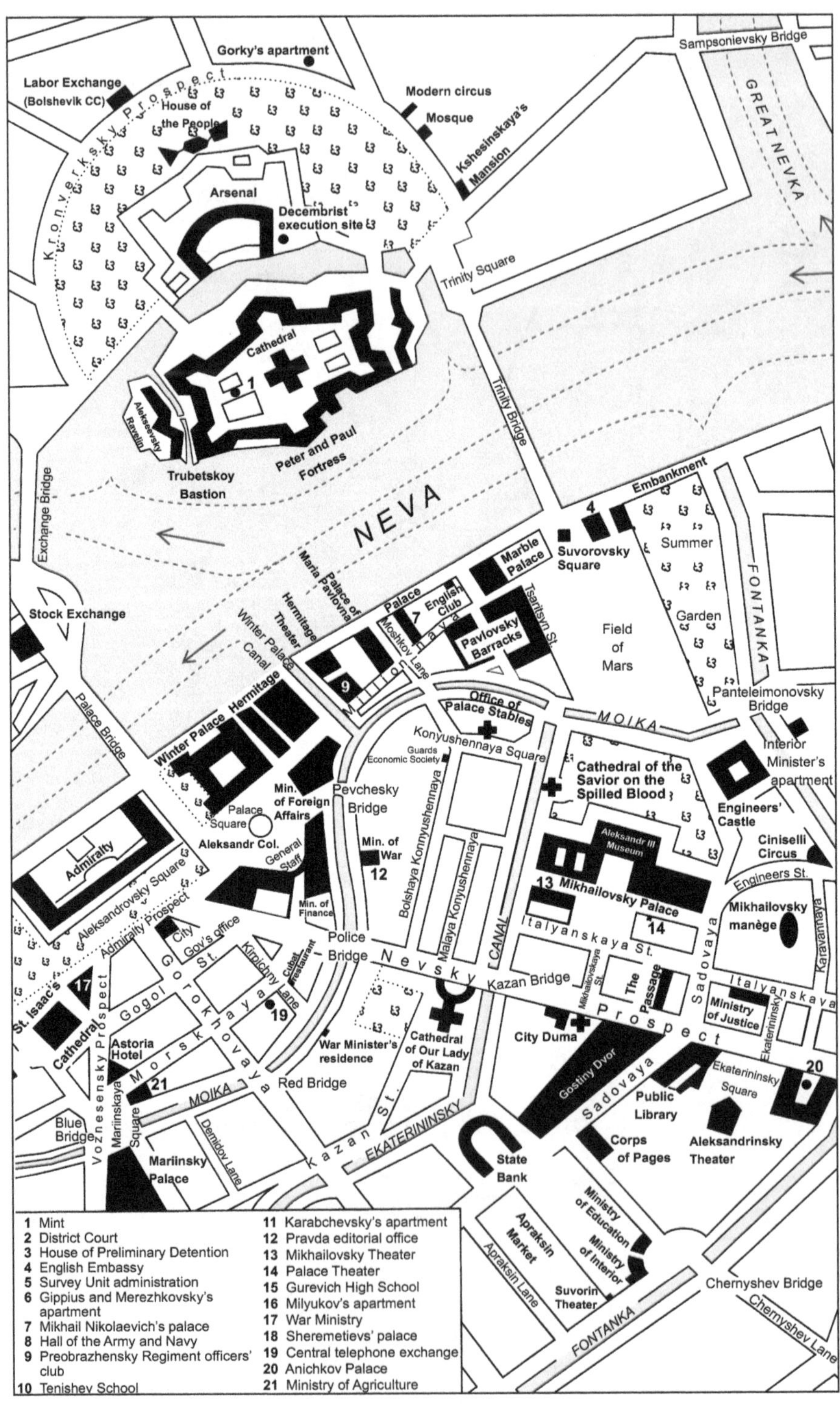
Gorky's apartment
Sampsonievsky Bridge
Labor Exchange
(Bolshevik CC)
House of
the People
Kronverksky Prospect
Modern circus
Mosque
Kshesinskaya's
Mansion
GREAT NEVKA
Arsenal
Decembrist
execution site
Trinity Square
Cathedral
Alekseevsky
Ravelin
Trubetskoy
Bastion
Peter and Paul
Fortress
Trinity Bridge
Exchange Bridge
NEVA
Embankment
Marble
Palace
Suvorovsky
Square
Summer
Garden
FONTANKA
Stock Exchange
Palace of
Maria Pavlovna
Hermitage
Theater
Winter Palace
Canal
Palace
English
Club
Moshkov Lane
Millionnaya
Pavlovsky
Barracks
Tsaritsyn St.
Field
of
Mars
Panteleimonovsky
Bridge
Palace Bridge
Hermitage
Winter Palace
Office of
Palace Stables
MOIKA
Konyushennaya Square
Guards
Economic Society
Interior
Minister's
apartment
Cathedral of the
Savior on the
Spilled Blood
Engineers'
Castle
Palace
Square
Min.
of Foreign
Affairs
Pevchesky
Bridge
Aleksandr Col.
General
Staff
Min. of
War
Bolshaya Konyushennaya
Malaya Konyushennaya
Aleksandr III
Museum
Ciniselli
Circus
Engineers St.
Admiralty
Aleksandrovsky Square
Aleksandrovsky Prospect
Admiralty Prospect
Min. of
Finance
Mikhailovsky Palace
Mikhailovsky
manège
Italyanskaya St.
Karavannaya
City
Gov's office
Kirpichny
Lane
Cubat
Restaurant
Police
Bridge
CANAL
Nevsky
Prospect
Kazan Bridge
St. Isaac's
Cathedral
Voznesensky Prospect
Gogol St.
Gorokhovaya
Morskaya
War Minister's
residence
Cathedral
of Our Lady
of Kazan
Mikhailovskaya St.
The
Passage
Sadovaya
Ministry
of Justice
Italyanskaya
Ekaterininsky
City Duma
Astoria
Hotel
Red Bridge
Ekaterininsky
Square
MOIKA
Gostiny Dvor
Public
Library
Blue
Bridge
Mariinskaya
Square
Demidov Lane
Kazan St.
EKATERININSKY
Corps
of Pages
Aleksandrinsky
Theater
Mariinsky
Palace
State
Bank
Ministry
of Education
Ministry
of Interior
Apraksin
Market
Apraksin Lane
Suvorin
Theater
FONTANKA
Chernyshev Bridge
Chernyshev Lane
1 Mint
2 District Court
3 House of Preliminary Detention
4 English Embassy
5 Survey Unit administration
6 Gippius and Merezhkovsky's apartment
7 Mikhail Nikolaevich's palace
8 Hall of the Army and Navy
9 Preobrazhensky Regiment officers' club
10 Tenishev School
11 Karabchevsky's apartment
12 Pravda editorial office
13 Mikhailovsky Theater
14 Palace Theater
15 Gurevich High School
16 Milyukov's apartment
17 War Ministry
18 Sheremetievs' palace
19 Central telephone exchange
20 Anichkov Palace
21 Ministry of Agriculture

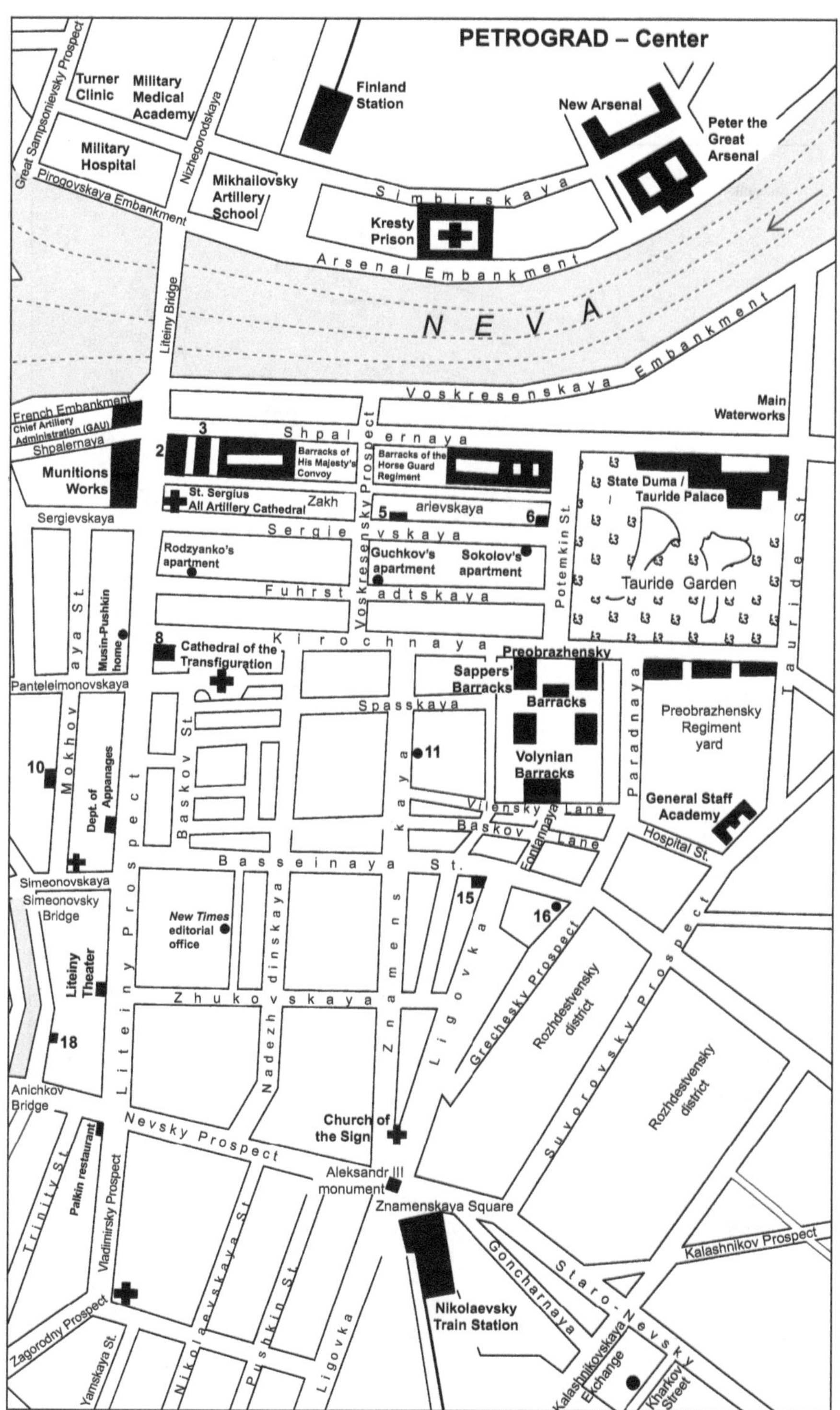
PETROGRAD – Center
Great Sampsonievsky Prospect
Turner Clinic
Military Medical Academy
Military Hospital
Pirogovskaya Embankment
Nizhegorodskaya
Mikhailovsky Artillery School
Finland Station
Simbirskaya
Kresty Prison
New Arsenal
Peter the Great Arsenal
Arsenal Embankment
Liteiny Bridge
NEVA
Voskresenskaya Embankment
Main Waterworks
French Embankment
Chief Artillery Administration (GAU)
Shpalernaya
Munitions Works
2
3
Barracks of His Majesty's Convoy
Barracks of the Horse Guard Regiment
Voskresensky Prospect
St. Sergius All Artillery Cathedral
Zakharievskaya
5
6
Sergievskaya
State Duma / Tauride Palace
Tauride Garden
Potemkin St.
Tauride St.
Rodzyanko's apartment
Guchkov's apartment
Sokolov's apartment
Fuhrstadtskaya
Kirochnaya
Mokhovaya St
Musin-Pushkin home
8
Cathedral of the Transfiguration
Preobrazhensky Barracks
Sappers' Barracks
Panteleimonovskaya
Spasskaya
Paradnaya
Preobrazhensky Regiment yard
10
Dept. of Appanages
Baskov St
11
Volynian Barracks
Vilensky Lane
Baskov Lane
Fontannaya
General Staff Academy
Hospital St.
Basseinaya St.
Simeonovskaya
Simeonovsky Bridge
New Times editorial office
Nadezhdinskaya
Znamenskaya
Ligovka
15
16
Liteiny Theater
Liteiny Prospect
Zhukovskaya
18
Grechesky Prospect
Rozhdestvensky district
Suvorovsky Prospect
Rozhdestvensky district
Anichkov Bridge
Nevsky Prospect
Church of the Sign
Palkin restaurant
Trinity St.
Vladimirsky Prospect
Aleksandr III monument
Znamenskaya Square
Nikolaevsky St.
Pushkin St.
Ligovka
Goncharnaya
Staro-Nevsky
Kalashnikov Prospect
Nikolaevsky Train Station
Zagorodny Prospect
Yamskaya St.
Kalashnikovskaya Exchange
Kharkov Street

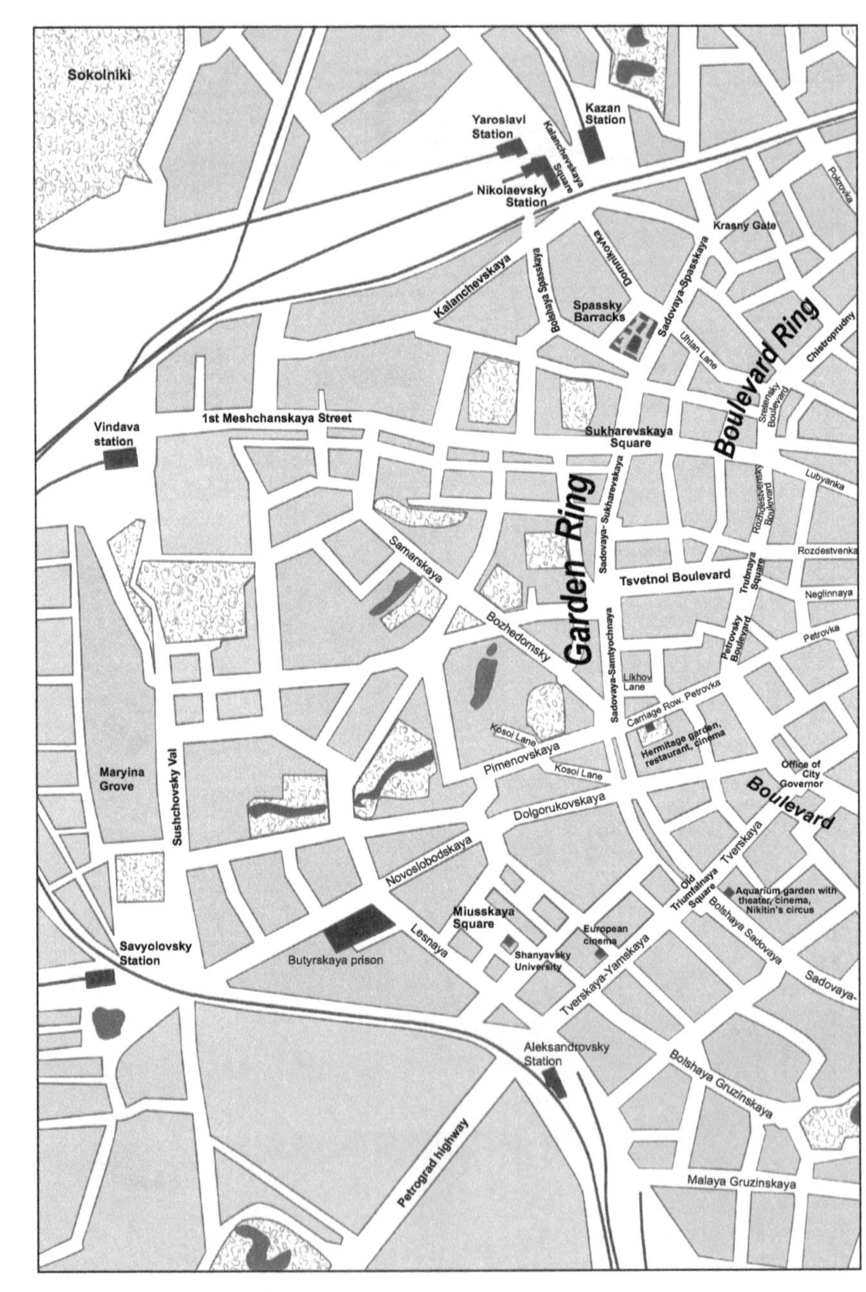

Sokolniki
Yaroslavl Station
Kazan Station
Kalanchevskaya Square
Nikolaevsky Station
Pokrovka
Krasny Gate
Domnikovka
Kalanchevskaya
Bolshaya Spasskaya
Spassky Barracks
Sadovaya-Spasskaya
Uhlan Lane
Boulevard Ring
Chistoprudny
Sretensky Boulevard
Vindava station
1st Meshchanskaya Street
Sukharevskaya Square
Garden Ring
Sadovaya-Sukharevskaya
Rozhdestvensky Boulevard
Lubyanka
Rozdestvenka
Samarskaya
Tsvetnoi Boulevard
Trubnaya Square
Neglinnaya
Bozhedomsky
Sadovaya-Samtyochnaya
Petrovsky Boulevard
Petrovka
Likhov Lane
Carriage Row. Petrovka
Kosoi Lane
Hermitage garden, restaurant, cinema
Pimenovskaya
Kosoi Lane
Office of City Governor
Maryina Grove
Sushchovsky Val
Boulevard
Dolgorukovskaya
Tverskaya
Novoslobodskaya
Old Triumfalnaya Square
Aquarium garden with theater, cinema, Nikitin's circus
Miusskaya Square
Lesnaya
European cinema
Bolshaya Sadovaya
Savyolovsky Station
Butyrskaya prison
Shanyavsky University
Tverskaya-Yamskaya
Sadovaya-
Aleksandrovsky Station
Bolshaya Gruzinskaya
Petrograd highway
Malaya Gruzinskaya

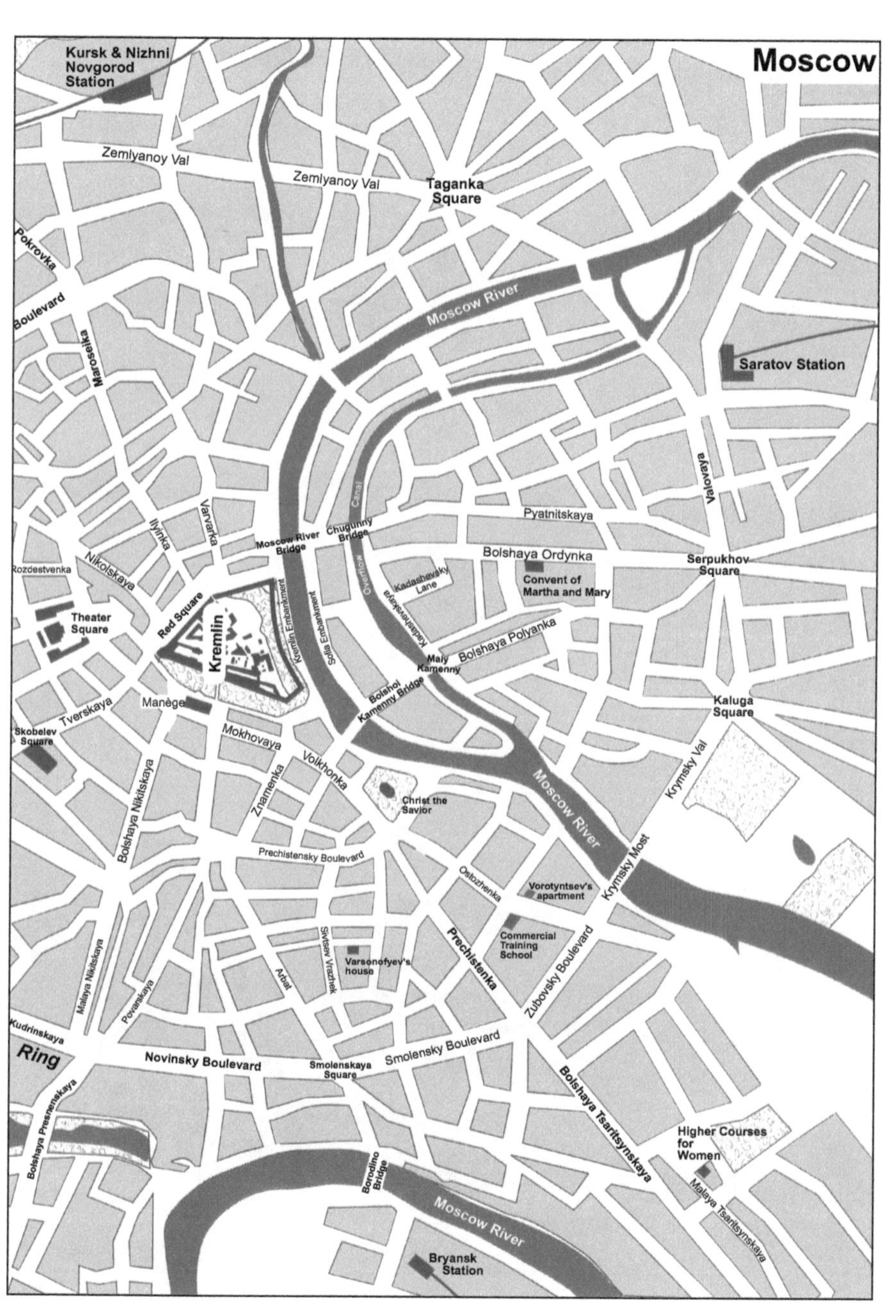
Moscow
Kursk & Nizhni Novgorod Station
Zemlyanoy Val
Zemlyanoy Val
Taganka Square
Pokrovka
Boulevard
Maroseika
Moscow River
Saratov Station
Canal
Overflow
Valovaya
Varvarka
Ilyinka
Nikolskaya
Rozdestvenka
Moscow River Bridge
Chugunny Bridge
Pyatnitskaya
Bolshaya Ordynka
Serpukhov Square
Convent of Martha and Mary
Kadashevsky Lane
Kadashevskaya
Theater Square
Red Square
Kremlin
Kremlin Embankment
Sofia Embankment
Bolshaya Polyanka
Maly Kamenny
Bolshoi Kamenny Bridge
Manège
Tverskaya
Skobelev Square
Mokhovaya
Volkhonka
Kaluga Square
Krymsky Val
Christ the Savior
Moscow River
Znamenka
Bolshaya Nikitskaya
Prechistensky Boulevard
Krymsky Most
Oslozhenka
Vorotyntsev's apartment
Commercial Training School
Sivtsev Vrazhek
Varsonofyev's house
Prechistenka
Zubovsky Boulevard
Arbat
Malaya Nikitskaya
Povarskaya
Kudrinskaya
Ring
Novinsky Boulevard
Smolenskaya Square
Smolensky Boulevard
Bolshaya Tsaritsynskaya
Higher Courses for Women
Malaya Tsaritsynskaya
Bolshaya Presnenskaya
Borodino Bridge
Moscow River
Bryansk Station

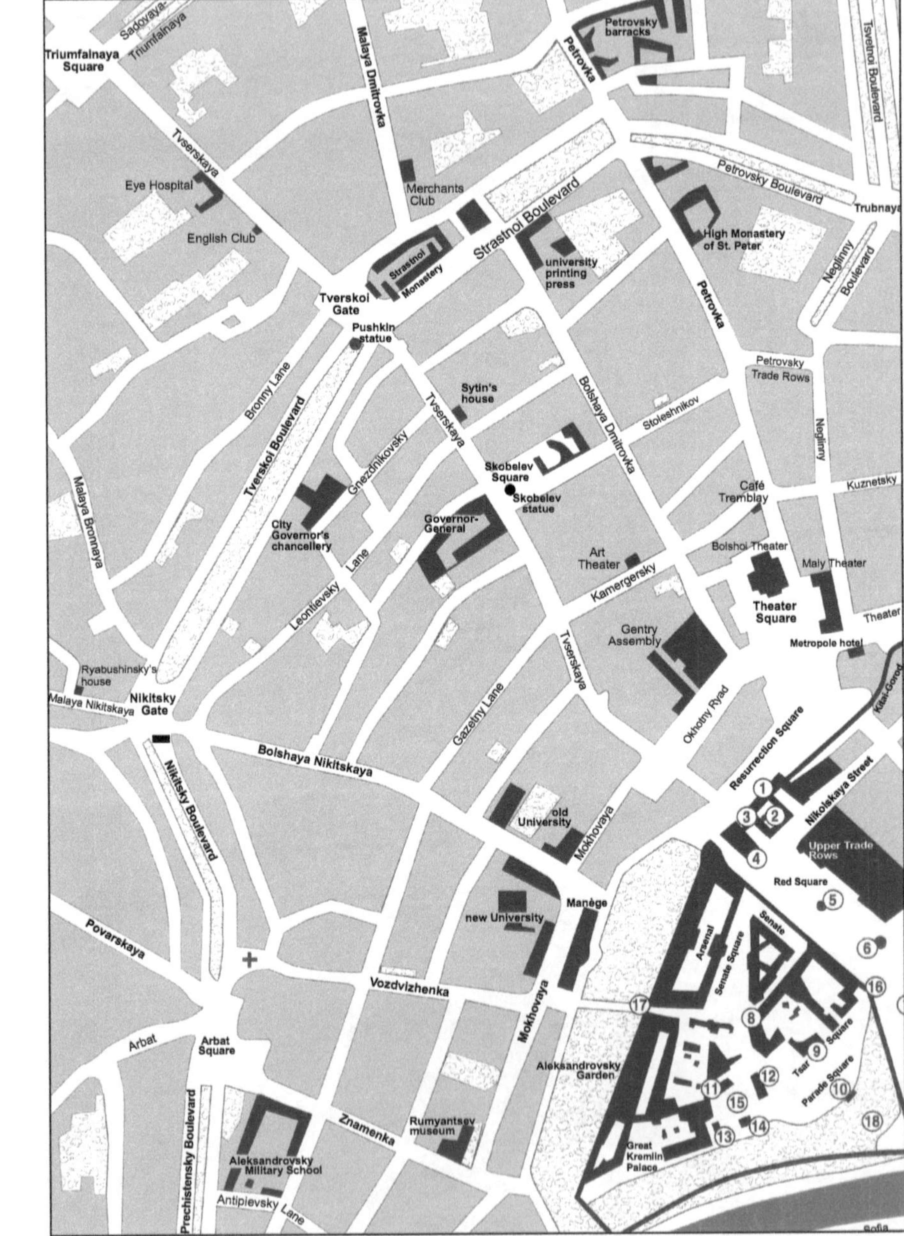
Triumfalnaya Square
Sadovaya-Triumfalnaya
Malaya Dmitrovka
Petrovka
Petrovsky barracks
Tsvetnoi Boulevard
Tverskaya
Eye Hospital
English Club
Merchants Club
Strastnoi Boulevard
Petrovsky Boulevard
Trubnaya
High Monastery of St. Peter
Strastnoi Monastery
university printing press
Neglinny Boulevard
Tverskoi Gate
Pushkin statue
Petrovka
Petrovsky Trade Rows
Bronny Lane
Tverskoi Boulevard
Sytin's house
Tverskaya
Bolshaya Dmitrovka
Stoleshnikov
Neglinny
Malaya Bronnaya
Gnezdnikovsky
Skobelev Square
Skobelev statue
Kuznetsky
Café Tremblay
City Governor's chancellery
Governor-General
Lane
Art Theater
Bolshoi Theater
Maly Theater
Kamergersky
Leontievsky
Theater Square
Theater
Gentry Assembly
Tverskaya
Metropole hotel
Ryabushinsky's house
Nikitsky Gate
Malaya Nikitskaya
Gazetny Lane
Okhotny Ryad
Kitai-Gorod
Resurrection Square
Bolshaya Nikitskaya
Nikitsky Boulevard
Nikolskaya Street
old University
Mokhovaya
Upper Trade Rows
Red Square
Manège
new University
Povarskaya
Senate
Arsenal
Senate Square
Vozdvizhenka
Mokhovaya
Arbat
Arbat Square
Tsar Square
Parade Square
Aleksandrovsky Garden
Prechistensky Boulevard
Znamenka
Rumyantsev museum
Aleksandrovsky Military School
Great Kremlin Palace
Antipievsky Lane
1
2
3
4
5
6
8
9
10
11
12
13
14
15
16
17
18

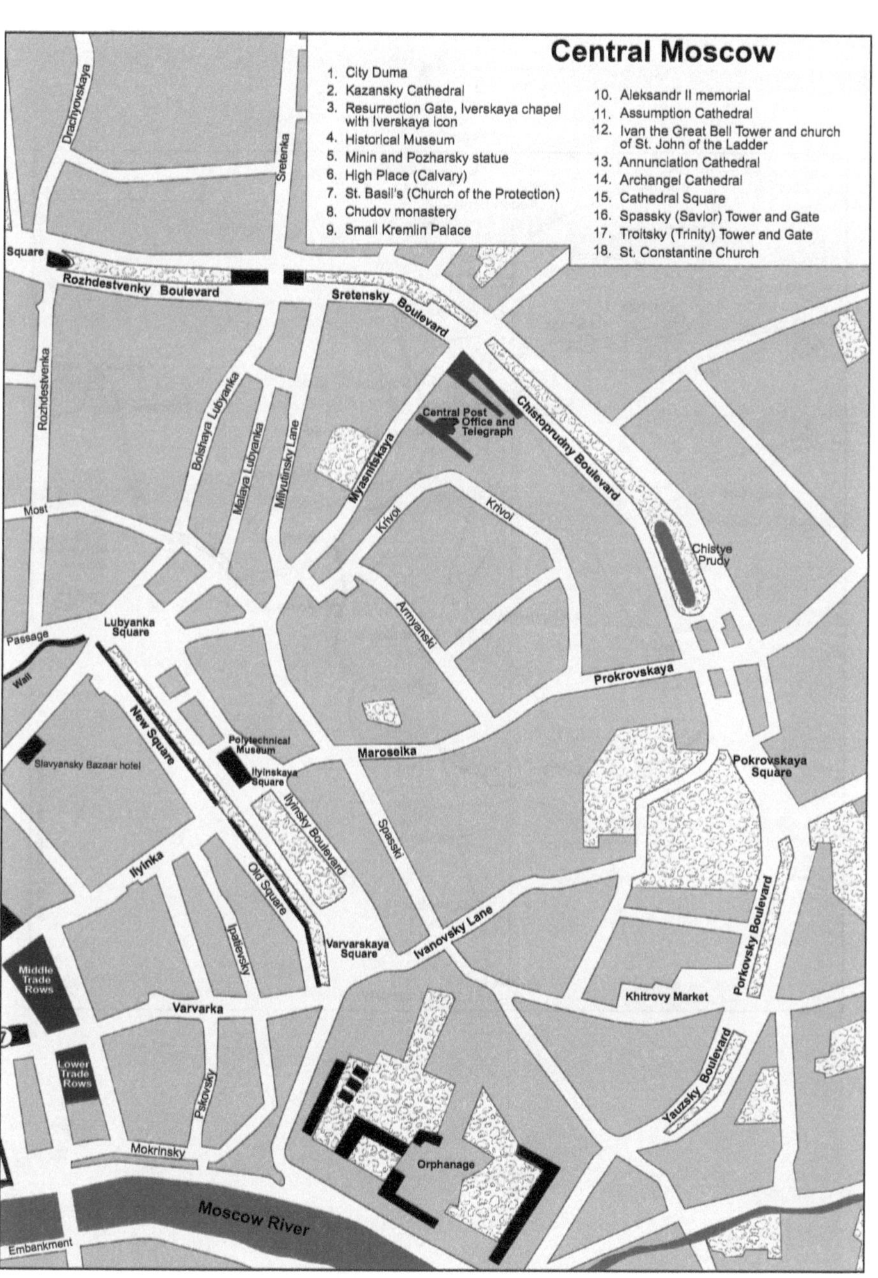
Central Moscow
1. City Duma
2. Kazansky Cathedral
3. Resurrection Gate, Iverskaya chapel with Iverskaya icon
4. Historical Museum
5. Minin and Pozharsky statue
6. High Place (Calvary)
7. St. Basil's (Church of the Protection)
8. Chudov monastery
9. Small Kremlin Palace
10. Aleksandr II memorial
11. Assumption Cathedral
12. Ivan the Great Bell Tower and church of St. John of the Ladder
13. Annunciation Cathedral
14. Archangel Cathedral
15. Cathedral Square
16. Spassky (Savior) Tower and Gate
17. Troitsky (Trinity) Tower and Gate
18. St. Constantine Church
Drachyovskaya
Sretenka
Square
Rozhdestvenky Boulevard
Sretensky Boulevard
Rozhdestvenka
Bolshaya Lubyanka
Malaya Lubyanka
Milyutinsky Lane
Central Post Office and Telegraph
Chistoprudny Boulevard
Myasnitskaya
Krivoi
Krivoi
Chistye Prudy
Most
Armyanski
Lubyanka Square
Passage
Wall
New Square
Prokrovskaya
Polytechnical Museum
Maroseika
Slavyansky Bazaar hotel
Ilyinskaya Square
Ilyinsky Boulevard
Spasski
Pokrovskaya Square
Ilyinka
Old Square
Ipatievsky
Varvarskaya Square
Ivanovsky Lane
Porkovsky Boulevard
Middle Trade Rows
Varvarka
Khitrovy Market
Lower Trade Rows
Pskovsky
Yauzsky Boulevard
Mokrinsky
Orphanage
Moscow River
Embankment

railways
to Vyborg
Beloostrov
Aspen Grove
Sestroretsk
Assumption military cemetery
Pargolovo
Shuvalovo
Ozerki
Udelnaya
Okhta
Kotlin Island
Lisi Nos
Kronstadt
Lakhta
Gulf of Finland
Petrograd
Gunpowder district
Fortress
Lake Ladoga
Schlüsselburg
Oranienbaum
Archangel Michael settlement
Novo-Saratovskaya colony
Peterhof
Strelna
Chesma
Neva
Ust-Izhora
to Vologda, Arkhangelsk, Murmansk
Mga
Kolpino
Krasnoye Selo
Aleksandrovka
Royal Pavilion
Tsarskoye Selo
Pavlovsk
Izhora
Gatchina
Semrino
Tosno
to Reval
Susanino
Vyritsa
to Luga, Pskov, Riga, Dvinsk, Warsaw
to Vitebsk, Mogilev
to Moscow
© ENVOL Cartographie - FAYARD

Index of Names

Adzhemov, Moisei Sergeevich (1878–1953, USA): Deputy in Second, Third, and Fourth Dumas. Prominent member of the Kadet Party.

Aizman, David Yakovlevich (1869–1922): Russian writer whose works often addressed Jewish themes.

Akselrod, Aleksandr Efremovich (1879–1954): Banker and Bolshevik revolutionary; would go on to hold finance and economic posts in the USSR.

Aleksandr II (1818–1881): The "Tsar Liberator," presided over the emancipation of the serfs, the introduction of the zemstvo system of local government, modernization of the judicial system, easing of the burden of military service. Assassinated 13 March 1881 by members of the Narodnaya Volya (People's Will) organization.

Aleksandr III (1845–1894): Became emperor following the assassination of his father, Aleksandr II. Discontinued and in part reversed his father's program of reform. Father of the Franco-Russian Alliance.

Aleksandr Fyodorovich (Fyodorych). *See* Kerensky.

Aleksandr Ivanovich (Ivanych). *See* Guchkov.

Aleksandra Mikhailovna. *See* Kollontai.

Aleksandrovich. *See* Dmitrievsky.

Alekseev, Mikhail Vasilievich (1857–1918): Infantry general, chief of staff, first on the Southwestern, then on the Northwestern Front. From September 1915, chief of General Staff. On sick leave 21 November 1916 to 7 March 1917. Advised the Tsar to abdicate in March 1917. Supreme Commander until 3 June 1917. After the October Revolution organized the first White Army on the Don.

Aleksei (1904–1918): Son and youngest child of Nikolai II and Aleksandra Fyodorovna, hemophiliac. Murdered together with his parents and sisters by the Bolsheviks.

Aleksinsky, Grigory Alekseevich (1879–1967, France): Had been a Bolshevik member of the Second Duma, stayed abroad after its dissolution in 1907 to avoid arrest. By the time he returned to Petrograd in April 1917, he actively opposed the Bolsheviks, resulting in his emigration in 1919.

Amfiteatrov, Aleksandr Valentinovich (1862–1938, Italy): Russian satirist who pilloried the imperial family, welcomed the February, but not the Bolshevik, Revolution, emigrated in 1922.

Andreev, Leonid Nikolaevich (1871–1919, Finland): Famous writer, author of dark and violent plays and novels; in 1916–1917, as editor of *Russian Will,* welcomed the revolution.

Andrei Ivanovich (Ivanych). *See* Shingarev.

Andrusov, Vadim Nikolaevich (1895–1975, Paris): Sculptor, grandson of Heinrich Schliemann. After the Revolution fought on the side of the Whites in the Civil War.

Anna Sergeevna: Refers to **Milyukova** (née Smirnova), **Anna Sergeevna** (1861–1935, France), wife of Pavel Milyukov.

Anya. *See* Timireva.

Armand, Inessa (née Steffen) (1874–1920): Bolshevik. French wife of the industrialist Armand and subsequently of his brother. Close friend and ally of Lenin from 1909. Buried in Red Square.

Asquith, Herbert (1852–1928): British statesman and leader of the Liberal Party; prime minister from 1908 to 1916.

Asya: Diminutive of both Anastasia and Aleksandra. *See* Vyazemskaya.

Avksentiev, Nikolai Dmitrievich (1878–1943, USA): Revolutionary socialist. He returned to Russia in April 1917 to defend the new government; opposed the Bolsheviks, briefly headed a socialist provisional government based in Ufa in 1918, which was deposed by Kolchak, with Avksentiev emigrating.

Axelrod, Pavel Borisovich (1850–1928, Berlin): A co-founder with Plekhanov of the first Russian Marxist party, the Liberation of Labor group, in 1883. Moderate populist, then Menshevik. Staunch supporter of the Provisional Government. Left Russia after the October Revolution.

Azef, Yevno Fishelevich (1869–1918, Germany): Terrorist. Double agent of the Socialist Revolutionary Party and the Okhrana; ousted by Vladimir Burtsev.

Bakunin, Mikhail Aleksandrovich (1814–1876, Switzerland): Principal theoretician and ideologue of anarchism; left Russia in 1840, participated in the revolutions of 1848, escaped from Siberian exile in 1861.

Balabanova, Angelica (1878–1965, Italy): Born in Russia, became active in revolutionary politics in Italy, returned to Russia as a Bolshevik in 1917, left USSR in 1922.

Balfour, Arthur (1848–1930): British political figure, conservative leader, Minister of Foreign Affairs (1916–1919).

Baryshnikov, Aleksandr Aleksandrovich (1877–1924): Architect, engineer, State Duma Deputy. Served under Provisional Government, then emigrated after October revolution.

Bazarov (pseud. of Rudnev), **Vladimir Aleksandrovich** (1874–1939): Social Democrat from 1896, first a Bolshevik but in 1917 a Menshevik Internationalist, like Himmer; perished in the purges.

Bebel, August (1840–1913): One of the outstanding leaders of the German Social Democratic Party.

Beilis (affair): The trial of Menahem Mendel Beilis, accused in 1911 of the ritual murder of a Christian infant; he was acquitted in 1913 after a violently anti-Semitic campaign and a vigorous counterattack by the intelligentsia (Gorky, Korolenko).

Beletsky, Stepan Petrovich (1873–1918): Police official and Vice-minister of the Interior; arrested in March 1917, and later shot by the Bolsheviks.

Bennigsen, Emmanuil Pavlovich, Count (1875–1955, Brazil): State Duma member, Red Cross official, emigrated in 1919; author of historical memoirs.

Benois, Aleksandr Nikolaevich (1870–1960, France): Celebrated Russian painter, graphic designer, and theater decorator, co-founder of the *World of Art* movement and magazine, a leading figure of the Russian Silver Age; left the USSR in 1926.

Bestuzhev-Ryumin, Aleksei Petrovich (1693–1766): Chancellor of the Russian Empire (directed Russian foreign affairs) from 1744 to 1758.

Bestuzhev-Ryumin, Konstantin Nikolaevich (1829–1897): Historian who in 1878 became the first professor and academic chair of a new institution for higher women's education, which came to be known as the Bestuzhev Courses.

Bezobrazov, Vladimir Mikhailovich (1857–1932, France): Cavalry general. Commander of the Guards Army.

Binasik, Myacheslav (Mieczyslaw) **Stepanovich** (Stanislavovich) (1883–1938): Lawyer and Menshevik, member of the Petrograd Soviet and of the All-Russian Executive Committee; arrested twice in the 1930s, executed.

Blanc, Louis (1811–1882): French socialist politician ("Utopian"); participant in the Revolution of 1848 and exiled between 1851 and 1870; author of *The History of Ten Years*.

Blok, Aleksandr Aleksandrovich (1880–1921): The best-known Russian poet of his time; Socialist Revolutionary supporter, secretary of the Extraordinary Commission of Inquiry of the Provisional Government.

Bogdanov, Boris Osipovich (1884–1960): Menshevik, secretary of the Workers' Group, defensist; after the October Revolution spent forty years in and out of prisons, labor camps, internal exile.

Bogdatiev (Badatiev, Bagdatyan), **Sergei Yakovlevich** (Sarkis Gaykovich) (1887–1949): Bolshevik activist, one of the leaders of pro-Lenin street actions in April, June, July 1917.

Bograd-Plekhanova, Rosalia Markovna (1856–1949, France): Revolutionary, wife of Plekhanov, returned with him in 1917 to Russia, then lived abroad, contributed Plekhanov's papers to the Public Library in Leningrad, where she also lived in the 1930s.

Bolotnikov, Ivan Isaevich (1565?–1608): Led an unsuccessful siege of Moscow on behalf of the second False Dmitri during the Time of Troubles, was defeated and executed. Soviet historiography described these events as an uprising of the have-nots.

Bonch-Bruevich, Mikhail Dmitrievich (1870–1956): Military leader who was the first to join the Bolsheviks after their coup, brother of the revolutionary Vladimir Bonch-Bruevich.

Bosch, Evgenia Bogdanovna (1879–1925): Bolshevik. Nicknamed "the Japanese" because of her escape (with Pyatakov) from Siberia via Japan. Fought on the Red side in the Civil War. Accused of "Trotskyism," committed suicide.

Bramson, Leonti Moiseevich (1869–1941, France): Lawyer, representative to the First Duma, Populist Socialist.

Brătianu, Ionel (1864–1927): Romanian politician; served five terms as prime minister, including from 1914 to 1918.

Breshko-Breshkovskaya (née Verigo), **Ekaterina Konstantinovna** (1844–1934, Czechoslovakia): The "grandmother of the Russian Revolution," her first activities dated back to the 1870s; prison or banishment, 1874–1896, then 1907–1917; ardent militant of the Socialist Revolutionary Party. Emigrated in 1919.

Briand, Aristide (1862–1932): Six-time prime minister of France, including 1915–1917; also long-serving Minister of Foreign Affairs.

Brik, Osip Maksimovich (1888–1945): Russian writer, literary theorist, scriptwriter; friend, publisher and collaborator of Mayakovsky.

Broido, Mark Isaevich (1877–1937, England): Menshevik, member of Petrograd Soviet, opposed Bolsheviks in 1917; emigrated in 1919.

Bronsky, Moisei (Mieczyslaw), alias Warszawski (1882–1938): Polish Social Democrat. Later Bolshevik, close collaborator of Lenin before the Bolshevik Revolution, modest career afterward. Executed.

Brusilov, Aleksei Alekseevich (1853–1926): Cavalry general, commander of the 8th Army, then of the Southwestern Front, responsible for the offensive of June–August 1916 ("the Brusilov breakthrough"). Served in the Red Army after the Revolution.

Bublikov, Aleksandr Aleksandrovich (1875–1941, USA): Deputy of the province of Perm, progressivist. Last name refers to a bagel (*bublik*). In March 1917 summarily took control of the railways and telegraph and thus ensured the revolution would spread from Petrograd.

Buchanan, Sir George William (1854–1924): British ambassador in Russia 1910–1918. Close to the leaders of the Kadet Party.

Bukharin, Nikolai Ivanovich (1888–1938): Bolshevik since 1906; Marxist theorist, publicist, member of Politburo. Executed after one of the show trials during the purges.

Bulavin, Kondrati Afanasievich (1667?–1708): Head of a peasant and Don Cossack uprising against the strictures imposed by Peter the Great's Northern War; was killed trying to take the fortress of Azov.

Burtsev, Vladimir Lvovich (1862–1942, France): Socialist Revolutionary, exposer of Tsarist double agents in his review *Byloye* (The Past); opponent of the Bolsheviks; emigrated after the Revolution; specialized in revealing discreditable episodes in the history of Bolshevism.

Cachin, Marcel (1869–1959): French socialist and later Communist; traveled to Russia in 1917; editor of the daily newspaper *Humanité* from 1918 until 1958.

Catherine II (Ekaterina II) **the Great** (1729–1796): Became Empress in 1762 after a palace revolution deposing her husband, Peter III. Led Russia through a golden era of military might but exacerbated Russia's inequality, granting ever more privileges to the nobility and entrenching serfdom of the peasantry.

Cavaignac, Louis-Eugène (1802–1857): French general who put down the workers' uprising of June 1848.

Chaikovsky, Nikolai Vasilievich (1850–1926, England): Important populist; émigré between 1874 and 1906; Socialist Revolutionary Party; arrested and imprisoned (1907–1910), broke with politics and turned his activity toward cooperation.

Director of Zemgor during the war; active opponent of the Bolsheviks after their coup; president of a short-lived White government at Arkhangelsk during the Civil War; emigrated in 1920.

Chaliapin (Shalyapin), **Fyodor Ivanovich** (1873–1938, France): World-famous opera singer (bass); left Soviet Russia in 1922, never to return.

Chernomazov, Miron Efimovich (1882–1917): Member of the Bolshevik Party, editorial secretary of the *Pravda* (1913–1914), in 1917 revealed as an agent of the Okhrana, arrested, found poisoned in prison in August.

Chernov, Victor Mikhailovich (1873–1952, USA): A founder and leader of the Socialist Revolutionary Party, joined the Provisional Government, opposed the Bolshevik coup, emigrated in 1920.

Chernyshevsky, Nikolai Gavrilovich (1828–1889): Philosopher, literary critic, inspirer of populism, educator of several generations of revolutionaries. Arrested in 1862 for having participated in the writing of a revolutionary proclamation, he spent two decades in prison (where he wrote *What Is to Be Done?*), forced labor, or exile.

Chkheidze, Nikolai Semyonovich (1864–1926, France): Menshevik leader, deputy at the Third and Fourth Dumas; in February 1917, president of the Petrograd Soviet. After October, president of the Georgian Constituent Assembly. Emigrated in 1921, committed suicide.

Chkhonia (Gurieli-Chkonia), **Archil** (1895–1955, USA): From a noble Georgian family; left behind his cameo role as jailer in Petrograd during the Revolution and became an active socialite in Paris and New York, married cosmetics queen Helena Rubinstein, was a friend of Salvador Dali.

Clodt von Jürgensburg, Peter (1805–1867): Sculptor and foundryman; creator of the statue of Emperor Nikolai I on St. Isaac's Square, and of the four groups in bronze on the Anichkov Bridge (the "Horse Tamers").

Cui, César Antonovich (1835–1918): Russian composer and specialist in military fortifications.

Dan (Gurvich), **Fyodor Ilyich** (1871–1947, USA): Menshevik; in 1917 was one of the "defencists" among the revolutionary leaders; doctor in the Red Army; opposed Lenin and was banished in 1922.

Danilov, Yuri Nikiforovich (1866–1937, France): "Black" Danilov, to distinguish him from a red-haired namesake. Quartermaster general at Grand Duke Nikolai Nikolaevich's headquarters. Chief of staff of the Northern Army Group.

Denikin, Anton Ivanovich (1872–1947, USA): Military commander, served as a colonel in Russo-Japanese War and as a general in the First World War, commanding the 8th Army Corps on the Romanian front; supported the February Revolution, was appointed army group commander; but was arrested for his support of Kornilov in August 1917; became one of the main leaders of the Whites in the Civil War, commanded the Volunteer Army; emigrated in 1920; wrote memoirs.

Deutsch, Lev (Leo) **Grigorievich** (1855–1941): Russian revolutionary; a populist and then a Social Democrat; organizer of the Chigirin conspiracy; cofounder of the Liberation of Labor group; arrested several times and evaded arrest; upon his return in 1917, he collaborated with Plekhanov's Unity group, arguing against the Bolshevik call for a socialist revolution and civil war; was untouched during the purges.

Disterlo (Düsterloh), **Yuri Romanovich** (1895–1975, France): From a baronial family, son of a lawyer and statesman; graduated law school in 1916, serving under Kutepov saw action against German forces as late as summer 1917; was arrested but avoided execution and joined Whites in Civil War, serving under Kolchak. Emigrated. Wrote memoirs.

Dmitri Pavlovich, Grand Duke (1891–1942, Switzerland): Son of Pavel Aleksandrovich, cousin of Nikolai II. Accomplice of Rasputin murderers.

Dmitrievsky, Pyotr (pseud. of Aleksandrovich, Vyacheslav) **Aleksandrovich** (1884–1918): Left Social Revolutionary, internationalist. Member of the Executive Committee of the Petrograd Soviet, later head of the CheKa (secret police); executed in July 1918 for participation in an anti-Bolshevik coup attempt.

Dobrolyubov, Nikolai Aleksandrovich (1836–1861): Literary critic, poet, one of the forerunners of the revolutionary intelligentsia; died of tuberculosis at age 25.

Dolgorukov, Pavel Dmitrievich (1866–1927): One of the founders of the Kadet Party; émigré after the Revolution but returned in secret to the USSR in 1926; immediately arrested and then shot the next year as a reprisal for the assassination of the Soviet ambassador in Warsaw.

Dragomirov, Abram Mikhailovich (1868–1955, France): Army general, commanded Third and Fifth armies during the First World War; then fought for the Whites in the south of Russia; evacuated in 1920.

Dubrovin, Aleksandr Ivanovich (1855–1921): Doctor, founder, and leader of the far-right organization Union of the Russian People; arrested in March 1917, shot by the Bolsheviks.

Dzhughashvili. *See* Stalin.

Eberhardt, Andrei Avgustovich (1856–1919): Russian admiral; commander of the Black Sea fleet until 1916, when he was replaced by Kolchak; arrested in 1918 but released; died in Petrograd.

Efremov, Ivan Nikolaevich (1866–1933 or later, lived in Switzerland): Deputy of the Don Cossacks in the Third and Fourth Dumas, a leader of the progressivists; held various ministerial portfolios under the Provisional Government.

Elizabeth (Elizaveta; daughter of Peter the Great) (1709–1762): Became Empress in 1741 after a palace revolution. Led Russia in Seven Years' War.

Eltsin, Boris Mikhailovich (1876–1937): Revolutionary, active in 1917–1918 in southern Urals, thereafter in Moscow; part of Trotsky's "Left opposition"; executed in the purges.

Epstein. *See* Yakovlev.

Erlich, Henryk Moiseevich (1882–1942): One of the leaders of the General Jewish Labor Bund. In 1917 a member of the Executive Committee of the Soviet of Workers' Deputies. Lived in Poland, fled to Soviet territory in 1939, where he was sentenced to death for espionage.

von Essen, Nikolai Ottovich (1860–1915): Admiral; distinguished himself in the Russo-Japanese War; commander of the Baltic Fleet from 1911.

Evert, Aleksei Yermolaevich (1857–1918 or 1926?): Infantry general, commanded 46th Army, then Western Front (from 1915). Recalled by the Provisional Government; murdered.

Fedya: Diminutive of Fyodor.

Ferdinand I of Bulgaria (Ferdinand of Saxe-Coburg and Gotha) (1861–1948): Elected prince of Bulgaria in 1887; proclaimed himself Tsar of the Bulgarians (1908); allied with the Central Powers in 1914, abdicated in 1918.

Figner, Vera Nikolaevna (1852–1942): revolutionary; arrested in 1883, she spent twenty years in Schlüsselburg; émigré (1906–1915). After February–March and then October, she spent most of her time on literary work; tried to help victims of political repression.

Filatiev, Dmitri Vladimirovich (1866–1932, France): Professor at the Nikolaevsky Military School, in 1917 joined War Minister Guchkov as an aide; dismissed by Kerensky; during Civil War was part of the White government under Kolchak; emigrated; wrote a book on the causes of the White failure.

Filippovsky, Vasili Nikolaevich (1882–1940): Navy lieutenant, Socialist Revolutionary. Died in a labor camp.

Filosofov, Dmitri Vladimirovich (1872–1940, Poland): Influential literary critic; close to Gippius and Merezhkovsky; emigrated in 1920.

Frederiks, Vladimir Borisovich, Count (1838–1927, Finland): Vice Minister of the Court 1893–1897, Minister from 1897.

Friedman, Napthali Markovich (1863–1921, Germany): Lawyer; deputy of the province of Kovno in the Third and Fourth Dumas.

Fyodorov, Mikhail Nikolaevich (1886–1940): Bolshevik, returned from Siberia after February Revolution, was active in forming Bolshevik militias.

Galliffet, Gaston, marquis (1830–1909): French general notorious for the force with which he suppressed the Commune.

Gegechkori, Evgeni Petrovich (1881–1954, France): Georgian Menshevik; Minister of Foreign Affairs of short-lived Georgian Republic, 1919–1921; emigrated.

Gendelman, Mikhail Yakovlevich (1881–1938): Lawyer; Socialist Revolutionary; principled opponent of Bolsheviks, was arrested and sentenced to death in early 1920s, a sentence that was replaced by exile; he and his whole family were arrested and executed in the purges.

Georgi Evgenievich. *See* Lvov, Georgi Evgenievich, Prince.

Georgi Valentinovich: Plekhanov.

Gershuni, Grigori Andreevich (1870–1908): One of the organizers and leaders of the Socialist Revolutionary Party; organized assassination of several high officials in 1902–1903; sent to prison, escaped, emigrated.

Gessen (Hessen), **Iosif Vladimirovich** (1865–1943, USA): Lawyer, member of the Second Duma, advocate for Jewish rights. In the 1920s and 1930s, in France, published 22-volume *Archive of the Russian Revolution*.

Glazunov, Aleksandr Konstantinovich (1865–1936, France): Russian composer, taught Shostakovich, director of St. Petersburg Conservatory from 1905, stayed in that post until 1928, when he did not return from a trip to Vienna; settled in Paris; reburied in 1972 in Leningrad.

Glinka, Mikhail (1804–1857): First national composer of Russia, particularly famous for his operas *Life for the Tsar, Ruslan and Lyudmila*.

Gnedich, Pyotr Petrovich (1855–1925): Writer, literary and theater critic, art historian, memoirist; died in Leningrad.

Godnev, Ivan Vasilievich (1854–1919): Octobrist deputy of Kazan Province; during 1917 comptroller general of the Provisional Government.

Goldenberg, Iosif Petrovich (pseud. **Meshkovsky**) (1873–1922): Revolutionary, contributor to Trotsky's *Pravda* in Vienna, Menshevik, defensist, later joined Bolsheviks, died of a heart attack.

Goloshchokin, Philipp Isaevich (pseud. of Shaya Itsikovich) (1876–1941): Bolshevik revolutionary; organized execution of Nikolai II and his family in 1918 on the instructions of Lenin and Sverdlov; organized confiscation of farms and collectivization in Kazakhstan in the early 1930s, leading to mass famine; arrested in 1940 and executed.

Gorbatovsky, Vladimir Nikolaevich (1851–1924, Estonia): Infantry general, commanded 10th Army on the Northern Front. After revolution fought for the Whites, emigrated.

Gorchakov, Aleksandr Mikhailovich (1798–1883): Scion of a princely family, classmate of Pushkin, skilled Minister of Foreign Affairs (1856–1882).

Gorky, Maksim (pen name of Aleksei Maksimovich Peshkov) (1868–1936): Major Russian writer. Supported the Bolsheviks financially and as a publicist. Disapproved of Bolshevik coup, but cooperated with the regime from 1919. Emigrated to Italy 1921, returned to the USSR in 1928, and became an apologist for Stalinism and the head of the Writers' Union established in 1932. Died mysteriously.

Gotz, Abram Rafailovich (1882–1940): One of the leaders of the Social Revolutionaries Party; returned from Siberian exile in March 1917; became an opponent of the regime after the Bolshevik coup, arrested in 1920 and condemned to death in 1922 (commuted to five years of detention); amnestied; re-condemned in 1939; died in the camp.

Gotz, Mikhail Rafailovich (1866–1906): Active in People's Will revolutionary group in the 1880s, became one of the main Socialist Revolutionary leaders, ideologue as well as financial organizer of the SR Combat Organization, which led a terror campaign assassinating high state officials. Older brother of Abram Gotz.

Grandmother. *See* Breshko-Breshkovskaya.

Gredescul, Nikolai Andreevich (1864–1941): Lawyer, journalist, broke with the Kadets in 1916 in a rightward shift; then shifted leftward and served the Bolshevik regime.

Grey, Edward, Sir (1862–1933): British politician, Minister of Foreign Affairs in 1905–1916.

Grigorovich, Ivan Konstantinovich (1853–1930, France): Admiral. Battleship commander at Port Arthur in the Russo-Japanese War. Minister of the Navy 1911–1917. Emigrated in 1923.

Grimm, David Davidovich (1864–1941, Latvia): Liberal lawyer, professor at the University of Saint Petersburg, specialist in Roman law, member of the State Council; Kadet; arrested and then released by the Bolsheviks in 1919; emigrated.

Grimm, Konstantin Davidovich (1896–1919): Son of Prof. David Grimm, fought for the Whites in the Civil War, died in combat near Poltava.

Grimm, Robert (1881–1958): Swiss Social Democrat leader. Presided over the international Zimmerwald and Kienthal conferences (1915 and 1916).

Grinevich (pseud. of Shekhter), **Konstantin Sergeevich** (1879–?): Social Democrat, member of the Soviet of Workers' Deputies.

Groman (Grohman), **Vladimir Gustavovich** (1874–1940): Russian Social Democrat, Menshevik, and economist. Sentenced in 1931 for an alleged Menshevik conspiracy, died in a labor camp.

Grushevsky (Hrushevsky), **Mikhail Sergeevich** (1866–1934): National historian of Ukraine, the independence of which he declared in 1918. Emigrated, then returned to the Soviet Union.

Gruzenberg, Oskar Osipovich (1866–1940, France): Famous lawyer for political and Jewish causes.

Gruzinov, Aleksandr Evgrafovich (1873–1918): Moscow nobleman, military officer, pilot. Embraced the revolution in Moscow, assumed control of the Moscow Military District; soon fell out with the Soviets, joined the Whites, died in the Civil War.

Guchkov, Aleksandr Ivanovich (1862–1936, France): Founder of the Octobrist Party. President of the Third Duma, March 1910–March 1911. Chairman of the All-Russian War Industry Committees. Minister of War in the first Provisional Government, February–May 1917. Emigrated in 1918.

Guesde (Bazile), **Jule** (1845–1922): French socialist; one of the organizers and directors of the Second International; turned to wartime patriotism, serving in a unity government after 1914.

Gurevich (Ber), Boris Naumovich (1889–1937?): Menshevik, would be repeatedly arrested during the 1920s and 1930s; died in prison.

Gurko, Vasili Iosifovich (1864–1937, Italy): General. Participant in the Anglo-Boer and Russo-Japanese wars. After two years of fighting in the First World War, served as chief of staff during Alekseev's illness (November 1916–March 1917), returned to command Western Army Group March–May 1917. Dismissed and exiled by the Provisional Government.

Gvozdev, Kozma Antonovich (1883–1956): Worker, Menshevik leader, defensist, president of the central Workers' Group. Member of the Central Committee of Petrograd Soviet, then Minister of Labor under the Fourth Provisional Government. Imprisoned from 1930 on.

Habsburg: Reigning dynasty in Austria (emperor) and Hungary (apostolic king).

Hamsun, Knut (1859–1952): Celebrated Norwegian writer; Nobel Prize winner in 1920.

Hanecki, Yakov Stanislavovich (Jakub Fürstenberg, pseud. Kuba) (1879–1937): Russian-Polish socialist; collaborator of Lenin and party financier; after October held financial and commercial functions. Victim of the purges.

Herzen, Aleksandr Ivanovich (1812–1870): Writer, philosopher, and Russian publicist, first revolutionary to have lived half his life abroad, editor of the journal *The Bell*; emblematic figure of the intelligentsia.

Herzenstein (Gertsenshtein), **Mikhail Yakovlevich** (1859–1906): Economist. Kadet deputy in First Duma. Professor at Moscow Institute of Agronomics; assassinated in Finland by Black Hundreds.

Himmer (Sukhanov), **Nikolai Nikolaevich** (1882–1940): Menshevik theorist, Zimmerwaldist, and important memorialist; shot after many years in prison and exile.

Hindenburg, Paul von (1842–1934): German field marshal, victor in East Prussia (see *August 1914*); in 1917 was head of the German Supreme Command.

Hohenzollern: Prussian royal and German imperial dynasty from 1701 until 1918.

Hopner, Serafima (Sima) **Ilyinichna** (1880–1966): Bolshevik revolutionary, during Civil War fought to establish Soviet power in Ukraine; represented Ukrainian communists in the Comintern; became a historian of the Communist Party.

Ilovaisky, Dimitri Ivanovich (1832–1920): Publicist and historian, the author of numerous classroom textbooks.

Inessa. *See* Armand.

Iosif Vladimirovich. *See* Gessen.

Irakli. *See* Tsereteli.

Ivanov, Nikolai Iudovich (1851–1919): Artillery general. Commanded Southwestern Army Group August 1914–March 1916. Charged by Nikolai II in March 1917 to reestablish order in Petrograd but did not even reach the city. Died of typhus during the Civil War.

Kaiser. *See* Wilhelm.

Kalinin, Mikhail Ivanovich (1875–1946): Worker from a peasant family; formally the head of state (Russian, then Soviet) from 1919 to his death.

Kamenev (Rosenfeld), **Lev Borisovich** (1883–1936): Bolshevik from 1903, one of the top leaders after the October Revolution, negotiator of Brest-Litovsk treaty. Allied, then opposed, to Stalin, sentenced to death and executed in 1936.

Kantorovich, Vladimir Abramovich (1886–1923): Prominent journalist and historian, published the *Jewish News*, chronicler of February Revolution, and subsequently the pogroms in Ukraine during the Civil War.

Karabchevsky, Nikolai Platonovich (1851–1925, Italy): Lawyer; president of the St. Petersburg bar association; known for his fiery speeches on behalf of revolutionaries and other defendants.

Karl I (Charles I) (1887–1922): Emperor of Austria and king of Hungary; he succeeded his great uncle Franz Joseph in 1916 but abdicated in 1918, ending the Habsburg monarchy. Beatified by the Catholic Church in 2004 for his peacemaking efforts during his reign.

Karpinsky, Vyacheslav Alekseevich (1880–1965): Social Democrat and then Bolshevik; emigrated to Geneva where he lived until 1917; held minor posts after the Revolution.

Keller, Fyodor Arturovich (1857–1918): Lieutenant general; commander of the Third Cavalry Guard Corps; resigned after the abdication; killed by the Bolsheviks.

Kerenskaya (*née* Baranovskaya), **Olga Lvovna** (1886–1975, England): From 1906 to 1917, wife of Aleksandr Kerensky. Arrested in 1918, left Soviet Russia under a fake Estonian passport, lived and worked in England.

Kerensky, Aleksandr Fyodorovich (1881–1970, USA): Lawyer. Social Democrat, then leader of Labor group (Trudoviks). In Fourth Duma. In 1917, successively Minister of Justice, Minister of War, and Prime Minister in the Provisional Government. Emigrated in 1918.

Khabalov, Sergei Semyonovich (1858–1924, Greece): Incapable and overwhelmed commander of the Petrograd Military District.

Kharitonov, Moisei Markovich (1887–1948): Social Democrat, close to Lenin, returned with Lenin; headed Petrograd militia and held provincial posts; arrested and died in labor camp.

Khinchuk, Lev Mikhailovich (1868–1939): Socialist militant since 1890, in 1917 a centrist Menshevik; later held posts in trade and commerce in the USSR. Executed in the purges.

Khrushchov, Aleksandr Girorievich (1872–1932): Kadet, member of First Duma, signatory of Vyborg appeal; in March–July 1917 served as Shingarev's deputy both in Agriculture and Finance ministries, staying on to run the Finance portfolio until the Bolshevik coup; was arrested but later freed and worked in the 1920s for the State Bank.

Kiesewetter, Aleksandr Aleksandrovich (1866–1933, Czechoslovakia): Historian; one of the founders of the Kadet Party; anti-Bolshevik; exiled in 1922.

Kirpichnikov, Timofei Ivanovich (1892–1917/1918): After leading an insurrection in the Volynian regiment was hailed as the "first soldier" of the Revolution and promoted to officer; but after October, when he joined the White forces against the Bolsheviks, was shot on the order of Aleksandr Kutepov.

Kislyakov, Vladimir Nikolaevich (1875–1919): General, in charge of military railroad logistics; his inaction helped ensure the spread of revolution; later, supported the Kornilov insurrection, joined the White forces, was shot by the Bolsheviks at Poltava.

Klembovsky, Vladislav Napoleonovich (Vladimir Nikolaevich) (1860–1921): Infantry general; turned down Supreme Commander appointment in 1917, supporting Lavr Kornilov against Kerensky; was held hostage by Bolsheviks, then joined Red Army as a historian; arrested as scapegoat for Red Army's defeat in Poland; starved in prison.

Koba: One of Stalin's *noms de guerre*.

Kokoshkin, Fyodor Fyodorovich (the younger) (1871–1918): Jurist, one of the founders of the Kadet Party, member of the First Duma, signer of the Vyborg Appeal; Minister of State Control in 1917; arrested, murdered together with Shingarev at the Mariinsky Hospital.

Kokovtsov, Vladimir Nikolaevich, Count (1853–1943, France): Minister of Finance (1904–1905, 1906–1914), prime minister (1911–February 1914), banker; jailed in 1918, then escaped Soviet Russia; a notable émigré figure, left behind important memoirs.

Kolchak (née Omirova), **Sofia Fyodorovna** (1876–1956, France): Wife of Aleksandr Kolchak, from whom she was separated in 1917. Emigrated in 1919.

Kolchak, Aleksandr Vasilievich (1873–1920): Polar explorer, vice admiral and commander of the Black Sea Fleet, which he was able to keep in order throughout the spring of 1917. Exiled by Kerensky, Kolchak returned via the Pacific during the Civil War and from 1918 to 1920 led the White armies in Siberia, was recognized by all White forces as the supreme ruler of Russia. His advance against the Red Army was stopped at the Volga, his armies were pushed back, and he was captured by the Bolsheviks and executed at Irkutsk on 7 February 1920.

Kollontai, Aleksandra Mikhailovna (1872–1952): Menshevik; companion of Shlyapnikov. Theorist of "free love." Novelist. In 1917, member of Bolshevik Central Committee. In 1920–1921, with Shlyapnikov, one of the leaders of the "Workers' Opposition." From 1923 to 1945 a Soviet diplomat.

Kolya: Diminutive of Nikolai.

Kon, Feliks Yakovlevich (1864–1941): Polish socialist, Bolshevik, in Switzerland (1914) and then Russia from 1917; worked in the Comintern; prolific writer (history of the revolutionary movement), wrote memoires.

Konovalov, Aleksandr Ivanovich (1875–1949, France): Industrialist; deputy in the Fourth Duma. Leader of the Progressive Bloc. Vice chairman of the War Industry Committees. During 1917 held commerce and industry portfolio in the Provisional Government.

Kontorovich, Nikolai Lazarevich (Natan Leizerovich) (1877–1921): Social Democrat, participant in 1905 revolution, imprisoned; freed in March 1917 and became head of Sevastopol Soviet.

Kornilov, Lavr Georgievich (1870–1918): Infantry general in March 1917, then appointed Commander of the Petrograd Military District; in July became Supreme Commander. His attempt to forestall the Bolshevik coup was frustrated by Kerensky. Kornilov was arrested but succeeded in escaping to the south, organized the White armies after the death of Alekseev. Killed in battle in the Civil War.

Korolenko, Vladimir Galaktionovich (1853–1921): Journalist, short-story writer, humanitarian activist, publisher; opposed Tsarist strictures and then Bolshevik repression.

Korovichenko, Pavel Aleksandrovich (1874–1917): Military lawyer, trusted deputy of Kerensky, who appointed him to oversee the arrested royal family; was then given military posts and assigned to quell a September uprising in Tashkent, where he was killed.

Kossior, Stanislav Vikentievich (1889–1939): Leader of the Ukrainian communist party, Politburo member, one of the officials implementing collectivization and mass famine in Ukraine; arrested and executed in the purges.

Kotovsky, Grigori Ivanovich (1881–1925): Revolutionary and gang leader; became a Soviet politician, but was killed by his close associate. Mythologized by the Soviets.

Koussevitzky, Serge (Sergei Aleksandrovich) (1874–1951, USA): Composer, conductor, and double bass player; organized an orchestra in Moscow (1908); emigrated in 1920 to France; led the Boston Symphony Orchestra from 1924 to 1949.

Kozma Prutkov: Satirical writer invented by the celebrated poet Aleksei K. Tolstoy (1817–1875) and the three Yemchunikov bothers, who published their "works" (poems, comedies, aphorisms) between 1851 and 1864. The aphorism that is paraphrased is number 18: "Tell me this: were it not for tailors, how would you spot the civil servants?"

Krasikov, Pyotr Ananievich (1870–1939): Old friend of Lenin, Bolshevik, lawyer, member of the Executive Committee of the Soviet in March 1917. After October, played major role in Soviet legal system.

Krasin, Leonid Borisovich (1870–1926): Engineer-electrician, Bolshevik, expert in conspiratorial techniques, the making of explosives, armed attacks; after October, was a commissar for Foreign Trade, then Roads and Railways; as a diplomat, participated in the Brest-Litovsk negotiations and was later ambassador to the UK and to France.

Krasnov, Pyotr Nikolaevich (1869–1947): Cossack general, led an unsuccessful counterattack against the Bolshevik coup in November 1917; fought for Whites in Civil War; emigrated in 1920. A prolific and talented writer (historical novels, memoirs), he was an ardent anti-Bolshevik, joining Second World War on the side of Nazi Germany. He was handed over to the USSR in 1945 by the English and Americans and executed.

Krotovsky (pseud. Yurenev), **Konstantin Konstantinovich** (1888–1938): Socialist, leader of the Interdistrict group from 1913, joined Bolsheviks in 1917, became a Red Army commissar in the Civil War, then a Soviet diplomat. Executed during the purges.

Krylenko, Nikolai Vasilievich (1885–1938): As a Bolshevik law student, participated in 1905 revolution; continued underground revolutionary activity; unsuccessfully tried to dodge military service, but when at the front was an effective propagandist against the war; one of the plotters of October coup and war commissar; as Justice commissar he was a leading prosecutor at the political trials of the late 1920s and early 1930s; was himself arrested in the purges and executed.

Krymov, Aleksandr Mikhailovich (1871–1917): General. Corps commander, associate of Guchkov and the Octobrists. Committed suicide in September 1917 after the failure of General Lavr Kornilov's attempt to forestall the Bolshevik coup.

Kshesinskaya, Matilda Feliksovna (Mathilde Kszesinska, 1872–1971, France): Ballerina of Polish origin. Girlfriend of Tsarevich Nikolai Aleksandrovich before his marriage and ascent to the throne as Nikolai II; then of Grand Duke Sergei Mikhailovich; then wife of Grand Duke Andrei Vladimirovich. Her private mansion in Petrograd, of refined and modern architecture, was requisitioned by the Bolsheviks, who made it their first headquarters.

Kurlov, Pavel Grigorievich (1860–1923, Germany): Director of the Police Department; in 1911 headed the Okhrana; the Stolypin assassination occurred on his watch. Arrested and released after the Revolution, emigrated.

Lasalle, Ferdinand (1825–1864): German social reformer, one of the early proponents of Social Democracy, but without the rigid class theory of Karl Marx.

Lavrov, Pyotr Lavrovich (1823–1900, France): Artillery officer; simultaneously managed philosophical, literary (author of the lyrics of the *Worker's Marseillaise*), and revolutionary careers (links to "Land and Freedom"). Arrested in 1866, wrote his *Historical Letters* in exile. Fled from Russia in 1870, never to return.

Lazarev, Yegor Yegorovich (1855–1937, Czechoslovakia): Member of People's Will, then Socialist Revolutionary. Escaped from exile in 1890 and lived in USA and a number of European countries, was in Russia for the 1905 Revolution. Rejected

Dmitri Bogrov's request to use the SR party's name for the planned assassination of Stolypin. Lazarev was deported in 1910, returned in 1917, opposed the Bolshevik coup, emigrated.

Lechitsky, Platon Alekseevich (1856–1921): Priest's son; enlisted in 1877; climbed the ranks by merit alone; infantry general in 1913; commander of the Fourth Army from the war's start; freed from his command for reasons of health in 1917; arrested and died in prison.

Lenin (Ulyanov), **Vladimir Ilyich** (1870–1924): Bolshevik revolutionary and Marxist theorist; was caught by surprise by the February Revolution but took advantage of it, famously making his way to Russia in a sealed train to Finland Station; led multiple efforts to overthrow the Provisional Government and ultimately succeeded; announced the Red Terror, War Communism, backtracked by creating the New Economic Policy; was the founder of the USSR.

Lermontov, Mikhail (1814–1841): Celebrated romantic poet; the action in his poem *The Demon* takes place in the Caucasus.

Lesch, Leonid Vilgelmovich (Pavlovich) (1862–1934, Yugoslavia): General, commander of the Third Army, played a major role in what became known as the Brusilov offensive. After the revolution, joined the White forces, evacuated via Odessa.

Lev Borisovich (Borisych): Kamenev.

Lidia. *See* **Vasilchikova** (née Vyazemskaya).

Lieber (Goldman), **Mikhail Isakovich** (1860–1937): Social Democrat, one of the leaders of the Bund from its foundation; returned to Russia in March 1917, joined the Soviet and its Executive Committee as a Menshevik; opposed the Bolshevik coup; was repeatedly arrested throughout the Soviet period, spent time in prison and camps; executed.

Liebknecht, Karl (1871–1919): German Social Democrat. Leader with Rosa Luxemburg of the left-wing, antiwar Spartacist faction; assassinated after a failed attempt at revolution.

Linde (popular nickname: "Lindya"), **Fyodor Fyodorovich** (1881–1917): Aspirant of the Finland battalion, Menshevik, commissioner of the Provisional Government at the Southwestern Front, killed by soldiers whom he urged to go into combat.

Lloyd George, David (1853–1945): British politician; prime minister, 1916–1922.

Lomonosov, Yuri Vladimirovich (1876–1952, Canada): Russian railway engineer; cooperated with the Bolsheviks during the Civil War and early Soviet period, designed the first Soviet diesel locomotive; decided in 1927 not to return to the USSR, became a British citizen.

Lordkipanidze, Ivan Nestorovich (1889–1937): Member of SR party, finished medical school and served as medic in World War; headed Odessa city duma in 1917; then served in the government of Georgia during its independence (until 1921); executed in the purges.

Lossky, Nikolai Onufrievich (1870–1965, France): Religious philosopher, entered the Kadet Party after 1905; was dismissed after 1917 for his religious beliefs; exiled in 1922, lived and taught in Czechoslovakia, France, and USA.

Ludendorff, Erich (1865–1937): German general, Hindenburg's chief of staff and then first quarter-master general of the German army; conceived the military operations of 1918 on the French front.

Lukomsky, Aleksandr Sergeevich (1868–1939, France): General; participant in the First World War and the Civil War; was one of the organizers of the White Volunteer Army; continued to serve until 1920, and thereafter in emigration was a leading military figure and memoirist.

Lunacharsky, Anatoli Vasilievich (1875–1933): Journalist and writer, variously with the Bolshevik and Interdistrict factions, returned to Russia by way of Germany (like Lenin, but after him); indefatigable Red propagandist during the Civil War, commissar for education until 1929.

Lurie, Mikhail Aleksandrovich (pseud. of Yuri Larin) (1882–1932): Social Democrat who joined Bolsheviks in 1917; widely published after October coup.

Lvov, Georgi Evgenievich, Prince (1861–1925, France): Kadet politician. Chairman of the All-Russian Union of Zemstvos (1914–1917). After February Revolution, Prime Minister until replaced by Kerensky in July.

Lvov, Vladimir Nikolaevich (1872–1930): Deputy in the Third and Fourth Dumas; Octobrist. Served as Procurator of the Synod in 1917, played a role in provoking the Kornilov Affair; after the Civil War returned to the USSR, led the Communist "living church," and became an anti-religious activist. Arrested; died in prison.

von Mackensen, August (1849–1945): German marshal; major victories on the eastern fronts, in particular the Russian in 1915 and the Romanian in 1916.

Makari (Macarius, civilian name Mikhail Nevsky) (1835–1926): Bishop of Tomsk, from 1912 metropolitan of Moscow and member of the Synod. Canonized in 2000.

Makarov, Aleksandr Aleksandrovich (1857–1919): Interior and later Justice Minister; executed by the Bolsheviks.

Makarov, Stepan Osipovich (1848–1904): Commander of the Pacific Fleet at the beginning of the Russo-Japanese War; died when his ship hit a mine.

Maklakov, Vasili Alekseevich (1879–1957, Switzerland): Lawyer, leading member of the Kadet Party, brother of Nikolai Maklakov. Ambassador of the Provisional Government to France in 1917.

Maksimov, Andrei (1866–1951): Vice admiral (1914); different commands in the Baltic Fleet; elected commander of this fleet (March 16–June 15, 1917). Vice minister of the oceans (December 1, 1917); passed into the service of the Soviet government; retired 1927.

Malinovsky, Roman (1876–1918): Bolshevik who turned out to be a double agent, worked for the police from 1900; protégé of Lenin; resigned from the Duma in 1914 and fled Russia; returned (lured back) in 1918 and stood trial, in Lenin's presence, following which he was summarily executed.

Mandelberg, Viktor Evseevich (1869–1944, Mandatory Palestine): Doctor with revolutionary sympathies, member of Second Duma, went abroad after its dissolution in 1907; returned in 1917, emigrated to Palestine in 1920.

Mandelstam, Mikhail Lvovich (1866–1939): Lawyer on the left wing of the Kadet Party, sparred with Milyukov; famous for politicized defense of terrorists at trial;

emigrated after October to Paris; returned to the USSR in 1927, where for some time he practiced law; arrested during purges, died in prison.

Manuilov, Aleksandr Apollonovich (1861–1929): Economist, professor, rector of Moscow University; entered politics as a member of the Kadet Party, was briefly Minister of Education under the Provisional Government. Under Bolshevik rule, participated in language reform and was an administrator of the State Bank.

Manukhin, Ivan Ivanovich (1882–1958, France): Doctor noted for his innovative methods in treating tuberculosis and pneumonia, friend of Gorky; investigated Tsarist officials after the revolution, left Soviet Russia in 1921.

Maria Pavlovna the elder ("Aunt Miechen") (née Marie Alexandrine Elisabeth Eleonore von Mecklenburg-Schwerin) (1854–1920, France): Wife of Grand Duke Vladimir Aleksandrovich, held high influence at court.

Marks, Nikandr Aleksandrovich (1861–1921): Archeologist, military officer, headed the Odessa Military District; would in 1919 be convicted by a White tribunal of serving the Reds, but was spared punishment; served as first rector of Kuban State University in 1920.

Marshall, Louis (1856–1929): American lawyer and defender of civil rights; conservationist; and a founder of the American Jewish Committee.

Martov, Yuli (pseud. of Julius Zederbaum) (1873–1923, Germany): Principal leader of Menshevism; during the war, internationalist (Zimmerwald), but also refused the transformation of foreign war into civil war; returned to Russia in May 1917, but then opposed the Bolsheviks and emigrated in 1920.

Masha: Diminutive of Maria.

Mentsikovsky, Albert Leontievich (1871–1919): Practicing doctor since 1895, and a Socialist Revolutionary; adopted defencism in 1917; died of pneumonia.

Mikhail Aleksandrovich, Grand Duke ("Misha") (1878–1918): Younger brother of Nikolai II, refused the crown in March 1917 after Nikolai's abdication. Murdered by the Bolsheviks.

Mikhail Vasilievich (Vasilich). *See* Alekseev.

Mikhail Vladimirovich. *See* Rodzyanko.

Mikhailov, Aleksandr Dmitrievich (1855–1884): Revolutionary (Land and Freedom and then People's Will); participated in attacks against Aleksandr II; died in prison.

Mikhailovsky, Nikolai Konstantinovich (1842–1904): Sociologist, publicist, the most influential literary critic of the last quarter of the nineteenth century, proclaimed a liberal populism.

Miller, Evgeni Karlovich (1867–1939): Lieutenant general in 1915, one of the leaders of the White movement. Emigrated in 1920; kidnapped in 1937 in Paris by Soviet agents, transported to Moscow, executed.

Millerand, Aleksandr (1859–1943): French politician, socialist who joined wartime "bourgeois" government; stigmatized by the Bolsheviks as a revisionist and opportunist.

Milyukov, Pavel Nikolaevich (1859–1943, France): Politician and historian, professor at the University of Moscow, dismissed in 1895; emigrated (1895–1905); main founder of the Kadet Party (1905) and its recognized leader; editor-in-chief of *Rech*

("Speech"); leader of the Progressive Bloc and its spokesman in the Duma; Minister of Foreign Affairs in the first Provisional Government; emigrated in 1920.

Misha: Diminutive of Mikhail.

Mitya: Diminutive of Dmitri. *See* Vyazemsky, Dmitri Leonidovich.

Molotov (real name Skryabin), **Vyacheslav Mikhailovich** (1890–1986): Bolshevik since 1906; for a long time Stalin's right-hand man; untouched in all the purges. Foreign minister before and during World War II.

Morgenthau, Henry, Sr. (1856–1946): Leading Jewish American figure; real estate developer, lawyer; as ambassador to the Ottoman Empire, he brought attention to the plight of Armenians and other minorities.

Muranov, Matvei Konstantinovich (1873–1959): Bolshevik railway worker, deputy at the Fourth Duma, arrested in 1914 and banished to Siberia with Kamenev and Stalin; thereafter a middling official.

Muravyov, Nikolai Konstantinovich (1870–1936): A prestigious lawyer involved in all the great political processes before 1917; in March 1917, president of the Extraordinary Commission of Inquiry. After October, worked again as a lawyer in the processes started by the Bolsheviks against their opponents; resigned from the Moscow bar in 1930; died of natural causes.

Muromtsev, Sergei Andreevich (1850–1910): Professor of law at Moscow University. One of the founders of the Kadet Party. President of the First Duma, signatory of the Vyborg Appeal in 1907.

Myasoedov, Sergei Nikolaevich (1865–1915): Military intelligence officer, accused by Guchkov of espionage in favor of Germany, convicted (by most accounts, wrongly) and hanged. The "Myasoedov Affair" is described in *November 1916*.

Nabokov, Vladimir Dmitrievich (1869–1922, Germany): Lawyer. Active participant in Zemstvo congress 1904–1905; one of the founders of the Kadet Party. Signer of the Vyborg Appeal. Secretary general of the Provisional Government. Emigrated, assassinated by a Russian right-wing extremist. Father of the writer Vladimir Nabokov.

Nakhamkes (Steklov), **Yuri Mikhailovich** (1873–1941): Early Social Democrat; from 1903 close to the Bolsheviks, contributor to the *Social-Democrat* and *Pravda*; after February, a "Revolutionary defensist," then returned to Bolshevism; after October 1917, active in journalism and historical works; died in the purges.

Natanson, Mark Andreevich (1850–1919, Switzerland): Populist, one of the founders of "Land and Freedom" in the 1870s. Socialist Revolutionary during the war, internationalist; sided with the Bolsheviks.

Natasha: Diminutive of Natalia.

Nazhivin, Ivan Fyodorovich (1874–1940, Belgium): Russian writer, already well-known before the Revolution, emigrated in 1920; he wrote many novels devoted to the revolutionary years, and his memoirs.

Nekrasov, Nikolai Alekseevich (1821–1878): Celebrated Russian poet, director of the most important journals of his time. Held populist, revolutionary views.

Nekrasov, Nikolai Vissarionovich (1879–1940): Kadet deputy in Third and Fourth Dumas. One of the organizers of the Zemgor. Held ministerial posts in the

Provisional Government, left Kadet Party and allied with socialists. Arrested in 1930, worked as a hydraulic engineer building canals and dams; freed; arrested and executed in the purges.

Nemirovich-Danchenko, Vasili Ivanovich (1845–1936, Czechoslovakia): Russian writer (brother of the celebrated theater director); wrote novels, ethnographic descriptions, and war correspondence; emigrated in 1921.

Nepenin, Adrian Ivanovich (1871–1917): Admiral, decorated for bravery in Russo-Japanese War. Led Russia's Baltic Fleet during the First World War.

Neratov, Anatoli Anatolievich (1863–1938, France): Deputy Minister of Foreign Affairs from 1910 until 1917, served Provisional Government but refused to serve Bolsheviks; represented Whites under Denikin and Wrangel.

Nikolai I (Nikolai Pavlovich) (1796–1855): Youngest son of Paul I; the premature death of Aleksandr I and renunciation of the throne by his older brother Konstantin made him Emperor in December 1825; repressed the revolt of the Decembrists on the day of his crowning. His reign was conservative and firmly authoritarian.

Nikolai II Aleksandrovich (1868–1918): Last emperor of Russia. Murdered with his wife and children by the Bolsheviks.

Nikolai Andreevich. *See* Gredescul.

Nikolai Gavrilovich. *See* Chernyshevsky.

Nikolai Iudovich. *See* Ivanov.

Nikolai Mikhailovich, Grand Duke (1859–1919): Older brother of Grand Duke Aleksandr Mikhailovich; a historian of note. Shot by the Bolsheviks without trial.

Nikolai Nikolaevich (the Younger) ("Nikolasha"), **Grand Duke** (1856–1929, France): Supreme Commander 1914–1915. Viceroy of the Caucasus (September 1915–March 1917). Was again named Supreme Commander by Nikolai II at the moment of abdication, but not confirmed by the Provisional Government. Emigrated in 1919.

Nikolai Semyonovich. *See* Chkheidze.

Nivelle, Robert (1856–1924): French general; distinguished himself at Verdun; following setback in April 1917, he was replaced by General Pétain.

Nobel: Dynasty of Swedish industrialists. The father Immanuel established a factory for mechanical construction in St. Petersburg; his sons Alfred (created the Nobel Prize), Ludvig, and Robert also founded a refinery at Baku in 1879.

Nogin, Viktor Pavlovich (1878–1924): Bolshevik revolutionary active in Moscow; first people's commissar of Commerce and Industry.

Nolde, Boris Emmanuilovich, Baron (1876–1948, Switzerland): Jurist and historian; Kadet; emigrated in 1919; author of noted historical works.

Novitsky, Vasili Fyodorovich (1869–1929): Promoted after February Revolution to become assistant to the Minister of War (Guchkov); later joined the Red Army.

Oberuchev, Konstantin Mikhailovich (1864–1929, USA): Served in military through 1906, retired as a colonel; was also a Socialist Revolutionary, deported in 1913; returned in 1917 and became head of Kiev Military District; but left Russia in 1917.

Olga Lvovna. *See* Kerenskaya.

Osorgin (Ilyin), Mikhail Andreevich (1878–1924): Socialist Revolutionary; arrested in 1905, emigrated; returned in 1916 and became widely published following the February Revolution; hostile to Bolshevik coup; exiled in 1922 and was a well-known émigré writer.

Ostermann, Andrei Ivanovich (Heinrich Johann Friedrich) (1686–1747): German in the service of Peter the Great; was at the peak of his power from 1723 to 1741, led Russia foreign policy; exiled by Elizabeth to Siberia.

Pahlen, Konstantin Ivanovich, Count (1830–1912): Leading government official and reformer under Aleksandr II, served also under Aleksandr III.

Paléologue, Maurice (1859–1944): French ambassador to Russia 1914–1917.

Panin, Nikita Ivanovich (1718–1783): Russian politician and diplomat; directed foreign policy between 1763 and 1781.

Parvus, Aleksandr Lvovich (nom de guerre of Israel Lazarevich Helfand) (1867–1924, Germany): Played prominent part in 1905 Revolution. Invented theory of "permanent revolution." Successful businessman; funded revolutionaries (especially Bolsheviks).

Paul I (Pavel I Petrovich) (1754–1801): Son of Peter III and Catherine the Great, emperor from 1796. Tried to undo his mother's policies elevating the position of the nobility. Murdered by a palace conspiracy in March 1801. The Pavlovsky regiment and military school were named after him.

Pavel Nikolaevich. *See* Milyukov.

Pepelyaev, Viktor Nikolaevich (1884–1920): Lycée professor, deputy of the province of Tomsk at the Fourth Duma; Kadet. In March 1917, commissar of the Provisional Government in Kronstadt, and then voluntary combatant at the front. Reached Siberia in 1918; prime minister of the government of Admiral Kolchak, with whom he shared his destiny and execution.

Pereverzev, Pavel Nikolaevich (1871–1944, France): Lawyer, minister of justice in the provisional government.

Perovskaya, Sofia Lvovna (1853–1881): Daughter of vice-governor of St. Petersburg. Member of People's Will. Organized assassination of Aleksandr II in 1881.

Peshekhonov, Aleksei Vasilievich (1867–1933, Latvia): Social populist, banished in 1922, buried in Leningrad.

Petrov, Grigori Spiridonovich (1866–1925, France): Priest, advocate of socialism, ardent preacher and reformer; moved to create an alternative church, for which he was defrocked in 1908. Welcomed the revolution, but emigrated in 1920.

Petrunkevich, Ivan Ilyich (1843–1928, Czechoslovakia): Lawyer. One of the organizers of Zemstvo congresses. Prominent member of the Kadet party. In 1904–1905, president of the "Union for Liberation"; deputy in the First Duma, signer of the Vyborg Appeal, editor-in-chief of *Rech* ("Speech"). Emigrated in 1920.

Pirogov, Nikolai Ivanovich (1810–1881): Famous doctor and surgeon (especially military); the "Pirogov Congress" regularly reunited medical personnel.

Platten, Fritz (1883–1942): Locksmith, then designer, secretary of the Swiss Social Democrat Party; at the Zimmerwald and Kienthal conferences; organizer of and companion in Lenin's return to Russia. Founded the Swiss Communist Party in 1918; from 1923 lived in the USSR, where he died in exile.

Plekhanov, Georgi Valentinovich (1856–1918): Major figure of Russian social democracy, first Russian Marxist, sometimes for and sometimes against Lenin; during the war, a defensist; unitarist; played only a symbolic role after his return to Russia in 1917.

Pleve, Pavel Adamovich (von Plehwe, Wenzel) (1850–1916): One of the brightest strategists and most decisive Russian generals in the World War; died of illness after a military career spanning nearly half a century.

von Pleve, Vyacheslav Konstantinovich (1846–1904): Headed the Police Department in the 1880s, put down the terrorism of the People's Will organization; in 1902 was named minister of the interior and pursued a hard line against revolutionaries; murdered by a Socialist Revolutionary.

Plyushchik-Plyushchevsky, Yuri Nikolaevich (1877–1926, Yugoslavia): Colonel and then general, assigned in 1917 to GHQ; took the side of the Whites in the Civil War, served under Denikin; emigrated.

Pogulyayev, Sergei Sergeevich (1873–1941, France): Chief of staff of the commander of the Black Sea fleet (1916–1917); emigrated in 1919, continued to serve as liaison between Allies and White forces.

Pokrovsky, Nikolai Nikolaevich (1865–1930, Lithuania): Last Foreign Minister of the Russian Empire. Banker. Emigrated, taught finance at Kaunas University.

Polivanov, Aleksei Andreevich (1855–1920): Infantry general, close to Guchkov, dismissed by General Sukhomlinov; Minister of War 1915–1916, overcame the munition crisis, offered his services to the Red Army, died of typhus.

Posern, Boris Pavlovich (1882–1939): Bolshevik and president of the Minsk soviet in 1917; commissar during the Civil War; henchman who led purge in the 1930s, then in 1938 was himself arrested and shot.

Prishvin, Mikhail Mikhailovich (1873–1954): Well-known Russian writer since before 1914 for his ethnographic essays and stories.

Protopopov, Aleksandr Dmitrievich (1866–1918): Deputy in the Third and Fourth Dumas, Octobrist, vice president of the Duma in 1914; accused of spying for Germany. Last imperial Minister of the Interior; incarcerated by the Provisional Government, shot without trial by the Bolsheviks.

Pugachev, Yemelyan Ivanovich (circa 1740–1775): Head of a powerful Cossack-peasant insurrection from 1773 to 1775; executed.

Pumpyansky, Leonid Moiseevich (1889–1942): Social Democrat, Menshevik, arrested in February 1917 together with the Workers' Group; after the February Revolution served under the Provisional Government. Left Soviet Russia in 1922 and came to Estonia in 1925, where he was an economist and manager in the machine-building and oil shale industries. With the 1941 invasion he evacuated to the USSR. He is believed to have died of natural causes.

Pushkin, Aleksandr Sergeevich (1799–1837): National poet of Russia; creator of the modern Russian literary language.

Pyatakov, Georgi Leonidovich (1890–1937): Bolshevik leader in Ukraine; became part of internal opposition in the 1920s; eventually executed in the purges.

Rachmaninov (Rachmaninoff), **Sergei Vasilievich** (1873–1943, USA): World-famous composer, pianist, and conductor. Emigrated after the Revolution.

Radek, Karl Berngardovich (Sobelsohn, Karol) (1885–1939): Social Democrat revolutionary, arrived in Russia with Lenin; later a leader of the Communist International, part of the intra-party opposition to Stalin; deposed, restored, perished in the purges.

Radko-Dmitriev, Radko Dmitrievich (1859–1918): Bulgarian general who served in the Russian Army, commander of the Twelfth Army on the Northern Front. Murdered by the Bolsheviks.

Rafes, Moisei (Moishe) **Grigorievich** (1883–1942): A leader of the Jewish Labor Bund, revolutionary; joined Communist Party, was an overseer of Soviet cinema; arrested in 1938, convicted, died in labor camps.

Rakovsky, Christo Georgievich (1873–1941): Bulgarian revolutionary, whose activities spanned western Europe, the Balkans, and Russia. Held key posts during civil war and afterward, de facto governed Ukraine. Arrested in purges; executed 1941 in Oryol shortly before Wehrmacht reached the city.

Ramishvili, Isidore Ivanovich (1859–1937): Georgian Menshevik leader; 1918–1921; member of the government of independent Georgia.

Rappoport, Semyon Akimovich (pen name S. An-sky) (1863–1920, Poland): Writer in Russian and then Yiddish; ethnographer who studied Jewish life in Pale of Settlement; one of the founders of the SR party; member of Constituent Assembly; opposed Bolsheviks and escaped after they came to power.

Rasputin, Grigori Efimovich (pejorative "Grishka") (1864–1916): Siberian peasant; self-proclaimed as a mystic with healing talents and ability to predict the future; a humble holy peasant at court, preaching and practicing licentiousness outside it. Met the imperial couple in 1905 (through the Montenegrin sisters) and eased the hemophiliac heir's suffering, probably by his hypnotic powers. Exerted growing influence in 1915–1916 over the imperial family and affairs of state; murdered in December 1916 by Yusupov and Purishkevich.

Ravich, Sarra Naumovna (1879–1957): Social Democrat from 1903 on, arrested in Munich while exchanging banknotes stolen in Tiflis. Was Zinoviev's first wife. Returned to Russia with Lenin. Survived the purges.

Razin, Stepan Timofeevich (Stenka) (circa 1630–1671): Don Cossack and leader of an insurrection in 1670–1671.

Redrov, Mikhail Aleksandrovich (1864–?): Served for over 30 years in the Corp of Gendarmes in the Caucasus and other regions, was assigned to Sevastopol when he was pushed out by Kolchak in 1916; further fate unknown.

Reichesberg, Naum Mosieevich (1869–1928): Early revolutionary who left Russia at a young age and became a Swiss economist and university professor; socialist reformer.

von Rennenkampf, Pavel Karlovich (1854–1918): General. Distinguished himself in Boxer War. His inaction in East Prussia was held responsible for the loss of Samsonov's army in August 1914. Equally ineffectual at Lodz in November 1916, he was dismissed. Shot by the Bolsheviks in 1918.

Rittikh, Aleksandr Aleksandrovich (1868–1930, England): Last Minister of Agriculture of Nikolai II.

Rodichev, Fyodor Izmailovich (1854–1933, Switzerland): Jurist. Kadet leader, deputy in all four Dumas, after February Commissar of the Provisional Government for Finland.

Rodzyanko, Mikhail Vladimirovich (1859–1924, Yugoslavia): Octobrist. President of the Duma 1911–1917; emigrated in 1920.

Rolland, Romain (1866–1944): French writer, musicologist, anti-war socialist. Showed some initial misgivings about Lenin's regime, but from the late twenties onward, became an increasingly fervent and uncritical admirer of the USSR.

von Romberg, Gisbert (1866–1939): German ambassador to Switzerland.

Rosalia Markovna. *See* Bograd-Plekhanova.

Rosenwald, Julius (1862–1932): One of the leading American Jewish businessmen and philanthropists of the early twentieth century.

Roshal, Semyon (Solomon) **Grigorievich** (1896–1917): Firebrand student revolutionary, arrested for spreading Bolshevik propaganda at the front in 1915; led Bolshevik takeover of GHQ and the killing of General Dukhonin in November 1917; was killed a month later in Romania in revenge.

Rubanovich, Ilya Adolfovich (1859–1922, Germany): Member of the People's Will, and then associated with the Socialist Revolutionary Party, lived in France from 1882 onward. A leading socialist figure, yet ardently backed the War. Returned to Russia for a very brief period in 1917.

Rubets-Masalsky, Fyodor Vasilievich (1865–1918 or later): Following a four-decade military career, by 1917 served as staff general; after the Bolshevik coup served on the Caucasian front in 1918; fate unknown.

Rumyantsev, Nikolai Petrovich (1754–1826): Russian diplomat, historian, collector, and patron; Minister of Foreign Affairs from 1808 to 1813; interested in numismatics, ethnography, manuscripts, old books, and paintings. Advocate of Russian presence in the Pacific and North America.

Ruzsky, Nikolai Vladimirovich (1854–1918): General, commander of the Northern Army Group, was instrumental in securing the abdication of Nikolai II. Executed by Bolsheviks during the Civil War.

Safarov, Georgi Ivanovich (1891–1942): Revolutionary émigré; returned to Russia with Lenin, led the Red Terror against Russian farmers in Central Asia; opposed Stalin in the late 1920s and was eventually arrested and executed.

Sakharov, Vladimir Viktorovich (1853–1920): Commander of the Romanian Army Group, dismissed from service after March 1917, retired, executed during the Civil War.

Samsonov, Aleksandr Vasilievich (1859–1914): Cavalry general, Cossack origins. Commanded the 1st Army in East Prussia in August 1914, which suffered a crushing defeat by the Germans at Tannenberg; committed suicide after the battle.

Sanya: Short and colloquial name for Aleksandr.

Sashenka: Short name, term of endearment for Aleksandra. *See* Kollontai.

Saveliev, Maksimilian Aleksandrovich (1884–1939): Socialist, member of German Social Democrat party, then Bolshevik; economist; historian.

Savinkov, Boris Viktorovich (1879–1925): One of the leaders of the Socialist Revolutionary Party and of its combat organization, responsible for a number of terrorist assassination attempts; served with Kerensky in 1917; sought to organize the fight against the Bolsheviks, organized the Union for the Defense of Motherland and Freedom. Clandestinely crossed the Soviet border, arrested, tried, died in Soviet prison, reportedly by suicide.

Schiff, Jacob (1847–1920): American banker and philanthropist; born in Germany. Prominent leader of the Jewish community and opponent of Russia's policies toward her Jewish population.

Schmidt, Pyotr Petrovich (1867–1906): Ship's lieutenant in the Black Sea fleet, with revolutionary sympathies; one of the leaders of the Sevastopol uprising in 1905; shot after its failure. Lionized in Soviet times.

Sergei Aleksandrovich, Grand Duke (1857–1905): Uncle of Nikolai II, governor-general of Moscow, assassinated by a Socialist Revolutionary in February 1905.

Sergievsky (also spelled Sergeevsky), **Boris Nikolaevich** (1883–1976, USA): Decorated military officer; in 1917 was responsible at GHQ for communications infrastructure; fought for the Whites in the Civil War; emigrated and published articles and several historical books.

Shakhovskoy, Dmitri Ivanovich (1861–1939): A founding member of the Kadet Party; member of the First Duma and signatory of the Vyborg Appeal; minister in Provisional Government; abandoned all political activity in 1923 to focus on work of literary erudition; arrested in the great purges; executed.

Shcheglovitov, Ivan Grigorievich (1861–1918): Jurist; Minister of Justice 1906–1915; President of the State Council. Shot by the Bolsheviks with Khvostov and Nikolai Maklakov as part of the Red Terror.

Shchepkin, Dmitri Mitrofanovich (1879–1937): Lawyer, writer, economist, member of Zemstvo Union, close colleague of Prince Georgi Lvov; then worked against Bolsheviks, was arrested, sentenced to death, had sentence commuted, worked in Soviet agriculture, was arrested again in 1930, then again in 1937, and executed.

Shcherbachev, Dmitri Grigorievich (1857–1932, France): General, commanded the 7th and then the 11th Armies on the Southwestern front (April 1915 to April 1917); succeeded Sakharov in April leading the Romanian front; fought in the Civil War on the side of the Romanians, Ukrainians, and Whites. Emigrated.

Sheideman, Sergei Mikhailovich (1857–1920): Russian general; remained in the service of the Red Army but was arrested and died in prison.

Shekhter. *See* Grinevich.

Shingarev, Andrei Ivanovich (1869–1918): Physician and head of a zemstvo hospital. Deputy to Second, Third, and Fourth Dumas. Member of Kadet Party leadership. Minister of Agriculture in the first Provisional Government, then Minister of Finance in the second. Imprisoned by the Bolsheviks, murdered together with Kokoshkin at the Mariinsky Hospital.

Shkuro, Andrei Grigorievich (1887–1947): Cossack officer who became one of the White generals during the Civil War; emigrated in 1920; in 1944 sided with Nazi Germany against the USSR, and in 1945 was handed over to the USSR by the English and Americans; executed.

Shlyapnikov, Aleksandr Gavrilovich (Gavrilych) (1885–1937): Born into a family of Old Believers. Bolshevik from 1905. Worked in factories abroad, 1908–1914. Collaborated closely with Lenin during the war, returned clandestinely to Russia via Scandinavia on various occasions, oversaw the work of the Bolshevik Russian Bureau. Trade union leader; first Commissar of Labor after the Bolshevik Revolution. One of the leaders of the Workers' Opposition movement in the Party, 1920–1922. Expelled from the Central Committee in 1922. Held minor posts subsequently. Excluded from the Party in 1933, arrested 1935, executed.

Shulgin, Vasili Vitalievich (1878–1976): Duma deputy, leader of the right. Member of the Progressive Bloc. With Guchkov, received Nikolai II's abdication. Emigrated, made a clandestine trip to the USSR. Captured in Yugoslavia in 1944, spent twelve years in a prison camp, welcomed by Khrushchev, lived out his days in the USSR.

Shuvaev, Dmitri Savelievich (1854–1937): Infantry general; intendant general of the armies. Minister of war, March 1916–January 1917. Served, taught courses in Red Army after the Revolution. Retired after 1927; arrested in 1937 and executed.

Skobelev, Matvei Ivanovich (1885–1939): Social Democrat from 1903; Menshevik, deputy in the Fourth Duma. Patriot during the war. Minister in Second Provisional Government July 1917. Joined Bolshevik Party in 1922. Worked in foreign trade organization. Expelled from the Party in 1937; died in the purges.

Skobelev, Mikhail Dmitrievich (1843–1882): Infantry general; distinguished himself in particular in the Russo-Turkish War (1877–1878); liberator of Bulgaria; conqueror of Turkmenia. His statue stood in the square in front of the governor-general's home (today's city hall), and the square was known as Skobelev Square before 1917.

Slutsky, Anton Iosifovich (Naftali Grigorievich) (1884–1918): Revolutionary since 1905, organized the Bolshevik Party in the Obukhov works; during the civil war, he was shot in Crimea.

Smirnov, Vladimir Vasilievich (1849–1918): Infantry general, Commander of the Second Army. Killed while held hostage by the Bolsheviks at Pyatigorsk.

Sofia Fyodorovna. *See* Kolchak, Sofia Fyodorovna.

Sokolov, Nikolai Dmitrievich (1870–1928): Lawyer, Bolshevik sympathizer. Drafted Order No. 1, which in effect destroyed discipline in the Russian army in March 1917. After the Revolution worked as a lawyer in various Soviet agencies.

Solovei, Don Markovich (1883–1954): Husband of Evgenia Solovei, also a banker, participated in the Bolshevik coup, Civil War, and was later a Soviet bureaucrat.

Solovei, Evgenia Markovna (1887–1976): Bolshevik revolutionary, worked in banking until 1917, participated in October coup, thereafter headed the State Bank's foreign operations and held other posts.

Sophie (**Sophya Vyazemskaya**) (née Vorontsova-Dashkova): Wife of **Vyazemsky, Vladimir**.

Stal, Lyudmila Nikolaevna (Zaslavskaya Lea Froimovna) (1872–1939): Bolshevik revolutionary; became a Soviet official, active in the Comintern, responsible for propaganda among women in the USSR.

Stalin (pseud. of Dzhughashvili), **Iosif** (Joseph) **Vissarionovich** (1879–1953): Militant Social Democrat from 1898, several arrests-escapes, co-opted by Lenin in 1912 to the Bolshevik Central Committee. Banished to Siberia in 1913, returned in March 1917. Would never again leave governing bodies; after the death of Lenin, would become the absolute leader of the USSR, responsible for innumerable deportations and executions.

Stankevich, Vladimir Bogdanovich (Vlada Stankevicius, Vladas Stanka) (1884–1968, USA): Lawyer, philosopher, military engineer, publisher of a textbook on fortifications; one of the leaders of Russian military efforts during 1917; arrested by Bolsheviks, emigrated; settled in Berlin, then Kaunas; after World War II worked in Berlin helping displaced persons; then left for USA in 1949.

Stasova, Elena Dmitrievna (1873–1966): Niece of the celebrated art critic Vladimir Stasov; from 1917 to 1920, secretary of the Central Committee; from 1921 to 1937, she worked in different organizations of the Comintern.

Steklov. *See* Nakhamkes.

Stepun, Fyodor Avgustovich (in German **Friedrich Steppuhn**) (1884–1965, Germany): Well-known philosopher who had, by 1917, studied philosophy in Germany and fought for Russia in the First World War; supported the Provisional Government; was exiled by the Communists in 1922 along with other intellectuals and proceeded to live, teach, and write in Germany, opposing both the Nazi and Soviet dictatorships.

Stolypin, Pyotr Arkadievich (1862–1911): Minister of the Interior and Prime Minister, 1906–1911. Initiator of important land reforms aimed at a stepwise elimination of the oppressive rural commune and fostering individual initiative among peasant farmers, giving them the means to work for their prosperity. Defeated revolutionary terrorism (mainly in 1906–1907) through a system of field courts-martial. Dissolved the first two Dumas, and worked with the Third Duma, which was elected on a limited franchise. Survived multiple assassination attempts but was felled by an assassin's bullet in Kiev.

Straus, Oscar Solomon (1850–1926): American diplomat, ambassador to Ottoman Empire; was also the first Jewish U. S. cabinet secretary, holding the Commerce and Labor post under Theodore Roosevelt.

Struve, Pyotr Berngardovich (1870–1944, France): Publicist, philosopher, writer. Began as a Marxist; became a liberal. Edited (abroad) the liberal journal *Liberation*. Became leader of the right wing of the Kadet Party. From 1917 to 1920 actively opposed Bolshevism, was sentenced to death in absentia. A leader of the emigration; founded and edited publications in Sofia, Prague, Belgrade, Berlin, Paris.

Stuchka, Pyotr Ivanovich (1865–1932): Latvian lawyer and journalist in Riga; Bolshevik party member, participant in October coup; leader of short-lived Latvian Socialist Republic (1918–1920); later minister of justice, president of the Supreme Court of the USSR.

Stürmer, Boris Vladimirovich (1848–1917): Member of the State Council from 1904. Protégé of Rasputin. Held power during 1916 as Prime Minister as well as Minister of the Interior, then of Foreign Affairs. After February, arrested and imprisoned in the Peter and Paul Fortress, where he died in September 1917.

Sukhanov. *See* Himmer.

Sukhomlinov, Vladimir Aleksandrovich (1848–1926, Germany): General, chief of staff, and war minister (1909–1915); arrested May 1916, freed thanks to Rasputin; rearrested by the Provisional Government in 1917, amnestied in 1918. Died in Berlin.

Suvorin, Aleksei Sergeevich (1834–1912): Man of letters, publicist, owner of a theater in St. Petersburg, founder and director of the journal *New Times*, evolved from liberal to right-wing.

Suvorin, Boris Alekseevich (1879–1940, Yugoslavia): Son of Aleksei Suvorin, edited the *New Times* after his father's death; during the Civil War he joined the Whites and published papers in areas they controlled; subsequently lived abroad; published memoirs.

Svechin, Aleksandr Andreevich (1878–1935): General, military historian, military theorist, served in the Russian Imperial Army, and then switched allegiance to the Bolsheviks; professor at the Frunze Military Academy; arrested repeatedly during the 1930s; executed.

Tarle, Evgeni Viktorovich (1874–1955): Historian; member of the Academy of Sciences (1927, excluded from 1931 to 1938); wrote extensively on Napoleon's invasion of 1812 and on the Crimean War.

Tereshchenko, Mikhail Ivanovich (1886–1956, Monaco): Major landowner, industrialist, and financier (progressive). Finance minister, then foreign minister of the Provisional Government. Arrested by the Bolsheviks, then released; emigrated.

Thiers, Adolphe (1797–1877): Politician, publicist, historian (*History of the French Revolution*); crushed the Paris Commune.

Thomas, Albert (1878–1932): French socialist who supported the World War and joined the wartime government; supported Russia's revolution; in 1919, became the president of the International Labor Office.

Tikhobrazov, Dmitri Nikolaevich (1886–1974, France): Served at GHQ, then as colonel in White Army in Civil War; emigrated.

Tikhomirov, Lev Aleksandrovich (1852–1923): Populist revolutionary (People's Will), emigrated in 1882, publicly renounced in 1888 all revolutionary activity and returned to Russia; publicist, conservative and religious thinker.

Timireva (Knipper-Timireva, née Safonova), **Anna Vasilievna** (1893–1975): Daughter of composer Vasili Safonov, became common-law wife of Kolchak, whom she accompanied until his execution in 1920; thereafter lived through multiple arrests, prison, and labor camps.

Tkachev, Pyotr Nikitich (1844–1885): Russian populist of the most radical wing; arrested in 1869 but escaped abroad; partisan of the "revolutionary dictatorship."

von Toll, Eduard Vasilievich (Eduard Gustav), baron (1858–1902): Baltic German, geologist, and famous arctic explorer; disappeared during an expedition to Bennett Island.

Tolstoy, Aleksei Nikolaevich (1883–1945): Writer known since 1908; emigrated between 1918 and 1923, returned to USSR and became a major; endlessly loyal establishment figure in Soviet literature; wrote science fiction and historical novels.

Tomsky (Efremov), **Mikhail Pavlovich** (1880–1936): Rose from among workers in the Bolshevik party to become a labor union leader in the USSR; excluded from political leadership in 1929; committed suicide during purges.

Trotsky (pseud. of Bronstein), **Lev Davidovich** (1879–1940, Mexico): Revolutionary Social Democrat from 1897. Chairman of the Petersburg Soviet during the 1905 Revolution. Returned to Russia after February and engineered the Bolshevik seizure of power in October 1917. Founded Red Army and led it through the Civil War. Lost struggle for power and expelled from USSR in 1929; murdered by a Soviet agent.

Trubetskoy, Evgeni Nikolaevich (1863–1920): Philosopher and religious thinker, professor at the University of Moscow; one of the founders and leaders of the Kadet Party. Died of typhoid during Civil War.

Tsereteli, Irakli Georgievich (1882–1959, USA): Social Democrat; deputy to second Duma; exiled in 1913, returned after February Revolution; important Menshevik leader. Emigrated after the sovietization of Georgia.

Tsiperovich, Grigori Vladimirovich (1871–1932): Economist, man of letters, publicist. Revolutionary from 1888; in 1917, editorial secretary of *Izvestia* alongside Nakhamkes-Steklov. Joined Bolsheviks, made his way in Soviet economic institutions.

Tulyakov, Ivan Nikitich (1887–1918): Deputy in the Fourth Duma, Menshevik; killed in Civil War.

Turgenyev, Nikolai Ivanovich (1789–1871): Economist, Decembrist (condemned in absentia, staying in France); amnestied in 1856; throughout his career he advocated for liberation of serfs and civic reform.

Ulyanov: Lenin's family name; Anna Elizarova-Ulyanova (1864–1935) and Maria Ulyanova (1878–1937) were Lenin's sisters and active Bolshevik party members; Maria Aleksandrovna Ulyanova (née Blank) (1835–1916) was Lenin's mother.

Uritsky, Moisei Solomonovich (1873–1918): Socialist; emigrated in 1914 and returned in 1917; became Bolshevik; head of the St. Petersburg CheKa (March 1918); assassinated by student Leonid Kannegisser.

Vasilchikova (née Vyazemskaya), **Lidia Leonidovna** ("Dilka") (1886–1948, France): Worked in the Red Cross in the Russo-Japanese War and First World War; two of her older brothers, Dmitri and Boris Vyazemsky, were killed in 1917; emigrated in 1919, lived in Paris, then Lithuania, Italy, Germany, Bohemia, and again France. Died tragically, run over by an automobile.

Vatsetis, Ioakim Ioakimovich (1873–1938): Military officer who at first supported the Provisional Government but later joined the Bolsheviks; during the Civil War he was commander of the "Latvian riflemen," a division that conducted punitive missions; carried out important functions in the Red Army; executed in the purges.

Vengerov, Vsevolod Semyonovich (1887–1938): Revolutionary lawyer, Menshevik, member of the Executive Committee; took part in Civil War in Red Army; thereafter repeatedly arrested and ultimately executed in Kazakhstan exile.

Venizelos, Eleftherios (1864–1936): Greek politician; Prime Minister several times (notably from 1917 to 1920).

Verkhovsky, Aleksandr Ivanovich (1886–1938): Lieutenant colonel; supported the February Revolution; war minister in last Provisional Government; then joined Red Army; military theorist in 1920s; twice arrested in 1930s, was executed in the purges.

Vesyolkin, Mikhail Mikhailovich (1871–1918/9): Rear-admiral, commandante of Sevastopol fortress; forced to resign in 1917; executed by the Bolsheviks.

Vinaver (Winawer), **Maksim Moiseevich** (1863–1926, France): Lawyer born in Warsaw, founder of the Kadet Party, deputy in the First Duma, signer of the Vyborg Appeal; in 1919, member of a White government in Crimea; emigrated to France that same year.

Vinnichenko, Vladimir Kirillovich (1880–1951, France): Ukrainian nationalist, productive writer; vice president of the Ukrainian Rada in 1917, proclaimed Ukraine's independence in January 1918; during and after Civil War tried to form an alliance between Soviet Communism and Ukrainian nationalism.

Vladimir Bogdanovich. *See* Stankevich.

Vladimir Ilyich. *See* Lenin.

Vogt, Carl (1817–1895): German naturalist; agent of Napoleon III in the 1850s; attacked by Marx in a pamphlet.

Voitinsky (Woytinsky), **Vladimir Savelievich** (1885–1964, USA): Economist and socialist, migrated from Bolshevik to Menshevik; member of the Executive Committee; emigrated; published memoirs.

Volodya: Diminutive of Vladimir.

Vorovsky, Vatslav Vatslavovich (1871–1923): Revolutionary, publicist, and diplomat; Bolshevik from 1903, led Soviet delegations to the conferences of Genoa (1921) and Lausanne, where he was assassinated by a Russian émigré.

Vorshilov, Klim (Kliment) Efremovich (1881–1969): Bolshevik, commander during the Civil War; helped purge the Red Army of competent officers in the 1930s; head of state from 1953 to 1960; belonged to Stalin's close entourage.

Vtorov, Nikolai Aleksandrovich (1866–1918): Very important financial and industrial magnate, known as the Russian J. P. Morgan, owner of a variety of businesses. Killed in Moscow in May 1918.

Vyazemskaya (née Shuvalova), **Aleksandra Pavlovna** (Asya) (1893–1968, Italy): Spouse of Dmitri Vyazemsky.

Vyazemsky, Boris Leonidovich, Prince (1883–1917): Personal secretary of Stolypin, heir and owner of the exemplary Lotaryovo estate, which was destroyed in September 1917 by revolutionary mobs, who beat Prince Boris to death.

Vyazemsky, Dmitri Leonidovich, Prince (1884–1917): Younger brother of Boris Vyazemsky. Organized a field hospital and treated wounded during the First World War. Was killed in Petrograd in March 1917 by a stray bullet.

Vyazemsky, Vladimir Leonidovich, Prince (1889–1960, France): Emigrated after the murder of his brother Boris; worked in France as a horse-breeder; was a historian and an amateur artist.

Vyrubova (Taneeva), **Anya** (1884–1964, Finland): Lady-in-waiting to the Empress. For some years her closest friend and intermediary between the imperial couple and Rasputin. Victim of a railroad accident in 1915, arrested in 1917, liberated, rearrested, emigrated.

Weinstein, Aron Isakovich (1877–1938): Leader of the Jewish Labor Bund and later the Communist Bund; executed in the purges.

Wilhelm: Wilhelm II (1859–1941), the Kaiser, emperor of Germany, king of Prussia (1888–1918).

Wilson, Woodrow (1856–1924): President of the United States from 1913 to 1921.

Witte, Sergei Yulievich (1849–1915): Minister of Finance 1892–1903. Urged civil reforms and modernization. Prime Minister October 1905–April 1906, when he resigned (replaced by Goremykin). Author of an important memoir.

Yakovlev (pseud. of Epstein), **Yakov Arkadievich** (1896–1938): Joined Bolsheviks in 1913, organized revolutionary militia following the February Revolution; later was the Communist party boss in Ukraine, Commissar for Agriculture, architect of 1930s collectivization and mass famine; executed in the purges.

Yanushkevich, Nikolai Nikolaevich (1868–1918): Infantry general; in 1914, Chief of Staff to the grand duke Nikolai Nikolaevich, whom he accompanied to the Caucasus; retired after March 1917; arrested in 1918 and assassinated by the convoy that brought him to Petrograd.

Yudenich, Nikolai Nikolaevich (1862–1933, France): Infantry general, veteran of Russo-Japanese War and World War I, where he led Russian troops in gains against the Ottomans; after the Revolution, led the Northwest Army, a White contingent based in Estonia, but was unsuccessful in attacking Petrograd.

Yuzefovich, Yakov Davidovich (1872–1929, Poland): General, veteran of Russo-Japanese and First World War; fought for Whites in Civil War, was an aide of Pyotr Wrangel.

Zak, Samuil Sergeevich (1868–1930): Economist and publicist; left-wing Socialist Revolutionary; he collaborated with the political and literary collection *Zavety* (1912–1914); left politics; worked in USSR's central planning agency, Gosplan.

Zarudny, Aleksandr Sergeevich (1869–1934): Lawyer, Populist Socialist, one of the ministers of justice in the provisional government; career as jurist in the USSR.

Zaslavsky, David Iosifovich (1880–1965): Menshevik Bundist (since 1903), defensist, fought the Bolsheviks from 1917 to 1918, but soon joined to become one of the leading propagandists of the Soviet regime and its policies on literature.

Zasulich, Vera Ivanovna (1849–1919): Populist terrorist, tried in 1873 for an attempt on the life of the governor of St. Petersburg, acquitted, fled abroad, became one of the Menshevik leaders, opponent of the Bolshevik regime.

Zavadsky, Sergei Vladislavovich (1871–1935, Czechoslovakia): Senator, jurist; in 1918 joined the government of Skoropadsky in Ukraine; then the White forces; after emigrating taught Russian law in Prague.

Zeeler, Vladimir Feofilovich (1874–1954): Governor of Rostov-on-Don in 1917; during the Civil War, served as president of the Committee of the Don and Minister of Foreign Affairs of the Government of Southern Russia. Had sympathies for the Kadets, emigrated to France, one of the founders in Paris of the newspaper *Russian Thought.*

Zenzinov, Vladimir Mikhailovich (1880–1953, USA): Hailed from a family of wealthy merchants. Member of Social Revolutionary Party, active in 1905 Revolution. Elected to Constituent Assembly, opposed Bolshevism, emigrated. Worked as a correspondent.

Zhelyabov, Andrei Ivanovich (1851–1881): Leading member of the revolutionary People's Will party; organized the assassination of Aleksandr II; executed.

Zinoviev, Grigori Evseevich (pseud. Radomyslsky, Ovsei-Gershon Aronovich, born Apfelbaum, Hirsch) (1883–1936): Bolshevik from 1903. Chairman of the Petrograd Soviet after the October Revolution, Politburo member, leader of the Comintern. Helped depose Trotsky, then was deposed by Stalin, expelled from the Party, tried and executed in 1936.

Zurabov, Arshak Gerasimovich (1873–1920): Socialist from the Caucasus; emigrated from 1908 to 1917; close to the Mensheviks; after October 1917 was back in the Caucasus on the side of the Bolsheviks.

Principal Non-Historical Characters

Alina. *See* Vorotyntseva.

Andozerskaya, Olda Orestovna: She was said to be the most intelligent woman in Petersburg. Professor of world history, she nonetheless supported the monarchy, a rare case in learned circles. In November 1916 she met Colonel Vorotyntsev, who was passing through Petrograd. They began a passionate affair, which continued through correspondence during the winter of 1916–1917.

Anton Lenartovich: Uncle of Sasha and Veronika Lenartovich, brother of aunts Adalia and Agnessa. Born in 1881, the year Aleksandr II was murdered by a member of the People's Will organization, Uncle Anton participated actively in the events of 1905. After the failure of this first revolution, he turned to terrorist action. Arrested and tried, he was given the death penalty and hanged.

Asya: Diminutive for Anastasia. Wife of Father Severyan.

Chernega, Terenti: Sergeant major in Sanya Lazhenitsyn's artillery battery. He is worldly, the happy warrior, one who sees life in simple terms, in contrast to Sanya's intellectual and spiritual quests.

Dmitri Ivanych. *See* Kharitonov family.

Dmitriev, Mikhail Dmitrievich: Engineer. Author of a trench gun project that the workers' strikes prevent him from realizing.

Fedya: Diminutive of Fyodor.

Kharitonov family (based on a real-life family, the Andreevs): **Aglaida Fedoseevna**, stern headmistress of the best high school for girls in the Russian south, in Rostov, holder of progressive views. But her children defy her: older son **Yaroslav (Yarik)** by becoming an officer; daughter **Evgenia (Zhenya)** by marrying **Dmitri Ivanych Filomatinsky** while pregnant with their daughter, **Lyalka**; younger son **Yurik**

dreams of becoming an officer like Yaroslav when, aged 14, he encounters the Revolution.

Korzner, Susanna Iosifovna: Wife of a well-known lawyer in Moscow, David Korzner. Jewish, she militated for the improvement of the life of Jews in Russia. Specializing in "lectures and proclamations," Susanna forged a friendship with Alina, who offered to become her page-turner for musical concerts for the troops.

Kotya: Diminutive of Konstantin.

Kovynev, Fyodor Dmitrievich: Originally from the Don, he lived in Petersburg. His prototype is Fyodor Kryukov, believed to be the real author of the novel *And Quiet Flows the Don*, whereas Soviet officialdom ascribed the novel to Mikhail Sholokhov.

Ksenia. *See* Tomchak, Ksenia Zakharovna.

Lazhenitsyn, Sanya (Isaaki): From the North Caucasus, a student before the war, he was seduced by Tolstoy's ideas. In 1914, he fought in eastern Prussia, where he met Colonel Vorotyntsev and Arseni Blagodarev. He was still at the front when the troubles of March 1917 erupted. Sanya Lazhenitsyn is the prototype of the author's father, Isaaki Semyonovich Solzhenitsyn.

Lenartovich, Aleksandr ("Sasha"): Student, enrolled in the army at the beginning of the hostilities. Raised by his aunts in the revolutionary tradition of the intelligentsia and in respect for his uncle Anton's memory, he militated against the aristocracy and was opposed to war. In August 1914 he met Colonel Vorotyntsev at the front, where he did not display courage or military valor.

Likonya (Yelenka, Yolochka): School friend of Veronika Lenartovich, although their friendship was broken. A devotee of the arts, she is the opposite of the ideal of revolutionary militancy.

Mikhail Dmitrievich (Dmitrich): The engineer Dmitriev.

Olda Orestovna. *See* Andozerskaya.

Pavel Ivanovich. *See* Varsonofiev.

Sanya: Short name for Aleksandr, as well as Isaac. *See* Lazhenitsyn.

Sasha: Short name for Aleksandr. *See* Guchkov (historical names); Lenartovich.

Savitsky, Dmitri Sergeevich: Shown in *August 1914* and again in *March 1917, Book 4*, Savitsky is the composite image of an officer who understands everything and is willing to speak truth to power, with little hope that power will listen.

Tomchak, Ksenia Zakharovna: Daughter of self-made landowner Zakhar Tomchak. Completed her secondary studies in Rostov-on-Don at Kharitonova's high school, where she discovered a thriving intellectual environment. Ksenia Tomchak is the prototype of the author's mother, Taisia Shcherbak.

Varsonofiev, Pavel Ivanovich ("Stargazer"): Aging thinker, seer of enigmatic dreams, whose meetings with Sanya contain riddles, and some answers, about duty, war, society, revolution, the fate of Russia, and the meaning of hope. Divorced from wife Leokadia (Lyoka), who repeatedly haunts him in his dreams.

Vera (Vorotyntseva, Vera Mikhailovna): Sister of Colonel Vorotyntsev. Lived in Petersburg with their old nurse. Worked at the Public Library. Fourteen years younger than her brother, she spent her childhood without him and was very influenced by the traditional peasant world of her nurse. In love with the engineer Dmitriev, she led a solitary life, while he was embroiled in a complicated love affair.

Vorotyntsev, Georgi Mikhailovich: Graduated at the top of his class from the military academy. Colonel. After his studies in Petersburg, he and his wife Alina lived in garrisons in the Vyatka region until he was sent to Moscow. After a brief rise that took him to GHQ (General Headquarters), he was sent on a mission in East Prussia. He escaped the encirclement of the Samsonov army at Tannenberg in August 1914. Eventually he was "exiled" to a regiment because of his positions on war strategy. In early November 1916, on a mission in Petrograd, he met Professor Andozerskaya and they began a passionate affair.

Vorotyntseva (née Siyalskaya) **Alina**: Wife of Colonel Vorotyntsev. Trained as a pianist, she devoted herself entirely to her husband's career during the eight years of her marriage preceding the 1914 World War. When he was sent to the front, Alina, who had no children, was left alone in Moscow and became extremely active, organizing concerts for the troops. During the war, she felt she had come alive again as a person, until she learned that her husband was having an affair with a famous woman from Petrograd.

Yarik: Diminutive of Yaroslav. *See* Kharitonov family.

Yegor: Georgi (Vorotyntsev).

Yurik: Diminutive of Yuri. *See* Kharitonov family.

ABOUT THE AUTHOR

Aleksandr Solzhenitsyn (1918–2008) is widely acknowledged as one of the most important figures—and perhaps *the* most important writer—of the last century. A Soviet political prisoner from 1945 to 1953, he set himself firmly against the anti-human Soviet system, and all anti-human ideologies, from that time forward. His novel *One Day in the Life of Ivan Denisovich* (1962) made him famous, and *The Gulag Archipelago*, published to worldwide acclaim in 1973, further unmasked communism and played a critical role in its eventual defeat. Solzhenitsyn won the Nobel Prize in 1970 and was exiled to the West in 1974. He ultimately published dozens of plays, poems, novels, and works of history, nonfiction, and memoir, including *Cancer Ward*, *In the First Circle*, and *The Oak and the Calf* (a memoir that is continued in *Between Two Millstones*). Few authors have so decisively shaped minds, hearts, and world events as did Solzhenitsyn.

www.ingramcontent.com/pod-product-compliance
Lightning Source LLC
Chambersburg PA
CBHW020505310726
48979CB00016B/2786/J
9780268210526